FOR MY BROTHER'S SINS

Sheelagh Kelly was born in York in 1948. She
attended Knavesmire Secondary School for Girls,
left at the age of 15 and went to work as a book-
keeper. She has written for pleasure since she was a
small child, but not until 1980 were the seeds for her
first novel, *A Long Way from Heaven*, sown when
she developed an interest in genealogy and local
history and decided to trace her ancestors' story,
thereby acquiring an abiding fascination with the
quirks of human nature. *A Long Way from Heaven*
was followed by *For My Brother's Sins, Erin's Child,
My Father, My Son, Dickie, Shoddy Prince* and *A
Complicated Woman*.

SHEELAGH KELLY

For My Brother's Sins

HarperCollins*Publishers*

For 'Our Kid', Robert Day
– with no aspersion in the title

HarperCollins*Publishers*
77–85 Fulham Palace Road,
Hammersmith, London W6 8JB

This paperback edition 1999
3 5 7 9 8 6 4 2

First published in Great Britain by
Century Hutchinson Limited 1986

Set in Ehrhardt

Printed in Great Britain

PART ONE

1867

CHAPTER ONE

It could have been a street of great beauty, for the buildings which formed its route spanned many centuries – medieval, Tudor, Georgian. Here had once stood the palace of one of the noble families of England. This street had witnessed the passage of kings – but no more. The once-handsome edifices had been allowed to slip into an undignified senility. The façades of the Tudor and medieval residences were crazed and ravaged, their timbers seemed to groan with an arthritic despair. Even worse, there were those whose ancient craftsmanship had been obliterated beneath an incompetent layer of modern improvisation – rough coats of plaster daubed over their elegant framework. To add to their ugliness two dirty lines marked the place where the street loafers leaned: one produced from their shoulders, the other, at the foot of the wall, caused by their boredom-induced boot-tapping. And the only heraldic banner which now graced Walmgate Bar was a line of washing, draped incongruously over the fortification that had once boasted the grisly remains of traitors. Nor were things any better at the tail-end of Walmgate, for the water beneath the unimpressive bridge that arched the Foss was choked with a carpet of green slime and foul-smelling refuse, dead cats and effluence.

Yet all this was not to say that the street was uninteresting or lacking in style; indeed, it was a street of much charm, having a very definite style of its own. Apart from the period buildings and odd assortment of shops that squatted between them – a saddler's shop which boasted harness of the finest quality, an umbrella maker, butcher, fishmonger, shoemaker, chicory-grinder and pawnbroker – the most common type of building could be easily identified by the names on the colourful signs that creaked over their entrances: The Fighting Cocks, The Hope and Anchor, The Shakespeare Tap, The Spotted Dog, The Spread Eagle . . . inns, taverns and ale-houses appeared at every step of the way. Even a blind man could not mistake his location, for each breath one took was tainted by the overpowering scent of processed hops, belching out from the ever-open doors of these abundant watering holes and from the breweries that supplied them.

There were less cheerful places, too, dotted out of sight along this street; dingy courtyards where the most impoverished of York's inhabitants – the Irish immigrants – resided. Filthy, disease-ridden yards containing flea-infested hovels, where babies played amongst the piles of excrement that spilled from the two privies which had to serve a hundred, maybe two hundred people.

Patrick Feeney knew all about these courts. After the Great Hunger had driven him from his beloved Ireland in 1847, it was here that his first child had been born. And here that he had lost his young wife, Mary, when the cholera epidemic had wiped out dozens of his ilk.

But all that was in the past. Now he was housed in comparative style in one of the many terraced dwellings that snaked off Walmgate like veins from a main artery, and instead of being under the landlord's rule was well on the way to owning his own property.

Patrick yawned and raised his arms above his head, gripping the iron rails of the bedstead and stretching his long, lean body between sleep-warmed sheets. His determined, tanned jaw rested against the white linen, his eyes blinking away the mist of sleep. The invading flecks of old-age had rapidly increased with each birthday and now, at forty-seven, the once coal-black hair was an iron-grey – his eyebrows too, but beneath them those pale-blue lights which had always been his most attractive feature could still summon up a youthful twinkle.

His brain began to function – what day was it? His befuddled thinking told him Sunday and he grinned with satisfaction, snuggling down close to the sleeping figure beside him, slipping a calloused, though gentle, palm over his wife's naked stomach.

Thomasin Feeney groaned as the searching hand forced her into wakefulness. Her auburn hair lay coiled in thick braids around her neck and shoulders with the burnished vibrancy that delights a child's eye when he peels away the spiky protective layer of a horse chestnut ... rather like her character, too. As if unwilling to expose to the outside world the true kernel of her nature she had super-imposed upon it a rough and ready, often prickly, outerc-asing. Her eyes, when they fluttered open, were grey, dark-lashed and clouded with sleep.

'It's not Sunday,' she mumbled as the fingers ventured further, her sensitive skin detecting every blemish on his hand.

He checked, disorientated, then grimaced. There were no churchbells. The abnormal quietness which had lulled him into believing it was a day of rest was because he had woken an hour earlier than normal. It was Friday. That's what summer does to ye, thought Patrick resentfully as he rolled onto his back, though his hand still lingered on her belly. The sun rose early in summer, thereby waking the sparrows and starlings which roosted under the eaves, and sparking off a discordant dawn chorus. Today a song-thrush had perched upon the chimneypot, his melodic tune piercing the usual monotonous twittering to which Patrick was accustomed and probing his sleep-clogged mind.

'The sound of summer,' he sighed, shifting the position of his long legs which he could never totally straighten in this cramped bed. 'Would that I had a little gun – I'd shoot the bloody thing.'

'Now just because yer've been cheated of yer slice o'Sunday comfort don't go taking it out on t'poor little bird.' Thomasin snuggled up to him, laying her palm upon his chest, and felt the heat burn deep into her hand. Their bodies became gummed together in the sultry morning.

'Little bird my eye,' complained her husband. 'By the sound he's making he must be the size of a turkey. An' the varmint's been twittering up there for an hour or more. Sure, I'd like to go up there an' pull off all his feathers one by one.'

Thomasin chuckled and rubbed his chest. 'By, it's gonna be another scorcher today.' She pulled away, sucking in her breath as their skin broke the sweaty vacuum. 'Well, I suppose I'd best get up; if I turn over I'm bound to sleep in.'

'Ah, don't go, muirnin!' He caught her wrist and pulled her against him. 'Can't ye feel I'm aching for ye? Just a quick one. There's not a sound out there; we'll not be late for work. Come on, Tommy, just five minutes won't harm.'

She buried her face in the muscles of his shoulder, inhaling the sharp scent of him. 'You're a randy old devil.'

Her fingers excited him and he groaned. 'Ah, I know 'tis horse-whipped I should be, but I can't leave ye alone.' He shuffled round to face her. Gusts of heat rose from the blankets and he threw them off impatiently. 'God, will ye ever look at the woman,' he breathed, propping himself on his palms and gazing down at her glowing body. 'A veritable goddess – a Venus. A body like a young girl's – an' her all of five and sixty.' He howled as she wound her fingers into his pubic curls. 'Ah, Jesus I was only coddin' ye!' He collapsed on top of her as she released him with an admonishing moue. 'Woman, ye get wickeder with age. See the tears ye've brung to me eyes?'

'Then I'll have to make it better, won't I?' she murmured sensuously.

A muffled complaint rose from beneath the bedclothes in the adjoining room. 'For pity's sake, our kid, will ye stop doing that? How's a fella to get any sleep while you're shaking t'bed as if yer've got St Vitus' Dance!'

Richard Feeney gave a low, shuddering sigh of release, then tugged his shirt down. 'Sure, I'm sorry if I've offended his lordship, but what with all that grunting an' groaning in there I just grew a stalk.'

'Yer disgusting,' grumbled his brother John, who was always referred to as Sonny. 'There's no need for it.'

'Hah! I like that,' exclaimed Dickie, then clapped a hand

10

over his mouth as he realised he had shouted. He lowered his voice. 'You're as bad as the rest of us – if not worse.'

Sonny did not answer. This was a sensitive subject for him. He knew that it was a sin to spill one's seed on the ground – though perhaps bedclothes didn't count? Father Kelly was very strong on self-abuse; it could do terrible things to a boy, he said. For a long time after Sonny's first experimentation the boy had examined his palm at frequent intervals for any sign of growth, and could recall only too well the terrible apprehensive prickle every time somebody asked him a question which he couldn't quite catch – *Mother o' God I've gone deaf!* Even after the gradual realisation that his physical and mental well-being was unimpaired by these nocturnal crimes his guilt remained unassuaged.

His brother nudged him. 'Come on, let's have a contest to see who can get the biggest.' He pushed the covers down to his knees.

Sonny immediately tugged them back into place. 'Ye'll burn in Hell! Ye'll deform yerself!'

'Sure, ye don't believe all that clap, do ye?' The accent was a curious amalgamation of Yorkshire and Irish – the product of a mixed marriage and shared by them both – but in Dickie it was the Irish which was predominant. He tucked his hands beneath his head and stared resignedly at the ceiling where a spider kept lowering itself on a slender thread, beleaguered by indecision. His tone was somewhat scathing. 'Course, I don't suppose you get the same urges as me – not having had a woman, like. Jaze, 'tis awful painful for a man to have to listen to those two in there when he's not had a woman himself for ages.'

To be precise, it was exactly twelve hours since fourteen year old Dickie had made his first conquest – if such a word could be ascribed to his inexperienced fumblings.

'I still don't believe ye about that,' muttered Sonny, rubbing the sleep from his eye-corners. 'Yer wouldn't be so tight-lipped if ye'd really done it. Ye keep crowing and strutting but yer not very forthcoming with the details, are

11

ye?' He kept his voice low in order that his sister, who slept behind the curtained partition, might not overhear.

Dickie grinned wickedly and curled his long Irish upper-lip. 'Sure, I can't be getting too basic, can I? You're far too young.'

'Dammit!' Sonny was fully awake now, brimming with the lust for enlightenment. 'I'm only a year and a bit younger than yourself. Come on, Dick, be a sport – I'll thump ye!' he added threateningly, at his brother's soft laughter.

Dickie's blue eyes closed in ecstasy as he journeyed into his memory. His lashes curled long and dark upon the sun-toasted cheek, so thick and abundant like the sweep's brush that pops from the chimneypot. 'Ah, Sonny,' he sighed, wriggling his bottom into the mattress. 'Can ye imagine every Christmas, all your birthdays and holy days, Mam's ginger parkin an' all yer favourite things wrapped into one? Well, that's what it's like. 'Tis like ... ah! ... drowning, I suppose; drowning in pleasure, till ye don't know which way is up. Or being held upside down so's all the blood rushes to your head; or when ye think old Bacon Neck is going to catch up wi' ye and slit your throat an' yer legs all turn to jelly.'

Sonny wasn't interested in analogies. 'But what's it really like? What d'ye *do*?'

'Ah, now that's for you to find out, little boy,' smiled Dickie patronisingly.

There was a frantic creaking from their parents' room, followed by a short period of silence, then the sound of their mother and father going downstairs. Sonny turned away abruptly from his brother and pummelled the pillow. 'A pox on ye! Anyroad, you're not so clever even if you have done it, 'cause Bertha Sunday goes with anyone – she's the communal mare.'

'Ah, now you're jealous!' laughed Dickie. 'I'll wager she wouldn't let you do it to her.'

'I wouldn't touch her with a barge pole,' scoffed the more discerning Sonny. 'Sure, ye can get all sorts o' nasty

12

things from people like her, I'm told. I prefer to steer clear of her sort an' confine my attentions to the ladies.'

Dickie smirked, pulled the covers over Sonny's head and broke wind. 'Mm! Sweet as a nun's drawers.'

'You're the filthiest pig I ever met!' Sonny pressed his heels against Dickie's back and ejected him from the bed to land with a thud on the well-worn rug.

Dickie dusted himself off, laughing, and tugged on his trousers and stockings. He padded over to the window and pulled aside the curtain, allowing the sun to stream in and coat the room with a golden warmth. ''Tis a grand class of a day; not the sorta day to waste on workin'.' He dropped the curtain and the sun reverted to its muted glow. After tucking in his shirt he cupped his hands into the bowl of water that stood on the washstand and sloshed it onto his handsome face.

'Mind you don't get your face wet,' observed Sonny from the bed, then rolled over swiftly and sat for a few minutes on the edge of the mattress, waiting for the burning stars in his head to settle.

'Anyways,' said Dickie, from behind a towel, 'I don't know what ye expect to gain from me telling ye about my experiences – sure ye'll never get a woman with a skinny little thing like that. They'll think ye've got a loose thread hanging from the tail o' your shirt.'

Sonny glowered. His brother had a singular capacity for cutting remarks. 'I'd rather have me brain in me head than in me prick,' he answered haughtily and began to pull on his clothes.

Dickie chuckled and raced him to the staircase but Sonny, as usual, was there before him. From their appearance one would have imagined Sonny to be the elder – though not as tall as his brother he was a good deal heavier and always emerged the victor in feats of strength or stamina. Dickie may have been blessed with the looks, but Sonny was the strong one both in body and character. The dependable one.

Downstairs, in the back room where the fire crackled in the black-leaded range, the appetising smell of cooking teased their nostrils. There was something about this room despite its modest furnishing – a table and four chairs, a battered horsehair sofa, a couple of old armchairs, a stool and a rag rug – an aura of utter contentment and friendliness that made one feel at home the minute one entered.

Their mother was in the process of doling out five portions of breakfast and smiled as they sat beside their father at the table and again a few minutes later when their half-sister, Erin, appeared. 'We are all bright and early this morning. I think somebody must've slipped summat in t'water. I've never known you boys up before your sister.'

Erin, neat and prim in her blue cotton dress, her black hair plaited into a crown and her complexion a blend of buttermilk and roses, scraped a stool up to the table and carved a slice of bread from the loaf. ''Twould be all the same if I'd wanted a lie-in,' she complained. 'I get no peace nor privacy from these two. God knows what they were at this morning but there was a terrible amount o' giggling going on.' The boys glanced at each other.

Patrick looked up as his wife placed a helping of fried bread and egg before him. Dear Tommy, her hair had lost none of its lustre despite the tribulations they had all heaped upon her – though perhaps there was just a hint of silver at the temples, making one remember that she had been forty-one years on this earth. Tiny wrinkles and character lines had begun to appear on the small face, but could in no way detract from the vivacity that so attracted the opposite sex; rather they added to her handsomeness.

He bowed his head and offered a prayer of thanks for the food he and his family were about to eat, then set upon his meal, spearing the yolk and painting his bread with gold. Funny, how the sight of a good meal always plunged him deep into the past, to the blackened putrid fields of his homeland, the months of famine, of dining on nettles, grass – anything. That was why he always made his prayer of gratitude for the happy, well-fed times they lived in now, marvelling at his stubborn inability to keep faith with his Catholicism during those famine years – and for a long time afterwards come to that. The maturity of his forty-seven years had brought him even closer to the God he had once denied.

He chewed thoughtfully and looked into each of their faces. Erin, with her raven-haired beauty and great eyes the colour of a Mayo sky, was the image of her dead mother, her face etched in the same delicate piquancy. At twenty she was still unmarried and showed no inclination to be so – though not for the want of admirers. Patrick had seen the way the young men looked at his daughter. But it would be a lucky man who got past the Irishman's stringent inspection.

He opened his mouth for another section of fried bread and turned his attention to Sonny. Despite the fact that he and his younger son were often at loggerheads, Patrick never doubted his love nor respect. He would make a fine man. His shoulders were well on the way to being as broad as his father's – though in looks there was not a drop of paternal blood in him. The red hair, the candid grey eyes and the generous mouth were all inherited from the boy's mother. Perhaps that was why Patrick felt so strongly for him – because of his son's resemblance to the woman he loved. Once, years ago, Sonny had been the one to bring them together when they had believed their marriage to be irretrievably shattered: he had staged a fake accident in the hope that their meeting over his inert body would rekindle their affection, but Fate had instituted a real one, nearly killing him in the process. He had succeeded in reuniting his parents but had almost paid for it with his life – a fact which neither Patrick nor Thomasin ever forgot. How childish they had both been then. How young and selfish, indifferent, he himself must have seemed. He hoped he had matured a lot since then.

His other son was a different proposition altogether. As handsome, sleek and slippery as an otter, his eyes held an invariable mixture of laughter and guile. He would stand oh, so contritely while being reprimanded for some fall from grace, then off he'd be like a wayward colt with a toss of his dark, crisply-haired head. Patrick felt a vague

15

unease about this beautiful son of his. Perhaps it was the beauty itself that made him balk, for no man should be so fair of face. People had remarked on how like his father the boy was, but whilst Patrick was undoubtedly handsome, his son had some strange extra quality about him. It was as though, thought Patrick, the fairies had been witness at his birth and had touched him with their magic, bestowing upon the child the power to charm and endear himself to all he encountered. But for all his assets Dickie would never be half the man his brother was. He used his endowments to attain his own ends. Patrick knew this, for did the boy not employ those same tactics on himself?

Thomasin finally sat down to her own meal. 'What's on the agenda for today, then?' she enquired of no one in particular.

'I'll be working up Fulford today,' supplied her husband. 'So I may or may not get home for dinner.'

'Aye, well I'll pack plenty of snap so yer can take yer choice.'

'I wish I could,' said Erin. 'It'll be the same as any other day for me: do that, Miss Feeney, do this, Miss Feeney, have you made quite sure that the tables all have clean cloths? We cannot have the customers dining on soiled linen *can* we, Miss Feeney? No, Mrs Bradall, kiss my bum, Mrs Bradall.'

Erin finished her meal and carried her plate to the scullery to rinse it. For the past five years she had been employed as a waitress in a small café in the centre of York – though how she had been able to endure it for so long was due more to her persevering nature than any affection for her employers. The work was almost as tiring and monotonous as when she had been a scullery maid at the Cummings' household, and the manageress as lazy and supercilious a person as one could wish not to meet.

She stood in a dream at the sink, wondering what they would be doing at the Cummings' house now, remembering Miss Caroline as a child and the lessons they had taken together. That had been the happiest part of her employment, the lessons, but they had brought with them

16

a complacency. She had imagined they would last forever and of course they hadn't; they had lasted only as long as Mrs Cummings remained unaware of what was going on. When that time ended, Erin was made to realise that the friendship she had thought belonged to her and Caroline was nothing more than a novelty to the latter and a pipe-dream on her part.

'Away, lass! Stop woolgatherin', you're going to be late!' Thomasin's words cut through her daydreaming and she went to take a last minute inspection of herself in the mirror over the range before setting off for another dreary day at the café. Where now was the dream she had once prized of becoming a governess?

Patrick, too, made ready for work, pulling on his dusty jacket and lime-caked boots. He encircled his spouse's waist as she tied a knot in the cloth which held his lunch, and planted a kiss on top of her head on his way through the back door. When the clomp of heavy boots across the yard had died away, Thomasin started to side the table, then addressed Dickie, who sat, now that his father was gone, in Patrick's chair with his feet propping up the range. 'Hadn't you better be makin' a move an' all?'

'In a minute,' he mumbled from behind the newspaper.

'Now!' She slapped his long legs, sending his feet bumping onto the fender. 'An' no nippin' into that Mrs Cesspit's or whatever her name is.'

'Nesbitt,' corrected Dickie, unperturbed by her reprimand. He hunched over to pull on his boots.

'Aye, well I reckon first name's more apt, things I've been hearin' about her from Miss P. You stay away from her, 'cause I shall hear about it yer know if yer in there for more than five minutes.'

'Sure, an' what would I be wantin' with a fat old besom like herself?' His Irish ancestry always sprang to the fore whenever he wanted to cajole. 'An' me a foine specimen o' manhood.' He bounced to his feet and twined his arm around her. 'Now, if she was as goodlookin' as me mother . . .'

'Aye, well just mind yer helm, blatherskite,' warned his

mother, immune to some extent from his charm. 'Yer gerrin' too clever by half.' She reached up to fasten the top button of his shirt. 'Good grief! Look at the muck on your chest. Stand there while I get scrubbin' brush.'

'That's not muck!' Dickie was offended. ''Tis hair. I'm a man now, ye know. Look at that.' He pulled down his shirt, causing his mother to put a hand to her cheek in mock surprise.

'Good Lord, so it is! By, there must be at least, ooh . . . half a dozen hairs there.'

Dickie knocked away her exploratory hand with a snort and unhooked his jacket from the peg, slinging it over his arm.

'Goodness knows where yer get that lot from,' added Thomasin, beginning to pile the crockery in the stone sink. 'Yer father's chest is as smooth as a baby's bum.'

Dickie could not resist getting his own back. 'Ah, I reckon ye must've had a secret admirer then, Mam.'

'What! By, just you let yer father hear that – he'll knock yer into t'middle o' next week.' She gave him a playful cuff round the ear. 'Now off to work.'

'I'll walk down wi' yer.' Sonny leapt up and grabbed his jacket.

Thomasin placed her hands on her hips. 'Godfrey Norris! Are yer sure yer feelin' all right? I've never known yer so eager for school. Yer'll be hangin' around for ages before t'bell goes.'

Sonny, eager to milk the details of the previous evening from his brother, replied that he liked to be in good time. Though he did not particularly enjoy school as such, this was the only way in which he could gain access to so many beautifully illustrated books, from which he would attempt to duplicate the pictures when the kindly Brother Francis allowed him to bring them home. Painting had always been his passion. He had amassed quite a few pictures now with the aid of his modest box of paints. If nothing else they helped hide the cracks on the bedroom walls. Hurriedly, he donned his cap and followed Dickie out into

18

the street where they mingled with the masses on their way to work.

'Well – are ye goin' to tell me about Bertha or not?' he demanded when the other remained unduly silent. Dickie never did have much to say on a morning but today Sonny felt the silence was cultured deliberately to provoke him.

Dickie chewed the inside of his cheek to prolong the agony. 'Eh, I don't know whether I ought to, Son – I mean, you're a bit young, aren't ye, to be learnin' my bad ways.'

'All right, cleverclogs, be like that! Just wait till ye want me to do anything for you.' Sonny forged ahead, then called over his shoulder, 'Any road, I know all about it really. I was just testin' ye to see if ye were lyin'.'

'Gerraway!' scoffed Dickie. 'Ye wouldn't know where to put it.'

'Course I do,' contradicted Sonny and waited for his brother to catch up.

'Tell us, then,' challenged Dickie.

'There y'are, yer don't know yerself, that's why ye wanted me to tell ye. Ye haven't done it at all, yer just showin' off.'

'Ah, now you're tryin' to rile me so I'll tell ye,' laughed Dickie. 'Well, it won't wash.'

They had reached the school gates and Sonny stepped inside, peering sullenly through the iron bars like something in a menagerie. His brother marched on, whistling blithely. 'Any road, yer don't have to tell me!' he shouted after Dickie. 'Any fool knows yer stick it in her bellybutton.' He stamped off into the deserted schoolyard and tried to blot out his brother's derisive merriment as Dickie proceeded on his way.

Perhaps, the older boy reflected, it was unfair to keep Sonny in the dark. After all, his brother had always defended him whenever he got himself into an awkward corner. He decided that he would tell Sonny when they met at lunchtime – though maybe not the full story.

CHAPTER TWO

He had noticed her slyly watching him at the travelling fair which had stopped for a couple of days outside the city walls. It was only a modest version of the huge annual fairs that were normally held in the middle of town, but nevertheless the shooting gallery had given him the opportunity to show his prowess to his friends – and more importantly, to the girls. She had pretended to be unimpressed by his marksmanship, making out that she was deep in conversation with her companion and absently sifting the contents of her reticule – at the same time making sure he was still watching her. Later, when she and her friend wandered back to the city, Dickie and his partner had shadowed them, tormenting the girls with the tickling brushes they had purchased – lengths of wire bound with strands of gaily-coloured wool. Their victims had feigned affrontery at first, but soon, after a few choice compliments from Dickie, they had paired off and both couples had gone their separate ways.

Bertha, although only seventeen, had her own apartment quite nearby and invited him to accompany her there. He did this eagerly, but could not help wondering what her reaction would be when she discovered he had no money. For he knew what Bertha was – her name cropped up frequently in the sniggering conferences he shared with his friends and he had often puzzled over it. Sunday – what sort of a name was that?

Bertha Sunday had soon come to realise, when she was old enough to leave the orphanage that had been her home since birth, that the most profitable way to earn a living was with her body. As bodies went it was not such a bad one – which was just as well, for her face would never have kept her from the workhouse door. Her eyes were

20

of a nondescript colour, situated too close together above a nose that looked to have been modelled from clay and stuck on as an afterthought. The mouth below held little appeal, apart from housing a full set of incredibly-white teeth, ever ready to flash an encouraging smile at a prospective customer. Also, the outfit she wore today did scant credit to her figure, but at least it was clean and neatly-pressed.

Despite her lack of beauty, Bertha was never short of clients, preferring to select them from the middle classes, men who could afford to pay generously for their pleasure. She had seen how the majority of her peers – less selective girls who had underpriced themselves – had ended up, and it was not going to happen to her. Unlike them, she had no bully-boy to answer to; therefore if, like today, she spotted a handsome face and felt like forgoing the payment and indulging herself, she was quite at liberty to do so.

They skirted the grim walls of York Castle and sauntered into Castlegate towards a notorious brothel district. The buildings here were dilapidated, the people seedy and unkempt. There was a certain effluvium about the place, but Dickie seemed unconcerned at entering an environment which was pretty much like his own and chattered happily in his boastful manner about his prowess with the ladies.

She curled her lips at his assuredness. 'It's funny I've never heard your name mentioned if you're that popular.'

'I've heard of you, though,' he replied suggestively.

Her smile began to look a little fixed and she turned her face away. Wasn't this always the outcome? She had hoped this boy could make her forget about her profession, for a little while at least. 'And just what have you heard?' She tried to make her voice sound casual.

The arm that encircled her waist pulled her closer. 'That ye like to do it.'

She turned back to face him, her expression blank. 'Do what?'

'You know.' He still wore the confident grin.

'But I'm sorry, I don't. What d'you mean?'

21

His self-assuredness collapsed. 'Well, er, you know, er . . .' he nodded exaggeratedly. 'Ye know!'

'You keep sayin' I know – I don't know.' She pretended to grapple with his words for some time, then a look of understanding flooded her face. 'Oh! You must mean indoor games,' she exclaimed, a gleam in her eye.

'Aye – that's it, indoor games.' Mentally he rubbed his hands.

'Oh yes, I'm quite fond of those,' said Bertha nonchalantly as they turned off Castlegate into one of the Water Lanes which ran down to the Ouse.

Dickie now started to show slight apprehension. There were some odd characters about. He jumped as an old slattern popped out of the shadows and leered drunkenly into his face, choking him with gin fumes.

Bertha seemed unaffected. 'Go find yer own Roger, Sall,' she told the street-walker. 'This'n's mine.' She gripped Dickie's arm. 'Stay close by me, you'll be all right.'

'I'm not afraid,' replied Dickie unconvincingly. He eyed a rough-looking man who was sharpening a knife on a doorstep. Indeed, his eyes were busy taking in all the sights and sounds. Overhead, the doxies called to one another from their tenement windows. Shifty-eyed pimps lounged across doorways, waiting for the sun to go down and business to begin in earnest. A couple rutted in a shadowy corner, a pair of grimy ankles locked around an ill-clad back.

Bertha had stopped. Dickie looked up wonderingly at the tall house. 'Is this all yours?'

She smiled. 'No, just two rooms – an' soon as I've saved enough money I'll be out of it an' all, to a more respectable district, Dringhouses maybe. You been there?' He shook his head. 'S'lovely. I don't normally bring me friends back here; we usually go to a tavern or someplace. This slum'd scare the pants off anyone – but I reckoned you didn't look the type to mind it.'

At the top of the first flight of stairs she fished a key from her purse and unlocked a door. It opened onto an oddly-shaped but comfortably-furnished room. Not a whore's room at all, thought Dickie, quite tasteful in fact, notwithstanding the damp and peeling walls. The curtains and upholstery were in a matching Regency stripe and the furniture, though quite scarred from age, had been well-chosen to give the room a hint of elegance. The bed in the corner added just the right touch to make one feel at home, and the empty beerbottle on the table took the edge off the rather unnerving ambience her attempt to good taste had created. There was one odd thing he noticed: there were no photographs on the mantelshelf. How strange, for almost everyone he knew, however poor, had at least one picture of the family.

She slipped out of her jacket. 'Right, shall we get down to it?'

He couldn't believe his luck. 'That's fine by me.'

'Good!' she said brightly, then disconcerted Dickie by moving in the opposite direction to withdraw a large box from a cupboard, prising off the lid. 'Now, which d'you prefer? Checkers, chess or, more fittingly, brag?'

'What?' He stared uncomprehendingly at the pack of cards she held.

'Didn't your mother tell you it's rude to say what? And you did say you liked to play indoor games, didn't you?'

His disappointment was acute. 'But I didn't mean . . . I thought . . .'

She slammed the lid noisily onto the box, sweetness and light vanished. 'Aye – I know bloody-well what you thought! You thought you were gonna get something else, didn't you? All full of self-importance. Cock o' the North, droolin' like a randy dog. Well, all right, fella-me-lad, you can have your bit o' fun.' His face brightened. '*If* – she emphasised the word – 'if you've got a sovereign.'

'A sovereign? Why, 'tisn't worth more'n five bob – an' dear at that.'

'Why, you little pinchfist! You'd not even get a sniff for five bob. I doubt you've even got half o' that, have you?' Scornful eyes raked him.

Bludgeoned down to size he shook his head and looked at his boots to hide his bitterness. The bitch. The teasing, tantalising bitch. She had known all along that he had no money.

'Well, you didn't think you were gonna get it for nowt, did you?' she asked incredulously. Dickie gave no answer, still smarting over her dirty trick. 'I can tell by your face that you did! Now let me tell you something, young man: you'll never get anywhere in life if you're always expecting summat for nowt.' There was a badtempered crease between her eyes. ''Specially not wi' me!' Though she had never intended to take any payment and would not contemplate his leaving even now, his arrogance badly needed planing.

Dickie decided that he was not going to take this from the likes of her; treating him as dirt when she was little better. He swivelled on his heel and strutted to the door. 'Have it your own way, but ye don't know what you're missing. I'll have ye know there's plenty would pay *me* a sovereign.'

'Oh aye, still bragging, are we?' She folded her arms under her plump bosom and challenged him. 'All right, then – show us! Give us a demonstration o' these manly charms an' let an expert be the judge.'

His sulk was cast off like a dirty shirt. 'But what about the money?'

'I don't think it'll break me if I let you off this once. I mean, I don't want to miss such a good thing, do I? If what you've been telling me is right, that is.' She placed a hand on one hip and thrust it forward suggestively.

He grinned and ran his tongue over his dry lips. 'Of course it's true! Do I look like the kinda fella to tell a lie?' He moved over to her quickly before she had time to change her mind and placed a bold hand on her breast.

She stood motionless, gazing mockingly into his face as his lips pecked her cheek and his hands explored her, then asked, 'Well, what comes next, pray tell?'

The hand hesitated. 'We take our clothes off?'

'Very astute.' She began to unbutton her bodice, then paused to ask, 'You're sure now?'

Dickie wasn't sure of anything any more, but answered

24

in the affirmative. He slowly shrugged off his jacket, eyes growing wider as Bertha stepped out of her dress and folded it over a chair. His movements became slower and slower as she attained a state of nakedness, feeling his body respond accordingly as the marshmallow breasts burst free of her stays. She wore no unmentionables. He jumped as she asked if he was going to stand there all day and hurriedly stripped off his shirt. She smiled at his reluctance to remove his trousers and stepped forth to help him.

'I can do it!' He took a step back, suddenly embarrassed to let her see what her nudity had done to him.

'How old are you, Dickie?' she asked gently at the awkward fingering of his trouser buttons. Lying, he told her sixteen.

'Truthful now!'

'Oh, all right . . . fourteen – but I'm nearly fifteen!' he blustered.

'This is your first time, isn't it?'

He was about to lie again, but after a slight hesitation nodded. He looked so sorry for himself, standing there with his chin tucked into his chest, those long, dark lashes whispering his discomfiture, that tenderness stirred inside her. She put her arms around him and hugged him fondly. There was something about this boy that moved her, despite the brashness. Beneath that handsome face and the twinkle of youthful exuberance, something that made her want to cry – and Bertha could never recall having cried in her life.

She patted her hands against his back, then pulled away and said softly, 'Come on, love, I'll show you what it's all about. But first,' she produced a sympathetic smile, 'will you rinse yourself off in that bowl? Forgive me, but I have to ask. I have my business to consider, you see.'

He hesitated at the bowl, unsure, embarrassed. She smiled reassuringly again and helped him.

His friends had never told him, in their furtive sniggerings, that it would be like this. He allowed her to take the lead, for he didn't know where he was going, felt himself drawn into the warm, clinging flesh that seemed to suck

25

him in and devour him. She could not have fit him better had she been made to measure; a moist, silken glove. She moved beneath him just once and it was all over. Bright lights burst across his eyes as he exploded in noisy accompaniment to her pleased chuckle.

'Surprised you, did it?'

He muttered his answer into the soft flesh of her shoulder. Then, still trying to collate his senses, he propped himself on his elbows, clasping his hands across her chest and looked down pensively into her face. There was now another facet to the expression she had read in his eyes: a gleam of triumph, of discovered manhood. 'Bertha?'

'That's me name.'

'Well, that's what I wanted to ask you about – your name; not Bertha, I mean your surname. 'Tis an odd sorta name, Sunday.'

'Aye, as odd as the bugger that gave it to me,' sighed Bertha, shifting her body beneath him and stroking his back. 'By, a right old bastard he was. The bloke in charge o' the orphanage I'm on about. I've seen him take a stick to one o' the lads and knock him near senseless for summat so paltry I can't even recall what it was. An' yet with us girls he was almost human, takin' the little uns on his knee to comfort their tears.' She laughed without amusement. 'Though if his missus had caught him doing his comfortin' she'd've given him a thrashin'. It taught me though, showed me that he weren't alone in his need for "comfortin'". I soon came to see that all men are the same – that's how I came to be in this lark. Not that I've been in it all that long, mindst; couple o' years in all. I came here from Leeds after I got done once too often for indecency – tut! I'm getting off the track: you asked me how I got the name. Well, it's simple: Sunday was the day some kind soul found me on a rubbish pile and took me to the orphanage.'

He felt he ought to say something. 'I'm sorry.' Though he wasn't. All he could think about was that which he had just experienced.

26

'No need.' She brightened and cupped his face between her hands. 'So, the boy's a man, is he? Tell me what it feels like.'

He grinned and wiggled on top of her. 'Terrific.'

'Well, I shouldn't get too cocky about it,' she dampened his enthusiasm. 'You're not much cop when it comes to pleasin' a lady – too quick, you see. Still,' she whispered, nibbling his earlobe, 'I reckon we could make summat useful out of you if we tried. Have you time for another?'

His face lit up. 'I've time for six more at least.'

'Quality, dear, not quantity,' said Bertha firmly. 'You young coves are all the same – never think a girl likes to enjoy herself an' all. A few quick thrusts an' you're there. Let me show you how to really please a lady.'

He was quick to learn. She sighed with pleasure as he practised what she'd taught and thrust her pink tongue deep into his ear. He was reminded of the sound of the sea whispering in the whelk shell on that one lovely day his father had taken them to the seaside, with the hot sun and the tang of salt, thrusting his fingers into the warm gritty sand . . . but there was nothing gritty here. Hot like the sun, yes, but smooth, smooth as melted butter, like dipping one's fingers into the secret rockpools with their dark recesses, not knowing what one might find.

After a convulsive shudder Bertha relaxed. 'I'll say this, boy, you're no dunce.' Affecting an approbatory grin she pushed him onto his back and straddled his knees with fleshy thighs. He tried to pull her on top of him. 'Ah, no!' she laughed, her teeth shining white as the sheets. 'It isn't often I get myself a succulent young virgin to pleasure me. You, my lad, are going to get the full treatment.' And as her smiling mouth folded itself around the part of him that least expected it, Dickie closed his eyes and dreamed that every day which followed could be like this.

They slept afterwards and the sun was turning red when they awoke. She drew in a noisy breath. 'Christ, I'll have to be getting to work!' Then she stretched beneath him, cuddled up again and begged sleepily, 'Say summat nice before you go.'

He grinned sheepishly and rubbed his cheek against her breast. 'What shall I say?' He didn't want to go, feeling warm and sticky and content.

'Well, you could start by saying I'm pretty – even if I'm not.' She looked past his eyes to the ceiling as if seeing someone else there. She always seemed to be looking at ceilings while some unfeeling dolt pounded at her body. Fat ones, thin ones, fancy ones, plain ones – but never one like this; he was beautiful, really splendid. 'A girl doesn't like to feel used,' came the plaintive addition.

His fourteen year old mind could not yet conjure up the rousing phrases that were to come as second nature in years ahead. He told her in a brief, stumbling monologue how beautiful she was, using the lie to worm his way into her one more time. This was to be the pattern of his life.

Dickie emerged from his dream and entered the grocery store where he was employed, laughing to himself at Sonny's false assumption. Hah! Bellybuttons, was it? Poor Sonny, he would have to let him into the secret: all one had to do was to tell a girl she was pretty and she was yours for the taking.

CHAPTER THREE

Thomasin made to enter the store in Goodramgate which had been her place of work for the past eight years, then frowned as the door handle resisted her pressure. She shielded her eyes and peered into the darkened shop. How strange – Mr Penny was usually there by the time she arrived. Not to worry though, the old man, having great trust in his assistant, had issued a spare set of keys for such an occurrence. Selecting the right one she inserted it into the rusting lock and gave a sharp twist.

Inhaling the aromatic tang of rosemary and sage, bayleaf

and dried fruit, she reversed the 'Closed' sign and hung up her shawl. After this she used another of the keys to unlock the safe and withdraw the day's float which she put in the till. This done, she positioned herself behind the counter, donned a fresh apron from her basket and awaited the first customer. The store was of reasonable size, but the vast jumble of bins and cases, stone jars and bottles that Mr Penny insisted on stocking made it appear smaller than it actually was. 'If you throw it away there's bound to be somebody ask for it,' he had always replied to her frequent enquiries as to the purpose of some little-sought-after item. So, the odd assortment had stayed, building up with every year that passed, to hamper any attempt she might cherish of converting the store into some sort of order. Everything was so drab. Around the counter leaned sacks of currants, raisins, assorted nuts, chests of tea, everything dark and uninspiring, apart from the smell. It could be a really depressing situation, thought Thomasin, were it not for the cheery presence of her employer – where on earth was he?

The bell above the door jangled as the first customer arrived. 'Good morning, Mrs Ramsden!' Thomasin greeted the matronly, silver-haired woman. 'Looks like it's gonna be another mafter today.' A desultory conversation followed. When the cost was tallied Mrs Ramsden surrendered her payment, saying, 'Where's His Excellency this morning?'

Thomasin chuckled. 'He's probably having a sleep-in. Had one too many last night I shouldn't wonder. Mindst, he deserves it, he's gettin' on yer know. He'll be seventy-two next week.'

'He never is!' declared Mrs Ramsden. 'By, doesn't time fly? It only seems like last week he was telling me he was sixty-five.'

'It probably was,' replied Thomasin with a grin. 'He's always knockin' years off his age. Every time he has a birthday he takes another five years off.' She counted out the woman's change. Another customer entered and joined the conversation. 'Eh, you wouldn't think he was that old!

Wears well, doesn't he?' She hooked a finger over her lower lip as Mrs Ramsden left. 'Now then, what did I come in for? I get talking and it completely leaves my head.'

'You should make a list,' suggested Thomasin.

'I did – but I forgot that an' all,' joked the woman. 'Oh aye! that was it – treacle. ' She handed over a container.

Thomasin made use of a small step-ladder to reach the treacle and, holding the earthenware jar beneath it, operated the tap. 'D'yer know, I'm gettin' a bit worried about Mr Penny; he's normally 'ere by this time. I hope he isn't poorly.' The jar filled, she raised the hem of her skirt in order not to trip over it on her descent.

'I shouldn't worry over much,' replied Mrs Aysgarth calmly. 'As you said, he's gettin' on a bit, he's mebbe overslept.'

'Happen,' mused Thomasin. 'All t'same, if he isn't in by dinnertime I think I'll nip round an' see he's all right.'

Towards elven o'clock Thomasin, her tongue like a piece of dried leather, pulled aside the curtain, went through to the back room and picked up the kettle. The rush of water onto metal obliterated the sound of the shop bell as someone entered. She set the kettle to boil on a small stove, her back to the curtain while she selected a mug from the shelf, humming to herself.

'Excuse me.' The deep voice startled her and she spun round, juggling with the mug until it finally evaded capture and fell to the floor.

'Godfrey Norris!' she exclaimed at the uniformed figure who had pushed aside the curtain. 'What yer tryin' to do – gimme a seizure?'

'Beg pardon,' apologised the constable. 'Didn't mean to frighten you.'

Thomasin, suddenly filled with dread, left the mug where it had shattered. 'Eh, hang on! What's up? Is it me husband? Has owt happened to me bairns?'

The police officer reassured her as he took off his helmet and placed it on a shelf. 'But I do have a bit of bad news; it's about your employer, Mr Arnold Penny . . .

Would you care to sit down?' He waited until she had seated herself on a stool, the only piece of furniture in the room which was little more than a cupboard really.

'He's dead, isn't he?'

He nodded, relieved that she had guessed. Of all the duties that he had to perform this was one he loathed; the breaking of bad news. He left her to fumble in her pocket for a handkerchief while he arrested the steaming kettle and filled the teapot.

'When?' she asked, unable to find a handkerchief and wiping her eyes on a corner of her apron.

He searched for two more mugs, gave the pot a noisy stir and poured the tea. 'He appears to've died some time yesterday evening or very early this morning. One of his neighbours got worried when his curtains stayed closed. She sent for us and we had to break in. He must've died in his sleep. So, you needn't worry, he never suffered.' He used his boot to scrape the shards of pottery into a pile.

'I'm glad about that,' she sniffed. 'He was a grand old fella. A good friend.' A sudden thought struck her. 'Eh, there's all Thursday's takings still in t'safe; d'yer think I'd better bank it?'

He sipped his tea. 'I should, if you know the procedure.'

'Oh aye – I do all t'books an' that. I more or less run t'shop on me own come to that.' She sat upright. 'That's another thing: what's gonna happen to me?' The selfishness of her question pinkened her cheeks but the policeman seemed not to notice.

'I expect Mr Penny's relatives will sort all that out when we manage to find 'em – you don't know where we might get in touch with them, do you? We couldn't find any mention of next of kin when we searched his effects, that's why you're one of the first to know.'

'As far as I know he hasn't got any. No one at all.' She sighed, as much for herself as for her dead employer. What would she do for a job now?

'Well, if that's the case,' said the constable, 'I'd continue as normal until someone tells you otherwise. I imagine his executors will contact you sooner or later.' Wiping the ends of his moustache he pushed aside the curtain and stepped into the main body of the shop. Thomasin thanked him for his kindness and showed him out, then slumped back onto her stool to shed a few more tears for the loss of her old friend. The remainder of the morning was taken up with explanations of Mr Penny's absence to enquiring customers. She was therefore relieved when both hands of the clock pointed skywards and she was able to lock up for lunch. As she hurried home she wondered how Pat would accept the news that they would be one wage short very soon.

'Miss Feeney, did I or did I not request that you take a pot of tea to table three?' Mrs Bradall's pretentious articulation came as an added burden in this damnable heat. Erin rolled her eyes as she turned to voice her reply.

'Mrs Bradall, I only have the one pair o' hands! You've just this minute asked me to see to table four.'

'And now I am asking you to attend table three also,' commanded the sour-faced woman. 'Will you please do as you are told?'

With a resentful sigh Erin placed a pot of tea, a jug of milk and another of hot water on a tray alongside two cups and saucers, then rattled her way across to table three.

The café was housed in a medieval building which, with its low ceiling and uneven floor, did not make for very pleasant working surroundings – especially in mid-summer. The tables were cramped together in order to fit as many as possible into the limited space and more than once Erin had been chastised for elbowing a customer on the head as she carried her tray backwards and forwards to the primitive kitchen. There was little respite from the open window; the lace curtain dripped lankly to the sill. The stifling climate affected both customer and staff alike.

The occupants of table three halted their conversation as Erin placed the items on their table. 'We ordered coffee,' complained one of the women, glaring at the teapot. Erin gave an unconvincing smile. It had been the most infuriating morning; at some point she was bound to blow. 'I'm dreadfully sorry, madam. I'll go and fetch it straight away.' Mrs Bradall stood at the entrance to the kitchen and watched Erin's stormy approach.

'They didn't want tea, they ordered coffee!' hissed the girl accusingly as she brushed past.

Mrs Bradall tucked in her chin and followed Erin into the kitchen. 'Then you should have paid attention to what I said.'

Erin rounded on her. The woman's dour-faced authoritarianism was just too much on a day like this. 'I like that! You told me . . .'

'Kindly do not take that tone with me!' exclaimed her superior, a hint of her Glaswegian ancestry slipping through the precise enunciation.

Erin deliberately turned her back and began to make a pot of coffee, pulling faces to herself.

'Miss Feeney, I have noticed for some time that you do not treat me with the respect that my position commands. Unless you change your attitude I'm afraid I shall have to dispense with your services.' Mrs Bradall had recovered her stature and switched back to her 'refeened' accent.

Erin bit back a rebellious retort and pranced hotly to table three to find that the customers had tired of waiting and had left. Oh, Jazers 'tis going to be one o' them sorta days, is it? sighed Erin to herself. As if it isn't bad enough listening to Mrs Bradall with her tartan voice moaning and wittering the customers are going to be awkward an' all.

'Miss! Miss!'

Here we go again, thought Erin grimly, but obeyed the summons and thankfully the pot of coffee she carried came in handy after all. She manipulated her shoulderblades beneath the sweat-dampened uniform. The material pulled away from the skin, then immediately clung again as she attended another table. She held her pad at the ready. Yes, what would madam require? A pot of arsenic? Sennapod wine? That should keep you on your toes.

'I would like a pot of tea for two – or would you like coffee, Annabel? No, tea would be more refreshing – and

33

a selection of pastries.' Erin was scribbling this down when the woman added sarcastically, 'If it is not too much trouble of course.' Returning the scathing expression Erin scribbled on her pad: six gallons of prune juice.

'Oh now, wait a moment, perhaps I would rather have coffee. Annabel, please help me, I do so hate making decisions.'

Annabel said that she would prefer tea. Erin looked back at the other woman who nodded and said, 'Yes ... yes, tea ... I think. Well, don't just stand there, girl, off you go!' Erin rushed off to the kitchen where an officious Mrs Bradall watched her every move. It had been absolute hell this morning with both of the other waitresses off sick – or supposedly sick. She could picture them sitting on the river bank dangling their toes in the water. But who could blame them? Mrs Bradall certainly extracted more than her fair share of their energies.

Having filled the teapot she returned to table six, puffing furiously at a wisp of hair that was stuck to her glistening nose and making her more irritable than ever. This heat magnified everything.

'I ordered coffee, I believe,' ejaculated the woman the moment Erin rested the tray on the table.

The girl frowned and consulted her notepad. 'No, I believe your last request was for tea.'

'I distinctly recall asking for coffee,' insisted the woman loudly. 'Annabel, did I or did I not ask for coffee?'

Annabel was quite sure that her partner did not, but Andrina Rowbotham was an extremely influential person; upset her and one would be wiped off the list of social engagements before one could blink. Annabel was not going to risk that for a grubby little waitress. 'You did, Andrina. I heard you quite plainly.'

'But tea is what I've got written here!' objected Erin. 'First ye wanted coffee then ye wanted tea, then ye wanted coffee then ye wanted tea – so that's what ye've got.'

The woman was livid at this backchat. 'Inform the management that I wish to make a complaint!'

'Can I be of assistance, madam?' Mrs Bradall had sidled

up and now fawned about the customer. Erin had visions of her bending to lick the woman's shoes.

'I sincerely hope there is someone in this establishment who can!' snorted the exasperated Andrina. 'This girl does not seem able to understand the most basic request. I ordered coffee and she has served tea.'

Erin refused to be browbeaten. 'She ordered tea! I have it written down here – look!'

'Miss Feeney, take it back to the kitchen and bring some coffee at once!' Mrs Bradall chivvied Erin away from the table, apologising profusely as she retreated backwards. Salaam, thought Erin disgustedly.

Back in the kitchen, the girl stood her ground. 'She did order tea, I know she did!'

'This is the second such mistake you've made this morning!' snapped her superior.

'That's not fair!' Erin slammed down the tray. 'The other one was your fault. I've been run off me feet this morning; there's only me to see to the tables. 'Tis all very well for you being hoity-toity when ye don't have to bother lifting a finger to help.'

'Miss Feeney, I do not like your tone.' Mrs Bradall hung onto her challenged superiority. 'I cannot be held responsible if the other girls don't turn up for work.'

'Well, then neither can I!' Erin ripped off her apron.

'What're you doing, girl?' cried the other in alarm.

Her vocal affectation had always irritated Erin, who now thrust the apron into the astounded woman's arms. 'I'll tell ye hhhwhat I'm doing!' she mimicked. 'I'm hoff, that's hhhwhat I'm doing.'

'Off?' Mrs Bradall reverted to her native accent. 'Wharrabootme? Ah'll nae be able tae see tae all this on ma ayn!'

'Whyever not?' asked Erin cuttingly. 'That's what ye seem to expect o' me. Ye've got two hands, haven't ye? And your head. That's room for three trays. If ye tie a duster on each foot and be very, very mindful o' them splinters on that broom ye'll be able to clean the floor at the same time.' With this she swept from the kitchen,

35

bubbling over with self-congratulation. It was high time someone knocked that one from her pedestal.

The pedant at table six accosted her as she squeezed past. 'And what, pray, has happened to our coffee?'

It may have been the heat, at least this was the excuse she would give later for her conduct, but all Erin saw now was an opportunity to wreak vengeance on all the customers who had ever mistreated her, using this one as a scapegoat for them all. She bent and whispered confidentially in the woman's ear, 'If I were madam I'd not be bothering whether 'tis tea or coffee ye get – what with the tomcat that pisses all over the kitchen they both taste pretty much alike. Enjoy your cakes.'

She giggled to herself as she emerged into the brilliant sunshine and pranced towards home. But the sobering thought soon came to her: what would her mother's reaction be when she heard the news?

CHAPTER FOUR

Dickie sang an Irish ditty as he trundled his handcart of groceries along Walmgate, peering alertly about him for a pretty face at which to direct his song. Shortly, he arrived at the penultimate delivery point of the morning – Mrs Nesbitt's. He wondered what she would have in store for him today, and the thought produced a grin. Ginger beer, rock cakes – or would today bring the reward that her eyes always offered? He lifted the brass knocker and tapped out his special code: rat, tat-tat-tat-tat, tat-tat!

Behind the door, Violet Nesbitt smoothed her clothes and took a last-minute look in the mirror before opening up. 'Why, it's young Master Feeney!' she exclaimed as if he were the last person she had been expecting. 'Do come in.' A most personable boy; she always looked forward to his visits. He was young, yes, but his complimentary chatter was most welcome to a woman on her own.

Dickie flashed his teeth and stepped through the doorway which opened directly onto the front parlour, a pleasant room, housing a high grade of furniture. The carpet, too, was of good quality and he politely wiped his boots before proceeding. Before him was a large mahogany circular table on which he knew he must not place the box of groceries but instead, as was usual, he carried it through to the kitchen. Once the box was out of his hands he took off his cap. 'I hope everything's to your satisfaction, Mrs Nesbitt?'

'I'm sure it will be, dear, it usually is. Now, sit down and I'll pour you a glass of refreshment; it's such a sticky day. What would you like?' She leaned towards him, the scent of violets drifting from the braided bodice of her dress. Her eyes rested briefly on the open neck of his shirt which he had adjusted to display the proof his virility. Mrs Nesbitt seemed suitably impressed. 'I think perhaps you're getting too big for ginger beer,' she decided. 'How would a glass of porter take your fancy?'

'Are ye trying to get me drunk, Mrs Nesbitt?' His recent exploits had made him bolder.

This new assuredness made her wonder whether it had been wise to offer alcohol. She sought to keep him in his place. 'What a thing to say, you cheeky boy!' Great emphasis was laid on the last word. Her hand inched towards the ginger beer.

'The porter will be fine,' he instructed firmly. She gave him a long look, then began to pour the ale.

She was quite a handsome woman, he decided, even if she was old – she must be at least thirty – and her sombre widow's weeds, heavily-draped with braid and tassels like a funeral hearse, could not hide the hourglass figure inside them. Her eyes, reflecting the colour of the violets she so lovingly nurtured in her windowbox, darted up occasionally to study him as she poured. Dickie took the drink from her, allowing his fingers to 'accidentally' brush against hers. He held the glass to his lips, then lowered it again.

'Mrs Nesbitt,' he tested the ground. 'Has anyone ever told ye that you're very pretty?'

My! he was growing up. 'Yes, as a matter of fact they have – quite often.'

Her answer threw him offbalance and he quickly raised the glass to his lips again. While he drank his mind searched for some other comment with which to ingratiate himself. Violet watched as he swallowed it down in deep, thirsty gulps. The glass drained, he placed it on the table and trained his eyes on her again. White froth dappled his upper lip and he curled out a pink tongue to lick it away.

The porter, consumed far too quickly, began to take effect. Dickie felt a new bravado flooding through him; it started in his chest where the liquid seemed to solidify into a burning concentration; it then spread down his arms into his fingertips, and from his legs to his toes. But he felt the effect most acutely in his head: a warm, happy feeling that made him want to say things he knew would get him hanged. His first request, however, was for another of the same.

She took in the flushed face, the added spark to his eye. 'You've had enough, young man. I don't know what your mother will think of me should you go home inebriated.' She reached over his shoulder to lift the empty glass from the table and as she did so, felt a warm pressure on her breast.

'I'll tell ye what she thinks of ye, Mrs Nesbitt – Violet,' whispered Dickie into her astonished ear. 'She thinks you're after havin' the trousers off me – an' I'm thinkin' she's right.'

Violet, her motion suspended by disconcertment, closed her eyes and a frantic argument took place inside her head. My God, it had been so long since anyone had touched her there; a man. But he's not a man, Violet, he's a child. What has got into you, allowing this to pass? But I want him. Don't be silly! Think of the scandal it would cause. Surely you could find someone nearer your own age? But no one will know! Oh, will they not? And what do you imagine will be the first thing he does when he leaves here? He'll go and tell all his friends. Think how you'll feel with all the neighbouring children queuing on your doorstep. Have you no shame, allowing a fourteen year old boy to behave so improperly?

With Violet's seeming reluctance to pull away, Dickie's confidence had swollen and now his hand began to trace the line of her curvaceous body, coming to rest on her hip. Unfortunately for Dickie this movement snapped Violet out of her trance. Looking into the face of the boy who was young enough to have been her son she felt a deep disgust with herself. The slap that she delivered to his face came so swiftly and so unexpectedly that he had no time to raise a protective arm. The fingers which had, a moment ago, been stroking her hip now flew up to his tingling cheek. His expression was one of surprise and accusation. Giving him no time in which to protest, she grasped him painfully by the ear, hauled him from the kitchen, through the parlour and shoved him from the house, slamming the door.

Shaken by his impromptu departure Dickie quickly picked himself up from the filthy gutter. He darted shame-faced glances about him, trying to ignore the pointed fingers of amused onlookers. With a token brush of his clothes he heaved his barrow towards his next port of call. The fervid air crept into every crevice of every courtyard, sucking up the wide variety of smells – rotting vegetables, rancid offal, dung, urine, people's midday meals – and forced the combined atrocity up his nasal cavities. Women! He would never understand them if he lived to be a hundred. He had been so sure about her . . .

Some time later, after depositing the final box of groceries, he returned to his base, the incident with Violet filed away at the back of his mind. 'Finished, Mr Hawksby!' he bawled as he burst through the door, setting the bell jingling furiously. 'Can I go for me dinner now?'

'One moment, young Feeney!' A grim-faced Mr Hawksby materialised from the back of the store, perching pince-nez on his Roman nose. 'I've just had Mrs Nesbitt round here.'

Oh, Jazers she's told him! Dickie's heart palpitated. The two-faced old witch. He tried to inject some neutrality into his reply. 'What did she want? Did I forget to give her something?'

'Don't play games wi' me, lad!' spluttered Hawksby, embellishing his whiskers with spittle. 'You tried to give her something she hadn't bargained for – an' we both know what that was.'

Dickie, realising the futility of denial, bore the accusation in silence, shuffling from one foot to the other.

'I can't have it, lad! I won't have you messin' around wi' my ladies.' The boy stifled a snigger and Hawksby crashed a fist onto the counter. 'And take that smirk off your face! I can't see owt to laugh at. You'll be getting me a bad name.' He began to march up and down in agitation, then swung round. 'What does it say above that doorway?' Dickie frowned and opened his mouth to speak but his answer was cut short. 'I'll tell you what it says!' Hawksby's whiskers were in danger of becoming swamped. 'It says: F. Hawksby, Grocer and Provision Merchant.' He started to walk away then spun back and wagged a finger under Dickie's nose. 'Not R. Feeney, Groper and Sedition Merchant.' He clasped his hands behind his back, tapping them impatiently. Tears of laughter formed in Dickie's eyes and he pressed his chin into his chest to try and contain a strangled laugh. 'Not funny, lad, not funny!' sprayed the grocer. 'You took advantage of a poor, helpless widow, abused her hospitality. I can't have such improprieties conducted in my employ. You've besmirched my good standing. I can't have it, I won't have it – you'll have to go.'

Dickie decided that it was time to defend his tarnished honour and assumed a look of boyish innocence. 'But Mr Hawksby, it weren't my fault! She's been shovin' herself at me for weeks.'

'Don't be coming that hiley-ho with me,' scoffed the grocer. 'I've seen you sniffing round t'lasses. If you're man enough to do what she accused you of you're man enough to own up to it.'

'But it was her, I tell ye!'

'Right! You've had your chance. If you'd've admitted it I might've overlooked it this time, you young lads being what you are, but you stood there and lied, let a poor, innocent widow take the blame. Well, I can do without your sort in my shop. You needn't bother to return after lunch – you're sacked.'

It was pointless to argue. With a resigned shrug Dickie took off his apron, laid it over the counter and with a last pleading look at the grocer left the shop. Christ, was his mother going to be mad!

The midday sun hovered directly above the space between the two rows of houses as Thomasin plodded down the street. It beat down upon her shoulders, causing her to whip the shawl away in vexation and use a corner of it to fan her crimson face. Her petticoats seemed to be weighed down with moisture, clinging to her stockings, catching round her ankles to hamper her movements. She laid down the heavy basket and ran a hand across her slippery brow, dragging away the stray hairs that clung to it. She then examined her palm, rubbing at the red criss-crossed imprints that the wicker handle had produced. Why did the passage to one's front door always seem twice as far when one had heavy baskets to carry?

A figure was coming towards her. The sun shone into her eyes making identification impossible. He seemed an odd shape with a tiny pin head on wide, square shoulders. It was only when she shaded her eyes that she could make out the sandwich board that swamped little Freddie Gash's frame. She did not have to read the message which was printed on it; she knew it off by heart – Prepare To Answer For Thy Sins, The Judgement Day Is At Hand.

She smiled widely as the diminutive Freddie took off his wide-brimmed hat with a sweeping flourish. 'Hello, Mr Gash, and how's the world behaving itself today?'

'I have very grave news to impart,' answered Freddie, ice-blue eyes glaring fanatically. 'Today will see the destruction of the entire human race.'

41

Thomasin lifted her eyes to the dazzling sky. 'Well, it's as good a day as any, I suppose.'

'Ah, you mock!' he breathed loudly. 'But you will not find it so amusing when the Lord vents His wrath on all the evils of this world. In one hour's time the sun will explode into a million fiery embers. Molten lava will spill from the great caverns that appear under your feet.' He swept his arms about dramatically. 'A plague of locusts will descend upon the countryside, devouring every last grain of wheat, every blade of grass until the earth is barren. Violent thunderbolts will bombard our helpless land. Torrents of rain shall cascade upon your . . .'

Thomasin cut in here. 'By, I'd best get home then – I've left me washin' out.' Picking up her basket she bade the eccentric Freddie a hasty good day. He was the last person she wanted to be saddled with, the way she was feeling.

On reaching the maroon front door, she unlocked it and limped along the dark passage. After swilling her face with cold water she took an ovencloth and lifted out the pot of stew that she had prepared before breakfast and which had been simmering while she had been at work. The thought of her dead employer returned. Every item upon which her eyes rested took on the wrinkled contours of Mr Penny's face. Poor old devil, she would miss him. He had been a grand old chap to work for.

'By, it's a bit cooler in here!' Sonny came in from school and flung himself on the well-punished sofa, raking grimy fingers through his brilliant hair. He caught her mood at once. 'What's up, Mam?'

She wiped her eyes briskly and shook her head. 'Nowt.' Flicking a cloth over the table she placed the stewpot on a mat in the centre. 'Go wash yer hands ready for dinner.' A burst of steam and rich aroma escaped the stewpot as she took off the lid, floating up to the ceiling and misting its cool surface.

There followed a look of surprise as Erin appeared in the doorway. 'What're you doin' home? You usually have your dinner at work.'

Erin leaned against the door jamb and twisted a lock of hair round her finger. 'I won't be having me dinner there any more.'

'Why not?' Thomasin rifled the drawer for an extra knife and fork, then set another place at the table. When Erin's answer was slow in coming she spun round sharply. 'I hope yer not going to tell me yer've lost yer job?'

The girl pulled at her lower lip. 'I had a row with Mrs Bradall and walked out. I'm sorry.'

'Walked out? Walked out!' screeched Thomasin. 'Did yer think we were that well-off that yer could waltz out when yer felt like it?' She pulled a chair away from the table and sat upon it heavily, placing a hand across her forehead. That was two wages short they'd be. She sighed. 'Oh well! I suppose what's done is done; my having a seizure isn't goin' to remedy it.' Resignedly she picked up a ladle and began to divide the vegetables – no meat today, being Friday. The door slammed. 'Here's another one home for his dinner.' Dickie slouched into the room. He looked at his mother's hot, flustered face, wondering whether this was the right time to break the news.

'Get them hands washed, yer look like summat off t'midden pile!' It was obvious his news would wait. He disappeared swiftly into the scullery.

'I don't know what yer father's gonna say,' Thomasin was muttering when he slipped back into the room and took his seat at the table. 'It's hard enough havin' to manage on what we have without another wage short.'

Dickie's fork paused in mid-passage: she knew! How could she have learned about it so soon? Drat! Miss Peabody must have told her, the old snoop. He gave a nervous cough. 'I'm sorry, Mam. I promise I'll get another as soon as I can.' He wondered how much of the story she knew.

Thomasin threw him an absent glance as she sliced into her meal. 'Another what?'

'Another jo . . .' he bit off the word as the realisation came that she had not been referring to his dismissal. But it was too late.

'What was that? What were you gonna say?' she asked sharply, then, at his reticence, uttered a mournful groan. 'Oh, God grant me strength! Not you an' all.' Her appetite completely soured she sent her knife and fork rattling onto her plate. 'Good grief! I'm beginning to think Freddie Gash was right when he said the end of the world is nigh. I thought it was too good to be true, us being comfortably off for once in us lives. I'm gonna need a magic wand to be able to manage on yer dad's wage alone.'

Erin ceased arranging the sliced carrots into patterns. 'What about your job?'

'You may well ask!' Thomasin propped her head in her hands and stared down into her stew. Trying to hang onto her patience she told them about Mr Penny's death.

Erin understood now why her mother had been so annoyed at her own admission. She leaned over and gripped Thomasin's arm comfortingly. 'I'm sorry, Mam, I wouldn't've done it if I'd known. 'Twas the hot weather made me lose my rag.'

'Me dad's here!' warned Sonny as the door slammed again and the sound of Patrick's boots thudded down the passage. On his entrance four expectant faces turned to him. 'I decided to come home after all,' he explained his presence, then added facetiously, 'just to see your smiling faces.'

His wife ignored the witticism. 'Before yer sit down, have yer anything yer'd like to tell us?'

He threw her a puzzled frown, 'Sure, an' what would I be havin' to tell yese? I've only been digging holes all morning.'

'Well, thank the Lord for that.' His wife relaxed and reached for another plate.

Patrick shook his head and went to wash his hands. 'Do I gather by that question ye've something to tell me?' he shouted from the scullery. His query was met by a wall of silence. Three guilty faces stared intently at the table as he returned for his meal. 'Well?'

'They've lost their jobs,' answered Sonny bluntly.

'What, all of yese?' cried Patrick, and at their dumb

nods, 'Jesus Mary an' Joseph! Is it so rich ye think I am that I can afford to support a load o' shirkers?'

They all spoke at once, explaining that it was not their fault, that they were innocent victims of one of Life's cruel twists.

'One at a time!' he bellowed, waving his hands and sinking onto a stool.

Thomasin began her excuse. She pulled out a handkerchief and dabbed her eyes. 'It's Mr Penny, poor old soul. He died through t'night. Goodness knows how long he'd've been lyin' there if his neighbour hadn't got worried and fetched bobbies. I nearly had a fit when t'policeman came in this mornin'. I thought you'd had an accident or summat.' She peeped slyly from the corner of her eye to see if her melodramatics had produced any sympathy, then blew her nose loudly. 'I don't know what to do about t'shop.'

'Three wages gone and she's worrying about the shop!' said Patrick, then addressed his next question to his daughter. 'An' what's your excuse, milady?'

Erin suffered a twinge of regret for her impulsive action as she related the episode. 'I'm sorry, Dad, if I'd known about the others losing their jobs I would've kept me mouth buttoned. I just got sick an' tired o' being treated like a slave. And this weather ...' she bit her lip. 'I suppose I could go an' apologise an' ask for me job back.'

Patrick shook his head. A flurry of brickdust peppered his stew but he seemed not to mind. 'I doubt ye'd get it.' He turned to Dickie who had been hoping his father had forgotten his presence. 'An' what've you been up to if I dare ask?'

Guilty eyes avoided his father's. 'Well, 'tis a long story.'

'I'm a good listener.' Patrick speared a forkful of potatoes.

Dickie cleared his throat. 'Well, ye see Mr Hawksby he's got this brother who's got a son, an' he's just left school an' he needs a job, an' what with him being family, like, Mr Hawksby thinks it's only fair that he gives him a

45

job, so he said I'd have to go 'cause he couldn't afford to pay the two of us.'

'Well, that's not right!' spluttered Thomasin, rising to her feet. 'He can't do that. I'm off to give him a piece of my mind.' 'No, don't!' Dickie pushed back his chair and shot upright.

'Why not?' asked Patrick suspiciously.

'Well . . .' stammered Dickie. Work, brain, work! 'This lad, his . . . his mam's just died! An' his dad can't work 'cause he's crippled. So there's only the lad what can earn the money. I couldn't begrudge him t'job, could I? He needs the money more than we do.'

Much to his relief Thomasin sat down again, enabling him to do likewise. 'Eh, when you hear of other people's troubles it makes yer wonder what yer've been complaining about, doesn't it?' sighed his mother, then added, 'But why did you have to leave right away? Why didn't you get any notice?'

'Well, Mr Hawksby did offer to give me some,' lied Dickie. 'He said he felt really bad about havin' to let me go and the least he could do was give me a couple o' weeks notice. But I said, no, I'm a big strong chap, Mr Hawksby, I'll easily find another job, you just worry about that poor lad o' your brother's. He was sorry to see me go, I can tell ye. Said he doubted his nephew'd do the job as well as I did.'

'I hope you haven't been spinning me a yarn,' warned his mother, eyes narrowed. 'If I find out there's been any jookery-pawkery your bum will draw sparks.'

'May God strike me dead, would I lie to you, Mam?'

She gave him a shrewd look and his composure slipped a little. 'I know you, remember. Anyroad, enough kallin. Yer can get yerself out after dinner, an' don't come back till yer've found a job. It's all very well you being charitable, but we have to live on summat.' She turned to Sonny. 'Tell yer what, you might as well take afternoon off an' join your brother. Not that I don't trust him, mind,' she winked, 'but seein' as you'll be leaving school an' needin'

46

a job yerself shortly today might be as good a day as any to start lookin'.'

Sonny felt something inside of him deflate. For some time he had been nurturing the idea of entering an art college when he left his present school. Now there seemed no point in even mentioning it.

'There's nowt wrong, is there?' asked his mother, noting his downcast expression.

Yes! he wanted to shout, there is something bloody wrong. Why should I be the one to suffer because the rest of you can't hold a job? But it was not in his nature to let anyone down when they were depending on him. 'No, 'course there's nowt wrong,' he answered, and smiled at her to show he meant it. 'Though I don't know what Brother Francis will think.'

'Brother Francis' thoughts don't put food in t'larder,' said Thomasin. 'Ah well, that's two of us sorted out. Now all we have to do is get Erin fixed up. That's a weight off my mind I can tell yer.' She stacked the crockery and carried it to the scullery. On her return she had an idea. 'Look, I know it'll not be for long, but I'll need some help at the shop if I'm to get organised for the new owner. How would you like to come an' help me, Erin? Wage'd tide us over.'

'I wouldn't't've thought it was any of your concern now,' opined Patrick.

'Well, it isn't really ... but yer never know, if the new owner sees it nice an' tidy he might decide to keep me on.' She went to brew the tea, leaving Erin to mull over her new employment.

CHAPTER FIVE

Receiving strict instructions not to go 'scrawmin' round that blessed slaughterhouse', the boys ambled down the street towards Walmgate. The heat had in no way abated. Once out of sight of the house Dickie reached over his shoulder to grasp a handful of shirt, pulling the garment over his head. He screwed it into a ball with which to wipe his gleaming face and armpits. Sonny warned what would happen if their mother caught him, then moved into the shade to sit down.

'Ah, nuts to her,' said Dickie scornfully, enjoying the exquisite coldness of the wall as he slid his back down it to join his brother.

'Not exactly gentry, are you?' responded Sonny.

'Ah, now there you're wrong,' said Dickie. 'In a few years' time I shall be a man o' means.'

'Huh! How can yer be a man o' means around here?' His brother gave a scathing gesture at the rickety buildings.

'An' who said anything about round here? As soon as I can I'll be out an' away to make me fortune. Ye'll not catch this one rotting his life away in this slum – ye can come with me if ye like,' he added generously. 'Be my business partner.'

Sonny shook his head, then laid it back against the wall of the public house. 'No thanks, I'd rather take my chances here than get meself mixed up in anything risky – for 'tis bound to be risky where you're involved.'

Dickie curled his upper lip and raked his thumbnail over the grille in the pavement from where rose puffs of beery perfume. 'That's your trouble, Son; ye've no sense of adventure, no wish to improve yourself.'

Coming from someone who had recently ruined any hopes Sonny had of bettering himself this was hard to stomach. 'Well, I don't see you makin' much effort to improve yourself either,' he said bitterly. 'Ye'll not find a job sat on yer backside.'

'Is that any way to talk to a fella who's gonna put ye right on the ways of women?'

'What's that supposed to mean?'

Dickie grinned widely. 'Bellybuttons, Son, that's what I'm on about. Ye did say this mornin' ye wanted to hear about the lovely Bertha.' He laughed as his brother leaned forward with interest. 'God love him! Look at the wee fella's eyes – like two glass alleys in a pig's arse. Ye can't wait, can ye? Right, pay attention – and put aside all notions o' bellybuttons.'

When he had finished, Sonny's face disclosed his dubiety. 'I think you're pullin' my leg!' He pushed his brother, then said thoughtfully, 'I can't imagine Mam an' Dad doin' it, can you?'

Dickie shook his head with a grin, then a period of speculation followed, after which he gave a groan. 'Mother o' God, I don't feel like hawkin' meself round in this heat, d'you?'

'I don't feel like hawkin' meself round at all!' snapped Sonny. 'There's things I'd much prefer doing than land meself with a stinkin' job.'

'Like painting, ye mean?' guessed Dickie with some sarcasm. That was all Sonny seemed to care about.

'Aye, like bloody painting! I was hopin' to go to art college when I left school, but you an' the others've put paid to that, haven't ye?'

'Why didn't ye say if it was so important?' asked Dickie mildly.

'How could I? After me mam's said how much we need the money. We're not all as selfish as you.'

'Ah well, perhaps 'tis for the best, Son.'

'For the best? For the bloody best!' yelled Sonny. 'Isn't there anything you've set yer heart on? Longed for so badly it's like a pain?'

Dickie grinned wickedly.

'God!' Sonny barked his disgust. 'You an' your bloody women. I'll bet there was one involved in your dismissal from Hawksby's wasn't there?'

'The boy's a mind-reader.'

'Sure, didn't I bloody-well know it? Couldn't I see ye were lyin' through yer teeth to Mam.' He cradled a badtempered scowl with his palm.

'Now ye didn't expect me to tell the truth, did ye?'

Sonny gave a snort. 'I never expect that – ye couldn't if ye tried.'

49

'Ah, begob now I've upset the boy.' Dickie laid a friendly arm over his brother's shoulder and hugged him. 'Will ye not believe me when I say I love ye like a brother?'

'You *are* my brother.'

'An' because o' that I'm goin' to fix ye up with my friend Bertha.' Sonny couldn't stop the laugh that escaped his lips and asked if Dickie had no interest in anything else. 'What else is there – apart from money?' Dickie ruffled his brother's hair. 'Are ye still mad at me?'

Sonny shook his head and smiled despite himself. One could never stay mad at Dickie for long.

'Good!' Dickie planted a wet kiss on the other's cheek.

'Ye big soft Mick!' Sonny laughed and wiped his face, then looked to the road where a man was calling for someone to hold his horse.

Dickie was first to the scene, holding the horse's head and flirting with the man's pretty wife while he was absent at the post office. Before the carriage moved away Dickie was given a tip which he accepted with a servile tug of his forelock. Once the man's back was turned, however, he stuck his middle finger in the air. 'That's the way to treat 'em, Son.'

His brother gestured as a gaunt-looking individual approached. 'Good afternoon, my fine fellows! And why are we not at our work?'

'Ah, just the very chap, my good pal Bones!' Dickie fell into step beside the newcomer, sprawling an arm across the angular shoulders. 'Would ye kindly tell us if there's any work to be had at your place by any chance?'

Martin Flaherty – 'Bones', because of his extremely undernourished appearance – gave a derogatory leer. 'Not for the likes o' you, Feeney. Ye'll not find many skirts to sniff around there – not to take your fancy anyways. Besides, I thought ye had yourself a good job.'

'I did – but it seemed I was putting too much into my work.' Dickie grinned at his brother who loped alongside.

'Do I detect some sordid undertone to that remark?' queried Bones. 'Would there happen to be a lady involved in all this?'

'Ah, God the boy's too quick,' sighed Dickie. 'Aye, Bones, I'm afraid my fatal charms deserted me on this occasion – with Mr Hawksby I mean, not with the lady concerned.' His face split into its familiar roguish grin.

One could almost hear Flaherty's bones rattle as he shook with amusement. He dipped into the bag he carried and pulled out a pig's tail, stripping off the meat with his unhealthy-looking teeth then tossing the remaining gristle into the gutter.

Dickie poked his nose towards the paper bag. 'Giz one, Bones.'

'Sorry, I've only got twenty-three left.' Bones showed his teeth then offered the bag to his two friends. 'Don't be takin' a handful, mind.' Sonny's reminder that it was Friday was met by uncaring grins. Bones made great play of enjoying the meaty titbits. 'Well now, ye mentioned a lady – anyone I know?'

'Sure, a gentleman doesn't tell,' reproved Dickie, nibbling at the pig's tail, then added slyly, 'But if ye want to know the answer I suggest ye recite that flowery little verse to yourself. Ye know, the one that goes: "*Roses are red . . .* "'

Bones mentally recited the rhyme for a moment, then the allusion hit him. 'God almighty!' he exploded. 'Not Violet?'

Dickie swiftly pounced on him and clamped a hand over his mouth. 'Ssh! D'ye want to get me a rope necklace? By the by, how did yourself do with our little friend from the fairground? I wonder, was she as tasty as her companion?'

Bones shrugged and, as they reached the entrance to the iron foundry, started to veer away. 'She was all right, I suppose.'

'That means he never got anything,' explained Dickie to his brother.

'That's all you know,' replied Bones. ''Tis only that it's beneath my dignity to talk about such things. Anyhows, you're not going to tell me you had enough money to buy Bertha's favours. If y'are then I'll thank ye to return that threepence I lent ye for the sideshow.'

51

'I'd not tell ye that 'cause it'd be a lie. For I didn't have to pay a brass farthing. The girl fell in love with me the minute she set eyes on my gorgeous face.'

Bones and Sonny exchanged sickened glances. 'I can believe it an' all, can't you?' said Bones, coming back to stand with them. 'The slimy bastard.'

Dickie laughed, unoffended. 'Come on now, Bones, how about seein' if ye can get your pals a job?'

The youth scratched his nose thoughtfully and asked, 'I suppose it's no use asking if I get a fee?'

'I could introduce ye to Bertha,' offered Dickie. 'T'would make up for your wasted night with her friend.'

'Didn't I tell ye she was all right,' complained Bones, then deliberated for a while before saying, 'I could ask the foreman about a job for ye – though 'tis no use ye comin' today, we're hellish busy; he'll not have time to see ye – come on Monday.'

'Hey look, Bones!' Dickie digressed. 'Isn't that one o' your cousins, they're attacking?' He pointed to a band of grubby, tousle-haired children who hauled between them a near-complete skeleton which they had just disinterred from an ancient graveyard. A helpful dog took possession of a jawful of phalanxes.

'Look! ye'll get no help from me if ye continue with these insults,' snapped Bones.

Dickie, pinging pebbles off the works' sign, apologised, then made the suggestion that all three of them take a trip to the country tomorrow.

Bones was pensive. 'I suppose I could ask me dad to pick me wages up an' tell the master I'm sick – though you're not to call at our house, the mammy'll skin me alive if she finds I've dodged off from work. There'll be holy murder when she discovers my wage is short as well. I'll have to tell her they've docked our rate or something.'

Their arrangements completed, the boys parted company, the Feeneys spending the remainder of the afternoon splashing in the open sewer known as the Foss. Hours later, after being chased off by a policeman for their naked cheek, they made their way home, boots laced around neck, damp hair awry. The pavements sizzled beneath their bare padding feet. Sonny's head hung down to face his toes where the still-moist spaces between them had collected the little puffs of dirt that eddied under his pounding soles. Before reaching home, however, the boys thought it expedient to smarten themselves up. Dickie used his fingers as a comb for his crinkly black hair, employing a shop window as a mirror.

'My, who's the handsome-lookin' fella in the shop?' he quipped, then: 'Why, bless me! 'tis me own reflection. God, but you're a handsome brute.' He blew a kiss to the female assistant inside.

The woman waved a deprecating hand. 'Go away!' she mouthed. Sonny joined his brother to press his face against the glass, flattening his nose and crossing his eyes. The woman pursed her lips as she went about her work, trying to ignore the grimacing expressions, but they would not desist. Finally, she gave an exasperated cry and flounced to the rear of the shop to ask the fishmonger to chase them off. In a flash Dickie had leapt through the doorway and whipped up a piece of yellow fish which slipped and slithered through his fingers as he tried to tuck it down his shirt front.

When the woman returned with reinforcements the boys were gone.

Edwin Raper sat outside his brother's butchery soaking up the dregs of the afternoon sun. To say that Raper was fat would be to understate the matter; he was an enormous man whose girth increased with every year. His eyes were pig-like. He had close-cropped gingery hair and skin the colour of boiled bacon – ergo his nickname – 'Bacon Neck'.

It was doubtful if one could find a single person who would confess to liking Raper; not the Feeney boys certainly, for if he was not shouting insults at them about their Irish ancestry then he was threatening to cut out their tripes. In truth he was harmless – a fat man with a big mouth – and no one took his threats seriously. On the contrary, his obnoxious displays had made him an attractive target for the younger generation's pranks.

The chair groaned as Raper shuffled his posterior into a more comfortable position and laid his head heavily against the doorpost of the shop. The ensuing vibration stirred up a cloud of bluebottles which buzzed over the blood-clotted joints that hung outside. They soon resettled, rubbing hairy little legs over their grotesque heads. His grubby, blood-caked apron stretched taut across the great mound of his belly. He snuggled his tongue into the roof of his mouth like a great bull chewing the cud. His piggy eyes flickered, then closed. The sausage-like fingers slipped from his chest to dangle somnolently at his side. He snored contentedly – for a while.

Alas, the butcher was suddenly jerked into rude awakening by something cold, wet and smelly wrapping itself around his head. In his panic he almost fell from the chair, his fingers scrabbling wildly at his face. The piece of stinking fish slipped down to his chest to land on his apron and, seizing it, Raper leapt up from the chair, his face boiling with rage.

'Who done it?' he bellowed, waving the reeking fish in the air and drawing amused glances from passers-by. 'I'll kill 'em! I swear I'll 'ave their bloody guts on my slab!' He glared angrily around him trying to locate the direction of the stifled sniggers.

Sonny bobbed up once too often. 'Oy, come back 'ere!' Raper ran into the road, hopping from one foot to the other as a hansom cab rumbled towards him and danced agitatedly until it had passed. Dodging the rest of the traffic he stormed across the road to pursue the escaping culprits, thundering after them with the fish still in his hand.

Laughing breathlessly the boys suddenly wheeled into a side street. The sweat trickled down their foreheads and gusts of warmth pumped from the open necks of their shirts. Still running, Sonny turned and thumbed his nose at the lumbering Raper, then he and Dickie swerved yet again into another side street and ran – straight into their mother.

After Thomasin had caught hold of her sons' shirts and given them a shaking, she folded her hands across her dark green skirt and asked, 'Now then, would either of yer like to tell me why yer in such a hurry?' She looked up sharply as Raper shambled stertorously around the corner, almost colliding with the three of them.

'I've got a bone to pick wi' these two,' Raper panted and propped himself against the wall to regain his breath, the sweat pouring into his tiny eyes.

'Don't tell me they've been up to mischief again, Mr Raper,' said Thomasin calmly, wondering what had sparked off the conflict today.

'Mischief? I'll give 'em bloody mischief!' Raper brandished the fish under her nose, causing her to move her head distastefully. 'Chucked this in me bloody face, they did. Just havin' a bloody nap, scared me out o' me wits. Listen, I'm just about sick of all these bloody filthy Irish tricks.'

Thomasin, well-used to Raper's bigotry – enough to know not to waste her breath on him – turned to her sons as if to admonish them. 'That was a silly thing to do,' she said sternly. Raper nodded his agreement. 'You know very well it was wrong without me havin' to tell yer.' Raper nodded vigorously. 'Didn't I say this dinner-time that we'd all have to tighten our belts, an' what d'you go an' do? You go an' waste a nice bit o' fish by throwin' it at the likes of him, when you know very well we could've eaten it.'

Raper stopped nodding and pointed a finger. 'Now, look 'ere . . .'

Thomasin gave the boys a push towards home, then addressed the butcher. 'I'm sorry I can't stop an' have a chat wi' yer, Mr Raper, I've got things to see to.' She followed her sons, leaving an incensed butcher waving the fish in the air.

'What am I supposed to do wi' this?' he bawled.

Thomasin looked back, then retraced her steps to

specify, 'Well, yer see yer get a pan, an' then yer fill it wi' water . . .'

Raper spat an expletive and marched away, still clutching the fish.

The intransigents looked up apprehensively as Thomasin's diminutive shadow fell across the doorway, but after being hastily informed that Martin Flaherty was going to get them a job at Victoria Foundry their mother forgot her annoyance.

Shortly, Erin entered carrying a parcel of stale teacakes which she had bought cheaply, intending to toast them for their evening meal. 'Is this all we're having?' Dickie stared down at them. 'I should've kept that mucky bit of fish.'

His mother's lips twitched. 'When you start bringin' money in then we'll be eatin' a bit better, but till then I'm afraid His Lordship will 'ave to make do wi' those – oh, an' another thing! I shall want you two lads to help me wi' stocktakin' one night next week.'

'Oh, Ma-am!' chorused the brothers.

'Never mind, "oh, Mam!", yer'll do as yer told. Me an' Erin can't manage all on our own. An' yer never know, yer might earn yerselves threepence if yer do a good job.'

'If ye think I'm killin' meself for threepence then ye're mistaken,' answered Dickie rashly.

Thomasin dealt him a stinging blow to the ear. 'You'll do it for nowt if I have any more o' your cheek!'

'When d'ye think ye'll have to leave, Mam?' asked Erin.

'Well, I should think me job'll be safe for a couple o' weeks. After that . . . we'll have to wait an' see.'

CHAPTER SIX

The three boys sauntered beneath the leafy palisade, slitting their eyes as the morning sun glinted intermittently through the treetops. It was so quiet here, far from the bustle of Walmgate with its dray carts and carriages, hansoms and gigs tearing up and down, high-stepping horses kicking up the dust, harness jingling, hooves ringing, and the bawls of draymen and street vendors.

Yet the countryside had noises of its own; gentler, more melodic noises. A hundred birdsongs heralded their intrusion, bursting out from the trees and hedgerows in tuneful waves.

Sonny raised his face to the green canopy and tried to distinguish the different breeds. 'There's a yellow hammer!' he whispered, and pointed to a thorny bush as the song rang out – '*A little bit of bread and no-o cheese!*' And then another – '*teacher, teacher!*' 'That's a great tit,' informed Sonny, causing Dickie and Bones to collapse upon each other with hilarity.

Sonny reproved them. 'Jazers, can ye think o' nothin' else? Here we are surrounded by beauty an' all you can think about is that.'

They left the track and forged a trail through a patch of woodland, thigh-deep in pungent grasses and wild flowers: red and white campions, wood anemones, alive with the drone of honey bees. Insects with long, stick-like legs whirred from the grass under their intrusive feet, whispering against their bare forearms, dancing and floating above their heads. Sonny filled his lungs with the heady scents and paused to wait as his brother twisted a branch from an elder bush.

They strode on, Dickie lashing out at the irritating swarms of insects which hovered at face level. 'God, these bloody flies are eatin' me alive.'

'I think it's lovely,' murmured Sonny as he plodded behind the others, stopping occasionally to cup a wild flower to his nose.

'You would!' shouted Dickie over his shoulder, and a startled pheasant broke cover with a colourful whirr of wings. 'Will ye look at that!' Dickie lowered his voice accordingly. 'Tomorrow's dinner handed to us on a plate almost.'

'An' how d'ye propose to catch it?' asked Bones. 'When ye've no gun.'

'Sure, I've no need of a gun when I've got brains,' said Dickie scathingly. 'They're bloody silly creatures, pheasants. Anyway, didn't I come prepared?' He thrust his hand into his pocket and produced a handful of raisins which he had sneaked from Thomasin's store cupboard. 'This is how we're goin' to catch it.' He smiled knowingly at Sonny who was immediately transported back to the days when they were little more than babies, sitting upon Uncle John's knee and listening to his tales. Dear, sly, cunning Uncle John who had one day disappeared and had never been seen again. Sonny recalled the times when he would bring them up here or to Low Moor for walks and try to teach them his poacher's tricks. The method of catching pheasants for those without benefit of firearm, was to lay a lure of raisins soaked in brandy for the foolish, unsuspecting birds, then when they were drunk enough one snared them, twisted their necks and dropped them neatly into a sack. That was the part which always spoilt it for Sonny, a sensitive soul for all his brawn. But Dickie had no such scruples.

'How did ye come by the brandy?' asked Sonny.

'I didn't. The cupboard door was unlocked so I drained off a little poteen.' Dickie grinned and began to lay the trail of raisins among the bark parings and pine cones.

'Jesus, is it pickled pheasants you're after?' breathed Bones. 'That stuff would burn a hole in a tin bath.'

'I didn't think your family knew what baths were, Bones,' responded Dickie.

They secreted themselves behind a rotting log, lying on their bellies to wait for the pheasant's return, perfectly quiet. The air was heavy with the persistent whine of gnat and bee-hum. They lay there for some time. Sonny watched the stumbling passage of a family of woodlice over the crest of the log, then turned away in despair as his brother proceeded to squash them one by one. The scent of the crushed pine needles beneath their sprawled bodies began to make him feel lightheaded. He sifted a handful of them through his fingers and said hopefully, 'He's not coming.'

'Is he not?' murmured his brother, and nodded at a nearby clump of bracken where a beady eye rotated suspiciously.

Their breath suspended they watched the bird place one tentative claw in front of the other. It pecked warily at first then, as the poteen did its work, became bolder, greedily gobbling up the raisins as fast as it could find them. The more he ate the more relaxed his gait became. Dickie hooked his fingers into the rotting bark as the intoxicated bird staggered towards them making drunken stabs at the raisins. Nearer, he staggered, nearer. Sonny bit his lip as his brother crouched ready to strike, his strong, widely-spaced teeth gripping so deeply that they almost drew blood. Go back! he wanted to shout. Go back!

Nearer. Nearer – and then he was caught! Scooped up in a struggling flash of plumage, his neck gripped between Dickie's large hands and twisted sharply. Twisted, twisted . . . oh! Sonny thought he was going to be sick, with the beady eye bulging at him, imploring . . . the grisly snap . . . and then it was all over. The pheasant, its head lolling uselessly on the rag-like neck, was thrust into Dickie's shirt front and the boys were once more on their way.

They did not speak for some time, swishing through the long grass, ducking under a low-hanging branch. Dickie felt the still-warm body against his own, the bird's hard beak tapping at his chest. It was the first time he had killed anything bigger than an insect. His heart was still beating rapidly with the thrill of the hunt. He had liked it; liked the feeling of power in his hands; liked the way his whole body had been infused with a chilling superiority. The bird had offered no resistance, had placidly succumbed to his effortless pressure.

Behind him his brother's heart was beating also; not with excitement but rather with regret. And yet more worrying than the sad demise of the handsome bird had been the look on his brother's face as he committed the deed; as if he had enjoyed it. He *did* enjoy it, thought Sonny, experiencing a sudden chill.

The sun grew brighter as the three boys neared the edge of the wood, and suddenly they were no longer shielded by a verdant canopy but standing on the brink of one of the most wonderful sights that Sonny had ever seen.

The clearing was very large, fringed by elder, hawthorn, rowan and silver birch, their contrasting foliage whispering and bending to the breeze; a warm, inviting breeze. Speechlessly the boys stripped off their shirts and absently hooked them over their shoulders as they stepped further into the clearing, gazing admiringly about them – then starting as a cloud of butterflies rose as one from a clump of Ragged Robin, lifting in a multicoloured swoosh! into the balmy air. A galaxy of wings – Red Admiral, Tortoiseshell, Painted Lady, ascending in a deviating flutter, now coming to land, now rising swiftly as the boys disturbed them once again; brushing, petal-like, against cheek and breast.

In the centre of the clearing was a lake, fondled by the zephyr into a gently rippling stretch of deep green satin, and ringed with bullrush, yellow flags and slender golden reeds. Strange great insects performed a ballet above its glassy waters; dragons and damsels in aerial courtship, their lapis lazuli bodies shimmering in the sunlight.

Sonny, with his artist's eye, lingered at the water's edge, held speechless by the beauty, while his two companions whooped and charged around the clearing like barbarians. Sacrilege, thought Sonny and sat down to unbuckle his knapsack. Withdrawing his modest tin paintbox and crumpled pieces of paper he set out to capture the scene, using water from the lake to mix the colours. Why, when they had journeyed up here many times before had they overlooked this beauty spot? Perhaps it had appeared by magic. Years hence the same thought would plague him, for try as he might he never found it again.

After their initial burst of steam the others, too, flopped down at the lakeside, chests heaving. They propped themselves on their elbows to watch the dragonflies' erratic passage. Sonny, his brush in retirement for the moment, leaned on his knee and thought how reminiscent of his brother these insects were; darting over the pool of life, making frantic grabs at everything within reach. One minute here, next minute gone. A gaudy, random dragonfly.

There were swallows too, skimming the sun-dappled water, scything through the nebulous hordes of midges with knife-like wings, wheeling acrobatically to display the rubies at their throats. Towards midday the breeze dropped and the clearing became a sun-trap. Dickie groaned and turned to look at his brother whose finished painting lay anchored by the paintbox, and at Bones who still lazed in the grass, a straw clenched between his teeth.

Dickie raised a hand to wipe away the sweat that stood in plump, shining beads on his bronzed forehead. 'Well, I don't know about your intentions but I know what mine are!' He jumped up and began to unbutton his trousers.

Sonny opened one eye to squint up at his brother who was now naked and looking as if he was wearing a brown mask and elbow-length gloves with the rest of his body – barely touched by the sun – ridiculously white. 'I'm with ye!' He sprang and tore off his own clothes while Bones followed their lead.

Dickie swaddled the pheasant in his shirt and placed it at the foot of a tree; it was beginning to attract the flies. He strutted round like a bantam cock, hands on hips. 'Jazers, I wish we could walk round like this all the time, 'tis a whole lot cooler.'

Sonny left his clothes in a crumpled pile. 'So do I. I wish Miss P. could see us an' all – she'd really have summat to goggle at, wouldn't she?'

They were diverted as Bones caught his foot on a thistle and swore. 'Oh, Mary Mother o' God!' guffawed Dickie, pointing at his thin friend. 'Will ye ever look at the cut of him? Sure, there's more meat on the bones me mam chucks in t'soup.'

Sonny doubled over at the sight of Bones' long, matchstick limbs and jutting breastbone. Almost every bone in his body was visible. 'I shouldn't cross your legs, Bones, it's too hot for a fire.'

'Ah, 'tis only jealous ye are of this,' retorted Bones, thrusting his hips forward.

Dickie wept with laughter. 'Ah, God, 'tis a fine specimen I'll grant ye. Seems a shame not to put it to any better use than for peeing over high walls. Grab him, Son! We'll stake him out an' use it as a sun-dial.'

A fight ensued with skewbald bodies coiled around each other, gleeful, tickling, thumping, grasping, rolling together in a mass of arms and legs. Sonny managed to grab Bones' ankles and Dickie, laughing heartily, took his arms and together they staggered to the lake and hurled him in, leaping joyfully after him, and disturbing the satin-like water with their thrashing.

For a long time they splashed and played the fool, taking it in turns to duck each other under, their hair plastered down into dripping caps, while the dragonflies and nymphs darted overhead. A flurry of airbubbles dotted the water as Sonny bobbed to the surface and nipped the water from his nose.

He shook his head and held aloft wrinkled fingers. 'I'm beginning to look like a prune. An' I feel awful peckish – let's go have our dinner.'

The others pantingly agreed and lunged out for the bank. As their floundering hands touched the muddy bottom they stumbled to their feet and switched to wading, the water boiling around their thighs.

It was then that they saw her; a doe-eyed, honey-braided creature seated provocatively on the bank with one knee raised beneath the white muslin dress and – if you please – one of their sandwiches poised at her mouth. She chuckled as their immediate reflex was to duck their lower halves under the still choppy water and observe her with open mouths.

'If you could see your faces,' she teased, taking a bite from the sandwich, her left hand disappearing into the long grass to brace her body. 'What's up, haven't you ever seen a girl before?'

Sonny gulped and looked at his brother. 'How do we get out? She's sittin' on our clothes.'

Dickie's mouth had begun to curve into a knowing smile. 'D'ye think she doesn't know that? She's doing it on purpose, thinks we'll have to stay in here till she's taken her fill. Well,' he emerged from the water, 'if she wants it that way she can have it.' Without further ceremony he stood upright, the water streaming from his supple young body, and walked towards her.

If he had hoped to disconcert her then he was to be disappointed; far from showing embarrassment she seemed positively indifferent to his nudity, and crammed the reminder of the sandwich into her mouth as he stood dripping above her.

'D'you mind not standing too close? You're getting my dress all wet.'

'It'd be a pity to do that,' said Dickie, adding boldly, 'Why don't ye take it off like us've done?'

'I might do,' she answered lightly, licking a crumb from the corner of her generous mouth. 'When I've dined.' She reached for another sandwich.

'Aren't you the cheeky wench,' breathed Dickie. There was no need for flattery here; she was ripe. He cupped his hand to his mouth and shouted towards the lake, 'Ye'd best come out before she eats all our snap!'

He flopped down on the grass beside her, leaning on his elbow, somewhat incredulous that she could behave so coolly in the presence of his nakedness. He glanced lazily at the lake where the others still squatted too embarrassed to come out. 'They're afraid of ye,' he told her. 'Surely ye'd not take advantage of little boys an' eat all their sandwiches. An' them not able to defend themselves.'

She sank her teeth into the bread and flashed her eyes seductively. 'I wouldn't take advantage, no – but I wonder whether you would if I should decide to take off my clothes an' join the three of you. You don't look like little boys to me.'

'Sure, I wasn't including meself in that statement,' answered Dickie.

The water that dripped from his forelock to trickle idly down the side of his nose seemed to transfix her. 'Does that mean I'm to watch out for myself, then?'

'Me, take advantage of a lady?' he said innocently. 'Never.'

She threw him a sultry look and, still chewing, rose and began to unbutton the flimsy white dress.

Sonny and Bones were calcified. They watched the girl pull the dress from her shoulder. She was completely naked underneath. Sonny felt something happen to him as he feasted his eyes on the golden triangle at the vee of her thighs, the rose-tipped globes which bounced and jiggled as she ran towards the lake. It was not the first time he had seen a naked female – he and his brother had made a spyhole in the curtain which divided their sister's sleeping quarters from theirs – but he had only ever managed to catch Erin's rear view with its slim, boyish hips, and was unprepared for the quivering mountain of flesh that plunged into the lake and paddled towards him. She disappeared momentarily as the bank sheered away beneath her feet. All the boys could make out were the shadows of her serpent-like braids beneath the viridescent water. Then up she came, spluttering and laughing, sucking in the summer air and striking out for them again.

'Come on, don't be shy!' She circled them, floating on her back and pointing a narrow foot at the sky while they rotated nervously. 'What's to do? Are you frightened I might eat you?'

'Frightened of a lass?' blurted Sonny scornfully.

'Oh – it does speak. Well, come on out an' show yourselves,' taunted the girl and made for the bank, shouting over her glistening shoulder, 'Else I'm going to sit and eat all your bait.'

Sonny and Bones shared a questioning glance, then simultaneously they followed her, stumbling in their eagerness as the water frothed around their calves.

Dickie, still sprawled unselfconsciously where she had

left him, introduced himself as she deposited her streaming body nearby.

'I'm Beth.' She ran her eye over Sonny and Bones who had seated themselves beside her, and who dropped their gaze from her curves on encountering her amused inspection. 'Well, now we're all here am I to share your victuals?'

'Looks like ye've been sharin' them already,' observed Dickie, but nevertheless dipped into his haversack and drew out his own packed lunch. He peeled back the wrapping and offered her a sandwich.

'Oh, they weren't yours I was eating then?' She leaned over to take one, her whole body a-tremor with the movement.

'No, they were mine,' answered Sonny, trying to keep his voice steady. He picked up the untidy parcel she had made of his lunch. 'But ye can have another if ye like.'

'I might do later,' she replied, then turned her attention to Bones who had broken into a fit of consumptive coughing. 'You've been in the water too long, my lad.'

'No, I've had the bark for a long time,' he replied between choking. ''Tis that bloody ironworks; it'll be the death o' me.'

'You look as though you're on the way out already.' She wrinkled her nose. 'Crikey! Aren't you skinny.'

He set his mouth and unwrapped his own lunch, coaxing from her more derogatory comments. 'Lumme! No wonder you're thin. Is that all you're having?'

Bones took a savage bite of the stale-looking sandwich. 'It's all I could sneak out. Anyway, 'tisn't my fault if me dad doesn't make enough to feed us,' he muttered. Not to mention the fact that Dad had usually disposed of his wages by the time he got home. To Jimmy the thought of passing a pub was anathema. She asked how many of them there was. 'Dunno, I've lost count. I think the mammy has too. Some of us're married. About eleven of us are still at home.'

'I'm not surprised your mother can't feed you.' Beth delved into Dickie's knapsack, bringing out an apple into which she inserted her teeth with a noisy crack.

'Doesn't look as if anyone feeds you either,' remarked Dickie. 'An' that's Bones' apple you're eatin' I might tell ye.' His mother had packed an extra one, knowing the Flaherty boy received very little fruit at home. He brought out a stoneware bottle and took a hearty swig of water, then passed it to his brother who, after wiping the neck with his palm, did likewise.

'Bones doesn't mind, do you?' said Beth with juice running down her chin. Bones did mind and said so. Beth seemed unoffended. 'Here you are, then.' She tossed the half-eaten apple at him and he fumbled for it. 'Got anything else?' Sonny offered her a slice of plum bread with quivering fingers. 'Thank you. What's your name?'

'John,' said Sonny, handing the bottle to Bones.

'But we call him Sonny,' provided Dickie, earning a cutting glare.

Beth picked up the painting, holding it this way and that. 'Who's t'artist?'

'Here, yer'll get butter on it!' Sonny snatched it from her and hid it in his knapsack, sharing Bones' opinion that she was too forward by half. She shrugged and pulled off a mouthful of plum bread, poking it into her mouth with nailbitten fingers. The boys ate slowly, watching her all the time. The drops of water that clung to their shoulders acted as tiny magnifying glasses, leaving red patches as they evaporated with the scorching sun. Dickie asked where she lived.

She flung her arm in the direction of the woods. 'Over there.'

'An' how old are ye?'

'You're a nosy devil, aren't you? I'm fifteen if you must know. How old are you then?' He told her, following which a host of other details was exchanged.

After the food was devoured Beth lay with her arms framing her damp, honey-toned locks, her ankles crossed and her white body turning pink. Dickie shuffled his body next to hers and began to trail a strand of grass over her belly, raising goosebumps. She did not stop him. The others watched, experiencing a strange churning in their

66

bowels. Dickie slowly dragged the grass downwards to where the golden hair sprang wild, like mustard and cress. She's sure to tell him to stop now, thought Sonny. But she didn't.

'What're you staring at?' she murmured lazily, eyes amber slits under barely-perceptible lashes.

Sonny, thinking she addressed him, tore his eyes away hastily. But it was Dickie who answered: 'Ye've got a greenfly caught in your curls.'

'Ugh! I can't stand creepy crawlies.' But she did not rise. 'Get it out for me.'

The churning in Sonny's bowels now enveloped his whole being. He stared with flaming face as his brother's fingers poised over the stumbling greenfly. Oh, Jesus! Oh, Blessed Mary! They were almost there. Dickie's fingers were almost touching her. It was as it had been with the pheasant, with the boys crouched alert, hardly daring to risk a breath. I'm going to burst, thought Sonny desperately, his eyes swimming and hot. In his mind he was in his brother's place, touching her.

And then somehow, Dickie was flat on his back as the girl with a gleeful shriek leapt over him in a flash of white thighs, giggling and screaming, great breasts bouncing as she made her escape. She ploughed through the long grass, the flesh on her thighs shivering and quaking like blancmange.

Dickie was first to free himself of the ensuing confusion. 'Come on!' He leapt up, galvanising the others who had been paralysed with excitement. 'If ye want to know what it feels like to be a man now's yer chance.'

Further persuasion was unnecessary. Sonny and Bones sprang to their feet, scattering the pile of screwed-up paper and clothing and charged after him. Beth's limbs sliced through the undergrowth as she laughed breathlessly over her shoulder to make sure that they were not too far behind. Around the glittering lake they pounded, with the hot sun toasting their youthful bodies, the butterflies and gnats fulminating in startled disarray as they ran, swerving and shying to avoid the clumps of thistles.

It happened so suddenly. One minute Sonny was haring eagerly after his quarry, his senses alive with the thrill of things to come, and the next a searing pain was shooting from his ankle into every crenel of his body. Down he went with a nerve-grinding thud, disturbing a clump of dandelion clocks, and the air was filled with a thousand fairy parasols. He curled up in agony, gripping his twisted ankle as the others thundered away.

His cry of, 'Wait on!' went unheeded. All that was to be heard was the faint sound of their lustful merriment as they vanished into the woods.

CHAPTER SEVEN

'Is there anything left to eat?' was Beth's question when the three returned from their sortie a good half-hour later.

'I shouldn't think so the way you've been troughing,' said Sonny petulantly, sitting, still naked, on the bank with his throbbing foot dangling in the water.

Dickie upturned his knapsack and rifled the contents. 'No, there's only paper.' He planted himself beside his brother who looked the opposite way. 'Ye should've come, Son,' he hissed. 'What happened to ye?'

Sonny turned on him angrily. 'I fell, that's what happened! Didn't ye hear me shoutin'?'

'Can't say I did, Son. Sorry. Still, ye didn't miss much – she's not a patch on Bertha, she wouldn't . . .'

'I'm not bothered! Go 'way an' leave me in peace.'

Dickie returned to where Beth and Bones were sitting and squatted down next to them. He could not help grinning at Bones' face. The lad was besotted. Look at him, massaging her back to smooth away the impression of the bark splinters. Dickie snapped off a handful of wild barley, using the heads as darts to aim at Beth's hair.

'Stoppit!' She pulled them from her hair and flung them

away, unfastening then replaiting her braids before lying on the flattened grass to soak up more of the sun.

'Ye were told to stop it, Feeney,' warned Bones as Dickie threw more. He lovingly caressed the pale-blonde hairs on her arm.

'Will we go for another swim?' suggested Dickie, aiming the darts at Bones instead.

'You three go,' she mumbled, eyes closed. 'I don't want to get my hair wet again. I'll have to go soon.' She noticed Bones' unwillingness to leave her. 'Don't think you're getting anything else. You've had enough from me. Go have your swim, that'll cool you off.'

He reluctantly joined Dickie and the two padded to the lakeside, coming to stand on either side of Sonny. 'Away, our lad, stop sulkin' an' come an' have a splash. Sure, I've telled ye, ye didn't miss nothing.' Dickie plunged in. Sonny threw up his hands to avoid a faceful of water.

'An' I've said I wasn't bothered!' With a grimace he hobbled after Bones who had also leapt in, and let the water cool his anger.

It wasn't long before they were friends again, uprooting a cluster of reedmace and using them to engage in a swordfight. They beat each other about the shoulders, ducking under the threshing surface and taking it in turns to sit on one another's shoulders, playing King of the Castle on a sandy shelf, one minute men, the next children.

When they came out she was gone. Bones tried to hide his disappointment by saying it would be a good idea for them to get moving too. He felt once again the plump cushion of her body and hurriedly pulled on his trousers as his body began to mirror that remembrance.

'Aye, my guts are tellin' me it's close to tea-time,' agreed Sonny, glad to see the back of her; she had quite spoilt his day. 'Come on, I want to pick some flowers for me mam on t'way home.'

Dickie rubbed down his body with a handful of dried grass and grinned devilishly at Bones. 'What did ye think to it then, Bones?'

'What?' asked the other nonchalantly, pulling on his shirt and tucking it into his trousers.

'What, says he,' scoffed Dickie. 'Your first fuck, that's what.'

'Who said anything about it being my first?' replied Bones indignantly, then his face cracked sheepishly at Dickie's prompting. 'Christ, wasn't it bloody marvellous! D'ye think she'll be here next week?'

Dickie waved his hand disparagingly. 'Nah! Ye don't want to waste your time on her again. There's plenty of tail if ye know where to look for it.'

'The voice of experience,' growled Sonny, circling his foot to test the strength of his ankle.

Dickie chortled. 'He's still mad 'cause he didn't get owt. Poor Son. Tell ye what, I'll see if I can arrange anythin' wi' Bertha. She's bound to be generous if I tell her it's me brother's first time. She likes virgins.' He pulled on his trousers.

Sonny cheered up a little. 'D'ye think so?'

'I do; she's got a soft spot for me has our Bertha.'

'She's got a soft spot for everybody,' answered Bones gleefully. 'But I won't say where it is.'

'Listen, she's all right is Bertha. She gave me the full treatment an' I didn't have to pay a sou – an' 'twas a lot better than I've had this afternoon.'

'I thought Beth was nice,' returned Bones. Absently he put his hand to his nose and inhaled deeply, imagining her smell still clung to his fingers. With a sigh he dropped his hand to his pocket. He patted it. 'Oh, bugger! I had a pocketful o' copper when I came; it must've slipped out when I pulled me togs off. Help me find it, will ye?' He knelt down and parted the grass.

'How come you're so prosperous on a Sat'day?' quizzed Dickie.

Bones crawled about on his hands and knees. 'I took some skins to the tannery.'

'Ah, so ye've been robbin' our pal again, have ye?' said Dickie. It was their habit, should Bacon Neck be careless enough to leave any hides lying unattended, to spirit them away to the tannery. 'Well, this is God's punishment for your dishonesty. Ye wouldn't catch me doin' a rotten trick like that.'

'Catch being the catchword,' muttered Bones, still searching.

Dickie watched his performance and his hand went unconsciously to his own pocket. He frowned. 'Eh, mine's gone too! I saved that tip the toff gimme, for a drink an' summat to eat on the way home. What about you, Son?'

'I didn't have any. Serves ye both right anyroad.' Sonny picked up the stoneware bottle and upturned it to his mouth – it was empty. He shoved it into his knapsack, then turned at his brother's exclamation of rage.

Dickie surged back from the place where he had stowed the pheasant, flourishing his shirt. 'The bitch! 'Tis her what's taken our money – an' she's pinched my bloody bird an' all!' He kicked angrily at a grassy hummock while Sonny set his mouth and shouldered his knapsack. 'Would ye bloody credit it,' continued Dickie. 'We share our dinner with the wench an' this is how she repays us.'

Bones shrugged sadly. 'Well, I suppose she was generous in her way.' He started to lope miserably in the direction of the woods, Sonny after him.

'Generous? Hah!' spat Dickie from his angry stance, hands on hips, legs apart. 'She didn't tell us we'd have to pay for it, did she?' He watched the others wend their way across the clearing, simmering with indignation, then with a last impulsive gesture he cupped his hands to his mouth and bellowed, '*Je-ze-bel!*' And the afternoon was filled with the whistle of startled wings as a pair of wood pigeons broke from the shelter of an oak tree.

Dickie threw his shirt over his arm and bent down to catch hold of his boots, using them to swing badtemperedly at the undergrowth as he followed the others.

Beth perched in the crook of a sycamore branch watching the three disappear into the woods. She wore a huge grin.

The sun was still mercilessly hot as they trudged down

the stony cart track. Their hair hung limp with sweat, their throats were parched, their tongues seemed swollen to twice their size and had taken on the texture of sandpaper.

'How's your ankle?' asked Dickie, adopting the role of legionnaire with the arms of his shirt tied around his forehead and the rest of it hanging in a cape to protect his burnt shoulders.

Sonny licked his lips. ''Twasn't too bad when we set off, but it's startin' to throb like the very devil now.' He hooked his hand over his shoulder to rub at the soreness that the sun had created. The moisture from the burst blisters trickled between his shoulder-blades to soak into his shirt. 'Jazers, could I do with a drink though.'

Bones flapped his shirt-front and blew down the inside. 'If I recall we passed a tavern on the way out here; it shouldn't be far now.'

'It may as well be a hundred miles for all we'll get from it,' replied Dickie. 'We've no money, remember?'

'But there's sure to be a pump or a horse-trough,' said Bones, and felt his throat turn even drier at the thought of cool, refreshing water.

Bones turned out to be right; around the next bend was a tavern, sparkling white with black timbers, which beckoned welcomingly. On reaching it Dickie sank gratefully onto a mounting block and flung down his boots and sack as the others lowered themselves to the cobblestones.

A buxom pot-wench appeared. She wore a peasant-style blouse which exposed pink shoulders, a brown skirt, its material far too heavy for this time of year, and a mob cap with which she had tried to contain her wild black hair. 'And what can I do for you three gentlemen?' She clutched a large jug of ale which the boys coveted greedily.

Dickie turned on his charm. 'Good day to ye, colleen. I wonder, could ye find it in your sweet person to help three young lads who've just been waylaid an' robbed of every farthing?'

The wench raised untidy black brows. 'Robbed, you say? Would you recognise the culprit?'

'Ah, God that I would. He was the biggest fella ye ever saw. He . . .'

'Only the one? Against three strong chaps like you?' she asked disbelievingly.

'Ah, but, lady ye oughta have seen the size of him. Why, he must've been all of seven feet tall, with hands like shovels an' a cruel wicked look about him.'

'Was he, by thunder? Seven feet tall, you say. My, it's a wonder he ever got into that pretty white dress, isn't it?' She laughed loudly at his discomposure. 'Oh, dear! I'm afraid you've been tangling with our Beth, young sir. She can see a half-wit coming a mile away, can Beth. Told me all about it only ten minutes ago.' She smiled at the recollection of the plump, white-clad figure who had come tripping gaily across the pastures and had slapped a handful of coins onto the bar top. The girl's invalid father would likely be enjoying his jugful of best ale right now. She was a rum one, was Beth. The pot-wench turned away still cackling to herself.

'Ah, come on, girleen!' begged Dickie. 'Would ye see a young fella die o' thirst?'

'Nay, I wouldn't. You're welcome to as much as you can drink.' She pointed to a water pump. 'From that.' She smiled archly and left them.

'Cow,' muttered Dickie and slipped from the mounting block to stick his head under the pump. The others, laughing at his failed tactics, also took their turn, one scooping his hands underneath the flow while another worked the handle, appreciatively gulping the lukewarm water.

Sated, they sank down once again, each turning their head in the direction of home. 'Why is it always further on t'way back?' grumbled Sonny, pulling his stockings from his haversack and picking at the knot in his bootlaces. The flowers lay upon the dusty cobbles, a limp and unattractive bouquet.

Bones, too, had picked some, if only as an afterthought. It had perhaps been asking too much of his father to keep the secret. Once Jimmy was in his cups he would likely

73

blab about his son's absence from work. The flowers might act as a palliative when dealing with his mother. He pulled on his stockings and laced his boots.

'Bones should be home in no time in his seven-leagued boots,' observed Dickie wryly.

Bones sighed patiently. 'I know they're a mite too big . . .'

'A mite?' laughed the other. 'They're like battleships.'

'Sure, 'tis all right for you who doesn't have to wear hand-me-downs,' objected Bones. 'Our Brendan grew out o' them an' me mother isn't likely to be throwin' them out, is she? Anyways, I'll grow into them.'

'When – in eighteen-eighty?' Dickie was in the process of donning his shirt when the sudden sound of music made him cock his head. 'Listen! There's somethin' goin' on round the back there.'

Inquisitively they crept around to the rear of the tavern to investigate. In the ale-house's rose-hedged garden men in white shirts and trousers danced in formation to the accompaniment of fiddles and a squeezebox. Their clothes were decked with long trails of red and green ribbons, their hats embellished with flowers. Each man held a stick which, in accordance with certain notes in the music, they laid across the opposing man's stick with a hearty thwack.

There was also another man but dressed differently to the rest who went among the good-natured crowd of villagers and beat them about the head with a pig's bladder on a stick. They seemed to enjoy this greatly for when the music ended they voluntarily dipped into their purses to supply the dancers with ale. The three boys watched agog at the Morris Dancers' mode of drinking; well-seasoned in this art they simply poured the entire contents of the tankards down their throats with barely a trace of resistance from an Adam's apple. Then with an appreciative gasp and a wipe of their upper lips they were off and entering yet another formation dance.

The boys sat down on the grass to watch the show, keeping well back from the main body of the crowd so that they would be in no danger of being asked for money.

The Morris Dancers tripped up and down the sun-baked lawn to the sound of the squeezebox and the jingling bells which encircled their knees. They danced in pairs, bearing between them a pliable hoop of flowers with which they weaved in and out of the other dancers. At the close of each dance the men swilled down the ale that the crowd had provided, thus making it inevitable that with each new dance their movements became a little merrier. By the seventh or eighth dance Dickie noticed that the tankards were not being drained so expertly; the men would leave an inch or two at the bottom. He pointed this out to his partners and suggested that they move around to the table which bore the dancers' tankards, in the hope that the men would soon be too drunk to notice if any was missing. His idea was rewarded. By the time the Morris Dancers were onto the twelfth dance of the afternoon – due to the crowd's demand for encores – they had imbibed so freely that one could almost hear it slopping about in their bellies as they danced.

The idea of going home soon left the boys as they sat down to share the dregs from the tankards, sniggering at the hilarious antics of the dancers. The Morrisers pranced leadenly up and down, their eyes like frosted glass. One of them made a wrong move, throwing the whole routine into confusion and making the crowd howl as the inebriated 'fool' swooped down upon the dancers and laid into them with the pig's bladder. Sonny thought his sides would split and the fun dissipated all bitter thoughts of Beth.

The flustered pot-wench slammed more foaming tankards on the table as the Morris Dancers swore and bickered at each other's inability to keep to the practised routine. Those foaming vessels were just too inviting to be left alone. While the crowd's attention was focused upon the fiasco on the lawn the three boys hooked sly fingers into the pewter handles and vanished behind a laurel bush.

Finally, amid a great deal of argument, the dancers staggered across to claim their drinks. Here another row broke out when it was discovered that three tankards were missing. The pot-wench swore they were there a minute ago, which led the intoxicated dancers to start accusing members of the crowd. The culprits listened, unrepentant, to the vociferous outburst and smiled into their tankards as the sharp ale struck the backs of their throats. Before long the disagreement had evolved into a full-blown battle with tankards being dented over heads and tables over-turned. With the residue of ale licked from their lips the boys thought it expedient to take their leave and slipped unnoticed back to the road, laughing uproariously at the trouble they had stirred up.

Further along the road they came upon a haywain, trun-dling mirage-like through the heat-haze. They summed up what little energy remained to run after it and throw themselves into the sweet-smelling hay.

Dickie chewed on a stalk and chuckled. 'Begod, what a bloody good lark that was!'

Bones agreed, his recumbent form draped over Sonny's knees, his long spindly legs dangling over the side of the cart. He imagined the hot sun on his naked skin, the smell of crushed pine – crushed by Beth's body, as he had crushed hers. 'Ah, it's been a grand day altogether,' he smiled, fingering the pathetic bouquet that lay on his chest. 'I don't think I'll ever forget it as long as I live.' The sun peeped through the leafy barrier, dappling his radiant face as they were slowly transported back towards reality.

The hay cart turned off before it reached the main road into the city, leaving them still quite a fair way to travel. The street was quiet and bathed in shadows when they finally reached it; everyone was having tea.

'Bye, Bones!' shouted Dickie cheerfully. 'See ye at Confession.'

''Tis more likely to be my Requiem Mass ye'll see me at,' parried Bones. 'The mammy'll kill me when I get home. Goodbye!' He hoisted his haversack and loped away.

Thomasin and Patrick looked up as their sons entered. 'By, there's no need to ask if you enjoyed yerselves,' laughed their mother, then called Erin in from the scullery

76

to come and view her brothers. 'Have yer ever seen owt like these two?' she asked amusedly, pointing at the grimy, sweat-stained shirts, the burrs that clung to their trousers, the sun-kissed faces perimetered by tousled hair.

Sonny proffered the bunch of flowers which were now draped pitiably over his fist. Thomasin kissed him and tried to smooth the defiant red hair. 'Flowers, eh?' she said cynically. 'I hope that doesn't mean yer've been up to mischief. What 'ave yer been doin' with yerselves anyroad?'

'Oh, nowt much,' answered Dickie with ease, and vanished into the scullery to wash his hands.

How can he lie so effortlessly? thought Sonny, and was all at once deeply grateful for his sunburnt face as a blush swept up from his neck and turned his earlobes into throbbing beacons.

CHAPTER EIGHT

Monday hauled itself wearily over the embrasures in the city walls. It could almost have been a different season for the outlook was grey and miserable with a north-easterly wind creating dust devils in the rain-starved street.

Thomasin bustled in from the yard, cradling some tiny object on her outstretched palm. 'Eh, aren't sparrows careless mothers,' she said to Erin who was bringing her ebony hair under control and who now smiled sadly at the pathetic little corpse on her stepmother's hand. 'That's the seventh little golly I've picked up since Friday.'

Thomasin gazed down for a moment at the naked, ugly creature whose bulging eyes looked so out of proportion to its skinny body. Why should she feel so bogged down with sadness at such an insignificant death? Most likely because every summer with these numerous little corpses came the memory of the child she herself had lost. The child that had been of similar appearance to this naked sparrow when it had been torn from her body; unfinished, incomplete. Adjacent to the sadness was a feeling of anger. Why should she, a good and caring mother, be denied the right to bear any more children while the sparrows allowed theirs to die with indiscriminate ease? With a flick of her wrist she committed the dead sparrow to the flames and brushed her hands. 'Aye well, if yer about ready, lass, we'd best get down town an' open t'shop.' Erin was proving a great asset at the grocery. It was a pity the partnership would probably have to end soon.

Thomasin laid a coin on the table and addressed her elder son. 'That's for the men who empty t'closet. Take it round to Miss Peabody if it hasn't been collected by the time you go out – and don't go spending it.'

"Course I won't! Honestly, no one ever seems to trust me,' complained Dickie, pocketing the coin.

'I wonder why – an' don't sit lozzockin' all mornin' neither. Sonny, make sure he goes for that job, won't yer? An' the two of yer can wash up them pots when yer've finished quaffin'.'

Sonny acquiesced as his mother and sister left for work. Dickie rose from his seat at the table and selected a clay pipe from the mantelshelf, helping himself from his father's tobacco bowl. The pipe lighted, he flopped into the armchair and swung his legs over the arm, puffing inexpertly.

'Didn't me mam say we had to do these pots?' said Sonny, draining the teapot.

Dickie closed his eyes and snuggled back into the chair. 'Sure, I'm not lowering meself to do women's work. I'm takin' some beauty sleep before I go see about that job.'

'But me mam said . . .'

'Me mam said, me mam said!'

'You're a warty old prick! Ye never go out o' yer way to help anyone, d'ye? Ye deserve a good thrashin'.'

'But you'll not be the one to give it to me,' replied Dickie slyly, opening one twinkling eye. 'Else ye'll not be gettin' an introduction to Bertha.'

'I'll believe that when it happens! Ye keep promisin' but

78

I don't see any results. I think yer just using it as a way to keep me at your beck an' call.' Sonny dashed the plates together noisily and knocked a cup to the floor.

'If ye perform like that there'll be no need to wash 'em,' observed Dickie, then: 'Ah-ah!' as he staved off his brother's attack. 'Lay a finger on me an' 'tis a life o' celibity ye'll be leadin'. Now go wash up like a good little fella an' leave the man to get his rest.'

'I hate you!' said Sonny with feeling. 'An' it's *not* celibity, it's celibacy.'

Later in the morning, Dickie finally collected the energy to haul himself from the chair and go down to the iron foundry with his brother. They crossed the foundry yard where men shovelled great heaps of coal into trolleys and, after being given directions by the gateman, stepped inside the busy works. If they had thought the noise deafening from the outside then the stridency of the amalgamated forces inside almost shattered their eardrums.

'Jazers, are ye sure ye can stand to work in this?' yelled Sonny as he and his brother automatically slapped their palms to the sides of their heads.

His voice was lost in the medley of clanking and crashing, metallic hammering, the scraping of shovels that stoked the furnaces and the nerve-wracking *hisssss!* as the white-hot girders were lowered into troughs of cold water. Everywhere seemed bathed in an orange glow. In Sonny's observation every man appeared to have a turnip lantern stuck on his shoulders instead of a head, as though there were a candle implanted in each brain, lending the eyes a feverish inhuman glow. Sweat gushed from the men's brows. It marbled the grime-caked faces and fell from glistening noses to disappear into nothing as it dropped onto the hot metal on which the men laboured. Their arms strained with knotted sinews as they manoeuvred the great cast-iron boilers and machine parts, while others steered huge ladles of molten ore towards the waiting moulds.

The heat was indescribable. Even the very air seemed on fire. The boys were reluctant to breathe for fear of inhaling the angry red sparks that spurted like devil's spume from all directions. They wandered, sweating, further into the womb of the foundry in search of the foreman fettler, who had just emerged from a small office when they eventually found him.

'Could we be after askin' ye for a job?' bellowed Dickie. 'Our friend, Martin Flaherty, said he'd have a word with ye. Me an' me brother – have ye anything to offer us?'

To his surprise the man understood at once, which was more than could be said for his own response to the man's reply. The foreman gestured for them to step into the office he had just vacated, then closed the door behind them.

'There! Perhaps you'll be able to hear me better in here,' he told them, still shouting through force of habit. 'A job, you say? Are you sure you're up to it?' He eyed Dickie up and down. Though the lad was tall he had not much depth to his chest.

'I am,' replied Dickie stolidly.

'Aye well, I'll give you t'benefit o' t'doubt. Your brother wants work as well, does he?' He turned his attention on Sonny and gripped the boy's upper arms. 'Bit more meat on this'n. When can you start?'

Sonny was ready to answer, 'Today' when he felt his brother's nudge.

'Next week,' Dickie was saying. 'I have to work notice at my present employment.' Might as well cadge a week's holiday if it were possible.

'Why are you leaving there?' enquired the man, over whose appearance Sonny was puzzling. What was so odd about the foreman? Why, that was it! He had no facial hair; no eyelashes nor brows, and there was none protruding from his hat, either. Sonny unconsciously fingered his own bright hair. He did not relish this happening to him.

'I wanted a better job,' replied Dickie. 'More prospects. I heard it was good here.'

'Oh, you did, did you? Well, I don't know what else you heard, but I don't tolerate no tomfoolery; any o' that or any disrespect for myself and you'll be out. The hours are six till six with Saturday afternoon off.' The man opened the door and the clamour leapt back with a vengeance. 'Start Monday next. Six o'clock on the dot. Any latecomers or bilkers get some o' that!' He brandished a hefty fist.

Assured of a job, the boys set their faces to the exit, peering through the ochrous haze for a sight of their friend. In the event it was Bones who spotted them. He had been sent to fetch some water for one of the fettlers and came trotting over in his ungainly fashion, on his arrival offering the cup to Dickie. 'Have a drink on me.' Dickie studied the layer of oatmeal that floated gruesomely on the surface of the water – an addition that helped to ward off the stomach cramps – and not so politely declined. Bones caught the impatient glare of the foreman and returned to his post. Halfway there, he turned to grin at his friends, walking backwards and making gestures that involved testing the muscles of his right arm. The Feeneys, however, interpreted the action's true meaning, and grinned back; Bones was still full of himself over Saturday's escapade.

He continued to walk backwards, leering and making graphic signals that referred to the accommodating Beth, when Sonny caught the agitated mouthings of the men standing to Bones' blind side. If Sonny had shared their lip-reading skills he would have deciphered the cries of: 'Eh up!' So would Bones, if he had been looking where he should have been, but he wasn't – he was still acting the goat and walking backwards.

A second before the back of his heel touched the great mould of boiling metal, his play-acting gave way to a bemused frown as Sonny and Dickie, realising what the others were trying to convey, started to leap up and down, pointing, stabbing frantic fingers in the air. But their semaphore was insufficient to stop him taking one more step backwards. One fatal step.

Bones finally sensed the obstacle against his heel and turned suddenly. Too suddenly. His mouth flew open in terror. His hands flailed like windmills trying to regain his

81

balance as his knees began to bend into a sitting position – then the white-hot molten metal seemed to erupt and cascade over the sides of the mould as Bones plunged down into its searing folds.

The onlookers, their mouths tortured O's in the scorched faces were caught in a suspension of time. They saw the young apprentice swallowed up by the threshing lava, heard the hideous cry that pierced the hitherto impenetrable barrier of noise.

Dickie felt an excruciating pain in his arm. He lowered his astonished face to the source of the discomfort and saw his brother's fingers digging deep into the flesh. He prised open Sonny's grip and, rubbing at the crescent-shaped weals which oozed blood, ran over to the scene of the tragedy. The men, finally coming to their senses, had gathered round the huge mould searching for a way to save the boy. One of them seized a pair of giant tongs and fished about in the steaming liquid, taking care not to splash any onto his feet. Eventually the tongs bit on something and the man attempted to pull it free.

His revulsion and shock as the object bobbed to the surface made him hurriedly drop the tongs, and what remained of the Flaherty boy sank once more to the bottom of the mould. The men leapt back as the lava slopped over the sides.

The brief glimpse of Bones' face where the flesh had burst through the skin like plague buboes was too much to stomach. Dickie whirled away and was violently sick. The force of his retching made him feel as though he were bringing up his very boots. His eyes swam as the vomit forced its way into every tube in his face, burning, scalding – like Bones had been. Sonny was coming towards him. 'Go back!' he managed to splutter, flapping his hands at his brother. But Sonny, like some automaton, came on.

With the re-emergence of their senses, the men had begun to hack at the mould. The brick and sand construction caved in and the still-hot metal trickled thickly over the foundry floor. Dickie pulled out a rag handkerchief and wiped his face, staring hypnotically with his brother as the level of the liquid diminished.

They had joked yesterday about Bones' nakedness, saying that there was more meat on the bones their mother used for soup – and that was exactly what the object at the bottom of the mould could be compared to as the last of the liquid drained away. On the parts of his body unprotected by the leather apron and solid boots – his face, the vee of his open-necked shirt, his hands – the liquid had boiled and rendered what little flesh the boy had on him, causing it to fall away and expose the pearly white of his bones. The agonised cavern which had been his mouth was still filled with the molten iron; a metallic, solidifying pool in the unrecognisable face. Mummified into a silent scream.

I hope to God it's not soup for dinner, was Sonny's first illogical thought as the grotesque corpse was swiftly covered over with someone's apron. Even when it was hidden he could not tear his eyes away. Quite suddenly he realised that the clamour had stopped; there was now only the underlying roar of the furnaces as men came from all directions to join the horrified cluster. A desperate figure fought its way through the crush. Jimmy Flaherty – Bones' father – shook off the hands that tried to shield him from the horror. 'Come away, Jimmy! For pity's sake, come away!' and came to stand where his son lay like a baby in a cradle. A crib of death. He sharply pulled back the apron that hid Bones and drew in a tortuous breath.

'Oh, Mother o' Christ! Me son! Me son!' His fingernails clawed at his waxen cheeks and he drew up sharply, the whites of his eyes turning red as the tears formed. He dropped his hands to his stomach and rubbed heavily as though trying to soothe a terrible ache. He bent over with the agony, moaning in a strange, wild language. His anguished sobs gave way to a bout of consumptive coughing. He heaved and barked into a filthy rag that, when it came away, was spotted with red. And still he coughed. Coughed and coughed.

Someone set up a firm clapping between his shoulderblades. 'As if that'll help,' wept Jimmy. 'As if that'll shake out the filthy rot that's set into me lungs, that's killing me.' He held up a hand to ward off the thumping and Sonny dropped his hand to his side, watching helplessly as Jimmy's harsh, dry cough competed with the roar of the furnaces. He felt a tug at his sleeve and looked up as his brother bent his face to mutter, 'C'mon, 'tis best we go, there's nowt we can do here.' Sonny was about to lay a last compassionate pat on Jimmy's shoulder, then decided against it and followed his brother out into the welcoming fresh air.

Dickie once again pulled out his handkerchief and wiped his sweating face which had temporarily lost its healthy tan. 'Well, that puts paid to that,' he said, roughly shoving the handkerchief back into his pocket. 'If they need a new apprentice they can look elsewhere. I'd rather make love to a pox-ridden donkey than go back into that hell-hole.'

Sonny did not reply. Could not reply. He just kept seeing that appalling sight. It would not go away. Oh, dear God, Bones! I can't believe it. I can't believe we'll never see ye again.

'Mother o' Mercy, Son,' breathed Dickie. 'Did ye see it? One minute he's walkin' about, the next he's screaming like a crab that's been chucked into boiling water.' Sonny winced and his mind begged, *please don't!* But he couldn't coax the thought through his lips. 'And his face,' Dickie went on, regardless of the mental pain he was inflicting. 'There was nothin' left of it, was there? Ye could see all the bones an' stuff . . .'

'Don't!' Sonny finally managed to squeeze out.

But his brother appeared not to have heard. 'Did ye see his mouth open as he went under? All that boiling liquid must've poured straight into his lungs. God, didn't he look horrible with the skin all meltin' off him like lard? And did . . .' He did not finish the sentence. Sonny grabbed hold of his shirt and rammed him up against a wall, his eyes brimming with moisture in the lobster-red face.

'Will ye shut your cruel mouth or will I shut it for ye?'

he rasped. 'That's Bones you're talking about – our friend – not some lump o' bloody meat!' – Though God knows that's what he looked like, came the anguished thought.

Dickie laid pacifying hands over the palsied fists that imprisoned him. 'Hey, you're tremblin'.' He felt the vibrations from Sonny's body run into his own. 'God, I'm sorry, Son. I didn't mean . . . it was just . . . I can't believe what I saw.' He too began to feel shaky. 'It's the shock of it . . . I keep seeing him going in there over and over again.' He disentangled Sonny's fingers from his shirt and patted his brother's cheek. 'C'mon, what we need is a drink.'

Sonny fell in beside him again and the pair slipped into the first public house that they encountered. Dickie slammed a coin on the counter and asked for two nips of gin, then rubbed his hands briskly over his face in an effort to rid himself of the vision.

'That's the money me mam gave ye to pay the men who empty the sugar-house,' Sonny pointed out in a dull voice. 'Ye were supposed to take it round to Miss P.'s.'

Dickie summoned a grin despite his queasiness. 'Then Miss P. will get the blame if the closet overflows before the next time 'tis emptied. Anyroad,' he nodded at his brother's glass where the gin slopped about with the boy's trembling, ''tis not as if we squandered it but, like, spent it on medicine. Don't we need something to calm our nerves after that lot? Knock it all back at once, Son, else ye'll not feel the benefit.' He followed his own advice and slammed the glass onto the bar. ''Fraid I've not enough for another. Have you any money?'

Sonny shook his head. He threw the contents of the glass down his throat and fought back a cough as the gin burnt its way down his gullet.

'Christ, I still can't believe it, can you?' Dickie played with his glass, upturning it on the counter and making a pattern of wet rings. ''Tis such a terrible way to die. When I go . . .'

'Please,' snapped his brother. 'Do we have to talk about it?'

'Oh, no . . . no . . . 'course not. Well, if we've no money

we might as well be off.' Dickie led the way out of the saloon and into the street where they made for home.

'Did ye mean it about not startin' at the foundry?' asked Sonny, then side-stepped to avoid a quack who had planted his display case upon a trestle in the centre of the footwalk and who was in the motions of persuading a householder to purchase one of his patent remedies. His presence had attracted a number of street arabs who were doing their utmost to disrupt his smooth patter by their impertinent enquiries: "Ave yer gorrowt for a boil on the bum, mister? Gorrowt to mek me cleaver grow?' until the housewife grabbed a besom and chased them off. On any other occasion Dickie and his brother would have joined the urchins in their torment of the quack, but today the scene passed almost unnoticed.

'I meant it all right,' answered Dickie. 'Sure, I'm not ending up like a boiled shrimp.' Sonny glared at him threateningly and he shrugged his apologies.

They took a short-cut through an alley where they stumbled upon a game of pitch and toss. The group of players looked up sharply at their approach then, satisfied the intruders were harmless, continued their game.

'You're not gonna tell me that you're still startin' on Monday?' continued Dickie.

Sonny screwed up his mouth in indecision. 'I don't want to – but what will me mam say when we tell her we don't want to work at foundry? She was banking on us.'

'Don't you worry none about Mam,' said Dickie. 'When I've finished tellin' her about poor Bones she'll not be lettin' the pair of us within fifty yards o' the place.'

CHAPTER NINE

Dickie was correct; he had only related half of the grisly catalogue of Bones' injuries when Thomasin begged him to stop and he relaxed into a chair with a triumphant wink at his brother.

– Well, what little sympathy you had for our friend was short-lived, thought Sonny, feeling the familiar rush of aversion which was common to their relationship.

'Oh, that poor lad!' Thomasin could not get over the horror. 'An' his mother . . . I'll have to go see her, Pat.'

'Should we go right away, d'ye think?' he asked concernedly.

His wife thought for a moment, then decided, 'No, we can't afford for you to be getting the sack for being late back to work – an' I daren't abandon the shop in case t'new owner turns up . . . anyhow, we'll probably be in the way this afternoon. We'll go directly we've had tea.'

'Anyways,' Dickie went on casually, 'I forgot to tell ye, Mam, – the foreman says we can start on Monday next.'

'You'll do no such thing!' Thomasin downed a plate on the table ready for dinner as Erin leaned over her to position the cutlery. 'I'd be worried out o' me mind every time yer went out o' t'door in case it were t'last time I'd see yer.'

Patrick was quick to agree. 'An' now I've given it more thought I don't much care for the idea o' Sonny leavin' school, neither. It seems such a waste of his skills, him being so brainy-like. I would've preferred for him to find something more worthwhile than the iron foundry.'

'There's lots o' things I'd like an' all,' retorted his wife as she arranged the table. 'But we can't afford 'em now, that's why he's got to leave an' find a job. I told the same thing to Brother Francis when he cornered me about Sonny's absence.'

'Just hold on!' Patrick waved his pipestem. 'You're not thinking any further than the end o' this week, woman. Just consider . . . if Sonny's allowed to continue his education there'll be a better job at the end of it.'

'It's all very well for you to talk, you don't have to make the money spin out.'

An argument ensued, at the end of which it was decided by Patrick that Sonny would take a little time from his studies to find a temporary job, but the minute the others found work he would go back to school.

His wife nodded. 'Sounds reasonable enough – but I wasn't doin' it out o' selfishness; yer know. Way you're going on yer'd think I enjoyed makin' him miss his education. I think it's just as important as you do.'

'Good! Then perhaps we might have our dinner? If we spend any more time jawing I *am* going to be late back for work. An' then we really would be in the you-know-what.'

Thomasin sighed and struggled with a large saucepan on the hob. 'Right. Come on, Erin – get rest o' them spoons laid out.' She took off the lid and, with a pair of tongs, began to stir about in its depths, eventually withdrawing a steaming chicken carcase. 'I can't say I've very much appetite after hearing about poor Martin but starvin' ourselves won't help him, poor lad. Anyway, it's only a bit o' soup.'

She turned bemusedly at the noisy scraping of chairs that greeted her innocent statement. There were now only two persons seated at the table. The others were out in the yard – retching their boots up.

'Anybody home?' rang out the cry and the family's response came as a combined groan, knowing what the visit would entail.

'Where the hell does she think we are?' muttered Patrick. 'There's nobody escapes this house without herself knowing about it.'

The family had just had tea. Patrick normally liked to relax with a good read at this time of day, but there was more serious thoughts to consider this evening. A wizened squirrel face peeped around the inner door and Nelly Peabody insinuated herself into the unenthusiastic gathering.

'I just thought I'd come round for a little chat,' she told Thomasin as she seated herself next to Dickie on the sofa. Thomasin's son rose and made to leave the room.

'Sit down!' commanded his mother. She knew from

experience that one by one the room would be vacated, leaving her to listen unsupported to Nelly's non-stop gossip. If she had to suffer Nelly then so would they. 'You too!' she ordered Erin who had edged towards the scullery.

'Sure, I was only going to wash up,' offered the girl lamely.

'I know what you were gonna do,' answered Thomasin sternly. 'Now sit down.'

Even Miss Peabody was taken aback by Thomasin's curtness; she seemed unusually on edge this evening. 'I can see you've got a new vase,' – she moved her head towards the one which held Sonny's bouquet. No one answered; she always began her conversations like this, starting with the insignificancies and progressing craftily to more pertinent issues. Tonight, Thomasin cut her short. Nelly's gossip was all very well when it didn't involve personal friends but she was damned if she was going to listen to that awful compendium of young Martin's injuries again. 'If yer've come to tell us about Molly's boy, Nelly,' she said bluntly, 'then yer can save yer breath, we already know. Dickie and Sonny were there, and we're going round to see her the minute I've stitched this hole in Sonny's shirt.' She continued with her sewing, temperamentally weaving the needle in and out of the fabric.

Nelly's face advertised her disappointment. 'Oh . . .' she replied weakly, 'then they'll also have witnessed Mr Flaherty's sad demise . . .' She broke off with a triumphant smirk as Thomasin's face told her they had not. She would now enjoy herself for a while – strike back at Thomasin for her rudeness. She rose, shaking the creases from her skirt. 'Well, as you apparently know all the details I shall leave. It's obvious my presence is an intrusion.'

Thomasin threw aside the shirt and leapt up to grab Nelly's arm. 'Did I hear you say that Jimmy Flaherty is dead?' It emerged in a disbelieving whisper.

Nelly took great satisfaction in her reply. 'But, my dear Mrs Feeney, I understood you to say that you'd been fully informed of the incident.'

Patrick too had risen and, catching hold of Nelly's other

89

arm said, 'Don't be taking us all around the houses, woman! Tell us what ye know.'

Nelly freed herself and gave him the most disapproving look she could muster. 'Mr Feeney, I will not be spoken to in such a manner.'

'Oh, Nelly for God's sake!' shouted Thomasin exasperatedly. 'I'll get him to clean your doorstep with his tongue for the next week if yer like but please, *please* tell us what yer know.'

'I'm sure you don't have to go to those lengths, Thomasin,' said Nelly airily. 'All I ask is to be treated in a civil manner. You made it very clear that you don't wish to listen to what I have to say.'

Thomasin could see that she was going to get nowhere until she had made amends for her brusqueness. She levelled her voice. 'Nelly, I apologise for being so sharp with you. It's simply that I was feelin' rather upset about poor Martin. I didn't intend to be rude.'

'Very well, I accept your apology.' Nelly was duly appeased and smoothed her skirts again before beginning, 'There are very few details. As you know, Mr Flaherty suffered with consumption . . .'

'He was coughin' awful bad when we left,' confirmed Dickie.

'Shush!' commanded his mother. 'Proceed, Nelly.'

'Well, he was wailing and carrying on to Mr Coulson – you know, he's the one with the gimpy leg that lives . . .'

'Yes, yes, Nelly! Go on!'

'Well, as I said there isn't much to tell. He was talking to Mr Coulson when instead of words out came all this blood – covered in it Mrs Coulson said her husband was – she wasn't too pleased because she had to set to and wash . . .' She caught Thomasin's glower and reverted to the subject. 'Yes, well, the main of it was that they called a doctor but it was too late. Mr Flaherty died of heart failure before ever the doctor put his hat on. Of course that's always the case, isn't it? Never around when you want . . .'

'Oh, dear God, poor Molly!' Thomasin sat down

heavily. 'And there's me thinkin' I've got worries; they're nowt compared to hers.' She rose again almost immediately and flicking her shawl from a hook laid it round her shoulders. 'We'll have to go now, Pat.' She shepherded Miss Peabody out as she spoke. 'She must be nearly out of her mind – oh, I wish I'd gone earlier, she'll think we don't care.' Her mind went back to the time when Sonny was lying near to death; when no one came to visit and she had thought it was because they did not care. Such silly thoughts went through one's head at times like these. She snapped the cotton from Sonny's shirt and tossed it back at him. 'That'll have to do until later.'

He put it on and asked, 'Do we have to come?' dreading that he would be asked to look upon that grotesque facsimile of his friend.

'Yes, I'm afraid you'll have to come and pay yer respects,' replied his mother. She began to fill her basket with bereavement gifts for the widow, items with which Mr Penny had rewarded her on his last visit to the shop. – He's always spoiling me, thought Thomasin, bundling the packages into her basket – or should I say *was;* there would be no more little extras now. But at least there would also be no more worrying about which two people were going to complete the triad of death. Births, deaths and marriages – they always came in triplicate, and it always worried her senseless whenever a friend died, waiting to see who the others would be.

To add to the family's misery, it had begun to rain and by the time they reached the courtyard where the Flahertys resided their clothes were sodden. Patrick cast grim eyes around him as he and his family picked their way through the piles of stinking excrement and bloody puddles that had gathered in the unpaved yard; it was like a swamp here when it rained. A pig was tethered outside Raper's abattoir, a ring through its nose. The look in its pink-rimmed eye was one of abject misery as it huddled against a wall to escape the deluge; a look which, for Patrick, summed up the whole insalubrious environment.

He gave a perfunctory tap at the door of the Flaherty

dwelling and, without waiting for an answer, opened it to step inside, almost knocking over the person who stood directly behind it. ''Tis sorry I am, Brendan,' he apologised as the young man made room for the Feeneys to enter. 'We just came to pay our respects to themselves.' He squeezed in between Brendan and Norah, shouldering his way through the prodigious Flaherty tribe – James, Michael, Thomas, Stephen, Malachy, Mary, Julia, Ellen and a horde of younger ones whose names he could not for the life of him remember though he was Godfather to at least half a dozen of them. All had congregated around the two open coffins in the unwelcoming room, leaving scant space for movement.

The candles which stood sentry around the paupers' coffins guttered deliriously in the moist draught that blew in from the tiny open window. They added little cheer to the mawkish gathering but rather boosted the eeriness. The room blossomed with the mingled odours of wet wool, decaying foundations and death. Thomasin blanched on finding both coffins open; she would not have insisted on her children's presence had she known that Martin was to be viewed also. It was one thing to look upon an unmarked body – quite another to confront the disfigured wreck of a child. Thankfully they were not yet close enough to be able to see into the coffins. She would try to keep it that way.

Patrick folded his cap into his pocket as the widow Flaherty glanced up at him. Molly's once fine bone-structure had been eroded to a gaunt mask with the pressures of incessant childbearing and poverty. Her skin, due to years of neglect, was wrinkled and seamed with dirt and could have been chiselled from bog oak. Around her scrawny shoulders and covering her flattened, sagging breasts was a sloppily-made and stained bodice. The drab, tattered skirt was draped with a piece of equally soiled sacking, secured in a knot over one bony hip. Her black slitty eyes were red with weeping, also from the quantity of whiskey she had consumed.

''Tis awful sorry we were to hear about your loss, Molly.'

Patrick took the basket from his wife's arm and proffered it to his old friend. 'It must've been a terrible blow to have the two o' them taken at once.'

''Twas, Pat – ah, God love ye for your kind thoughts.' The scent of liquor was strong on Molly's breath. She gestured for one of her daughters to take Patrick's gift. ''Tis needing them we'll be an' no mistake with two wages gone.' Of Molly's children, four were married and only three of the ones still at home had been wage-earners. 'I've had to scratch about for the pennies to put on their poor darlin' eyes. An' shall I tell ye a strange thing? Ye know how my Jimmy used to have his wages drunk by the time he got home? Well, Saturday dinner he comes in sober as a grave an' puts his full wages on that table. "Molly," says he, "I've seen the error of me ways. I was going into the King Willie when who should I meet coming out? 'Twas meself, an' no word of a lie. All togged up like a royal retainer, I was an' all. Fair shook me up. An' never another drop'll pass me lips for 'twas goin' mad I thought I was."' She tugged out a grubby rag and began to wail. Those nearest to her pressed supportive hands to her shoulders. ''Twas a sure sign, was it not, Pat? An' to think I laid into poor Marty for skippin' off work on Saturday – I could cut off these cruel hands that beat me wean.'

Patrick's sons and daughter were crushed behind their parents, dreading the moment when they would be asked to pay their respects to the dead. Dickie's eyes flitted around the assembly. Normally he avoided visiting Bones' hovel; there could be no avoidance today, but he wished they would get on with it and let him out into the fresh air. Always in search of humour, even in the most unlikely places, his lips twitched at the corners and he bent to whisper to his brother, 'Fancy some fried mushrooms?'

Sonny followed his brother's gaze along the running walls to where an ugly fungus grew in abundance. He felt a deep disgust at Dickie. How could he joke at a time like this?

Molly gave a noisy sniff and weaved the rag through her fingers. 'Ah, 'tis a terrible wicked thing to happen to me poor darlin' Marty – an' him little more than a babe. If it'd been only himself 'twould've been hard enough, but to have Marty taken too is more'n a heart can bear. An' didn't I know the very minute he was summoned? Didn't his young ghosteen come a visitin' at the very moment they tell me he perished, God be good to him.' There was another brief interlude while Molly further dampened her hanky. 'An' I'll get no constipation from the fettlin' works. 'Twas his own fault, they say – though not to me face o' course. Sure, I never would've known I was a widow if Mrs McMahon hadn't passed on the message.'

'Bloody typical!' snorted Thomasin, then leaned over to comfort the woman. 'If there's owt we can do, Molly, yer know you only have to ask.' She shivered and rubbed her hands over her upper arms. 'By, it's turned right cold, hasn't it? Wouldn't we be better wi' t'window shut?'

'Sure, an' how would their souls be escapin' if we shut it?' asked Molly, then indicated the coffins. 'Would ye care to pay your respects now?'

Patrick shuffled up to stand over Jimmy's coffin. The face below looked oddly at peace despite the harrowing death he had suffered. ''Tis very well himself looks,' he told the widow, then turned to his wife. 'D'ye not think so, Tommy?' She nodded with the barest of smiles. Would she ever become used to the mad Irish and their customs?

'Ah, 'tis right y'are, Pat,' agreed Molly. ''Tis the healthiest I've seen him in a long time.' She tugged at Erin's sleeve. 'Come by me, girleen an' pay your respects to your Uncle Jimmy.' A tiny hand hooked its way into the coffin and made for the pennies on the dead eyes; a larger hand slapped it down.

Erin, her face like parchment in the candlelight, looked into the box and racked her brains for something nice to say. 'He's looking very smart, Aunt Molly,' she finally provided.

'He is, pet, he is.' Molly thrust the reluctant Feeney boys up against the coffin. ''Twas real generous o' Mrs O'Brien to lend me her Declan's suit. Though perhaps 'tis a mite short in the arm – what d'ye think, boys?'

Dickie shook his head violently, gagging at the odour from the coffin. 'Seems like a perfect fit to me, Aunt Molly. Right dandy.'

Sonny hastily nodded his agreement and Molly, not noticing Dickie's expression of disgust, seemed content. 'Sure an' we have to have him spruce for his viewin'. 'Tis a pity it'll have to go back after the wake. Well, boys, come say goodbye to your little pal.'

This was the moment they had been dreading. Thomasin saw her younger son's pale face beseech her and rapidly intervened. 'Oh, heavens! I think I left kettle on t'fire,' she exclaimed, hand over mouth. 'Sonny, you an' Dickie run home an' check, will yer? Else it'll be like a collander when we get back. Hurry now.' She pushed them through the press of sour-smelling bodies and out into the yard before anyone could object. She was only sorry that she could not spare Erin in this manner but she could see that Molly was rather miffed already and sending three people to see to one kettle would be overdoing things.

'Does it take the two o' them to look after one kettle?' asked Molly peevishly.

'Well, I worry about 'em if they're out on their own at night,' explained Thomasin, knowing it sounded a lame excuse for two such strapping youths. 'Yer never know what might happen to 'em.'

'Sure, the size o' your Dickie I would've thought him well able to take care o' hisself.'

'Well, it were more t'bobbies I'm scared about, Molly. They're that edgy they'd brain anybody just for being out after dark. If anybody'd cop it yer can be sure it'd be our Dickie. I feel safer if Sonny's there to see to him. I know he's big but he's nobbut a bairn really.'

'Almost the same age as my poor Marty,' sighed Molly, and began to weep again. 'It is frightened to look at him y'all are? I know he's a fearful . . .'

'I *told* yer, I left kettle on.' Thomasin edged up to Patrick who stood ashen-faced at the foot of Martin's coffin. Her innards seemed to liquefy with the shock of that first sighting. The horror leapt within them all but somehow, each managed to pass the compliment that custom demanded.

Molly, satisfied with their tributes, said, 'Will ye be takin' tea with us Pat – or would ye prefer something stronger?'

'Ah, thank ye, no, we'll not intrude on your grief any longer.' Patrick steered his wife and daughter towards the door, stepping over the pale-faced babies who crawled between the forest of legs. He asked when the wake would be, telling Molly that they'd all be there.

They edged their way out into the foul-smelling yard and made for home. None of them spoke for a while, speechless with what they had seen. It was left to Thomasin to break the silence. 'Poor little skite.' Her voice held incredulity. 'Now I understand why our banes were so chary of comin'.'

'My sympathies lie more with Molly,' said her husband, lowering his head against the driving rain. 'I wonder how she'll cope with two wages short.'

'Aren't yer forgettin' summat?' asked his wife, then swore as she stepped into a puddle and the water soaked into her stocking.

'I'm not forgetting,' he replied sharply. ''Tis just thankful I am that we haven't all Molly's brood to feed.'

'We'll still be in a pickle though,' insisted Thomasin. 'It won't be long before t'new owner turns up at shop an' turfs us out – an' I'm not lookin' forward to tomorrow either.' Tuesday was the day of Mr Penny's funeral.

'Cheer up, woman.' Patrick caught her arm and tucked it through the crook of his. 'There's always clover growing round a cowpat. Haven't we been down before an' come springin' back up many a time? Who knows what could be round the bend?'

'It's you who's round the bend,' she replied sardonically. 'I suppose you mean I could be layin' a fire an' find a bag o' sovs stuffed up chimney?'

'Stranger things have happened, have they not?'

'My husband, the eternal optimist,' said Thomasin, but smiled.

CHAPTER TEN

During the next week Thomasin and her daughter made valiant efforts to bring the shop into order for the new owner, although they were still in the dark as to who this might be. Rather than cope with an inventory during working hours when they would have customers to distract them, they had decided to do it after closing time one evening. Workers were rushing homewards as Thomasin turned the sign to 'Closed' and locked the door, re-opening it a few minutes later to admit her sons who had been pressganged into helping. A couple of days ago they had both found employment – Dickie at a match factory, his brother running errands for a newspaper office – so life was not quite so bleak as it had been.

'We'll have some tea before we start,' Thomasin informed them at their complaints of slave-labour. 'I've bought us a pie each an' I've left yer dad's tea in t'oven so he'll not have owt to moan about – though doubtless he'll make a chore out o' lifting it onto table. Eh, I'm fair clemmed meself.'

The pork pies had just been unveiled and the tea poured when Sonny observed, 'There's a fella at the door.'

'Well he can just shift away from the door!' Thomasin craned her neck to inspect the personage. 'We're closed!' she shouted and turned back to her tea, but the man was insistent, tapping on the glass with his cane until she could ignore him no longer and had to open the door. 'We're closed!'

'Yes, I am quite capable of reading the sign, strange though it might seem.' The man appeared to be very put

97

out. 'May I come in? I have no wish to discuss business matters on the doorstep.'

Thomasin experienced a lurch in her stomach. Oh, my goodness! This must be the new owner and here she was treating him like dirt. Fat chance she had of keeping her job now. She made belated efforts to sound affable. 'Oh, do please come in! Would you do us the honour of joining us in some tea?'

He frowned at the three young people whose eye-whites shone from the shadows. Thomasin, seeing his questioning glance, explained that she had brought her family to assist with the stocktaking before handing it over and hoped that he did not consider it too impudent. He manufactured a cursory smile and said that it was of no consequence to him whom she brought into the store and that he was merely a messenger of sorts.

'Then you're not the new owner?' said Thomasin, somewhat confused.

'Do I look like a shopkeeper, madam?' he asked imperiously, then added, 'No, I am simply a representative of Ramsworthy, Duce and Saddler, solicitors at law, here to extend an invitation on behalf of Mr Ramsworthy. He would very much like to see you at your earliest convenience.'

The mention of solicitors worried Thomasin even further. 'You mean I have to come to your office to see someone? What about?'

'That I am not at liberty to divulge,' answered the man, as though her very asking had caused him deep offence. 'When shall I say you will be calling? Would tomorrow at ten am be suitable?'

'I suppose so.' She gave an absent nod and he turned to go, standing aside for her to unlock the door. As he passed over the threshold she asked suddenly, 'Is it all right for me to carry on with what I was going to do, then?'

'I assume it will be in order,' he replied, and left.

'Well, can anyone tell me what all that was about?' Thomasin picked up the mug of tea and finding it only lukewarm poured it away. 'Eh, mebbe Mr Penny's left me some money.' She nudged Erin and chuckled. 'He was always sayin' "I'll remember you in my will".'

'Maybe that's not as daft as it sounds,' replied Erin, washing the cups. 'Didn't ye say he was very fond of ye? I'd not be surprised if he left ye a few bob.'

'Eh, I don't know about that. It has been said about Mr Penny that he were that narrow-nosed he'd take the sneeze out o' the pepper before he'd part with it.' Thomasin mused, a finger to her chin. 'Still, happen yer could be right about him leavin' me summat. He were never stingy where I was concerned. It would be nice if he left us a fiver. At least it'd tide us over till I find another job – 'cause if His Holiness what was just here is representing t'new owner I've not much chance o' keepin' this'n.'

'I'll bet ye were relieved when he said he wasn't the new owner,' laughed Erin.

Dickie joined in to mimic the visitor. ' "Do I look like a shopkeeper, madam?" Silly old fart.' He received a cuff round the ear.

'Don't you let me hear you using language like that, young man, else it's a wagon to Wetwang for you.'

They proceeded with the stocktaking, the boys stacking each commodity into piles for easy counting whilst Erin and their mother toured the shop with a clipboard and counted each item, giving an occasional screech as a disturbed spider ran from between the boxes. The lamplighter came and went proclaiming the lateness of the hour. After the last stack was counted they straightened their aching backs, the boys swept up and everything was left neat and tidy.

'I'll take the books home wi' me, I think,' yawned Thomasin, as they all brushed the patches of flour and dust from their clothes. 'Solicitor'll no doubt want to cast his beady over 'em.' She gave a last sad look around the shop – she had been very happy here – then locked the door on another episode of her life.

It had taken twenty minutes to reach the solicitors' offices in High Ousegate. She was early for her appointment;

better early than late. Turning the brass handle she peered nervously around the door, expecting it to open onto an office. Instead, there was a dark and dingy corridor leading up to a flight of stairs. Closing the door behind her she made her way slowly up these stairs and, on reaching the top, was confronted by two more doors. On one was a sign saying: *Geo. Ackroyd, Chartd. Acc.* The other bore a brass plaque which stated: *Ramsworthy, Duce and Saddler, Solicitors and Attorneys.* With a tentative knock she entered the office.

The clerk whom she had encountered the previous evening sat at a high desk which immediately faced the door, so that she had to make the long walk up to it under his disapproving sneer.

'Ah, Mrs Feeney!' The man forced a brief smile then reverted to his former grandiloquence. 'I shall inform Mr Ramsworthy of your arrival. Pray take a seat.'

He disappeared into another office while Thomasin seated herself and nervously examined her surroundings. The dark, unfriendly room smelt of ancient manuscripts, dust, pipe-tobacco and male sweat. Besides the clerk's desk, on which was spread a ledger, two inkwells – one red, one black – and a selection of writing implements, there was an aged table where, between the rolled and bound documents, she could detect the carved initials of apprentices long past, and the ink blots disgorged from troublesome quills. In one corner of the room was an umbrella-stand housing one battered gamp, presumably left by a forgetful client. In another corner was a coat-stand swathed with garments.

Thomasin began to perspire, due more to the thought of what awaited her in the other office than to the warm weather. If a humble clerk could be so formidable then what sort of ogre would his master be? She was about to find out; the clerk emerged from his superior's lair and informed her that Mr Ramsworthy would see her now. With a downwards tug at her grey zouave jacket she straightened her shoulders and swept into the solicitor's office with more confidence than she actually felt.

But instead of an ogre she was greeted by a white-haired, pink-featured old gentleman with a stomach that bespoke its propensity for suet puddings and port wine. He shook her hand warmly as if she were an important and valued client, putting her immediately at ease. He bade her take a seat and spoke with a voice that made her imagine that his collar was fastened far too tightly and the words had to force themselves through the constricted aperture.

'Now, Mrs Feeney, as you are the only person to whom the will pertains I shall without further ado attempt to convey to you the deceased's wishes.'

'I'm sorry,' stammered Thomasin. 'Did you say will?'

He responded with perplexity. 'Did not my clerk inform you of my reasons for this meeting?'

She shook her head and thought – no, but I'll have that little so-and-so given the opportunity. 'But do go on, Mr Ramsworthy.'

He unrolled the last will and testament of Arnold Penny and, putting a paperweight on the top edge, held a pair of spectacles to his eyes and read: '*I, Arnold Geoffrey Penny, being of sound mind etcetera do hereby bequeath all my properties, the chattels within the said properties including all outbuildings, and all monies owned by me to my trusted friend and employee, Thomasin Feeney, to do with as she so wishes and . . .*' he paused here and squinted over the spectacles, noting the startled expression. 'Mr Penny did not give you prior warning of his intentions?'

She barely heard him, so absorbed was she with what she had just heard. When he asked if she was all right and repeated his question she shook her head, knowing that she must present a pretty picture sitting here gaping like a fish but oh – what a surprise!

'You know of course that he had no family?'

With some difficulty she regained her power of speech. 'Well, yes but I never thought . . . I mean, yer wouldn't, would yer?' The words leaked out in an incoherent jumble. She was finding it impossible to digest the revelation.

'Yet you must have had some inkling of his fondness

for you?' pressed the solicitor, who had not only acted as Mr Penny's lawyer but as friend and confidant. Arnold had often spoken of his employee in the most effusive terms. Looking across his desk, Mr Ramsworthy could see why he had been so enamoured; Mrs Feeney was a handsome woman. With the help of this inheritance she would be even more attractive, clad in fashions that would do more justice to her looks than the modest garments she wore now.

'Yes, I was aware of his affection,' said Thomasin with a sad smile. 'But, dear me – this! It's the sort o' thing that only happens in books.'

Ramsworthy leaned forward. 'But we are in a book of sorts, Mrs Feeney – the book of life. If you have ever read a good novel you will know that the story will take an unexpected twist from time to time. There are some boring passages, of course, and some exciting ones – this is one of your exciting passages, Mrs Feeney.'

She shook her head. 'Things like that just don't happen to me. I admit that it did cross my mind that he might leave me a few bob – he was always sayin' "I'll remember you in my will ... " ' She broke off as Ramsworthy nodded and said, 'There you are! He did offer you an intimation.'

Thomasin took a deep breath. 'But I never once dreamed he'd be this generous. I don't know what to say. It's got me completely stumped.'

'There has not been an inventory of his possessions,' went on the solicitor. 'But you can be assured that you have inherited a considerable sum.'

'D'yer mean it could be as much as hundreds?' she had the temerity to ask.

He laughed and his cheeks crinkled like pink crêpe paper. 'My dear lady! Considering the fact that Mr Penny owned a profitable business apart from a very roomy house I think you can safely say that the gross bequest will run to four figures rather than three – indeed, it could be even more.'

She was aghast. 'But surely the grocery trade alone

wouldn't produce such an amount; at least not one so modest as Mr Penny's?' Her speculation was founded on experience; she knew every penny that went through the till and it certainly did not add up to that sort of money. She had often wondered what she would do to improve the takings had she the chance; well, now she had.

Mr Ramsworthy replied, 'You are of course correct in your assumption, Mrs Feeney, although the shop does have a fine potential, its central position being one of its attributes. It will be breaking no confidence now to tell you that Mr Penny was himself the beneficiary of a similar bestowal some years ago, indeed that was how he came to be in possession of the property in Goodramgate. The house in Monkgate was also included in the bequest, left by a maiden aunt – the lack of a direct heir seems to be a family trait.' He began to lift up papers on his desk, looking for something. 'Alas, I'm unable to give you the keys at present as I've temporarily mislaid them. I shall send my clerk round whenever . . . tut! I'm sure they were here.' He finally gave up. 'Anyway, you'll find that one of the doors needs a new lock. The police had to break in. They boarded it up afterwards.'

'Does all this mean it's all right if I take me wages from t'shop till, then?' she asked, having wondered at the legality of such an act.

The solicitor obviously found her naïvety delightful. 'Mrs Feeney, do you not understand? It is now your shop, you may do as you wish.'

The full extent of his statement did not hit her until she was halfway home then, in mid-step, she stopped and a surge of excitement seemed to emanate from her boots. It forged up her legs and finally gushed from her mouth in a great whoop. She began to skip, lifting her swirling skirts to expose a well-shaped calf and drawing whistles from a gang of navvies. She laughed and broke into a run, intent on one thing: to tell Patrick the good news. She pulled up abruptly. Fulford was a fair walk and she might not be back to get the children's dinner. Oh, how disappointing. Then she berated herself. – Well, you daft clot!

You're in money now, you can get the omnibus and be back in time for dinner. No! a cab. That would really set tongues wagging. Seeing a hansom speeding towards her she leapt into the road and waved him down.

'What're you tryin' to do?' bawled the cabbie. 'Get yerself killed?'

She placed her hands on her hips. 'Kindly show me some courtesy, my man. I will have you aware that you are talking to a woman of means.'

He gave a warped leer. 'An' I'm Lord bleedin' Carlton.'

'I require your services,' said Thomasin ignoring his manner, and before he had a chance to move off she climbed into the cab.

He banged on the roof. 'Oy! I hope you've got the money to pay for this.'

'Of course I have,' returned his passenger. 'Now shurrup gasbaggin' an' take me to Fulford.' As the cab pulled away she hastily examined the contents of her purse to make sure she could fulfil her boast.

Her arrival at the building site caused a minor sensation. Patrick's workmates gathered round the cab as she alighted and addressed the cabbie. 'Be so good as to wait here, my man. I shall require your services further.'

The cabbie snorted and gave the workmen a look that said – she's mad!

'Michael O'Leary, what're ye doing?' hissed Patrick as she flounced importantly up to him.

'Mind your manners, Feeney. I've already put one lout in his place this morning. Kindly employ the deference you would show to a person of distinction.'

'The Lord preserve us, 'tis mad the woman's gone.' Patrick was undergoing a severe bout of embarrassment at his wife's odd behaviour in the presence of his friends, who seemed to be greatly enjoying his discomfiture.

The conversation was interrupted by the foreman who had stepped from the site office when the cab had drawn up, thinking it was his superior. Though he was relieved to find it was not, he was angry at being drawn out of his comfortable seat for nothing. 'Oy! What the hell's going

104

on? I'm not payin' you lot to stand chatting to bawds all day. Get back to work!'

Patrick, already aggravated by his wife's eccentricity, turned on the man. 'Bawds, is it? I'll have ye know that's my wife you're talkin' about.'

'I couldn't give a damn if it's the Queen o' bleedin' Sheba, just get your arse back to work!'

The man turned his back and Patrick was about to follow him when Thomasin halted them both. 'Wait on! Don't you go talking to my husband as if he's a clart; you address him properly – an' while yer at it don't go callin' me no bawd neither.'

The foreman threw up his hands in mock consternation. 'Oh, I beg your pardon if I've offended madam,' he spat sarcastically. 'Now, bugger off an' let these men get some work done.' He assumed this to be the end of the matter, but knew differently when he felt a large hand grasp his collar.

'Ye'll watch your mouth in front of my wife, Burns,' growled the Irishman.

'I can stick up for meself, thank yer very much,' cut in Thomasin, and took a swing with her boot at the man's shin.

Dancing about on one leg, the man snarled at Patrick, 'Can't you keep your drab under control?' And his foolish tongue earned him an impulsive blow to the jaw which sent him sprawling onto a pile of sand.

'That's it!' stormed Burns, spitting out a mouthful of sand and blood. 'That's bloody-well it! You've finally done it now. Go on, bugger off! You're sacked.'

'He's not sacked – he quits!' retorted Thomasin, and with ruffled hauteur pushed her fuming husband into the cab and shouted instructions to the cabbie.

'Oy, I don't want mud all over my seats!' he complained.

'Oh, get on with yer,' snapped an impatient Thomasin and clicking her tongue set the horse in motion.

'Oh, after my job an' all, are we?' shouted the cabbie. 'You'll be climbin' up here an' drivin' the blasted thing next.'

'I will if you don't stop your infernal complaints and allow me to talk to my husband,' she threatened, then turned to Patrick and planted an enthusiastic kiss on his muddy cheek.

'Stop that!' He pushed her away. 'Has the devil got into ye today? Ye come an' make a fool of me in front of all me friends, kick the gaffer, then get me sacked. Is it mad ye are? What are we going to do for money now?'

'Nowt,' she answered smugly, cuddling up to him.

'Ah, Jazers,' he sighed, then to the cabbie: 'Forget the previous directions. Take us to the asylum – the woman's off her head.'

'You keep going,' she warned the driver, then took hold of both Patrick's hands and shook them. 'Silly boy! D'yer think I'd be actin' like this if I didn't have summat up me sleeve?'

'Sure, I never know with you. When there's a full moon anything can happen.'

'Has it escaped your notice that it's broad daylight? Not a full moon in sight.'

'Then please, please, Tommy will ye tell me why you're acting so?'

To his growing disbelief she related word for word what had transpired at the solicitor's office. When she had finished he merely sat there with his mouth open. 'Well, are yer gonna sit there catchin' flies?' she demanded.

'Mary Mother o' God!' he gasped. 'Tell me again for I can't take it in.'

'Nay, I'm not goin' through all that again.' She linked her arm through his and snuggled delightedly against him. 'But in short, Mr Feeney, in a pixie's earhole – we're rich!'

'Rich,' he repeated to himself, then laughed stupidly. He tore off his cap, threw it to the floor of the cab and sprang up, banging his head in the process. 'We're rich!' He craned his neck over the half-doors of the hansom which rocked and swayed precariously. 'We're rich!' he shouted to every passer-by. 'We're rich, hah! The Feeneys are rich!'

'Christ, he's mad an' all,' muttered the cabbie under

his breath. The horse pricked its ears as though to say – aren't you all?

When the cab deposited them at their front door, Patrick helped his wife down and unlocked it while she paid the cabbie, needing all the money in her purse to do so. But then, she could draw her wages this afternoon. Eh! she reminded herself with pleasure, they wouldn't be wages now. All the money in the till would be hers; all the money in the safe; all the money in the bank.

She emitted a delightful whoop then, seeing Miss Peabody's curtains move, she pressed her nose against the neighbouring window in devilment. 'Have a good geg, Nelly!' she called, as her neighbour bobbed out of sight, then giggled and followed her husband indoors.

Inside they both hugged each other tightly. 'Oh, Pat.' She laid her auburn head against his dusty shoulder. 'I can't believe it's true. Am I dreamin'?'

He pinched her bottom, bringing forth an indignant squeal. 'No, ye can't be dreamin'.' He rubbed his rough hand over the spot he had nipped. 'Best do that to me; it might be me who's dreamin' all this.' He leapt back at her groping hand. 'Hey, you're not supposed to nip me there! Ye've got me all het up now – d'ye think we've time for a bit o' sport before the spoilers get home?'

'I don't see why not,' she murmured into his ear, teasing the lobe with her teeth.

'Is me dinner ready yet?' Dickie came in and flopped down on the rug to pull off his boots. 'Jazers, these crabshells are killin' me.'

His parents regretfully pulled apart. 'Them's not all as'll be killin' yer,' grumbled his mother. 'Yer really pick yer moments.'

'Ah, now ye'd miss me if I didn't come home, Mam.' Dickie's blue eyes crinkled at the corners, then looked towards the door as his brother and sister entered.

'I went to see how Aunt Molly was faring and found this young fellow hanging round Raper's place,' said Erin, receiving an accusing glower from Sonny.

'What 'ave I told you about messin' round that slaugh-

107

terhouse?' demanded Thomasin. 'Haven't you upset ol' Raper enough for one week?'

'I wasn't messin' round,' objected her younger son. 'I had the same idea as Erin; I went to see how Aunt Molly was.'

'Aye well, that's all by the by – I've summat much more important to say to you all.' She then told the children her exciting news and watched each face react as it sank in.

Erin was the first to congratulate her parents on their good fortune. The piquant face softened into a jubilant smile as she hugged them both sincerely. It was high time they had the reward they deserved after so much hardship.

'You'll be pleased, Sonny,' laughed his father as the boy shook his hand and kissed Thomasin. 'Now ye'll be able to go back to school.'

His son smiled, biding his time before putting forward his request. Maybe now he would be able to pursue the education he had in mind. However, his gladness did not stem wholly from self-interest – he was immensely pleased for his parents. He wet his mother's cheek with an impulsive kiss and she hugged him, laughing. Then she looked expectantly at Dickie's handsome face, trying to guess what lay behind that inscrutable meditation, and waiting patiently for him to offer his congratulations as had the others.

But Dickie was thinking of all the things that the money would buy. He was thinking that now he would not have to endure the sulphurous stink of the match factory. But most of all, he was thinking that his mother's newfound wealth would buy his way into any bed that he wanted . . .

CHAPTER ELEVEN

That evening Patrick's suggestion that they should all go to Mass to give thanks received a mixed response. Thomasin, although not of the Catholic persuasion, often accompanied her husband and children to Mass, but tonight said that there were more pressing affairs to see to. She had not yet balanced the books after stock-taking and would like to put them in order if he did not object.

Erin, the Catholic teachings instilled in her from birth, accepted Patrick's proposal without question. The boys, however, did not so readily share her faith and argued that they, like their mother, had more urgent matters to attend to. 'Mam isn't going,' Dickie complained at his father's insistence.

'Are you aspiring to mutiny?' came his father's peremptory reply, to which Dickie shook his head. He was not yet mature enough to engage in full battle with Patrick but felt that at least he must make these occasional token gestures at independence. 'I'm glad to hear it, 'cause you're going whether ye like it or not. Is it a couple o' heathens I've raised?'

Thomasin changed her decision. 'Maybe I'd best set a good example. I can always do t'books when we get home.' She went to smarten herself up then, commanding her sons to wash behind their ears before daring to come out of the scullery, she unwound her hair and ran a brush through its gleaming strands. Winding it back into a bun she took the hairpins from between her pursed lips and secured the glossy chignon.

When all were ready and decently-attired they set off on foot towards the other side of town. Though a church had been built not fifty yards away, Patrick and his family would sooner seek the friendship and understanding of Father Liam Kelly who, over the years, had become a dear and trusted friend as well as confessor.

Later, when Mass was over, they waited for Liam to change into less formal garb before interrupting his homeward stroll to acquaint him of their good fortune. Liam was delighted; his cherubic face became crazed in wrinkles with his smile. 'Why, that's the best bit o' news I've had all week!' he cried, his green eyes alight with genuine gladness. 'I'll be round with me begging bowl the very first thing. I hope, though, that ye'll not be too rich to talk to the likes o' me.'

Patrick pulled down his lower lip. 'Sure, I'll talk to anybody, Father, but I can't vouch for her ladyship here. The money's gone straight to her head. 'Tis cabs she's been hiring to run her all over the place – an' her only feedin' us bread an' scrape for our tea. How d'ye like that?'

'Ah, 'tis a terrible thing, Pat, avarice,' sang the priest. 'I'm thinking 'tis a penance I'll have to be setting her. What d'ye say to seventy-five Hail Marys? Is that steep enough d'ye think?'

'I'll give you Hail Marys,' retorted the woman irreverently. 'I was going to ask you round for a meal when we move into our new house, but I'll think twice about it now.'

'New house?' Patrick interrupted the priest's laughter. 'What's all this? I didn't know anything about a new house.'

'There y'are yer see – yer don't know everything,' replied Thomasin. 'Mr Penny's house, that's what I mean. It all falls to me, so we might as well take advantage of it.'

Liam asked where it was. 'Monkgate, I believe,' answered Thomasin, watching the expression on her husband's face slowly alter, knowing what was going through his mind. Monkgate was where Roland Cummings used to live – still did as far as she knew. She had not heard of him in years.

'I can see I'll have to be paying a sovereign before I can speak to you.'

The priest's voice infiltrated Patrick's thoughtfulness and he smiled suddenly. 'Now, ye know the money'll never alter us, Father, an' ye'll always be welcome – 'specially if ye bring along a few bottles o' the old golden mixture.'

Liam spread his hands in mock indignation. 'Has nobody any respect for the priesthood any more? I shall expect to see ye at the next Confession for that slander. Ah! and speaking of Confession,' he wheeled on the boys who had been trying to make themselves small, 'I haven't noticed your faces outside the confessional lately. Is it saints ye are?' Liam, very observant of his flock, was always quick to put a name to absentees.

'Saints, Father?' scoffed Patrick. 'Ye wouldn't say that if ye had to live with them. An' did they not come to Confession last week? For that's where they purported to be off.' He tossed a recriminatory glance at his sons.

'We did come,' lied Dickie. ''Twas Father White's turn to hear Confession.' Father White was a young priest who was here to learn how to run a church.

'Ah well, that could be the case,' allowed Liam charitably. 'Well, I'll no doubt be seein' ye this week as 'tis my turn to hear everyone's sins, God protect me.'

'Don't worry, Father,' Patrick promised. 'They'll be here if I have to drag them along personally.'

'Ah yes, I was about to mention that.' Liam's green eyes were cynical.

'Me, Father?' Patrick made a circular motion with his finger over his head. 'Can ye not see that little gold hoop? Sure, the amount o' sinning I'm allowed to do would be very tame compared to some o' the things I bet you hear.'

'Tame or no, I'll see you here!' Liam stabbed a finger at the ground. He then went on to ask if either of them had seen Molly Flaherty. 'She hasn't been to Mass since poor Jimmy was taken. I wondered, is she all right?'

'I saw her the other night,' replied Patrick. 'Ah, she's still in low spirits, the poor soul. An' she'd given the vinegar bottle a right belting too.'

Liam sighed knowingly. 'I must go round meself an' have a talk to her.'

'Aye, well I'll tell her to expect ye,' said Patrick as the family made to depart. 'I was thinking to call on her this evening but on second thoughts I'll leave it till the morning. With me wife doing me out of a job I'll have the day to meself.'

They took their leave of Liam, but before going home they called at Monkgate to see the house, if only from the outside. Patrick gained some relief from the fact that it was situated at the opposite end of the road to the Cummings'

111

residence though he was very quiet as they strolled home to a supper of shortbread and cocoa.

Later, as the dark shadows enfolded them in their own private dreams, Thomasin snuggled up to her husband's febrile torso, trying to find a comfortable niche in the lumpy mattress. 'What're you thinkin' about?' she asked as he trailed his fingers up and down her arm, obviously deep in thought.

'Oh, I was just wondering what I'm going to do about a job now ye've got me sacked.'

She chuckled softly. 'Soft 'aporth. It still hasn't hit you, has it? Yer don't need a job now. I've got a shop, an' all t'money in t'bank, so why would yer need a job?'

He hesitated before replying. 'I'm not sure I like the idea of me wife doing the supportin'. . . 'tis not decent.'

'Oh, here we go again!' She sat up sharply. 'Proud Harry. The money's just as much yours as mine, yer know. In fact in the eyes of the law it's all yours.'

'It was left to you. I want nothing I haven't earned.'

'Look!' she cried exasperatedly. 'If it'd been t'other way round you wouldn't've kept it all to yerself, would yer?'

'No, but . . .'

'But nowt! That money's for all of us. You, me, the bairns, all of us – an' there's an end to it.' She lay down again.

'Yes, ma'am,' he answered meekly and she pushed him in playful reproach.

A short silence followed, then she said, 'Yer could come an' help me run t'business if yer like. I'm gonna need help.'

She sensed his reaction rather than saw it. 'I'm no businessman, ye should know that by now.'

She curled her arm round his nakedness, sorry that her words had resurrected memories of the Debtors' Prison. 'Tell me what yer'd really like to do.'

He did not have to think for very long before replying. 'What I'd really like is what I promised myself when I first came to this country as a youngster: a plot of land to put me name to – somewhere I can be what I really am.'

His answer seemed to take her by surprise. 'I would've expected yer to say shares in a brewery or summat like that ... I'd no idea.' With his reply she had suddenly been brought to realise that there were still so many things she had to learn about this husband of fifteen years. 'Well, if that's what yer want that's what yer shall have,' she promised. 'An' what will yer do with this here land?'

He rolled a drowsy face across the pillow. 'Why, grow things – what else?'

'Well, I don't know, do I? Yer might've wanted to build on it or summat.'

'Sure an' why would I be wantin' to spoil a fine piece of earth by stickin' up some monstrosity of a building? No, I'd use it how God meant it to be used: to grow food.' He could already smell the newly-turned soil, black and fertile, clothed with the white flowers of healthy potato plants. Now he must endure the life of a labourer no longer. His wife's murmured tones broke into his reverie. 'Sorry, what did ye say? I was miles away.'

'I was just sayin' that we'll be able to pay t'mortgage off,' repeated Thomasin. At first they had rented the property but when circumstances had permitted it they had opted to buy.

'We'll no doubt make a bob or two when we sell it an' all.'

'*If* we sell it,' came her answer.

'Sure, I thought ye wanted to move into that big house ye've inherited. Have ye changed your mind?'

She was sorry to disappoint him, hearing the note of expectant hope. She knew he was loath to move to Monkgate and knew the reason why. 'No, yer misconstrue. What I meant was, we might make more money by renting it rather than selling, in the long run.'

'Ye'd make a landlord of me?' He was incredulous.

'I thought we could help Molly at the same time, offer it to her at a lower rent – say a shillin' a week.'

He was again amazed. '*Rent* it to her?'

'Well – you're surely not suggestin' we *give* it to her?'

'She's done a lot for us.'

'Aye, an' we've done a lot for her, an' she's going to get her share of our good fortune. I'm not thinkin' to leave her penniless. But Patrick, nobody gives houses away – not unless they're dead anyway. I thought I was bein' rather generous, offerin' her a better house for less rent.'

'Well aye, but it just sounds so . . .' he couldn't think of a word. 'After we've known her so long.'

'Yer think I'm being mean I know,' she replied. 'But I can just see what would happen if I let you look after our interests. You'd be doling it all out amongst your friends and we'd be back in Britannia Yard within a week. I'm not sayin' it's wrong to think of your friends first – I've said we'll make sure Molly's comfortable – just that we've been given this opportunity to make something for ourselves and we mustn't waste it.'

'I recall a time when ye swore ye only wanted me an' my children, said ye weren't bothered where we lived as long as you had us.'

'That still holds,' she told him firmly. 'If we hadn't received this windfall I'd be quite content with what I've got. But we *have* been given it an' no one in their right minds would turn aside such a chance. It won't change anything, we'll still be the people we are, but just a little better fed an' clothed, an' more comfortably housed.'

'I suppose so . . .' but his tone was not very convincing.

His display of ill-humour caused her to rethink. 'If yer really an' truly can't bring yerself to live at the house in Monkgate I'll understand, yer know. I don't want to force yer into a move where yer won't be happy. We've had some good years here . . . we don't have to leave.'

In the moments that followed the lurid picture flashed through his mind of his wife and that Cummings fellow together, naked and sweating, fornicating . . . then he said softly, 'If you've set your heart on going there I'll not be the one to steal your wish. It isn't as if we'll be living next door to . . . Besides, all that business is over an' done with now.' But was it? When she had all that wealth, a big house and fancy clothes, would he, a poor Irish labourer, still be good enough for her? Or would living in such close proximity to the man whose mistress she had once been set the relationship in motion again?

'I'd like to think yer believe that, Pat – that it is all over. I didn't ever love him, yer know.' How easily she could read his thoughts, even though the darkness hid his eyes. She gave him an encouraging squeeze and he turned to her, the passion thudding inside. 'There's only one man I've ever loved,' she added sincerely. 'An' surely I don't have to tell yer who that is, do I? Not after all these years.'

'Tell me.' The soft lilt of his brogue breathed warm upon her ear and she mouthed the words he wanted her to say. Then intertwining they became as one, a sensuous, writhing beast beneath the bedclothes.

The next morning, Patrick suggested his wife go with him when he went to see Molly to tell her the good news.

'Sorry, you'll have to go on yer own, love,' Thomasin told him as she stood before the mirror winding her hair. 'I've a business to run, remember?'

'Oh, aye,' he nodded and, groping under the chair for his best boots put them on. 'I'm clean forgetting you're the provider now.' Properly attired he stood. 'Will I at least give her your regards then?'

''Course.' She put in the last hairpin. 'An' tell her I'll be round to see her soon as I can.'

'How much're we going to give her, then?'

'Oh, we'll 'ave to wait till we get everything sorted out before we know that – you can take her what bit we've got saved in the tin if yer like.'

Patrick, pocketing the two sovereigns from the tin, set out for Britannia Yard. When he got there he had to wait while Raper cleared the alleyway of sheep before proceeding to Molly's. 'I may as well say my goodbyes now, Mr Raper,' he called above the bleating and cursing. 'I'll be leavin' the area shortly an' knowin' how much the parting is going to break your heart I'd not like to leave it till the last minute, there's always tears, isn't there?'

'Off back to the bogs are we?' bawled Raper, kicking a sheep up the rear. 'Best bloody place for thee.'

115

'Er, no – I'm off to live among the nobs actually,' returned Patrick lightly. 'We've come into money, don't ye know. Got ourselves a nice big house over the other side o' town.'

'I think I know it,' said Raper. 'Got bars on the windows an' padded walls.'

Patrick gave a heartrending sigh. 'Ah, there y'are ye see, I knew ye'd be upset at us going.' The sheep out of his way, he entered the Yard and came up to the butcher. 'But never mind. I've sent for two dozen o' my cousins from the ould country just so's ye don't feel too lonely. Told them there's this nice little place called Britannia Yard where they'll be made to feel most welcome.' He cupped his ear as Raper swore. 'Best o' luck, did ye say? Why, thank ye, Mr Raper. Oh, here! Let me give ye something just to show my regard.' He thrust his hand into his pocket and followed Raper up to the doors of the slaughterhouse. The butcher held out his hand to accept Patrick's offering – a button. 'That's for your lip. I'm sure it'll come in very handy when my cousins get here.'

He was still chuckling as he poked his head round the door of Molly's dingy hovel. 'God save all here!'

Molly was sitting listlessly in a corner, a cup in her hands. Around her on the bare floor small children frolicked. With a child every year Molly's house had never been a peaceful place. Though these were not her own children, for even if Jimmy had still been alive there'd have been no more; she was past all that, God be praised. No, these were her grandchildren whom she tended while their parents worked. Her own youngest, born five years ago, was at school now so things were not quite so hectic. Seeing the identity of her visitor she brightened and gave a pathetic gesture of admittance. 'Just the very fella I need to lift me spirits.'

He came up to her and peered into the cup. 'Ye don't seem to be doing too badly without my help.'

'Sit ye down an' stop your preachin'. Will ye take one with me?'

''Tis a little early in the day for the hard stuff, Blossom,

116

even for a celebration. I'd not say no to a cup o' tea, though.'

She squinted at him as she clambered over a child to spoon the tea into the pot. 'Celebration is it? I'm glad somebody's got a reason to curl their mouth corners.'

He tousled a small head, found a stool and pulled it up beside her chair, waiting with a smile while she poured boiling water into the teapot. 'Here, come sit down now an' let me tell yese.'

She did so, waiting patiently while he sat with a big smile on his face. 'Well? Are ye going to sit there lookin' like ye've swallowed a sickle?'

He chuckled and pulled his earlobe. 'God, now I'm here I don't know how to say it.' Another brief pause, then: 'The long an' the short of it is, Molly, that me an' Tommy we've come into money.'

'Oh, that's nice for yese, Pat.' She smiled fondly, then reached for the teapot, swilling its contents before pouring. 'A win on the horses, was it? How much?'

'Oh . . . a few hundred I expect when it's all . . .'

'Hundred? *Hundred!*' She'd spilt the tea, her slitty eyes wider than he'd ever seen them.

He laughed loudly. 'Aye, my love! An' the first thing I'm going to do is see my old pal Molly gets her fair share.'

'Oh, I don't want none!' she said hurriedly and used her sleeve to mop up the spills. 'Oh, no . . . no.'

'Begod, whyever not?'

'I never had no money . . . I wouldn't know what to do with it.' She put the cup to her lips, hiding behind it.

'Hey, I wasn't thinking to give ye the whole lot, ye know,' he joked. 'I'm talking coppers.' Then he cuffed her. 'Ye soft old biddy! Wouldn't know what to do with it. Ye spend it! Get yourself a nice bit o' furniture, some fancy clothes, things ye've never had. Soon as we get sorted out I'll be round with a sackful o' sovs.'

'Oh no, I couldn't take it!'

'Have I come to the wrong bloody house?' he asked himself, then grabbed her hand. 'Aw, Molly ye've had a terrible time of it lately what with your losses. I couldn't help ye more at the time but I can now. Please let me.'

'God,' she breathed, shaking her head and gazing at him. 'My Pat a rich man. To be sure the sky'll turn green.'

'Isn't it raining peas out there.' He gave a laugh. 'Don't worry – I had trouble taking it in myself. I still find it hard to believe.'

'Well ... where's this money come from?' she asked weakly.

He told her of Thomasin's inheritance and of the house in Monkgate. 'Actually, with the house and the business it'll amount to a bit more than a few hundred. So ye see, we'll be moving out o' the old place ... going over there. Tommy thought we should rent our old house, thought maybe you might like first refusal – we'd not expect the full rent o' course, a shilling a week Tommy suggested. Sure, I'd give it to ye if I could, you know that but ...' He inwardly berated Thomasin for causing him such embarrassment. Renting a house to an old friend indeed! It sounded terrible after saying they'd come into a fortune. But then Tommy was right. If he had charge of the inheritance there'd be nothing to leave their children.

'Ah, 'tis a kind thought, Pat,' tendered Molly. 'But I have to say no. I couldn't deprive yese of the rent ye could be getting.'

Guilt made him look for sarcasm in that remark but he found none. Molly seemed genuinely pleased for his good fortune. 'But why?' he pressed her. 'Ye'd be much more comfortable there, more room ... is it that ye think we're being tight-fisted asking for rent?'

'God, no! How could I ever call ye tight-fisted when ye've just told me you're bringing me a sackful o' sovs.' She clutched his hand. 'I wouldn't dream of expecting it rent-free, ye have to think o' the future ... 'tis just that I don't think I'd feel right round there, ye know. I'm not sure I'd want Nelly Peabody for a neighbour, nor her me come to that.'

'Ye'd be away from Raper,' he tempted.

'An' who would I have to slaver at? No ... no. 'Tis best I stay put.'

He gave a sigh. 'Ah well, if ye won't, ye won't, I can't force ye. But ye will accept the money won't ye?'

'Sure, have y'ever really known me turn down money?' she asked.

'An' you're to spend it on something sensible, not go buyin' crateloads o' this stuff.' He pointed at the cup from which she had been drinking when he had come in. 'Ye could get a little place somewhere else, away from here.'

'We'll see, we'll see,' nodded Molly. 'Now, less o' what I'm going to do, and tell me more about this inheritance o' yours.' She continued to press him for details for at least an hour, until one of her grandchildren poked his fingers through the bars on the grate and had to be hastily attended to.

'Well, I'd best leave ye to tend to the wounded, Molly me love.' Patrick raised his voice over the screams of pain and rose to shove the stool under the table.

'Right, darlin' – holy Saint Anthony will ye stop that bawlin', boy!' she told the child, trying to smear butter on his throbbing fingers. 'An' ye'll not desert us now? Ye'll come an' see us from time to time.'

'Sure, we've not gone yet,' he laughed. 'Can't ye wait to see the back of us? It'll be a few weeks before we move I expect. I'll be round to see ye before then. Clear all them moths out o' your purse to make way for the dibs.'

'Ah, God love ye!' Molly slung the screeching child around her hip and came up to grab Patrick's arm, eyes threatening tears. 'I'm that glad for ye. It couldn't fall to a nicer man than my Pat. Tell Tommy I think 'tis great. God, I feel like I've swallowed a bagful o' frogs I'm so excited. I still can't believe it.'

'Nor can I.' He kissed her. 'Take care, Molly – oh, Christ! Here's the eejit forgetting the reason he came round.' He took the sovereigns from his pocket and pressed them into her hand. 'That's to tide ye over till I see ye again.'

'Oh, good. For a moment I thought that's all I was

119

getting.' She laughed as he scolded her. 'Ah, thank ye, darlin'. I'll light a candle for ye. Goodbye!'

As the door closed Molly looked down at the gleaming coins on her palm and smiled broadly for the first time in a week. 'Well now, isn't that grand?' she said to a grubby-cheeked infant – grubby-cheeked both ends for he wore nothing but a little shift. 'My Patrick . . .' And then she gathered them all together and warned them to stay put whilst she went out for 'just a second', and bearing a jug scampered across the yard in the direction of the nearest pub.

The boys had tried to wriggle out of it but Patrick had been adamant: they must go to Confession. Strolling through the town centre with a warm breeze ruffling their hair Sonny asked his brother if he was going to tell Father Kelly about Bertha and Beth.

'An' why not indeed?' answered Dickie lightly. 'It'll put a little sparkle in his life. I don't suppose he'll even know what I'm talkin' about. I can't visualise him going with a woman, can you? Still, there's his housekeeper . . .'

Sonny sprang to Father Kelly's defence. 'I suppose ye know that's blasphemy? Priests aren't even allowed to think of things like that. They're above it all.' Liam Kelly was one of the few people outside his family whom Sonny respected.

'Who're ye tryin' to cod?' his brother asked cynically. 'I'll bet they're as bad as the rest of us. Sure, how can any man go without a woman? I could never manage more than a few days without. 'Course,' he could not resist a taunt, 'it wouldn't bother you, seeing as you've never had it.'

Sonny stooped suddenly, pretending to tie his bootlace – anything to stop his hands from closing round his brother's throat.

'Ye see, you're not tryin' hard enough,' Dickie was saying.

Sonny straightened and proceeded on his way. 'What're you on about now?'

'Dipping your wick. You're not goin' about it the right way at all. 'Tis no good waiting for it to come to you, ye've got to play it clever.'

'Like you did with Violet, ye mean?' came the sarcastic reply.

'What's that mean?' demanded his brother.

Sonny tapped his nose, a mannerism picked up from his father. 'Your cleverness didn't get ye very far with her, did it? Chucked ye out on your backside, I heard. A bit different from the way you told it.'

If this was an attempt at retaliation it did not have the desired effect. Dickie burst into uproarious laughter. 'Oh, Son – did I get an earful from her! An' a couple o' good rattles round the head for luck. Jaze, she was like a woman gone mad!' He shook his head and laid an arm across Sonny's shoulders. 'An' d'ye know the funniest thing was, after Hawksby gave me the push an' slung me all that humbug about turning his store into a house of ill-repute, I find out he's been after tupping her himself, the two-faced old ked.' Sonny involuntarily joined his laughter as Dickie added, 'Anyways, I'm stayin' away from the mature ladies for a while; they can't be trusted. God, if ever I thought there was one ripe for pickin' it was Violet, but there y'are. See now, ye've diverted me from my topic, which was: how do we go about making a man of you?'

Sonny shook him off and straightened his collar. 'Don't you concern yourself about me. I'm not bothered about women.'

''Course y'are! You're a male aren't ye? Look over there.' Dickie stopped and pointed to two young girls who hid giggling faces behind their hands and whispered to each other. 'I think it's the carrot-planting season.'

'Ye can't just go up to people in the street an' ask 'em for it!' hissed Sonny.

'Sure, do I look that indelicate? Ye've got to give 'em the old sweetener first, boy. Stay by me, ye'll learn something.'

'But we have to go to Confession,' Sonny reminded him.

Dickie halted in his tracks. 'Christ, the boy's a saint!

121

Ye're not going to tell me ye'd rather go to Confession than get your little bit of cotton in, are ye? Leave it till later, then ye'll have something worthwhile to tell him.'

Sonny bit his lip, torn between the two. 'Me mam'll kill us if Father Kelly says we haven't been.'

'She's not bothered about that stuff. It's me dad who's the Bible-champer. I can always get round him. Come on, Son.'

'I don't think we'd better.'

'Huh! Weeks he's been pesterin' me to tell him what it's like an' when his chance has come to find out he's got cold feet.'

'I have not! Anyroad, how d'ye know they'll be game? They don't look the type to me, too prim.'

'Never believe it, Son. They're usually the worst kind – or the best, depending on which way ye look at it. Personally I don't waste much time looking.' He gave an exaggerated leer, hoping to humour his brother into agreement.

Sonny was not convinced. 'I'm not so sure – anyway they're off, look.' He nodded towards the girls who, tired of waiting, had started to move away.

'It's a game – they want us to follow. Away, Son.' He lolloped after them, dragging his brother with him.

Sonny struggled free. 'I'm off to church.'

'Oh, do as you will,' said Dickie testily. 'Listen, do us a favour, will ye?'

'Another one?'

'Ah, come on now, ye know ye'd do anything for your brother. Will ye confess my sins for me?'

'Will I *what!*' spat Sonny. 'You're not serious?'

'Look, if you confess in my place 'tis not so bad as me not goin', if ye see what I mean. 'Tis like I'll be there but speakin' through you. D'ye take?'

'Oh, I take all right! Ye want me to take the blame for all your filthy goings-on.'

'No honest, I wouldn't expect ye to pay the penance . . .'

'Oh, thanks.'

122

'. . . just tell me what he gives ye an' I'll carry it out gladly.'

'That's very noble of yer,' replied Sonny bitterly. 'Has it occurred to ye how Father Kelly will think it's really me who's the lecher?'

'He's going to think that anyway, isn't he? *Well* – aren't ye goin' to confess ye've been in the company of a naked female?'

'That doesn't count! I never actually . . .'

'Tut! Of all the little hypocrites.' Dickie shook his head in disapproval. 'Pretending to be a saint, going to Confession an' all the time he's keepin' the best bits back.'

Sonny was deep in thought now. This point had been troubling him since it had happened. Dickie mentioning it had brought it back to prominence.

'So, ye may as well do my sins while you're at it,' Dickie told him. 'Save the both of us getting a trouncing.'

Sonny was only half-listening. 'Sling yer hook.' God, this was going to be terrible. He was blushing even at the thought.

'I'll give ye a shilling.'

'What?' asked Sonny absently, then as Dickie repeated his offer, 'You haven't got a shilling.'

'Me mam has,' said Dickie. 'Oh, come on, Son! Look, if ye like I'll do the same for you next week.'

'Dickie, yer missin' the whole point o' Confession. How can yer cleanse yer soul if ye don't do it in person?'

'You're my brother, aren't ye?' argued Dickie in desperation. 'Me own flesh an' blood, part of me. When you speak it'll be like I'm speakin', only through your lips.'

'You are bloody incredible!' Sonny turned and stormed away. After a few steps he turned to see if his brother was following, but Dickie, with a girl on each arm, was walking in the other direction. 'There'll be trouble when me dad finds out!' he yelled after his brother.

'He won't find out unless you tell him!' retorted Dickie. 'An' saints don't tell on their brothers.'

For a few maddening seconds Sonny considered surrendering to the feet that itched to carry him after the trio.

But then he swore, spun round and marched off to church, rehearsing the dreadful speech that he would soon be forced to make.

Father Kelly was ensconced in the confessional, yawning as the sinner behind the grill mouthed a boring soliloquy. 'Go on, my son,' he murmured absently and took a sip from his tea cup which had been laced with a drop of Irish – I'm getting too old for this, he told himself. One day 'tis bound to get me. I'll either die of boredom, or shock from the sordid confessions some of my less-respectful parishioners serve up.

He tried to turn over the pages of his newspaper without rustling them as the sinner droned on. Where were those dratted racing results? Ah, that was more like it. He settled back to discover whether or not Rafferty's tip had been well-advised. The sinner fell silent and Liam dealt out a stiff penalty for imposing so much boredom. The curtain wafted as the sinner left. Liam hoped that the next trans-gressor would have something more entertaining to say.

The distinct dialect percolated the grille and Father Kelly, lifting the curtain a fraction, detected the flash of auburn that bespoke the sinner's identity.

'Bless me, Father for I have sinned . . .' Sonny reeled off the words in an automatic monotone, divesting them of any sincerity as he approached the moment of confession. Liam put down his newspaper and leaned his ear close to the grille, waiting for Sonny to provide him with the material for a good laugh. The last time, he had admitted to seeing his sister's navel. He knew that his colleagues would thoroughly disapprove of his amusement, but sure, the boy was only thirteen, still a child, what did he really know about sinning? Liam couldn't abide those who filled an innocent head with the fear of eternal damnation; there was time enough for that when they got down to some really bad stuff. 'I'm waiting, my son.'

Sonny considered it prudent to confess the lesser sins before touching on his more serious crimes. 'Father, I found threepence in the street an' didn't tell anybody. I spent it all on meself.'

'Then ye've doubly sinned,' reproved Liam. 'By not trying to discover to whom the money belonged you acted dishonestly, an' by spending it all on yourself were guilty of total selfishness.'

'Yes, Father. Sorry, Father.'

''Tis not to me ye owe your apologies, my son. Is there anything else?'

Sonny gulped. 'Father, I ...' – oh, dear God. 'I committed a terrible sin ... with a girl.'

Liam's green eyes twinkled in the kind, leathery face. 'Would ye like to enlarge on that?'

There was another pause, then: 'I saw her naked.'

A short delay from Liam, then: 'Might it have been by accident that ye saw her?'

'In a way ... that is, I tried to shut my eyes ... but they kept opening.'

'What I mean is, what were the circumstances of her being in this state?'

'Well ... it wasn't just her that was naked, Father ... I was too.'

The spark of amusement fizzled out. 'You're not telling me that ...'

'No, no, Father! I was just sort of there ... where she was ... with no clothes ... by the lake.'

'I think you'd better confess all,' demanded Liam, the paternal tone gone.

Sonny had never felt so ashamed. He confessed the whole sordid adventure, face on fire. At the end of it there was a prolonged silence.

Then Liam, cheek cupped in palm, said leniently, 'Well, if ye did nothing more than look at her ... perhaps 'tis not too heinous.'

Sonny bit his lip. God could see into his head. He would have to tell. 'No ... but the thing is, Father ... I wanted to.'

Liam closed his eyes as though weary. An overwhelming sadness came over him, not for the confession as such, but for the passing of a childhood. He might have expected it from the other one, but not from Sonny.

The boy's fingers curled tightly around the edge of his seat, waiting for Absolution. Before it was granted, Liam asked, 'Was there anyone else involved in all this?' He was sure the boy had been led.

Sonny deliberated for a long time. 'Saints don't tell on their brothers', came Dickie's parting shot. 'No, Father, just me,' the boy finally lied, and even as it slipped out, he thought – oh no! that's another sin, and silently prayed to God to add this one to His list.

Liam was quiet for another few seconds, then abruptly gave a penance and told Sonny to go and sin no more. Sonny could tell by the tone of voice that he had shocked his old friend deeply. He emerged from the confessional cursing his brother for letting him carry the blame; at least Dickie had got something out of it – like he was probably getting it now. Damn him!

CHAPTER TWELVE

Thomasin lifted the glass cowl from the oil lamp and applied a taper to the wick. The room was gradually infused with the smell of fried bacon, due to her economical measure of using the stale fat from the frying pan to fuel the lamps. Patrick furrowed his brow as he turned over another page of his *York Herald*. 'Sure, 'tis still light, what d'ye want to go wastin' fuel for? The sun's not gone down yet.'

Thomasin settled herself beside the lamp and opened a book; even without benefit of a full education this joy had not been lost to her. 'I've been watchin' yer squintin' an' screwin' up yer eyes for t'past half hour. Yer'll be goin' blind if y'aren't careful, tryin' to read in that light. Anyroad, yer talkin' as if we're still poverty-stricken. We'll soon have enough brass to keep ten lamps goin'.' She was about to begin her book when another idea struck her. 'Eh, I wonder if we'll have gas lamps at this new house? I'll bet there are, yer know. By, won't we be grand! Happen there'll be a lotta things we'll find different – like proper hankies instead o' these scraps o' rags.' She wiped her nose and wriggled her stockinged toes in eagerness. 'Oh, I can hardly wait to see inside.'

He smiled indulgently. 'An' I can't wait to see ye invested as mistress, God love ye, ye deserve it.' He crumpled the newspaper into an untidy heap and stood up to reach his pipe from the rack on the mantelshelf. 'Lord, but I wish it were sorted out now, though. I'm bored stiff with no work to lay me hands to.' Added to the bacon fat was now the smell of tobacco as he stoked his pipe. 'Where's her ladyship an' the rapscallions? Did they not come in from Confession yet?'

'Erin's out in yard putting some newspaper in closet. Lads came in while you were doin' that job for Miss P. then went straight out again. I think they'd been fightin'; Sonny's face was like thunder. I gave 'em money for a haircut. Dickie said they were off down to tannery afterwards wi' some rabbit skins. He's becoming a dab hand at catchin' bunnies is our Dickie – an' we both know where he got that from.'

They smiled fondly at each other. Dear, crafty John – dead many a year now but his questionable skills handed down to their sons. Patrick puffed on his pipe and made to sit down when a movement in the yard caught his eye. An annoyed scowl took over his face. He strode quickly through the scullery and into the yard. His daughter, who had been chatting to someone over the wall, turned swiftly at his angry instruction.

'Erin, go into the house at once! And you!' The person with whom Erin had been conversing bobbed hastily behind the wall. 'Stay away from my daughter – unless ye want to know what a broken neck feels like!' He stormed back into the house and slammed the door. Erin had flown upstairs to her room. 'Erin, come down here this instant!' he bellowed.

'What's all racket about?' demanded Thomasin, placing a strip of paper in the book to mark her place.

''Tis that lecher from next door!' Patrick informed her noisily.

'I don't think Miss Peabody would appreciate being called a lecher.'

'Less o' your sarcasm, woman! Ye know very well who I mean – that tousle-haired no-good lout from the other side. He's been payin' too much attention to our Erin of late.'

'Gregory?' said Thomasin amazedly. 'He's nobbut fifteen. Besides, he's no lout, he's a respectable young lad. And apart from anything else, I don't think that was any way to talk to a young boy – you'll have his mother on to me.'

The temper which Patrick had been so successful in curbing still flared occasionally. 'Fifteen or no, I don't like him pestering my daughter. Erin, come down here now!'

'Nay,' scoffed his wife. 'There's nowt goin' on there. Our Erin'd run a mile if she thought that. Yer know how shy of men she is. She looks on Gregory as a bairn, like her brothers. An' will yer please stop shoutin' at poor lass to come down. She'll not come; she can be as stubborn as her father when she's a mind. Anyroad, yer've embarrassed her.'

'Me, embarrassed her? Better that than some young buck takin' advantage of her.'

'Now yer being silly,' reproved his wife. 'Sit down.'

'Oh, 'tis you who're giving the orders now, is it?'

'Way I look at it, t'one who gives the orders should be t'one wi' sense – an' you're showing precious little o' that. Leave the lass alone, will yer? God help her if yer gonna go on like this every time a young man talks to her. She'll never get wed.'

'Are ye trying to marry her off an' her little more than a child?'

128

'Nonsense! She's twenty. There's many a girl got three bairns by the time they're her age.'

'That's exactly my point, Tommy,' he said emphatically. 'These young rakes they have no intention of marriage. All right ye can laugh, but I've seen the way they look at her. I was that age once. I know what's going through their minds.'

'Then that doesn't speak very well for you, does it?' she replied. 'Now, d'yer think I could continue wi' me book?'

An hour of calm followed with the two sat contentedly reading, one on either side of the black-leaded range like a couple of Toby jugs. When the last ray of sun had dwindled over the roof of the privy a subdued Erin finally came down to join them. No mention was made of the earlier disturbance.

Thomasin stretched and yawned noisily, then placed her book on the table. 'I suppose I'd better start makin' cocoa.' She pushed herself up from the chair. 'By, it's gerrin dark. I wonder what them lads are up to.'

Her query was to be answered shortly by the sound of the front door opening and her sons making their boisterous entrance. 'Talk of the Devil,' started Thomasin, then placed her hands on her hips, her eyes suspicious slits. 'You've been drinkin', I can smell it wi' me eyes shut.'

'Ah, Mother dear!' Dickie, his eyes like glittering zircons with the effects of the liquor, draped his arm across her shoulders. ''Twas a terrible funny thing, was it not, Son? We were just walkin' past The Spread Eagle, mindin' our own business, when this great hand reaches out an' grabs Sonny by the collar an' starts to pull him into the pub. Try as he might he couldn't escape the pull of it. He was dragged kickin' an' screamin' right into that tavern an' the door bolted fast behind him.'

'An' I suppose you were fastened in as well, were yer?' said his mother.

'Well, I couldn't see him in such a stew, could I? I mean, he *is* me brother. I had to go in an' rescue him. My, we had the very devil of a time gettin' outta that place, didn't we, Son? Still, we're home safe an' sound ye'll be glad to see an' no harm done.' He kissed her. 'What's for sup?'

She pushed him away. 'Tongue – the edge of mine if yer gimme any more o' that flim-flam. Eh, yer want puttin' in a bag an' shakin' up. I reckon we wouldn't've seen hide nor hair of yer if you hadn't been hungry.'

'Ah, that's not strickly true,' corrected Dickie, ignoring his father's darkening face, feeling bold and warm. He could twist them all round his little finger. Sonny had been absolutely furious when he had returned from Confession, especially when Dickie had told him what he had missed, but a quick dose of his brother's magic had cured Sonny; they were the best of friends again now. And Mam, underneath that expression, was not really mad at him. 'We were ready to come home anyway, an' ye can thank the Bible-thumpers for that. Gob! Why can't they leave a fella alone? Going on about the virtues o' temperance – 'tis enough to drive a man to drink.' He yelped as Patrick, with two quick strides, dealt him a stinging blow to the ear.

'What was that for?'

Patrick gave him another to match at the other side. 'That one was for daring to question my authority, an' if ye want to know what the original one was for I'll tell ye. When I came to this country those Bible-thumpers as you so disrespectfully call them were the only ones to help me. They housed me an' fed me, while others in this city would've seen the lot of us cast out to die. So don't let me hear ye speaking so scornfully about them again. The Quakers are good people an' if it weren't for them you wouldn't be here to malign them.' He relit his pipe and spoke through the cloud of sweet-smelling tobacco. 'Apart from all that, I don't care for my sons making a habit of frequenting such places. You're far too young to be wastin' your lives like that – ye coulda been out doin' something more constructive. An' another thing, your mother tells me she gave ye both the price of a haircut before ye went out. Was the barber unavailable or has he taken to cutting it with his teeth?' He surveyed the raggy ends where his

130

sons had attempted to cut each other's hair using a knife. 'There's no need for me to ask where ye got your ale money from, is there?'

Dickie scowled. 'Sure, you're always slapping us down, isn't he, Son? Treatin' us like bairns an' us almost men.' Sonny hung his head and swayed.

This remark seemed to alter Patrick's whole outlook on the matter. His tone brightened considerably as if nothing untoward had gone before. He clapped his hands and rubbed them together briskly. 'Why, God love us an' save us. The man can't see what's under his very nose. 'Tis right you are, son, I've been treatin' ye both like weans for too long, 'tis time I saw ye for the men you are. Well now, why don't we three sit down an' have ourselves a little parley, man to man like.'

The youngsters grinned inanely at each other and sat at the table expectantly as Patrick ordered his wife to bring forth a jug of poteen. Some years ago he had installed his own private still in a large cupboard off the scullery, but this was the first time he had shared his illicit brew with his sons. They watched as he selected a couple of pipes from the rack and tossed them and his tobacco pouch onto the table. 'Will ye take a pipeful with me, lads? All men together, right?' His sons reached eagerly for the pipes, plugging the patterned bowls with tobacco.

'Didn't I tell ye it'd be all right?' slurred Dickie to his brother as Thomasin dubiously placed the jug of poteen on the table and her husband poured three glasses. 'Sonny was thinkin' maybe we'd be in for a roastin', but I told him, "Dad's all right – he understands that a man needs a drink from time to time to soothe all the troubles o' this world." Am I right?'

'Oh, that you are. There's nothing I like better,' said Patrick levelly, then indicated the glasses. 'An' now ye can take that drink with your father.'

Dickie tapped the glass against Patrick's then disposed of its contents, thinking smugly what a dummy his father could be at times, so malleable. Most fathers would have given them a beating for their misdemeanour and here was theirs plying them with drink. Only Thomasin saw the dangerous glint in Patrick's eye. She passed a mug of cocoa to Erin who wished everyone a goodnight and carried the mug up to her room. Thomasin sat back in the chair to watch her husband's performance. A silverfish scuttled from under the fender and ran over her foot; she did not notice.

'Another, boys?' Patrick grasped the handle of the earthenware jug and refilled their glasses, ever watchful. His sons knocked back the poteen as though it were water.

The hour grew late and the level of the jug grew lower. Patrick tilted it towards him to examine the contents. 'Looks like we'll be needing a refill, Mother. Would ye do the honours?'

Thomasin rose and carried her empty cup to the scullery, muttering in passing, 'I don't know what game you're at, but I'll not be party to encouraging those lads to become drunkards. If yer want a refill yer can get it yerself.'

'Ah, women,' sighed Patrick, pushing himself up from his seat at the table. ''Tis nothing but trouble they are. I ask ye, what's the use o' keepin' a dog an' barking yourself?' He followed her into the scullery, winked at her frown, then returned with another jug.

Sonny was making his third attempt to rise from his chair. 'If ye'll excuse me, Dad, I think I'd rather go to bed.'

'Ye'll surely not be deserting your father?' Patrick pressed him back into the chair. 'Not when we're having such a good time.'

Sonny turned bleary eyes on his brother who was beginning to look rather pale. Their father pushed the tobacco pouch at them. 'Come on, fill up your pipes. I'm feeling generous the day. 'Tis a great experience when a father discovers his sons have become men.' He waved away their pleas of tiredness. 'Away with ye! The night's still young, an' ye'll not leave a man to finish the jug on his own.' He filled their glasses to the brim. 'Come on, sup up, as your mother would say.'

Thomasin made a face as she took the breakfast pots from the cupboard.

'I just hope you aren't gonna be clutterin' up that table all night, 'cause I want to set it for mornin'.'

'Plenty of time. There's no work for me to go to so I might as well enjoy meself,' said Patrick calmly, then to his sons: 'What's the matter with ye? Ye've not touched your drinks.'

'I don't think I can drink any more,' replied his elder son thickly, his pipe resting on the table.

'Hey, that's good baccy you're wasting!' Patrick tugged the pipe from Dickie's fingers and pressed it to his son's mouth. Looking decidedly bilious Dickie slowly took the pipe between his lips and made a token puff.

'It's gone out,' declared his father and leapt up to light a taper from the dying coals. 'There! Take nice big puffs an' ye'll soon get it started again.' He kept the flame at Dickie's pipe. 'Ah no, you're acting like Soft Mick. Big puffs, I said. Come on, let's see that baccy glow. Suck, boy, suck!'

Dickie's face took on the colour of the green tablecloth as the clouds of tobacco-smoke enveloped it. His brother, too, was looking extremely unwell as his father forced another glass of poteen upon him. 'C'mon now, a toast,' decided Patrick, holding his glass at arm's length. 'To your mother, the finest woman on two legs.'

Thomasin, purse-lipped, pushed him aside in order to set the table for morning. 'I hope 'tis something substantial you're going to be feeding us, me darlin',' he told her. 'For 'tis three men ye've got on your hands now. Aye, they're not boys any more, look at them. They really know how to hold their drink. What's it to be then, Tommy? Three plates full o' bacon an' eggs? Something nice an' greasy to line the stomach, an' the eggs all runny as I like 'em. Three apiece, an' I think I'll have six rashers o' nice fatty bacon, with plenty o' greasy dip.' He leaned towards the boys. 'Sure, I like the way the plate looks just before ye mop it up with a big wad of bread; all mixed with egg yolk an' black juice from the mushrooms an' lovely greasy

133

fat, don't you, boys? An' then we'll have a gallon o' tea to wash it down with. Gob!' He smacked his lips. 'I can almost feel my belly full to bursting with it, slopping around with all that tea . . .' His voice petered out as his sons charged from the table, through the scullery and into the yard, both with hands clapped across their mouths.

Patrick grinned at his wife as he replaced the bung in the jug and gave it a triumphant slap with the heel of his palm. 'That took a little longer than I anticipated. I was in danger o' becoming slewed meself.' He forced his grin into a frown as his sons staggered back into the house clutching their aching stomachs. 'Men, ye say? Hah!' He prodded Dickie's shoulder with his finger. 'Ye'll need a few more years on your back before ye can call yourself anything resembling a man, me boyo. It takes more than a few jars of ale to make a man.' He shook the jug under their noses so that the liquid slopped about inside it. 'Fancy another before I put it away? No? Then ye'd best be off to beddy-byes.' They stumbled groggily to the stairs, then turned at his shout of: 'Here!' He emerged from the scullery bearing a bucket. 'Ye'll most probably be needing this through the night. Anyone who isn't quick enough to use it gets a hiding; ye'll not make any extra work for your mother.'

'That was a bit drastic, wasn't it?' observed Thomasin when her sons had staggered up to their bed.

'It was. They've used almost a week's supply o' baccy between them. Can ye lend me a few bob for some more?' He jumped out of the way as she made to cuff him. 'Ah, I'm taking your meaning sure enough, but it worked did it not? I doubt they'll be able to even walk past a pub for a long time without that old heave-ho feeling. I've nothing against a man taking a drink – sure I like a drop meself – but they've got to learn how to moderate the bending of their elbow. If I'd said nothing they'd've thought I condoned their behaviour, an' I don't. No son of mine is going to grow up a drunkard.'

CHAPTER THIRTEEN

'Oh, isn't it lovely!' Thomasin clapped her hands together as she stood in the hall of her new home, eyeing it with near disbelief, the unexpected grandeur of it robbing her of a more laudatory comment. This evening the solicitor's clerk had delivered the keys of Mr Penny's house and the moment the family had eaten Thomasin had whisked them off to see it.

'Well, if tha'd let us in happen we'd all be able to say that,' complained William Fenton, her father who, along with his wife, had been invited to share the unveiling ceremony but was still confined to the doorway.

Thomasin hastily moved aside to allow them entry then whirled back to appraise her surroundings, eyes bright with anticipation. 'Well, what d'yer think?' she pressed everyone. 'Isn't it absolutely grand?'

'Very nice, dear,' understated her mother. 'Very nice indeed. I always said that one day you would find your true position and I was correct, was I not? Of course,' she sniffed disparagingly, 'I also knew that whatever good fortune befell you would be of your own making and not of your husband's.' Hannah Fenton had always despised Patrick. She felt her daughter had married beneath her and fifteen years of familiarity with the man had not changed her opinion. Neither had her advancing years brought any sweetening of character. 'It is as well, dear, that one of you at least had some sort of social connection. I had visions of you ending your days in that terrible little house.'

Thomasin laughed. 'I'd hardly call Mr Penny a social connection, Mother. He was a grumpy old bugger at times.'

'Really, Thomasin dear,' reproved her mother, limping

about the hall – she suffered greatly with rheumatics nowadays. 'You will have to moderate your deplorable language if you are to move into wider circles. It is all very well being liberally-minded when one is living among people of a lower bearing than oneself, but I imagine that your new neighbours will take great exception to such gutter language.'

'Blimey, don't start on about the neighbours already,' sighed Thomasin. Despite much leg-pulling her mother still retained that superior air. 'Giz yer hat an' let's have a nosey round t'old place.'

'It stinks,' provided Dickie as Thomasin led the way.

'By, yer can always rely on kids to put the dampers on things, can't yer?' answered his mother. 'It's only fusty 'cause it's been shut up for a while – like you ought to be.'

'He must've been old,' speculated Sonny. 'Old people's houses always smell.' He lowered his eyes on incurring a vitriolic glare from his grandmother.

'If yer tryin' to put me off yer goin' the right way about it,' complained Thomasin. 'Any more an' I'm gonna chuck the lotta yer out. Ooh, Lord look at this!' She swept, sparkling-eyed, into the front parlour. 'He's got a pinanna.'

'Reet, let's 'ave kettle on an' mck a bloody do of it!' bawled William, rubbing gleeful hands, as rough and ready as his wife was aloof.

'William, language please,' objected Hannah. 'And do keep your voice down, none of us are deaf.'

William leaned towards Patrick. 'She's freetened neighbours'll hear,' he chuckled. 'By, have they gorra shock in store for them. They won't know what's hit 'em when we move in.'

'I wasn't aware that I was takin' in lodgers,' said Thomasin whimsically.

'Tha knows what I mean, clivver bugger! We will be visitin' thee, won't we?'

'That's debatable,' said his daughter with a crafty wink at Patrick. 'I don't know as I want my new house cluttered up wi' riff-raff, showin' me up.'

'Eh, just 'cause tha's gorra piano there's no call to get uppity. We've enough shirty buggers in t'ouse wi' tha mother. Anyroad, what about purrin' that whatsit on?'

'How doest expect me to boil t'kettle when there's no bloody fire?' His daughter matched his basic commentary.

'If ye wait a couple o' minutes longer,' murmured Patrick, 'ye'll be able to boil it on your mother's head. Will ye look at her face: red as a farmer's bum.'

Hannah's cheeks were suffused with ill-temper at having to listen to this repartee. She had hoped Thomasin's new status would have reformed her unladylike behaviour, but the last few minutes had doused that expectation.

'I think me father's right,' Thomasin was saying now. 'We oughtta make a do of it, just to warm t'house up a bit; have a bit of a sing-song round t'piano. What d'yer say, Pat?'

'I second the motion. Will I go out an' fetch us a couple o' bottles?'

'Why not?' Thomasin ignored her mother's disfavour. 'Me father can help yer carry 'em.'

'O' course, ye'll be wanting a proper housewarming later on,' said Patrick. 'With all our pals.'

'Oh, please!' ejaculated Hannah, wringing her hands. 'Not that dreadful Mrs Flaherty.'

Patrick set his mouth and waited for Thomasin's usual retort of: 'Oh, don't be such a bloody snob, Mother!' But oddly, and much to his disquiet, it did not come. 'Ye'll surely not be forgetting Molly an' the rest just 'cause ye've come into a bit o' money, Tommy?' he prompted.

There was the briefest delay, then she answered airily, 'Whatever made yer think that? Naturally they'll all come. But just let's get settled in before yer start inviting 'em round, I'll have enough to do without parties.' – The longer we wait, hoped Thomasin with a vague sense of betrayal, maybe he'll forget the idea. Molly was a good sort and Thomasin did pity her circumstances but the mind came up with all sorts of visions at what impression the Irishwoman would create in this select neighbourhood.

137

It was going to be hard enough being accepted here without Molly. Best if she and Patrick visited their old friend instead of the other way round.

– Perhaps she *is* learning after all, smiled Hannah to herself, then said aloud, 'Are we to be allowed to finish our tour of the house before the men indulge themselves?'

'Aye, away then,' said Thomasin. 'Let's see what's hidden away upstairs.' She caught her father's expression. 'The ale won't run dry in five minutes, yer know. That's all it'll take us to inspect t'bedrooms. After all, that is what we're 'ere to do, not test quality o' t'local brew.' She led the way up the blue-carpeted stairway and stopped at the first landing, off which there were two bedrooms. Craning her neck around the door of the room to her right she uttered a moan of disappointment. 'S'empty,' she explained to those behind her and opened the door wider for them to see. 'Fair-sized rooms though, aren't they?'

While her family was still commenting on the spaciousness of the empty room, Thomasin investigated the other and her wondrous cry brought them all rushing to crowd into the doorway at her shoulder. 'Well, the old bugger!' she exclaimed, then laughed delightedly as she pounced upon the splendid papier mâché bed. 'He's really done himself proud wi' this lot, hasn't he? What a bed! I wonder if he ever entertained in it?'

'Thomasin!' Hannah almost fainted. 'If I have to listen to any more of your vulgarities I shall leave. If you have no respect for your benefactor do have a care for your poor mother's sensibilities.'

Thomasin was undaunted. '*We-ell*, yer not gonna tell me that a man who lives alone is gonna buy a bed like this just to sleep on, are yer? Just look at it.'

The bed was fitted with an eight-feet high canopy which was fringed with red wool and draped with curtains of deep crimson, these edged with gold cords and tassels. The foot and headboard were shining black papier mâché, embellished with gold-painted flowers and inlaid with mother-of-pearl. The pillow slips, though a mite wrinkled at present, were of best quality linen and edged with thick lace. There was a frilled valance to match the damask coverlet on which Thomasin now lay back contentedly, ankles crossed, hands behind head, and feeling extremely shabby against this plush backdrop.

'Didn't tha say he died in bed?' asked William innocently, making her leap up with a curse.

'Don't do that to me!' she chastised him, suppressing an involuntary shiver. 'Yer've put me right off now.'

William chuckled. 'Lig down, soft 'aporth! Look at number o' folk that've snuffed it in my bed before it were handed down to me, an' I'm still walkin' around – just. Away, can't we go an 'ave that ale now?'

Erin had opened the door of a huge mahogany wardrobe. 'There's all his clothes still here, Mam.'

'Let's have a gander!' Her grandfather edged her aside. 'There might be summat that'll fit me.' He lifted out a navy-blue frockcoat and held it against himself.

Erin urged him to try it on and reaching into the bottom of the wardrobe lifted out a pair of boots.

'Nay, lass.' William waved his hand positively. 'A coat's one thing, but I draw t'line at wearin' dead men's boots. I'm gerrin too old to tek risks like that. By, I look a reet toff in this.' He searched for a hat to cover his bald pate then studied his reflection in the wardrobe mirror. 'Well, I wouldn't know meself if I didn't know it were me.' He spat on his hands and smoothed down his side-whiskers. 'Aye, a proper gent.'

Hannah was examining a japanned box which she had found in a drawer. 'Why, this is full of jewellery!' she exclaimed, lifting out a cameo brooch.

'Aye, it'd belong to his late wife.' Thomasin came to stand beside her. 'There's some nice stuff, isn't there?'

Hannah agreed and held the brooch against the lace at her collar, admiring the effect in the cheval mirror that stood in the corner.

'Yer can have it if yer like,' said her daughter generously. 'Erin, perhaps there's summat you might fancy here.'

Patrick stared at his family, and was imbued with the picture of the women at the foot of the Cross haggling over

139

Christ's clothes. There were the three females hunched avariciously over the jewellery casket, his father-in-law preening himself in his new outfit, Sonny opening and shutting drawers as if there were no tomorrow and his elder son bouncing on the bed in a most peculiar fashion. 'For God's sake will ye look at yourselves!' he accused. 'The poor ould fella's hardly cold an' here y'all are rifling through his personal possessions as if it were a free-for-all. Tommy, I thought better of you. After all, he was your friend.'

His wife spun to face him with a sound of guilt. 'Eh, yer right! Poor Mr Penny, what would he say if he could see us? I got carried away with it all. Still,' her mien changed to one of business-like resignation, 'it's got to be done sometime, Pat, and he is dead and buried. I can't really see t'difference whether we do it now or in a month's time. We'd still be intruding into his private memories.'

'Aye, that's true,' allowed Patrick grudgingly. 'Come on then, are we going to look at the rest o' the house? Ye've plenty of time to go through all that another day.' He headed the procession up the next flight of stairs where they found two more empty bedchambers, and up yet another flight to the top of the house and two attic rooms, one of which was piled almost to the roof with old books and pictures, furniture and trunks. After the hastiest examination they returned to the ground floor where Thomasin ushered everyone back into the parlour.

It was decided that the boys should be sent for the refreshments and in their absence Thomasin invited all to be seated while she herself went to check on the contents of Mr Penny's larder. She reappeared bearing a tray. 'There's some fruitcake here. It looks all right; I can't vouch for its taste though. Some biscuits too.' Selecting an armchair she seated herself happily, placing the tray on the occasional table beside her. 'I also found this.' She indicated a half-filled bottle of Madeira. 'That should be more to your taste than beer, Mother.'

'Well, perhaps just a thimbleful, dear if I may. Will you join me? One really cannot consume ale you know in a house such as this.' Hannah cast her critical eye over the furnishings. Besides the cottage piano there was a sofa and two armchairs upholstered in striped silky material of green and white. In the opposite corner to the piano was a heavily-carved mahogany bookcase, the contents of which seemed to be providing great interest to Patrick, and a little to its right stood a reading stand, also carved from mahogany. Apart from the occasional table which bore the tray there were two others; on one was a composition of wax fruit and flowers under a glass dome, and on the other, also protected by a glass dome, was a pathetic tableau of stuffed goldfinches. 'They're out for a start,' decreed Thomasin. 'They give me the creeps.' The remainder of the pleasant room's decor was provided by dozens of embroidered cushions, runners, mats, antimacassars and framed samplers, a firescreen painted with a sailing ship and a good many gilt-framed pictures, bedded on gold flocked wallpaper. The carpet's pattern was a mixture of green and beige, and the curtains were of dark green velvet, with tassels the thickness of a man's wrist.

'Mr Penny was a widower, you say?' enquired Hannah of her daughter.

Thomasin captured her line of thought. 'I was thinking the same thing: everything seems too neat and orderly, too well-furnished to have belonged to an old widower, doesn't it? Not to mention clean. Although I expect t'rooms haven't altered much since his wife died, he probably only used t'back room, an' he was at work best part o'day, so he'd hardly time to make a mess had he? And happen he could've had someone in to clean for him, that'd account for it. The only other option is that he had a fancy woman tucked away somewhere, an' I don't believe that for one second, otherwise why would I have been the only benefi- ciary in t'will?' Mr Ramsworthy had reassured her that the will would stand uncontested. Being well-acquainted with the deceased he would have known had there been anyone of this nature in Mr Penny's background.

At this point the boys returned with beer-filled jugs, grumbling at the long walk they had had to the nearest public house. So used were they to Walmgate with its surplus taverns that a walk of more than five yards seemed excessive to them.

'A toast, then,' put forward William, when his glass had been charged. 'To Tommy an' Pat an' their well-deserved prosperity.'

'Thanks, Dad,' smiled Thomasin. 'Everyone. And here's to your continuing good health too.' She sipped appreciatively at the Madeira.

'Chuck us one o' them thingys over will yer, Pat?' William's son-in-law passed the plate of biscuits. 'Ta! Right then, who's gonna give us first turn?'

'Eh, give us a chance to have our sup first,' pleaded his daughter. 'We've got all night for fun an' games.'

'Well, if I'm not gonna get to sing tha can oblige by tellin' us what tha's gonna do wi' all this brass tha's got comin' to thee,' said William through a mouthful of crumbs.

'We haven't rightly decided yet,' replied Thomasin, then to her elder son who kept nudging her in the ribs: 'Will you please stop interrupting while I'm tryin' to talk! What d'yer want, anyroad?'

'Can I have another piece o' cake, please?' asked Dickie.

'Oh, here y'are then, gutsy. Pass the plate round first.'

'Want a bit o' cake, Grandma?'

Hannah sighed inwardly. No matter how often she had reminded them that she was not 'Grandma' but 'Grandmama' or 'Grandmother' it seemed to go in one ear and out the other. 'No thank you, dear,' she told Dickie. 'The cake is a trifle heavy for my fragile digestive system.'

'Grandad?'

William selected a hefty wedge and addressed Thomasin again. 'Tha must have some sorta notion what tha might like to do. Esta gonna keep shop or sell it, or what?'

'Oh, I shall keep it on,' said Thomasin decisively. 'Our Erin's goin' to help me run it, it'd be too much on me own, if I want to make a real go of it.'

'That'll be nice for her,' said William, prising a cherry from the cake and handing it to his grand-daughter.

– Will it? Erin took the cherry resentfully. – I notice no one asked for my opinion.

Hannah had noticed this omission too. 'And what does Erin have to say to your plan?'

'Oh, it's a lot better than workin' in the café, isn't it?' said Thomasin before the girl could answer. 'An' she's been a great help to me this past week. I don't know where I'd've been without her. An' now she won't need to go lookin' for another job; she's got a ready-made one right here.'

'Erin?' persisted Hannah.

Erin would have liked to answer that – no, she didn't like the arrangement at all. But how could she when her stepmother had just said how much she relied on her help? Erin wasn't the sort to let anyone down. Besides, what was the point in telling them of her true wish? The eight months of education she had received at the Cummings' household had not provided her with enough experience to call herself a governess, and she was far too old to attend college now. Even if she were not, Father would never countenance wasting money on a girl's education. Wonderful though Patrick was in many ways he was very narrow-minded in this respect.

'Mam's right,' she told her grandmother with no hint of the bitterness she really felt. 'It seems the obvious thing for me to do; help in the shop. Why hire an assistant when there's two willing hands at home?' – And besides, came the resentful thought, for what else would I qualify? But even as she passively accepted her fate she was determined that should she ever be lucky enough to have daughters they would never suffer the same deprivation as herself.

'An' what about thee, Pat?' enquired William. 'What's this lass o' mine got lined up for t'maister?'

'Ah, that's one thing we're definite on,' replied Patrick confidently. 'I'm going to purchase a piece of land an' grow my own produce.'

'Be a farmer?' Hannah was aghast. The man had just

143

been presented with enough wealth with which to cultivate a worthy reputation and still he seemed unable to uproot himself from his lowly origins.

'There are such things as gentlemen farmers, Hannah,' Patrick informed her.

'There are – but I'm sorely afraid you would not number among them,' said his mother-in-law scathingly. 'Gentlemen farmers employ labourers to do their work for them. You, I think, will not be happy unless you are grovelling about in the dirt yourself. However,' she condescended, 'I am most pleased to hear that my daughter will not be entrusting the maintenance of the store to you.'

Patrick shook his head and chuckled deep in his chest, though more from annoyance than amusement. What did one have to do to earn this woman's respect?

'There's method in all this, Mother,' said Thomasin. 'After Pat told me that that was what he wanted – a plot o' land – I got to thinking – why not widen my own horizons by selling not just provisions but greengrocery too? Grow all our own produce so there's no middle man to worry about. It would all be on a soil-to-shelf basis, and with Pat doing the cultivating there's no labourer to pay either. Heaven knows there are enough people makin' money out of us without handin' it to 'em on a plate. There're all sorts of possibilities it would open up.'

'Aye, yer could start yer own greengrocery round,' suggested William.

'There y'are, Pat – I told yer he weren't just for slingin' nuts at,' cried Thomasin. 'My thinking exactly, Father. We could put our Dickie in charge o' that.'

– Oh, you're too kind, thought Dickie and sipped morosely at his ale. If ye think I'm going to idle me precious time away humping crateloads o' stinking cabbage then ye can think again. If my father doesn't want to be a gentleman here's one that'll not turn up his nose at it.

'I thought tha said tha'd not given it much thought,' said William, smacking his lips as he finished his ale. 'Seems to me tha's got everyone neatly sorted out into their little pigeonholes. There's only Sonny left without a job. What about thee, lad? What might thoo like to do wi' thissen?'

Sonny placed his glass of ale on a runner and leaned forward intently. 'Well,' he began carefully, tenting his fingertips, 'seeing as how the subject has been broached ...' What he was really thinking was – Seeing as how nobody else seems to have been given a choice in the matter, I'll get my two pennorth in while I'm able ... 'What I'd really like to do is to go to art school. I'm sure I'm good enough to get a scholarship and it's summat ...'

'Art school!' exploded William and Patrick in unison, their disdain and condemnation undisguised.

Somewhat aggrieved that his idea had been met by such contempt Sonny pressed home his request hurriedly. ''Tis not just painting, ye know, they teach designing and architecture an' all sorts ...'

'That's no sorta job for a man!' declaimed William. 'Hangin' about wi' a bunch o' puffs, paintin' flowers an' whatnot. God! I've never heard owt so daft. Art school, he sez, puh! tha gurt fooil. Tha's thirteen, lad, time tha were purrin aside all these soft ideas. I thought tha'd grown outta that be now.'

''Tis right your grandfather is,' confirmed Patrick. 'No son of mine is going to waste his life painting pictures. Fortune or no I'll not squander good money on such an addle-brained idea.'

'If that's the amount o' respect ye show for my opinion,' was Sonny's tart response, 'I'm surprised ye even asked for it. After all, ye gave none o' the others a chance to voice theirs, did ye?'

Patrick looked uncomfortably at his wife. Even taking into consideration that the boy was getting very assertive that made him no less right. Dickie and Erin had been sort of dragooned into things. This had been justifiable with the former, for if it were left to Dickie he would spend his days sat on his backside, but perhaps Erin should have been given the opportunity to speak her mind. She was, after all, old enough to form a sensible opinion.

'I meant what I said,' she told him when asked. 'Only,

I've just been thinking . . .' she paused for Patrick's approval, 'instead of just being a general dogsbody . . .'

'Oh, Erin!' cut in her mother. 'Nobody's asked yer to be that.'

'No, I know that,' Erin appeased. 'I didn't mean for it to sound recriminating, and I'm quite happy to help ye, Mam, truly I am. Only . . . well, ye know how I like cooking an' baking – I mean I'd really have liked to do it for a living – well, I was wondering: how about turning all this produce that me Dad's going to grow into fruit pies? They'd sell ever so well, I'm sure of it, an' ye said yourself ye wanted to widen your horizons . . .'

'Whoa! Whoa!' Thomasin's wide mouth stretched into a smile. 'Don't get hosses in a foam. We haven't even got fruit trees planted yet an' here you are havin' them all sliced up an' baked in a pie. I know what I said, but there's more than just hot-air needed to fly a balloon . . .' She smiled sympathetically at the disappointment on her daughter's face. 'Still, it were an illuminatin' idea. Come up with more like that an' I might give yer a seat on the board. You are a smashing little cook – much better than me – and the minute yer Dad starts to harvest his fruit we'll implement your suggestion. All right? Happy now?'

Erin nodded. If she could not have her first wish come true then her second would do. Rose Leng, the cook at the Cummings' house, had passed on along with countless recipes her own love of cooking and Erin had been a very good pupil. She would not mind helping in the store half so much now.

'I suppose I'm going to get the same treatment, am I?' said Sonny rather impudently. 'Patted on the head and told: "There, there. Father knows best. Be a good boy an' we'll see in a few years' time," hoping I'll forget about it. Well, I won't! 'Tis the most important thing in my life, painting. Why should it be denied me just because Father thinks it's womanish?'

'By, God I'd've got a clipped ear'ole if I'd spoken to my father like that!' burst out William. 'An' there's not just yer dad thinks it's 'feminate neither.'

Patrick's comment was ripe with parental indignation. 'Ye've overstepped the mark, Sonny. Ye'll show more respect an' apologise at once.' Sonny, with bowed head, complied. 'And,' said his father, 'what's all this rubbish about being denied your pleasures? There's no one says ye cannot do your painting in your spare time as usual. I've never stopped ye, have I?'

'But yer don't understand . . . I want to make a career of it.'

'You're damned right I don't understand!' barked Patrick, annoyed at his son's persistence. 'And I'm blowed if I'm going to try. Now, I've told ye, if ye want to spend all your free time painting that's all well an' good. But the rest of us are each contributing something to this business an' tis only fair that you should too. I've been giving serious thought to the question of your education and I've decided that your talents should be given their due – which is not happening at your present establishment, fine though the Brothers are. So, ye'll be going to another school, not art school, but a proper college where your brain will be put to full use. If your mother is set on making a go of this business then she'll need someone with a bit of acumen to assist her.' He glanced at Thomasin. 'What you have in mind will take more running than the poky little shop does at present, it needs brains. I'm not saying I don't think you're able to handle it, Tommy . . .'

Here, Hannah interjected caustically, 'I should hope not, Patrick. I would have thought that a failed businessman is the last person to advise anyone how to run their affairs.'

Patrick bypassed this sarcasm and continued to address Sonny. 'It may mean your spending some time away from home: are ye willing?'

Sonny directed his eyes at his brother to catch an amused twinkle. Still, if he could persuade Mam to talk his father into sending him not to just a business college but a school where there might be a generous quota of art instruction on the curriculum, he would consider himself to have fared a lot better than his siblings. He nodded his agreement to his father, and the atmosphere lightened somewhat.

With the cake devoured and the ale almost depleted, there followed an hour of lightheartedness around the piano. After Hannah had exposed them to a slice of culture by expertly fingering some Mozart, it was the turn of Patrick and his daughter. With Thomasin at the keyboard, Erin sank to her knees, pawing at Patrick's trousered leg with one hand, the other pressed to her brow in suitable melodrama, and sang:

> Oh, landlord I humbly beseech thee,
> Serve my father no more evil brew,
> Heed the plea of his poor abused daughter,
> Ere the blame for her death lies with you.

'Most apt,' murmured Hannah under her breath.

Once Dickie and his brother had taken their turn, there was only William who had not performed, and since the monologue on which he embarked with gusto was turning out to be another of his shameful, homespun compositions, Hannah decided enough was enough and called a halt.

'William, the hour is growing late.' She consulted her fobwatch. 'We had better make ready for home.'

'Nay, I haven't finished yet,' he complained. 'I'm just gerrin' to best bit.' Suddenly he clutched his chest and sat down; his face had turned quite grey. At once his family were around him voicing their concern. 'It's nowt. I'll be all reet in a minute.' He waved them away. 'Just gimme some air.'

'William, what is it?' begged Hannah, flapping round him. 'What ails you?'

'Nowt. Don't pother, woman! I just got this stabbin' pain 'ere.' He prodded his breastbone. 'S'gone now, there's nowt to fuss abaht.'

'Shall I go for a doctor, Billy?' said his son-in-law. 'Ye don't look at all well.'

'Nay, I'm not havin' no piss-prophet pokin' round wi' me. I've never been to one in me life an' I don't aim to start at my age. It's nobbut a bit o' wind – that cake musta been off.'

'It tasted all right to me,' said his daughter dubiously. 'Dad, yer look awful. Please let us send for a doctor.'

'Wilt tha stop natterin'!' The colour was beginning to return to William's face though he still breathed deeply and there was a slight tremble to his fingers. 'I'll be reet, I tell thee. Yer mother'll put me to bed when we get home an' I'll be good as new in t'mornin'.'

Hannah asked for their coats. 'We'd better be on our way all the same. I don't like the look of him one bit.'

'Well, that's nowt new,' said William. 'Eh, anybody'd think I were on me last legs.' He attempted to divert attention from his discomfort. 'Listen, we haven't seen rest o' house yet. What abaht back parlour? I like to get me full quota, tha knows.'

Thomasin laid down the coats that she had fetched and shepherded everyone through the hall. 'Very well, but just a quick look. Don't think changin' t'subject is gonna stop me packin' you off home to bed.'

'I don't know who she reckons she's talkin' to,' said William to Sonny, then leant on him. ''Ere, give us hand, lad.' They moved with the others through to the back parlour. 'Eh, tha's a good'n. Happen I were a bit hard on yer before, I were just tekken aback, like. Doesta really want to spend tha life paintin' pictures? Seems a queer occipation to me, but if that's what tha's set thy heart on I could have a word wi' tha father. I can see t'grocery trade might not be everybody's cuppa tea.'

Sonny smiled his forgiveness as he assisted his grandfather through the doorway. 'Thanks, Grandad but I wouldn't risk it if I were you; ye saw how it affected Dad. If we keep natterin' at him it might make him worse. No, I think I'll just cut my losses an' be thankful for what I've got.'

William winked at him. 'Good lad.'

'You will have to employ a maid, Thomasin,' said Hannah when they stood in the back parlour. She ran a finger along the marble mantelshelf. 'If you insist on running the store personally then you will certainly need assistance with the upkeep of the house.'

'Me, employ a maid?' Thomasin laughed out loud. 'Nay, our friends'll think we've gone soft in t'head.'

'Even with Erin's help, dear, you could not hope to run such a large establishment unaided. You can be sure that your neighbours have a staff of at least three. I should have thought a maid would be the least you could allow yourself.'

William was back to his old form now. 'Oh aye, an' yer'll have to have thissen one o' them varlets, Pat, to help thee put tha togs on. Eh, what next! Our Tommy wi' servants.'

'May I remind you that your other daughters employ staff, William,' said his wife. 'Please don't make it sound like such a novelty to this family.'

'How do I know what they've got? I never get bloody invited there,' replied William strongly.

'Nay, don't let's be going into all that,' begged Thomasin, afraid that any discourse about her sisters might lead to a nasty argument, and that would do her father no good at all.

'Esta gorra back yard?' enquired William, running a handkerchief noisily under his nose.

'A garden, Papa, if you please,' quipped Thomasin pompously. 'But I'm afraid I can't serve tea on the lawn today, it's over dark.'

'Ee, short o' nowt we've got!' responded William, then pointed. 'What's through that door theer?'

His daughter wrinkled her brow. 'I can't say as how I've had time to look.'

'Well, tha should! I expect thee to keep me informed on such matters.' He twisted the knob and threw open the door. There was a collective gasp as the family crowded round to admire the *pièce de résistance* – a water closet.

'By God, that's a gradely piece o' work!' claimed William, bending to scrutinise the necessity, and responded in his usual blunt fashion when Thomasin pulled the handle and a shower of water sluiced the bowl.

'We'll all be shadowin' one another to t'closet to watch this. We won't be able to call it privy any more – it'll be about as private as a public hangin' in 'ere.'

They all laughed, even Hannah, as each eagerly awaited their turn to pull the handle. And then what they had thought to be the house's crowning glory was eclipsed by Thomasin's next discovery.

'Eh, look at this!' She reverently lifted a box from the lavatory floor and held it aloft for them all to see. 'Real toilet tissue – now I know the Feeneys are really on the way up!'

Moving day came, though it was more a question of moving bodies than furniture. They would be taking one or two items with them, such as beds, but as Mr Penny's furniture had far more class then theirs they were going to leave the latter where it stood and rent the old house as partly-furnished, thereby getting more rent than if it were unfurnished. Hence it was only necessary to make one journey, the cart they had hired carrying them and their possessions quite comfortably.

Patrick was first to alight in Monkgate, helping Thomasin from her perch. The boys and Erin jumped down from the back and waited to be told what to carry and where to put it. Patrick went to unlock the front door.

'Let's have these crates off first,' ordered Thomasin, 'so we can get this fella paid, or we're gonna run into another hour.' The man and his cart had been hired by the hour.

The family began to lift everything onto the pavement – beds and boxes, pictures and pans. With only a few seconds to spare the cart was finally evacuated and the driver, with a shrewd smile for Thomasin's Yorkshire thrift, flicked the reins and pulled away.

'Right,' said Patrick, rubbing his hands. 'It'd better be the beds in first or our neighbours'll think we're in the habit of sleepin' on the pavement. Oh, I'm terribly sorry!' He had stepped back and landed on someone's foot. He now spun round fully to offer more apologies but was robbed of speech. The man's grimace of pain had smoothed into an expression of recognition and shock . . . and something else.

'Thomasin.' Roland Cummings' hand went to his hat which was slowly raised and lowered, his eyes fixed affectionately on the red-haired woman who had once been his mistress. 'How . . . lovely to see you.'

'Hello, Roland.' Thomasin heard the words but couldn't quite tell if they had emerged from her own mouth. Her skin prickled. She finally tore her eyes away. 'Er, have yer met my husband? Pat, this is Mr Cummings, an old friend.'

Roland held out his hand. Patrick ignored it, staring into the man's face, intense dislike on his own.

'An' these are our sons an'. . . oh, yer know our daughter, don't yer?'

Roland, eyes still grappling defiantly with Patrick's, now looked to where Erin stood holding a box. 'Hello . . . Erin, isn't it?'

She smiled hesitantly and, with a snatched glance at her father, said, 'Hello, Mr Cummings, Miss Caroline . . . Alice.'

Thomasin noticed for the first time that Roland was not alone. Accompanying him was a young woman in a wheelchair, attended by a maid.

'My daughter Caroline,' Roland introduced her.

Thomasin smiled politely, feeling a nerve twitching her lip. She dared not look at Patrick. She didn't have to. Patrick, seizing the nearest crate, carried it up to the front door of his new home with no word of excuse. The boys, having little interest in these people, followed.

Erin approached the girl in the wheelchair with what she hoped was a friendly smile. 'I'm sorry to see you're not in the best of health, Miss Caroline.'

The ravishing young woman looked at her vacantly, staring so long that Erin was forced to look away uncomfortably and turn her attention to the maid who had control of the wheelchair. 'Alice, how're you keepin'?'

Her old workmate nodded and smiled. 'Not so bad, Erin. How're you?'

'Oh, can't grumble.' Erin looked at Caroline again.

'You will have to forgive my daughter for her apparent unfriendliness,' Roland told her kindly. 'She has not been well since her mother died.'

Erin nodded but did not look at him, her interest trained on the girl who appeared to be in a permanent trance. Once again, Erin was standing in the Cummings' household, seeing the beautiful blonde girl work herself into a frenzy because her mother was about to send her best friend Erin away. The mother who, with the aid of one hysterical hand, had plunged to her death over the banisters: Caroline's hand. The girl had obviously never recovered from that dreadful night.

'I trust it won't be long before you're restored to full health, Miss Caroline,' Erin said quietly then, with a look at her mother and a nod for Roland and Alice, she followed the others into the house.

Roland looked at Alice, his unspoken order causing her to manoeuvre the wheelchair around the pile of the Feeneys' belongings – having to go onto the road to do so – and carry on up the street.

'My daughter will never be fully recovered, I fear,' sighed Roland.

'I'm sorry,' replied Thomasin genuinely. 'Well, how's old Roly been, then?'

'Oh, quite well,' he smiled. It was all so polite.

They stood looking at each other for a while, his face filled with a remembered ache, hers friendly but awkward.

'It's good to see you again, Tommy.' The face was ugly, but Roland had some inner quality that attracted the females – a quality he had always played upon. She wondered if he still gave rein to the old weakness.

'Good to see you too, Roly . . . I'm sorry, we've blocked your path haven't we? As yer see we're in the act of movin' in.' She told him about the inheritance. She could see that he wasn't really listening, but remembering the times they'd spent together. 'I'm sorry if it's gonna be a bit awkward,' she said after she had finished telling him.

'Not for me, it isn't,' he answered. 'But I suspect very awkward for you.' A glance at the house.

153

'Aye . . . he wasn't best pleased when he knew where we were movin'.'

'I'm a little surprised he consented.'

'He did it 'cause he wants me to be happy.'

'So do I.' His eyes flickered over her.

'Do you?'

'Of course.'

'Then don't try to see me, Roly.'

'How can I help but see you when we're to be neighbours?'

'Yer know I didn't mean in passin', I meant don't come to the house.'

'As if I'd be so foolish.'

'I just thought to warn yer. We're settled now. It would only cause trouble if you were to keep actin' the good neighbour. I don't want you here, Roly.'

'Still the same old Tommy. You don't mince words, do you?' It was said in cheerful tone, but she had hurt him.

'I'm just warnin' yer 'cause I don't want anything else to be minced – namely me.' She glanced at the door of her house where a dark-faced Patrick was on his way back to the cart. 'Well, it's been nice seein' yer again, Roly,' she said brightly. 'I must go now an' get the house straight. Goodbye now.'

Roland wanted to take hold of her, to keep her there, but instead he doffed his hat, smiled and said, 'Goodbye, Thomasin, so nice to have met you. I trust you'll soon be settled into your new home. You must all come and take tea with us some time.'

'That'd be nice,' she said artificially, then picked up a couple of bags and went into the house.

Roland was about to move on, but Patrick stopped him. 'A word in your ear, Cummings,' he muttered softly, pretending to be involved in the sorting of his possessions. 'I don't know what ideas our moving in here has put into that ugly head o' yours but ye'd be wise to keep them there.'

'You're a damned fool,' issued Roland contemptuously and made to walk away.

Patrick grabbed his arm. 'An' so are you if ye think she'll be comin' to take tea with yese. Just keep your distance.'

'Hard when one lives in the same road.' Roland could appear very arrogant when he wanted to. It was unfortunate for him that his face chose this moment to advertise just how much he despised his opponent.

'A long road – an' I suggest ye don't try to shorten it.'

'Perhaps Thomasin does not share your views.'

Both hands reached for him. 'I'll break your bloody . . .'

'*Patrick.*' Thomasin stood once again in the doorway, staring hard at both of them. She hadn't raised her voice but the mere tone of it was enough to stay his arm.

Face still seething, Patrick strode back into the house. As he brushed past her, his wife gave him a look of loving reproach.

Seeing that look and the rejecting stare that was in turn directed at him, Roland pocketed his briefly-rekindled hopes, bent his head and wandered off up the street. Yes, he would keep his distance. Since taking silk, Roland had been trying to decide whether to take his talents as a QC away from York and set up chambers in the capital. He was gaining quite a reputation for himself and perhaps there could be even wider possibilities in London.

That look had just decided him. Thomasin and her Irishman had no further cause to worry.

PART TWO

PART TWO
1870

CHAPTER FOURTEEN

Well, it's finally happened at last, thought Patrick as he perched on the fence and viewed the product of his labours with great satisfaction. After twenty-three years in these alien climes I've finally got my piece of land. Two hundred acres to be exact, a couple of miles out of York on the road to Malton. Yet his pleasure was slightly marred by the fact that the land had not been purchased by his own endeavours. He had still to prove his worth to these people. A new set of clothes and a big house could not, for his neighbours, erase his Irishness. He remembered their ill-disguised concern at the thought of an Irish family coming into their midst.

One good thing, though – that which he had feared most from the move had proved to be without substance. Within days there had been a 'For Sale' notice outside the Cummings' residence. A couple of weeks later a gratified Patrick had watched the removal firm carry his rival's belongings to another place. Patrick hoped it was far away. There had been no comment between him and Thomasin but he sensed her relaxation at the departure.

He dropped from the fence and squatted on his heels, enveloped by the smell of rain-dampened earth. He yielded to the impulse and clawed up a handful of the moist soil, pressing it to his face and breathing in the rich pungency of life. His mind was immediately swamped by indelible memories ... the sing-song voices of the peat-cutters as they dextrously sliced and stacked the turves, speaking in a language which had not tripped from his own tongue in years; the girls with their skirts tucked up to expose red flannel petticoats, pounding their washing on the banks of the stream; the granite mountain that sheltered his home; the endless swathes of purple heather

. . . and then his memories turned black. Acre upon acre of steaming, putrid earth, ravaged like its people. Death everywhere – corpses piled high, matchstick legs sticking out at grotesque angles . . .

'Ah see tha's got mole trouble!'

The broad accent startled Patrick and he spun round smiling, expecting to see his father-in-law, but instead of William's jolly countenance was met by a rather miserable, weather-beaten character who leaned on the fence and let his rheumy eyes wander over the horizon.

'Sorry, what was that?' Patrick straightened and advanced carefully over his neat rows of infant cabbages.

The rustic ceased puffing on his pipe and pointed with the long curved stem at the orchard that ran parallel to the cabbage field, which also belonged to the Irishman. 'Moles. Ah can rid thee of 'em for a fair price.'

Patrick screwed up his eyes against the sun and surveyed the orchard. All he could see were ranks of young apple trees which he had planted last spring – slender green maidens who, in years to come, would bear the fruit that would line Thomasin's shelves. Everything seemed as it should be, healthy and flourishing. He frowned at the man. 'I'm sorry, ye've got me puzzled.'

The man returned his frown. 'Look, s'no good thinkin' tha'll gerrit done cheaper by anybody else. Tha won't. Anyroad, this is my territory – no bugger else is allowed to mole on my patch.'

Patrick gave a confused laugh and scratched his head. 'Look, Mr . . .'

'Catch.'

'Mr Catch . . .'

'Not Mr – just Catch,' provided the stranger. 'Me name's Newton Catermole, but folk bein' what they are, an' what wi' my profession bein' what it is, they changed it to Catchermole – sithee? Then it got shortened to plain Catch.'

'Look, I know ye must think me an eejit,' said Patrick, endorsing the man's opinion, 'but I've as much understanding of what you're talking about as I have of the workings o' the female mind.'

The man's weak blue eyes toured Patrick's face, then he spat. 'Thinkin' o' catchin' 'em thasel' then, esta? Doin' a poor owd man out of his livin'.'

'Catch what, for God's sake?' Patrick was beginning to be irritated by this conversation.

'The bloody moles for God's sake!' shouted the man, stabbing his pipe stem at the orchard.

'An' would ye kindly explain to me what these moles are when they're at home? Is it something wrong with the trees you're tryin' to tell me?'

Catch was about to produce another biting retort when he realised from the total absence of duplicity in Patrick's expression that the Irishman's confusion was genuine. 'Well, Ah'll be . . . what doesta think all them mounds of earth are, dotted all ower thy orchard – fairy bloody castles?' He slung his leg over the fence and began to walk towards the orchard, keeling from side to side. He had the bandiest legs Patrick had ever seen, encased in leather gaiters.

The Irishman tagged on behind like a stray dog. 'Sure, I've been wonderin' what the hell they were! The very morning after I planted them trees I came back to find a dozen o' them with their roots pushed right out o' the ground. I thought somebody had a down on me. In fact I've sat here many a night waiting for the varmints to show themselves so I could give them a hiding, but never a thing did I see. An' ye say 'tis these moles that're responsible? What sort o' creature would they be, then? Obviously some sort o' burrowing insect, but they'd have to be pretty big to do this much damage.'

Catch began to chuckle. Wait till he told the lads down at The Black Bull about the looney who thought moles were insects. He carried a sack over his shoulder and now let it drop to the earth and dipped his horny fingers inside. 'That there's what a mole is, lad,' he explained, offering the tiny velvet corpse to Patrick. 'Don't they have 'em where you come from then?'

161

The other turned it over on his palm. 'If they do they've been keepin' them well hidden.' It was true, there were no moles in Ireland. 'Sure, I've never seen the like of such an oddity in all me life, an' there you are with a bagful o' the little demons. Ye wouldn't think a creature so small as himself could do so much damage, would ye? An' what might ye be going to do with them now?'

Catch retrieved the mole, dropped it back to join the others and shouldered the sack. 'Do, lad? Well, I'm off home to see if there's any o' the buggers worth skinnin', an' if there is then they'll go towards makin' them breeches what I've been promisin' meself.' He fingered his waistcoat proudly. 'Natty piece o' work, eh? Not bad wi' a needle isn't my sister. Mindst,' he shook his sack. 'I doubt I'll have enough for a pair o' breeches in here. May, tha knows.' He could tell Patrick didn't understand him. 'They'll've moulted! Proper time for skins is just afore Christmas – 'course that's when tha gets best prices an' all so tha still doesn't get tha moleskin breeches. 'Ave to sell 'em while tha can.'

'But ye still catch them all the year round?'

'Oh, aye, more or less. Except for where there's crops growin'. Ah can fettle that there orchard for thee though.'

'I'd be pleased if ye could. They're unsightly things. Are them your traps?' Patrick gestured to the collection of metal that partnered the sack.

'Aye. Ah can't start right now though, I've others to collect. Tomorrow'll do.'

Patrick kept his new friend talking for a long time, gleaning as much knowledge of the land as Catch was willing to impart. In the old country Patrick's crop had been limited to potatoes and he was grateful for any tips the old man might give him. It transpired that Catch was a hedge-layer too, amongst it seemed a hundred other occupations and he told Patrick that he would be willing to undertake anything the Irishman might throw his way.

'Live nearby, doesta?' he asked.

'No, I live in York.' Patrick became alert. 'An' I'd best be makin' my way there. My son's coming home today.

He's been at college these last three years. His mother an' me only see him at high days an' holidays, so I'd like to be home to greet him.' He headed for the road home. Catch followed.

'One o' them boardin' schools, eh?' he grunted. 'Don't hold wi' too much schoolin' meself. Leavin' t'masters to do t'work o' t'father. Ah should think it costs a pretty penny to send him there an' all.' The tone of his statement conveyed his view that he had thought this beyond Patrick's pocket.

As the light shower ceased and a rainbow arched its way to the heavens, Patrick found himself telling Catch all about Thomasin's inheritance; how in three short years his wife had transformed a reasonably profit-making shop into a flourishing business.

It failed to impress the countryman who waddled beside him, traps rattling. 'Can't say as how I hold wi' women in them sort o' positions,' he muttered, tugging at the peak of his cap to shield his eyes from the sunshine.

Truth to tell, neither did Patrick, but he would not go so far as to demean his wife's accomplishments before a stranger. 'I think she's done remarkably well in such a short time,' he defended. 'She's doubled her custom.'

'Nay,' Catch argued stubbornly. 'A woman's only fit for birthin' a man's sons an' fillin' his belly wi' good grub, not gallivantin' off doin' t'job a fella should be doin'.'

'Ah no, not this fella,' replied Patrick with a firm shake of his head. 'I'm not getting meself involved in the running of a business for anybody. Me – I'd rather be out in the open air, doin' the donkey work than in a stuffy shop, panderin' to a lot o' bickerin' women.'

'Aye well, tha's said summat sensible at last,' Catch nodded, then asked how much land Patrick owned, and when told, said, 'That's a fair bit for one man to work – not that I haven't done it meself, mind, but then I'm used to it. Instead o' that son o' thine wastin' his time at school why dun't tha get him to help thee? How old is he anyroad?'

'Sixteen,' answered Patrick. 'But no, if I'd need of help

163

I've another son. Me wife'd skelp me for wasting the younger one on the land. Besides, I wasn't thinkin' to get it done all at once.' Catch asked where the other son was. 'Dickie? Ah well, we decided it might be a good idea to have a travelling grocery to boost the earnings even further. Ye know, going door to door so's people don't have to lug all those heavy baskets home. Ye'd be surprised at the trade it's brought us.'

'Nay, I wouldn't,' sniffed Catch. 'Lazy buggers. They'll be fittin' folk wi' wheels next. All they want to do is sit on their backsides these days an' let other folk wait on 'em. Why, when I were a lad nearest village were ten mile away an' before I were barely out o' frocks I'd 'ave to be up at five, rain or shine and down that road wi' a basketful of eggs to sell. An' woe betide me if Ah weren't home afore Father had his ten-thirty's. By, Ah can still feel that stick round me legs! Our lass an' all, poor bairn. Eh, Ah've seen her fingers like ten blue sausages swollen up wi' t'cold, but she still had to do t'milking, froz or no. An' did she complain? Never! Neither of us'd ever've dreamed o' questionin' me father's orders. His word were law. Even me mother bowed an' scraped when he gave command. 'Course, times've changed now. Womenfolk've started wearin' t'breeches an' youngsters don't seem to want to do nowt for nobody or have any respect for their parents. Our lass's boys are a load of idle buggers. Ah'm glad I nivver wed.'

'Oh, I don't know,' smiled Patrick. 'Ye can miss a lot by staying single. An' mine aren't such bad lads. Dickie's coping admirably with the grocery round an' Sonny's masters speak very highly of him. D'ye know, half the things he says to me now go right over my head.'

Catch's normally doleful face cracked again as he and Patrick went their separate ways. It wasn't very often Catch laughed but by golly! he chuckled now. It wouldn't take very much to go over the Irishman's head. Are moles some sort of insect indeed! By, he'd be able to milk a few quarts of ale from his pals tonight with that tale.

*

When Patrick arrived home his younger son was already there and the hall cluttered with his trunks and cases. 'Is there no one else here to greet ye save me an' your mother?' Patrick bear-hugged his son and remarked on his maturing appearance, as he did every time Sonny came home.

'Dickie came in half an hour ago and vanished like a genie,' donated his wife. 'I've sent Erin round to Mother's to ask if she and Father would like to come to tea tomorrow, what with Sonny being home; they like to see him.' She had taken a seat by the fire and was toasting two marshmallows on a fork.

'Oh, Tommy did ye have to!' Patrick flopped onto the sofa joined by his son.

'I shall inform Mother what a high opinion you have of her.' Thomasin prodded the browning marshmallows with her fingertips.

'She knows. Listen, what about all of us going down to the King Willie to celebrate Sonny's homecoming?'

Thomasin teased the marshmallows from the toasting fork onto a dish. 'You've been out in the sun too long, my lad.'

'An' I'm desiccated – hence the suggestion. What's wrong with wanting to go to the pub for a little relaxation? D'ye realise the both of us have been workin' so hard that we've never been near the old place in . . . God, 'tis almost a year! They'll think we've deserted them.' At first he and Thomasin had gone back regularly to see how Molly was and to have a chat with friends. On each visit Patrick had slipped Molly a few pounds, though she never seemed to use it for anything other than to drink herself silly. Nor did she have much to show for the original sum they had given her which had not been insubstantial. It appeared she'd given most of it to her married daughters and sons before buying a few items of furniture for herself and drinking the rest. When Pat had scolded her for not investing it more sensibly she had said: 'Ah, what's the point? I could be dead tomorrow,' and had poured another drink to toast his health. Still, she had seemed happy

165

enough and that was what counted. At least she had been a year ago – God, was it that long, Patrick asked himself ashamedly. How time flew. It wasn't that he was sick of going to see her, just that when he got home after working all that land he was so damned tired he'd just fall asleep in the chair, couldn't be bothered to shift. Well, he would definitely go tonight and Tommy must come too, as he now told her.

'But how can I go like this?' Her hand swept over the blue silk dress.

'Looks all right to me,' said her husband. 'What's wrong with it?'

She tutted. 'There's nothing wrong with it! Only I'm going to stick out like a bishop's corporation, aren't I?'

'Haven't ye got an old dress ye could put on?' he persisted.

'Patrick, this *is* an old dress – at least the oldest one I've got. Besides,' she put two more marshmallows on the fork, 'women of my standing do not frequent public houses.'

'Standing? I'd've said leaning – leaning towards snobbery.' Patrick snatched one of the marshmallows from the dish and rolled it petulantly around his mouth. 'It was good enough for ye before.' His wife had begun to annoy him lately. It was only natural that primarily the tremendous jump in finances should drive them all a little crazy. No one had enjoyed the initial spending spree more than Patrick himself, and not the least of his pleasure had been derived from watching his wife – freed of her restrictive budget – fill the house with new furniture and fine clothes. Once the novelty had palled he had expected her to return to earth, to be exactly the same as before, but she hadn't. Somewhere on her fanciful flight she had changed. He was not certain he liked it.

'Look, can't you see?' She turned around too quickly and one of the marshmallows fell onto the ash-smeared grate where it oozed and bubbled stickily. 'Oh, damn! Now look what you've made me do.' She put another sweet on the fork. 'What I mean is, it's a different life we lead now. We don't fit in any longer round there. Besides, our neighbours think badly enough of us as it is without me visiting the boozer.'

'Well, they're not going to stop me enjoyin' meself,' said her husband positively, and turned to his son. 'Surely you'll not let your father drink alone?'

'I had hoped to have an early night,' was Sonny's excuse. 'I'm sorry, Father, but I'm really worn out with all that travelling. A hot bath would be more appreciable to a quart right now.' Thomasin told her son she would arrange it.

'Then I'll go by meself an' bugger the lotta yese!' Patrick slapped his knees and stood up. Dammit, his son had changed too, no longer referring to his parents as Mam and Dad but as Mother and Father. Had he been doing it all along or had Patrick's impatience at his wife suddenly made all these tiny points more noticeable? 'Do I get something to eat before I go?'

'Supper will be on the table when you come back down,' promised his wife.

'Who said I was going up?'

'Well, I presume you are getting changed. You'd hardly be going out dressed like that.' It was an order rather than an observation.

Patrick looked down at his ragged, dirt-stained workclothes, his soil-embedded nails. He had not given it a second thought and had indeed been going out like this. What harm could a bit of honest grime do? It had never mattered in the old days. But at his wife's edict he went upstairs to wash and change.

'And you may as well collect the rent while you're down that end,' she said before he left. 'They weren't in when I called this morning. I don't see why we should leave it another week.' Then an afterthought: 'Give my regards to Molly if you see her.'

'Ye didn't think to call on her while ye were round that way this morning?' He had stopped at the door.

'I didn't have time,' she replied. 'I don't like to leave the store too long.'

'Aye, an' of course it would have rather taken you out of your way,' he answered sarcastically and left.

After collecting the rent from the occupants of his previous home he called at The King William then, finding none of his old friends there, sank a quick tankard and retraced his steps to visit The Spread Eagle. At his entrance Molly Flaherty raised her glass and bared ochre-hued teeth. 'Well, if it isn't that rascal who deserted us! Hey, Michael, Jimmy, look who's here!'

Patrick grinned widely and awaited the buzz of greeting; it was strangely subdued and bewildered him. But he strolled across the sawdust-covered floor and sat beside the inebriated Molly, putting his arm around her to deliver a squeeze. 'Ah, Molly me old flame can ye ever forgive the miserable wretch that's neglected ye?'

'I can if he's a mind to fill this.' Molly shoved her empty glass at him.

Patrick's nostrils flared at her smell as she swayed against him in pleasure at seeing him, but he remained smiling. ''Tis hollow legs ye have, woman.' He went to order two whiskies, then returned to ask how life was treating her.

'Oh, terrible, Pat, terrible,' she slurred after the first pull. 'Did ye hear I lost another o' me babes? Aye,' she nodded at his shock, 'the angels took young Sile – that's our Norah's eldest, last Friday. The measles it was.'

'God, I'm so sorry, Molly. That's tragic ... I knew nothing.' He shook his head and sipped his drink, looking round at the poorly-clad assemblage, their faces drawn and undernourished. How come he had never seen them in this light before? Was it because once upon a time he himself had looked like that? He was still troubled by the lack of interest from his old chums. A year was a long time to stay away but surely it didn't make him a stranger?

'Little Paddy O'Kelley dropped dead on Monday an' all,' Molly continued, 'An' him just bringin' me a jug of ale across the yard as a treat. He was awful taken with me was Paddy since Himself passed over.'

168

'God save us, he was younger than me!' Patrick experienced a flash of vulnerability. 'What happened, Molly?'

'The ale splashed all over the yard that's what happened,' bemoaned his partner. 'Sure, I never got to taste a drop for Raper's pigs got every lick. Such a cruel waste.'

Patrick had to smile. Still the same old Molly. Some things never changed. 'I really meant what killed Paddy, Molly.'

'Oh! Well, I can't say. Some queerfangled name it was they called it, but what I think it boiled down to was his heart gave out. It comes to us all.' She pushed her empty glass gently towards him. 'I don't suppose ye'd care to fill that up again, Pat? An' you lookin' so effluent.'

'An' what have ye done with all that brass I gave ye?' he chided. 'I hope it hasn't all been liquidated.'

She gave him a look both guilty and beseeching. He tut-tutted and slipped her a sovereign before going for refills. 'What about you, lads?' he shouted to his old pals. 'Will ye join me?' They swapped glances. 'Come on now. Aren't I good enough to buy ye a drink now?'

'God!' exclaimed Molly. 'Here's the man throwing money about like a banker with palsy an' not one taker. Well, ye don't have to worry, Pat. I'll drink with ye all night if needs be.'

Fran Nolan spoke up grudgingly at Patrick's repeated offer. 'Go on, I'll have a drop o' that bilge-water he calls beer.'

The landlord pointed. 'Oy, you, watch your tongue.'

'What about you, Michael?' said Patrick to Flynn, who also capitulated, albeit with some reluctance. 'All right. I'll have the same as Fran.'

'Come on now, do I have to ask each an' every one o' yese?' shouted Patrick. 'It's been ages since I've seen this motley gathering an' I want to buy ye a drink to make up. Speak now an' let's be having your orders. Sure, ye need something to oil them tongues o' yours, not one o' ye's asked me how I am.' His eyes flicked to the door where another old pal had just entered. 'Ah, thank God! Ghostie, will ye come an' stir up these spalpeens with your fiddle? 'Tis like a wake in here. What're ye having?'

The man with the mournful, spectre-like face did not even grant the other a glance as he moved across to the bar. 'If ye expect me to doff me hat I'd as soon buy me own.'

'Have I come to the right place?' joked Patrick, but the humour was tinged with concern. This was not the welcome he had expected after such a long absence. 'I thought, I'll just saunter down to the old place an' have a wee drop with all me pals, an' what do I find? A funeral parlour. There's only Molly what's had a kind word for me.'

'She'd kiss the Devil's arse if she thought it'd fetch her a drink.' It was Ryan who spoke, one of Patrick's workmates from the past. A deathly hush fell over the normally congenial atmosphere.

'What did you say?' Patrick stared hard at the man.

'Has the money sent ye deaf too? I said . . .'

'Sure, I heard what ye bloody said!' returned Patrick. 'Would you be placing me lower than Old Nick? 'Cause if y'are I'll be calling ye out.'

'Aren't ye afraid o' messin' up your nice new clothes?' sneered Ryan, hands gripping the edge of the table, poised for action. 'I mean – look at ye, dressed up like a pig's prick. Coming in here acting the swell, making out you're better than everybody else. Motley gathering indeed!'

'That was only a figure o' speech,' protested Patrick. 'Ye should know me by now.'

'I thought I did, but not any more. Ye made a big play at first of being the same, but we all know ye couldn't wait to see the back of us once ye got your riches. Well save your money, we'll buy our own drinks. We don't want your bloody charity, Lord Crapper, so just go back to your own kind – you're fetching the place a bad name.'

The place erupted as Patrick made a dive for Ryan. 'Stand up an' fight ye waster! I'll not have anyone throw my friendship back in me face,' and knocked him off his feet.

170

Ryan scrambled up and charged headlong for Patrick's stomach, knocking the wind out of him and throwing him to the floor. They rolled about in the sawdust, pummelling and kneeing and grunting. Ryan was on top, pounding at the other's face. Patrick wedged his boots under Ryan's belt and heaved. The smaller man now hurtled backwards over the tables, smashing glasses and splintering wood. The place was a-boil as Patrick sprang up and delivered another punch to Ryan's jaw as he closed in again. The receiver grunted and made a counter-attack, laying open the skin beneath Patrick's eye. The landlord pleaded for someone to fetch a priest to break up the fight but his entreaties were drowned in the exhortative roar as the taproom became a boxing booth. Molly punched at the air with one hand while the other tipped her glass as the fight effervesced around her.

'Please, please boys, leave me a glass or two!' begged the landlord, wringing his hands.

The two men fell to the floor again, grappling with each other, Ryan's hands around Patrick's throat. The heel of Patrick's palm found Ryan's chin and forced it backwards so that his oppressor eventually broke his grip and fell away. They were standing toe to toe, two middle-aged men hammering and punching at each other, both showing signs of weariness, when at last Patrick swung a hefty right hook and caught Ryan a beautiful smack on the jaw – more through luck than good aim, his exhausted arms flailing anywhere. Down went Ryan, rolling over and over, his ragged jacket caked in sawdust, and came to rest with his head clattering against the spittoon.

'Jaze, I'm getting too old for this,' wheezed Patrick as he stumbled to lean on the bar. 'Gimme a whiskey, quick.'

'Who's gonna pay for all these breakages, then?' demanded the ruffled landlord.

'Will ye hold your whinnying an' get me that drink? Then I may consider reimbursing ye for our sport.' Patrick knocked back the whiskey, snorting at the burning goodness of it. 'Ah, God that's nectar!' Then went to grab

Ryan by the arm and haul him to his feet. '*Now* will ye let me buy ye a drink?'

Ryan's legs wobbled and he cradled his bleeding jaw in a red-knuckled hand. 'God deliver us, will somebody remind me not to open me mouth, an' me so short on teeth.' He allowed Patrick's hand to remain supporting him. 'Your persistence is to be rewarded, yer honour. For that ye can buy me a treble Irish.' Then he raised a chuckle at Patrick's dishevelled state. 'Will ye look at himself – the beautiful butterfly's splitting out of his cocoon.'

Patrick grimaced at the sawdust-covered frockcoat whose seams had burst under the arms. 'If ye thought I packed a devilish punch wait till Tommy sees this – she'll pulverise ye.' His eyes toured the grinning faces, and his own split with good humour. 'Don't tell me I have to go through all this rigmarole every time I want to stand me friends a drink?'

Ryan clapped him on the back and steered him to the bar amid a murmur of unanimity. 'Ah, 'tis sorry I am, Patrick. I don't know what got into me. 'Twas just the sight o' them togs an' the fact that ye haven't been near for so long that set me ranting. I should've known the money'd never alter ye.'

'Well, ye know now to your cost,' said Patrick severely. 'Landlord, drinks all round!'

Patrick felt as though he hadn't enjoyed himself so much for ages as he staggered home three hours later, his head still reeling with the whine of Ghostie's fiddle and the joking, familiar banter of his kindred. He felt his pocket. It had been an expensive evening. But it had been well worth it once he had whittled away their understandable suspicion. The recollection of being treated like an interloper came as a sobering thought as he reached Monk Bar. Though he had weathered the experience he couldn't help feeling that he didn't truly fit in anywhere now. Here, in Monkgate, he was an outsider because he was Irish, because he was not, and never would be, a gentleman. There, in Walmgate, he was viewed – albeit in a less hostile fashion – as an outsider because of his wife's good fortune. Hitherto it had been his poverty which had bought his inclusion to the clan and without it, his membership was forfeit. He had to face up to the fact that life was never going to be the same again.

He drew in a chestful of air as he crossed the road. Better get smartened up before he got home else Tommy would have his hide. She was well on the way to becoming as bad as her mother.

CHAPTER FIFTEEN

This was Sonny's fourth day at home and already he was wishing himself back at college. It was not that he didn't enjoy being reunited with his family – he did – it was simply that here he felt guilt whenever he had the compulsion to pick up a paintbrush. All the family seemed so involved in the business and so, even though this was supposed to be a holiday, Sonny had felt obliged to pitch in too, helping his father with the planting of new crops. Following an afternoon spent in the company of Patrick's new and crusty acquaintance and having to defend his reasons for being at school to Catch, he decided that if he volunteered for duties again it would be to assist his mother with the book-keeping, which after all had been the main reason for his going to college in the first place.

It was seven o'clock on Tuesday morning. He lay, half in, half out of the covers and wondered what today had in store for him. Normally at this hour he would be far from his bed and entrenched in the military bustle of school life. He found it quite difficult to adjust to the quietness of this house, having spent most of the previous three years at college. He also had to get used to sleeping alone – something he had never done in his life. He had always shared a bed with his brother, and even at school he was expected to share a room. Now, in this spacious residence each had his own private quarters. It was rather ironic that even in his newfound privacy he felt unable to pursue his lifetime's passion; his brush had been in use but once since he came home and would probably not come out again till it was time to leave. For that reason alone he'd be glad to get back there.

He had already accumulated dozens of worthwhile land-scapes, culled from the picturesque countryside in which the college was situated. It was too far to contemplate coming home often at weekends so, after Mass, his Sundays were filled with the heady scents of linseed oil and turpentine. Besides the landscapes he had also portrayed on canvas a great many of his schoolfriends and, secretly, the masters. Everyone agreed that Feeney had a superior talent. His canvases had travelled home with him, propped now against his bedroom wall.

Sonny's thoughts were shattered by the entry of his sibling who planted himself on his brother's bed and pointed at the light sheet that covered Sonny's body. 'Talk about tent-poles. Are ye still going short of it, Son?'

Sonny dragged himself into a sitting position and laid his hands over his lap. 'Still the same old Dickie with his crude humour. Do you never alter?'

'Why should I alter when I'm already perfect?' Dickie bounced from the bed and padded around the room in his stockinged feet, hands in pockets, chest bare.

They had both noticed a difference in each other's stature during Sonny's time at college. Some time in his brother's absence Dickie, though still of wiry build, had equalled his father's height. Sonny, too, had gained inches in that direction but had added even more to his chest and the muscles of his arms – probably due to the gymnastic lessons he received.

Dickie stopped and looked at the painting on the easel then stepped back to appraise it, nodding approvingly. 'Ye know, you're a damn good painter, Son. That lake is so convincing I could almost feel my fingers would come away wet if I touched it.'

'They would – it's just been varnished,' said Sonny straight-faced.

'Don't they teach you how to take a compliment at that fancy school?'

Sonny smiled. 'I get so few from my brother.'

'Well, I'm giving ye one now – you're good. Look at this.' He moved away from the easel to point at a portrait of one of Sonny's schoolfriends that headed the stack by the wall. 'Ye'd think he was goin' to step right off the canvas any minute. S'bloody clever.'

'Your praise is much appreciated,' said Sonny. 'But really, I'm no Leonardo Da Vinci.'

'Who?'

'You know, Lenny O'Davinchy, the fellow from County Cork who painted our front guttering last year.'

'Oh, him,' nodded Dickie, and moved on. In his pacing about he noticed an unfinished letter on the dressing table and casually picked it up. '*Dear Rupert,*' he began, then broke into rude laughter. 'Rupert! Oh, God help us! *Dear Rupert, I arr... arrived home saf... safely,*' – Dickie's reading was not very good and he tackled the letter with great difficulty – '*after a wearisome journey of almost five hours. I find that I am missing your company already and there are still ten more days to go before we meet again ...*' He broke off again. 'Eh, I'm beginning to think Grandad was right about you.' He winked and went back to the letter. '*I trust your arrival at Greensleeves found your family in good health ...* where's Greensleeves?' Sonny told him it was the name of Rupert's house. 'Bloody stupid names these people have ... *in good health, especially Agatha.*' Here the letter finished and Dickie waved it at his brother. 'Hello, what's all this? Has me baby brother got himself a little mopsy tucked away an' never a word to me?'

Sonny, instead of flying into a rage as he might once have done, remained calm and aloof. If the college had taught him one thing it was how to control his temper. He had made the discovery on his first day that one could not fight everybody. 'What a way you have with words, brother. Agatha, for your information, is the sister of my best friend.

175

I was introduced to her when Rupert kindly invited me to visit his home last year.'

Dickie scowled. 'Ye never said anything to me about it.'

Not revealing the immense pleasure he derived from getting one over on his brother Sonny shrugged. 'Why should I?'

'What's this sister of his like then?'

'She's charming,' smiled Sonny, a warm look in his eye.

'She's certainly got you at it,' observed his brother. 'Did ye get anything?'

Sonny's placidity was short-lived. He began to rise menacingly from the bed. 'I'll not have you speak that way about Agatha, or any of my friends. They're decent, respectable people, something you wouldn't understand. One more word in that direction and you're in for a hammering.'

'All right, keep your hair on! Just 'cause she's tight there's no need to take it out on me.'

– He's irreclaimable, thought Sonny, settling back against the carved oak headboard. He truly believes that all females are the same. But Agatha was different, her mind unsullied by the thoughts that occupied the heads of working class girls. She was a lady.

Dickie turned the letter over. 'What else are ye goin' to write? How about: *"My handsome brother has expressed his desire to meet with your ravishing sister . . . "* '

Sonny grew tired of lying there listening to his brother's prating. He leapt out of bed and began to dress. 'Or more fittingly: *"Dear Rupert, it is such a bore being at home and not having anyone of your intellect to converse with. My brother, who imagines himself to be God's gift to women, is a total philistine. His manners are atrocious, his language gross in the extreme. It is a great pity that he does not have as much between his ears as he imagines is between his legs . . . "* '

Dickie tossed the letter back onto the dressing table, crossed his arms and watched his brother tug a comb through his unruly red hair. He had laughed at Sonny's remark but now his tone was serious. 'Ye know, ye've changed, our kid,' he said pensively.

176

'Why, because I refuse to be party to your dirty conversations any more?'

'No, it's not that – ye've never taken much gorm of anything I've said anyway – if ye had ye'd not still be a virgin.'

'I don't remember saying anything about that,' snapped Sonny.

'Oh, so ye did get something after all.'

'No! I meant . . .'

'D'ye know how many women I've had since last we met?' asked his brother suddenly. 'Twenty-four. Ye'd do well to take a leaf out o' my book, Son. Remember that plump little bird I got lined up for ye last time ye came home? If ye'd've only listened to what I said an' given her a bit o' the old blarney, but no, you had to go at her like a bull at a cow, an' where did it get ye?'

Sonny had no wish to be reminded of the sordid venture. 'Go to Hell!'

Dickie waved his hand. 'Ah, it's nothin' to do with that anyway; 'tis more the way ye talk to us – snobby like – as though you're too good for us now.'

Sonny turned from the mirror to examine his brother for some seconds before his face split into a conciliatory grin. 'I suppose I must sound that way to you – I don't mean to. It's just that when I first went to Cravenshill the others treated me as something of an oaf for the way I spoke and my lack of manners. They goaded me when I showed my ignorance over which piece of cutlery to use, or mopped my plate like I would at home. At first I got into lots of fights, had to defend my origins, you see. I saw no reason to alter my outlook or speech just to fit in with them.'

'Yet ye have changed all the same,' said Dickie.

'Yes,' frowned Sonny. 'I can't say when it happened, because I haven't consciously made an effort – I wouldn't've given them the satisfaction of knowing their prodding got to me. It's possible that rubbing shoulders with them for so long has taken the edge off my accent without my being aware of it happening.' He clutched

Dickie's arm in a fraternal gesture. 'I was only joking, you know, about you being a philistine. You're not mad at me, are you?'

'Why – I am one, aren't I? Aren't ye always tellin' me so? Just 'cause ye've altered your voice doesn't mean to say I set any greater store by your words than before.'

'Of course not,' said Sonny, turning back to the mirror. 'It was bloody stupid to think that anything I said would have the slightest effect on you.'

'Now to more important issues,' said Dickie, uncrossing his arms and bringing his hands together in a loud clap. 'How about you an' me having a saunter down to the Cattle Market this morning? Ye know, like the old days.'

'I was thinking to help at the shop,' answered Sonny. 'Besides, I understood you had your grocery round to attend to.'

'So I have, but if I whip round quick I can be done for nine o'clock or so.'

'And what will you tell Mother?'

'Ah, I can always get round Mam. Come on, our kid, what d'ye say? Let's have a laugh like we used to – auction old Bacon Neck off at the fatstock mart.'

Sonny laughingly agreed and suddenly began to feel at home again. His brother could always be relied upon to provide the amusements, even if they were usually at someone else's expense. Later in the morning, with Thomasin's permission, they set off down Goodramgate towards their old haunt. Although Dickie professed to have risen above the inhabitants of Walmgate here was where he was most at home. Both had dressed in their best attire – Dickie in a navy-blue serge suit, Sonny in checked worsted jacket and brown trousers – which seemed rather foolhardy to Sonny in retrospect, but the sartorially-minded Dickie insisted that his brother was not going to let the side down by dressing like a tramp.

Instead of going directly there, Dickie expressed his wish to watch the cattle's journey to the market, so they positioned themselves beside the Barbican on Walmgate Bar. To their right running parallel to the city walls, was a row of pens already occupied by bleating, wild-eyed sheep which jostled and baahed, their dainty hooves skittering on the urine-soaked floor. Several interested buyers toured the row of pens, poking and prodding at a fleecy rump with a gnarled stick or crook, sometimes climbing into the pen to grasp a sheep by the nose and roughly examine its teeth.

Soon, a cloud of dust hovering above the buildings foretold the arrival of another herd being driven in from the outlying pastures. The two boys leaned with their backs to the limestone wall, idly watching the dustcloud get nearer. Fifty yards' progress and added to the cloud was the sound of a far-off storm, a low rumbling, and soon too could be heard the faint yelps of the drovers' dogs and the harsh 'Goo ahn!' of the drovers themselves.

The wind was blowing in their faces; it carried the rich smell of dung. Another fifty yards and instead of a dustcloud came a many-legged beast that lowed and echoed a mournful song. Now each beast became discernible – red and white with long, curving horns, their eyes rolling in terror as they were herded towards an unknown fate, their hooves lost beneath the swirling sea of dust. They filled the entire street, those at the flanks stumbling on the cobblestones that edged the road. The dogs yapped and snarled at their heels, darting, tongues slavering, in and out of the threshing heave of limbs. Now and then an excited steer would rear up to break the rippling pattern and attempt to mount the beast in front, then fall back, rewarded only by a jarring blow to its chin from the other beast's rump. Their hocks were caked with dung. Festoons of saliva dangled from pink, slimy muzzles, swinging like frail elastic to cling to stumbling forelegs. One could almost smell their breath, fetid in its terror.

Sonny was laughingly trying to fight his brother off. Dickie had stolen a hat that one of the farmers had hung on a post and was now imitating its owner, talking gibberish whilst trying to force Sonny's jaws apart to examine his teeth. The herd was almost on them, when

Sonny to his horror realised there was something else in the road – a tiny child.

'Jesus Christ Dickie – d'ye see there!' He lanced a finger at the tow-haired infant who was playing happily with a pile of pebbles right in the cattle's path.

Dickie voiced concern, but made no attempt to move. At his side Sonny swayed agitatedly from one foot to the other. The child had seen the cattle now and had risen excitedly to his feet, jumping up and down and pointing a stubby finger at the clamorous mob that was bearing down on him. Sonny looked frantically to right and left. No one else appeared to have noticed, too engrossed in their business. And the cattle were still coming.

The child was perhaps twenty-five yards away from where the boys stood and an equal distance from an horrific crushing death. With no regard for his own safety or for his best clothes, Sonny dashed out into the road, shouting and calling to the child. He could hear his brother issuing words of encouragement from the safety of the footwalk. 'Go on, Son, you're nearly there!'

Sonny hailed the child again and this time the infant turned. His smile inverted when he saw the man running towards him. To him the flaming red hair and determined expression spelt one thing – trouble. He too started to run – towards the herd.

'Come back, ye stupid little tick!' Sonny tore breathlessly after him. The cattle were very near now. He could hear the rasping of their breath, smelt it, imagined its rancid heat on his face. The boy fell, rose to his feet, and then suddenly he realised his danger as the beasts bore down on him. They looked bigger from here. In the instant he turned Sonny swept him up, spun round and wheeled away from the danger, pelting back to his brother as if the very Devil were on his heels.

'Mother o' God, I thought I was gonna have to scrape y'up with a shovel!' Dickie prised the struggling child from Sonny's rigor mortis-like grip and pinioned it firmly under his arm.

Sonny warily opened his eyes and stared at his brother

as if at a stranger. His heart had somehow shifted position and now beat furiously in his throat. His mouth was bone-dry and filled with the acrid taste of fear. He swallowed and gradually his heart began to descend to its natural habitat. A look at his suit produced a groan; it was ruined. The clean shirt, too, bore signs of the hostilities, smeared by the grubby hands and mouth of the infant.

He took a deep breath and blinked at the perpetrator of the disaster who was now inquisitively quiet under Dickie's arm and returned his scrutiny with undisguised ill-feeling, the ungrateful wretch. Paradoxically, a sparkling white handkerchief still stood to attention in Sonny's top pocket. He shook it out and ran it over his sweating face. Looking around him he noted with sinking spirits that everything was as it had been five minutes before. No one, apart from his brother, had noticed his heroism. 'God, I could do with a drink!' He crumpled the handkerchief and rammed it tetchily into his trouser pocket.

Dickie fished into his own pocket and pulled out a silver threepence. 'Here, nip into that pub an' have a drink on me. Ye deserve it after such a deed. Wait till I tell Mam her son's a hero.'

'She'll not be too pleased about the suit,' replied Sonny unhappily. He refused the coin from his brother, saying he had enough. 'What about the mawk?'

'Sure, don't worry your head none about him,' answered Dickie. 'I'll go see if I can find its mother. You get yourself a dram an' brush yourself up.'

When the other had retired to the tavern Dickie set the child on the footwalk and said, 'Now then, young spadger, an' where would you be livin'?'

The infant's response was to turn down his mouth and start to snivel, just as his not unattractive mother arrived. She had, in fact, just vacated the very tavern into which Sonny had gone and now demanded to know what Dickie had been doing to upset her son. He hastily explained the situation: how the child had been snatched from the jaws of death, supplanting his brother's part in the rescue with

181

his own. Here was a woman who looked as if she would show her gratitude.

When Sonny stepped out into the sunlight some ten minutes later, his brother – like the will o' the wisp he was – had disappeared.

The auctioneer's magnetism was beginning to fade. Sonny elbowed his way through the crowd of ruddy-faced York-shiremen and strolled back to the road. He wondered briefly what had befallen his brother and the child, then leapt aside as two drovers manhandled a protesting ewe from a pen. It fell at his feet and was bleeding heavily from beneath its tail, the wool around its haunches pink. The men grabbed fistfuls of fleece and hauled it away. Sonny lingered sympathetically and shouted to the men to take more care with their charge, then went on his way. The place abounded with life. His ears were crammed with bellows and bleats and grunts, plus the often unintelligible dialect of the farmers; his nose with the overpowering stench of ammonia and excrement. He sliced a passage through the final cluster of farmhands with their linen smocks and dung-streaked gaiters then turned homewards via Fishergate Bar.

He was preoccupied with ridding himself of the rusty iron parings that his clothes had attracted whilst leaning over the pens, and examining his ruined jacket when, with half an eye, he observed a young girl sitting at the kerb. She was hunched dejectedly, head in hands, her drab skirt bunched untidily around her thighs. He saw on drawing closer that there were pink channels down each dusty cheek.

He halted close to where she was sitting. 'Can I be of any assistance?'

She snatched a tear-stained glance, then hid her face once more. 'That depends.'

'On what?'

'On whether you've got half a crown goin' spare.' The dullness of her tone implied her pessimistic assessment of the untidy youth. 'Me da's gonna kill me when I see him.'

Sonny smoothed back his red hair and deliberated. She was very pretty, even the tattered dress could not hide that. He wanted to help her. He hated to see anyone so unhappy. Yet half a crown was an awful lot of money. His fingers strayed to his pocket and played with the coins he had saved from the money his parents had forwarded while he was at college. Apart from his paints there was little else he needed and he had accumulated a fair amount. He had felt rather guilty at his reluctance to leave his savings at home but his brother, sad to say, could not be trusted. Thoughtfully, he stroked the milled edge of a coin with his thumbnail. She was very pretty. Surrendering to compassion he took out a florin and a sixpence and squatted down beside her.

She stared at the coins on his palm, then quickly snatched them up and tucked them into the warm cleft that disappeared into her bodice. 'You needn't expect any reward,' she accused.

Deeply offended he blushed and rose swiftly. 'I want none! If that's your gratitude, madam, I'll be off!' He had taken four strides before her voice called him back.

'I'm sorry!' He turned and glowered as she added: 'It's just the way you were lookin' at me. I thought . . .'

'I was admiring your prettiness, that's all.' Sonny reddened again at his own forwardness.

'Thank you . . . and thanks for your generosity also. I can't say when I'll be able to repay it.'

He waved aside any question of reimbursement. She rose and came to stand beside him, her head level with his shoulder. 'Are you always so trusting? I mean, you don't even know me . . . neither did you ask me why I needed that money.'

'You said your father would kill you when you saw him,' answered Sonny. 'That seemed good enough reason to me. A pretty girl like you doesn't deserve such a fate.'

She grimaced. 'Aye, well it weren't just a figure o' speech neither, I'm afraid. If I'd've gone home without that egg money he'd've taken me to wipe the floor with.' She curled her lip to display a gap in her teeth. 'See that?

He did that 'cause I was too long in fetching his ale from the tavern — badtempered cove he is.'

Sonny expressed his disgust, then asked what had happened to the egg money.

'Uh?' She seemed miles away. 'Oh, that. I never got it in the first place. Got as far as Fishergate Bar an' this little arab comes harum scarum knocks the basket right outta me hand an' smashed the blinkin' lot. I've been sat here worrying summat awful – 'til you came along.' She smiled happily and, hooking her arm through the empty basket, added, 'It'll be ages before me da gets finished selling his porkers. Shall I walk with you awhile?'

Sonny replied that it would be his pleasure to continue his journey in her charming company. He walked slowly, so that his dream might not be over too fast. She asked his name; he asked hers. By the time they reached the end of George Street Sonny was hopelessly in love with her. Gone were all thoughts of Agatha. Agatha didn't even exist any more.

Annie was from out Naburn way. She often came into York, she told him, to sell her eggs or to visit the market. She was Sonny's age – sixteen. She had three brothers. Her mother was dead. Her father was frequently drunk. No, she answered Sonny's question, he wasn't always violent, it was only after her mother had died that the beatings had started.

'But why d'you stand for it?' asked Sonny, wanting to beat the living daylights out of the brute who had struck that pert face.

She gazed up at him with bright eyes and said simply, 'He needs me.'

He felt a rush of tenderness and a great need to put his arms around her, to show her that he understood. Dickie would have found no difficulty in such an act, but Sonny's arms remained twitchingly at his sides.

They were in Walmgate. The sun was gentle on their shoulders. Sonny felt very happy. Oh, she was lovely . . .

Dickie slouched despondently down Walmgate, hands in

184

pockets, stock awry, kicking viciously at every stone in his path. The child's mother had shown her gratitude not in the manner which he had expected, but by providing him with the reward she fancied every boy his age would most appreciate – a slice of plum pudding. Had he guessed that this would be the outcome he would not have bothered to desert his brother. Sonny had probably had a more satisfying morning at the market.

He had just reached Violet Nesbitt's house where the windowbox overflowed with tiny magenta blooms, when he spotted his brother not twenty strides away – and the girl who accompanied him was quite a looker. They had stopped in the middle of the footwalk to watch a dancing bear which had been tethered outside a public house while its master drowned his thirst. There were no shadows on this side of the street in which to escape the pitiless sun and in its thick coat the creature was boiling alive. It reared up onto its hind legs and began to pirouette, clawing frantically at the leather muzzle which had begun to chafe terribly. The bear's giant paws scraped feverishly at its ears, trying to dislodge the strap. It danced agitatedly all the while, only stopping to charge at the urchins who tormented it as far as the chain would allow. The crowd which had gathered thought this splendid entertainment. Not so Sonny, who found it appalling that anyone could find pleasure in a creature's sufferings. He glanced down at Annie whose pixie-like face was wreathed in smiles and felt a touch of pique.

'Will you excuse me while I go see if I can find its owner? The poor thing is going to lose its mind if it's left any longer in the sun.'

Annie showed surprise that Sonny wanted to spoil the fun, but said that she would wait for him.

Dickie watched his brother cross the road and disappear into a tavern. It was obvious that Sonny had no idea how to treat a female. With a saturnine grin he straightened his stock, dipped his hand into Mrs Nesbitt's windowbox and uprooted a fistful of violets. Suitably equipped he made a beeline for his prey.

185

Sonny emerged from the public house in time to see his brother bearing down upon his lady-love. He left the irate man to tend to his equally irate bear and rushed across the road to Annie, reaching her at the same instant as his brother.

'Trying to beat me to it, are we, Son?' said Dickie amiably, hand behind back. 'Well, I can't say I blame you. She's a prize worth winning.'

'As a matter of fact,' said Sonny hotly, 'Annie was already with me.'

'Ye don't say? Ye mean to tell me ye've been familiar with this pretty young damsel for some time an' never introduced her to your brother?'

'We've just met today actually,' provided Annie, undisguisedly taken up with this charming, handsome fellow. She forced herself to spare a glance for Sonny. 'Are you going to introduce us, John?'

Sonny dismally acquainted Annie with his brother who grinned and brought the tiny bouquet from behind his back. 'As I have no drink with which to toast your beauty, ma'am, may I be allowed to present you with a humble token of my undivided admiration. You are indeed the most ravishing creature I ever set eyes on in all me life.'

Annie uttered a delighted gasp and buried her face in the purple blooms. 'Oh! but no one's ever given me flowers before.'

'Is that right? Then 'tis a wicked cryin' shame that the men in these parts go around with their eyes shut. They must be blind not to honour such beauty.' He took her hand and laid it in the crease of his arm.

Sonny scowled as his brother coaxed Annie away, and obstinately clung to her side. Her face was turned away. She seemed to have completely forgotten his presence and the fact that it was his half-crown that was to save her a beating.

Dickie mouthed his practised oratory, entrancing the girl and further enraging his brother. – I'll kill you! raged Sonny, I'll bloody-well kill you.

Towards midday, after the couple and their gooseberry

friend had taken refreshment in a small café, Annie begged leave to go. 'My da will be finished with his business now. I must leave or there'll be trouble.'

'If there is,' replied Dickie, pulling out her chair, 'just refer your father to me. I'll take any blame that's coming.' He steered her to the door, leaving his brother to settle the bill.

– Oh, I'm sure you will! flared Sonny. Since when have you faced up to any trouble? He tapped his foot impatiently while the waitress counted out his change, and watched them through the window. They were talking earnestly, their faces almost touching. He pocketed his change and rushed out into the street.

'Annie!' he blurted awkwardly. 'If you come to York next week perhaps we could meet and . . .'

She never even allowed him to finish his sentence. 'Oh, I'm sorry, John.' She didn't appear to be at all sorry; her eyes remained glued to Dickie's face as she answered. 'I've already promised to meet your brother. You should've said before.'

'It doesn't matter,' he replied quickly, too quickly for sincerity. 'Really, I just thought . . . but if you're . . .' He glared at his brother who was smiling that arrogant smile of his. – Why, he's done it on purpose! he exclaimed to himself. He knew all along she was with me – he must've seen us. He isn't really interested in her the way I am, he only did it because I saw her first.

He made a vain attempt to salvage the situation. 'We could all meet and go somewhere . . .'

Dickie was quick to intervene. 'Son, I'm sure Agatha wouldn't be too pleased if she thought ye were giving your attentions to another young lady,' he said slyly, preempting any other bid.

Agatha. How could he have transferred his affections so glibly, when the object of those affections was about to disappear on the arm of his brother – a situation that was to be a recurring feature in Sonny's life. He could have gone after them, but he didn't. Once Dickie had had his hands on her, things would never be the same. He stood outside the café, trembling with outraged passion and watched them walk away.

CHAPTER SIXTEEN

Sunday afternoon invariably found Thomasin poring over her accounts, comparing the figures with those she had inherited from Mr Penny. The results were very uplifting. The business had undergone a transformation in these three short years, and the once dingy store had evolved into a competitive business. Thomasin's first instincts on becoming the proud owner had been to rid the shop of its dowdy image by decorating the interior. This had been done in light blue and dove-grey, and these instincts had proved to be well-founded, judging by the number of compliments she had received from her customers.

The one thing that remained almost unaltered was the name over the shop's façade – *Penny's*. When Patrick had expressed surprise at this, assuming her first act would be to place her own name above her property, she had smiled shrewdly and said, 'That name is going to be our trade-mark, a symbol of our competitiveness.'

'You're certain there isn't a more devious reason?' was his reply.

She asked what he meant. 'Ye know quite well what I mean, Tommy. Are ye afraid that if ye put your own name over the shop ye'll lose your trade?'

She had been surprised and hurt that he should think her capable of such disloyalty. 'It never even crossed my mind. Besides, I don't imagine people would give two hoots if an Irish name were over the shop – or a Jewish name, or a French name. You're far too touchy. All they care about is the quality and price of the goods inside.'

Patrick had then pointed out, not unkindly, that the

prices would hardly bear comparison with those of the market stallholders'.

Thomasin had been forced to agree. 'But the market isn't here every hour of the day – also I intend this to be a shop renowned for its quality rather than cheap prices. Though I do plan to have a bargain corner to get rid of all the stuff Mr Penny was bent on hoarding, and to boost my liquid assets.'

'I could do to boost mine an' all,' he joked. She had made him get rid of the illicit still when they had moved to the new house.

'Things are going to change around here, Pat – drastically,' she had said, and they had. Thomasin had begun by approaching each of her suppliers, armed with an ultimatum: they either renegotiated their terms, or she would take her custom elsewhere. The few who had not been swayed by her persuasive nature and had taken exception to these upstart tactics had regretted it, for in that first year of business Thomasin had doubled her orders to those with faith in her. To these firms Thomasin was now one of their best customers.

Another way she had found to bolster her stock was to visit stores which were about to go into liquidation and purchase leftover items at rock-bottom prices. In such dealings her bank manager, Mr Eade, another captive of her vivacious nature, would tip her the wink when he heard of any impending bankruptcy, allowing her to be first on the scene with her cheque. The outcome of these lucrative meanderings was arranged in the window to lure in more customers who, lulled by the low prices in the bargain corner, would often purchase their entire grocery order there.

Sonny had returned to college now, but on previous vacations had applied his artistic flair to the window display, making it even more alluring by his clever play with colour. In the centre of the window was a sugarloaf which he had painstakingly chiselled into the shape of a fairy castle. Cherries and angelica served as doorknobs and windowpanes, with marzipan battlements upon crystalline turrets. It was this that brought the local children flocking to the window, dragging along their mothers or nurses who, eyeing the high quality fare which completed the fairytale scene – neatly-sculptured pats of butter, rich amber sultanas, dewfresh fruit and vegetables depicting the castle's grounds – decided that here was a shop worthy of their patronage.

Sonny had not only been the motivator of the interior design but also that of the outside, and while he agreed with his mother's decision to keep the original owner's name, he thought that it looked that little bit better when he had personally repainted the name in gold copperplate and had amputated the *s*, leaving it simply *Penny*.

Thomasin's growing clientèle was positive proof of the efficacy of these small amendments, for never was there a moment in the day when the store was completely empty. Also, her custom covered a wider spectrum than had visited the dingy little shop before. Overnight, it seemed, it had become fashionable to be seen at *Penny's* – for despite Sonny's alteration people would insist on calling it that, the habits of the shop's lifetime dying hard.

The grocery round was proving to be very beneficial too and would be even more so when Patrick's fruit trees came to maturity and another middle-man was deleted. It was part of Dickie's job to deliver weekly orders as well as running the travelling shop; people were inclined to buy more if they did not have to struggle home under the weight of a heavy shopping basket.

Thomasin reclined in her chair and touched the hilt of the pen speculatively to her lips. Patrick sat opposite reading one of Mr Penny's books and making frequent referrals to the dictionary at his arm. He felt her gaze and looked up. She smiled and stretched her legs under the grey silk gown. It rustled invitingly and Patrick experienced the usual rush of warmth whenever he looked at her. If there was one thing above all else that had stemmed from their good fortune it was to see those dowdy, homespun dresses cast away. For all he worried about her overstepping her limits she did look beautiful.

190

In the beginning she had put on quite a lot of weight – they all had, but Thomasin had exceeded moderation. This was due to the fact that she could not bear to see food left on anyone's plate – each crust had counted in the old days – and had insisted on consuming all the leftovers. It was an obscenity to waste good food, she had told them. But the sly digs from her husband, and the rolls of fat which oozed over the stays that her improved status had warranted, soon communicated the impracticality of her conviction and lately she had shown a marked reservation at the table. Patrick's only wish was that she would find no need for the stays once the excess fat had dissolved, but sadly it was not to be granted. Instead of the warm squash of flesh when he put an arm around his wife, these days all it encountered was an unyielding barricade of whalebone.

'Not now, Mr Feeney.' She intercepted his question and pinched the bridge of her nose, squeezing shut her eyes which ached from the surfeit of figures.

'Now, how did ye know what I was going to say?' protested her husband, who had changed from his uncomfortable Sunday best after Mass and now wore more casual attire. 'Sure, I never opened me mouth.'

'You didn't have to,' she replied. 'You always get that look in your eye when there's something you're after.' The broad accent was still there but had been tempered to fit in with Thomasin's new lifestyle. She had found that people tended to look down on her at first, assuming that because she spoke that way it meant that she was a poor gullible peasant to be cheated. The strong-minded Tommy had soon altered their ideas for them, but had also decided, if only from good manners, to try to moderate her speech. After all, it was difficult to do business with someone who had to keep asking you to repeat yourself. One was still able to detect that she hailed from Yorkshire, but there was little doubt in anyone's mind that this was no country bumpkin to be manipulated.

A faint jingling conveyed that someone was paying them a visit. Obviously it was not one of their neighbours; no

191

one had been near since the Feeneys had moved in. Patrick half-rose to answer the door. Thomasin leaned forward and touched the shaft of her pen to his knee, keeping him in his seat. 'We've got somebody to do that now, remember?'

'Ah, so we do.' The reflex took some curbing. 'Three years an' I'm still not used to it. Doesn't seem decent somehow.' He relaxed as the maid, Amy Forsdyke, wiggled into the room.

'Yes, Amy?' Thomasin always reckoned she must have been suffering from a brainstorm on the day that Amy came for her interview. For what else would have persuaded her, a seasoned judge of character, to employ such a sly, lazy baggage? Especially one with no references. But then Thomasin had been determined not to be one of those employers who treated people like minions. She knew what it was like to be in such a position and decided from the start that she would not expect Amy to do all the dirty jobs; the workload would be divided between herself, Amy and Erin. At first she had shied away from Hannah's suggestion to hire a maid; it seemed so ... pretentious, as if she, Thomasin Feeney, was now too good to lift her hands to menial work. But as her expanding business took her farther and farther afield, and kept her engaged until all hours – Erin too – she had finally made the move that gave just acclaim to her new prestige.

Amy ignored her mistress and addressed herself to the master. 'There's a young man at the door, sir. Says could he have a word with Miss Erin?' Her eyes brazenly toured the length of Patrick's body. What a way for the master of the house to dress – soiled breeches, a baggy, shapeless tunic – anyone would think he was the odd-job man. What a waste, because he was really a fine figure of a man, and very handsome, even if he were twice her age and Irish too. She always went weak at the knees when he turned those speedwell eyes on her.

Patrick's mood changed. He rose abruptly and the book fell from his lap as he reached for a pipe and tobacco.

'Tell him she's not at home,' was his blunt response as his teeth clicked on the pipestem.

Amy retrieved the book and laid it on the table. She ran her eyes over him again, inclined her head at Thomasin's request for tea and left the room.

'You'll have to stop doing that, you know.' Thomasin brought the two halves of the ledger together with a heavy thud and laid it on the carpet at her feet.

'Stop what?'

'Don't play the innocent with me. You know very well what I'm talking about. This is the third one you've sent away. Your daughter is going to end up a crabby old spinster like Miss Peabody.'

'God forbid.' He slung his leg over the chair arm and reached for the book. Erin's beauty had always attracted male attention, with young men openly ogling her, but he had thought to leave the worst of that behind when they had moved to a more respectable district. Not so – he had still to put up with it at Mass. And not content with making sheep's eyes at his daughter over their prayer books the young buggers had had the audacity to follow her home. The first time a young man had called, Amy had unwittingly let him into the drawing room where Patrick sat. When the fellow had had the gall to tell him that his daughter was so beautiful he had just had to follow her to see where she lived and had blithely gone on to ask permission to take Patrick's daughter out, the Irishman had told him that if he ever followed Erin here again he'd better hire crutches to carry him home. After this, when told by Amy there was a young man at the door, he had always instructed her to send them away.

Erin was sauntering through the hall when she heard these instructions conveyed: 'Miss Erin's not at home, sir.'

'Yes, I am,' she said in a puzzled tone and came to the door to see who was calling. She blushed then. It was the young man she'd seen at church this morning, the one who'd kept smiling at her. He was rather nice-looking.

'Mr Feeney says you're not at home, Miss Erin,' contradicted Amy.

'But you can see I am, Amy,' replied Erin forcefully. 'And why did ye go to my father if it was me the gentleman came to see?'

"Cause you know it's me what'd get the stick if I let him in,' retorted the maid. 'If he says you're not to 'ave followers then who am I to argue? Now you clear off an' leave this girl alone,' she ordered the young man.

Erin, suffering from the double embarrassment of being treated like a child by her father and being spoken to in such a tone by the maid, gave an exclamation and promptly fled up the stairs to her room where she burst into tears. Oh, the humiliation of it all!

Meanwhile, the conversation in the drawing room was still about her marital state. 'Mark my words, I'm right!' Thomasin was saying. 'Look, the next time one calls, instead of booting him out, why don't you invite him in for tea? Get to know him.'

He raised a badtempered face from the page. 'I don't need to know them, they're all the same – rakes.'

'For pity's sake!' issued his wife exasperatedly. 'Why should you think of them all in that light?'

'Because who but a rake would admit to following a respectable girl home?'

'Well I ask you! How else is he going to meet her? Would you prefer that he approached her in the street? He couldn't've been that bad if he sought your permission to walk her out. You never gave him a chance.'

'Look, Thomasin, we've been through this a dozen times. I will not give my permission for her to go walking out with someone I don't know.'

'God help us!' Thomasin fought with her temper. Calmer, she said, 'Look, Pat, you know how shy she is, and between that and your intractability she's going to end up on the shelf if we don't do something about it.'

'I have this feeling you're going to suggest something.'

'You say you won't allow her to walk out with men you don't know. Right, well – let's start by listing the ones you *do* know.' There was silence. 'Exactly!' she threw at him. 'So just where does that leave Erin?'

He sighed. 'Someone'll come along eventually.'

'Aye, he'll probably have silver hair an' be on walking sticks by the time you've decided to let her out of your sight. Come on now, talk sensibly about this. There must be a nice young man somewhere.'

'An' where do ye suggest we find him? Our neighbours aren't going to let their little darlings mix with us, are they?'

She waved dismissively. 'We don't need them. I have a wide circle of business acquaintances, most of whom have families. Would you object if I invited one of their sons for tea?'

'Erin might.'

'Leave Erin out of this. It's nothing to do with her.' She laughed then and so did Patrick. 'Oh, we'll have to help her along, Pat. She's ripe for marriage is the lass – you should see how she handles the bairns that come into the shop. A natural mother if ever I saw one. Come on, what d'you think to my suggestion?'

He drew thoughtfully on his pipe, fighting himself. 'I'd want to be here when he called. We wouldn't leave them on their own.'

'I wasn't implying we would. I thought you could start by stringing him up to that curtainrail by his earlobes, then pull out all his fingernails one by one till he promised he wasn't going to besmirch your daughter's honour.'

'Behave,' he puffed, 'I'm thinking.'

'Well, think a bit faster.'

Finally he said, 'All right, invite your man – but have a care, Tommy, I'd not see her hurt.'

'And I would?'

'No, no, but ye might get carried away in your enthusiasm. Ye get these ideas into your head . . .'

The conversation came to an end as Amy appeared with the tea. She placed a stand, on which hung a small silver kettle, at Thomasin's right elbow, and laid the tray containing teapot, cream jug, sugar bowl and a plate each of macaroons and bread and butter on an occasional table.

'Will that be all?' She looked at Thomasin with barely-

195

veiled contempt. Jumped up nothing! she was thinking. There she is acting the lady when she's no better than me. That was quite apparent from the way, when Amy had commenced her duties, the mistress had always referred to luncheon as dinner and had also shown great ignorance over the times of afternoon tea and supper. She had tried to cover her slips but Amy had seen them, oh yes. Even if she had not learnt it from the servants of neighbouring households it would have been crystal clear – the mistress was just a nobody who had been left a fortune by some fancy-man and now thought she could walk all over her own class. And it wasn't as if she knew how to handle all her wealth, otherwise she would have employed a cook at least. But no, the mean bitch, she had to leave all that to Amy. Oh, she had been ever so fair when Amy had first started, saying, 'Leave that to me, Amy, I'll do it,' or, 'Miss Erin will see to supper tonight, Amy.' Well, that hadn't lasted long, had it? And now here was poor Amy doing the bloody lot. And to rub it all in she was looked down on by everyone else's staff because she worked for an Irishman, a nowt.

'Haven't you forgotten something, Amy?' The comment was iced with officiousness.

'I don't think so,' replied the maid, knowing full well what was implied, then dropped her eyes from Thomasin's penetrating stare and added a sulky, 'Ma'am.' The mistress always got the better of her, but one of these days Amy would have the last word. She did not see why she should add this deference to one of her own class. Just to show she had not been completely cowed, Amy allowed her eyes to rest insolently on her master for a few seconds before curtseying and leaving the room.

'She's a sly-looking piece,' muttered Thomasin as she handed a cup of tea and a plate to her husband. 'I shall certainly have to review her employment. I wouldn't've hired her in the first place if there'd been any other applicants. She's far too cocky.'

'Why, because she's set her cap at me?' grinned her husband, and reached for a macaroon.

'Oh, you did notice, then? And why, might I ask, didn't you reprimand her?' Thomasin selected a slice of bread and butter.

Patrick sank back into his chair and laughed. 'An' what should I say? Will ye please stop lookin' at me as though ye'd like to ravish me?'

'You could make it clear that you don't approve, instead of treating it like a joke,' reproved his wife.

'Now that's a shame – 'cause I rather like it. 'Tis very flattering, ye know, for an ould fella like me to draw such youthful attention.' He gave an expletive as his efforts to bite into the macaroon were repulsed. 'What the hell is this she's giving us? I almost broke me teeth on it. It's like a lump o' rock.'

'It was her afternoon off yesterday,' provided his wife dryly. 'She probably used it to go chiselling fossils on the east coast – it saves on the baking. Well, can you tell the difference?' she asked at his look of disdain.

He shook his head. 'I think ye could be right. Either that or she's getting a percentage from the tooth-puller. My God, I'm sure I've damaged something.' He threw the uneaten cake onto the fire where it soon resembled just another piece of coal. 'I think ye were right in wanting to be rid of her,' he said, rubbing his jaw. 'She's no great shakes as a cook, is she?' He dangled a piece of wafer-thin bread and butter between thumb and forefinger. 'An' will ye look at this? 'Tis like eatin' bits o' lace.'

'That is what my mother would term genteel refectionary,' answered Thomasin. 'You can't be expecting doorsteps now, a man of your standing. Still, I agree with you about her being a poor cook. And it's not only her culinary art that's suspect neither.'

Patrick raised his eyebrows. 'Ye think she's on the hey-diddle-diddle?' She nodded. 'But if that's so why is she still working for us?'

'Because, my dear, she doesn't look upon what she's doing as thievery – selling odds and ends at the back door to supplement her wages – it's considered perks of her trade. She'd look at me daft if I were to dismiss her on those grounds.'

'I never thought I'd hear the day when anyone put one over on my wife an' got away with it.'

'And you won't.' She set her mouth. 'Why do you think I pay her such a low wage? I worked out beforehand just what she was likely to pilfer from me each week and docked her wages accordingly. She gets three shillings per month less than I'd pay to someone honest. A little integrity would've bought her a rise after a few months, but I'm afraid that is not one of Amy's qualities. Things even themselves out quite nicely all said and done. What she thinks she's fiddling from me is really her due.'

'You're a bit of a slyboots yourself,' chuckled Patrick. He reached for two more pieces of bread and butter and stuck them together. 'It'll be a very clever person who gets the better of my wife.'

CHAPTER SEVENTEEN

The person who had accredited himself with that title was, as they spoke, cleaning out the stables. Things had not worked out exactly as Dickie had forseen. The riches he had anticipated when his mother inherited the business had not materialised. Three years on and he was still in the same position in which Thomasin had cast him; a glorified barrowboy, with an allowance of a few shillings per week. To Thomasin, who had always had to keep a strict check on the purse-strings – disregarding her own brief spate of flamboyance – it had seemed grossly extravagant to pay him more when he had little expenditure. After all, Dickie, his brother and sister would each receive a share in the legacy when their parents expired, and though she did not necessarily agree with the adage of money being the root of all evil – it had, after all, brought her great pleasure – in Dickie's hands it might bring an element of truth to the saying.

Dickie found it impossible not to equate his mother's caution with parsimony. In his view, it was just her way of keeping him tied to her apron-strings. So, he had been forced to resort to Amy's underhand tactics to make up for his mother's stinginess. The extra sixpence that his customers thought they were paying as a delivery charge was in fact going into young Feeney's coffers, secreted behind a loose brick in the stable wall. Once his nest-egg was large enough, this bird would spread his wings and fly.

'Get over, Polly!' He slapped the mare's chestnut rump, pushing her over to the far side of the stable in order to rake up the droppings. It was a job he detested, gathering manure for his father's land. The only reason he was doing it now, and so late, was that his father had paid a visit to the stable a short time after lunch and had discovered the horse almost knee-deep in soiled bedding. He had been furious, saying that he would return in an hour expecting to see the job completed.

True to his word Patrick strode in now as Dickie shovelled another pile of manure into the barrow. 'What, not finished yet? What the devil have ye been playing at, boy? Ye've had ample time to clean twenty stables out.' His pale-blue eyes visited every corner of the stable.

Dickie countered his father's annoyance by suggesting he might get the job done quicker by a stable lad. Surely they could afford one? This in turn was met by his father's derision.

'Of course we can afford one! But I'll be damned if I'm employing someone else when I've got a healthy son to do it.' Patrick kicked viciously at the evil-smelling straw. 'How d'ye expect your horse to do her work if she's got diseased hooves from the filth you're too lazy to shift? I pay out a hefty sum each week to keep this animal – I suppose ye have fed her, by the way?'

'Of course I have!' objected his son. 'What d'ye take

me for? I just forgot to muck out that's all, what with having to go to Mass.'

'Is it blaming your Maker y'are then for the horse's predicament?' snapped Patrick.

'No more I am. But I've that many things to see to, I only have time to do one or the other. If ye think the horse is more important then perhaps next Sunday ye should go to Mass without me. I can't see the point in it anyway.' He threw another shovelful onto the barrow and paused to straighten his back.

'Oh, no, my lad!' Patrick took a step forward. 'Ye needn't think you're using the horse to escape your other duties. If ye've not sufficient time then ye can rise an hour earlier, for both are equally important. Ye need to go to Mass for your spiritual well-being, for 'tis obvious that you're in grave danger o' becoming one o' these folk who couldn't give a damn about anybody, man nor beast. And ye need the horse because without her ye couldn't do your job, and where would ye be then? Certainly not sponging from my pocket. That horse obeys every command ye throw at her, pulls that heavy cart all over town without a word of protest. She deserves more reward than you're intent on giving her.'

'Rather like someone else I could name,' muttered Dickie sullenly, his bending back towards Patrick.

Patrick grasped his shoulder and turned him around. 'And what meaning am I to put on that? Come on, out with it! If ye've any complaints I'll hear them now.'

Dickie rested the spade at his side and leaned on it. 'Well, what sort o' reward do I get, I'd like to know?' he demanded petulantly. 'Sure, there's not only the horse that slogs all over town, ye know. 'Tis no picnic for me neither.'

'Ye get paid for it don't ye – 'tis more than the horse gets.'

'Hah! A few measly bob. I'll hardly get rich on that, will I?'

'Rich is it? An' what might ye be needing a fortune for, might I be knowing? Don't your mother an' me feed an'

200

clothe ye? Ye've no rent to pay, no creditors. I think the money ye receive is sufficient for a lad your age.'

''Tis all very well for you to talk when you're not exactly going without. Anyway, how would you know what I need?'

'Sure, I have been seventeen meself once ye know.' Patrick relaxed his severe frown as he drew on his memories. 'If I remember rightly the only things I was interested in at your age were a regular supply of whiskey an' pretty women. The money you get paid is well able to keep ye in drink for more than a week if ye choose to squander it that way. An' ye don't need to spend any on women ...' He caught the change of expression on Dickie's face and said sharply, 'You're not trying to tell me that I'm paying good money for the upkeep of a brothel? For if ever I thought ye were frequenting those kinda places I'd hold back every penny. I'm not saying this to spite ye, son, but for your own welfare. Ye see, those women are riddled with terrible diseases ... I don't know if you're understanding my meaning ...' He looked awkward. 'Catch a dose o' that an' you're in deep water. Will ye tell me honestly that you're not spending your money that way?'

Dickie manufactured a look of puzzled innocence, finding it hard to keep a straight face at his father's unworldliness. 'What way is that, Dad?'

Patrick had the uneasy feeling that beneath that bland exterior his son was mocking him, yet decided to accept that bemused frown as answer. 'Never mind. I'd not put ideas into your head that aren't already there.' He smiled and patted Dickie's shoulder. 'I know how hard it is for a young fella, son; I've been there meself. But ye must try an' wait for marriage if ye can – God! that sounds hypocritical coming from me. I'd not have ye believin' I'm a saint, but ... well, a man needs a wife if he's to do himself justice an' not fall into unsavoury ways. You're almost grown; ye'll likely be thinking about it yourself soon.' He turned away from those inscrutable eyes. Why did he feel as if he were talking to a stranger and not his own flesh and blood? Why could he never feel the comfort with Dickie that he did with his younger son? No, he corrected himself, that was no longer true – he didn't even feel comfortable with Sonny any more since he had gone to that college. His sons were strangers to him. He was pensively silent for a while, then asked, 'While we're being open with each other, are there any more complaints? I'd not like to be at the centre of this feeling of exploitation. Ye see, your mother thinks – an' I tend to agree with her – that it'd be foolish to supply ye with a lot of money when none of ye are used to handling it. Apart from anything else she thinks it might spoil ye.'

Dickie scuffed his boot against the edge of the idle spade. Spoil me indeed!

'Still upset at having to do a bit o' dirty work, are we?' Patrick sensed the reason behind the sullen countenance. 'Ye talk about being rich – how d'ye expect to get rich without dirtying your hands, tell me? Is it that ye think it's beneath your dignity to do such a menial task? Afraid that it might sully your peacock image?' At first it had been a bit of a joke when Dickie went out to work dressed as for a party. Now it was not so amusing.

'All right! If ye'll allow me to give a straight answer without clouting me I'll tell ye. I do think it's beneath me,' declared his son. 'I thought we were supposed to have gone up in the ranks. I'll wager there's not many young gentlemen that're expected to do the work of a labourer.'

This remark angered his father even more greatly than the one about the lack of wages. He launched into a vociferous diatribe about how he had come to this land penniless and starving and had been derided and spat upon by his so-called betters. The acquisition of mere money did not give anyone the right to think a job beneath him. 'Ye know what your trouble is, son? Ye've never been hungry – I mean *really* hungry. Ye see your meal upon the table an' never spare one second's thought as to how it got there.'

Dickie had heard it all before, had been weaned on tales of the Great Hunger, but instead of instilling in him any sort of sympathy or compassion it had had the adverse

202

effect. Dickie thought his father was a fool. If it had not been for his mother's friend they would most likely have been in the decrepit little house for the rest of their lives, with Father getting the egg, Father getting the meat from the stew, Father getting this that and the other, quite content to see his children go without because that was the way of things around there. Mother, now, had obviously known there was a bob or two to be made from the old man and had worked on him. She at least had her head screwed on right, if one overlooked her tight-fistedness. Father had no spirit about him, apart from when he was spouting the tedious old story about what it felt like to be starving.

Patrick spoke again. 'You're not going to achieve any sort of maturity by letting less-fortunate people do your dirty work, ye know.'

'What about the maid?' Dickie was swift to parry. 'Why does there have to be one set o' rules for Mother an' another for me?'

'Amy is not simply there so's your mother can delegate her less-tasteful chores,' corrected Patrick sternly. 'Your mother does a hard day's work. No one could expect her to run a large house like ours single-handed, yet she still finds time to do her share.'

Here Dickie enjoyed an inward smile. This contrasted greatly with Amy's grumblings. She was always moaning about his mother – he didn't know what she expected *him* to do about it. 'I do a hard day's work too,' he argued stubbornly. 'But I've no one to help me.'

Patrick tilted his jaw. 'Your idea of hard work does not tally with mine or your mother's, Dickie. An' despite your argument 'tis my thinking that if I were to employ a stable-hand you would spend your time doing nothing more strenuous than giving orders, and there's an end to it. As for your line of thinking that the money has somehow promoted you to the rank of gentleman, a word to the wise. You're Irish – or half Irish – and to the majority of the populus that renders you less than even working class, less than human, perhaps. The Irish have no status except in their own country – and even there most of them are kept in check by poverty. Maybe 'tis a good thing that we've moved away from Walmgate where most o' the people were the same as us. Out into the real world. Here ye'll get a better picture of how our kind are judged. Don't ye even notice how none of our neighbours deign to call on us? How they can barely bring themselves to nod hello when our paths cross – virtually collide – on our way to our separate places of worship?'

Dickie had genuinely not noticed. His world was centred around himself and he rarely bothered to observe how others behaved towards him unless they were pretty females. He had, of course, submitted to a great deal of abuse from Edwin Raper – Bacon Neck – but then he was a badtempered old swine with everyone. No, it was Dickie's opinion that his melodic brogue was one of his best assets when courting the ladies. If his father's theory were correct, then the moment Dickie opened his mouth the girls, by rights, should turn up their noses and walk away. And that wasn't the case at all – not by any measure. He was slightly amazed, even while holding the opinion that his father was a simple peasant, at the lack of pride in Patrick's statement about the Irish being without class. Where was the man who, from the time they were no higher than his knee, had drummed into them the importance of national pride, had imbued all his stories with a patriotic moral, had weaned them on the knowledge that a man's heritage was as vital as life itself?

'Just give it some careful thought, Dickie,' added Patrick as he made his way out of the stable. 'Everything you see – the business, that big house – will all fall to you children one day. The more ye put in the more ye get out, even you must see that – unless you expect the others to do your share for ye, in which case ye'll be disappointed, for I'd not allow it to happen.'

'I don't hear ye having this conversation with my brother,' replied Dickie, stopping Patrick in his tracks.

His father speared him with a glare. 'There's no call to lecture Sonny. He's doing his bit.'

'Oh aye, sat on his backside wielding nothing heavier than a pen,' spat his son.

'He's working with his brain – seeing as how he's the only one of my sons to have any. And he works damned hard. Perhaps if you'd put a little more effort into your schooling you might've been the one to go to college. You're not an unintelligent boy, Dickie, if ye'd steer your brain on the right course instead of entertaining all these fanciful notions about being rich.'

His son's face was hard. 'Ye think I'm dreaming – but I will be rich one day,' he promised.

Patrick sighed. 'I've no doubt ye will. But I'm equally certain it won't come through hard work – and of course there are differing degrees of richness. Even when we lived in what most people would term poverty I considered myself rich to have a wife like your mother and three normal, healthy children. Though I doubt you'd count these things as wealth. To you there's only one rich, an' that's money. Well, I'll underline what I already said – even though I can see from your face it bores the hide off ye – however much money ye succeed in totting up, be it thousands or millions, to them you'll still be Irish.' He gave his son a long searching look, then left.

Dickie's lip curved into a sneer. He discounted his father's words as so much hot air, the rumblings of an old man whose life was almost over – and what had he to show for it? Patrick set himself up as a proud man but did not contribute anything to alter people's views when they classed him as an oaf. Well, no one was going to look down on Dickie.

CHAPTER EIGHTEEN

Lack of punctiliousness from anyone – least of all her suppliers – was something for which Thomasin would not stand. After several late deliveries from one such quarter she broke off relations and set to work in finding a replacement. When Erin smilingly waved her off that drizzly morning she little guessed that this was to be the start of a very uncomfortable period in her life.

Thomasin drew up outside King's, wholesale purveyors of fine quality confectionery and, stepping from her carriage, asked where she might find Mr Joseph King, the head of this organisation. The labourer doffed his cap and himself showed her to King's office, leaving her at the door.

She knocked and went straight in. 'Mr King? I'm afraid I do not have an appointment but trust you will take pity on my dilemma. My name is . . .'

'Don't tell me!' King's pince-nez dropped from his nose as he leapt from the leather chair to shake her hand effusively. 'You are the lady about whom I have heard so much – the genius behind the revitalization of *Penny's* – am I correct?'

'Such praise is gratefully received, Mr King.' Thomasin felt as though her shoulder was about to be wrenched from its socket in the violent handshake and diplomatically pulled her hand away. 'But really, it's no genius you see before you, simply a woman whose hard work has paid dividends.'

'Your modesty causes you to understate matters, madam. Here, allow me to take your coat.' King ripped the damp garment from her back and hurled it onto a coatstand then, directing her to a chair, all but pushed her into it. 'Well, well. This is indeed a great compliment you pay me. And what, pray, can this humble family business do for you, dear lady? You mentioned a predicament.'

Thomasin, in a daze at this overwhelming reception, told him of the dispute with her previous supplier and added her thoughts that it would be beneficial to both parties if King should step into the vacated shoes.

'It would be an honour and a privilege, madam.' King admired her from his side of the desk. She was an extraordinarily handsome woman and obviously had a brain to match, judging by the way old Penny's shop was looking now. He heaved his great body in a sigh of pleasure then, witnessing her befuddlement, grabbed a handful of papers and spread them in front of her. 'There is a list of the commodities we stock, ma'am, plus the relevant prices. I trust you will find them competitive.'

Thomasin scrutinised the documents and murmured conservatively while King held his breath. Then she looked up with a smile. 'I see I ought to have been dealing with you all along, Mr King,' and he beamed elatedly.

'Does that mean I can look forward to your custom, ma'am?' At her affirmation he came around the desk to shake her hand again. 'Splendid, splendid!' He yanked at her hand and patted it roughly. 'Now, may I offer you something to drink as way of celebration? A glass of sherry perhaps?'

She tested her arm for damage, rubbing at her shoulder. 'Thank you, no – but tea would be appreciated, Mr King.' She stared out of the window through a rain-stippled coating of dirt to the street below where two draymen, soaked to the skin, rolled barrels down a plank to the cellar beneath the pavement. The great shires hung their heads, the rain trickling down their rounded haunches, each with one feathered foot crooked in boredom. 'What a day. It makes you feel cold just to look at it. A cup of tea is just what I need.'

'Tea it shall be!' King inserted his head round the door of another office. 'Walter, some tea for Mrs Penny and myself, if you please.'

'Oh, it's not . . .' began Thomasin, but King bumbled on, 'What relation were you to old Mr Penny by the way? His nephew's wife? I know he was childless.'

'Well, actually . . .'

'I always find it heartwarming to hear of a family business being perpetuated,' went on King. 'There is something so sad about a son's disinclination to continue in his father's footsteps. Have you sons, Mrs Penny?'

'Yes.' Thomasin gave up trying to correct the surname as King unfolded his family history. 'Five generations have run this business, Mrs Penny. It gives me such pride to be part of it.' He progressed in this vein until Thomasin was rescued some fifteen minutes later by the appearance of a young man bearing a tray.

'Ah, thank you, Walter!' King rose. 'Come along, put the tray down here. That's it. Look sharp, boy, look sharp! Mrs Penny, I should like to introduce my junior partner – who is also my son. Walter, this is Mrs Penny.'

'Actually it's . . .'

'I'm very pleased to make your acquaintance, Mrs Penny,' said Walter, putting down his tray and proffering his hand. She breached the gap warily but was pleased to find that King junior had not inherited his father's mania for dislocating limbs. Her hand came away unscathed.

'I have just been informing Mrs Penny of the history behind our business,' the young man's father told him. 'She agrees with me how important it is to have a son who will carry on the good work, don't you, Mrs Penny?'

Thomasin looked from one to the other. 'Er . . .'

'So, if you will not take your father's advice at least you must pay heed to such a distinguished opinion as our guest's. What say you, Walter, have you no tongue in your head?'

'I . . .' attempted his son.

'Good, good!' King picked up the teapot and tilted it heavily towards the cups, spilling much of it in his enthusiastic pouring. 'I'm glad you see sense at last. Very well, you may leave us to our discussion now, Walter.' The young man gave Thomasin a pathetic gesture, then wasted no time in escaping the office.

'I hope you did not take offence at my using you as a battering ram so to speak, Mrs Penny,' said King, handing her a cup of tea – half of it in the saucer.

'Well, I'm sure I wouldn't if I knew the purpose of it, Mr King,' Thomasin finally slipped in as her host filled his mouth with tea.

'Oh, did I not say?' He clashed the cup and saucer together. 'Well, dear lady it is like this: Walter refuses to find himself a wife – and without a spouse how can he hope to provide a son to carry on the business?'

'Ah, I see,' Thomasin nodded. 'But have you no other issue?'

'Alas, eight daughters,' bemoaned King. 'None of them, I'm afraid, blessed with your flair for commerce. All they want to do is find a husband. It's costing me a fortune. And the one I truly want to see married remains obstructive. He's really a fine chap, Walter, a good head on his shoulders and knows plenty about the running of things here – could take over tomorrow if I met with an accident. But, you see, the ladies just don't take a shine to him. I can't think why, I've tried my best to help him along in his courtships. He doesn't speak much, you may have noticed – had to do all the talking myself.' Thomasin smiled into her cup. 'In normal conditions the boy's mother would be there to aid matters but I lost my dear wife with the birth of our last child and I'm totally at a loss as to what to suggest for him. If you can offer any solution I would be most grateful.'

Thomasin expressed her regrets about the late Mrs King. 'But I'm afraid I'm not the best person to advise you in this problem, for I too have an unmarried child on my hands.' Suddenly the recollection of her discussion with Patrick came rushing back and her face became alert. King noticed this.

'May one enquire the gender of this unmarried child?' he said slowly.

Thomasin pictured Erin being swallowed up by King's over-enthusiasm. 'I'm not certain my daughter would thank me for interfering,' she said carefully.

King leapt up in his boisterous fashion. 'Nonsense! This is ideal. If we can bring the two together . . .'

Thomasin scraped the bottom of her cup against the rim of the saucer to avoid drips and thought about it. This was what she had been hoping for, a good match for Erin, and Walter was certainly that – if he decided to follow his father's lead, of course. And thereby lay the stumbling block – his father. When one married, one didn't just wed the man but his whole family. Could Erin, or Thomasin for that matter, endure King senior as an in-law? She looked up at his eager face. It was difficult to gauge a man's character from one meeting. The only way to find out the suitability of the match was to invite both father and son round to the house.

'I can hear your mind whirring away there, Mrs Penny,' laughed King. 'If it is Walter's qualification as a husband which deters you . . .'

'Oh, pray forgive my rudeness,' said Thomasin. 'My silence was not an indication of my reluctance. My only fear is that my daughter will see it as an intrusion into her private affairs. I would not antagonise her. I wonder, would you think it impertinent if I asked you to put on a little charade?'

'But I love charades!' exclaimed King.

'Well, this is what I had in mind: you could pretend to be calling on a matter of business and just happen to bring your son along, while I make certain that my daughter will be present. That way it will not seem too obvious.'

'Quite, quite,' replied King. 'And I shall be equally discreet when dealing with my son. He has inherited his father's sensitivity and if he felt he was being manipulated would be most upset.'

Thomasin pretended to be coughing to cover her hilarity – King was about as sensitive as a navvy's boot. 'I do beg your pardon. Now, Mr King, when shall this meeting be?'

'Oh, the sooner the better I say. Tomorrow would be admirable.'

'Tomorrow is Sunday, Mr King. Will your son not find it strange to be conducting business on the Sabbath?'

'It does not have to be business, Mrs Penny,' replied King. 'I could say you have invited us to take tea with you as a way of cementing our new relationship. What will your husband's reaction be to our machinations, I wonder?'

'Oh, I have my husband's blessing,' said Thomasin. 'He would like to see his daughter happily settled as much as I.' – Though I doubt he had foreseen it happening this soon, she thought to herself. She replaced her cup in its miniature pond and stood. 'Thank you for the refreshment, Mr King. I shall have to go now, I have much to attend to.'

King seized the cup from her and clattered it onto the tray, then tripped past her to open the door, bowing. 'Until tomorrow then, Mrs Penny.'

She smiled. 'Do you think I could have my coat?'

He shot upright. 'Oh dear, how foolish I am!' and grabbed the coat from the stand, spinning her round and thrusting it over her shoulders.

'Thank you – and, Mr King my name is . . .'

'Ah, Walter!' King spotted his son and waved him over. 'Direct Mrs Penny to her carriage, there's a good chap. Au revoir, Mrs Penny, until tomorrow!'

And that, thought Thomasin, finding herself standing on the wrong side of the door with a hesitant Walter at her shoulder, was that. She wondered, as she hurried beside him through the rain to her carriage, if she had made a mistake. Walter if anything was shyer than Erin, barely exchanging two words in the time they were together. But, looking at him over the carriage door she saw a young man with a pleasant smile and a willing manner. Even if this arrangement proved to be a waste of time, it would at least give Erin the chance to converse with a member of the opposite sex.

Thomasin told Patrick of her plan. He did, however, need strenuous assurances as to the suitability of the young man before reluctantly granting his blessing. After Sunday lunch, instead of his usual nap, he changed into his working clothes and said that he would fit in a few hours on the land to work off the heavy meal. He didn't want King to catch him in crumpled togs and bleary eyes.

Thomasin had not minded this. 'Only make sure you're back in good time,' she warned, rubbing her arm in memory. 'I don't feel strong enough to face the ordeal alone. I still think he damaged something yesterday.'

At four o'clock she sent Amy to fetch Erin from her room. 'I thought you might care to take this chance of

211

gleaning a few hints on how to entertain,' she told her stepdaughter when she came down. 'You'll have to learn some day, you know.'

Erin innocently accepted the offer. 'Will Dickie be coming to join us?'

Thomasin said no. She had made sure of no diversions from her wilful son by lining up an alternative tea party at her mother's. Hannah was also in on the secret and thought it a wonderful idea, though Thomasin doubted Dickie would see the tea party as such. 'Mr King will be here shortly. I hope your father doesn't forget what time it is – our guest does tend to get a wee bit overbearing.' She eyed Erin's outfit. 'D'you think that's suitable, love? Haven't you got anything newer? After all, the mistress of the house does have to make an impression on her guests.'

'Well, I didn't see the point of crumpling one of my best dresses: I've been scrunched up in a chair, reading. I was goin' to change later for church. Anyway, I'm not the mistress, you are, Mam. An' I'm sure in that dress you'll make a resounding impression on anyone.'

'Yes, but the object of this exercise is for you to see how the mistress of the house deports herself,' said Thomasin. 'Now, you've got that lovely pale-blue dress hanging in the wardrobe, why don't you run and put that on? You've ample time before our guests arrive.'

'Guests?' Erin frowned. 'I thought ye said there was just Mr King?'

Thomasin flustered guiltily at her slip. 'Well, he did mention he might bring someone with him but it was all very vague. Go on, hurry up, it's almost a quarter past four. I'll ring for Amy to help you.'

Without further harrying Erin did as she was asked and, with Amy's grudging help, rematerialised ten minutes later in the gown her mother had suggested.

'Oh, you do look bonny!' cried Thomasin happily. 'I'm sure Mr King will be delighted that you've gone to so much trouble to please him.'

'And why *are* we going to all this trouble, Mam?' asked Erin, her head tilted in confusion. 'I understood he was only one of your suppliers. This is the first time I've known you to entertain one of them in your home.'

'I know and it's high time I did,' replied Thomasin. 'You have to put yourself out in the business world, Erin. Butter 'em up a little – that way you get better service.' She looked at the clock again. 'It's nearly time. I think I'll ask Amy to make a start on the tea. If I get my order in early I'm more likely to get it delivered within the next three hours.'

Joseph King and his son stepped from the cab. The senior left Walter to pay the fare and ran to take shelter in the doorway, hauling on the bell-pull. The rain was coming down in sheets. Walter, having paid the cabbie, rushed to join his father. King was in the motion of grappling with the bell-pull yet again, this time more forcefully. 'Confound it! Is no one going to answer?' said the older man crabbily. 'We are going to get drenched.' At the moment he spoke he spied a figure dashing round the side of the house, head well down against the rain. 'You . . . man!'

Patrick had thought to creep in the other entrance without the guests spotting him. His heart had sunk when he had seen the cab arrive. His blasted watch had stopped at two-thirty and there he'd been digging merrily away. . . If it hadn't started to pour down he'd probably have been later still. He turned to meet his enquirer, eyes narrowed against the downpour, his collar up and his hands thrust into his pockets. Before he could offer apologies, however, the man snapped a question. 'D'you belong to this household?'

'I do. The name is Feeney.'

'Well, do you think you could inform someone that Joseph King is on the doorstep and no one appears to be attending the bell. Your mistress is expecting me.'

Patrick made his way up to the man, brow furrowed. 'My . . .?' and then he realised that the man thought he was a servant. 'Oh yes, sorr! Allow me, sorr!' He grasped the brass knob and pushed open the door for King and his son to enter. 'Please to go in, yer honour.' He bowed, the rain dribbling off the rim of his hat. He followed them into the hall and wiped his boots on the mat.

King turned in surprise. 'Does your mistress permit you to use this entrance?' He took off his wet cape and looked around for somewhere to put it.

Patrick divested him of his burden and draped it on a coatstand, Walter's too. 'Oh, I'm sure her ladyship wouldn't disapprove if she knew I was lookin' after her guests, sorr. She'll be madder than a wasp with toothache when she knows the maid ain't doin' her job roight.'

'Nevertheless, I doubt she would appreciate my allowing her servants to litter the carpets with mud from their boots,' said King, straightening his cravat. 'Be a good fellow and use the correct entrance.'

'I will, sorr!' Patrick backed away, bowing constantly. 'I'd not like to get on the wrong side of her ladyship, oh no.'

'Never worry, I shall inform her how helpful you have been,' said King and delved into his pocket. 'Here! Take this in reparation for the extra soaking you'll receive through helping us.' He gave Patrick a sixpence.

The Irishman bit it and tugged his forelock, enjoying himself tremendously. 'Oh, tank ye, sorr! May your son be as great a gentleman as his father. God bless ye. 'Tis that door ye'll be wantin'.' He pointed to the drawing room and watched King and his son enter before grinning, leaving his muddy boots where they stood and going upstairs to change.

'Mr King! What a pleasant surprise, you've brought your son.' Thomasin rose to greet them. 'Do come sit by the fire.'

'I regret having to force my way in unannounced, ma'am,' King came forward and embarked on his usual ritual, 'but no one appeared to be answering the bell.'

Thomasin expressed horror at their treatment. 'I'm most dreadfully sorry, Mr King. I assumed the maid to be answering it. I shall have to remonstrate with her.' She glanced at Erin to see what effect Walter's arrival was having on her. Oh dear, she was blushing already. Walter was obviously interested, though.

'No harm done, Mrs Penny,' said King, 'another of your servants was on his way to the rear entrance and very compliantly let us in.'

Thomasin looked once again at Erin, who raised one eyebrow. 'Another of my servants?'

'Yes, tall chap, odd-job man or gardener by the look of him. I must confess he was extremely accommodating for an Irishman – though I should be very wary if I were you of employing other Fenians. I myself made the error once of hiring a number of them. Thank goodness it was only on a temporary basis. As shifty and workshy a bunch of scoundrels as one could meet. And one never knows these days, all these bombings. . . Walter!' he clapped his hands suddenly. 'Don't stand there like a wallflower. I'm sure you're just as eager as I to meet Mrs Penny's charming daughter.' He trained appraising eyes on Erin, who had suddenly lost that shy smile.

Thomasin dared not look at her stepdaughter, whose animosity could be felt two blocks away. How could one so experienced have made such a blunder? She should have made her name plain from the outset – if only she could have got a word in edgeways. Recovering herself, she put on a charming smile and drew a tight-lipped Erin up to meet the guests. 'Mr King, Walter, I should like you to meet my daughter, Erin Feeney.'

'Charmed, Miss Feeney, charmed!' King was pumping her hand before the name made itself felt. He looked obliquely at Thomasin. 'But, Mrs Penny . . .'

'No, not Penny,' Thomasin was at last able to correct him. 'The name is Feeney, Mr King.' The door opened as she spoke. 'Ah! Here is my husband come to join us.'

King found it hard to turn, knowing what he would see when he did. Still shaken he accepted Patrick's falsely cheerful handshake with much less than his normal verve. 'Delighted, I'm sure,' he said weakly and looking at Patrick's change of outfit added plaintively, 'I must apologise for my former misconstruction . . . your clothes . . .'

'Yes, he is very elegant, isn't he, Mr King?' Thomasin produced a warped smile, guessing what had happened. 'For an Irishman.'

'My dear Mrs Pe . . . Feeney,' bumbled King. 'Do forgive me, I did not realise.'

'Of course you didn't,' soothed Thomasin, then added a sting. 'If you had you would not be here – is that not right?'

King shook his head strenuously, while Walter cast awkward glances at Patrick. 'I must protest. Had I been acquainted with your true surname I should never have made such remarks.'

'And then we should never have known what a viper we had in our midst,' responded his hostess.

'This is outrageous! I will not be insulted in such a manner.' King marched to the door.

'One moment, Mr King!' Thomasin stepped after him. 'You're very quick to take offence but not so quick to apologise for the offence you yourself have caused.'

'I did beg pardon of you!'

'Of me, yes, but I was not the one you slandered. I know that my husband and daughter must take great exception to your views on the Irish being workshy, especially as my husband broke the Sabbath to attend to his commitments.' She waited.

King, without looking at either of them, bowed stiffly. 'Feeney, Miss Feeney, I beg your pardon if my words provoked offence. Good day to you all.' With that he made a swift exit, Walter scuttling after him.

'Well, I must say! Mother, ye've done some surprising things in your time but ye've never before invited such a boor into our home.' Erin was furious. 'To be humiliated by outsiders is one thing, but in our own home . . .'

And if you knew that that boor's son was intended as your husband you'd be in even more of a lather, thought Thomasin. God! How could I have made such a slip? But she said calmly, 'I had no idea he held such views, Erin. You know I'd never've subjected you to that if I had.

216

Patrick, I'm really sorry.' She looked pleadingly at him. *Please don't tell her,* she beseeched silently.

He had no intention of adding further humiliation, still angry at his own, though he reckoned he had had his own back with his bit of play-acting. 'God! Did ye see how it hurt him to bring himself to apologise?'

'Well,' said Erin, 'unless ye've any more o' your guests for me to learn how to entertain I'll be off to my room.'

'Don't you want your tea?' called Thomasin.

'I really don't feel like any!' Erin banged the door.

'To think I trusted you,' pointed Patrick.

'Oh, I know, I know ...' she formed a sympathetic expression. 'I feel really bad about it. I should've got to know the man better before I invited him here. It's just that ... well, he does have this enthusiastic manner and I sort of got carried along with it.'

He nodded his understanding but was still not in the best of humour. 'Well, I think ye should give the old matchmaking a wee rest. God, to think that man's son was nearly married to my daughter!'

'I think that's highly unlikely from what he said, don't you?' A cryptic smile from Thomasin. Then she poked him. 'Oh, don't give up on me, Pat! I promise I'll be more careful the next time.'

'Next time!'

'Surely I'm allowed a few mistakes?'

'Not if they're all as serious as that. She didn't know about the lad, did she?'

'About him being invited for her? No, thank God. I wouldn't've told her anyway, you know how huffy she gets if she thinks people're trying to arrange her life. Anyway, listen! I've had a much better idea.' He groaned. 'Listen, I said! I've decided to give her a birthday party. I've got it all worked out. I'm going to send invitations to the children of all my business contacts.'

'An' what'll ye do if a cartload o' six year olds turn up clamouring for jelly an' custard?'

'Stop making fun!'

'Sure, I don't think it's funny.'

217

'I'll do my detective work first and only send invites to those with offspring Erin's age – if I can find any that aren't married. It beats me why I never dreamt of it before; inviting them altogether, I mean. It's a much better idea. En masse she can take her pick. Then it'll seem like the choice is hers.'

'You're not going to surround her with a crowd o' strange men!'

'Oh, of all the . . . of course I'm not! Do I look that stupid? I'll invite some girls too.' He asked if she was going to invite any of the family. 'No, this is Erin's do entirely. Besides, I wouldn't dream of unleashing our Dickie on a bevy of innocent young ladies.'

'Then who'll be there to see she doesn't fall prey to a rogue?' he asked.

'Me an' thee, lad. I wish you'd stop trying to blunt my preparations. This is much the best way I assure you. And you never know, you might even enjoy yourself.' She gripped his arm. 'Eh, but one promise. Please, please, no more party-pieces, there's a good boy.'

CHAPTER NINETEEN

With the party in full swing, Patrick was forced to admit that it had been a good idea; he had never seen his daughter so full of zeal as she sang with the rest around the piano – though the closed circle of admirers did tend to worry him.

'Stop chewing yourself,' muttered Thomasin, smiling and swaying to the music. 'If you keep hanging round like the heavy-handed father you'll put them off and all this will have been a waste of time. Come on, let's retire to the front parlour and let them get on with it. She's quite safe.' The piano had been pushed into the back room for the party as there was more space and the doors to the garden left open so that the guests could wander out onto the terrace.

Patrick was hard to convince. 'I just want to get the measure of them first. I'd not leave her to their mercy if I thought they were going to make fun of her.'

'And why should they do that?' enquired his wife.

'For one thing she's not had the education they've had – an' before ye ask whose fault that is I still stand by my views that women don't need educatin' the same as men do. All the same, I'd not expose her to their ridicule. I know what these young people can be like if they sense someone is different to them.'

'If I thought they were that way disposed then I would never have invited them,' answered Thomasin. 'I made doubly sure that each of their parents were attuned to our correct surname this time; if they'd held any objection their offspring would hardly be here tonight, would they? And tell me, does it look as if she's the centre of ridicule?' Erin's face glowed as she turned over the sheet of music for the young man at the piano. It was plain to see that shy or no she was blossoming under all this attention.

'She seems very taken with the young fellow who's playing,' said Patrick.

'And he with her,' smiled Thomasin behind her feathered fan. "He's a bonny enough lad too.' The man seated on the piano stool had curly brown hair and warm hazel eyes, and though he was encircled by other attractive girls his romantic song was directed solely at Erin.

'I think I'll just have that word before we leave them to it, though,' said Patrick doggedly, and sauntered up to the youthful gathering as the song finished. 'Everybody happy?'

They chorused their appreciation. 'I should say, Mr Feeney,' cried Stephen Hartas, the piano-player. 'A dandy party – and this punch is first class. It's thirsty work having to entertain this bunch of rowdies.' His words met with hoots as he reached for the cup of punch that Erin had been guarding for him.

'Don't let my daughter bully you into providing all the

219

amusement, Mr Hartas,' said Patrick amiably. 'As your hostess 'tis up to her to keep everyone happy – and she's a first-class entertainer in her own right. Ye must insist she displays her talents before the night is through.'

'She has displayed her talents already, sir,' replied Stephen gallantly. 'I have never had more enchanting assistance with my music.'

'She's a beauty sure enough,' said Patrick, his eyes twinkling at his daughter. 'But I refer to her talents with the harp – though I warn ye to have your handkerchiefs at the ready for she never fails to set the tears aflowing.'

'Erin, I demand that you bring your harp in right now,' cried Stephen, bringing forth a blush.

'No one wants to hear me,' said Erin bashfully. 'I'm sure they'd much rather listen to you play the piano, and I would too.'

Everyone shouted their disagreement. 'We don't want to listen to Stephen's amateurish plonking,' said the young man's sister with a smile. 'And please, Erin – don't tell him you actually *enjoy* it, or I shall never hear the last of it.'

Stephen shouted her down and took Erin's hand. 'There you are, you see how highly they rate my music? You must comply or I shall ask for a forfeit.'

'I rather hoped we could have some dancing first,' revealed Erin. 'Things tend to get maudlin when I play my harp, and 'tis ages since anyone asked me to dance.'

'Oh well, we can't disappoint her, can we chaps?' said Stephen to a murmur of accord. 'You shall have your way, Erin, but I must insist on that forfeit; if we are to dance then I claim the first and last with you.'

Erin's head swirled. 'But who'll play the accompaniment?' she asked.

'I shall, if I may claim the second dance,' spoke up a young man with Dundreary whiskers.

'I claim the third!' brought forth another, bringing a jocular comment from the girl at his side.

Satisfied that Erin would come to no harm, Patrick retired with his wife into the other room.

When everyone had a partner the man with the Dundreary whiskers – Alex – struck up a modern tune and set the room in motion. Erin accepted one of Stephen's warm, dry hands in hers, felt the other curve around her waist, and smiled shyly into his hazel eyes as they set off.

'I wish I'd had the foresight to claim every dance with you, Erin,' he told her breathlessly. 'But the others would never forgive me. You're the best dancer here – and the prettiest.'

She clung to him as he whirled her around the room, her lavender dress frothing around her quaking knees. Oh, he was lovely! So attentive, such a gentleman. She had never known anyone quite like him before. He was so much fun to be with.

The dance was not nearly long enough and to her dismay Stephen was torn from her grip to take his turn at the piano and his dear face replaced by Alex's who pulled her much too close and tickled her face with his whiskers. After that she danced with Laurence and Henry, Albert and Clarence, while her mind still danced with Stephen. Instead of Clarry's slippery palms she felt his smooth, dry ones hugging hers. Smelt his clean, gentlemanly smell, his breath against her cheek, lightly flavoured with punch. It seemed aeons until he came to claim his final dance. By that time she was out of breath, her legs were on the point of collapse and she badly wanted to sit down, but no amount of fatigue could persuade her to give up her precious partner and she fell gladly into his arms.

Finally, amid a great burst of clapping the dance broke up and everyone wandered off to a quiet corner with their chosen beau.

'Well, shall we be privileged to hear these unsung talents, Erin?' panted Stephen as they sat together on the sofa. 'Have I not paid for the honour? Wearing my fingers to the bone at that infernal piano when I would much rather have been dancing with you.'

She laughed, her eyes sparkling. 'The moment I recover I'll fetch it – but don't say you haven't been warned.

Parties are supposed to be gay affairs, ye don't really want to see everyone cryin' do ye – as Father would have ye believe my music has the power to do.'

'If your music is as beautiful as you then it will have the power to move mountains,' replied Stephen, his face – such a kind face, thought Erin – moving close to hers. 'I must tell you that you are the loveliest girl I have had the honour to partner.'

Inexplicably, Erin felt claustrophobic at his proximity and jumped from her seat. 'Listen, why don't you take a stroll on the terrace to cool off while I fetch my harp?'

Stephen regarded her with a bemused smile, then stood up to join her, flicking back the tails of his coat. 'Topping idea – if you will come and keep me company.'

'I can't keep you company *and* fetch my harp,' laughed Erin. 'You must make up your mind which takes precedence.'

The decision was made for him by calls from the other guests, asking when they were going to hear this harp of Erin's.

'It looks as if you'll have to do without my company for the moment,' she smiled.

'Alas! the maid deserts me,' cried Stephen, woebegone. 'Very well, I shall take with me a glass of that extraordinarily fine punch to drown my heartache.'

'Oh dear, I'll have to ask Mother for some more,' said Erin examining the crystal bowl. ''Tis almost empty. You wait on the terrace; I'll bring it out to you.'

'Very well.' He made for the open door. 'But don't leave me alone for too long or I shall pine completely away.'

Erin looked fondly after him for a moment, then went to find Thomasin to ask for more punch.

Thomasin told her there was more in the kitchen. 'Go tell Amy to fetch it in for you.'

Erin was about to go straight back out, when on impulse she turned to embrace them both with a radiant smile. 'Thank ye, both of ye, for this lovely birthday. I can't ever remember enjoying one so much.'

'I don't think that has so much to do with us as of the

exuberance of your guests,' replied Thomasin, reflecting her happiness. 'Mr Hartas especially.'

'Yes, he is wonderful, isn't he?' agreed Erin. 'I'll wager he's the life an' soul o' the party wherever he goes. Now, I must get back; I promised to play for him.'

Play for him, thought Thomasin with satisfaction – not the others, only him. Well, things had worked out a little better this time, hadn't they?

'You run along an' enjoy yourself,' said her father. 'An' mind, not too much punch.'

Erin collected the harp and left it in the hall until she was ready to play. When Amy brought in the fresh bowl of punch she filled two cups and wandered out onto the terrace. The garden was in darkness but the light from the house sprayed out over the crazy-paving merging into soft shadows at the outer edges where the terrace met a high laurel hedge. A cool breeze plucked at the lace on her bodice, lifting it to brush against the hollow of her neck. She shivered, raising a crop of goosebumps, and searched the terrace with her eyes, a cup in each hand. She smiled suddenly as Alex's broad tones bit into the silence of the garden, and made towards the laurel hedge from whence the voice came.

'I'd fancy a crack at her myself if I hadn't been landed with Sophie. She's a real spanker, isn't she? No wonder you agreed to come, crafty devil!'

Erin's flesh tingled with pleasure at Stephen's reply, 'She's a looker all right,' and paused before rounding the hedge so that she might hear more compliments.

Stephen added to his comment. 'It's a damn shame I'm not allowed to handle the goods – not that I'd get very far, she's as timid as a fawn. These Irish girls are all the same they tell me – model themselves on the Virgin Mary. Even if they were willing the fathers see to it that no one gets within ten feet of them. Beat the stuffing out of you if you so much as blow them a kiss. That's why I was surprised to be given so much leeway tonight.'

'Yes, Feeney presented himself as a pretty likeable sort of fellow,' returned Alex. Erin's blood had began to congeal in her veins. 'Not what I expected at all after the lecture I got from Mama.' He put on a feminine squeak, imitating his mother. 'Be most vigilant, Alexander, in your deportment. They may be a wild lot.' He laughed. 'I think she visualises me going home with a broken head. She'll be at the front door waiting with the bandages and liniment.'

Stephen shared his merriment. 'My parents are exactly the same. Bloody bigots. Did you hear about old King? Thought Feeney was the gardener and tipped him sixpence; bumbling old ass!'

'Who hasn't heard?' replied Alex amusedly. 'Still, one can see where he made his error. If Feeney had been dressed in the old togs that Walter described I'm sure I would've made the same mistake, what with his begobs and begorrahs.'

'He never said that!' reproved Stephen laughingly.

'Did he not? Well, I couldn't grasp half of what he said – proper bog-trotter isn't he?'

'Oh, I thought the chap was quite approachable,' defended Stephen.

'For a Fenian,' prompted Alex and burst out laughing again.

Stephen sucked in his breath. 'Poor old Kingy! What a blunder.' He lit a cigar; the smoke reached Erin as she stood there, paralysed with disbelief, the glasses of punch still clutched in her hands. 'You ought to have heard him going on to Pa about his darling boy's narrow escape.'

'Yes, I know, that's what I find so dashed amazing,' frowned Alex. 'Why, if our parents knew the purpose of this party, did they allow us to come?'

'It's not so amazing when you know the answer,' said Stephen, savouring the cigar.

'Well, if you know would you be so kind as to share it with me? I must say after the speech I received from Mama on the dangers of entering a Fenian stronghold I was taken aback when she and Father gave their permission for me to come.'

'Simple,' replied Stephen, blowing smoke-rings. 'Mrs Feeney is one of our best customers. Pater didn't want to offend her by turning down the invitation and advised all his contacts to follow his lead if they valued their client. Besides, what was the point of ruining a perfectly good business relationship? Just because we accepted the invitation doesn't mean that any of us are going to have to marry her.'

Erin gripped the cups so tightly that the crystal cut into her flesh. How could she? How could Mam disgrace me so?

'Naturally,' proceeded Stephen, 'I had to swear to a list of dos and don'ts before they'd let me out of the house. Number one – be politeness itself, do your utmost to cultivate good relations with our patron. Number two – lavish as much attention on the daughter as you feel able, *but* – Number three – on no account make any promises of betrothal.'

'So that was the reason for your little warning before we arrived?' breathed Alex. 'All that about being nice to her and making her feel one of us.'

'Well, someone had to make the effort, didn't they?' said Stephen. 'Poor girl, it would've been one hell of a birthday party if we'd all ignored her. And I didn't do it just because I was told to – I really like Erin. My only fear is that I may have overdone things. I should hate her to be fond of me and have to be told there's no hope whatsoever of our getting together. Damn shame, isn't it? She's such a beautiful girl. I could very easily have become attached to her. And her parents are jolly decent, too. It's all so damned hypocritical of Father; I wonder he can face Mrs Feeney thinking as he does of her husband.' He dropped his cigar butt and ground it with his heel. 'It's getting pretty cool out here, Alex old chap – d'you think we'd better go back in? I wonder where Erin's got to. She went off to find some more punch and to fetch her harp, been an awful long time. Come on, we don't want to miss the recital.'

Erin, physically sick with the shame of it, pressed herself into the shadow of the hedge as they came around it and crossed the terrace. She watched them enter, but did not

225

move herself. *Oh, Mam how could you?* She bit her lip hard to stop the tears, then slowly traced Stephen and Alex's steps, still clutching the cups of punch. When the light from the interior hit her she stopped and watched them all laughing amongst themselves. Oh Blessed Virgin! They must all know in there. If Stephen was aware of it then they all were. Erin, it seemed, was the only one who hadn't known that her mother had arranged this party to find her a husband. But the people in there wouldn't believe that – they would think that Erin was part of the conspiracy. Oh, how humiliating! And she had to go in there and face them. No, she didn't, she could slip away now – no one knew where she was. Let Mam sort out the mess that she had created. She hurriedly turned to face the garden.

'Erin! I've been searching all over for you.' Stephen caught sight of her and came to relieve her of one of the glasses. 'Oh look, your hand is bleeding! Where on earth have you been hiding yourself?' He pulled out a handkerchief and tried to dab at the wounded finger with one hand, balancing the punch in his other.

'I've been out here ... by the laurel bush,' said Erin, levelling her eyes to his.

There was the slightest check in his movements, but he continued to wrap the handkerchief around her bleeding finger. This done, he swapped his cup of punch into his right hand and put it to his lips. 'Mm, delicious! You should be more careful; we can't have you going wounded when you promised to give us a recital.' But she could tell by the way his eyes refused to meet hers again that he knew she had overheard.

Erin, in spite of her misery and the cut finger, kept her promise and brought the harp in to a spatter of polite applause. As Patrick had said, her music had the power to reduce people to tears, but in his fatherly pride he had forgotten that the Celtic souls who comprised her normal audience were tonight replaced by less emotional ones. When the music died away the only tears in the room belonged to Erin – and she alone knew that the haunting lament had nothing to do with them.

When Patrick softly enquired why his daughter's spirits were so low after such a good party, Erin did not immediately give the whole reason, knowing it would cut him as deeply as it had her. What made it worse was that Stephen's had not been the usual form of bigotry to which they were subjected. He had simply been nice because he felt sorry for the Feeneys, which in its way was as gross an insult as his elders' insularity.

But instead of burdening Patrick with this, she rounded on him. 'You want to know the reason I'm fed up? I'll tell ye; 'tis all this matchmaking o' Mother's – don't make out ye don't know what I'm talking about! You're in on it too, aren't ye? These "surprise" visits an' parties. I'm not daft, I can see what's going on.'

Patrick owned up to a small part in the plot. 'But I wasn't totally behind your mother's scheme.'

'No, because *you* don't want to see me married at all!'

'Of course I do!'

'Oh, so that's why ye keep sending all my admirers away, is it?' She caught his guilty look. 'Well, ye surely didn't think I was unaware of it. God! the bloody embarrassment it's caused me.'

'Hey now,' he wagged a finger, 'don't swear at your father.'

'Dammit, Father!' cried Erin, ignoring his outraged look. 'I'm not a little girl. I'm twenty-three years old, old enough to decide what is good for me an' what isn't. Ye seem to think we're still babies, all of us. Haven't I heard the way ye talk to my brothers.' – And if you could hear the things Dickie comes out with when he thinks no one's listening you'd not mistake him for any baby, she thought cynically.

'Erin, chi. . . all right! All right.' He held up his hands in despair. 'I take your point. 'Tis only a manner o' speech ye know, I can see very well you're a woman.' He wanted to go to her and fold her in his arms, but her rising temper dissuaded him. 'Erin, can't ye see we love ye an' we only want ye to be happy. That's the reason I sent those young fellas away. I didn't think they were good enough for

227

ye. That's why your mother's been arranging these little meetings, so's we could introduce ye to a more respectable class o' boy.'

The change of expression that followed that remark was ever so slight but he noticed before she turned her back. He came to stand behind her and, putting his hands on her narrow shoulders, touched his lips to her hair. 'You're not tellin' me everything are ye, darlin'? It isn't just your meddling old parents that've got ye this mad. I wasn't drunk at that party, I didn't imagine the effect young Stephen had on ye. What happened to take the smile off your face?' His voice became hard. 'He didn't . . . ?'

'No, no.' Still with her back to him she covered the large hands on her shoulders with her own dainty ones and leaned back against the comforting hardness. 'It was nothing like that. 'Tis not important any more.'

'If 'twas important enough to dim your smile 'tis important enough to share with your father. What's wrong?' She remained silent. He rotated her gently by the shoulders so that she faced him. 'What happened at that party?'

Erin lifted her eyes to that strong, honest face and after a pause asked, 'What is it about us that they find so loathsome, Daddy?'

He released his breath. 'Ah, so that's it,' then gazed down at her sorrowfully. Instead of an answer he murmured, 'God, you're so much like your mother.' A faraway look smoothed away the lines of anger. 'Your eyes especially – like two puddles out o' Lough Conn, I always used to say to her. I remember as clear as anything the day we came here, your mother an' me. She was barely sixteen and oh, so beautiful. I think 'twas herself that kept me going through the Hunger – that, an' knowing she was carrying you. If I'd known what she would've had to suffer in this Godforsaken country I'd rather have stayed to die with the rest. Ye can't begin to imagine what it was like, comin' from that wondrous land into the squalor of Walmgate. Ye can't imagine it 'cause you'd known no different; you were born among all that dirt an' disease.

228

Jaze! I often think 'tis a miracle ye survived all that ...
your poor mother didn't.' He stroked Erin's face and
stared at it, but his daughter knew it was his dead wife he
was seeing. He smiled. 'We made plans, ye know. We
were only gonna stay here as long as the famine lasted an'
then we'd go back. That's what kept her alive for so long:
knowing this degradation and all the insults that went with
it weren't going to last and one day we'd go home. Even
now, ye know, even though I've been here more'n twenty
years I still don't look upon it as home.'

'Why did ye never fulfil your plans if it was so bad?'
asked Erin, breaking his concentration.

He sighed and rubbed his bristly cheek against her
head. 'I did consider the idea when your mother passed
on, God rest her. When I recovered from the shock I
started savin' up with that aim in mind. But then o' course
I met Tommy an' the idea o' going home didn't seem so
appealing any more.'

'D'ye love Mam more than ye loved my real mother?'
asked Erin shyly.

He started. 'Now there's an odd sort o' question. Not
more, no ... in a different way, certainly. Your mother
was nothing like Tommy. She was fragile, soft an' gentle.
Where Tommy would take a shillelagh to me sometimes
if she could lay her hand to one, Mary would never've
dreamed of arguing. And she'd never see wrong in a
person, only the good things; she often got taken in. I
loved her very much, Erin.'

'So did I,' whispered his daughter, face resting on the
serge of his jacket, inhaling the impregnations of tobacco
and that special father-smell. 'I didn't ever think that I'd
come to love Thomasin ... but I do.' She raised a serious
face. 'I only wish she'd stop all this meddling in my life.
She's changed since she got the money. It's as if she wants
to run everyone's lives to fit in with hers. Don't you feel
it?'

Patrick was unwilling to voice his agreement, though he
knew Erin was right. Thomasin would never have made
mistakes like those of the past few weeks in the old days.

'She can't be blamed for what happened at the party, Erin,' he said charitably. 'She hand-picked those people in good faith. See, your mam, not being Irish, doesn't pick up the signs as quickly as we do – though I have to say that young Stephen had me fooled, too. I didn't take him for a bigot.'

'He wouldn't see himself as one either,' replied Erin. 'Nor would any of the others. But for all their affability they still look upon us as a different race, not British like them.'

'We *are* a different race,' said her father.

She chanced a risky question. 'Did ye ever wish ye weren't, Father? I mean, doesn't all this ever make ye more determined to go back where ye belong? Don't ye ever wonder what sort o' life ye'd've had if ye'd stayed in Ireland?'

He thought for a while, then answered, 'Life comes as God sends it to us, Erin. Oh! if ye could've seen the sufferin' that went on in those famine days ye'd not wonder why I stayed to weather all the insults. But still, I don't regret one drop o' my Irish blood.'

'Ye make me feel ashamed to have asked at all. I'm proud o' my birth too, an' I shall make sure my children are aware of their heritage. And that,' she said with a little smile, 'brings us back to my original protest. Please, *please* can't ye stop Mother's games?'

'She just wants ye to be happy,' said Patrick sadly.

'I'd be happier left alone,' replied his daughter firmly. 'I'm shy, Daddy, but if the right man comes along I won't need Mam or you to tell me, I'll know for myself.' She summoned another smile. 'Don't ye know I'm waiting for someone who's just like my dear father?'

'Ye'll definitely die a spinster then,' chuckled Patrick. 'This one's unique.'

She kissed and hugged him fondly. 'I know that Daddy, an' I love ye dearly – but the same goes for you too – stop interfering!'

He pulled away, smiling. 'All right, muirnin, ye've made

it plain how ye feel. I swear on the name of every saint
that I won't meddle any more.'

'An' ye'll speak to Mother?'

'Aye, we'll make sure she brings home no more waifs
an' strays.'

CHAPTER TWENTY

Sam Teale bellowed a hearty rendition of *Sweet Lass of
Richmond Hill* as he manoeuvred a side of beef onto his
able shoulder and transferred it from the slaughterhouse
at the rear of the butchery into the shop itself. Sam was
twenty-six years old, but appeared much younger with his
cheeky grin and spiky blond hair. There was nothing
muted about Sam's features: his cheeks were like bright
red apples and beneath the black brows that sprouted
willy-nilly as though stuck on with glue, shone candid blue
eyes. He also had healthy white teeth, due to an endless
supply of raw carrots and apples. Coming from the
countryside, such good food was easy come by.

Sam had been at Mr Simons' butchery shop in Goodramgate all his working life, first as an apprentice and now
as a qualified butcher. During this time he had learnt how
to get the minimum wastage when cutting joints, how to
talk customers into buying a piece of meat that had been
hanging there far too long, and had also learnt how to kill
swiftly and cleanly – a less pleasant task but one which
must be done and was better undertaken by someone
with consideration for the condemned beast than some
unfeeling lout.

Grunting, he backed up against the row of hooks that
gleamed from the tiled walls while Mr Simons slipped the
hook into the dissected beast's hamstring, thus relieving
the pressure and allowing Sam to bounce off for another
carcase. When each of the hooks, plus those outside, were

occupied, Sam sloughed the perspiration from his brow and stepped outside to take a breather. It was a grand morning, though chilly. He pulled a rag from his pocket and wiped the dewdrop from his nose, studying the over-hanging roofs of the medieval buildings opposite. It was a wonder, thought Sam, that they didn't fall down, the way they leaned at such a precarious angle over the footwalk. Unbelievable, really, that they were still standing at all after four or five hundred years. They must have been real builders in those days. Yet perhaps it was time they were pulled down to make way for something more modern, smarter. There was a plethora of such buildings in York and Sam considered this did nothing to enhance the mucky old place. Maybe this was unfair comment, for Sam was country down to his boots and would much rather be working on the land than in a sooty, noisy city. But his father had wanted him to have a trade and there wasn't much in that line where Sam came from – save the smithy; there was only labouring work. So, his dad had made arrangements with Mr Simons for him to come here.

Working so far from home meant that he had to lodge with Mr Simons and his good lady, and could only go home on a Sunday. But there you were, that was life, one seldom got what one wanted. One day, though, he mused, reaching under his apron to replace the rag in his pocket, one day he would have that rose-garlanded cottage filled with bonny kids and a wife who could cook like his mother. He would have some livestock too, though not to kill. No, he'd keep a cow for milk and some hens for eggs. Well now, perhaps he might have to have just one pig for meat; he was a bit partial to his pork chops was Sam. He'd grow fruit trees and his own vegetables so's he wouldn't have to rely on anyone but himself. And then ... his fanciful wanderings stopped in midstream as his haphazard gaze came to rest on a young woman who was sweeping away dead leaves and rubbish from outside the grocery store not a stone's throw away. Oh, my! what a little dream. With a smooth of his hair and a setting of his shoulders Sam made straight for her. But sadly, his intended approach came to a rude end as Mr Simons called from inside the shop, 'Away, Sam you've had long enough!'

Sam stood there for a few more seconds, hoping she'd look up and see him, but she seemed more concerned with her task. With one last hankering look he retreated into the butchery. How come he had never noticed her before? He must have something wrong with his eyesight – or else she was new to the grocery. A dazzling smile split his healthy face, drawing a questioning look from his employer, but Sam was too engrossed in his plans to notice. – Best get your best bib and tucker on tonight, Sam Teale, you're going a-courting. Hold on, was she wearing a ring? He'd go buy something at the grocery first just to make sure that the ground was uncluttered. Wouldn't do to go pestering a married woman. He'd go in his dinner hour. Roll on twelve o'clock!

Came noon and Sam whipped off his blood-soaked apron, laying it over a chopping block.

'By, you're on the dot today,' remarked his employer. Sam made no comment, other than to ask if Mrs Simons would mind if he went upstairs to wash his hands – the Simons lived over the store. 'Washing your hands at dinner-time?' said the butcher amazedly. 'There must be a skirt involved somewhere. Eh, you young lads are all the same – it must be working with all this fresh meat.' He was a good lad was Sam but he was a caution where the females were concerned. One of these days a customer would lean over the counter and bunch him one for the saucy things he said.

Sam's teeth flashed. 'Aye, a right smasher. She works at *Penny's*. I thought I'd go ask if I can walk her home this evening.'

'I wondered how long it'd be before you set your eye on her.'

'You mean you knew she was there?' chided Sam. 'An' you never told me?'

'I thought I'd try to protect her as long as I could,' replied Mr Simons, grinning. 'I might've known you'd sniff her out. Still, I have to agree with you – she is a stunner. Though I can't see her falling for your saucy chat; she seems like a very nice girl to me.'

Sam's eyebrows shot up. 'Mr Simons, are you trying to blacken my character? I'll have you know I'm a very nice boy.'

'Some say.'

Sam grinned and made for the door. 'When I come back I'll bet you a tanner I've been successful.'

'Don't waste your money lad, you're onto a loser – they close for dinner.'

Sam's smile faded but he retained a note of optimism. 'I might just catch her if I'm quick.'

'Aye, well if you miss her I don't expect you to be bringing a long face back with you this afternoon. I'm not having my customers suffering – and don't be asking if you can slip out during working hours neither, you know my ruling on that.'

'Yes, Mr Simons!' Sam rushed from the shop.

The butcher shook his head and chuckled, then drove a cleaver through the bloody joint on the block, severing bone and sinew in one clean swipe.

Eagerly Sam dashed up to the grocery, his boots skidding on the pavement. This side of the street, untouched by sun, was still moist with frost. His expectant smile evaporated – the shop was closed as Mr Simons had foretold. After staring for a few baleful seconds at the door, Sam shoved his hands into his pockets and slouched despondently round the corner to buy a pie for his dinner. How the hell was he going to meet her if her dinner-time coincided with his every day? The grocery would most likely be closed when he left work tonight as well. Disgruntled he bit into the pie, looked at it without relish, then held it out to a stray dog. He wondered again why he had never noticed her before. But one thing was certain; he was going to see her again.

The following day as Sam passed *Penny's* in his dinner-hour he glanced casually towards the sign in the door, expecting it to say Closed. He was almost past the shop before the awareness hit him that it had not said Closed – but Open. Open! He swivelled in his tracks and, without thinking what he was going to purchase, went inside.

'Yes, can I help you?' asked Thomasin.

Sam's expression of eager anticipation was replaced by one of dismay. He snapped his eyes away from her patient cordiality and rapidly flicked them over the shelves. 'Er, I'll have, er . . .' What was the matter with him? Acting like a blithering idiot. Why didn't he just ask where she was?

Thomasin spotted his preoccupation. It was as if he were searching the shop for something other than groceries. Could it be Erin? She was about to speak, then hesitated. Erin had made it palpably clear that her stepmother's interference would not be tolerated, and for the last four months Thomasin had managed to control her urges. But what a pity the girl was not present to see her pleasant-looking admirer – for Thomasin had satisfied herself that this was his status. However, she decided to mind her own business for once. 'Have you made your choice?' she asked politely.

'Er, I'll have some of that!'

Thomasin took a scoop to weigh out the tea. It was quite obvious he was only making the purchase to gather time. 'That's best quality,' she said kindly. 'Rather pricey I'm afraid. Should I weigh you two ounces of this one?' Inwardly she laughed at herself – what a saleswoman! Still, the poor lad didn't look as though he had money to waste, and if he was interested in Erin it was best if he received encouragement from the girl's mother.

'Oh, yes, that'll do fine.' Sam rippled a pile of pennies through his fingers. Should I ask where she is? Oh, hell!

Thomasin struck up a conversation while she weighed the tea, and in answer to his blurted query said that, yes, the grocery store usually did close for lunch but today she had introduced a new dinner-rota, thereby enabling the shop to remain open. Always eager to fillip sales she had questioned her lack of insight in closing the shop for the hour when most other assistants took their breaks.

235

'Does that mean that you and the other young lady take it in turns to serve on, Mrs Penny?'

Ah! So she had been right. Thomasin provided the correct surname – she really was going to have to do something about that name over the shop – then said, 'My daughter serves occasionally but mostly she's busy with the baking. She makes a cracking pie, does Erin.' She concluded her statement with a laugh. 'Oh, dear! Perhaps cracking is the wrong word.'

He smiled thoughtfully. That was probably the reason he had not seen her before, if she had been hidden away in the back.

'Yes, she'll certainly make someone a good wife,' went on Thomasin blithely. Sam loved her – that was another of his queries solved. She handed over his purchase and took the money. 'Thank you, sir. My daughter will be taking charge of the store tomorrow at lunchtime. If you should need any help with your purchases I'm sure she'll be only too pleased to assist. We do like to create a good customer relationship here, you know.'

'I can see that, Mrs Feeney,' he answered amiably, then his lips widened into the characteristic grin. 'And I dare say there will be something I need tomorrow. I work nearby and your shop is handy. I'd've paid you a visit much sooner had I realised what you had in stock.'

'Oh, then we'll look forward to seeing quite a lot of you,' smiled Thomasin, congratulating herself on her deft handling of the situation. No one could accuse her of matchmaking in this instance.

And if that wasn't an open invitation to court her daughter, thought Sam happily as he left, I don't know what is.

Next day Erin, unaware that her mother had been up to her tricks again, took control of the store while Thomasin slipped home for lunch. That was one of the beauties of living so close to the shop – one could go home to a real meal instead of relying on a snack. She seated herself behind the counter and nibbled from a handful of raisins, making mental calculations of the items which needed restocking.

As usual, business was rarely slack and within seconds of her stepmother leaving two customers entered. The first of them, a young man with spiky yellow hair, said that he was in no hurry and the lady could take her turn first. The woman nodded graciously and handed over her order to Erin. Sam shuffled his feet, sighed and Um-ed and Ah-ed, pretending to search the shelves for his requirements, all the while making surreptitious glances at Erin. It had thrown him at first, the way she had plaited all that lovely hair and reduced it to a gleaming knob on the top of her head. But her face was even more exquisite than he remembered. His spirits began to flag. She's too lovely, he thought sadly. She'll never entertain a plain old hobnail like me. Yet, he argued with himself, you must have thought you had a chance else you wouldn't't've come in here. I wish I hadn't, came the glum response. She'll not have me, not in a million years. I'll bet she's been proposed to hundreds of times and turned them all down. She can afford to be choosey, looking like that.

The woman departed and Sam was just summoning the courage to approach the counter when another customer foiled his plan. He backed away to resume his pretended search and to recoup his tactics. This was to happen so many times that Erin began to be suspicious, thinking he might be a thief. Sam too was becoming concerned. Looking at the clock beside the giant containers of treacle he found he had been there almost twenty minutes. He decided that there was only one way to achieve his objective. When the final customer had gone he stalked briskly to the door, rammed home the bolt and turned the sign to Closed. 'Now don't be alarmed, I'm not gonna hurt you,' he reassured a panic-stricken Erin who had backed up to the wall as he approached, glad that the counter was between them.

'What are you after?' she stuttered, eyeing the long, sharp knife that Thomasin used to slice the ham. Could she grab it before he reached her?

'Now don't fret thisself! I just want to talk with you for five minutes, that's all.'

'Then why did ye lock the door?' she demanded.

Her tremulous sing-song voice touched Sam's heart. She was absolutely terrified. He had better state his intentions immediately to show he meant no harm. 'I wondered, would you do me the honour of allowing me to walk you out one evening?'

'No!' cried Erin, too hastily, then, frowning, '*What?*'

'I asked if you'd honour me by walking out with me one evening?' His fingers curled up to play with the frayed cuffs of his shirt.

Her panic subsided but her defensive position did not. 'Why?'

Sam remained calm. 'Well, why not?'

''Cause I don't want to!' snapped Erin mulishly. 'Go find someone else.'

The young man was extremely hurt. She was scowling as if he were some sort of monster. Surely he wasn't that offensive? He had never had this response before. People usually took to Sam's friendly nature. He could have understood it if he'd been familiar with her, but here he was employing his best manners, and they didn't seem to be getting him anywhere. 'Tell me why you won't come out with me an' I'll leave you alone.'

Erin's face softened at his hurt expression, but her tone continued to be stubborn. 'I've told ye, 'cause I don't want to, that's why. Now please open that door. Mother'll be back soon. I shouldn't cross her if I were you.'

'That's not good enough.' Sam could be obstinate too. 'Is it because you think you're too pretty to be seen with a clod-hopper like me?'

Erin forced a high-pitched laugh. 'Don't be silly!'

'Then why?' He decreased the space between them.

'Don't come any nearer!'

'For Heaven's sake! What're you so scared about?' Sam stared at her trembling shoulders and dilated pupils.

'You force your way in here and keep me prisoner an'

238

ye ask why I'm afraid!' shrilled Erin. 'Why, you could be a thief, a murderer – anybody.'

'But I'm not anybody.' His tangled brows puckered. 'I'm Sam Teale.'

'Well, ye never said, did ye?' she accused hotly. 'Anyhow, what difference does that make? How do I know Sam Teale's not a murderer?'

'Blimey! I'm beginning to wonder why I bothered,' replied Sam shirtily.

'Then why did ye?' she retorted, regretting it instantly.

'Because I thought what a beautiful young lady you were and how much I'd like to get to know you. I never once thought I'd get a reception like this. Would you at least have the decency to tell me what it is you have against me before I go?'

'I haven't got anything against ye, I just don't know ye, that's all.'

'An' I don't know you neither – you could leap on me when me back's turned an' throttle me.' He clutched his hands to his throat and made strangulated noises, noting with satisfaction that he'd made her smile.

Erin was starting to feel foolish. She was behaving like some adolescent instead of a woman of twenty-three. No wonder Father still treated her as an infant. 'I'm sorry, ye must think me very stupid.' Her eyes were lowered to the floor.

'I don't think you're stupid at all,' he said kindly. 'If there's anyone who's stupid it's me, barging in like that an' frightening you half to death. You were right to challenge me. Why, I didn't even give you a chance to tell me your name.' Though he knew it from her mother it provided an opening in this cheerless dialogue. She blushingly told him. 'Well, Miss Feeney, would it be in your power to wipe my slate clean and let me begin afresh? Might I even be allowed to call on you some time?'

There was silence while Erin dwelled on his question. He did seem so very nice now that she had overcome her qualms. 'When?' she heard herself say.

'Sunday?' He had completely forgotten that he usually went home on his day of rest.

'I go to church on Sunday.'

'So do I, but it doesn't take all day does it?' Actually Sam didn't often go to church; he preferred a lie-in.

She hesitated a moment longer, then with a shy smile told him, 'All right.'

He was delighted. 'Where shall we meet?'

Erin pondered. 'Come to the house.' If nothing else, his visit would show Mother that she was capable of finding a man by her own efforts, and anyway, if Father thought she was meeting someone secretly he'd go mad. 'Say, three o'clock?'

He suddenly remembered. 'Could we perhaps make that four? I normally go to see my parents on Sunday. It might be a bit of a rush to get back for three.'

'I'd hate to drag you away from your family if it's the only day ye see them,' said a concerned Erin.

'Oh, no! They won't mind. Will four be all right then?'

She nodded and gave him her address.

'Till Sunday then.' He glanced at the clock. 'Oh, Lord! I'd better dash or I'll be late back for work.' He gave her a wide smile then spun round ... straight into a display of tins. The pyramid tumbled. 'Oh, blazes!' he sighed in dismay.

But Erin burst out laughing and coming round the counter told him to get back to his work, she would soon have them righted. Sam continued to fumble with the tins and she grabbed the one he was holding. 'Sam, you'll be late!' One of her fingers touched his as she grasped the tin. Even Sam was unprepared for the shock of contact. Each drew their hand away quickly, then smiled. Erin, tin in hand, watched him go. He was really very nice.

A breathless Sam arrived back at his place of work, hurriedly donning his cap and apron. His first words to his employer were about Erin. 'You know,' he mused, picking up a sharp knife, 'I'm sure I've met her somewhere before, but I can't for the life of me think where.'

'I thought she had a face one couldn't forget,' teased Mr Simons.

'Ah, she has that! No ... it's just summat about her that's familiar; but if I have met her before it must've been a long time ago. Never mind,' he slid his knife through flesh, 'it'll come to me.'

CHAPTER TWENTY-ONE

'Now I want none of your meddling, Mam,' threatened Erin when she had broken the news to her surprised parents. 'Mr Teale's just a friend, that's all. Don't go putting any great meaning on this visit.'

'Did I say a word? Did I, Father?' Thomasin spread her hands at Patrick, but her husband was thinking too deeply to lend an ear. He began to fire question after question at Erin. Who was this young rake? How old was he? What was he doing sniffing round Patrick's daughter behind a man's back?

'Well, I like that!' said Erin. 'You've certainly lost some of your understanding since last we spoke on it. And how can he be going behind your back if he's calling at the house?'

Patrick tried to subdue his parental concern. 'I just want to make sure he's right for ye, that's all.'

'Well, ye'll be able to see that when he calls.'

Thomasin asked what time he was coming.

'Four o'clock.'

'Oh well, you must invite him to stay for tea.' Before her stepdaughter could voice a warning she added, 'Don't worry I'll not stick my oar in. I won't even mention marriage. I should like to see what this young man's like, though. He must be very special – privileged even – for our Erin to invite him home.'

'He seems very pleasant and polite.' Erin was giving

nothing away – or so she thought. Her mother, though, could tell by the secret expression that these were not the only attributes he had. Erin obviously liked him a lot.

After lunch, when she and Patrick were alone, Thomasin sought to add a few well-chosen words on the subject of Sam Teale. 'Pat?' He grunted from the sofa where he usually slept off his Sunday lunch. 'Will you open your eyes? What I have to say is important and I can't go on speaking to the wall.' When he had complied she went on: 'When he comes you will be nice to him, won't you?'

'Have I said otherwise?' He closed his eyes again. 'If that's all I'll get on with me nap.'

'No, that's not all! You've been crowing a bucketful about there not being any decent young men around for Erin to wed so now you're going to meet one I hope you aren't going to be laying down the law like you're in the habit of doing.'

'I'll just want to make it clear that he'll not be takin' liberties with my daughter.'

'Happen he doesn't want to. Happen he'll have something more permanent on his mind. I won't let you spoil her chances – and while we're on about it, it's a pity your fine sentiments don't extend to your own sons. Oh, our Sonny's fine,' she said at his look of dismay, 'but I'm beginning to get a bit concerned about the other one. He's out till all hours up to Lord knows what ... Think on that while you're railing about lechers.'

He relaxed and made his position more comfortable. 'Dickie's all right. A lad's got to sow a few wild oats. He'll settle down when he's a little older.'

'That's exactly the attitude I'm referring to,' she argued. 'You've got double standards, Patrick. You say you'll not have any lad taking liberties with your daughter, but you don't condemn your own offspring for doing just that with other people's daughters.' He had the grace to look chastened. 'Aye, that's something else for you to chew on while you're doing your bombasting this afternoon.'

'Sure, I never said I wouldn't give the lad a fair hearing, did I?'

'Before throwing him out you mean? Well, Patrick Feeney, before he comes, which will be any time now, just cast your mind back eighteen years or so – if it'll extend that far – to when a young Irish widower called to pay court on somebody's daughter and found himself the target of a certain lady's prejudice. Remember what it felt like to be an interloper, to sit there while my mother turned up her nose at your ideals and looked down on you because you weren't what she had intended for her daughter.'

'That's entirely different an' you know it,' he contradicted. 'Ye'll not try to discredit me with your mother's narrow-mindedness.'

'It's not so acute, I'll grant you, but the hostility is there all the same. Think how that lad will feel knowing you don't rate him good enough for your daughter.'

'I didn't say that at all.' He swivelled his body into a sitting position.

'Then just what *are* you saying, Patrick? I don't think you even know yourself.'

He sighed heavily. 'All I'm sayin' is I want to be sure of him before I let him loose on Erin.'

'My, you make him sound like a tiger.'

'An' well he may be!' Patrick sprang up and began to pace the room. 'I ask ye, what do we know about him?'

'We know his name, we know he's keen on Erin . . .'

'An' that's about all. We don't know where he comes from, what his business is . . .'

'I do,' she replied smugly.

'He's another o' yours?' Patrick had stopped pacing.

'Not exactly.' She told him about Sam coming into her store. 'There wasn't much need for matchmaking, he was obviously interested enough as it was. He works a few doors away at Simons' butchery. I spied on him when he left . . . nice young lad . . . So you see, he's not entirely a stranger.'

'But for God's sake 'tis not much, is it? I mean, we don't know what sort o' family he comes from, what his beliefs are – I'll wager he's a Protestant not a good Catholic boy like I would've chosen for my daughter.'

Here Thomasin gave a hollow laugh. 'Oh come on, Pat, talk sense! I seem to recall it was the "good Catholic boys" you turned away from our door! An' come to that, there were a good many years when you yourself were far from being a "good Catholic boy". The very mention of church set your teeth gnashing. You didn't give a damn about the ones I invited here being Protestant, you're simply nit-picking, trying to find an excuse not to like him because you can't bear the thought that your little girl is going to leave you.'

His anger was substituted by despair. 'Can you, Tommy?' he asked pitifully.

She reached for his hand and rubbed her fingers along the calloused palm. 'Of course I'm not saying I won't miss her. But, Pat she's got her own life to lead, you have to face up to that. Nothing will alter the fact that you're her father. She won't forget it simply because she's found someone else to share her love with.' She chuckled then. 'Eh, just listen to me! Erin'd kill me if she could hear me going on as if she's getting wed tomorrow. But it's silly to get worked up over it when she herself said he was only a friend.'

'You don't believe that though, do ye, Tommy?' he asked softly.

She smiled and squeezed his hand. 'No. I watched that lad's face light up when he knew he was going to see her. I've seen that look too many times not to know it means more than friendship. I see it every time I look at thee.' He smiled then and opened his arms, folding them around her. 'You will be nice to him Pat, won't you?'

She twined her arms around those which imprisoned her. He kissed the top of her head. 'For you, I will.' Lifting one of his great hands from her waist he touched her hair. 'Why, I do believe you're going grey, Mrs Feeney.'

She laughed and leaned her chin against his chest, looking up at him with sparkling eyes. 'One more word on that score and you'll find old-age taking a grip on you.'

'Not on the Lord's day,' he reproved, then pushed her hand away. 'Away with ye, woman! Erin'll be down any moment, ye'd not have her witness her mother's brazen ways?'

'Naturally her father is blameless,' scoffed Thomasin, at which point her elder son came in. 'Oh, it must be nearly tea-time! So nice of you to drop in.'

He flashed her a smile and settled himself into a chair.

'And will you kindly take all that straw out of your hair. We have a guest coming.'

'Who?' He searched for the bits of straw.

'A young man of Erin's,' his mother told him.

'He must be hard-up.'

'And I want no clever remarks like that, thank you very much! If you spoil this for her I'll clip your earhole.'

Erin entered then, wearing a deep-blue corduroy dress trimmed with lace and mother-of-pearl buttons. No sooner had she entered than the doorbell jangled. Her hand flew to her mouth, belying all her previous protestations that he was merely a friend. 'Oh, he's here! What will I say? What'll I do?'

'Do?' laughed Thomasin, cuffing her son for his imitation of Erin's flustered behaviour. 'You do nowt, lass. Just sit there and look pretty for your beau. Come on now, relax. Listen, Amy's letting him in.'

There was the faint sound of mumbling from the hall, then Amy entered. 'There's a young fellow here askin' to see Miss Erin, sir. I told him to go away but he says he's expected.'

Thomasin made a face of exasperation for her husband, then instructed the maid to show the visitor in. 'I'm sorry for your reception, Mr Teale,' she told Sam when he entered looking bemused. 'The maid must've been a little mixed up. Do come and sit by the fire, you look positively nithered, lad. Oh, you'd better meet the rest of the family. As you'll have gathered I'm Erin's mother,' she hoped he wouldn't mention their previous meeting, 'this is Mr Feeney, her father, her brother Dickie . . .' Sam shook hands with both men. 'My other son is away at college,' Thomasin explained.

'Sit down now, young fella,' grunted Patrick and reached for a pipe from the rack on the mantel. He proffered a bowl of tobacco to Sam. 'Would ye care for a pipeful, son?' Erin smiled at her father and relaxed a little.

'Thank you, sir, I don't,' said Sam, his cheeks glowing even redder than normal from the cold. He held his hands gratefully to the fire and gave an admiring smile to Erin who smiled back then lowered her eyes.

Thomasin made a prompting motion with her mouth and her daughter stuttered, 'My mother'd like you to stay to tea, Mr Teale – if ye'd honour us.'

'I'd be delighted. Thank you very much. I must say you're lookin' very pretty today, Miss Feeney – not that you don't always.'

'Have ye known my daughter long, young fella?' asked Patrick.

'No, sir. Unfortunately we only met the other day. But with your permission I'd like to get to know her better.' Again a smile was exchanged with Erin.

'Well, we'll have to get to know you a wee bit better, Mr Teale before we can grant our permission.' A spark of something like jealousy had occurred at the shared smile. Thomasin was right. It was serious. 'Anyway . . . will ye take a glass of sherry before we eat?' It was said as Patrick applied a flame to his pipe. 'Or, if your tastes are similar to mine, would ye prefer whiskey?' He motioned his son to fetch the decanter and glasses.

Sam looked awkward at having to refuse Patrick's second offering of hospitality. 'Well . . .'

'I suppose ye don't drink either,' said Patrick almost accusingly.

'As a matter of fact I don't, sir,' answered an embarrassed Sam. 'At least not spirits.' He stole another glimpse at Erin and flashed her an apologetic smile which she returned, making her father even more testy.

Dickie shook his head at all the coy actions and poured himself and his father a drink. Patrick flicked the taper against the fire wall, dousing the flame. 'Ye don't drink an' ye don't smoke,' he laid the taper on the mantel, 'so your vices must lay in other directions, Mr Teale.'

'Patrick!' admonished his wife. 'How can you be so rude? You make it sound like a sin to be clean-living.' She gave her support to the young man. 'I don't blame you, Mr Teale. Sometimes I think this house smells like a taproom.'

Sam smiled. He had liked Thomasin straight away. 'That's what my mother always says, Mrs Feeney. "I'm not havin' my house smelling like a tavern," she'll say. "If you want to take up the Devil's habits then you can do them elsewhere . . . " ' he finished lamely on encountering Patrick's scowl.

'She sounds a sensible woman, your mother, Mr Teale,' nodded Thomasin. 'I wish that sense would be more evident elsewhere.' A scathing look for her husband.

'Please Mrs Feeney – call me Samuel,' requested the young man. Thomasin inclined her head.

'I can't abide bossy women meself,' muttered Patrick, with a meaningful glare at his wife. He clamped his teeth around the pipestem, took the drink from Dickie and looked at Sam whose nose had started to run with the warmth of the fire and who kept sniffing noisily. 'Haven't you got a handkerchief, young fella?'

Oh, Father, Father! raged Erin. You promised!

Sam reddened and fumbled in his pocket. 'Sorry, sir. I've got a bit of a chill.' He withdrew his best spotted handkerchief and trumpeted into it.

'Seems to me ye'd've been better off stoppin' at home instead o' coming here an' sprayin' us with the stuff.' Patrick was sorry as soon as he had said it for the look on Sam's face was one of near-pain. He didn't know what had got into himself.

'Father!' Erin finally put words to her outrage, along with her mother's cry of admonishment. 'There was no call for such rudeness.'

'It doesn't matter, Miss Feeney,' Sam rose stiffly and

shoved his handkerchief away. 'I understand the reason for it; your father just doesn't like me.'

'I never said that,' replied Patrick uncomfortably, pretending that his pipe had gone out and bending to light another taper. What on earth had possessed him to say such a rotten thing? The lad was pleasant enough.

'You didn't need to. I could see from the way you looked at me the minute I set foot in here. You think I'm not good enough for your daughter.'

There! thought Thomasin angrily, I knew this would happen.

'Think if you keep insulting me I'll up and leave,' went on Sam, 'never bother you again. Well, you might be right about me not being good enough for your daughter, but you're completely wrong if you imagine that insults will get rid of me, for the more I see of Erin the more I'm determined to see of her and I refuse to be deterred by your animosity. Oh, no! I shall see her whether you approve or not – she's quite mature enough to make up her own mind. And while you're busy despisin' me an' thinking I'm abnormal 'cause I don't conform to your standards, here's something else to think about: I'm a bloody Catholic an' all! There, you can stick that in yer pipe with yer smelly old baccy.' He stood as if to leave. Erin, panic-stricken, rose too. But before Sam could show if he really meant to leave, a sound made all of them revolve in wonder.

It started as a low rumble and grew into a boom that almost rattled the china in the cabinet. Patrick, his eyes crinkled in mirth, was showing his teeth for the first time since Sam had entered.

'I'm glad you find somethin' to your likin', sir,' said Sam tartly. 'Even if it is my discomfort.'

'Ah, I'm sorry, me boyo!' chuckled Patrick, the tears trickling from the outer corners of his eyes. He threw the pipe carelessly onto the mantel, speckling the marble with burnt tobacco. 'I wasn't laughin' at your distress, or your show of spirit. Indeed I found the latter most heartwarming . . . 'twas just the bit about your faith that tickled me.'

'If you're goin' to make Papist jokes, then . . .'

'Sit down, boy! God, the man's got a quicker temper than me own. I know all there is to know about Papist jokes, Samuel – haven't I borne the brunt of them since I came to this country twenty odd years ago.'

'You're a Catholic yourself?' Sam's bushy eyebrows rose.

'And proud of it.'

Sam grinned embarrassedly. How could he have failed to notice the religious paintings and the plaster Madonna on the mantelshelf? Maybe because he only had eyes for Erin. 'You must think me a right numskull. Even armed with the knowledge that you're Irish I never stopped to consider that you might be Catholic too.' He thought to add that religion wasn't all that important to him, but as it obviously was to the Irishman he kept his mouth shut.

'The same could be said o' my attitude, son. Tell me, how come an English fella has the faith?'

'Well, there are one or two of us about, Mr Feeney,' said Sam amusedly. The Irishman's animosity seemed to have gone.

Patrick nodded thoughtfully. 'I suppose there must be, the same as not all Irishmen are Catholic – one just never thinks about it. Well now, isn't that a right piece o' luck for you?'

'In what respect, sir?'

'Why, in the respect that seeing as how you're a good Catholic boy,' here he gave a sly wink at his wife, 'I'm going to grant my permission for you to call on my daughter – provided that's what she wants.' He leaned towards Sam who appeared dumbstruck. 'Have ye lost your tongue? Isn't that what ye were after?'

'Oh aye, indeed!' Sam was overjoyed and pumped Patrick's hand vigorously.

'Er, there's just one thing we ought to get out o' the way,' said Patrick. 'I'd like to know here and now whether your intentions towards my daughter are wholly honourable?' Erin closed her eyes, as did Thomasin.

'Of course they are!' Sam looked injured. 'An' I don't mind sayin' I find it most offensive that you thought otherwise.'

'Ah well, then I apologise.' Patrick's features evened out into sincerity. 'But ye appreciate I had to know. Now sit yourself down. I promise I won't force any more o' me smelly old baccy on ye. Tommy, ring for that woman to bring the tea. I'm sure Mr Teale – Samuel – must be thirsty after his fiery speech.'

'Thank God,' muttered Dickie. 'I'm bloody starvin'.'

'You see what sort of household you'll be coming into, Samuel?' Thomasin gestured at her son. Sam grinned at Erin's good-looking brother, who made a face as if to say, 'Women!'

After they had taken tea and Dickie had sloped off elsewhere, Patrick at his wife's whispered suggestion, allowed the two young people to retire to the front parlour. 'But no funny business, mind. There's a brick wall separating us but any whiff o' foulplay an' I'll smell it.'

Thomasin laughed at him when the young couple had gone. 'You don't believe in diplomacy, do you, Pat?'

''Tis best he knows where he stands.'

'Well, I don't think he's in any doubt as to that. God, I thought we were in for a right time of it when you started on him. You really were rude, you know. Oh, don't worry,' she smiled at him, 'I understood why. He couldn't keep his eyes off her could he? So ... what do you think to him then? Now that you've asked all your questions.' Teatime had been abundant with the latter.

'Oh, he seems a nice enough young fella.' Patrick meant it.

'Nice enough to be your son-in-law?'

'We'd best leave that for Erin to decide.'

She smiled. 'Oh, I think our Erin has already decided.'

'Your father's a very strict man,' observed Sam now they were alone.

'He's very fond of me,' defended Erin. Though he wasn't really worthy of her defence after all the rude things he had said to Sam. Never mind, she could tell the rivalry was over now.

'Oh, I can see that,' responded Sam hastily. 'An' if you don't think it impertinent I can see why. It's very easy to be fond of you, Erin.'

He was looking deep into her face. The strange feeling that she had from time to time came over her now. She rose quickly from the sofa. 'Would ye like to join me in a game o' cards, Mr Teale?'

'Samuel,' he reminded her. 'An' what I'd really like to do Erin, is to sit here an' talk to you – all night if you'll allow it. I want to know everything about you.'

She risked a bold smile at his earnest face and sat beside him once again, not moving when he shuffled closer. 'I wish I could say the same about you but I think Father put paid to all that over tea. I'm sorry about all the questions. He does get a bit fatherish now and again. Well . . . what would you like to know first?'

'Is there anyone else? A man I mean? Anyone important?'

She shook her head.

'I find that surprising.'

'Do you – with Father?'

He laughed. 'Eh, I must be privileged then.'

'You don't know how much.'

'Have you ever loved anybody?' It came out of the blue.

'I'm not sure . . . I've sometimes thought I did, but . . .' an embarrassed shrug. Then she asked, 'Have you?'

'No . . . not till now anyroad.' He put his arm around her. She allowed it to lie. He sensed she was a bit nervous. 'Your dad won't mind, will he?'

She shook her head.

'Do you like working at the store?' he asked for want of something better.

'I'm not on the counter so often,' she answered. 'I'm through the back baking the pies – I like doing that.'

'Yes, your mother told me you bake an exceptional pie.'

'When did she tell you that?' Erin had not heard this mentioned throughout tea.

'The other day when I called in your shop.'

Erin's heart sank and she gave a loud sigh.

'What's up?' he asked puzzledly.

'You're another one of hers, aren't ye?'

'Sorry, I don't . . .'

'Did Mother ask you to call on me?'

'No, you did.'

'I mean before that! Did she arrange for you to call in the shop when I was on my own?'

'I'm sorry.' He took his arm away as it was apparently unwelcome at the moment. 'I don't understand what you mean.' This family really confused him. One minute they were nice as pie the next they were laying into you.

'Did you or did ye not arrange all this with Mother?'

'I didn't arrange anything except wi' you! The only time I've met her before is when I went into the store in the hope of seeing you. You weren't there so I came back another time: that day when I locked you in . . .'

'Oh, God I'm sorry . . . ye must think . . . 'tis just that Mother has this terrible habit of trying to pair me off with every man she meets. I thought when ye said . . . that she might . . .'

'I wouldn't've thought you'd've had any trouble in that direction,' said Sam. 'Can I put me arm back now?'

She smiled gratefully. 'I am sorry.'

'S'all right.' He grinned. 'Eh, won't it be nice us working close to each other? We'll be able to see each other more often.' After a period of nods and smiles he continued, 'You're not at all like your mother, are yer?'

She explained that Thomasin was her stepmother, that her own mother had died from cholera when Erin was two years old. 'But I still remember how kind an' beautiful she was, how she used to encourage me in my attempts to play the little harp over there.' She nodded to the handsome instrument with its intricate carvings and expert marquetry which stood in a prominent position in the room, as though placed there as a constant reminder of the family's Irish ancestry.

'I noticed that the minute I came in.' Sam pulled himself from her side to examine the harp more closely. 'It were a real craftsman what turned his hand to that.' He trailed capable fingers over the bowed forepillar, then made a small sound of dismay as he came across the terrible scars.

'Those were made by a very wicked person,' said Erin quietly, seeing Helena Cummings once again fall to her death. 'A long time ago. Some day I might tell you about it, but not tonight.' Not tonight when she was so very happy.

'I don't know as I want to hear of anyone being wicked to you, Erin.' He returned to the sofa and scooped up her hand. 'An' one thing's certain: now that I'm here no one is ever gonna hurt you again.'

CHAPTER TWENTY-TWO

Erin's body was outside the grocery store, sweeping away the weekend's debris, but her mind was engaged in matters far less mundane. The afternoon with Sam, though it had overspilled well into the evening, had been far too short and the hours between then and seeing him again seemed endless. However, Sam had been granted Patrick's permission to call on her again tonight. Hopefully there would be the usual stream of customers to occupy her and to shorten the day.

'Good morning!' she shouted to a passing knife-grinder as he trundled past. 'Isn't it a lovely day?'

The man lifted a quizzical eye to the overladen sky, through which only Erin could see the sunshine, then returned the pretty girl's smile. It seemed to Erin that everyone was smiling this morning. There were no nasty people in the world, just happy, loving ones. Dear, dear Sam.

She turned as a tapping drew her attention to the grocery window. Thomasin was making stabbing gestures at Erin's half-hearted attempts at sweeping the pavement. 'Come on, lovestruck!' she mouthed. 'I'm run off my feet in here.'

Sam Teale emerged from the butchery and stepped back to the edge of the pavement to scrutinise his expert display. His timely action meant that he just caught sight of Erin as she was about to retreat to the grocery. He shouted her name. She spun round joyfully as he pounded towards her.

'I'd best not stay too long,' he panted, reaching for her hand. 'Mr Simons'll talk about docking my wages if I stand here chatting. He likes his pound of flesh . . . oh!' He bent over and smacked his knee. 'That's a good one, that is. Him being a butcher, see?' he explained to Erin. But his voice petered out as he caught her expression. 'What's the matter? You aren't ill are you?' He sandwiched her hand between his bloody mitts and rubbed it briskly. 'You're frozen, lass. And here's me keeping you talking in this weather. But oh, Erin I just couldn't wait for tonight. Erin? Erin!'

She had snatched her hand from his and was now rubbing it frenziedly against her apron as if it were contaminated. Her chest was rising and falling rapidly. She seemed anchored to the footwalk by some unspeakable fear. But it was her face that disturbed him most – full of horror. The blue eyes were wider than they had been even when he had locked her in the store that day. She seemed unable to tear them from the blood-stained apron that he had seen no reason to change.

Erin's heart felt like a trapped sparrow trying to free itself from her ribcage, fluttering pathetically against her breastbone. She felt a strange, creeping tingle at her hair roots, and a prickling of her body. Her hand still rubbed itself involuntarily on her thigh, trying to rid itself of that clammy stickiness where his hands had fouled her. Those butcher's hands with their red-tinged cuticles and the small pieces of animal flesh beneath the nails. The blood on his apron. His face, last night so dear, now revolted her, with its pimples and splashes of blood. Always blood.

'Erin, dearest, tell me what I've done!' begged poor Sam, and reached out. Reached for her with those ghastly hands, to claw at her clothes, *to hurt her*.

And she screamed . . . and screamed . . . and screamed.

Then Sam remembered where he had seen her before. How a twelve year old child had stood almost on this very spot and looked at him as if he were the Devil incarnate and had screamed – like she was screaming now – and wouldn't stop. And people had looked – as they were looking now – pointing and accusing. And he didn't know how to cope with it. He just stood there, staring into that gaping hole in her face which emitted such a terrible, noisy fear.

Thomasin rushed out into the street, gauged Erin's hysteria and dealt her a sharp slap that cut off the scream abruptly. She clutched the now-sobbing girl to her bosom and addressed Sam over the racking shoulder. 'You'd best go back to your work, lad.'

'But, Mrs Feeney!' Sam grabbed Thomasin's arm. 'I didn't do anything. I swear by all that's holy. She just looked at me and started screaming.'

Thomasin's recriminative eye swept over him. 'You must have done something, Samuel. People don't go around screaming for nothing.'

'You've got to listen!' He wanted to tell her about the chance meeting all those years ago. 'She's done this before.'

But Thomasin steered a dough-faced Erin in the direction of the grocery where people craned their necks to see what all the commotion was for. 'I can't stand here listening to explanations, I have to tend to Erin.'

'May I still call tonight?' cried Sam anxiously.

'I don't think that's such a good idea,' said Thomasin over her shoulder.

'But please, I . . .'

'No, Sam!' she cut him dead. 'You've obviously upset her, whether intentionally or not. She isn't likely to want to see you for a long time – if ever.'

Sam was devastated. He watched Thomasin, her auburn head resting against Erin's raven-haired one, shepherd the girl into the shop and close the door on him. What would Mr Feeney's reaction be when they told him? That was obvious. He stood there for a while longer until Mr Simons shouted for assistance. Suddenly, everything was grey.

Sam did keep his appointment, however. Despite the fact that he was going to get his head chewed off he had to see her, to find out what he'd done wrong. He could not settle all day, earning a dozen rebukes from his employer for the laxity of his work. By evening his stomach was turned inside out with what was going to happen to him – and more importantly, to him and Erin.

Patrick had himself not been home long from work when Sam's knock came. Still in his working clothes, his face peppered with soil, he looked a formidable sight to Sam as the nervous young man was shown into the Feeneys' drawing room. He had the feeling the Irishman was about to reach for him, when he was saved by Thomasin's entry.

'Mr Teale, we weren't expecting you,' she said coolly.

'I oughtta belt you!' Patrick finally spluttered. 'What happened to those honourable intentions?'

'Mr Feeney, Mrs Feeney, please let me explain! I had to come, I couldn't let you go on thinkin' it was summat I'd done that made Erin scream.'

'So she was screaming for the fun of it, was she?' asked Patrick.

'Honest, Mr Feeney!' pleaded Sam desperately. 'We were just talkin' – least I was, natterin' away thirteen to t'dozen an' all of a sudden Erin let out this big scream. I swear I never said nor did anythin' which might upset her. I . . .' The door had opened and a waxen-faced Erin stood there. His face softened in concern. 'Erin . . .'

Thomasin took control. 'You weren't supposed to be

256

up, young lady.' At lunchtime she had closed the store in order to bring Erin home and put her to bed with a sleeping draught to calm her down. She had been absolutely hysterical, but she couldn't or wouldn't say what had happened, just kept saying, 'It's my fault . . . so silly,' over and over again. And when her mother had told her it was all right, that Sam wouldn't be allowed to bother her again she'd got herself into another state.

'I heard the door go,' murmured Erin. 'I hoped it might be Sam.' This morning was still hazy. She couldn't really remember what had happened, only that she'd stood there in the middle of the street screaming, but she didn't know why. All she could remember was blood . . . She shivered. But there was no blood now. Here was Sam with a look of concern on his dear face. 'I wanted to say I was sorry.'

'*You* were sorry?' said Patrick as Sam let out a sigh of relief. At least they knew it wasn't his fault now.

'I'm so embarrassed, Sam.' She found it hard to look at him. 'I don't know what came over me. Will ye forgive me?'

'Oh, Erin!' he laughed his relief, then nodded. 'Aye, 'course I do. It's just that I couldn't understand what I'd done . . . I mean, this is the second time, isn't it?' At her frown he said, ''Course you wouldn't remember, it was a long time ago, you were only a little girl . . . all I said was hello an' you burst out screamin'. . . frightened me to death.' He laughed. Erin, too, smiled, though she said she could not remember. 'Well, I couldn't expect you to remember me, but I remember you 'cause you were so pretty.'

'So, he never made indecent approaches?' said Patrick dubiously.

'Oh, Father of course he didn't,' replied Erin, still feeling muzzy from the sleeping draught. 'I've told Mother it was all my fault.'

'Ye'd better sit down,' advised her father. 'You too, young fella.' He made a face at Thomasin to show his incomprehension of the situation. She shrugged.

They all sat, but nothing much was said, Patrick still

257

annoyed at what he considered to be Sam's fault. Eventually Thomasin said, 'Well . . . we usually eat at this time, Samuel.' It had been prearranged to Sam to call after dinner, but naturally he hadn't been able to wait that long.

He stood. 'Oh, I'm sorry. I didn't give it a thought, I was so eager to . . .'

'Could Sam stay for dinner?' interrupted Erin.

Patrick, tight-lipped, exchanged looks with his wife.

'If you want him to,' replied Thomasin.

'I do,' said Erin. ''Tis the least I can do to make amends for causing him such worry.'

After dinner – though Patrick was again none too keen – Thomasin told the couple to retire to the front parlour. 'Well, they clearly found it a bit difficult speaking in front of us,' she told Patrick when they'd gone. 'And it gives us a chance to discuss things too. Dickie, are you going out?'

'I was thinking of having an evening in,' he smiled perversely.

'Well – have it in your own room,' she parried, and waited till he had slouched from the room before continuing. 'Right, Patrick. Let's decide.'

'Decide whether Teale is a lecher or our daughter is a looney,' he muttered, pouring a drink. 'God! I don't know what to make o' the whole matter. Tell me again what happened.' It was hard to digest when he had only learnt of it an hour or so ago.

She repeated the scene as she had witnessed it. 'Erin was just stood there screaming at him. That's all there was to it. Mindst, I reckon anyone would've screamed, he did look a sight. He must've crawled inside a carcase the amount of blood that was on him; it was all down his pinny, his hair was gummed up . . .'

He nodded thoughtfully, took a sip of his drink and then said in cautious tone, 'I think I may have an idea.' He waited to see if his words had provoked the same conclusion. When she frowned he had to explain.

'It can't be that!' she scoffed. 'It was years ago, she'd never remember that far back.'

258

'Tis the only explanation I can give: Jos Leach was a butcher, Sam is a butcher.'

'But she knew that yesterday! She didn't carry on like this.'

'No ... but he wasn't covered in blood then, just as he isn't covered in blood now – she didn't scream at him tonight, did she? Can you supply another answer for her behaviour other than that?'

She admitted she couldn't. But to suggest that a person could remember an incident that happened when that person was six years old and that it could have such a drastic effect at this stage in her life seemed plain silly. Especially since neither Erin nor her parents had ever discussed the horrifying incident since the day it had happened. Erin had surely forgotten it. 'No, I think it's more likely to be just the sight of the blood. I mean, she's always been a bit squeamish and there are lots of folk who can't stand the sight of blood. Our Erin must be just one of them. Eh, I do feel sorry for the way I snapped at that poor lad.'

'Me too,' he surprised himself with his alliance. 'He's really fond of her, isn't he?'

She nodded and smiled. 'It'd be awful if something so silly as a drop o' blood came between them. D'you think you'd better have a word with Sam about looking presentable before he sees her?'

He agreed, then looked at the clock. 'I'll tell him now before he goes. 'Tis getting late. We don't want to leave them in there too long on their own.'

Thomasin fetched the young couple back to the drawing room, then made a pretext of wanting Erin to help with a chore so that Patrick could give Sam the verdict.

'Don't look so worried, son.' Patrick motioned him to a seat. 'I just wanted Erin out o' the way in case the explanation I'm gonna give ye embarrasses her further. Has she mentioned any explanation herself?'

Sam said not. 'I thought it best to steer clear of that subject.'

'Well, Sam, we think we know why she screamed at ye

259

like that; 'twas the sight of all the blood on your clothes. She's always been a sensitive creature and . . .'

'Oh, blazes!' Sam threw up his hands. 'So it *was* my fault. Oh . . . I could kill meself.'

'No, don't do that, son or there'll be a bit more blood about, an' Erin wouldn't be too happy neither.' Patrick actually smiled at him – something he had certainly not envisaged doing at the start of the evening. But Sam had such a likeable personality. 'Just clean yourself up a bit before ye pay your visits – like you've done tonight – an' I think things'll be a lot smoother.'

'Oh, I will! How bloody insensitive of me never to give it a thought.'

'Well, you weren't to know.'

'No, but it wasn't very good manners anyway, was it? Presenting meself like that. Oh well,' he cheered, 'now that I know that's all that ails her I'll keep out of her way while we're at work an' make sure I'm well-scrubbed before I call on her. . . that's if you'll still give your consent?'

Patrick looked deep into the apprehensive face, then smiled and nodded his affirmation. 'I think you're goin' to be good for my daughter, Sam – but just watch your step, young fella else 'twill be a bit more than cow's blood getting spilt.' They both laughed.

CHAPTER TWENTY-THREE

Sam Teale became a regular caller at the Feeney house, always being absolutely scrupulous in his efforts to remove the last traces of his profession from his skin and clothes. He had never felt for anyone the way he did about Erin.

Having survived the embarrassment of that reunion, Erin felt the same way, and was now envisaging plans of a spring wedding. There had been no recurrence of that 'funny feeling', apart from once or twice when Sam had kissed her and she had found it hard to breathe – but then that was probably how one felt, being in love.

Christmas came and went and the new decade added a one to its number. Outside, there were two inches of snow on the pavement but the room where the family was assembled round the dinner table was a-glow. A great log fire sizzled and whined in the grate, with the hot resin hissing and bubbling onto the firedogs. Aloft, the picture-rails were still draped with ivy, laurel, myrtle and holly laden with plump red berries, an ill-omen, Thomasin had said, for any hope of a short winter. The gaslamps' yellow flicker made everything seem cosy and safe on this winter's eve. The meal was over and the table abuzz with conversation as Amy entered to clear the plates. Thomasin suggested they retire from the table to give the maid room to move.

'Have you been treating yourself to a new gown, Mother?' asked Sonny as he pulled out her chair.

Thomasin preened swankily in the pale-green dress. It was high-necked with a ruffle of lace at the throat, a tight-fitting bodice and the ubiquitous bustle. 'I'm glad somebody noticed.'

Patrick moved his head aside as she slipped from the dining chair and squeezed past him. 'How could a man not help noticing with that bumroll almost knocking his head off?'

'I can't ever foresee us making a gentleman out of your father,' replied Thomasin, choosing the armchair nearest the fire and placing a fire-screen before her face to shield her complexion. She toasted her hands. 'We'll take coffee in here, Amy; it's a better fire.'

'All right, ma'am,' said the maid uninterestedly.

Thomasin gave a heartfelt sigh. She had really persevered with this girl but still could not summon up one ounce of liking for Amy. There was no longer the need to remind the maid to address her correctly; however, Amy always succeeded in making the word ma'am sound like a much less savoury name. It incensed Thomasin.

What cause had she ever given Amy to despise her? It was only because of Patrick that she kept the girl on. The poor soul would never get a job anywhere else if they dismissed her, he had said – she was such a terrible cook.

'Oh, so I have to put up with her?' his exasperated wife had replied, after yet another meal had been ruined. Even so, Amy did stay, if only because Thomasin was always too busy in the grocery to get around to replacing her.

Now the maid piled the plates one on top of the other, making a surplus din with the cutlery. Still as crude as ever, she was thinking. Whoever heard a gent talking about bumrolls? But like Her Highness said, he'd never make a gentleman – and neither would she make a lady.

A loud burst of laughter as Patrick treated them to a joke made Amy's blood bubble. There they all were, sitting on their arses, watching her do all the work. It made her sick. She clattered the plates onto her tray, clashing and banging.

'Oh, Amy! Please be more careful!' cried Thomasin as the maid mishandled a tureen of leftover potatoes and succeeded in upturning it on the carpet.

'I couldn't help it,' snarled Amy cheekily, and crouched down to scrape the spilt food back into the dish. 'I'm tryin' to rush so's I could get your coffee an' not keep yer waitin'.'

'There's no need to rush,' replied Thomasin, more calmly than she felt, watching her beloved Staffordshire being filled with fluff-topped potatoes. 'No one's at your back with a whip.'

'I should hope not after I've slaved all day over you bloody lot. You seem to think I'm some sort o' machine what keeps going all day long.' The complaints were made under her breath but intended for Thomasin to hear. 'It's too bad.'

Thomasin lost her temper. 'You are quite correct, Amy, it is too bad – though it is the meal to which I refer. In fact the floor was probably the most suitable place for it, because we certainly found it much too difficult to swallow.'

262

Amy turned on her defiantly. 'If yer don't like it then yer know what yer can do!'

Patrick rose angrily from his seat. 'Amy! You'll keep a civil tongue in your head when speaking to my wife. I should inform ye that your mistress has been very patient in putting up with all your faults – and you must admit that ye've more than your fair share o' those. If you're to stay in my house then ye'll have to smarten your ideas up an' put a lot more effort into your work.' His eyebrows came together to make one black line over humourless eyes, a play of feature which warned Amy that she would get away with no more cheek. She curtsied and mumbled something which had to pass for an apology then, balancing the pots on a tray, returned to the kitchen. I'm not going to stick this much longer, she promised herself grimly. I've had it up to my stocking tops with the sanctimonious, lazy cow. She released her hold on the tray an inch or two from the table; several items rolled off and crashed to the floor. Her an' her bloody fancy dinner-set! She kicked the pieces petulantly. That's her idea, the old witch; she thinks if she works me hard enough and tosses enough insults around that I'll up and leave. Well, there's too much to keep me here yet. I'll go when I'm good and ready, and when I *do* go I'll enjoy rubbing her nose in it, by God I will.

The question of Amy's future was also being aired in the dining room.

'Well, I agree with Mam,' Erin said to her father. 'We should get rid of her and find someone else. She doesn't seem to know her place. I mean, I'm not a snob or anything, but when I worked at the Cumm . . .' She could have bitten her tongue for raising that subject, well aware what hurt it would cause, but it was out now. 'When I was in service I had to call the mistress ma'am, and wouldn't've dreamed of cheeking her like Amy does Mam. What do you say, Sonny?'

Sonny, home from college, glanced up from the Christmas card he had been reading and replaced it on the mantelshelf. 'Oh, well, seeing as how I'm hardly in the house and don't have to put up with her it's not for me to say. I must confess, though, that Christmas lunch was a let-down. I'd been looking forward to it for weeks after the scanty rations we get at college.'

'It would've been a darned sight worse if we'd left her to cope on her own,' Erin confided. 'We prepared the vegetables an' Mam did the brandy butter. That's the other annoying thing; me and Mam shouldn't have to work in the kitchen when we have Amy, that's what we hired her for. I don't mind lending a hand now and then but she seems to do less and less every day. I have my baking to do, I haven't time to be running around after her. That kitchen is a disgrace as well; I don't think she ever cleans it. I wouldn't mind but Mother paid out good money to have that new gas cooker put in, so her workload isn't anywhere near what she'd have to tackle in some other place.'

'Well,' sighed Sonny, 'you appear to be pretty firm in your views. What d'you think about it all, Dick?'

'No point asking him,' said his sister dismissively. 'He couldn't give a tinker's cuss. He's never in the house to notice.'

Dickie grinned and decided to return his sister's disdain. 'Will darlin' Samuel be payin' a visit this evening?'

Erin donned a panoply of indifference. 'I should imagine so,' she replied casually. 'What's it to you?'

Dickie pointed to a sprig of mistletoe which hung over the doorway. 'Well, 'tis almost Twelfth Night – ye'd best make the most out o' that while ye can. A couple o' days an' Sam'll have no reason to have to kiss ye. He'll be safe for another year.'

'Oh, you insolent creature!' Erin blushed and flew at him. He ducked away, laughing. 'It's for certain *you* don't need any kissing berry, the stories I've been hearing about yourself.' She clamped down her jaw, realising her blunder, and stole a glance to see if anyone else had noticed.

'Don't worry,' said Thomasin without looking at her. 'You've not let any cat out of the bag. I've been hearing one or two stories myself about that one.' Then turned her vexation on Patrick's complacent smile. 'And well you might laugh when you're to blame.'

'Me? Sure what have I ever done to encourage any misbehaviour?'

'You've done nothing to stop it though, have you? Allowing him to roam the streets at all hours, the dirty little tomcat.'

Dickie, unabashed, looked at his brother who diverted his face rapidly. 'I don't know who's been spreading rumours about me, but 'tis lies, all lies.'

'How d'you know when I haven't even said what I've heard?' challenged his mother.

'Ah, leave the lad alone,' said Patrick, surprising Dickie with his alliance. 'Didn't ye live next door to Miss Peabody long enough to know not to listen to gossip?'

'I'd like to write it off as gossip,' Thomasin replied. 'But somehow I tend to believe what I hear.' She tapped Erin's shoulder. 'Come on, I think we'd better go and see where that coffee's got to. She's taking an awful long time. If I stay here I might swing for somebody.'

When the women had departed Patrick poured out three small measures of whiskey. 'Despite what I said to your mother I'd not like to think ye were bringing this family into disrepute,' he told Dickie, handing out the drinks. 'I trust ye recall the few words we had on that score last year?'

'I do.' Dickie tipped the whiskey down his throat in one movement. He was damned if he was going to listen to any lectures tonight. His trip to replace the glass on top of the drinks cabinet took him to the door.

'Where are ye going?'

He turned and manufactured a smile for his father. 'I'm going out – with a young lady, if ye've no objections?'

'Isn't it a bit cold for courting?' asked Patrick, then added, 'Well, just mind ye behave yourself. Is she a decent girl then?'

'Oh, as pure as me own sister,' confirmed Dickie glibly. 'A good conscientious Catholic, and Irish to boot.'

This appeared to meet with his father's approval. Patrick nodded and smiled. 'Can we expect ye to bring her home one o' these days?'

'Not for a while I shouldn't think, she's awfully shy.' Dickie opened the door. 'Ah well, I'd best be off and get changed, I don't want to be late.'

'Wait a moment,' said Patrick amicably. 'You're giving no secrets away, are ye? Will ye not even tell me her name?'

'Ah, there's no secret in that, Dad,' said his son before the door closed. 'Her name is Lucy Fallon.'

Patrick's eyes were still glued to the door when his wife and daughter returned. He stared right through them, mouth slightly ajar.

'What's up with your dad?' Thomasin waved her hand in front of Patrick's face.

Sonny lifted his eyes from the sketchpad which held the rudiments of his father's portrait and shrugged. He put aside the pad and took the cup of coffee which Thomasin held out to him.

Thomasin had to ask Patrick three times if he wanted this coffee or not, and when he did look at her his face was considerably older than its true years. She asked if he was unwell and receiving no answer propelled him to a chair.

'It was just something Dickie said,' he eventually conveyed in a quiet voice. 'A name, just a name.'

She narrowed her eyes. 'What name?'

'Fallon.' He waited for the innocuous-sounding word to draw the same response from her as it had done from himself. 'He's going to meet someone called Lucy Fallon.'

The furrows on Thomasin's brow deepened. Here was another ghost from the past come to haunt them. Then her face relaxed. 'This is absurd! There must be other families with that name. Sonny, what do you know about this?'

'Nothing!' was his first response, but at his parents' firm prompting he put down the cup of coffee on the hearth and reluctantly divulged what his brother had told him.

Sonny was not a little annoyed about it; after poaching Annie from under his nose that time his brother had promptly dropped her – as he always did after he'd had what he was after. There had apparently been dozens of girls since Annie. Of course Dickie had wasted no time in telling his brother all about them when he came home from college. Lucy was his current attraction. When Sonny had told his parents about her he added, 'Grandma's not going to be very pleased about the relationship – Lucy's from a tinker family.' He saw the look that passed between his mother and father and was rather surprised at this show of snobbishness. It was commonplace from Hannah, and perhaps lately from his mother, but never Patrick.

'I can tell what you're thinkin', Son,' said his father quietly, 'but you're wrong.' He paused for a while, then went on, 'I don't know if this is the time to tell ye, but I've a terrible feeling that I helped to kill this girl's father.'

'If you're going to tell the story you might as well get it right,' corrected his wife, informing Sonny, 'In fact your father was the one who tried to save Fallon's life. It was your Uncle John who killed him.'

'Uncle John?' Sonny was now totally confused. He chewed the end of his pencil, waiting for a more comprehensive explanation.

'To tell it briefly,' sighed his father, 'this tinker, Fallon, was the one who maimed Uncle John before you were born. John waited years to take his revenge – it was all he lived for, I think – and when he finally got it he paid for it with his life. Both he and the tinker drowned in the River Foss. We never found the need to tell ye before, you being so fond o' the lad.'

So, that mystery was solved at last, thought Sonny. He stripped a splinter of wood from the pencil and flicked it into the fire. 'I can see your concern now.'

'So how long has it been going on?' asked Patrick.

Sonny was unsure. 'Not long, I suspect. Dickie . . .' he hesitated, feeling slightly treacherous. 'Well, he soon gets bored if he's with the same girl for too long.'

'Then let's hope an' pray he soon gets bored with this one,' said Patrick grimly.

Thankfully, when the time came for Sonny to return to college he was able to report that Lucy Fallon was no longer a danger to his parents' peace of mind. Dickie, as was his fashion, had moved on to fresh waters. It was a great weight lifted from both their minds. Thomasin had far too much to concern her at the store without having to worry about her wayward son; it was fast taking over her whole life. She threw herself wholeheartedly into her work, knowing that her industry would ensure that no member of her family would ever go hungry again.

At this very moment she was struggling with a home-cured ham, finally managing to suspend it from the hook over the counter. This was yet another commodity which Thomasin had introduced and which was moving nicely. Positioned at just the right angle over the customer's nose – 'well, perhaps just a sliver for my husband's tea' – and yet another credit to Erin's culinary expertise.

'Well, you ought to let me stay at home and cook the meals,' said Erin, when complimented. 'And let Amy serve on here.'

'What, and lose all my customers,' was Thomasin's droll reply, then she donned her hat and coat, said, 'I'll be back shortly,' and left Erin to cope alone.

Two hours later she had still not returned. Erin, puzzled by her long absence, was rather angry at her stepmother for leaving her alone like this on one of their busiest days. There were a number of large pies in the oven they had installed in the back room – so that there would be less conflict in the kitchen at home – and Erin could smell that they were on the turn, yet custom denied her the opportunity to rescue them.

Thomasin returned at last and with no word of explanation, just a secretive smirk, took off her coat and set to whittling down the long queue. 'There's something burning in there,' she told an infuriated Erin.

'Well, I know that!' shouted Erin from the other side

of the shop. 'I've been attempting to get through there for the last ten minutes. Where've you been?' She slammed the till drawer shut noisily. When Thomasin imitated the annoying habit that Patrick had of tapping his nose with a forefinger she became even more upset. 'Oh, come on, Mother! Ye can't leave me here to do all the horsework without so much as a by your leave. I demand to . . .'

'You demand?' said Thomasin gaily, with a wink at one of her regular customers. 'You demand! Eh, I don't know what children are coming to these days, do you, Mrs Falsgrave?'

'Mother!' Erin reined in her temper as another customer approached the counter. There were three more behind her and Erin impatiently took care of them all before making a trip to the oven then turning on her stepmother yet again. Thomasin pretended not to notice as she escorted the last of the customers to the door and put up the Closed sign, then she whirled around to confront her daughter.

'I can see you're going to be no fit company to work with if I don't tell you, so I'd better lock up if we're to do without these constant interruptions. Running a shop would be lovely if it wasn't for the customers.'

'Mother, I'm in no mood for jokes . . .'

'Who's joking?'

'I've ruined four good pies because of you. Now will ye please tell me – was it worth it?'

'Then take them home for tea – everybody'll naturally assume they're Amy's.' She laughed. 'All right, don't start throwing things! I shall reveal all – I've been to buy a shop.'

'But we already have a shop,' Erin pointed out.

'Well, now we've got another,' said Thomasin, as if this explained everything. 'Calm down, calm down!' She warded off another burst of inclemency. 'The shop next door is vacant – right?'

'Correct.'

'Not any more it's not. Your clever mother has just been to an auction and bought it.' She hoisted her shoulders in

269

an expression of delight. 'Eh, think of it, Erin. It's ideal. If we knock down that wall we've got a spanking new emporium. I've got all sorts lined up for us. We're not just going to be a grocery that sells the odd pie – your baking's too good for that. I'm going to put in a really big commercial oven so we can do it justice. We'll sell dozens. And I'm going to offer a service whereby people who shop with us can get their Christmas goose cooked free of charge. And I'm going to set up a Christmas club where people can save a small amount each week and by Christmas time have a nice big sum to spend on their yuletide fayre. And where d'you think they'll spend it?'

Erin's temper had long since fizzled out and she was now laughing full-bloodedly. 'I think ye'd better sit down, Mam. After doing all that thinking ye must be in need of a rest. But tell me seriously, how could ye afford the place?'

Thomasin sat down. 'When one has a friendly bank manager dear, one doesn't need money. Mr Eade is very astute. He knows that this,' she tapped her chest boastfully, 'is a person who is going to go far. These boys don't mind forking out if they think they're going to get a nice fat return. Besides, I'm not entirely without funds, you know.' At the outset Thomasin had instructed Mr Eade to invest a certain portion of her money in the manner which he thought most beneficial. She knew he had purchased some shares but was neither sufficiently versed in these matters nor interested enough to ask for details of her shareholdings. The store occupied ninety per cent of her time at the moment, too much to tax her brain with stocks and shares. Perhaps later when she had built up her business empire . . . She beat a rapid tattoo on her knees then rose from the stool. 'Still, I shall have to have some extra money to pay for the improvements. I've been giving it some thought on my way back here. Our delivery service is well-established now – I shouldn't think people will resent being asked to pay a small fee for the convenience in future.' There came a rapping on the door's glass window. 'Eh, you can't have five minutes can you?' She went to unlock the door. 'Never mind, I'll try this one out about the delivery fee.'

'Good day, Mrs Meldrum. Come to leave your next week's order, have you? I do trust that everything is to your satisfaction? No complaints?'

'Well, you nearly had one when I thought I'd come all this way to find you closed.' The woman stepped past Thomasin and up to the counter. 'But no, all in all I'd say we have an excellent arrangement. Very high quality merchandise and much better service than in the old days. And if I may say so what an extremely personable young man your son is, always ready to please.'

'As we all are, Mrs Meldrum,' said Thomasin, coming back around the counter. 'Any little item you might require we will be only too pleased to supply. I'm delighted to have your continued custom.' She ran her eyes over the woman's list when she next spoke. 'Having said that, it's rather embarrassing that I have to raise the question of money. You see with my increased expenditure I find myself forced to add a delivery charge of tuppence to your weekly order. I'm sorry to have to do this, but as I said my own outlay impels me to do so. I hope that we can still rely on your patronage?'

Mrs Meldrum pondered for a moment, then said uncertainly, 'We-ell ... eightpence does seem very stiff for a delivery charge, Mrs Feeney. But I suppose one cannot expect such a service without having to pay for it – especially one so punctual and efficient.'

'I think you misheard,' said Thomasin patiently. 'I said tuppence, not eightpence.'

'Yes, but tuppence increase makes the charge up to eightpence. You already add on sixpence, don't you?'

Thomasin was about to give a negative reply, then her adept mind summed up the situation and produced one sickening conclusion – her son was cheating her customers, and worse still he was cheating her. Covering her dismay she gave a stumbling excuse for this oversight, assuring Mrs Meldrum that there would be no increase on her bill.

It was a disgusted and furious Thomasin who left Erin to cash up the takings and wound up business an hour earlier than normal so that she might catch her son before he had the chance to disappear as was his habit on an evening. She stopped by the mews and, finding him rubbing down the horse ordered him to come home as soon as he had made Polly comfortable. Her tone implied that he was in for a roasting.

'Ah, I've a wee bit o' business to see to, Mam,' he lilted, sleeking the mare's coat with a bunch of straw.

'Like fiddling your mother out of her hard-earned money?'

He laughed a shade uneasily and kept on working, giving himself a few moments' grace in which to compose a virtuous expression. 'Sure, I'd never fiddle you, Mam.'

Her grey eyes regarded him contemptuously. 'You'd swear on the Bible would you?'

'As God's my witness,' he assured her levelly.

The anger went out of her face and she gave a humourless laugh. 'Then may that same God forgive you, Richard,' she said wanly, and turned away. Her sharpness reappeared as she reached the door. 'If you're more than fifteen minutes I'll send your father to fetch you. Oh, yes,' she wheeled back and surveyed him coldly. 'When you do come – bring your treasure trove with you.'

There was the slightest flicker in his unfathomable eyes. 'What treasure would that be?'

She continued to stare at him icily. 'You might think your mother is a halfwit because she's allowed you to pull the wool over her eyes for so long, but I can assure you, Dickie, I'm not. You've not had time to spend all the money you've stolen from my customers . . .'

There seemed little use in upholding the pretence. 'I didn't steal it! I thought it was only fair that they should pay me for my hard work. They were only too willing.'

'. . . that you stole from my customers,' she continued as if he had not interrupted. 'I know very well you must have it stashed away somewhere.' His eyes jumped involuntarily to the loose brick in the wall. 'So, that's where it is!' Her lips formed a hard line. 'That money is mine, Richard; you will bring it with you when you come home.'

'Will I?' He set his jaw refractorily.

Her eyes glinted as they held his face, but she said nothing further, merely turned and walked out.

When she arrived home it was a rather smug-looking Amy who attended her. She seemed unduly polite, though Thomasin was far too preoccupied to notice.

'There was a lady left her calling-card, ma'am.' Amy produced a silverplated tray. 'And this letter.'

Thomasin spared her a vague look, then ripped open the letter, allowing the marks of sabotage on the envelope to pass uncommented upon.

Mrs Feeney,
Your maid familiarised me with your name as I have not previously had the misfortune to make your acquaintance. However, current events have impelled me to call upon you to voice my protest. It was perhaps fortuitous that you should be out when I called as what I have to say is of a most unwelcome nature and is better dealt with in a letter. It concerns your son . . .

It would do, thought Thomasin tiredly, then read on:

. . . who on numerous occasions I have caught making advances to my daughter. On none of these instances was my permission sought, indeed had it been I would have quashed the request immediately . . .

At this juncture Patrick entered. He always came in by the kitchen entrance to avoid bringing soil into the hall, leaving his boots by the back door; in Amy's opinion another pointer to his lack of breeding. 'Hello, we're early today!'

She looked up distractedly. 'Oh, hello love. I thought you were Dickie.'

'Judging by the look on your face I'm glad I'm not.' He leaned over her shoulder. 'What's that you're reading?'

273

'It's a keep-off sign,' she replied cryptically. 'It appears our son is making unwelcome advances to one of our beloved neighbours' daughters. If we didn't know what they thought of us before, they make it crystal clear in here.'

Patrick read a few lines, then straightened, walked over to the fireplace and spat into the flames. 'Bloody snobs.'

'Well, be that as it may our son is upsetting them and they want him calling off. Otherwise,' she slowly reread the closing lines, 'they're going to call the police.'

Patrick began to rage against the pomposity of his neighbours, about their prejudice and bigotry.

'That's not all, Pat,' she said with creased forehead, during a lull in his anger. Folding the letter in half, she informed him bluntly, 'Our son is a thief.'

Patrick opened his mouth, but any enlargement his wife was going to make was halted by Dickie's appearance. He loomed, falsely cheerful, in the doorway. 'Has somebody died?' He alluded to their doleful faces.

'Your blarney won't work this time, young man.' Thomasin's palm shot out. 'Hand it over.'

'Hand what over?' He still maintained his breezy exterior.

'It's in your right-hand pocket, you're standing all lopsidedly. Now hand it over!'

Dickie dropped the façade and pulled the metal box from his pocket, placing it on her palm. It was much heavier than she had calculated it might be. 'Is it all here?' He nodded. 'I'll not ask you to swear on the Bible,' she said sarcastically. 'It'd be a bit futile, wouldn't it?' She rattled the box at Patrick. 'This is what our son's been doing over the last – how long is it, Dickie, two, three years? Stealing from his own parents. What do you make of that?'

Patrick sank into a chair, his face drained of any passion. 'What does a man say when he's told his son is a thief?' he breathed, then shook his head to rid himself of the confusion. 'Why, son? I know ye've always complained o' being short o' money, but to go behind our backs an' do a thing like this . . .' He ran a hand over his mouth and stared into the fire. Those words were the last he uttered for some time; it was Thomasin who went on to inform Dickie about the letter, and who doled out the punishment. 'First, get this straight, Dickie: under no circumstances will you pester this woman's daughter again.'

'Mam, I didn't pester her,' he complained. He made to sit next to his mother and put his arm around her but her icy look dissuaded him. All at once he seemed to have lost his wizardly powers. 'Look, the girl likes me. She wants me to call on her. Her mother is only being awkward because . . .'

'Be quiet! I have given my verdict and you'll abide by it. I hope I shan't have to reissue my warning?'

'No, Mother.' He hung his head, assuming subservience but feeling anger. Anger at his mother for laying down the law, and scorn for his father, the real reason for their neighbours' contempt. How could Dickie hope to impress anybody when his father insisted on wearing labourer's togs? Patrick's choice of apparel had helped to dub the whole family as peasants. They were never going to climb the social scale while his father clung to his origins. If a damn fool of a customer had not exposed Dickie's deception he would still have his secret kist and could have packed his bags and left them all to it. But the three bob in his pocket would not get him very far. He needed them a little while longer.

'Very well, after you've eaten you will spend the rest of the evening in your room, and also every evening for the next month.' Thomasin drifted over to the fireplace and dropped the letter into the flames. 'It seems to me you've been allowed far too much freedom and have abused it. A little self-constraint cannot but improve your character. Now, go to your room.'

'Had our legs smacked, have we?' smirked Amy as Dickie skulked morosely through the hall. He sucked in his cheeks and rolled his eyes despairingly. 'Making him stop in his room like a naughty boy,' she taunted, slouching gleefully against the door jamb where she had been listening.

'We'll see,' he muttered darkly.

But any attempt at mutiny that Dickie had been nourishing was quelled later in the evening when his grim-faced father caught him trying to sneak out through the side entrance. 'Very well, Richard,' he said stiffly, having recovered from his earlier speechlessness. 'If ye insist on behaving like a naughty schoolboy then ye'll be treated as such.' He escorted Dickie up to his room and saw him safely inside. 'Ye'll be confined to your room each evening until ye show some contrition for your disgraceful behaviour. And since ye cannot be relied upon to perform any self-discipline, then I will have to give ye a helping hand.' So saying, he locked the door.

CHAPTER TWENTY-FOUR

'Sonny! We didn't expect you till later this evening.' Thomasin tossed aside the sheaf of invoices through which she had been sifting and rose to greet her son.

'School broke up early,' he informed her as their auburn heads met. 'I've left my trunks and painting equipment in the hall. I hope no one trips over them.' Thomasin said she would send for Amy to take them upstairs. 'I'm not helpless,' he laughed. 'I can carry my own things, you know.' He began to retreat into the hall.

'Well, hold on before you go rushing off to your room,' said his mother. 'I'm afraid you'll find things slightly different up there. I've had to put you in with your brother.' She went on to explain the reason for this. Erin's wedding would take place in ten days' time and the house had to be rearranged to accomodate Sam's parents who would be staying over the Saturday night, as would Thomasin's own parents. Hannah wouldn't allow herself to be left out and always welcomed the chance to be a resident of this big house. 'I'm sorry about the inconvenience,' she offered on seeing the distracted frown.

He hastened to assure her it was no hardship for him to share a room with his brother. 'But you see it completely slipped my mind that the wedding was set for next Saturday. I've gone and invited Rupert and Agatha to visit on that day. I beg your pardon for not consulting you first, but I thought you'd want me to return all the hospitality they've shown me. Eh, I am sorry Mother, but it's too late now to let them know. Even if I sent a letter they wouldn't get it as they're spending most of the holiday with relatives.'

'You don't half land me with some problems,' she chided amicably. 'Never mind, as long as they don't expect to stay the night we'll be solvent. Two more mouths at the reception aren't going to make much difference anyway. Come Saturday morning and it'll be like a buggers' opera in here.'

He laughed. 'They must take us as they find us, which, knowing them, I'm certain they will – they're very decent. Right, I'll take up my things – oh, what time's the ceremony by the way?' His mother told him. 'Ah well, they're not coming until the afternoon so we should be back in plenty of time.' He indicated the otherwise empty room. 'All on our own, are we?'

'More or less. Your father's tilling God's good earth, Erin's round at Grandma's getting a final fitting for her wedding gown and Dickie's upstairs. I don't know what he's up to – I'm not sure I want to know, either.' She told Sonny about the distressing episode of Dickie's underhandedness. 'It really knocked the stuffing out of your father, I can tell you. It was a shame it took something so drastic to make him see his son's true colours.' She also told Sonny about the need to lock Dickie in his room. 'I think he's learnt a bit of sense now, though. I haven't had any more complaints from the neighbours. And he's bought me that lovely plant over there as his way of saying he's sorry. He can be such a loving boy at times, but I do

277

wish he could be more dependable like you.' She smiled at her younger son. 'I never have need to worry what you're up to.'

'I don't think he means to cause you so much trouble. It's just the way he is,' said Sonny, wondering where Dickie had stolen the plant.

'You don't need to make excuses for him, love,' she replied. 'I know all there is to know about that one.'

If only you knew the half of it, thought Sonny as she went on, 'He's well able to stick up for himself.'

'He isn't you know,' revealed Sonny. 'There's many a time I've had to get him out of trouble. He's big, yes, and he's also got the gift of the gab, but he's not a physical sort of person.' – Well, not in that sense, came the mischievous thought.

'Now, take heed, don't let him get you involved in his goings-on. He might not be able to use his fists like his brother but his fly tongue will always save him from a trouncing. Promise me Sonny, you won't let him take advantage of you like that, for it's even money that if anyone is going to land in trouble it won't be Dickie. It's a charmed life he leads.'

'You don't have to concern yourself about me,' said Sonny. 'There might have been a time or two in the past when I got myself into scrapes because of him, but not any more. Apart from anything else I'm hardly home long enough to get into anything.' He opened the door to go upstairs.

'By the way!' Thomasin called after him. 'You and he are ushers at the wedding. I'm relying on you to keep an eye on him.'

Sonny grasped the handle of his trunk, swinging it up onto his shoulder, and staggered upstairs. At the second landing he applied his boot to Dickie's door and kicked it wide open. There was a flash of white bottom and a startled expression, which melted into vast relief as Sonny hauled his trunk into the room.

'Jazers, Mary an' Joseph! Don't ye ever knock?' asked his brother impolitely, his trousers round his ankles and a

278

cut-throat razor poised in his hand. 'Sure, ye almost made me lose my manhood.' He reseated himself on the bed and resumed the task of shaving his pubic hair as Sonny hurriedly closed the door.

'What the blazes are you doing?' he asked Dickie. 'What if it had been Mother who came in?'

Dickie gripped his tongue between his teeth as he undertook his delicate work. 'She'd likely have done voluntarily what you nearly made me do accidentally. Will ye stand out o' me light?' He waved Sonny to the other side of him. His brother asked once again what was the purpose in shaving himself, sitting down on the bed to watch.

'Crabs,' came the succinct reply. Dickie paused to blow the shorn hairs from his razor. 'They've been drivin' me up the bloody wall. I've been itching and riving at me breeches all day. Please! Will ye stop moving the bed else I'll be without me hunting tackle.'

'How come you managed to get those when you've been locked up in your room every night?' asked Sonny genially. 'They can't jump *that* high.'

'Ah, ye heard about my incarceration?' replied Dickie, finishing his chore and hoisting up his drawers and trousers. 'They don't only come out at night, ye know. I do have one or two paramours on me grocery round. Besides,' he grinned, 'it'll take more than any locked door to keep this lad down. I've been climbing down the drainpipe, haven't I?'

Sonny had to laugh. 'You're absolutely incorrigible! Haven't they got any idea?'

'Who, them? They're far too busy counting their piles o' money to notice if I'm there or not. It makes me sick. There's Mam buyin' shops right, left an' centre and me with not a sou to scratch me backside on. I could do with a new suit. When I ask them, what do I get? "There's five years' wear in the one ye've got." How can I be expected to do me courting in rags like these?'

Sonny said they looked all right to him.

'Well, they would to you, you not being fashionably inclined. I'm not sayin' they're shabby, but Mother's

279

choice is so drab. She won't let me buy me own, doesn't trust me. So I'm stuck with this old sack.'

'I can't say I blame her,' said Sonny. 'I seem to remember the first time she let you buy your own – you came back with a bright purple jacket and mustard-coloured trousers. You looked like a nightmare.'

'A peacock can't attract his hens without his fine feathers,' retorted Dickie. He threw the razor on the bedside table, rubbing at his crotch through his trousers. 'Jeez, that's better. I can't wait to get me knife an' fork into some fresh meat. I tried all sorts before this, ye know. An old salt I met in The Red Lion told me to rub in a mixture of paraffin and sand. Talk about powerful, Holy Mother, did I do some dancin' that night!'

Sonny fell back onto the bed, laughing. 'It's good to tell I'm home!'

Dickie sat back next to him and clasped him affectionately. 'Ye know something? 'Tis great to have ye back, Son. There's not been many laughs lately. Ye'll not believe this, but I think you're the only true friend I've got.'

'Oh, I believe it,' said his brother drily. Dickie spent far too much time in female company to cultivate male companionship. It stood to reason that when Sonny went back to college his brother would have no one with whom he could share a joke or a tankard. 'But my friendship doesn't extend to sharing a bedroom with your livestock so will you sweep that lot up?'

'Aw, I'd begun to grow pretty attached to them,' answered his brother. 'They've all got names, ye know.'

Sonny threw himself around on the creased coverlet, laughing. 'You're a daft bugger!'

'Aw, Jesus, Son ye've just crushed poor little Billy!' Dickie laughed and laid back too. 'God, we're gonna have a right little shindig now you're home. Just you an' me like the old days. I'm sick o' bloody women – ye never know where y'are with 'em. I'd rather have the company o' me darlin' brother than all the bloody tarts put together.'

And at that moment, Sonny could almost have believed his brother was sincere.

*

Thomasin was not so reluctant to unleash her son on society knowing that his brother was there to supervise. During the daytime Sonny aided Dickie with the grocery round and spent the rest of the time in the shop. But came the night and the two young men would be out on the town dressed in their finery and ready to take whatever was offered.

By Friday evening the boys were looking rather worse for wear and their capital was considerably diminished. Dickie stood in front of the mirror over the fireplace and pulled down the lower lids of his eyes. Sonny, standing next to him, winced. 'Ugh! I wish you wouldn't do that; it makes me go all squeamish.' He tackled his fiery hair with a comb dipped in water. 'Tut! Whatever I do my hair always looks like a bloody haystack.'

'Sonny,' warned Thomasin through a mouthful of pins as she and Hannah knelt at the hem of Erin's wedding gown adding the final touches. 'Remember your grand-mother is present.'

'Sorry, Grandma,' offered Sonny.

'I do hope you will all feel able to keep a check on your tongues tomorrow,' pleaded Hannah, smoothing down the folds of the gown. 'It would be so belittling if the family is let down in front of Samuel's relatives. At least that dreadful Mrs Flaherty isn't coming; I suppose I should be grateful for small mercies.'

'That's not really fair, Grandma.' Erin threw an accusing look at her mother. She herself had only learnt of this fact yesterday, having left all the arrangements to her parents. They probably wouldn't have even told her if she hadn't asked. She thought it terribly mean of them not to include Aunt Molly, or any of their old Irish friends for that matter, and was surprised at Father for going along with what she knew to be Mother's idea. But then, self-examination had told her that she was as guilty as them, for her last visit to Walmgate had been even longer ago than her parents'. She was not in a position to throw stones. Besides, once you moved away from an area you did tend to grow apart. Oh, people said, 'Keep in touch!'

but they soon forgot about their old neighbours. Hadn't Aunt Molly illustrated this by not calling on them?

Thomasin shied away from Erin's glare and was glad that her husband was not present to witness Hannah's remark. There had been a hell of a row over the guest-list. She had eventually got around her failure to invite any of Patrick's old friends by saying that the house simply would not hold them all. Patrick had then suggested that they hire a room for the reception, then there would be no need to offend anyone. 'She was very good to both of us once upon a time, was Molly,' he had said crossly. 'Don't go thinking you're gonna make me throw up all my old friends just 'cause you think we're too good for them now.' Though he had blushed as he'd said it, for though he'd visited Molly once or twice since the night he'd had the shindy with Ryan, he hadn't gone as often as he could've done.

Then it had been Thomasin's turn to be angry. 'Do you remember what happened at our wedding?' she had hurled at him. 'Do you? A right fiasco that was. And who was to blame? None but your own dear Molly. All right!' she had granted at his objection. 'My own relatives were as bad, but it was Molly who started all the fighting. Do you want that to happen at your daughter's wedding?' He had fallen silent then. Molly, however filthy and untutored in social graces, was more like a relative than a friend. How hurt she would be if she discovered she had been omitted from the celebrations. 'And how will she know?' his wife had asked. 'We hardly ever see her nowadays – even at Mass. If we don't tell her she'll be none the wiser. And if it makes you feel any better I'm not inviting any of my sisters either, so you can't say I'm just singling out your friends for shoddy treatment.' And Patrick, wanting his daughter's wedding to go smoothly, though feeling not a little shameful, had had to be satisfied. Though God knew how he'd ever face Molly again.

His had not been the only concern over the arrangements. Hannah, too, had been irked to find that none of her other daughters would be invited. Yet she had to agree with Thomasin's statement that the Feeneys had neither seen nor heard anything from the others since their marriage – not even a Christmas gift to the children – and they probably wouldn't want to come anyway. Also, the honour of being requested to make Erin's wedding gown, plus a brand new sewing machine, had helped to heal the wound and now she was looking forward to the event as much as anyone.

'Oh, I do so love a spring wedding, don't you, Thomasin dear?' she said. 'It's such an opportune time; a season of new beginnings. Erin will make a beautiful bride.'

Erin caught her mother's smile and reflected it. She wondered if Thomasin was thinking the same as herself: there was a time when Hannah had labelled Erin something less than beautiful – that snotty little ragamuffin in the torn pinafore. She gave a high-pitched giggle. 'I'm so nervous! I haven't been able to keep my mind on anything for days. Do all brides feel like this?'

'Every one, dear,' answered Thomasin. 'But you'll find it's worth every shudder to be joined with the man you love. And Sam's a grand lad. There!' She tugged gently at the hem of the gown and sat back on her heels. 'Stand over and let's take a look at Grandmother's handiwork.'

The dress was simply gorgeous. It had a stand-up collar of scalloped lace, cream, like the satin bodice that hugged Erin's slim figure. There was a cape of the same thick lace draped around the top half of the bodice, secured with eight pearl buttons. At the waist, the sash, decorated with two cream rosebuds, curled around to meet the enormous bustle. This in turn fell to meet an underskirt of the same rich cream silk, made from yards and yards of material and a great deal of fingerpricking labour.

Even Erin's brothers admitted that she looked breathtaking. 'I could almost fancy her meself.' Dickie planted a kiss on Erin's cheek and she pushed him away goodnaturedly.

'She'll look even lovelier tomorrow with her satin slippers and her hair bound up with spring flowers,' said their mother, then pulled herself up with the aid of a chair.

'Right! Let's be having you menfolk about your business.'
She drove her sons to the door as Hannah began to help
undo the dozens of buttons down the back of Erin's dress.
'Get yourselves to the pub like your father, we've women's
work to contend with here.'

'Have ye heard her slandering our characters, Son?'
asked Dickie as he was shoved from the room. 'As if two
clean-living boys like us would visit the dens of iniquity
that our father frequents.'

'Oh aye, and where might you be going then?' Their
mother paused before shutting the door.

Dickie took his brother's arm and tapped his hat. 'We're
spending a nice innocent evening at the fair. I might just
bring ye back a coconut if you're nice to me.'

She patted his cheek roughly. 'Well, just think on.
You've got a responsible job to do tomorrow. I shall expect
you home sober.' She finally closed the door.

The city streets were a blown-up version of an ants' nest;
riddled with life. Though in contrast to the ants' regimen-
tation there appeared to be no pattern to the crowd's
passage; its components rushed hither and thither, from
merry-go-round to 'Gypsy Francesca', from the boxing
booth to the dancing bear. Children with pieces of toffee
apple adhering to their tatted hair drove their parents mad
for another go on the swing-boats, their gooey, red-ringed
mouths ever-open, wanting.

Dickie and his brother let themselves be carried by the
crowd. Their eyes reflected the bright array of torchflare,
their ears crammed with the competition between hurdy-
gurdy and merry-go-round, the cackle of geese and the
lowing of cattle, and the 'Roll-up! Come buy!' of the
stallholders. Their noses twitched. The air was thick with
the combined aromas of burnt toffee, sausages, onions,
muffins, parkin, all mingling into one. It was so heavy it
made them feel that if they stuck out their tongues they
would taste it on the air. They were soon both infected
by the invigorating atmosphere and purchased a set of

balls to hurl at a coconut shy, groaning when their attempts met with failure.

'I think the old bugger has 'em stuck on with glue,' said Dickie as they moved away from the shy in search of something more fruitful. He could not resist a parting jibe to the man who obviously regarded the public as mugs. 'I'll send me mam round with a shillelagh; she'll knock your nuts off all right.'

The man formed a rude gesture and smugly jingled their coins in the pouch at his belt.

Dickie's interest was soon diverted. 'Come on, let's take a geg at the freaks.' He was off, pulling his brother in the direction of a tent labelled 'Curiosities' where a slick showman accosted them for the entrance fee.

'I hope it's worth it,' grumbled Sonny as he handed over the admission for both of them. 'Funds are getting perilously low.'

'It'll be worth every penny, young sir,' proclaimed the man. 'What you see in there cannot be seen anywhere else in Her Majesty's Empire.' He lifted the flap of the tent and they stepped past him.

The interior was very dim but they were just able to make out a row of cages and went towards it. In the first was a goat which nibbled at a few oats amongst the droppings on the floor of the cage, and bleated forlornly as Dickie pointed to the fifth leg that dangled uselessly from its flank.

Sonny pondered momentarily over the unfortunate beast, then traipsed after his brother who had already moved on. The four adjoining cages housed animals with similar deformities. Sonny stared pityingly at the hapless occupants, then progressed to the bearded lady. At the end of the display was a booth with a curtain hiding its contents. Another showman stood beside it, taking more money from the dozen or so people who had assembled. 'Do the young gents want to take a look at the most exciting discovery this country has ever seen?' the man enquired loudly. 'Observe this fascinating creature, half man, half monster, who was found in the jungles of South

America where even the wild animals were afraid of him, and brought back to civilisation to titillate, amaze and astound!'

The boys looked at each other, then nodded, Dickie more eagerly than his brother. 'That'll be sixpence each then,' said the man.

Sonny puffed out his cheeks at this exorbitance, but at Dickie's coaxing handed over the money.

'Now, ladies and gentlemen,' began the showman. 'I must warn those among you of a more delicate nature that the sight of this creature has been known to cause some good people to pass right out.'

'Get on wi' it!' shouted someone.

'Very well, you've been warned!' The showman made a dramatic play of suddenly whipping aside the curtain and the crowd gave a collective gasp.

The man they saw was so grotesquely misshapen that it would have been almost impossible to tell what kind of animal he was had it not been for the glint of recognition in his eyes – but man he undoubtedly was in his nakedness. Sonny's heart went out to the poor, misused creature as he returned the man's stare, wishing he had not come here. This was no imbecile; beneath that scaly, wart-covered body there lurked the bright spark of intelligence which, though badly battered through years of abasement, remained undimmed. Sonny wanted desperately to reach out and comfort the man, to tell him that not all his fellows were as obnoxious as this gathering; but as his brother's voice came over the rest he realised it would not be true. He closed his eyes in a vain effort to blot out the man's suffering.

'What's up, Son?' His brother elbowed him. 'Are ye jealous? I know I am. It's just not right for a freak like him to have such a prick. I ask ye, what use will he ever put it to?'

'Shut up!' hissed Sonny through clenched teeth.

Dickie, too engrossed in badinage with the crowd to hear him, suddenly felt himself being roughly grasped by the collar and the next minute he was back in the hullabaloo of the fairground. He complained noisily that his weak-stomached brother might at least have allowed him to take full advantage of the extortionate price. But Sonny had vanished round the back of the tent and was splattering his boots with vomit. Angrily the younger boy wiped the tears from his streaming eyes and straightened, rubbing a hand over his strained diaphragm.

'Come on,' he said gruffly. 'Let's take a ride on the roundabout.' He set off.

'Are ye sure ye oughtta? I don't want ye spewing over my best clothes.'

Sonny ignored this. He was desperate to find something that would take his mind from those terrible eyes.

They fought their way through the hordes and Dickie threw his leg over a brightly-painted horse. His brother, still shaken, took the one beside him. The music burbled and the carousel filled up and began to rotate. Sonny embraced the metal pole that supported the horse and leaned his face against its coolness.

Dickie was quick to notice the action. 'Remember to turn the other way if you're going to be sick!' he shouted above the din.

The roundabout gathered speed. The sea of faces that watched its motion became a blurred swathe of colour. Dickie held his hands out before him, showing off as usual and trying to revitalise his brother who had become incredibly dull all of a sudden. He bandied witty remarks with anyone who would participate, tossed his handsome head about and laughed, full of his own self-importance. He was just in the process of placing his feet on the horse's back when two faces leapt at him from the crowd. He almost lost his balance and sat down awkwardly, straining to look over his shoulder as the faces sailed out of view, hoping that he had been mistaken. But when the merry-go-round completed another circuit and he picked out the faces again his heart sank. There was no mistake.

'Oh, God I feel sick. Oh, sweet Jesus!' he muttered, pressing his face into the hardness of the pole. The roundabout had started to slow. 'Oh, Christ!'

Sonny's grey eyes held a query that did not extend to words. He watched his brother's face grow pale as the merry-go-round got slower and slower.

Busy thinking, Dickie took no notice of the questioning look. 'Listen careful now,' he said eventually, his voice deadly serious. 'When your horse gets around to the other side jump off an' run like hell.'

Sonny came alive. 'Oh, stab me! What have you got us into now?'

'Don't argue!' hissed Dickie, ashen-faced. 'Just do it – an' make sure ye don't jump off the wrong side else we've had it.' With that he was gone, leaving his bewildered brother to watch him bullock his way through the crowd, pursued by two strapping tinkers.

The carousel whined to a halt and Sonny leapt off. There was still a wide rift in the crowd where Dickie and the tinkers had hacked their passage and Sonny was able to follow without much resistance. By the time he caught up with the trio the tinkers had Dickie cornered in the elbow of a shop wall. He skidded on a muddy patch, noting as he did the look of relief that flooded his brother's worried face. In one move he had pushed past the tinkers and stood shoulder to shoulder with his kinsman.

'Ah, now isn't that nice, Con?' sneered Garret Fallon softly. 'He's brought his nursemaid with him.' He and his brother were slightly older than the Feeneys. They were dressed alike in drab trousers – Garret's held up with twine – and jackets that were a size too large, the shoulder-seams coming well past the intended point. Garret was perhaps a trifle more flamboyant than his sibling, with a red neckerchief at his bronzed throat and a gold ring in his right ear. The important factor to the Feeneys, however, was that both looked equally able to use his fists.

''Tis a handy sort o' fella he is, judging by the size of him,' answered Conor with the same, quiet menace. 'Handier than the other one wouldn't ye say?'

'Oh, I wouldn't say that at all, Con. I'd say our friend was real handy in his own little way.'

'With the womenfolk, ye mean?' asked Conor.

'Ah!' responded Garret.

Conor addressed Sonny. 'If ye've come to save your friend from a beating I've a notion ye'll be sorry.'

'If you've any argument with my brother then let's be hearing it,' said Sonny defiantly.

'Ah, brother is it? Sure, they don't look much like brothers, do they, Gary? I mean, the two of us are pretty much a pair – but them? Oh no, they can't both have the same father; one o' them has to be a bastard.' He was looking straight at Dickie. 'Now I wonder which one.'

Sonny took a step forward. Dickie grabbed him and hauled him back.

'Ah, we's got ourselves a fighter,' breathed Garret, his eyes glittering. 'Well now, will I tell ye why we're after your brother before or after ye get your beating? It might as well be before; ye'll be in no fit state to listen afterwards. See, 'tis like this: this handy fella has been dallying with our baby sister, an' now he's left her danglin' on a thread.'

Sonny turned accusingly to his brother as Dickie spoke up. 'Will ye make up your mind what it is ye want? I thought it was your wish for me not to bother her in the first place?'

'So it was, boy! But ye see what we didn't know when we sent ye packin' was that ye'd leave her a little souvenir.'

Watching Dickie's jaw drop, Sonny realised that their escape could only be brought about by dirty methods. The tinkers, versed in the art of street combat, would have to be taken by surprise. He tensed in readiness.

'I can see ye take my meaning,' said Garret. 'So, are ye goin' to be good and . . .' His sentence terminated abruptly in the noisy rush of air that was forced from his gaping mouth as Sonny's fist sank into his gut. He doubled over, the instant before Sonny's boot found Conor's groin, streaking out like a fork of lightning.

Sonny made off, calling over his shoulder, 'Run, you soft bugger!'

Dickie only tarried to insert his finger into the retching Garret's earring, ripping it from the lobe and adding to the tinker's incapacitation, before dashing after his brother. They ran like the wind, angering people in the crowd as they carved their escape route through the packed street, clashing with a pyramid of acrobats and throwing the act into total chaos. They continued to run until their pumping legs had carried them round the corner into Pavement, away from the bright lights, and they were able to lose themselves in one of the many convenient alleyways. Dickie hunched over in the darkness and pressed his hands to his knees, his head hanging down, breathing heavily. When he eventually straightened Sonny saw, amazingly, his eyes gleaming and his white teeth bared in a laugh.

'That bloody tinker was right!' he hurled at Dickie. 'You are a bastard – leaving that poor girl with her belly full. You seem to think everything is a game. You nearly get our heads kicked in and all you can do is laugh! I don't know why I bothered to rescue you.'

Dickie guffawed loud into the night. 'Son!' He slapped his brother on the back, his gleaming teeth rending the darkness. 'Had I a medal I'd pin it on your chest, but I've nothin' in me pocket save a bent meg.' He pulled a half-penny from his pocket, flicking it into the air and catching it. 'But to show me eternal gratitude – an' if ye can loan me the funds – I'm goin' to give ye such an evening as ye'll never forget. This time, boy, we'll not go home till ye know what it's all about.'

Sonny shook his head, trying to hang on to his self-control as Dickie lured him towards the maze of public houses. 'What am I going to do with you?'

'We'll find something, brother mine,' grinned Dickie, wiggling a forefinger on which was looped the tinker's gold earring. 'We'll find something.'

That night Sonny lost his virginity.

CHAPTER TWENTY-FIVE

The wedding had gone smoothly. The bride, as do all brides, looked radiant, the groom uncomfortably smart in his starched collar and top hat. Erin clung to Sam's arm, deliriously happy as they and their guests spilled from the Gothic church and visited the photographic studio nearby. She couldn't believe it had all been so easy, so perfect. What had there been to be nervous about? Of course there was still tonight to face, but she was sure that would be dealt with as easily as the ceremony. Things could not have gone better.

Her brothers too had behaved impeccably; model ushers. Dickie caught his brother's eye as they waited on the footwalk and shared a conspiratorial grin. Sonny was that full of himself! Look at him, with his chest puffed out. You'd think he'd had the entire occupants of a harem instead of just the one. But then Dottie was a nice little piece and Dickie supposed that was the way he himself had acted after his first time.

Sonny tore his grinning face away from his brother's and fixed his eyes on the photographer's door, waiting for his sister and her husband to emerge. He still couldn't believe it – that he'd actually done it at last. He'd heard none of the wedding service. The altar and its figures had blurred into another stage with different players: a bare little garret with a bed, a patchwork quilt, two pillows in plain slips, one sheet on top one on the bottom, one blanket, one chest of drawers ... Sonny remembered everything, every single item in that room. He'd lain there afterwards and soaked it all up, so he'd always remember. He had known from the outset that she was only entertaining him as a favour to his brother and at first had objected to Dickie's treat. But then, he told himself, it wasn't as if he loved her and she was so very nice, so kind and instructive and it was after all her job, that he'd wiped aside his priggish doubts and for once had not turned up his nose at his brother's leavings. And how glad he'd been. He felt himself inside her again, over and over ... He had arranged to go back next week – not to participate in some of the same, but to paint her. His brother had roared with laughter when he'd found out. Dottie herself had smiled to show she thought he was cracked. But she had been flattered that he'd found her body so attractive and had agreed to pose naked in order for him to immortalise this important episode in his life – as long as he paid, naturally – she'd made it plain that there'd be nothing else free. He didn't mind paying for her services as a model, but he wouldn't be paying for anything else, that would have spoilt everything.

His thoughts went to Agatha then, a naked Agatha that made him blush and he shoved the vision aside. He shouldn't think of a respectable girl that way. He still felt guilty for the way he'd pushed her from his thoughts on meeting the shallow Annie. Agatha maybe wasn't as pretty, but she was worth ten of Annie. That was his real reason for inviting her and Rupert over today, to make up for his behaviour and to show how fond he was of her. The naked Agatha crept back into his head.

Someone nudged him and he blushed as he turned to his mother who indicated that the photographic session was over and he should attend to his duties as usher. He began to direct guests to the carriages which hemmed the roadside.

Sam helped Erin into the bridal carriage, then stood with one foot poised on the running board to admire his bride. 'You look beautiful, Erin,' he said sincerely. 'I'm right proud to be sharing this carriage with you.'

Erin, her face a-glow, sat with her skirts puckered around her like a huge gardenia. The landau had been decked with the same spring flowers that garlanded her hair, its impatient, stomping horses harnessed with white ribbons. She felt like Queen of the May. 'I'm the proud one,' she replied softly as he climbed in beside her and the driver whipped up the horses. 'And it's not only the carriage we're sharing, Sam,' she reminded him, 'it's the rest of our lives.'

He pressed against her and kissed her cheek, whispering, 'An' tonight we'll be sharing a bed, Erin. Won't that be wonderful?'

The blush spread like a bloodstain from the scalloped collar of the wedding gown. She veiled her eyes with lustrous dark lashes. 'Ssh! The driver will hear you.'

'Eh, I'm sorry,' he grinned, taking her hand in his. 'It's just I love you so much I can't help thinkin' about it. I think of it all the time.'

Erin's face was crimson, yet not without pleasure that he wanted her. She squeezed his hand. She was just a little worried about tonight, that was all. She'd thought perhaps Alice, the maid at the Cummings' house who'd told her all about 'it', might have been wrong. But no, Thomasin had told her much the same last night – at least she'd started to, before Erin overcome with embarrassment had told her mother that she already knew. Her mother had patted her hand and said kindly, 'Ah well, that's good, you'll know what to expect, then. I thought I'd just better make sure. I want you to be as happy as I am with your dear father.' Erin had replied that she was sure she would be, as soon as that was out of the way. Then her mother had laughed as though she'd said something hilarious and said, 'You'll learn!' God, there was so much to think about. Would she make a good wife, a good mother? For she wanted dozens and dozens of children, little Sams running about all over the place . . . She smiled up at him once more, then clung to his side as the carriage took them home.

Thomasin had engaged two temporary maids for the occasion, much to Amy's relief. The food had been provided by caterers – there was to be no danger of any of the guests breaking their teeth on Amy's baking. In the dining room the furniture had been moved and two tables placed together to accommodate the guests. The two maids, Fanny and Sarah, had been rushing back and forth with dishes all morning and now, as the guests trickled in from church, the completed wedding breakfast was spread out in all its glory.

After the meal the ladies retired to the other room while Patrick handed out claret and cigars to the men. He had read about this procedure in the book of etiquette which Hannah had more or less forced upon him but which, in the end, he had been grateful for. It was a shame Father Kelly couldn't be here to enjoy the fine claret. After performing the marriage ceremony he had had to rush off to keep an appointment with the bishop. But with a bit of luck he'd be able to catch the tail-end of the celebrations.

Half an hour later the menfolk went to join their wives and sisters. Hannah was in the middle of a discussion with Sam's mother when they filtered in and found themselves seats.

'At what time have you to return home, Mrs Teale? I understand that you live some fifteen miles away.'

'Sam's parents are to be guests for the evening, Mother,' provided Thomasin. 'I saw no point in them having to spoil their enjoyment of their son's wedding day by leaving early. They'll stay until after Sunday lunch.'

'Oh, then we will be seeing a lot more of each other, as we too are to be guests of my daughter.' Hannah sipped her sherry and put on her 'royal' face as her grandchildren had labelled it. 'It is fortunate that Thomasin has such a large house, is it not, Mrs Teale?'

Edith Teale, a thin, unassuming woman, smiled uncomfortably. Living in a two-roomed cottage whose roof leaked when it rained, she was unused to these plush surroundings. 'It's very grand, Mrs Fenton,' she said nervously. 'And so kind of Mrs Feeney to have us stay.'

'Oh, Thomasin please,' put in her hostess. 'After all, we're family now.' She had liked Edith, as she had done her son, on sight. It was clear that the poor soul was feeling out of place and Thomasin wanted to do everything she could to make Sam's mother feel at home. Inside, she

294

found it quite amusing that they were thought of by this humble family as 'nobs'.

Hannah spoke again. 'Yes, I expect it comes as rather a treat for you to stay in such a house after what you must be accustomed to. Sam is a very lucky boy to be marrying into this family – I hope you appreciate that, Mrs Teale.'

'Oh, well . . . we do,' stammered Edith, with an uneasy glance at her husband whose face had become a stiff mask.

Hannah forged on. 'By rights, my daughter could have selected someone far more eligible than Samuel – not that he isn't a dear boy, he is, we all dote on him – but you have to agree that as a butcher's boy he has not the prospects that I personally would have looked for when choosing a husband for Erin. Still, thanks to my daughter Erin is bringing a splendid dowry to her marriage.'

Thomasin made a gesture for Fanny to refill glasses in the hope that it might relieve the tension. But Hannah was undaunted. 'I expect your son will rise in the world now that he has Thomasin to guide him; she is a very astute businesswoman you know, Mrs Teale. Oh yes, it is Thomasin who has made that shop the thriving concern that it is.'

Patrick stepped forward, laughed and said bluntly, 'An' now y'all know what my mother-in-law thinks of my capabilities.'

There was a ripple of embarrassed laughter and Hannah's nostrils flared. Erin squeezed her husband's arm. 'Don't pay any heed to Grandma, Sam,' she whispered as the conversation changed course. 'Ye've heard her before. She's like it with everyone. I think she could even find fault with the Angel Gabriel 'cause his wings had a feather missing or something.'

Sam remained grim-faced. 'She can demean me all she likes, but if she keeps on belittling my mother like that I'm going to have to say something, Erin – that's if Father doesn't say it first; look at his face. Butcher's boy indeed! I like that. I'm a qualified tradesman, I'll have her know.'

Somehow, the topic moved around to the political situation and, with the former danger averted, Thomasin turned her attention to Sonny's guests, Rupert and Agatha, who seemed to be fitting in very nicely. Rupert was a nice young fellow, well-spoken and very fond of his sister. She studied Agatha, a not unattractive girl, who was hanging attentively onto Sonny's words. Thomasin, eager for any signs of romance, examined Sonny's expression. It would be lovely if another of her offspring could find a partner. He did seem to be paying the girl a lot of attention but whether it was out of affection or merely politeness Thomasin could not decide. She rose and went across to the youthful gathering. Sonny offered her his seat.

'Thank you, dear.' She spread the bouffant skirts of the lilac gown more evenly over the chair. 'I just thought I'd come and engage in a small chat with your friends while I have the chance. It's very difficult having to circulate – everyone wants to talk to the bride's mother. I'll become quite conceited before the day is through.' She smiled at Agatha. 'That's a very pretty gown you're wearing, Agatha.'

'Thank you, Mrs Feeney,' said the girl, whose sudden, disarming smile encouraged further conversation. Her face, bordered by dark-brown hair parted in the middle and caught up in an elaborate chignon, had erstwhile seemed very aloof. 'I'm very pleased to meet you.' She turned to Sonny. 'John, you are so much like your mother. Indeed, she hardly looks old enough to be your mother. If I had not been forewarned I should have taken her for your sister.'

'What a very charming person your friend is,' bubbled Thomasin to her son. 'Agatha, with compliments like that you are welcome in this house always.' Sonny smiled to show his attunement. His mother moved her body round to face Rupert who was the same age as her son but a great deal less robust. His complexion was sallow and Thomasin would have labelled him consumptive had he come from a poorer home. 'It grieves me that I can't offer you the same hospitality that you've shown my son, Rupert, but as you see we are rather overcrowded. As it is we'll very likely end up sleeping six to a bed.'

This odd comment from a lady produced a slight twitch

at the corner of one of Rupert's eyes. He was lost for words for the moment, then managed to stammer, 'Think nothing of it, Mrs Feeney. I quite understand. As a matter of fact we would be unable to accept your hospitality for our parents are giving a special luncheon tomorrow and expect us to be back.'

Thomasin asked Rupert about the college. Was her son a good scholar? Did he conduct himself well?

'Oh, admirably, you may be assured,' he smiled, harking back to the days when Feeney had fought with almost every boy in the school to defend his background. Rupert had been the new boy's only friend at that time. Having borne the pain of a lot of wigging himself he had felt compassion for this unfortunate boy. 'Feeney – that is, John – and I share a room,' he informed Thomasin. 'We're best friends.'

Thomasin smiled and said that she was glad, then her face altered as she saw poor Mrs Teale being once more harangued by her mother. 'Oh dear, it looks as if I must go to the rescue again. Please excuse me, Agatha, Rupert, but my mother can be a great trial at times.' She rose and went forth hurriedly, leaving Rupert thinking what an odd lady Feeney's mother was, and what a dreadful old snob his grandmother was, too. What right did she have to brag to that poor woman?

Dickie had been cornered by his grandfather. William, scorning the sherry that the maid had offered, had asked for a tankard of ale but had had to suffice with whiskey. He was well-saturated and speaking even more loudly than usual. Dickie saw Agatha's head turn at a particularly noisy outburst from William. He shrugged apologetically and watched her over the rim of his glass.

'What's all this I've been hearin' about thee?' shouted William in Dickie's face. 'Like a bloody tomcat the mother sez y'are. She's thinkin' of havin' thee seen to.'

'Ssh, Grandad! Keep it down.' Dickie ran a finger inside his collar and laughed into his hand. 'Anyway, I'll bet you were the same when you were my age.'

William guffawed and touched his glass to Dickie's

shoulder, sprinkling the youth with whiskey. 'By tha what! When I were thy age . . .'

Dickie charged one side of his face with attentiveness while his grandfather began to relate all the tales he'd heard before. With the other side of his face he surveyed Agatha who kept darting inquisitive glances in his direction. He didn't know what Sonny saw in her. The only thing to her credit was that she was gentry.

'Tha's not heard a word I've said, has tha?' William jabbed his grandson in the chest. 'Now don't be tryin' to tell me otherwise. Nay, I've seen thee makin' sheep's eyes at that bonny lahl filly ower there.' He slopped his glass at Agatha. 'I know tha'd rather be wi' her than thy own grandfather.'

'Ah, now you're only sayin' that to make me feel guilty,' smiled Dickie, and began to move away.

'I'm not bloody succeedin' though, am I?' shouted William. 'Listen, don't be slopin' off just yet, I wanted a quiet word wi' thee.'

Dickie's smile widened. His grandfather, missing the humour of his comment, proceeded loudly, "Ere, plant tha bum. I'm damned if I'm wanderin' round after thee.'

Dickie stopped pacing and sat beside his grandfather on a carved oak chest which had been brought in as extra seating and made more comfortable with cushions.

'Tha may've noticed I'm not gerrin' any younger,' said William, rolling the glass in his hardened fingers. 'I want to 'ave this chat wi' thee afore it's ower late.'

'Get away, Grandad! Ye can't be more than fifty. Ye'll outlive the lot of us.' Dickie swilled his drink around his tongue, his eyes still on Agatha.

'Well, there's one thing certain, I'll outlive thee, t'way tha's goin' on. Eh, y'allus were a smooth-talkin' bugger,' said William, shaking his head. 'Nowt's serious to thee, is it?' Have a talk with him, Tommy had said. He thinks a lot about you; he's more likely to listen than if we keep nagging at him.

'What's to be serious about? We could all be dead tomorrow.'

298

'That's what I'm tryin' to get through to thee, clog-head. At least, *I* could be dead tomorra – that's why I think it proper we should 'ave this 'ere chat.'

'Chat, or sermon?' said the other distantly. Agatha was holding out her glass for more elderberry wine.

'Tek it either way tha wants, but tha's gonna listen. Tha's a big worry to thy mother an' father, tha's well aware. I'm askin' thee to curb thissen. I know I made light on it afore, but happen it were a mite frivolous. Tha mother's reet concerned, tha knows.'

'I don't see what all the fuss is about,' said Dickie, paying his grandfather full attention now. 'I'm no worse than any other lad my age.'

'Happen not, but I want thee to promise tha'll not do owt to hurt 'em. Them's good folk, tha mother an' Pat, I don't like to see 'em mucked abaht. If tha'll tell me tha'll do nowt to mek 'em ashamed o' thee I'd be able to rest easier in me grave.'

'Grandad, don't talk like that,' said Dickie concernedly. 'You're too young for such twaddle.'

'Wilt tha promise?'

'Of course I wouldn't do anythin' untoward,' said Dickie. 'What d'ye take me for? Sure, I like a pretty girl on me arm, but who doesn't at my age?'

'At any age, lad,' grinned William, then meditated. 'I told tha mother much t'same thing,' he said, slurping from his glass. 'Tha's mekkin pumpkins out o' pimples I told her – he'll grow out of it. Eh, I don't know. It don't seem five minutes since I were tekkin pair o' thee on me knee an' tellin' bedtime stories . . .'

I could tell you a few now, thought Dickie, a sparkle in his eye. Agatha was eyeing him again. He had caught her that time, even managed to make her blush. 'We all get older, Grandad.'

'It's all reet for thee to say it so lightly, tha's barely eighteen! Tha'll not be so confident when tha gets to my age. So, before I kick me clogs,' William dipped into his waistcoat and unhooked his silver watch from its anchor, 'I'd like to see thee get this, bein' t'eldest like . . .'

299

Sonny chose to glance over just at the moment the timepiece changed hands; saw the watch that he had always played with as a little boy and had hoped would be his some day, cradled in his brother's palm. There was a cold knob of bitterness in the pit of his stomach as he watched Dickie turn it over to read the inscription that Sonny knew off by heart. What did his brother care for the watch? He who never allowed sentiment to meddle with his life.

'That's what tha gets when tha works hard,' William was saying proudly, after his grandson had read the inscribed words. 'That's not just a watch, it's a monument to my father's loyalty and industry – that wharrit sez: *To Septimus Fenton, in gratitude for thirty years' loyal service.* From a real lord, that is. I'm trustin' it to thee 'cause I want thee to follow his example an' work hard for our Tommy an' Pat; tha'll get tha reward in t'end.'

'This is reward enough, Grandad,' said Dickie sincerely, sliding the watch into his own waistcoat pocket. 'It's the most precious thing anyone's ever given me. I'll treasure it always.'

'Aye, well . . .' William rubbed his nose, bashful at the height the emotions had reached. 'Tha can bugger off now. I've said what I 'ave to. Where's that bloody woman wi' drinks?' He shuffled off in search of more whiskey, leaving Dickie to seek a more interesting conversationalist.

Hannah still had poor Edith Teale at her mercy; Thomasin had been sidetracked on the way to her rescue. 'I'll guarantee you haven't seen anything as elegant as this before.' Hannah fingered the tapestry hanging by the fireplace. 'It is my own mother's work,' Edith was informed. 'She was an expert needlewoman – as I am myself, I might modestly add – and came from a very distinguished family. Her maiden name was Barry and her ancestry travels right back to ten sixty-six when the Dubarrys, as they then were, came over with the Conqueror.' .

Edith's husband was engaged in talking to Patrick and was unable to offer his wife any assistance, but Sam overheard. 'Really? I always thought Barry was an Irish name, Mrs Fenton,' and earned himself a look of acrimony from Hannah. 'Then you have been labouring under a fallacy, Samuel! I can categorically state that none of my ancestors' blood was tinctured with that of the Celt.'

'Just French, eh, Mrs Fenton,' smiled Sam, and turned back to his bride who made a soft moue of reproach.

But Hannah was not to be deterred, and went on, and on, and on. Edith was feeling terrible. Mr and Mrs Feeney had seemed like such nice, ordinary people, despite the huge house, but Mrs Fenton was intent on making it plain that Erin, in marrying Sam, had married beneath her.

At last Thomasin freed herself and carried out her intention to rescue Edith. 'Come now, Mother,' she took a firm hold on Hannah's arm. 'The bride's grandmother is expected to circulate too, you know.' She noticed her father's unsteady gait and pointed it out to Hannah who hurried off to intercept him.

'I'm dreadfully sorry you've had to suffer for so long,' Thomasin told Edith. 'Every time I was about to rescue you someone collared me. Oh look, your glass is empty. Let me get it refilled.' She looked around for a maid; there was none in sight. 'Oh, dear where have those girls got to?'

'Please, don't worry on my account,' said Edith, rolling the stem of the glass between her thumb and forefinger then, noting that the action drew attention to her work-reddened hands, ceased.

Thomasin sighed loudly and stood to reach the jug of lemonade from the cabinet where Fanny had left it, without, she noticed angrily, a mat to protect the mahogany. There was now a white ring marring the glossy wood. Knowing Sam's mother's views on drink she had made the lemonade specially.

'I'll bet they're hiding in the kitchen.' She filled Edith's glass. 'I shall have to go and scuttle them in a moment.' Placing a mat under the jug she sat down again beside Edith and said sympathetically, 'If it's any comfort to you, Edith, my mother behaved in exactly the same manner to

Patrick when he wanted to marry me; acting as if he were marrying into royalty. I don't know why she does it. It only antagonises folk. We're not that grand, you know. I should imagine the houses we've lived in were a great deal more humble than your own ... that is ...' Oh, God's truth! she hadn't meant it to sound that way.

'Oh, I don't mind her comments,' said Edith unconvincingly. 'I dare say she was right in a lot of them. Sam is very lucky to be marrying your daughter.'

'Eh, now don't be giving me that,' rebuked Thomasin. 'The way I see it our Erin's the lucky one to catch herself a nice steady chap like Sam. He'll have his work cut out with her, you know. Oh yes, she's a right stubborn little jenny when she puts her mind to it. I hope you'll convey my apologies to Mr Teale for my mother's behaviour if I'm unable to get around to it myself. He looked awfully annoyed before.'

'Dominic's a very proud man,' Edith told her. 'He's worked very hard for what he has and hates for anyone to belittle it.'

'I can understand that, Edith. My husband is a proud man, too. You must tell him, though, that nobody in this family takes the slightest bit of notice of my mother. We're all that used to her sanctimonious speeches that we sometimes forget that strangers might be hurt by her attitude. Oh, dear, I really must see what those girls are up to – I can see a dozen people with empty glasses.' She excused herself and swished off to the kitchen to remonstrate with the temporary help. 'You're supposed to keep people's glasses filled,' she complained on finding them, and Amy, sat drinking sherry themselves. 'Not dallying here drinking yourselves sillier than you already are.' She shooed the temporaries back to their posts, then turned on Amy. 'And what might you be doing, madam?'

Amy, slightly tipsy, grinned. 'Oh, there's no need for you to call me madam, madam,' and clinking the glasses together carried them to the sink.

'I asked what you were supposed to be doing,' repeated Thomasin sulphurously. 'I did not ask for a load of cheek.'

'I'm washin' up, whassit look like?'

'Aye, and I'll bet you're making that spin out, aren't you? Just so you won't be called upon to help the others in there. Well, when you've finished – which had better not be more than five minutes – you can get your body in there and pull your weight. We shall have to reconsider your position after the wedding is over. I'm greatly displeased with your standard of work.' She returned to act as Edith's protector, leaving Amy to fume with pent-up frustration. Had the maid known that a quarter of the clock would bring her the revenge she had been praying for perhaps her rage might not have been so acute and Thomasin's crystal would have fared better.

Thomasin heard the doorbell sound and broke off her dialogue with Edith. 'That'll probably be Father Kelly. I'm glad the Bishop didn't keep him yapping.' She pulled the rope that worked the bell in the kitchen to indicate that Amy was expected to answer it, though holding out little hope of compliance. She was pleasantly surprised, therefore, when a flustered but civil-looking Amy appeared before her. Indeed, such pleasantry had never been forthcoming from this quarter before.

'Sorry to trouble you, ma'am, but there's a person outside says she's a friend o' yours. Says she's got a present for Miss Erin. I weren't sure whether to let her in, seein' as how she didn't have an invite.'

'Well, naturally if she says she's a friend then you must show her in, girl,' said Thomasin, craning her neck expectantly. She was pressed to imagine who could be calling halfway through the reception. The smug expression on Amy's face went unnoticed as the maid retreated to admit the guest. It was only when the latter appeared in the doorway that Thomasin understood the reason for Amy's smile.

Patrick, who had been enjoying several confidences from Dominic Teale, saw heads beginning to turn. He watched his elder son cover a smile with his hand. Heard Sonny mutter, 'Oh, crikey!' Saw his wife's blank mien and his mother-in-law's chagrin, and turned his own head with theirs.

And there stood Molly Flaherty.

CHAPTER TWENTY-SIX

The bog-oak face registered both surprise and hurt as her slitty eyes fell on Erin's wedding gown and the three-tiered cake by which the girl was poised. She looked from Thomasin to Patrick, then back at Thomasin. She said nothing, but they both knew what was going through her mind: she was Patrick's oldest friend and she had not been invited to his daughter's wedding.

And it had never crossed her mind. Even when Father Kelly had told her that Erin was getting married after Easter she hadn't thought it strange, them not mentioning it, for she hadn't seen Pat or Tommy for quite a while and anyway the Father hadn't said what date the wedding was set for. Sure, the boy would be rushed off his feet with all that land to see to. She'd go visit them herself and take the gift in advance of the wedding and they'd give her the invitation then. The shock of being so wrong was still on her face.

In her hand was a crumpled brown package. She now handed it falteringly to the girl to whom she had once been a surrogate mother. 'Sure, I didn't mean to barge in like this.' Her voice was faint. 'Father Kelly mentioned ye were gettin' wed after Easter but he didn't say what day. 'Twas only the thought o' wantin' to save your legs that brought me over with this. I thought ye must've been busy else one o' yese'd been.'

Agatha and Rupert were thunderstruck at this filthy old pauper with her ragged bodice exposing one grubby breast and the piece of sacking that was slung across her hips covered in something unmentionable. She lifted a claw-like hand to smooth her tousled hair, what little was left of it. Her fingernails were black with the filth of her habitat.

Patrick came forward then to greet Molly while Erin stood nibbling her thumbnail, feeling utterly wretched, Molly's unopened gift in her hand. Thomasin, too, recovered sufficiently to say, 'Sonny, why don't you and your brother take Rupert and Agatha for a turn round the garden? I'm sure they'll find the spring flowers a delight.' She then went over to Molly and led her to a chair as the young people filed into the garden, wincing at Agatha's confused question: 'Who is that funny old woman?'

''Tisn't much of a present.' Molly drew attention to the parcel, still clutched in Erin's hand, and the girl hurried to unwrap it. 'I don't expect 'tis as grand as your new friends've given ye.' She eyed the others with suspicion and dislike.

'It's just what I wanted, Aunty Molly.' Erin held up the cheap ornament for Sam to see and was gratified when her husband thanked Molly in the same manner. She bent impulsively and kissed the grimy, withered cheek. 'Er, ye haven't met Sam, have ye?' What an idiotic thing to say. 'Sam, this is my Aunt Molly – Mrs Flaherty.'

Sam nodded and smiled.

Molly looked him up and down. 'A bonny man ye've got yourself, Erin Feeney.'

Erin looked away to hide her guilt.

Hannah was on the point of collapse. As if Molly's intrusion was not demeaning enough on its own, Erin had to address the woman as 'Aunt'. She caught Dominic Teale's gloating expression and hurriedly took herself off to the dining room to weep her shame. Dominic smiled vindictively; his humiliation at Hannah's hands was about to be superceded by the woman's own.

Molly eyed the glasses which the guests were holding and ran her tongue over her lower lip – though from the aura of liquor fumes that whistled through her teeth it had not been a dry journey to the Feeney house. Patrick signalled to a maid to bring another glass for his friend.

'Well, 'tis pleased we are to see ye here, Molly. Are we not, Tommy?' Thomasin's pallid face belied his geniality. He went on hastily, 'We were only just talkin' about ye last night, sayin' as how we'd have to have a separate wedding party for our old friends 'cause our house isn't large enough to hold the lotta yese. But there y'are, ye'll be able to say ye've been to both parties now, won't ye? I'd not like ye to think we were going to leave ye out, ye know, but we've been that busy with the arrangements that between hoppin' an' troddin' we quite forgot to mention to Father Kelly to pass the message on if he saw ye at Mass. Well, as I said ye would've been getting an invite to the other do we're going to have but . . .' it all sounded so awful.

You're talking too much, Pat, thought Thomasin wretchedly. The more you try to convince her the less plausible your explanation sounds. She tried to inject a little credibility into her own remark. 'Erin will have to cut you some cake to take home with you, Molly. She helped make it herself. It's delicious.'

'Am I to leave already?' asked Molly, sniffing at the sherry before knocking it back in one go. She waved away Thomasin's denial. 'Ah, sure ye can't kid me, the pair o' yese. Ye didn't want me here I can tell. An' who could blame ye? I'm not very pleasant company for a gathering such as this, am I? I would've liked to have gone to the church, though, just to see my godchild wed.' She sighed as she inspected the fine array of clothing. 'Ah, 'tis a long road ye've travelled from Brit Yard, Patrick Feeney. I recall the days when ye hadn't a backside to your trousers nor a penny to your name – Tommy too. I'd never've recognised her in them fancy hangin's. I'll bet they never came from the pawnshop.'

Amy, peeping through the crack in the partly-open door, was loving every minute of Thomasin's mortification. She watched her employer grow more uncomfortable by the second as Molly waded through her memories.

The pauper woman cheered. 'Ah, but them were great days all the same. We'd have some right old shindigs, didn't we just? Singin' and dancin', old Ghostie with his fiddle ... Ah, but the best time,' she elbowed one of Sam's relations who was unlucky enough to find himself sitting on the chair next to hers, 'was when Pat an' my poor Jimmy – God be good to him – got into some sort o' argumentation with old Raper. Ye never saw such a spectacle as that butcher dolin' out the insults, callin' us fleabags an' suchlike. A right poltroon he was – still is. But Pat could sort him out, couldn't ye, Pat? A fine scrapper is my lad here.' She cackled. 'An' d'ye remember when Tommy pushed him into the pile o' shi ...'

'No, I'm afraid I don't!' jumped in Thomasin rapidly. 'Erin, go ask Amy if that cake is going to be cut up by next Christmas. Molly, let me give you another glass of sherry.'

'Maybes I'd better get moving an' let you folk get on with your party,' slurred Molly wistfully, and made great play of rising from her chair.

'Ye'll do no such thing,' said Patrick to his wife's horror. 'Now you're here, ye'll stay until the party's over.'

However, the wedding reception was destined to be over sooner than anyone had anticipated. Some minutes after a shame-faced Erin had returned with a wedge of cake wrapped in a napkin and Amy had repositioned herself outside the door, a pink-cheeked Agatha stumbled tearfully into their midst supported by her irate brother.

'This really is outrageous, Mr Feeney!' protested Rupert, and when coaxed for an explanation enlarged: 'My sister, as you can fully see, is extremely upset. Your elder son, under the pretext of showing her a secluded corner of the garden, has made the most improper advances to her.'

Patrick's temper flared instantly. 'Where are my sons now?' he demanded of Rupert who was mopping at his distressed sister's face.

'Richard, I trust, sir, is in the process of receiving a thrashing from his brother,' said Rupert, whose words were soon validated when Patrick looked from the window and saw the struggling figures razing the flower border.

His authoritative shout was followed by the appearance of both sons, one of whom held a bloody handkerchief to his nose, the other sullenly rubbing his knuckles.

'How dare you?' roared their father, striding up to them. 'How dare ye ruin your sister's wedding day with such juvenile behaviour?'

'I was defending my friend's honour,' argued Sonny.

'Silence! Whatever the reason you have both performed abominably in front of our guests. Ye'll both apologise forthwith, especially to your sister.'

'Pray, don't concern yourself on our account, sir,' said Rupert stiffly before Patrick's order could be carried out. 'My sister and I are leaving. Might one have one's hat, please?'

A maid was sent to fetch the hat and Agatha's jacket as he continued, addressing himself to Sonny now, 'I am a pretty tolerant sort of chap, Feeney, but I hope you will forgive me if I decline any future invitation you may have in mind to offer. I was quite ready to accept that your background was a little humbler than my own, but was not prepared for the company I would be expected to frequent,' – here he looked at Molly – 'or that my sister would suffer such indignities at the hands of your brother. My sympathies lie with you, Feeney, in having such a cross as this family to bear, but you will excuse me should I not choose to suffer it with you.' With this he wished them a curt farewell and, supporting his still-weeping sister, left the house.

'Funny friends ye've got yourself,' piped up Molly, gulping another helping of sherry. Her voice cracked the stunned silence. No one dared look at his neighbour. Sonny pushed past his brother and returned to the garden, totally sickened by the experience. He hadn't turned his back but one minute – one bloody minute! But that was sufficient for that lecher to get his hands on her, destroying another of his brother's dreams. Oh, God! how could he face her? A bitter laugh then – he probably wouldn't have to. There'd be no more invitations to her home. They wouldn't want *his* sort in the house. But he would have to face Rupert. He didn't know how he was going to cope with that. He cursed his brother: bastard, bastard, bastard!

Patrick tried to restore conviviality by handing out more cigars, most of which were declined. Dickie dabbed at his bleeding nose and looked around for a quiet corner. Hannah, who had unfortunately wandered back in at the height of the furore, fixed glazed eyes to the door through which Rupert and Agatha had disappeared.

'Goodness, look at the clock!' cried Thomasin, abnormally shrill. 'Erin, it's high time you were changing, the carriage will be around any minute.'

Erin remained where she was, looking into each uncomfortable face in turn. Her day had been ruined. Not just by her brothers, and her mother's treatment of Molly, but by her own thoughtlessness. Sam broke into her reverie, saying quietly, 'Come on, lass, I'll carry your trunk down. Let's get away from this lot.' They went upstairs.

All of a sudden it hit Thomasin that Erin would not be coming back. After their honeymoon she and Sam would be going to live in a village some eight miles from York in the little cottage recently purchased with the money donated by Thomasin. So far away! Had there been any need for that? But then, Erin had wanted to follow her husband's wishes, which were to live in the countryside he loved and in time raise some livestock. For the moment he was still employed at the butchery, however. But that didn't bring Erin any closer. Thomasin's eyes became misty and threatened to brim over. What a note for their daughter to be leaving home on.

Patrick saw the tears but made no move to comfort her; he thought she was crying with self-pity. Well, damnwell serve her right. Thinking she was too good to rub shoulders with the likes of Molly. He should never have allowed her to persuade him. Sonny could take some of the blame too for bringing his fancy friends here. And the other one . . . well!

When Sam and Erin rejoined the party the latter wore a deep-pink velvet gown and matching jacket trimmed with cream braid. Her eyes, also, were on the pink side.

It was quite apparent she'd had a good cry upstairs, but the veil on her feathered hat served to hide her unhappiness somewhat.

'Oh, what a picture!' beamed Molly and tried to rise, but failed. 'Oh, God – it looks like I'm here for the night.'

Erin bent and kissed her. 'There's no need for you to come out with us, Aunt Molly.'

'Ah well, I can as soon wish ye luck in here,' agreed Molly. 'Here's good health to ye once more, Erin. To you an' your Sam, may ye be blessed with a hundred children.'

'Oh, Molly I'm so sorry,' blurted Erin, but the woman shook her head and clicked her tongue.

'No need, pet, no need. Off ye go now – an' take care o' my baby, young Sam!'

'I will, Mrs Flaherty – Aunt Molly.'

They left her there, silly with drink, while the other guests flowed after them to the front of the house. It was then that Father Kelly arrived, breathless from his rush from the bishop's house.

'Oh, God love us! I'm here just in time to wave the happy couple off. Ah, isn't she the most beautiful bride y'ever saw?' Reaching Erin he promptly kissed her then turned to Sam and engaged in a warm handshake. 'You're a lucky fella, Samuel. I wish 'twas meself that was taking her away.'

'Shame on ye, Father.' Erin managed a laugh for her old friend. 'Trying to compromise a married woman.'

Liam sighed and addressed himself to Patrick. 'Ah, it doesn't seem like five minutes since I was baptisin' her.'

Patrick mouthed wistful accord, then said, 'There's another o' your lady friends in the house, Liam if ye'd care to go in.'

'God, can I never shake these women off?' bewailed the priest. 'Following me about all over the place. I'd best go see to her then.'

'There y'are deserting me already,' chided Erin, then kissed him again. 'Goodbye, Father. See ye when we get back. Goodbye everyone.'

Thomasin and Patrick took it in turns to hug their

daughter. Then Patrick, after a second's hesitation, clasped Sam's hand. 'I'm sorry it went the way it did, Sam. What with one thing and another it wasn't the smoothest of weddings, was it?'

'Oh, well.' Sam gave a smiling sigh at his bride. 'Upsets or no, it accomplished what it was meant to.'

'Ye'll take good care of her now?' Patrick couldn't help feeling a little resentful that Sam was taking her away, however much he liked the man.

'I will. She means everything to me, you know that.'

Erin impulsively threw her arms round her father's neck and clung on tightly. It felt so strange to be going.

Then all stood back to wave as the carriage rolled away. The members of the wedding party who were not staying overnight also took their leave and climbed into their carriages and carts, leaving the Feeneys standing alone on the pavement as the remaining guests stepped back into the house.

'I've never been so humiliated,' breathed Thomasin tearfully, watching the honeymoon carriage disappear from sight. 'It should've been one of the happiest days of my life, the marriage of our daughter. Instead, it was a disaster.'

'I've not felt such humiliation either,' responded Patrick coolly. 'But not for the same reasons as yourself.' He looked down at her, his eyes brooding. 'The look on that poor woman's face when she realised she'd not been invited – an' her a friend o' twenty-five years' standing. I hate to say it, Tommy, but say it I will: I was ashamed of ye, and of myself for allowing ye to talk me into leaving poor Molly off the list. I don't know how I'm ever going to reconcile with it.'

'Are we going to throw that second party you promised her?'

He looked down at her derisively, not crediting that with an answer.

'I'm sorry, Pat. I couldn't know it was going to turn out like this, that she'd get to hear of the wedding from Liam. Poor Molly . . . and damn that son of yours too!' she added vehemently. 'You can't blame that episode on me.

311

If you'd played your role when he was younger . . . It's about time you started laying down the law. You must tell him if anything like that happens again he'll be out. I don't trust myself to speak to him at the moment.'

Patrick led the way back into the house and sighed. 'I think Sonny will have a few words to say to Dickie on that score.'

But Patrick could not have been more wrong. Sonny had nothing whatsoever to say to Dickie for the remainder of that day, nor for any of the following day, either.

Sam's parents, having shared the Feeney's place of worship, and later their Sunday luncheon, left in the early afternoon. Thomasin and Patrick waved them off in their cart, then returned to the dining room where William snored discordantly. He was their only company. Sonny had not shown his face at lunch nor breakfast. They knew he was in his room, but decided not to disturb him. He'd come down when he'd a mind. Dickie and Hannah had gone upstairs after lunch, the latter because she could not bear to feel Dominic Teale's mockery every time she caught his eye. When she did come down her wrinkled forehead bespoke her concern.

Thomasin finished checking on the state of her dinner service and closed the doors of the china cabinet. 'What's to do, Mother?'

Hannah took a deep breath before answering. 'I hate to say this, dear – but someone in this house is a thief!'

Patrick looked up sharply from the book he had been reading as Thomasin called for elucidation.

Hannah flopped down into one of the Regency-striped chairs. 'It seems totally ironic. I bring my valuables with me for fear of them falling prey to burglars while my own house is unattended and promptly fall foul of them in my own daughter's house.' Patrick and Thomasin had laughed when she had arrived clutching her jewellery box the day before. They didn't laugh now. 'My cameo,' said Hannah. 'The one you gave me, Thomasin, it's gone missing.'

'Are you sure you brought it with you?'

'Thomasin, I had it on yesterday! Before I went to bed I replaced it in my jewellery box and it's no longer there. I only noticed a moment ago when I went to take another brooch out.'

'But you're sure you put it in the box?' pressed her daughter. 'Not on the dressing table – or maybe you left it down here?'

'Thomasin, it was in the box!'

'Well, maybe it's fallen underneath the other things.'

Hannah sighed heavily. 'How could it be underneath when last night it was on top? Unless someone has been rifling the box. It has definitely been purloined.'

After establishing that her mother could in no way be mistaken, Thomasin's first reaction was to blame one of the temporary maids.

'Well, if it was one o' them 'tis too late, they've gone,' said Patrick, then suppressed a smile as William made bodily noises in his sleep.

Hannah poked her husband frenziedly. 'William, wake up! We have a crisis.'

William moaned and rubbed his eyes, then squinted at their serious faces. 'What's all t'scrattlin' about?'

Hannah told him about the theft, then turned to Thomasin. 'There's only one thing for it, you'll have to fetch the police.'

'Now hold your rush,' replied her daughter firmly. 'Let's get Amy in here first and ask her if she noticed anything suspicious about these girls. I don't want to be bringing them into disrepute if they're innocent.' She rang the bell. 'And we don't want to be calling in the police unnecessarily. You know what the neighbours are like, Mother.'

Some minutes passed before Amy slouched in, up to her elbows in flour. 'I hope you're not gonna ask for tea,' she said impolitely. 'I'm in the middle o' bakin'.'

Thomasin ignored the discourtesy. 'I won't keep you, Amy, I just want . . .'

'Why, it's her!' screeched Hannah, leaping to her feet. 'Look! She's got the audacity to wear it.' She hobbled up

313

to the maid and pulled at the brooch which secured Amy's collar.

'Eh, what you up to?' shouted Amy rudely, knocking her hand away with floury hands. 'Get off!'

'Where did you get that brooch?' barked Thomasin.

'It were a present,' answered Amy, uneasy now. They were all staring at her. 'Why, what business is it of anyone else?'

'I'll tell you what business it is,' replied Hannah, before Thomasin had a chance to reprimand the girl for her cheek. 'It's my brooch.'

'No! It's mine. It were a present, I tell yer!' Amy put a protective hand over the brooch.

'Let me see!' Thomasin held out her hand.

The mistress' authority overruled Amy's disinclination to part with her property. Slowly she unpinned the brooch and handed it over. 'All right, but I'm tellin' the truth,' she emphasised stubbornly.

Thomasin looked from the brooch to her mother and then back at the maid. 'Who gave this to you?'

'None o' your business!' rallied Amy.

The menfolk rolled their eyes at each other and decided to stay well clear of this female disagreement. Besides, Patrick would not know one brooch from another.

Thomasin stepped closer to Amy and thrust the words into her face. 'It goes without saying, Miss Forsdyke, that you are no longer in my employ and as such are not beholden to answer my questions. However,' her eyes narrowed, 'if you choose not to answer mine, perhaps you will be more pliable when the Constable arrives.' Any involvement with the police was the furthest thing from Thomasin's mind, but Amy was not to know that.

The maid paled but stood her ground and her voice, though it trembled, bore a degree of victory. 'All right, then, call the police, I dare yer!' She chanced a smirk as Thomasin's confident expression faded slightly. 'Just what d'yer think they'll do? I'll tell yer: they'll laugh their bloody heads off. An' shall I tell yer why?'

Despite her failed bluff Thomasin retained her composure. 'I'm sure you will delight in it.'

'Too bloody right I will! I'm sick to death o' you pushin' me about, actin' like you're Lady Muck. It's about time that someone cut you down to size. I'll tell yer who gimme that brooch, Mrs High an' Mighty, it were your bloody son, so if anybody's a thief, he is!'

Patrick threw aside the book. 'I think if my son's to be accused he should be present. Thomasin, go tell Dickie to come down.' The damning thought occurred to him that without any name being mentioned he had known that it was his elder son who was the culprit. When Dickie made his entrance he summed up the situation in one glance and prepared himself for the onslaught. How could they think he would stoop to something so low as stealing his grandmother's brooch? Didn't Amy have more opportunity than he did to steal it when she was making the beds?

'Why, you lyin' little swine!' Amy went for him. 'You gave it to me. An' what about all that other stuff?'

'What other stuff?' asked Patrick.

'The stuff that's been buyin' his way into my bed for the past year! Aye, I thought that'd make yer prick yer ears up!' She nodded at Hannah. 'Look at her! Eyes like organ-stops.'

'That's enough!' interjected Patrick heatedly. 'Dickie, what have you to say on this?'

'I've no idea what she's talkin' about,' his son protested.

Amy was furious. 'Oh, I'm supposed to've imagined all them necklaces an' bracelets, am I? Was I also supposed to've imagined the fella that kept bouncin' on top o' me?' Hannah's bosom heaved and she collapsed into a chair. William sat with mouth agape.

'Would you care to show us these . . . gifts, Amy?' said Thomasin, but it wasn't an invitation.

Amy looked dubiously at the others. She'd really landed herself in it, hadn't she? She must've been mad not to see it . . . Nevertheless she was forced to bring them the articles – several brooches, two necklaces, a ring and a bracelet.

'I see,' Thomasin nodded, then said to her son, 'So, your deception doesn't merely extend to your grandmother, Richard.'

'They're yours, Tommy?' asked Patrick.

'Every one.' Thomasin had a jewellery box in which she kept her favourite ornaments. The ones here being a mite too heavy for her tastes had been stored away in a separate box in her wardrobe – at least they had been when last she had looked.

'So . . .' Patrick turned back to his son. 'Are ye going to tell us that Amy's lying about these also, Richard?'

Dickie toured a philosophical eye around the hostile assembly, then said equably, 'Ah, 'tis true in part what she says, I did give her the things – but 'twas her leading me on, saying she'd be nice to me if I brought her presents. Ye know how hard it is for a young fella to resist temptation, Dad. There was no malice intended in my taking them. Mam never used half o' that jewellery, never even missed it . . .'

'So ye thought your grandmother wouldn't miss it either,' interrupted Patrick.

Dickie looked suitably hurt. 'It wasn't a case of her not noticing. Amy said she'd tell about all the other things if I didn't get it for her, she knew they were Mother's. I'm sorry Grandma, but I was frightened.' His face was contrite but the sidelong glance he gave Amy was far from it.

'That wasn't the way it was at all!' yelled Amy. 'I thought he'd bought 'em.'

'Where would I get the money to buy things like that?' asked Dickie injuredly.

'That's true, you must've known, Amy,' said Thomasin sternly.

'D'yer think I'd be bloody soft enough to wear 'em if I knew they were stolen?' shouted Amy. 'I do know one thing, though – I was bloody stupid to think he'd bought

316

'em when all the time he's tellin' me what a tight cow you are.'

'Be quiet!' Patrick stared at his son then. 'May God forgive me for choosing to believe the word of this trollop before ...'

'Oy, just a minute!' objected Amy, and was silenced.

'As I was saying, may God forgive me for choosing to believe the word of a trollop before that of my son, but I do. Your conduct in the last two or three years has left me in no doubt that what she accuses ye of is completely feasible. There's no depth to which ye wouldn't stoop if ye thought it'd better your position.' He looked hard at his son for a full minute longer, then spun away in disgust and the room was heavy with his silent anger. 'Very well, Amy,' he said at last in disciplined tones, 'despite the fact that my son has apportioned blame to you, I find myself forced to exonerate you in the theft of the jewellery.'

'Dad, I ...' Dickie was silenced by a glare.

'However,' went on Patrick as Amy's shoulders gave way in relief, 'neither your behaviour with my son nor the manner in which ye spoke to my wife will be condoned. Whatever your grievances she's still your employer and as such deserves respect.'

'Respect – her?' flung Amy.

'I must warn ye not to proceed on this tack,' said Patrick coldly. 'Ye've been cleared of stealing the jewellery but should ye mouth one more insult about my wife then I should find no remorse in fetching the police and having ye questioned on the matter of several items of food and linen which have persistently gone astray since you entered my employ. We've been very fair with you, Amy and this is how ye repay us.' Amy lost some of her bluster as Patrick concluded, 'Ye will leave the room now and go pack your bags as quickly as ye can. When ye come down you'll be given a month's wages in lieu and will then depart this house for good. Go now.'

Fifteen tempestuous minutes elapsed before Amy, plus luggage, stood once more in front of him. Patrick handed over the envelope containing her wages. 'Ye may wish to count it.' When she shook her head and pocketed the envelope he went on, 'I trust that every item in your case is accountable for?'

Her lips, until now bloodless with compression, parted. 'You've got all the things he gimme,' she spat. 'An' don't be sayin' they're not all there 'cause if I know him he'll've whipped a hell of a lot more than he's given me.'

Here Thomasin stepped forth and took great pleasure in her spiteful retort. 'Don't worry yourself on that account, Amy. To retrieve those items we will just have to consult with his other harlots.'

If looks could kill there would have been mass murder committed in that room. As it was, Amy turned on her heel and flounced out, her only satisfaction coming in a violent slam of the outer door.

Night fell. The beds had not yet been returned to their normal positions and Sonny was still forced to sleep in his brother's room. Dickie sighed heavily into the darkness and revolved his head in the direction of his brother's bed. 'Are ye awake, Son?'

There was no answer. He had not expected one. He propped himself up and peered at the lumpy shape beneath the blankets. A strand of light escaped the closed curtains and illuminated a sprig of Sonny's hair, setting the pillow a-flame. 'Son, please talk to me. You're the only one that matters to me. I'm really in the shit with all the others.'

'And what makes you think you smell any sweeter here?' came the muttered reply. He was doing his damnedest to push Agatha from his head; there seemed no point entertaining idle dreams now.

'Ah, God love him he's talkin' to me!' Dickie laughed his relief. 'Have ye got over your mulligrubs?'

Sonny let out a noisy exhalation and rolled onto his back. His character would not allow him to keep up this adverse silence any longer. 'I can see I'm not going to be allowed to sleep until I listen to your prattling.'

'I'll not keep ye, Son. I just wanted to make peace

318

with ye. I'd hate us to fall out over a woman – an' a plain-lookin' one at that. Jaze, I've seen better-looking pigs.'

'If Agatha was so abhorrent to you then why did you have to press your unwelcome suit?' enquired Sonny acidly. 'And before you speak I can provide the answer. You did it because you supposed I was fond of her and you couldn't bear the thought of me having a girl that you haven't had first.'

'Ye've got it all wrong, Son,' pleaded Dickie. 'I can't even answer myself why I did it. It doesn't seem to matter what they look like, I just have to try. I don't know what it is about me . . .'

'I think you do and I think I got it right the first time,' insisted Sonny.

'Aw, Son – don't let's fall out over a silly thing like this.'

'Silly!' breathed Sonny forcefully. 'You don't seem to realise that besides insulting Agatha you've disgraced me in front of my schoolfriend. I don't have to face Agatha but I do him. You've ruined my whole life! He imagines that we're a bunch of clods . . .'

'If y'ask me 'tis him who's the clod,' remarked Dickie. 'An' after the way he looked down his nose at ye I'm surprised ye want to go back there an' share a room with him.'

'I'm not going back,' Sonny revealed.

Dickie became alert. 'You're staying with me?'

'Shit to you. I'm just not going back, that's all. I decided yesterday. You're right in part of what you say, he was a false friend – but don't think that excuses your behaviour, you were bloody detestable. Anyway . . . it was almost my last year there. I've learnt pretty much all I need to know. Now that Erin's gone her own way Mam's going to need my help, 'cause I don't forsee her getting it from any other quarter. I don't think Dad'll put up any objections after what happened with Rupert. So . . . it looks as though I'm here to stay.'

Dickie let his head drop to the pillow and snuggled his

arms under the covers, trying to see his brother's face in the gloom. 'I'm glad you're stayin', Son,' he said, with nary a hint of guile, then closed his eyes and went to sleep.

PART THREE
1871–1872

CHAPTER TWENTY-SEVEN

Thomasin, though sad that Sonny felt unable to return to college, was greatly obliged for his help in running the store. The course he had taken in Commerce proved a great boon. Together they went through the books and devised new ways of improving an already flourishing industry. The workmen had just finished knocking down the dividing wall between this shop and the one next door. By next Christmas the plans she had outlined to Erin should be a reality. And now that the wall was down and the choking dust dispersed she could reopen the store.

One of the plans already implemented came not from Thomasin's brain but her father's. William had for a long time felt the need to retire, but like most men of his years and status was unable to afford to do this. Undoubtedly, his other daughters would have contributed to his unkeep, if only to salve their consciences for the infrequency of their visits, but William wanted none of their gratuities; not even from his favourite daughter, whose proposed endowment had been politely, but firmly turned down. He didn't want to be a burden on anybody. He was a man accustomed to earning his own daily bread and would continue to do so until his body gave out.

But with his daughter's exciting concepts for the new store it came to him that there was a way round this. William had worked in the cocoa and coffee trade since coming to York half a lifetime ago; he could be a financial asset to Thomasin whilst solving his own need to take things a little easier. He put forward the idea that she should install a coffee roaster, of which he would be in charge, and produce their own blend of coffee.

'I could pass on all my knowledge to Sonny,' he said eagerly. 'Then he'll be able to do it when I'm gone. Oh, come on, Tommy! Don't let me down. It's the answer to an owd man's prayer.'

'You never said a prayer in your life!' But she laughed at his earnestness. 'Well, if we do put one in it'll be somewhere out of the way at the back of the store. I don't want your fruity language drifting in while I'm serving the ladies from the convent – you'll lose me all my custom.'

'Yer mean I can have one? Oh, champion!'

And that had been the start of his new career. It had been arranged that William should confine his roastings to the mornings thereby halving the twelve hours that he presently worked at the factory. He had had a few qualms about leaving his employers – they were good men and he would be setting up in a kind of opposition – but characteristically they had wished him luck in his venture and voiced their gratitude for the loyal service he had given them. There had also been a collection amongst his workmates which had resulted in William being presented with a plaque to commemorate his stay there, an unprecedented action and one which reduced this normally bluff fellow to tears.

Thomasin had been instructed that the coffee roaster would take four weeks to deliver, to which she had promptly retorted that if it did not arrive within a fortnight she would not be requiring it at all. Now, a fortnight later, here it stood in an area specially designated for it, begging to be stoked with wood and aching to churn out pounds and pounds of freshly-roasted coffee.

The woman watched her father put Sonny through the whole procedure of roasting coffee beans, rambling on about blending and tasting, and smiled felicitously. For a long time she had been trying to persuade him to retire – the pains he kept getting in his chest worried her, though William himself made light of them – but the stubborn old goat had constantly refused her 'charity'. And now the installation of this simple piece of equipment had done what she had been unable to do; lend him a sense of self-esteem for the remaining years of his life. Just look at him, she smiled, one would never dream he's in his seventies the way he's acting over that roaster. He's like a child with a toy train. So full of . . . here she laughed aloud at herself; she had been about to say *beans*. Likely they would all be inundated with blasted beans if her father's over-enthusiasm was allowed to run riot. She moved her smiling face onto her son's, whence an immediate frown took its place. Sonny, though trying valiantly to conceal it, was quite clearly bored by the entire business.

She stared at him for a while longer as thought took over. It seemed they had all been assuming far too much of Sonny. Father had assumed that his grandson would find as much enjoyment as he did in his trade. She herself had taken it for granted that the boy was happy working beside her – well, he had never given her any indication to the contrary. It was high time she and her son had a talk. Making some excuse to her father she left him clucking over his new toy and dragged Sonny over to the far side of the store.

'Sit down a minute, son,' she indicated a wooden crate. He studied her with mild surprise but did as she told him. She sat on the adjacent crate. 'I was watching you just now when your grandfather was showing you the ropes – you're not happy with all this, are you?'

He lowered his face so that she wouldn't see the truth. 'I'm not complaining, am I?'

'No, you're not. You're a good lad, better than I deserve I sometimes think. Is it what happened with Agatha that's still bothering you? I think you were very fond of her, weren't you?'

He nodded. 'Still, I'll get over it. I usually do.'

She curled tapered fingers round his shoulder and gripped him affectionately. 'Eh, son you've had a rough deal out of all this haven't you? You get sent away to a college where you don't really want to go. Then your brother upskells all that, like he upskells everything, and you find yourself stuck here with your old mother. It doesn't seem fair, does it?'

His grey eyes were solemn. 'And who would help you

325

here if not me? Erin's gone now and I doubt Grandad will be concerned with anything other than his coffee beans.'

'Aye, he's right taken up with that, isn't he?' she chuckled. 'But I can always hire an apprentice, you know. We're not exactly penniless.'

He shook his head, somewhat apathetically. 'And what would I do then? Anyway, if a fella can't help his own mother ...'

'How's that painting lark of yours these days?' she asked unexpectedly.

He shrugged. 'I don't seem to get much time for it now.' The store opened at seven o'clock in the morning and closed twelve hours later. What time was there left for painting? Only Sunday, and that was mostly eaten up by Mass.

'Would you like to?' The question startled him. 'What I mean, Sonny, is that back there with your grandfather I was suddenly overwhelmed by the fact that we're all doing something we enjoy – all except you. Me with my shop, your father with his land, Dickie ... well, Dickie's another matter, but Erin has her Sam. What have we left you with? Nothing. It's a bite late in the day for such exposures I'll admit, but I realise now you're not cut out for this work, even though I do appreciate your business acumen. You weren't at college long, but you certainly didn't waste your time there.' She patted him, then her hand left his shoulder to rest in her lap. 'I'm going to make a deal with you.' He watched her alertly. 'You can help me get this new store together and keep the place well-stocked, give me a bit of assistance with the book-keeping, and I'll give you the afternoons to spend doing your painting.'

He was flabbergasted. 'But you know Father's views on artists. He'd go up in the air if he thought I was slacking while my mother broke her back here.'

'You're telling me you don't want this deal then?'

'No! I'm not saying that at all,' he said quickly, making her laugh. 'I want it all right.' He dropped his face and picked at the splintered edges of the crate, then looked

326

up again to regard her with interest. 'Can I ask what made you change your mind?'

'Maybe it was just standing back and taking a really good look at my son,' replied his mother. 'You've an extra-ordinary talent, Sonny. I always knew that but I've just been too selfish . . .' She countered his objection. 'Oh, yes. I didn't wholeheartedly agree with your father when he scoffed at your choice of career, but in letting him have his own way I was just as guilty.'

'Well, I suppose as it turned out it wasn't much of a hardship to go to college,' said Sonny forgivingly. 'I did manage to get in a lot of painting between lessons, so you could say we've both benefited.'

'But if I'm not wrong you want to devote more to your painting than just in-between times? Make it more than a hobby, which is what it is at present.'

'I'd be less than honest if I denied that,' he answered. 'Ideally I'd use it to form my future.' He hunched forward, the points of his elbows resting on his knees. 'You see, Father doesn't understand what it means to me – I don't think anyone does.'

'Would you like to try explaining?' she ventured. 'Maybe if I were to put your case . . .'

'It's far too hard to describe. It's like . . .' he groped for a word that would dovetail with his feelings, but the only comparison with those was his brother's obsession with women, and that was unmentionable. 'Like an illness,' he decided, for want of more apt description. 'No . . . a compulsion. It's not just that I like to paint, but that I *must* paint. The magic that takes over when I pick up a brush . . . it . . . oh, it's inexplicable! I won't even try. I think, though, of all of you Erin would be best able to identify with it. The look on her face when she plays her harp is what I feel about my painting.'

His mother moved her head sadly from side to side. 'And to think I'm responsible for denying you that pleasure . . .'

He recovered his normal stance. 'Don't heap too much

of the blame onto yourself, Mam. It was Father's decision in the end.'

She came alive. 'Aye well, never let it be said that Thomasin Feeney was the one who robbed the nation of a major talent. I'll stick to what I've said: you give me the mornings and the afternoons are your own. As for your father,' she winked, 'what he doesn't know . . .'

'D'you know . . .' he kissed her '. . . I'm right glad you're my mother.'

'Aye, well you can show your appreciation by painting me some good pictures. If I'm going to employ a part-time assistant I'm going to make sure I get my full whack. I've been studying that wall over there. It's wasted space. I intend to put it to full use by covering it with an exhibition of your pictures. You must have a tidy few stacked away in that pigsty you call a bedroom. Somebody ought to be fool enough to buy them.'

'Why, you mercenary old bugger!' laughed her son. 'And here's me thinking you're getting benevolent in your old age, when all the time you're bent on making money out o' me.'

She gave a prim smile. 'Well, don't you want the opportunity to prove to your father that painting isn't as worthless an occupation as he makes out? If your work is making money he'll have to eat his words, won't he?'

'I don't know that they will sell, Mam. People are a bit wary when it comes to unknown artists.'

'Stuff and nonsense! If folk don't know a masterpiece when they see one that's their hard luck. Your paintings will be fetching thousands in ten years' time.'

'Well, perhaps twenty,' he joked.

'Not a word to your father about the afternoons off, mind. We'll just let him think we're selling the paintings you've done in the past.' She elbowed him. 'Isn't this better than humping sacks of currants around all day?'

'Owt's better than that,' he laughed, and squeezed her. 'All right, if you say so I'll dig out some of my better efforts and get them framed. Though I must say it'll be like selling part of myself.'

'Eh, you do talk daft,' scoffed Thomasin. 'Now, come on, let's use that coffee roaster to stick kettle on, I'm fair clemmed.'

Her comment brought another smile to his lips; it was ages since he had heard her use such an expression. As they approached the coffee roaster the sudden thought came. 'Eh, what about Grandad? His nose is going to be put out of joint when he knows about this.'

'About what?' William continued with his ministerings without looking up.

'That we want to boil the kettle on your new contraption,' provided Thomasin adroitly.

'Tha'll 'ave a bloody job – blasted thing's gone out.' William rammed in a pair of bellows and worked them furiously.

'Never mind, Dad,' said his daughter. 'I was thinking of locking up and going home anyway. Before I do, though, me and Sonny have been discussing the matter of this coffee roasting.'

'Oh aye?' He spared an abstracted look, then dropped his eyes back to his work, piling more wood into the roaster.

'And we thought it might not be such a good idea for you to honour Sonny with your expertise.' She eyed him carefully.

'Don't tha mean his talents are too good to waste on a soft article like me?' answered her father sourly.

'I didn't mean that at all. My point being that you'd be better off with a boy who could devote all his time to learning the trade, without the distractions that Sonny would have. How would that suit you? An apprentice all to yourself.'

'All to missen, tha sez?' William stopped feeding wood into the roaster and perked up. 'To do with as I like? Givin' orders an' that?'

'Aye – you can whip him six times a day if it suits you,' answered his daughter. 'Provided you limit your teaching to coffee roasting and don't pass on your expert vocabulary.'

'Eh, tha gets more like tha mother every day,' commented William, saying to Sonny, 'There were a time when thy mother could match everything I said – an' better it. This business is goin' to her head.'

'You're right it is! And I'm learning more sense. You don't win custom by telling people to bugger off like you'd do given a chance. Now, do you want this apprentice or not?'

'Eh, I do indeed! Fancy, William Fenton a maister, with a lad to do his biddin'. Eh, I'm dead chuffed.'

Thomasin winked at Sonny. Would that everyone was as easily pleased as her father. 'Are you coming home with us, Dad or are you going to play with that all night?'

'Nay, you go 'ome. I think I sh'll stop a bit longer, get t'hang o' this blessed thing. It's a bit more newfangled than I'm used to.'

When Thomasin and her son arrived home, Josie Flowers, the maid whom Thomasin had been fortunate enough to engage within a short interval of dismissing Amy, met them with a cheery welcome. 'Good afternoon, ma'am, Mr John. I've got the kettle on to boil. You go rest your legs an' I'll whip it in there in two shakes of a lamb's tail.'

'Oh, God bless you, Josie.' Thomasin handed over her jacket which the maid slung over her arm. Once in the drawing room she kicked off her shoes. The warm weather had made her ankles swell. I'm getting old at both ends, she thought, examining her hair in the mirror before sinking into a chair. Her feet troubled her something awful in the summer nowadays and the auburn in her hair was fast being replaced by silver. 'Wouldn't you know I'd start going grey just when red hair is all the rage,' she complained to her son.

Josie entered with the tea. 'There y'are, ma'am, an' I've made some o' them little cakes you like an' all.'

'Are you trying to fatten me up for Christmas, Josie?' asked Thomasin, eyeing the great pile of cakes and scones. She liked Josie.

'Fatten you up? Why, I should say so, wouldn't you, Mr

330

John?' Josie said breezily. 'You're nothing but skin an' bone, an' no wonder the way you're working yourself. You should take it easy at your age.'

Thomasin covered a smile. Josie, at sixteen, thought as most young people did: once you were over thirty you were ready for the boneyard. She placed her throbbing feet on a bead-embroidered footstool. 'Happen you're right, Josie. I have been overdoing it lately – but no one else is going to mind the shop. My son's a great help but if he could do the baking I'd be set up.'

'Well, you will find work for yourself, Mother,' said Sonny, munching one of Josie's 'Fat Rascals'. 'And you'll have even more to do now you've given me the afternoons off.'

Fortunately Josie missed the look of reproach that Thomasin threw her son for mentioning their secret. 'Now, you know I offered to do Miss Erin's job,' she said plainly. Thomasin had told her of Erin's aptitude and how she would miss her. 'I've got into a nice routine now. I'm certain I could manage a few extra pies an' all.'

'It'd be more than just a few, Josie,' said Thomasin, gratefully sipping the tea. 'Everyone seems to have taken such a liking to our pies that I sell dozens every week. And if I get this new oven installed it could run to dozens per day. Besides, I don't imagine you'd find much joy in splitting yourself between home and shop.'

'You're ahead of yourself, Mrs Feeney,' scolded Josie. 'No wonder you always look so tired. You haven't even got the oven in yet. We can meet that when we come to it. 'Till then I'm sure I'm capable of turning out a few pies at home. If you could've seen the workload I had to cope with at my last job then you'd not doubt me.'

'Doubt you?' said Thomasin. 'Never. You're a gem, Josie. I consider myself most fortunate to have found you. And if you're intent on doing that extra baking then you must have extra money to make it worth your while.'

'Oh, ma'am, there's no need. It's so much easier here than at my last place that I sometimes feel ashamed to accept such a good wage.'

'Nevertheless, you will get a pay rise,' insisted her employer. 'I had enough accusations of being tight-fisted from our last help.'

'Oh, I'd never call you that!'

'I'm sure you wouldn't dear, but all the same I think you're worth more than you're getting and therefore you're going to get that rise.'

Josie was in the middle of mouthing suitable credit when the doorbell sounded and she bustled off to answer it, leaving Thomasin and Sonny smiling over her enthusiasm.

'Ah, you must be Miss Erin and Mr Sam!' Josie exclaimed on opening the door to a surprised couple. 'Or should I say Mr and Mrs Teale?' She ushered them into the hall, fussing over their coats like a broody hen. 'The mistress told me all about you, ma'am. You must go straight in, I know she'll be delighted to see you both looking so well.'

'Well, fancy ringing the doorbell!' Thomasin leapt up as Erin and Sam were shepherded in and flung her arms wide.

'We thought we'd surprise you.' Erin received her hug then stood aside while Thomasin wrapped her arms around Sam.

'You did that! Oh, it's lovely to have you back. Are you both well? You certainly look it. What sort of weather have you enjoyed – or were you too busy to notice?'

Erin blushed and pushed her mother away with a sharp laugh, answering the barrage of questions with one statement. 'We're both perfectly fit and well, Mam. Now, tell me who in the world is the girl who showed us in? She talks as though she's known us for years.' She returned her brother's uneffusive, but sincere greeting and made way so that Sonny could shake hands with Sam. Thomasin led them to the sofa and, seating one on either side of her, told them all about the sordid affair with Amy. When she had finished Erin conveyed her disgust. 'I don't know why you put up with my brother, I really don't. He disgraces the whole family.' It was easy to see she had not forgiven Dickie for spoiling her wedding.

'There's more,' said Thomasin wearily. 'To cap it all, the other day a policeman knocked at my door and informed me that Dickie had been making a nuisance of himself with our neighbour's daughter again. Said if it didn't cease forthwith he would have to arrest him for making a public nuisance of himself. I was so ashamed.'

'Why don't ye throw him out?' said Erin viciously.

'I have seriously considered it, believe me.' Thomasin's face was awash with despair. 'But he's my son, Erin, I can't just cast him out like I did Amy. I know he's a despicable creature – a cheat and a liar – but I only have to look at his face to know I could never be so callous. All this has hit your father very hard; Dickie being a thief especially. The lad protests it was because we didn't pay him enough, and at one time I did consider raising his allowance. But then we both came to the conclusion that he'd be an even worse philanderer with money in his pocket. By curtailing his funds we can at least keep some sort of control over him.' She brightened and gestured at Sonny. 'But I shouldn't be complaining. This one makes up twofold for his brother's sins. You ought to see the shop now, Erin, you wouldn't recognize it. The wall's down and your grandfather's set up a coffee roaster ... Oh, now listen to me full of myself! I haven't even asked if you've settled into your new home?'

Erin said they had, even though they had only been back off honeymoon a couple of days. The house felt like home already. 'Sam's finding it hard to get up so early in the morning though,' she added. 'I don't know why he doesn't find work nearer home instead of travelling all the way to York every day.'

Sam made his first donation to the conversation. 'We've been through all that,' he said patiently – too patiently. Thomasin at once sensed some sort of friction. 'Mr Simons has been good to me. I can't just up and leave like that, not until his apprentice has served his time, or at least has grasped the gist of the trade, enough to save Mr Simons doing all the heavy work.'

'But that'll be ages,' protested Erin.

'Not really. Just a couple o' years. By that time we ought to have saved enough to buy those animals we've been talking about.'

'*You've* been talking about,' corrected his wife. She told her mother, 'He's getting so ambitious – even talking about buying more land. As if you haven't been generous enough.'

Thomasin said that this sounded like a fine idea and straight away offered financial help. 'Always leave room for expansion, that's my motto. That cottage is very cosy for two, but there'll come a time when you want to build on.'

Erin laughed, but the sound was without humour. 'Mother's got expansion on the brain. Here we are only just married and already she's got us saddled with a family.'

Sam remained silent and looked down at his hands. Thomasin noticed that perhaps Sam didn't look as happy as she had at first thought. There was a worried crease dividing his forehead and the hint of a shadow under his normally sparkling eyes. It could, of course, be put down to rising extra early for work, but Thomasin was not so sure. She addressed Erin. 'Well, isn't that what you got married for? And if you think my comment is premature, why, let me tell you that I gave birth to Dickie in my first year of marriage.' She chose not to divulge that Dickie had been conceived *before* the wedding.

'I've changed my mind,' replied Erin airily. 'I'm not sure that the world is any fit place to bring children into. There's no future for them. Just look at all the wars and other terrible things that're going on all over the globe. I couldn't inflict that on a child of mine.'

Thomasin smiled indulgently. Wasn't it funny how every generation of prospective mothers wrestled with this agonising decision? Nevertheless, looking at Sam's preoccupied face she felt that there was more behind it. But it was none of her business; Erin was a married woman now and must solve her own problems. 'Eh, I'll be a lot happier when these lads of mine have made as good a match as you,' she sighed to Erin. 'One of them's too busy dividing his attentions to be caught with one girl, and the other shows no inclination whatsoever to make his mother happy. I was just thinking, I'm not getting any younger. It'd be a tragedy if I were to die without seeing all my children happily married.'

'We'll have to see what we can do then, Mam, won't we?' Sonny winked at Sam, his spirits having been raised enormously by his mother's generosity. But his brother-in-law did not seem his usual self at all. The cheeky grin was nowhere to be seen, and the normally youthful face looked all of its twenty-six years and more.

Thomasin bit her finger thoughtfully. If that was the face of wedded bliss, then she was Queen Dick.

CHAPTER TWENTY-EIGHT

Having the afternoons to do with as he pleased did more than anything to help Sonny over the Agatha incident. By the summer he found himself able to think of her without it hurting. In fact he rarely thought about her at all, being involved so much with his other passion.

Today, the family was at Mass, sitting in their habitual pew six rows from the front. Thomasin elbowed Dickie sharply to end his devious survey of the congregation. Wherever he goes, thought Sonny, seeing the action, he's always on the lookout. He knelt down with the others and drew his rosary from the pocket of his smart donkey-brown frockcoat, lowering his head in a brief prayer: 'please, God, make her be here.' Peeping discreetly over the top of his clasped hands he shot a quick glance at the pew where he had seen her sitting last week, that lovely girl with the dimples and the doe-like eyes who had intruded on his thoughts even while he was painting.

His stomach did a tipple-tail at the sight of a cherry-coloured bonnet. She was here! He was certain it was the same girl, though he could only see the back of her head from his position. It must be her; the bonnet was the same. The artist in him was always susceptible to colour and contrast. Apart from which, on the last occasion his observant eye had spotted a tiny mole just beneath her right earlobe. If she would just turn her head slightly so that the ringlets which now obscured it would . . . yes! It was her.

Sonny started as his parents and brother rose from their knees and settled back to wait for Father Kelly. He sat back with them staring at the cherry bonnet, willing her to turn round. For once in his life he didn't want Mass to end. He just wanted to sit here and feast his eyes on her.

But inevitably Mass did end and people began to shuffle from their pews. Sonny felt a dig in his back. It was Dickie. 'Get a move on, Son, I'm bloody famished. We'll be here all day if ye let everyone else past. Go on now, after this old biddy. Push!'

Behind Dickie his parents waited patiently for Sonny to lead the way, but their son had no intention of leaving the pew until the girl who was moving slowly down the aisle came level with him. He held onto the backs of the pews on either side of him to stop his brother from pressing him out before he was ready to go.

'Will ye bloody shift!' hissed Dickie. 'I've got things to see to.' He leaned on his brother hard.

Sonny strained to keep his position. He looked directly into her face as she neared him. Look at me! he pleaded – and she did. Those molasses-brown eyes settled briefly on his red hair, then dropped to take in his own. At the contact she lowered her lashes demurely, suitably proper as she drew level with him.

Dickie was still pressing his weight against him. When Sonny released his grip on the pews to move forward, he went sprawling into the aisle. The girl gave a high exclamation as he crashed into her. Thomasin, who had seen it happen, gave Dickie a reprobatory prod in the back, while Sonny stuttered his profuse regrets to the girl.

And then she was lost; at least to Sonny. He could still see the top of her cherry bonnet as he shuffled shoulder to shoulder with the congregation, but when he finally slipped into the blinding sunlight she was gone.

After a disconsolate breakfast, during which he ate hardly anything, he told his parents that he was going for a walk. Thomasin folded her napkin and dabbed at her lips. 'Well, please remember it's the Sabbath, I trust you won't be undertaking anything strenuous.'

'Just walking, as I said, and maybe I'll do a little sketching. I'll be back for lunch.'

'Would ye be knowing the whereabouts of your brother?' Patrick asked before his younger son left. Dickie had wolfed down his breakfast then had hurriedly excused himself. 'On second thoughts, don't bother to answer that. I'm sure I wouldn't like it.'

Sonny had not the slightest interest in where his brother had gone; he had only one person on his mind. He wondered whether she would be at Mass this evening – though his parents would think it highly suspicious that Sonny had actually volunteered to go to Mass twice. He must see her; he must.

Going upstairs he collected a fistful of pencils and a sketchpad then, as an afterthought, a small box of watercolours. Immersion in his favourite pastime might take that gnawing hunger away.

He strolled to the centre of town where he occupied himself for a short time pencilling sketches of various buildings or portions of architecture that caught his interest. But as he found that each sketch turned into a doe-eyed girl in a cherry bonnet he soon gave up. He would have liked to take off his coat – the sun was awfully hot – but felt that his mother might not approve of her son in his shirtsleeves on a Sunday.

Housing the pencil in his top pocket and the sketchpad under his arm, he strolled on. He wondered what she was doing now, and kicked a rotten apple along the pavement until it rolled out of reach of his feet and into the gutter. There was nothing in the windows to interest him at all. All he saw were cherry-coloured bonnets. Like as not he'd be seeing them in his sleep. There was yet another over there.

He sighed and walked on – then checked swiftly to stare at the girl who was sauntering towards him. Oh, no! Yes! I mean yes, don't I? His mind would not function. What do I say? Say something, you fool! Anything to stop her walking past. But she was already past, her sprigged cotton skirt swaying from side to side and never a look in his direction.

And then he saw it: a tiny scrap of white lace on the footwalk. Deftly he snatched it up and hared after her. She graced him with questioning eyes at his rude approach. 'I think this must be yours, miss.' He breathlessly proffered the glove.

She gave an expression of surprise and examined her small hands with their tapered fingers and pink nails. One was wearing a glove, the other was naked. 'Oh, how careless of me.' She took the glove from him. 'I'm most indebted, Mr . . . ?'

'Feeney,' said Sonny. 'John Feeney – and it was my pleasure to oblige such a charming lady as yourself.' Good heavens he was beginning to sound like Dickie! He rifled his mind for something intelligent to say, anything to keep her there. But there was no need – she appeared to be in no hurry to go.

'I recall now taking the glove off to pick up a pin from the footwalk. Well, it's good luck, you see,' she explained. 'See a pin, pick it up, and all the day you'll have good luck.' Sonny nodded adoringly. 'The glove must have slipped to the pavement. How fortunate that you were there to save me the trouble and expense of purchasing a new pair. You must be my piece of good luck.' She laughed gaily, then leaned her head to one side and studied him. 'Haven't we met before?'

He was encouraged by her lack of inhibitions and soon lost his own. 'I'm afraid it wasn't a very favourable meeting.

It was my clumsiness that caused you some discomfort in church this morning.'

'Ah,' she smiled. 'I did wonder if you'd done it on purpose just to get to know me. Well, it is the sort of trick some young men employ,' she said as he reddened and pulled in his chin. 'Oh, dear! I hope I haven't offended you.' She bent her knees slightly in order to see into his hidden face. 'I was only teasing. I'm afraid that's one of my faults. I'm always upsetting members of my family with it.'

He forced his eyes to meet hers, though they burnt with embarrassment as he spoke. 'You were right.' She repeated her trait of putting her head to one side. 'I mean . . . I did do it on purpose,' he blurted. 'Well, not actually. . . what I mean is . . . I did . . . I do want to get to know you.' It was said. He breathed a sigh of release.

'Well, I must say, Mr Feeney you can be very persuasive in your ambitions. You almost bowled me over.'

Sonny was immediately at pains to specify that it had been his brother who had pushed him. He would have made his approach more gently had he been allowed. 'I'm glad we've met again. The apology I gave this morning was hardly sufficient.'

'I agree it was most opportune, Mr Feeney,' she smiled. 'Not because I fancied your apology to be unsatisfactory, but because I too was eager for us to know each other more intimately.' He gaped speechlessly as she added lightly, 'Do you believe I'm always so careless with my gloves?'

'You dropped it on purpose?' said Sonny, though more amazed that his feelings had been reciprocated than at her blatant act.

'I know it was terribly forward of me,' she pouted. 'But, dear Mr Feeney, I've been thinking of you all morning since church. I kept inventing different ways of getting to know you, never suspecting that I would be able to carry out my plan so soon. When I saw you not twenty paces away I had but a few seconds to make up my mind. It was a very old ruse I chose I must admit, but effective all the same. I was, though, a little troubled that my precocity might deter you, that you might think me terribly fast.' Her lashes fluttered modestly against her cheek.

'Oh, my dear Miss ... why I don't even know your name,' exclaimed Sonny.

She provided it. 'Margaret Clancy.'

'Dear Miss Clancy, I'd never hold you in such low regard. Indeed, my own thoughts throughout the morning have been on a similar par with your own. I, too, had devised methods of meeting you, but I'm too great a coward ever to have carried them out.'

'I'm sure that's not true,' she chastised gently. 'Besides, now we've been properly introduced there's no more need for devious action. We can be open and honest with each other, can't we?'

Sonny eagerly agreed. 'Can I walk with you awhile?'

She said that she was going to visit her aunt and that he might walk as far as King's Square with her. 'I should hate for my aunt to look from her window and see me arm in arm with a gentleman, unchaperoned; she'd deem it most immoral.'

He took this as the hint it was and linked his arm with hers. 'I hope you'll excuse my asking, but isn't Clancy an Irish name?' He felt a slight stiffening of her arm and added swiftly, 'You have no trace of an accent.'

'My father and mother came from Ireland,' she explained. 'I was born here.'

'So was I,' said Sonny. 'But only my father is Irish.'

'You have managed to rid yourself of the accent too,' said his companion.

'You speak with some bitterness, Margaret ... oh! I'm sorry, may I call you Margaret?'

'No, but you may call me Peggy,' she smiled. 'Everyone does. Yes, you are right about my wish to hide my ancestry wherever possible. You too must be aware of the bigotry directed at us. As a young girl it quite upset me.'

He laughed softly. 'You are still young.'

'I am seventeen, Mr Feeney ... John.' She was quite serious.

So accustomed was he to hearing his childhood nick-name that when she spoke his real name he felt his skin tingle with delight.

'I trained myself to speak properly so that if one were not acquainted with my name one would never know I was Irish.' She did not reveal that she had accomplished this while in service, listening carefully to each of her employer's commands, not out of conscience but so that she would be able to repeat them accurately to herself later. It had worked; there was no trace of sing-song to her sentences now. She only wished her family would be so easily disposed of. They were going to prove a great handicap here. 'Surely, you too must have entertained similar ideas, John? I mean, you obviously had to alter your accent.'

'Not consciously,' said Sonny. 'It just happened when I went away to college. I'm not ashamed of being half-Irish, Peggy. I'm proud of my father; he's a good man. If people want to slander us then let them. I'll not relinquish my heritage for the sake of prejudice.'

'I'm sure you're a very noble sort of person, John,' she sighed. 'Beside you I must appear so shallow and conceited. Do you know, there was a time, quite recently, when I even toyed with the idea of marrying someone simply to change my name.'

He was aghast. Was that a hint for him not to mention the subject of marriage? That she would in no way coun-tenance swapping one Irish name for another?

But Peggy went on: 'I understood in time of course that my motives for marrying the person concerned were quite wrong. It would have been cruel of me to marry him purely for his name. Now that I am more mature I have dispensed with such fancies. When I do marry, John it will be for love. And I shall not care what his name is. I may be an idealist but I do believe that love is paramount when choosing a partner for life. Don't you agree?' She tightened her grip on his arm.

'Oh, yes,' breathed Sonny.

*

They met every Sunday after that – in secret naturally, for Sonny, much as he wanted to show her off to his family, knew what would happen the moment she spied his brother. In church they behaved as total strangers, only later in the afternoon could they share their true affections. Eventually, though, his parents began to comment on his regular absences and he was forced to tell them.

The moment that Sonny introduced his mother to his sweetheart Thomasin knew that this girl was not for her son. She watched those liquid brown eyes pour over her elder boy to whom the girl was now being introduced. Peggy was indisputably good-looking, albeit in a blowsy sort of way, but was more the kind that Thomasin would have associated with Dickie than with her younger son. And that terribly pretentious voice! I know you all right, lass, thought Thomasin shrewdly. The sort that dresses immaculately on top, but underneath her garments are crumpled and grimy – rather like her nature. And much as I want to see my son settled you'll not be the one to get your hooks into him if I have my say.

She waited for Josie to lay down the tray of tea before she began her grilling. 'Where do you live, Peggy?'

Peggy accepted a cup of tea. 'Goodramgate,' she replied but did not go into detail. Probably Bedern, thought Thomasin, though her fine clothes would have me believe otherwise. Bedern was as notorious an Irish ghetto as the one from which the Feeneys had sprung. She asked if Peggy had regular employment.

'I have indeed,' replied the girl. 'I am a lady's companion.' Well, that sounded more impressive than a maid-of-all-work, and it was not exactly a lie. She did keep her employer company – she and the old girl were the only two people in the house.

Patrick, too, had his questions. 'Do I know your father, Miss Clancy?'

'I think not, Mr Feeney,' she responded after disposing of a mouthful of cake. 'He is familiar with your identity of course, being a regular churchgoer himself. He and my

342

mother are always voicing their admiration for the way you have improved old Mr Penny's store.'

'I'm afraid that's to my wife's credit an' not mine,' answered Patrick pleasantly. 'I only produce the fruit an' vegetables for her to sell.'

'Then it's you I must congratulate on the grand appearance of the store,' said Peggy to Thomasin. 'My mother always shops with you, I believe, although I am hardly ever at home due to my work.'

Thomasin could not reply that she was acquainted with Mrs Clancy, for much as she would have liked to know every customer by name to cultivate her reputation of good service, her clientèle was now so large as to make this virtually impossible.

Patrick then asked in what line of business was Peggy's father.

'He is in the building profession,' disclosed Peggy.

'Ah, didn't I used to be in the building trade meself,' said Patrick. 'I like the outdoor life. Though I must say I prefer to work the soil than a pile of mortar.'

'So, you find no interest in retail, Mr Feeney?' enquired Peggy matter-of-factly. 'I find it all fascinating myself, and envy Mrs Feeney her skill.'

Thomasin put the record to rights. 'I did have a lot of help from my family. In fact, now that Sonny is no longer at college he probably puts in as much work as I do.'

'I daresay it will all be good practice for when his time comes to take over,' replied the girl, without thinking.

Yes, he is a good catch, Miss Clancy, isn't he? thought Thomasin intuitively, but smiled evenly and said, 'I have three children, Peggy. When the time comes for my husband and I to meet our Maker the property will be divided equally.'

Peggy was contrite. 'Oh, I didn't mean to imply . . . oh, dear, how rude you must think me. I'm sure you have many years ahead of you yet. I simply meant that John appears to be the one most directly concerned in the running of the store. I assumed . . .' her voice trailed away and she hurriedly hid her face in her teacup.

Thomasin finished her tea, placing the cup and saucer on the tray. 'Sonny, I'm sure that you and your friend would like a bit of privacy. Would you care to take Peggy into the front parlour?'

Sonny rose, trying not to look too eager, and led Peggy through to the other room, leaving behind a mother whose opinions were quite infrangible; this must be allowed to go no further.

'I fear your mother doesn't like me,' said Peggy plaintively when they were alone. 'I believe my innocent remark about you and the grocery led her to think that I am only interested in you for the fortune you will inherit.'

'Oh, I'm sure you're wrong,' said Sonny earnestly, seating himself beside her. 'Mother doesn't think that way at all.' He was blissfully unaware that the Peggy he saw and the one his mother saw were two different creatures. His Peggy was the sweetest thing he had ever met. He was so glad that his mother had suggested bringing her in here, having found the way Dickie had been examining her quite unnerving. 'I think she's very pleased that I've found someone of my own.'

'Well, your father seemed to like me,' said Peggy thoughtfully. 'He was very charming, and your brother – does he have anything to do with the grocery trade?'

He nodded, wishing she would not show so much interest in his brother. 'He runs the delivery service.'

'I didn't know. I must speak to Mother; she will be very interested. Is your brother not spoken for, then? I believe he is older than yourself.'

'A year, that's all. No, Dickie is unattached. He hasn't yet found anyone who is willing to put up with him.'

'I would have thought that a handsome fellow like him would've been snapped up ages ago.'

'For someone who professes to be very fond of a chap you show an inordinate amount of interest in my brother,' scowled Sonny, and stood up to pace the room agitatedly.

'Oh, John you're jealous! How could you think I would set my cap at him when I already have a handsome, caring beau of my own?'

He caught hold of her hands. 'Do you really think that? I've always been in my brother's shade in that sphere.'

'Oh no, you are far more attractive than he is,' soothed Peggy. 'He's too flashy by far. I wonder you can even think such a thing after we've been seeing so much of each other.' She led him back to the sofa and changed the subject. 'Tell me, why does everybody call you Sonny?'

He winced. 'It's just a name I've had since childhood that seems to have stuck. It was given to me initially so I wouldn't be confused with my Uncle John who used to live with us. I'd rather you didn't use it.'

'Nonsense! I think it suits you. The way you were looking at me a few moments ago reminded me of a little boy whose favourite toy has been taken from him. Most appealing.'

'But I'm not a little boy – and I don't regard you as a plaything, Peggy.' He hung his head. She always made him feel so juvenile.

'Oh, there I go again. I can't seem to let two minutes pass without teasing someone. Dear Sonny – for that is what I'll call you despite your reservations. I think it is a charming name. You will be my own dear Sonny and I promise not to tease you ever again.'

Sonny gazed into her winsome face, his own burning with love and admiration. 'Can I kiss you, Peggy?' he asked without notice. It had taken all these weeks to pluck up the courage even to ask.

She avoided his beseeching face as if shocked. 'I made myself a promise, Sonny,' she whispered. 'That I would only allow myself to be kissed by the man I am to marry.'

'Then I ask you again,' came the husky response. 'Can I kiss you, Peggy?'

She turned wondrous eyes to meet him. 'Are you then asking me to be your wife?'

'I am.' His nose was almost touching hers.

'Then you may kiss me, Sonny,' she answered, the second before his warm, dry lips pressed clumsily on hers.

CHAPTER TWENTY-NINE

Summer was on the wane. There was a doleful scruffiness about the garden now that the herbaceous borders were past their best. It was in that awkward transition period, when the summer flowers are dead but the flame of autumn has not yet been ignited. Thomasin paused in her toilet to look from her bedroom window into the garden. She had always hated this time of year. The state of the garden mirrored her mood. She should have been quite contented with her business growing more prosperous by the day, her daughter married and her younger son promised . . . but she wasn't.

The dying summer instilled in her a vague unease. If only her elder son would find himself a nice girl then perhaps that feeling would subside. Or perhaps it was the rift that had set in between herself and Sonny, always so close, that had produced this despondency. Her attempts to dissuade him from being too hasty in his choice of partner had been a failure. More than that, there had been displays of temper from him that had been under restraint for many years. It wasn't right; at this time in her life she should be allowed a little peace. She sighed, and answered the summons of the breakfast gong.

Once breakfasted the family prepared for work.

'Don't forget to go round to the wholesaler's first thing this morning,' Thomasin reminded Dickie as he made for the front door. 'There're a lot of items I've run down on. I'd hate to be completely without.'

'I've said I'll go, haven't I?' He slammed the door and made his way to the mews. Once there he harnessed up the mare, whom he had earlier groomed and fed. He was a lot more conscientious nowadays, as far as the horse was concerned. He climbed onto the cart, feeling unusually depressed this morning. He put it down to being robbed of his brother's companionship; Sonny spent all his time with Peggy now. Being stuck all day in this dead-end job didn't help. There was no incentive to anything. His mother had clamped down on his money-making activities, demanding to go over the takings for the grocery round time and time again until they balanced. He had yet to find a loophole which allowed him to make a few bob on the side. Oh sure, he didn't need the money for his women, they were easy enough to come by. But Dickie wanted something else. Something of his own that would furnish him with more and more money. For money was power.

Sadly, he was powerless today – his pockets were devoid of even a farthing. Money had a habit of slipping through his fingers like water. He had not even a pipeful of tobacco in which to take comfort.

The cart rumbled past a pawnbroker's. Somewhere in the back of his mind a chord was plucked. After a further revolution of the wheels he suddenly hauled in the reins, leapt down to the pavement and went into the pawnshop. When he re-emerged his right-hand pocket was ten shillings heavier and the pocket which had held his grandfather's heirloom had lost its bulge. The moment the watch crossed the counter was the last that Dickie thought of it. He shoved the screwed-up ticket into his pocket and went straight into the tobacconist's next door.

But even the expensive pipeful of tobacco could not alleviate his mood. His less than genial arrival at the wholesaler's prompted an enquiry from one of the labourers. 'What's up, didn't yer get none o' yer usual exercise last night?'

When the typical rejoinder was unforthcoming the labourer, Albert, clapped him on the back and laughed, 'God's truth! You are in a way wi' yerself. Away wi' me an' I'll show yer a bit o' summat as'll cheer y'up.'

Dickie grimaced and followed him lethargically through a maze of stacked crates to where a batch of workers were engaged in loading boxes onto a wagon. 'There, what d'yer think to that?' queried Albert, pointing out a girl whose pretty print frock was mostly obscured by a rough, unattractive apron and who was busily ticking off items on an invoice.

'Is that your surprise?' asked Dickie detachedly as they drew nearer.

'Well, don't sound so interested,' chided Albert. 'What's up wi' yer this mornin'? Yer must be sickenin' for summat. We can't usually keep yer away from t'lasses. Don't yer think she's a smasher?'

'I've seen better,' answered the other uncharitably, and knocked away Albert's hand as the labourer sought to feel his forehead.

'You *are* sick,' said Albert. 'Anyroad, I suppose it's just as well 'cause yer'd not get anywhere wi' her. She's a bit out of our class.'

'Is it lumpin' me with the likes o' you lot ye are?' was the corrosive answer. 'Have ye not known me long enough to know that all I have to do is sit on this here crate, snap me fingers an' she'd come running.'

They had moved into earshot now. The girl's nostrils flared with annoyance at his self-opinionated assumption, but her eyes never wavered from the invoice. 'There's two sacks of lentils short,' she informed one of the boys who was stacking crates. 'Go see where they've got to – and while you're at it nip into the office and fetch that clipboard that's on my chair.'

'Will ye listen to it givin' orders,' muttered Dickie to his partner. 'An' her not the size of a flea's earlobe. There's not much on her to cushion the bedsprings, is there? Is she like this with everyone? D'ye want I should put her in order for ye?'

The girl turned on him and her face was furious. 'The possibility of you "putting me in order" is about as likely as someone nominating you for Prime Minister! You may not have anything better to do than sit there sneering but we have.' She walked up to him, the invoice crumpled in her balled fist. 'Kindly give Albert your order and then

348

we'll have you about your business. I can't have you keeping my staff tittle-tattling all day.'

'Gob, have ye heard the woman?' laughed Dickie to Albert who had begun to look uncomfortable and now tried to silence him.

'I'd better tell yer who you're talkin' to before yer get in any deeper,' murmured the labourer, ill at ease.

'Don't bother, Albert!' snapped the girl. 'Just get on with what you are supposed to be doing. I'll deal with this person.' Before a slack-jawed Dickie could speak she was at his throat again. 'Now, I don't know who you are . . .'

'The name is Feeney, ma'am!' Dickie sprang to life and bowed. 'Richard Feeney esquire at your service.' The turbulent interchange had whetted his curiosity in this undersized virago, whose rather bland exterior had meta-morphosed with the onset of her temper. Slanting green eyes blazed from beneath the frizzy chestnut hair which had been scragged back into an unprofessional chignon. She had the look of a cat whose tail had just been trod on.

'. . . and I'm not really concerned,' she fobbed off his gallantry. 'What does take my interest is how you have the gall to come in here with your unfounded insults . . .'

'I'm sorry, I . . .'

'. . . we've never even met and there you are making the most derogatory remarks in front of my staff . . .'

'Well, it was that remark I found funny, ye see,' supplied Dickie. 'You referring to "your staff" .'

'Then your humour must be easily satisfied. What gives you cause to doubt that I have every right to address them as such?'

'Well . . .' he groped lamely for an answer. She had thrown him completely out of kelter with her attack.

'My father happens to own this warehouse, Mr Feeney and from time to time in his absence I deputise for him. Therefore I think even you would agree that I have every right to label these people as "my staff" ?'

'Well, yes of cou . . .'

'So! If you would kindly surrender your order and we may all continue with our work?'

'Look, I'm sorry if I offended ye,' said Dickie. 'A beautiful lady like yourself.'

'You didn't seem to hold the same opinion a moment ago. If my memory doesn't fail me you found my lack of physical attributes a source of ridicule.'

'I didn't mean . . .'

'It doesn't matter one jot to me what you meant,' she answered loftily, her cheeks still pink with temper. 'As far as I am concerned your disgusting conceptions are irrelevant. I . . .'

Dickie jumped in desperately. 'Look, I'm trying to apologise. I was in a foul humour an' I took it out on you. I humbly crave your pardon an' beg ye to let me make it up to ye.'

'And how do you propose to do that?' enquired his opponent guardedly.

'Well, I'm askin' ye to do me the honour of dining with me. Would tonight be convenient? I'll come an' pick ye up at . . .'

Before his last offering the girl had been prepared to be mollified – he was an extremely attractive young man – but the fact that he had not awaited her reply, had merely taken it for granted that she would accept his invitation produced an incendiary effect in her. Her eyes flashed. 'I'm sorry, I have another engagement this evening,' she said curtly.

'Tomorrow, then?'

'No,' she replied bluntly, coldly. 'I accept your reparation but I do not wish to associate with you further. Your infantile preamble might make some of the more gullible of my gender swoon at your feet but it does not impress me. I can see straight through you, Mr Feeney. I know your type. That kind has always repelled me.'

He was astonished. She gave him a wintry smile and, at his speechlessness, pressed home her attack. 'I can see you are more used to silly females who faint into your arms. I am sorry to disappoint you but I am not of that

350

persuasion. I have far too responsible a position here to indulge in such foolish practice. So, if you'll excuse me I'll proceed with my work.' She started to walk away as Dickie found his tongue.

'Talk about me having a high opinion of meself!' he shouted after her. 'I'm a poor second behind you. Well, suit yourself but ye don't know what you're missing, lady.' He laughed acidly. 'Or maybe ye do. Perhaps that's what you're afraid of. Ye've probably only been courted by milksops afore. Never been out with a real man. Oh, well,' he threw his mother's list onto a bench, 'I'll leave that with ye. When ye realise what a mistake ye've made the address is at the top of that list.'

She regarded him contemptuously from the office doorway. 'Why should you think I've made a mistake in refusing your offer?'

He hooked his thumbs into his waistcoat and strolled over to her nonchalantly. 'Ah, it's been done before. Girls are sometimes overwhelmed by my presence, but they soon realise what they're missing an' come running. Ask around, anyone'll tell ye what a fine asset I am to a lady's boudoir. I'm thinkin' o' taking out a patent.'

She angled her shoulders. 'No, Mr Feeney I do not need to ask around, because if your intellect is any indication of your unbreeched prowess then I doubt I shall be missing very much at all. Good day!' She closed the door firmly in his face.

Dickie stood looking at the closed door, dumbfounded, until the furtive titters pierced his shock. The only way to compensate for his loss of face was to join them. He threw back his head and to his surprise the laugh that boomed out was genuine. She really had the measure of him.

'I did try to warn yer what yer were lettin' yerself in for!' cackled Albert. 'By, she's a right caution, isn't she? She might 'ave the airs of a lady but by God she don't mince her words. Now yer know why none of us lads dare to mess with her.'

Inside the office the girl pressed her back to the door and tried to listen to what was going on at the other side, but was rendered deaf by the unaccountable rushing in her ears.

Each time Dickie visited the wholesale merchants he looked for her, but was invariably disappointed. A sly survey of the office revealed only the dour-faced Mr Miller, her father. He tried going to the warehouse at different hours of the day, but not once in the ensuing fortnight did they meet. He began to feel disillusioned and not a little angry at himself for this alien role. No woman had ever affected him like this. He tried to name one item that made her so desirable and could not come up with a single one. Her hair was like a bird's nest, her mouth was too big – definitely too big; he prickled at the way she had got the better of him. And there was nothing about her figure that made him want to crush it to him. So why could he not forget her? Why, when he was stowed away in a cosy corner with someone twice as attractive as the shrewish Miss Miller, did his mind always wander? He must see her again, if only to reassure himself that she was not worthy of all this self-flagellation.

And see her he finally did. Some three weeks after their first encounter he arrived at the merchant's to find her seated in the office, knitting and sipping tea. He paused outside the open door and peeped around it. 'Hello there! I was beginning to think ye'd dropped off the edge o' the earth.'

She glanced up briefly, then dropped her eyes back to her knitting, seeming to find more interest there. 'Yes, it stands to reason that a pea-brain like you would still believe the earth was flat. I should not imagine that it would be of any consequence to you if I had dropped off.'

'Oh, but it would.' He slipped into the office and closed the door behind him, regaining some of his self-esteem at the flicker of apprehension in her green eyes. 'Ye see, I was desperate to make amends for the way I discredited ye the last time we met.'

There was a derisive arch to her eyebrow. 'I rather thought that I was the one who did the discrediting.'

'You're right!' he burst out crossly. 'Ye were very rude. There was no need for it, none at all. No one's ever spoken to me like that before.'

'Oh, I'm quite sure they haven't,' she smiled knowingly. 'And that's what attracts you to me, Mr Feeney, is it not? You find it most unnerving that I am not another little goose to add to your list of conquests, and your male ego has been deflated. You won't until you have compromised me.'

He looked positively decimated. 'Miss Miller! I don't know who's been dirtying my good name, but sure I'd never take advantage of such a lady.' She's right, by God, she's right, the wee bitch. Of course that was the reason he found her so alluring. He had grown so used to getting his own way that it was all too easy, lacked excitement. But not now – damn her. She excited him. He would never rest now until he had got what he wanted. Just let her see how long she could hold out, the officious wench, and afterwards how much she'd have to say for herself. He rested one of his buttocks on her desk and leaned over to insert one of his fingers through a chestnut curl, not minding that she jerked her head away. 'Miss Miller,' he embarked, then sighed. 'Look, I can't keep callin' ye Miss Miller.'

'Why not? That's my name' she said lightly, finding his attempts at seduction very entertaining. She completed the row of knitting and started another, tucking the needles under her arms.

'Your first name,' he prodded. 'Please, if ye'll not consent to anything else at least give me your name to console myself with.'

'It won't do you any good,' she answered. 'But I can't see the harm in it. My name is Dusty.'

'Sure, now what sorta name is that for an immaculate vision like yourself?'

'That's what everyone calls me,' she replied, going back along the row to pick up a dropped stitch. 'Because of the surname.'

'Ah, I see now – Dusty Miller.' He nodded. 'Still, a

strange name for one so fair. Your beauty could blind a man, Dusty.'

'So could these knitting needles. Now will you please stop sprawling all over my desk?'

'But will ye not tell me your given name?' he begged.

She shook her head. 'No one uses it except my father.'

'Tell me,' he persisted.

'It's a ridiculous name,' she snapped from embarrassment. 'Oh well, if you must know . . . it's Primrose.' Her glare said – laugh if you dare!

But he did not laugh, he sighed rapturously. 'Begod it suits ye, so it does, sitting there in your bonny yellow dress, with your hair the colour of autumn leaves an' your eyes belonging to some sorta wild creature. Mother Nature herself. Primrose, you're like a breath of spring . . .' he broke off as she started to laugh.

'Oh, young Feeney you're a tonic!' She set down her knitting and giggled. 'You sound just like one of those Penny Dreadfuls!'

'I'm glad ye find me so funny – an' not so much of the young.'

'Well, you are young – if you could hear yourself.' She started to cough with laughter.

He was reaching a state of desperation. 'Ye'll be sorry if I tire of your indifference an' walk out. Come on, admit it – you'd miss all these compliments I'm tryin' to pay ye.'

She cocked a humorous eye. 'Is that a pig's nest I see on that chimney pot?'

He straightened haughtily and laid a docket in front of her. 'Very well, when ye've finished havin' your laugh at my expense maybe ye'll be good enough to have one o' your lackies get this order ready?' He turned and marched away, anticipating the cry of apology before he reached the door. But it did not come.

He could still hear her laughter after he had slammed the office door. Damn the woman. He would have her, so he would. The last laugh would be reserved for him.

In the office Dusty was feeling sorry for the way she had mocked him. But oh! he deserved it. She had heard the labouring girls whispering amongst themselves about this Casanova. It appeared there was not one among them who had escaped his persuasive chatter. Well, he had not got very far with Miss Miller, had he? So much for his infallible Irish charm. Though he was deliciously hand-some. No one as handsome had ever paid her so much attention before. If he had not been so ridiculously shallow she might well have found it all very flattering.

Still, she had to feel sorry for the fellow. He had looked so taken aback, so pathetic when she had laughed at his ludicrous monologue. Was that the type of prattle that moved others to relinquishing their virtue? It certainly hadn't impressed Dusty. Even so, she had hurt him and having put him in his place could afford to be magnani-mous. When next he called she would apologise.

And one week later apologise she did, though her recti-tude did not bring the response she had visioned. She was testing some samples of the tea just delivered by the brokers, liquoring them against those already in stock. Due to ten years of her father's instruction she had attained a keen palate – the slightest difference and she would be quick to spot it. She rolled the sample round her mouth then discreetly spat it into the waste pot. It was during this action that she saw Dickie arrive with his cart and, setting the tasting spoon upon a saucer she dabbed at her lips and made her way across the warehouse.

Dickie hardly seemed aware of her presence as he strug-gled to load his cart, taking scant notice of her rehearsed speech.

'Well, now I've passed on my regrets,' she said lamely at this neutered reception, 'I'd better get back to my work.'

'Aye, you do that,' he grunted. 'I'd hate to keep ye from your precious work.' It had been his decision to employ different tactics and to match like with like.

There was a strained silence punctuated only by his gasps as he heaved the boxes and sacks onto his cart. She still hovered, watching him. 'Look, I have apologised,' she said captiously.

'An' I acknowledged it,' was his equable response. 'Now, if there's nothing else?' He turned his back.

'Would you care to call for tea tomorrow?' she said unexpectedly, and marvelled at where her words had sprung from; they were the last she had intended.

He swore as a splinter from one of the crates embedded itself under his nail.

'Well, I'm sure my invitation didn't warrant such language!' she retorted, the lynx eyes growing hard.

He started to explain, trying to shake the pain from his hand. A glob of blood flew onto her turquoise dress and she gave an exclamation. 'Oh, let me see!'

''Tis nothing.'

She grabbed hold of his hand and examined the finger. 'It'll have to come out. Come along!' She dragged him into the office.

He followed her, unusually meek, and stood dutifully while she fished in her purse for something that might remove the splinter. Laying her hands upon a pair of tweezers she beckoned him over. 'Rinse off the blood in that bowl.' After he had complied she wedged the offending hand under her arm to steady her task. 'This may hurt.' She applied the tweezers to the protruding tip of the splinter. It was removed in seconds. 'There!'

She waited for him to take his arm back and when it adhered to her side she made great show of removing it herself. 'Rinse it off again then we'll put on a bandage.'

Dickie blessed the fragment of wood that had brought about this apparent change of heart and sat on the desk while she bandaged his finger. She could be really quite feminine if she put her mind to it.

'Ye do that expertly, Primrose.' He watched her snip the ends of the bandage and tie them around his wrist. 'Healing hands ye have. It feels better already.' He took a chance and moved his hand in her lap, feeling the heat of her thigh against his knuckles.

She patted his hand as one might a child's and said reprovingly, 'Now we don't want to start all that again, surely, Mr Feeney?'

'Dickie.'

'Dickie then – and do stop calling me Primrose, I can't stand it. It makes me sound like a delicate little flower.'

'Ah, that you're most definitely not!'

She tucked the remaining bandage and scissors into the first-aid box, replacing it in the cupboard. 'Would you like a cup of tea?'

'You've certainly changed your tune,' said Dickie, his handsome features flexed in smiles. 'Ye sure 'tis tea you're giving me an' not hemlock?'

She furrowed her brow but her eyes remained friendly. 'I don't think there's any need for that now that you know your place, do you?' She filled a kettle and placed it on the gas-ring.

Bide your time, boy, Dickie told himself. Just chalk up all these insults on the slate and one day she'll suffer for them.

Later, when they sat side by side drinking tea, she asked him, 'Would you care to answer my original question?'

'Which was?' His startlingly-blue eyes wandered over the boyish figure.

'I asked if you'd care to call to tea tomorrow?'

'You're sure about that? I should hate to think ye were only asking me out o' charity.'

She set down her cup. 'Mr Feeney . . .'

'Dickie.'

'. . . Dickie, I'm sorry if we got off on the wrong footing, but you've only yourself to blame, you know. If you weren't so arrogant . . .'

'Me, arrogant!' he laughed astoundedly. 'Sure, you're not so hot on humility yourself.'

'All right, I admit I did get a bit officious, but . . . for God's sake, man! I can't keep atoning for my sins, and I don't see why I should, I shan't do it any more. We'll start anew. Forget about all previous encounters. When you come to tea tomorrow it will be as if we are meeting for the first time.'

'Isn't that taking things for granted?' mocked Dickie. 'I mean, I never said I'd come.'

She knotted her brows, annoyed at being caught practising Dickie's tricks. 'No, you didn't, did you? I'm sorry.'

'Ye said ye weren't going to say that again,' he goaded.

She bristled, then composed herself, realising how silly this was becoming, and answered, 'You're testing my patience, which happens to be very fragile. Nevertheless I'm going to ask you very nicely once more, and only once: will you kindly come to tea tomorrow?'

He rose, bowed and answered, 'Miss Miller, how could any red-blooded male refuse such a delightful request? I should be honoured.'

'Good, that's settled then.' She gathered up the cups and saucers and took them away. He trailed her, standing very close, and began to sing quietly, making up the song as he went along:

There was a Dusty Miller once lived on the river Dee,
... Though she might try to hide her flame I know she
*   pines for me,*
... And when I ask her for her hand ... she will have
*   one reply-y ...*
There is but one place you belong ... and that is in a sty!

'There, I made ye laugh.' Dickie used the opportunity of her laughter to move even closer. Her gaiety reverted to the canny smile and she eyed him.

'Hadn't you better be loading your cart?'

'I should – but I'm loath to tear meself away from your side,' he told her throatily. 'I rather hoped ye'd feel the same way.' He inched his face to hers.

Unperturbed she placed a hand in front of her face so that he kissed not her lips but her palm. 'Ah, Dusty! How can ye be so cruel?'

'Oh, I can be a lot more cruel than that, Mr Feeney,' she answered, her slanting green eyes full of mischief. 'The invitation was to tea only, not an invitation to help yourself. If you think that you're going to seduce me like you did all the others ...'

'Miss Miller, ye make me sound like a lecher!' he objected, hurt.

But Dusty laughed, neither embarrassed nor outpaced by this exchange. 'You may think you're very clever, Richard Feeney but you don't fool me with your blarney. I'm not like all the others you've met. It'll take more than a few compliments to put me on my back. You're a fine, handsome lad I'll grant you that, but I value my chastity too highly to go melting under those beautiful eyes. For I know what would happen if I did. So, if you've nothing more on your mind than to take my virtue and run, you'd best be on your way right now, for the answer to that would be a very definite No.'

He was forced to admire her, however much she irked him with her bossiness. He studied her unblinkingly until her cheeks began to turn pink knowing what was on his mind. But her lynx eyes never wavered. He could walk out now and still retain some of his pride, or he could stay and forget about the slate – there was no way he was going to get around this one without the firm promise of a wedding ring. And not just a hollow promise either – this one would see through subterfuge right away. So, did he want her badly enough to put a ring on her finger? There was nothing much about her that he couldn't get elsewhere, and more easily. But what was in those strange, feline eyes ... he had never seen that before, and that was what he wanted. That intangible thing he could not put a name to. And above everything, she produced in him a feeling that no one else had ever created before. He didn't know what it was. It worried him.

'You're a hard woman, Dusty,' he said at last. 'Ye know very well I couldn't walk out of here if I wanted to.'

'And do you want to?'

'No – though God help me I don't know what sorta spell ye've worked on me.' They were all going to laugh their heads off when the news circulated that someone had cornered the irrepressible Feeney at last.

'And what about all the others?' she asked.

'What others? There's only you from now on.'

'I'd like to believe that, Dickie.'

'Believe it. From today I'll never look at another woman.'

'It's not the looking I'm worried about.'

'Dusty,' he reproved, 'I swear there'll be no more than that.'

'Come here then.'

'What?'

'Are you deaf? Come here.' And she raised her face to his, kissing him full and long on the lips. It fell a long way short of the most passionate kiss he had ever tasted, but the fire in her green eyes when she broke away verified its sincerity.

'Heaven help me, I must be mad,' she breathed wonderingly. What had happened to the convictions she had been spouting before?

'Ye voiced my very thoughts, Dusty,' he tasted her again. I must be mad. Bloody mad.

'And if you so much as blink at another woman we're finished. Do you understand?'

'I do,' he replied contritely, and suffered another twinge of self-mockery at his choice of words.

CHAPTER THIRTY

As the leaves turned to crackling ashes in the gutters the buds of romance welled and burst forth into blossom. Dickie was welcomed into the Miller household just as Dusty was enveloped into his. Probyn Miller was a widower and unlike Patrick Feeney remained totally uninvolved when it came to his daughter's choice of partner. With a realistic shrug he had decreed that Dusty was quite capable of mapping out her own life, and if Dickie was her chosen one then so be it. He was not a well man and it had often worried him that he might expire leaving his only daughter to cope with the wholesale business unaided. Not that he didn't think her capable, but he would hate to see the business turn her into a hardened spinster. She needed a man to take the edge off her forceful nature. Now it looked as if he would see her safely married before he succumbed to his weak heart.

Patrick and Thomasin, at first astonished when their wayward son had brought in this rather homely-looking girl, had after half an hour in her company realised what he found so attractive in her, and had immediately taken Dusty to their hearts. This was the sort of wife that Dickie needed to keep him in line. Would that Sonny had been so fortunate. Thomasin's attempts to dissuade him from marriage until he was older had only served to strengthen his resolve. But, Sonny was happy and that was the main issue. Thomasin for one would be glad if Peggy proved her wrong and made a model wife.

The thought that all three of her children would soon be settled down did wonders for Thomasin, and not the least important factor in her revitalisation was that Dusty would one day be the owner of a large wholesale business. Allied to her own fast-expanding trade it would make the Feeneys well-nigh self-sufficient. She had coveted a wholesale warehouse of her own for a long time, but as yet had not the temerity nor the experience to move into this sphere.

She smiled at Dusty and offered a plate of small cakes which the girl refused. 'Thank you, no. If I eat any more I'll be like a harvest frog. I think that'd spoil the cut of my wedding gown somewhat.'

'Wedding gown?' said Thomasin. 'So it is serious, then?' The two of them were alone for the present. Dickie had slipped round to the stables with his father to seek Patrick's advice about a sore on the mare's flank. Sonny was upstairs getting ready to meet Peggy. 'You really love my son?'

Dusty raised a quizzical eyebrow at the disbelief in Thomasin's voice. 'You make it sound as if he's virtually unlovable, Mrs Feeney.'

The other laughed and poured herself more tea. 'Well,

no I wouldn't say that — he can be very affectionate. But I must be honest, I never expected to see him married, especially to a nice girl like you.'

Dusty pulled a face at the description.

'Now I didn't mean it how it sounded,' said Thomasin. 'You're a bonny lass as well. But our Dickie needs someone with her head screwed on right. He's a bit of a handful, you know.' She appraised Dusty meaningfully, wondering if the girl understood.

Dusty's wide mouth turned up at the corners. 'You mean his fatalism for the opposite sex?'

'Well, just as long as you realise what you're letting yourself in for,' replied Thomasin seriously. 'You're a lovely girl, Dusty. Patrick and me have a great deal of respect for you — rather more, I'm afraid than we have for our son. We love you and welcome you as a daughter. I hope with all my heart that he's going to make you happy, dear. But I couldn't in all honesty guarantee it. He's been such a trial to his parents.'

Dusty leaned forward and covered Thomasin's hand with her own. 'I understand what you're trying to tell me, and I'm grateful that you seek to protect me.' She gave a little laugh. 'I often think it was madness on my part to allow this relationship to develop. It wasn't as if I was bowled over by your handsome son, however charming he might think himself to be. It'd take someone a great deal less transparent to take me in. No, I know exactly what I'm letting myself into. I accepted his promise of matrimony with open eyes. If things go wrong there's none to blame but me. You don't know what a time I've had since I consented to the relationship, wondering if I'm going to regret it. But despite his roving eye I'm positive that his feelings for me are genuine. If I didn't believe that then I wouldn't be sitting here. So, there's no call to worry on my behalf, Mrs Feeney. The boy says he loves me and I trust him.'

'Oh, I'm inclined to agree on that,' Thomasin nodded vigorously. 'He does love you. I've never seen him apply himself to anything with such enthusiasm.' She clasped

362

her hands delightedly. 'Oh, won't it be lovely! Two weddings to look forward to next year.'

Dusty wholeheartedly agreed. 'Though I've never been to a wedding in my whole life. I've no idea of how to conduct myself.'

Thomasin found this unbelievable. 'Never been to a wedding?'

'Never! Twenty-three years of age and never a grain of rice has left my fingers. The only rice I've ever thrown is the pudding I once emptied over Father's head when he said it was burnt.' She winced at the recollection. He had whipped her soundly and locked her in her room for a week. 'So, I'd welcome any advice you could give me on the ceremony and about married life. My mother died when I was small so I've never had an example to follow.' She interpreted Thomasin's uncomfortable expression and chuckled without embarrassment. 'Oh, don't worry. I'm not going to ask about what to do on the wedding night. I've not led that sheltered a life. Besides, I've picked up enough snippets from our employees to serve me in good stead for that. No, I meant more in the domestic field. I desperately want to be a good wife to your son, Mrs Feeney. If a man doesn't have a secure background then he's more likely to stray. I won't stand for that.'

Both women looked to the door which had just opened.

'Oh, sorry, Mother. I didn't realise ye had company.' Erin lingered on the threshold.

'Hello, love! What're you doing here through the week?' Thomasin gestured for her to come in and looked surprised when Erin closed the door after her. 'Are you on your own?'

Erin came forward. 'Sam decided he'd mend the shed when he came in from work, so I thought I'd pop over for a little chat rather than sit on my own. Sorry if I barged in.'

'Rubbish! It's only our Dusty.' Thomasin smiled at Dickie's bride-to-be. 'You're not intruding on anything. In fact you might be a bit of a help.'

'Oh?' Erin perched on the edge of a chair.

Dusty got the feeling that Erin wasn't too happy to see her. 'Perhaps I'll have a wander down to the stables to see what Dickie's up to.'

'Nay, they'll be back any minute,' said Thomasin. 'Don't waste your legs. We were just discussing wedding plans,' she told Erin, who smiled her congratulations. 'Dusty's been picking my brains about how to be a good wife, but I don't know as I'm the right one to ask.' A chuckle, then: 'You should be more useful, still being in the first flush of marriage yourself.'

'I think she'll need wiser instruction than mine to deal with my brother,' said Erin, a little unkindly.

'Well, that's a nice way to welcome Dusty to our family, I'm sure!' said her mother in surprise.

Erin apologised immediately. 'I'm sorry, Dusty I didn't mean it like that . . . it's just that I don't think I'm a very good person to give advice on marriage, that's all.' Though Dusty was a very nice girl she was the last person Erin had hoped to see. It was her mother who had been the target of this impromptu visit. Though what she was going to say to her . . . It had been mostly Sam's idea. 'Go talk to your mother,' he had told her. 'Maybe she can put you straight. I won't come with you, you need to be on your own, talk woman to woman.' It didn't look as if there was going to be much chance of that; the door had opened again and the rest of the family spilled in.

'Erin! What a sight to brighten my day.' Patrick, still in working clothes, kissed his daughter. 'An' where's that husband o' yours?' She told him she had come alone. 'Oh great! I've got ye all to meself.' He squeezed her. 'But how did ye get here?'

'Sam cadged me a lift on a villager's cart that was coming into town. I'd be grateful if one o' ye could give me a ride back, though.'

'Oh no! Now we've got ye here we're going to keep ye, aren't we, Tommy?'

'Tell him he's a soft devil,' said Thomasin. 'She's not likely to be captivated by a poor old duffer like you when she's got herself a strapping young lad at home, is she?'

Erin smiled weakly and looked at the happy couple opposite. Dickie had gone directly to Dusty's chair where he now sat beside her on the chair arm. He kissed her fondly. 'An' what've ye been plotting, the three o' yese while me back's turned?'

'Oh, nothing important,' Dusty replied casually. 'Just a small matter of a June wedding, nothing for you to worry your head about – it's all in hand.' They laughed lovingly at one another, foreheads pressed together. It was plain to all that their adoration was mutual. Thomasin marvelled at the change in Dickie. She glanced at her daughter. There had been a change in Erin too, but not for the better. If anything she looked even more unhappy than on her last visit. Thomasin had tried to winkle it out of her what was wrong, but after Erin's repeated 'nothing, nothing', she had stopped asking, not wanting it to look as if she was interfering again. She knew how Erin detested that.

Her eyes went back to the young couple. 'One thing we didn't discuss,' she told them, 'was where you'll be living after you wed. You too, Sonny. There's ample room here should you choose to make your home with us.'

Sonny was unsure. Peggy was full of grand plans about what type of house she wanted, and those plans didn't include living with her in-laws. He didn't know where she expected him to get the money to fulfil these fancy ideas. 'I rather think Peggy would prefer us to have our own place,' he informed his mother.

I'm sure she does, thought Thomasin.

'Of course, it'll be a lot smaller than this,' he added appeasingly.

Will it? thought Thomasin. I think you're wrong to expect a two-roomed cottage to satisfy Miss Adventuress. But she said charitably, 'Of course I can understand Peggy wanting a house of her own. It's only natural that she'd want to be mistress of her own household. What about you?' she asked Dickie, who looked at his Intended. 'There'll be plenty of room if you want to postpone buying your own place.' She had promised each of her sons a substantial settlement on their marriages, just as Erin had had.

The girl smiled, entwining her fingers with Dickie's. 'That's very kind of you, Mrs Feeney. We'll be delighted to take up your generous offer. I've no ambition to stay at home and be mistress of my own household just yet. Perhaps later when we have a family, but just now I'm too involved in helping my father with the warehouse.' Her happiness turned to gravity. 'And if anything should happen to him, God forbid, then I'll be running it on my own. So I shan't have too much time to run a house as well.'

'Not alone, darlin',' Dickie reminded her. 'Ye'll have me, remember?' The grocery trade would not seem so dull with Dusty at his side.

'Of course, I'm sorry.' She squeezed his fingers. 'But Dickie, you'll still be required to help with your parents' business and won't have a lot of time to spare for mine.'

'But you're forgetting,' said Thomasin. 'When you wed there won't be any "mine" and "yours" – it'll be "ours". Heaven help that I should bury your poor father before his time, but I do think there's a lot to be said for merging the two businesses when that time comes.'

Dusty nodded. 'I'm sure you're right. I hadn't given it much thought, but that would seem the logical solution. I trust, though, that my father will last a good many years yet.'

Thomasin inclined her head, not wanting to press the point and have it sound as if she were only welcoming Dusty for her inheritance, for that was not true. 'Shall I ring for more tea, Pat – if you can take your eyes off your future daughter-in-law, that is.'

Patrick looked startled. He had been studying Dusty and thinking how like his wife the girl was in a lot of ways, especially her candid manner. He laughed and declined the tea. 'I was just thinking how it's going to be with two headstrong women in the house. Us poor lads'll be doing all the fetchin' an' carryin' no doubt. Gone is the day when a man is master in his own house. I don't know what things are coming to.'

'You poor old soul,' derided his wife, then turned serious for a while. 'Getting back to the subject of weddings, Dusty, I suppose you are aware that you'll be marrying into a Catholic family?'

Dusty replied that she was. She gave a sidelong glance at her Intended. 'I think we ought to tell you now that we'll be marrying in my church.'

Patrick was instantly alert. 'Richard, why have ye not mentioned this before?'

'Because I knew what a stink it'd cause,' Dickie told him, then spread his hands. 'Look, Dusty's father is a very easy-going man, but one thing he won't have is her gettin' wed in a Catholic church. So, I told him there was nothin' to worry about . . .'

'Oh, ye did, did ye?' stormed his father.

'There isn't Dad,' replied Dickie. 'Ye know very well that going to church means nothin' to me, absolutely nothin'. I can't see the difference if we get married in a Catholic church or a Protestant one or a register office or the middle of a bloody field. I'm marryin' Dusty, not the bloody church.'

'Richard!' commanded his father.

'I'm sorry, but 'tis no use you goin' on about it, 'tis all fixed.'

'Mr Feeney – we don't want this to cause a split in the family,' said Dusty. 'I wouldn't have brought it up had I thought that.'

'Well, I'm glad ye did, Dusty,' answered Patrick heatedly. 'At least now we know how highly our son prizes his faith.'

'Not my faith, Dad, yours,' said Dickie. 'I've always made it plain how I felt but ye insisted on my being there. Well, no more. Once I get married in Dusty's church I'll be excommunicated an' that'll be that.'

'You hypocritical little toad!' Patrick scowled witheringly. 'Forsaking one church for another as simply as changing your socks an' neither of them meaning a toss to ye.'

'You're right they don't. I'm only doing it for Dusty's sake. If she says we get married in a Protestant Church then we do.'

'Protestant or no the lass has more sense of responsibility than you,' snapped Patrick. He moderated his tone to address Dusty. 'Don't think all this is directed at you, colleen. I respect you for your loyalty to your own church. I just wish my son had the same quality. Father Kelly isn't going to be too pleased. 'Tis as well we won't have this trouble with Sonny.'

Thomasin was thinking unkindly that she would rather have Sonny marry against his faith than marry Peggy any day, but asked, 'What date do you and Peggy have in mind, Sonny?'

'Peggy'd like a June wedding too,' he replied. Sonny of all the family was the most relieved that Dickie had found himself a partner. He also wished his mother would be a little less hostile towards Peggy. One might say it was understandable that a mother should be overcritical when faced with her son's choice of partner, but then she wasn't that way with Dusty, was she? One could also be charitable and say that it was different in Dickie's case – Mother would be pleased to see him married to anyone. Even so, he could not help feeling a little disappointed in Thomasin for her glaring favouritism. He stood.

'Right, I'm off to collect Peggy. I'll be back in time for supper.'

Before he could reach the door, though, Josie entered looking a trifle apprehensive. 'Don't go, Mr John,' she waylaid him in a softer voice than she normally used. 'Miss Peggy's here.'

Sonny's face broke into smiles. 'Peggy? Why, I was just . . .'

'She's not alone, Mr John,' cut in Josie, and turned to Patrick. 'Her father's with her, sir. He asked to speak to you.' She chose not to repeat the man's exact wording; such language was beneath her dignity.

368

'Well – show them both in, Josie.' Patrick rose. 'I'm sure we'll be delighted to meet Peggy's father.' It was something he would have preferred to take place before this, but Peggy had always been cagey about her background.

'I did invite them in, sir, but the gentleman says he'd prefer to see you in the hall – alone.'

Patrick exchanged glances with his wife. 'Very well . . .' he began, but Sonny interceded. 'Don't be silly!' he cried, thinking Mr Clancy was standing in the hall from courtesy. He had never met the man either, always picking Peggy up from her employer's house. 'Show them in, Josie.'

At the maid's uncertainty he tutted, edged past her and threw open the door. 'Peggy! Mr Clancy! Don't stand out there, come in, come in!'

But Clancy remained aloof. 'I'll stay right here if 'tis all the same to you. I've words to say to your father I'd as soon not to have to say in front o' the womenfolk. Ye'll no doubt learn about it in due time. Hah! What am I sayin'? To be sure ye know about it already.'

'About what?' Sonny peered at Peggy who stood with bowed head behind her father. She had not even acknowledged him. 'Peggy?' He approached cautiously and put out his hand – and found it gripped by hairy fingers.

'You lay another finger on her, me boyo, an' I'll tear it off,' hissed Clancy menacingly.

Consternated, Sonny awaited Peggy's explanation and saw now that her eyes were red from weeping. 'Peggy, what is it?' He ventured forth again.

Clancy was in the process of twisting the boy's arm when Patrick strode into the hall.

'What the Devil . . . take your hands off my son, Clancy if ye don't want the same done to you! What's all this about might I ask?'

'An' well ye might!' Clancy thrust aside his victim and stalked up to Patrick. He was a head shorter but twice as wide, with a great beer belly falling over the heavily buckled belt. His voice was still thickly accented though he had been in this country longer than Patrick. 'I'll tell ye what 'tis all about: I'm here to make weddin' plans, that's what 'tis about.'

Thomasin had drifted into the hall to stand beside Patrick. 'Why, we were only just talking about . . .'

''Tis more than talk I be wantin', missus!' interjected the man rudely. ''Tis action. Ye're goin' to have to bring them weddin' plans forward, 'cause that filthy young buck ye call your son has been a bit previous.' He hung back while they digested his words, then nodded violently when they looked tellingly at each other. 'That's right – she's up the spout!'

Thomasin recovered first. 'Oh, Sonny! How could you?'

Sonny broke his astonished stare away from Peggy to look unseeingly at his parents. 'But . . . I didn't,' he stammered.

'No good tryin' to wriggle out of it, boyo,' said Clancy viciously. 'Ye were clever enough to put a child in her belly, ye're well able to put a ring on her finger.'

'My son will stand by his promises, Clancy,' guaranteed Patrick stiffly. 'Shall we go into the parlour . . .'

'Peggy! Peggy!' Sonny tried to get near but was held at bay by the girl's father. 'Tell them it can't be true.'

'It's true enough, Sonny,' she whispered into her bosom. 'I'm going to have a baby.'

'But that's impossible!' Sonny threw up his hands in despair and implored Clancy. 'I swear, Mr Clancy nothing like that ever took place between us. I love Peggy. I wouldn't let a thing like that happen.'

'Well, happen it has, an' you're responsible.'

'No! I won't have you saying things that aren't true. Peggy, you must have made a mistake. You can't possibly be having a child.' Perhaps Peggy in her innocence thought that babies came from kissing.

This suggestion was received with crude hilarity from Clancy. 'I think me wife is experienced enough to be sure of her daughter's condition, her havin' dropped a dozen or so of her own.'

Sonny was desperate. 'But I swear before God that I never touched her, Mr Clancy.'

'Well, unless she's been playing doctors an' nurses with the Archangel Gabriel, I'm gonna have to call ye a liar.'

'I'll have no blasphemy here, Clancy,' ordered Patrick severely. 'I'm sure we can settle this in a more civilised manner. After all, our children were pledged to each other anyway; 'tis only a case o' bringing the wedding forward.'

'But I didn't do it!' shouted Sonny angrily.

'Then who did?' demanded Clancy.

In the ensuing speechlessness Sonny, watching Peggy's face, saw her eyes flicker over the hallway and followed them. Then, suspicion nosed its way into his brain like a venomous snake and suddenly bafflement turned to rage. '*It was you!*' He hurled himself bodily at his brother who stood in the doorway alongside Dusty, his arm around her, unprepared for the hail of blows that rained down upon him.

Dusty cried out as Sonny's assault knocked her roughly aside and Dickie fell to the floor with his brother's hands curling into his black hair. Erin, too, raised alarmed hands to her cheeks. By the time Patrick had hauled Sonny off, Dickie's head had been pounded against the marble-tiled floor several times and a cut was welling blood from his checkbone.

Patrick fought to restrain his younger son. 'Help me, Clancy!' while Dickie looked up bemusedly, rubbing the back of his head.

'Let me at him, Father!' Sonny struggled with the two stronger men, trying to shake them off. 'I'm going to kill him!'

'Sonny, for Christ's sake!' panted his father. 'Calm down, else I'm gonna have to resort to your methods an' knock ye out. Ye don't know for certain your brother is responsible. Nothing was said.'

'Don't I?' yelled Sonny, his face red with fury. He nodded vigorously at Thomasin. 'Look at Mother. She knows, don't ye, Mother?' Thomasin's eyes were riveted on her elder son. They travelled briefly upwards to take in Sonny with a compassionate look, then lowered themselves back to his brother. 'Let me go, I'll bloody slaughter him!'

371

Sonny lashed out at Dickie with his boots. His brother tried to drag himself out of the way.

'Sonny!' commanded Patrick, the sweat standing on his brow. 'Am I going to have to floor ye? How can we get to the bottom of this while you're behavin' like a madman? Give me your oath that ye'll not try to attack him while we find out the truth.'

'Mother knows the truth, don't you, Mother?' shouted Sonny. 'Oh, and Peggy of course! An' how many other people, eh? I'll bet I'm the only bloody one that didn't know what was going on under my nose. What about you, Dusty? You're very quiet. Did you know what sort of fellow you promised to wed?'

Dusty regarded him, outwardly calm, trying to curb the trembling fingers that were twisting her stomach inside out. 'We haven't yet heard what Dickie has to say. Don't you think it would be more sensible to do so before accusing him?' Please, please let it all be a dreadful mistake, she begged.

'Oh, certainly!' cried Sonny. 'Do let's hear what my dear brother has to say; it'll be a real eye-opener.' He twisted round to look at Patrick. 'You can let me go now, Father. I give my word that I won't try to kill him till dear Dickie has had his say.'

Patrick and Clancy slackened their grip and Sonny shook himself free. Everyone stared at Dickie who, after being regarded expectantly for what seemed like ages, shrugged and gave a brittle laugh of resignation. 'Well – it looks like I've no option but to own up.'

At his words Sonny sprang into action again and was immediately hauled off. 'Dickie, ye'd best disappear if ye know what's good for ye,' choked Patrick, fighting to contain Sonny.

Dickie, his head still throbbing, struggled to his feet to face Dusty. 'Dusty, I . . .'

'Oh, there's no need to explain,' she forestalled him, fighting back the tears of disappointment and betrayal. 'After all, I'm nothing to you, am I? Why should you worry about excuses?'

'But ye must let me speak, Dusty! I'm sorry.' It sounded so insincere.

'Sorry? Yes, so am I. Sorry that I was foolish enough to think I could change you. Silly of me, wasn't it? Ridiculous for me to think that I could monopolise your attention for even a few months. It's obvious that one woman is not enough for the insatiable Mr Feeney.'

He had hold of her by the shoulders, speaking frantically. 'Dusty, I promised ye I'd not look at another woman an' I've kept that promise.'

'Yes, well I blame myself for not studying the wording of that proposal more closely.' She looked so splendid in her feral indignation. Her lips pulled back in an animal snarl, her eyes green fire. He couldn't lose her. He couldn't.

'Listen to me, please! It happened before I met you, please believe that. I love you, I wouldn't do a thing like that to you.'

'But you would to your brother,' said Dusty hollowly.

'Aye, well I'm sorry about that.' Dickie had the grace to hang his head, but it was not long before his eyes sought hers again. 'It was a filthy trick. I don't know what gets over me sometimes. But I swear it's all in the past. It'll never happen again.'

'It makes no difference to me,' she replied evenly. 'For I won't be here.'

'No! Ye can't mean that. What about the wedding?'

'God's teeth you're the limit!' She was really angry now. 'You don't appear to understand that it's not just me you've hurt, it's everyone: your mother, your father, but most of all your brother.' She had deliberately excluded Peggy from this list. That slut had not needed much encouragement, had most probably engineered the whole thing. Dusty had never liked her from the moment they'd met. 'I couldn't remain friends with anyone who'd do that to his own brother, let alone marry him.'

'Aye, well, maybe that's all to the good,' Clancy spoke up. 'For he's going to have to do his duty by my daughter.'

Dickie faced him scornfully. 'Ye surely don't think I'm going to marry *her*?'

'I don't think – I know,' replied Clancy darkly. 'Unless ye want to find yourself in deeper water.'

'Mr Clancy is within his rights,' confirmed Patrick. ''Tis only proper that as you are the one to wrong Peggy you must make amends.'

'I'd as lief marry Connely's pig!' flung Dickie spitefully. 'Anyhow, she's Sonny's girl.'

'Damn you! You despicable, spineless brat, you should have thought of that before,' said his mother passionately. 'I side with your father and Mr Clancy – you will marry the girl!'

'I won't!' Dickie gripped Dusty's shoulders more tightly and spoke pleadingly into her face. 'Dusty, please don't listen to them. This doesn't have to make any difference to us. We can go away together, forget it ever happened . . .'

'How can you stand there and say that?' she breathed disbelievingly. Then, 'Let go, Dickie, I wish to go home.'

'I'll take ye! We'll talk!'

'No! I must go alone. I don't want to talk to you, ever again.' She tried to disentangle herself but his grip tightened. She closed her eyes impatiently. 'Please, you're hurting me.'

'Richard, haven't you hurt her enough?' said Thomasin. 'Let her go.'

'Damn what you say!' shouted Dickie. 'I'm going to marry her. Dusty, please don't go.' But what he saw as she opened her eyes caused him to release her at last. She gave him a long, searching look, trying desperately to keep her real feelings from her eyes. She succeeded. The glittering orbs, now cold as jade, registered only contempt. He dropped his hands from her as if burnt. Once, in a bout of childish cruelty, he had applied a lighted match to a beetle and had watched it contort in agony. That was how he felt now – and the lighted match had been self-inflicted.

His recovery came too late. Before he could reach out for her again she was gone.

'Can we let ye go without ye going for him again?' Patrick asked Sonny, who nodded smoulderingly, and rubbed his arms where Clancy's fingers had bitten deep.

'I've got to get out,' he muttered, and stumbled for the door, declining to spare a glance for his lost love. His parents were too relieved not to have another fight on their hands to stop him. They both looked to Dickie who was staring marble-eyed at the wall.

'So, I can take it your son is gonna make an honest woman of me daughter,' said Clancy, breaking the silence.

'You can,' vouched Thomasin with great surety. 'Because in refusing he would forfeit his claim to a share in my business. I shall cut him off without a penny. My son places money too highly to risk that – don't you, Dickie?'

And though at that moment he wanted to shout and rail his hate for her out loud, his mother's words dispelled any resistance he might have offered and he nodded submissively. Dickie knew when he was beaten.

CHAPTER THIRTY-ONE

He was in a daze, his mind overwhelmed by the events of the previous evening. He sat atop the cart, the eyes beneath the bowler hat dark and brooding, staring benightedly over the horse's rump, trusting her to take the correct route. Deep inside him was a raging sore for which there was no salve. The sparkling November frost anaesthetised his extremities but did nothing to numb his inner pain. His mind replayed the tragic scenario over and over relentlessly. Dusty's whipped expression at his betrayal, mouthing accusations – but the words she spoke were his brother's: *I'll kill him! I'll kill him! I'll kill him!* Peggy feigning innocence, letting him take the worst of the blame. Devious, suffocating Peggy. Coy and demure in his brother's company, but in his . . . an overpowering, rutting sow. Throwing herself at him. More, more and yet more until he had felt desiccated. God! how was he ever going to escape? For escape he must. He could not, would not ebb out his life tied to that termagant.

Dusty, oh, Christ, Dusty! Her name stabbed repeatedly at his brain. Why couldn't she understand that it had meant nothing? They had all meant nothing, 'til her. But the pain in those glazed angelica eyes betold the lie.

Damn that slut! How many more men had she tried to entrap? There must have been more. One man was not enough to pleasure dear, innocent Peggy. How did they even know the child was his? His mind became suddenly alert. Exactly! He had been too shocked last night to respond to their accusations – had arrogantly accepted paternity – but now he glimpsed a chink of light in his hitherto inescapable predicament, and he'd be damned if he'd marry her. Dusty. He must see Dusty now. Tell her. Beg her forgiveness. She'd surely understand, after a night in which to mull things over. She'd surely be regretting walking out like that. She loved him, didn't she? Dusty, oh, Dusty!

The mare laid back her ears in confusion as he jerked on the reins to deviate her from the normal track. 'Damn the round, Polly!' he laughed. 'Damn them all. We're going to see Dusty.'

He slapped the reins, urging her to go faster and the mare broke into a trot. The crates on the cart began to vibrate and odd items toppled off the back, falling prey to a lucky scavenger, but Dickie was unconcerned. His objective was to reach Walmgate as fast as he could.

Polly kept throwing back her head peevishly, unused to such a pace. She was accustomed to doing her rounds at a leisurely gait, with plenty of stops along the way where ladies would pet her and push titbits between her velvet lips. The cart rumbled and clattered over the cobblestones – it made her nervous, made her want to run.

Suddenly, something leapt at her. Rough hands clawed at her bridle and heaved savagely on the bit. She gave a high whinny of pain as the metal dug into her. There was shouting and confusion and the sound of a struggle somewhere behind her.

'Get him, Con!' Garret Fallon applied his weight to the bridle as the mare tried to rear. His brother Conor was balanced on a spoke of one of the cartwheels, reaching up to pull Dickie from his seat.

Dickie was overcome by a weird paralysis. His mind, until a moment ago, filled with thoughts of Dusty, now fought to regain his reasoning. He stared into the swarthy face of the tinker, trying to put a label to it. Fallon, that was it. Weren't the Fallons out to kill him? He could not move. He watched Conor's hand reaching. He was going to die and he couldn't move. Oh, God save me!

There was a sudden jolt as the frightened horse wrenched the bridle from Garret's fingers. The cart lurched hindwards, unbalancing Conor from the wheel and pitching him into the gutter. Dickie was unseated, tumbling backwards against the pile of groceries, his feet in the air. The movement served to jerk him from his insentience. In a trice he had rolled from the cart, onto his feet and began to run.

Garret released the terrified mare, shouted to his brother and both tinkers thundered down the street in pursuit. The cold air slashed at Dickie's lungs. He flung a haunted glance over his shoulder, gasping with exertion and fear, praying that his long legs would outmatch theirs. There was an alleyway not far ahead. He knew it led onto a maze of back lanes. Once there he could lose them with ease. But he had to reach it first.

He looked frantically over his shoulder again, looked back in front . . . and crashed headlong into a woman who was carrying a stack of parcels from a haberdashery store. Down they both went, the parcels flying out in every direction, the woman rolling undignifiedly beneath her assailant, skirts up to her knees. With no time for apologies

Dickie scrambled to his feet, leaving behind his bowler on the pavement as he ran on.

They were almost upon him now. His terror was having a detrimental effect on his limbs; like a horrible nightmare where one is running like mad but not getting anywhere and the pursuer is inches behind, reaching, reaching . . .

There it was! The alleyway. A few more strides and he would be free. He dashed in . . . and realised his error straight away. Oh, Jesus it was the wrong alley! In his panic he had taken the wrong turning. This alley led not to the network of outlets, but to an enclosed courtyard; a dead end. Dead.

He continued to run, though it was futile to do so, then finally stopped, his back to the wall, his breath coming in painful, rasping clouds on the frosty air. The tinkers stopped also, blacking the exit, and smiled breathlessly. Garret thrust his hands deep into his pockets and surveyed the figure that awaited them so conveniently. 'Well, now wasn't that thoughtful of him, Con? Saves us running all over the shop, don't it?'

They swaggered towards him. Dickie's heart pounded at his chest wall. He pressed himself to the sagging brick-work as if in the hope that it might swallow him up. He wanted to speak, to plead for his life, but his terror had taken his tongue.

'I do believe the poor fella's frightened,' gloated Con.

'Sure, he's got cause to be,' said Garret portentously. He reached inside his jacket. When his hand emerged the weak sun snatched at something silver.

Dickie's blood turned to jelly at the sight of the knife. He could not tear his eyes from it. An acute trembling took over his limbs.

'Hey, brother them's awful dangerous things is knives,' said Con, feigning concern. 'Hadn't ye best put it away before somebody gets hurt? Ye're makin' the young fella terrible nervous.'

'Look, I'm sorry about your sister!' Dickie's vocal chords finally freed themselves, escaping in a high-pitched tremor. He fumbled deliriously in his pockets, pulling out the money he had taken as a float. He scrabbled on the icy ground for the coins that slipped from his grasp. 'Here! Take this for her.' He thrust a handful of silver and copper at them.

'Well now, that's not much reward for our sister's pain, is it, Con?' said Garret reproachfully, counting out the money that Dickie's trembling fingers had poured into his hand.

'Take the horse!' said Dickie eagerly. 'The cart too.'

'Anything – just so long as we don't hurt your pretty hide, eh?'

Dickie did not answer, too obsessed with the knife that the tinker kept turning in his fingers.

'How about it, Con?' said Garret lazily. 'D'ye think we should let him go?'

'We-ell, he has been kinda generous, givin' us the horse an' cart, an' a couple o' pounds too. An' we never axed him for anythin', did we? Still,' he drawled, 'it don't seem much to pay for our sister's lost virtue, do it?'

'That's exactly what I thought,' nodded Garret. 'So I think we'll just do what we set out to do, Con. All right?'

'Right.' Conor, too dipped into his pocket and brought out a knife.

Dickie screamed, squirming against the unyielding wall. *Dusty, help me!* His eyes rolled as the knives advanced upon him. He screamed again. '*No!*' A cloud of ammonic steam wafted under his nose and his trousers suddenly bore an extra weight. The sun flashed on a knife-blade. There was the sharp application of steel to flesh. Then, no more.

Josie bustled in, startling Thomasin from her meditation. For the first time in months she had been forced to close the store at lunchtime. Sonny had not appeared for work this morning which, though hardly unexpected, meant that she had to cope at the counter alone. She had made several attempts to gain access to his room. Apart from a gruff 'Go away!' only the smell of linseed oil betrayed his presence. He was using the room as a coffin, and who could blame him?

'Sorry, Josie,' she said absently, playing with the braid on her dress. 'I'm afraid I've not done justice to the lovely meal you prepared me.'

But Josie had not come to remove the half-eaten meal, instead she said quietly, 'There's a policeman in the hall, ma'am.'

Her employer sighed and placed a hand over her eyes. 'What now?'

'He didn't say, ma'am.' But Josie knew it undoubtedly concerned Mr Dickie. He was a proper nuisance to his parents. So different from his brother. She had been quickly ushered away at the first sign of trouble last night but was aware that something of great import had taken place.

He doesn't have to, thought Thomasin cryptically. As if we haven't enough trouble. 'Show him in, Josie.'

When the officer entered Thomasin asked him to be seated and offered refreshment. He sat down but declined the offer of tea and pulled out a notebook.

'And what has my son been up to this time?' she asked tiredly, before he had disclosed his reason for being there.

He fluttered through the pages of the notepad. 'You speak as if your son is an habitual offender, madam.'

She was quick to rectify the assumption. 'But I can't think of any other member of my household who would warrant your presence. It is about my son?'

'Your son may or may not be implicated in this matter, ma'am,' he said. 'But I am primarily concerned about a horse and cart which I believe belongs to you. It is – or should I say was, for it has been removed – causing a traffic hazard in Walmgate.' Thomasin frowned and asked him to be more detailed. 'There was no driver in the cart,' he told her. 'The mare decided she would like to quench her thirst, spotted a trough on the opposite side of the road, turned into the path of an oncoming vehicle, nearly causing a nasty accident, and finished up with the cart blocking the entire street. The address of your business premises was painted on the side of the cart but as I got no answer there I had to look up your home address.'

Thomasin's mind had gone no further than his words 'No driver in the cart'. 'But my son?' she said abstractedly.

'He was in charge of the vehicle?' queried the policeman, at which she nodded rapidly. He asked for a description of her son which she quickly provided. 'Well, I can't say if the two incidents are related and I should hate to alarm you unduly but we received another complaint at the same time from a lady who was knocked to the ground by a young man of a similar description to the one you've just given me. He was being pursued by two men who appeared to be gypsies . . .'

'And I hope they bloody caught up with him!' Sonny had entered the room unnoticed, his face strikingly tallow beneath the flaming hair.

'I beg your pardon, sir?' The police officer became alert. 'Would you be able to enlarge on my information, Mr . . . ?'

'I'm sorry, officer,' said Thomasin flusteredly. 'This is my younger son. Sonny, what did you mean? Do you know what's happened to Dickie?'

'I can guess.' Sonny flopped into a chair and leaned his head back, regarding them sardonically.

'May we be privy to this information?' asked the policeman politely. Sonny's lips remained compressed.

'Sonny, if you know anything please tell us.' Thomasin wrung her hands. 'Who are these men? Where is your brother?'

'With a bit of luck, Mother,' he said bitterly, 'my brother will be dead and I will have been spared a job.'

'Sonny!'

'Mr Feeney.' The officer grew impatient. 'If you have reason to believe that a crime has been committed . . .'

'Oh, there's a crime been committed all right!' spat Sonny. 'It's a crime he was ever born. Very well!' He sprang up and trod the fireside rug. 'I have no definite evidence but I believe the two men who were chasing my brother were named Fallon . . .' At this, Thomasin gave a sharp cry and sat down. Sonny continued, 'It appears that my dear brother – as seems to be his pastime – was rather too free with his wild oats and impregnated the Fallons' sister. Yes!' he tossed sarcastically at his mother. 'Another one!' He went on to tell her about the episode at the fairground. 'So, the tinkers have caught up with him at last,' he concluded. 'Let's trust they've done a good job.'

'Oh, Sonny.' Thomasin put her hands to her cheeks. 'Don't.'

'Why not? Why should I care if they kill him?'

'He's your brother.'

'That fact only makes me hate him all the more. I'll be glad if he's dead. How could he do it to me, Mother? To me, who always defended him?' His face beseeched her, but she could not answer him. Because she did not know the answer.

The policeman had done nothing to interrupt the flow, but now he reclaimed the initiative. 'Look sir, are you certain that these two men were the same?'

'Of course I'm not certain,' said the other testily. 'I've been here all morning. Anyway, there must be any amount of people wanting to kill him.'

'But you think there may be a distinct possibility of them being somehow connected with this incident?' persisted the officer.

Sonny nodded, and the man turned to Thomasin. What had set out as an insignificant inquiry had developed more sinister proportions. 'I shouldn't be too quick to jump to conclusions, Mrs Feeney. We've had no reports of a ... well, of anything of an unsavoury nature. It's most probable that your son escaped these men. Did he happen to be wearing a bowler hat by the way?' He had suddenly recalled that the woman who had been assaulted had clung grimly to the bowler hat as 'evidence'. Thomasin could not see the relevance in his question but answered, 'Why, yes he was. Is that significant?'

He evaded answering by consulting his watch. 'At what time does he usually return from his work?'

Thomasin said that it varied, but Dickie was normally in for his evening meal. 'He's never been one to miss a feed hasn't Dickie,' she answered, making herself all the more anxious. If Dickie did not appear at the table they would know that something had definitely befallen him.

'These young fellows are a bit unpredictable,' soothed the officer kindly. 'I've sons of my own. I know they can be a handful at times. Leave it with me. I'll ask around, see if anyone's seen anything. I'm sure he'll turn up, but if he doesn't you might get in touch with me at the station. Ask for Police Constable Darley. I can't treat him as a Missing Person officially 'cause he's not been gone but a few hours – we don't even know if he has gone, anyway. I think he'll turn up myself.' He folded his notepad into his breast-pocket and retrieved his helmet. 'If you would be so good as to send someone along for the horse and cart?' Thomasin nodded and rang for Josie to show him out. When he had left she gave way to her feelings. 'God . . . what are we going to do now?'

'You heard the policeman,' he replied, abnormally harsh with her. 'He'll probably turn up like the unwelcome visitor. Well, when he comes – I go.'

'Aw, Sonny.' She sank down next to him and tried to draw him out. 'I know it was a dreadful thing for him to do to you, and I know how you felt about Peggy. But surely it was better for you to find out what she is before you married her?'

'What *she* is!' said Sonny venomously. 'It's my brother that's the villain in this, Mother. I won't have you shifting the blame onto Peggy. You know his morals. No woman is safe when he's around. God! I was so complacent; thinking that now he'd found his own girl Peggy would be safe. I never learn, do I?'

'I know, I know, love,' sighed his mother. 'But do try to see things sensibly. He's not a brute for all his failings. If she hadn't been willing he would never have forced her, I'm sure. She must have been agreeable.'

'Please, be quiet.' He became sullen. 'I don't wish to listen to any more.'

'I wish you'd try to see . . .'

'No!' He sat bolt upright, facing her. 'I wish *you* would try to see. This wasn't just another tart whom my brother has been tupping. She was almost my wife; the girl I loved; still love . . . oh, Christ, help me!' He dropped his head to his hands and began to sob noisily. Coming from one who had always contained his tears as a child his grief horrified her. She laid her hand on his brilliant hair and stroked it. His own came up to knock it away. 'Get away from me! Leave me alone!' He leapt up, still sobbing and ran from the room, at the same instant that Patrick came in from work. They collided with each other. Sonny recovered first and ran on.

'Let him go!' cried Thomasin as her husband made to go after him. 'Pat, please sit down, there's something I have to tell you: it's about Dickie.'

'Jazers, not again,' muttered Patrick.

The church was empty, the way thought Liam with not a little shame, he liked it best. Maybe he was being a bit rough on himself, for the pleasure he experienced when the undercurrent of two hundred supplications wafted up to his pulpit was certainly very real. It was just different, this emptiness. Silent – no, more pronounced than silence, and in this quietude the presence of the Lord seemed all the more acute. At this time of day Liam felt able to talk with the Lord not as the Deity, but on a friendlier basis. Man to man. He was sure that his Maker would forgive this blasphemous familiarity, for in this instance it bred not contempt but a joy that deepened with each passing year.

After genuflecting he sat in his usual place – the altar steps – and stared pensively at the great crucifix. 'Ah, Lord,' he began, rubbing a wrinkled, blue-veined hand up and down his shin. 'I don't want to sound ungrateful for it's taken us twenty years to achieve it, but this grand new house o' Yours is a terrible cold hole. Ye know what a decrepit old eejit I've become, could Ye not persuade some of our parishioners to donate a new stove?' He bent his grizzled head and was silent for a time, still rubbing his aged limbs. Then, as a humorous thought came to him his shoulders began to shake and when he looked up once more to the rood he was smiling broadly. 'What did Ye make of Fanny Dolan's confession today? Strange? I'll say it was. 'Tis enough to make a man give up the drink, er, always supposing he's that way inclined o' course. Did I do right to give her the penance I did? Were Ye satisfied with it? Ah, I can hear Ye. A bit on the steep side, Ye say. Getting hard in me old age, You're thinkin'. Ah well, Ye could be right. I was only sayin' to meself the other day . . .' His gaze fell on the ranks of pews. The church was not empty as he had previously surmised; there was a solitary figure sitting not four rows away from Liam, forehead pressed to the pew in front. An' that's another thing, Lord thought Liam – the old eyes aren't what they used to be. What must he be thinking, that lone worshipper? 'Tis the first sign, they said: talking to yourself.

His joints groaned as he levered himself from the altar steps to pad along the aisle. The bowed head did not rise at the sound of the approaching footsteps. Only when Liam recognised the auburn thatch and spoke its owner's name did Sonny heed the priest.

Liam, perturbed by the lack of animation on this usually friendly face, slid into the pew and sat beside him. Gazing for a moment into the dough-like features with the red band across its forehead – the imprint of the pew – he said, 'Am I right about this place, or is it only me that feels the cold? Me an' my poor crackling bones.'

'You're not wrong, Father,' mumbled Sonny. 'I feel it too.' *A deathly, numbing cold. But in my case the cold stems from within.* He blinked at Liam who had spoken again. 'Sorry, Father?'

'I said is there any way I can help?'

'Do I look as if I need help?' asked Sonny.

Liam did not give an answer, knowing that Sonny did not expect one.

'I'm beyond help, Father,' whispered the young man.

'No one is beyond help,' said Liam. 'Not in this place.'

Sonny straightened and said spontaneously, 'Will you hear my confession?'

Liam studied the tight mask and sensed the pain beneath it. He leaned towards Sonny conspiratorially, 'Official or unofficial?'

The lozenge of comfort was lost on Sonny who shook his head apathetically. Something awesome had happened to this boy. Liam patted him kindly on the shoulder. 'Come, my young friend. I don't suppose it matters where I take your confession for God will hear it, an' 'tis a darned sight warmer in my study.' He led the youth from the church and into his welcoming, book-lined study where a blazing log fire licked the chimneyback. 'Will ye look at that? Warmer than Beelzebub's backside.'

Sonny sat in the chair which Liam indicated and watched the old priest with his shaking hands pour out two measures of whiskey. 'I suppose I'll be in trouble with your mother for encouraging ye in the evils of drink.' Liam handed over the glass. 'But by the look on your face a wee drop wouldn't go amiss.'

'I wanted to kill my brother,' said Sonny, as simply as if he were confessing to stealing the last cake off the plate.

Liam contemplated his whiskey, waiting for the outpouring he knew would follow. It came in a jerky, incoherent deluge, the tale of his brother's treachery, verbalising the rage he had felt, the murder, but worst of all the pain. Only when he had exhausted the flow did he drink from the glass, pouring the whole measure down his throat like a veteran. And here was I, thought Liam, imagining I was corrupting the boy. He set down his own glass and went to refurbish Sonny's. He glanced at the well-built young man whose maturing frame overtaxed the strength of the old easy chair. The chair in which, fifteen years ago, a minute, red-headed toddler had sat leafing through one of Liam's picture books, his grubby, bare toes dangling a good nine inches from the carpet.

Having refilled his young friend's glass he sank back into his chair and took a sip of his own whiskey. 'I remember once,' he initiated, 'oh, a good few years ago it would be, a rather strange confession. Strange, because it was totally out of character with the person who delivered it. Oh, 'tis a fact I'm not supposed to know the identity of the sinner shoved away at the other side of the box, but when a man knows an' loves every one of his children 'tis hard for him not to recognise the voices. I recall being terribly saddened at the time, for the loss of a childhood, and even more surprised that it was this young fella that was confessing and not his brother. But then an old picture formed itself in my mind: that of two boys, one dark an' beautiful, with a smile that'd put Lucifer to shame, the other smaller boy following him about like a sheepdog. Then I realised that ye'd rather take the lot on your own shoulders than implicate your brother who was probably the main culprit in the deed. 'Tis my betting ye carried the blame a lot more times than that.'

'You're right,' snorted Sonny. 'Many's the time I swore I'd kill him. But don't think I'm a saint. I was mad as anything that it was me who had to confess while he was committing more sins.'

'An' what happened after ye'd cooled down? I'll bet ye forgave him, didn't ye?'

'Look, I know where all this is leading, Father – and I won't do it.'

'Did I ask ye to do anything?'

'You didn't need to. You want me to forgive him.'

''Tis you who's saying those words, not me,' said Liam, then leaned forward earnestly. 'Sonny, he's still that same brother ye forgave all the other times. I'll wager ye could've killed him a hundred times over yet he's still walkin' the earth.'

'No! This time he's gone too far. He knew I loved her – worshipped her – yet he deliberately ruined everything we had. How could he do it to me, Father? Me, his brother, who looked after him, loved him more than I loved anyone I think till Peggy . . .'

'Ah, I know what you're going through, son,' groaned Liam, then noted the look of scorn. 'An' I know what you're thinkin' too: how can this woodwormed old codger with his brewer's belly, this priest with no knowledge of women, begin to know how I feel. An' ye'd be right in part – I never had a woman's love, saving my mother's which I fully realise is not the same thing at all. But I do understand your pain, because that same pain affects me. An' 'tis my thinkin' Dickie's hurtin' too.'

Sonny exhaled bitterly. 'Oh, now that is taking understanding a shade too far. Him, feel pain? He's insensible to anything except his own lecherous appetite.'

'I disagree. I believe if you reject him it'll affect him more than you imagine. Despite his apparent selfishness he's not a boy without emotions; they're just slow in coming to the surface. Did you ever consider why he does these things to ye?'

'It doesn't take very much considering. It's simply that he can't bear the thought of me being happy with a woman.'

'Could it not be that he loves ye so much that he can't bear the thought o' sharing that love? Well, 'tis a point to consider,' he added to Sonny's derision. 'He still has a lot of growing up to do, Sonny. In a lot o' ways you're more mature than him; in fact I think ye were born old.'

'If that were true I'd have the wisdom that goes with age and I'd've seen all this coming.'

'So . . . now that it has come, what's to happen next?' sighed Liam.

Sonny retreated into his depression like a morose hornet. 'There's talk of the wedding being brought forward – with a slight alteration to the name of one of the participants.'

'I was referring more to your feelings. D'ye still feel ye want to kill him?'

Sonny stared into the fire and shook his head. 'I don't feel anything. Just empty. Besides,' he smiled unpleasantly, 'I forgot to tell you: even if I still had that inclination I'd not be able to purge it. He's gone missing.' He related the facts that the policeman had told him. 'And if he's not turned up by the time I get home I know what'll happen – Mother is going to ask me to join the search party.'

'An' will ye?' asked Liam softly.

Sonny shrugged. 'Can you give me one good reason why I should?'

'I'll give ye the one your mother will give ye: he's your brother.'

'Ah,' nodded Sonny, 'and that's supposed to make everything all right, is it? I'm meant to fling my arms around him and smother him with kisses. Oh, welcome home, Dickie, all your sins are forgiven! Have you got a best man yet? No? Oh, well we can't have that, can we? Me? Oh, I'd be honoured to stand beside you while you wed the girl who was supposed to wed me. Me, hold it against you? Why, whatever for? Just because you've successfully ruined my life that's no reason for me to feel any bitterness, is it? After all, you are my brother. That makes everything just perfect. Ask Father Kelly, he'll tell you.'

'You're quite in order to vent your spleen on me if ye're so disposed,' said Liam quietly when the verbal flaying had ceased.

Sonny moved his head wearily and stood. 'I'm sorry, Father. I came here to offer my confession and end up giving you the battering that Dickie should have had.'

'Forget about me,' replied Liam, rising with him. 'What're ye going to do about your brother?'

'Well, Father.' Sonny was at the door now. 'If you're asking me if I'll join the search, then yes I'll probably go, if only to please Mam and Dad. But if you're asking if I'll forgive him when we do find him, then the answer is an emphatic No. I'll never forgive him for this, Father. Never.'

CHAPTER THIRTY-TWO

They knew that the tinkers' camp must be very near by the mixed odours of boiled cabbage and woodsmoke that drifted down the lane to meet them. It was a bitterly cold and forbidding night, the blackness of the sky rent only by an insipid slick of moon. They had much difficulty in negotiating their path but had not dared to bring a lantern with them, unwilling to forewarn the tinkers of their coming.

Soon, though, they saw the campfire crackling and shooting sparks into the murk, throwing dancing shadows over the cluster of caravans that surrounded it. Over the fire, suspended on a tripod of branches, was a steaming cauldron, but there was no sign of life.

Patrick froze, laying his hand on his son's forearm, and squinted into the shadows for signs of danger. He whispered into Sonny's ear, his lips almost touching the skin and irritating the youth. It was very easy to vex Sonny these days. 'You take the two at that side,' he indicated the wagons, 'I'll take those three. Look out for dogs.' He sidled into the encampment, feeling his way along the edge of the first caravan, assisted by the soft light that spilled from within. The iron wheel was icy cold to his touch as he hoisted himself up to snatch a glimpse over the half-door.

The interior took him by surprise; it was like a miniature palace, with fine porcelain jugs and ornaments, shining brasses and copper sparkling under the lantern that hung from the ceiling, and luxurious scarlet hangings as rich as could be found in any stately home. His astonished eyes raked along the walls taking in the finery; and then the hairs at the nape of his neck relayed the feeling that there was someone in there. He ducked down involuntarily, only rising again slowly when there was no shout of alarm. Snug in the let-down bed with its needlepoint coverlet lay a child asleep. A slumbering angel with dark, tousled locks, its parted lips producing a soft snore.

No sign of his son here. Patrick climbed down and felt his way to the next caravan, trying his best not to tread on any frost-brittled twigs. He squatted to peer under the caravan before he chanced to view the inside. During this action someone came slowly down the caravan steps and

Patrick hurriedly rolled under the wagon. He watched the legs make their way to the campfire, accompanied by four more. The old man stooped to pull a lighted stick from the fire and applied it to his pipe. The face illuminated by the flare must have faced the elements for many a year for it was the colour of tanned hide, the chin stubbled with silver. His hair was grey, but apart from this gave no intimation of his age for it was thick and wavy, curling up over his collar.

The tinker threw the stick back into the fire, gave a cursory stir of the cauldron, then sat down with his back towards Patrick, pulling a blanket around himself. The dog lay beside him, its grizzled head on its paws. Its coat bore the same signs of age as did the man's hair. Patrick remained beneath the caravan, watching, wondering if he dare move. He peered to his left to see if he could spot Sonny.

Sonny was watching the scene too; the old man and his dog huddled by the campfire, with the transient light playing over their mellow features. His mind automatically transferred the scene to canvas.

'If 'tis murder ye have in mind ye'd do well to get on with it!' Both Patrick and his son jumped as the tinker's throaty observation reverberated off the iron cartwheels and shattered the silence. The man had not turned his head. The movement he made now was only to fondle the dog at his side. 'We may be old but we're not stupid. There's one of ye under the yellow wagon an' another skulking behind the midden pile. Ye'd best come out an' show yourselves.'

Patrick and his son guiltily emerged from their supposed hiding places to slowly approach the fire.

'Come closer an' let's see your faces. Don't worry, the others are away for the time, there's only me an' the child here.'

They dropped to their hunkers beside him, grateful for the warmth of his fire and the patch of frost-free grass. 'Now, would ye like to explain why you're creepin' around pokin' your noses into other people's homes?' The man turned and fixed cloudy blue eyes to Patrick's face.

'We had no harmful intentions,' mumbled Patrick, juggling with a twig that had escaped the fire. 'We came to speak to the Fallons.'

'An d'ye always approach someone's front door between the cartwheels?' countered the man. 'Can I be after askin' ye if the Fallons are friends o' yours?'

Patrick smiled tightly. 'I could hardly lay claim to that.' He snapped the twig over his middle finger and tossed the pieces onto the fire.

'I thought not,' nodded the tinker and directed his eyes back to the blaze. 'An' what would ye be wantin' with Gary an' Con?'

'I think they may have my son,' Patrick told him. 'He's gone missing. We believe he was attacked by the Fallons.'

'But what makes ye think they brung him here?' asked the man, puffing on his pipe. 'If those boys attacked him ye can be sure he's dead; they don't waste punches.'

Patrick tingled at the man's words and found his own hard to form; his tongue kept sticking to his teeth. 'There was no sign of . . . a body, or anything. He just vanished into thin air. We think they musta kidnapped him.'

The tinker gave a throaty chuckle. 'An' tell me, why would two fine tinker lads want to kidnap themselves a buffer?'

'I should say they've good reason,' said Patrick noncommittally, then at the old man's searching stare added, 'My son got their sister into trouble.'

'Ah, God I'd not give much for his chances then. If Garret an' his brother don't fix him the mother will. 'Tis her ye want to watch out for.'

Patrick's temper flared and he bunched his fists. 'If they've harmed my boy then I promise there'll be nothing left o' this camp but matchwood when the police arrive.'

The tinker looked at him sharply. 'The runners are coming?'

'They are. But don't worry, they'll not be here for a day or two yet. Ye see, my son is not "officially" missin'. Now will ye kindly point me to the Fallons' caravan or do I have to turn each one o' them inside out?'

The man pulled the sleeping dog's ears. Poor old Tasker was not even aware of the strangers' presence when they were virtually on top of him. He'd get his backside kicked if he belonged to anyone but Paeder. But his owner knew what it felt like to be old and useless. 'I'd point it out to ye if I could,' he told Patrick good-naturedly. 'But I can't. See, they're not here, the Fallons.'

'Not here? Then why didn't ye say something before? Where are they?'

The man hoisted his shoulders. 'Who knows? Here, there . . .'

'Ah, come on, man!' Patrick leapt to his feet, at last waking the dog who bristled and uttered a low warning growl.

'Ah, ye've decided to wake up, have ye?' The man ignored Patrick's threatening stance. 'I coulda been dead six times over for all you care.'

'Damn ye, man! They have my son, now where are they?'

The lurcher seemed to shake off his old age in an eye-blink. He rounded, hackles rising, his yellowed teeth bared. Sonny rose slowly to stand with his father.

'Easy, Task!' The man dropped the blanket from his shoulders and used the dog to pull himself up. He stood facing Patrick, or rather looking up, for the younger man was considerably taller. 'This is your boy too?' Patrick nodded. 'Then listen, mister, if I was yourself I'd be thankful I'd one son left an' forget about the other. For if those Fallon boys really have a down on him, ye've as much chance of seein' him again as I have to crack walnuts with me teeth.'

He smiled widely – there was not a tooth in his head.

Dickie had been gone for more than two months now and neither the police nor Patrick could find any trace of him. Thomasin was frantic with worry. For all she had threatened and berated and disowned he was still her

393

son; if anything had befallen him she would never forgive herself. For it was she and Patrick who were to blame. Somewhere in his upbringing they had failed. Her mind would not concentrate on anything, always straying back to her wayward son. Christmas, usually a rumbustious occurrence in the Feeney house, passed almost without celebration. Even poor Josie's attempts at festivity by decorating the room with holly and myrtle only earned her a severe ticking off for fetching the household more bad luck by carrying in the greenery herself. Traditionally, it should have been left to the men whose thoughts, understandably, were far from mistletoe.

Thomasin knew that it must be worse for Patrick than for herself. At least she had the store to occupy her. His land could afford him no relief under six inches of snow. For the most part of the day he was out combing the streets for his son. When not doing this he was prowling around the house like a caged beast, getting under Josie's feet and being generally bad-tempered.

It was on a day such as this that yet another shock was to come. Patrick, chided from all quarters, stated that it was a poor thing if a man could not release his frustrations in his own house and informed them that he was off where he might be allowed some peace. It was a filthy day. The heavy downpour was turning the snow to a grey slush that sprayed up from the carriage wheels as they sped past. He trudged blindly on through the streets and out towards the countryside, regardless of the saturated condition of his clothes and the bone-chilling cold. He had no idea where his feet were taking him; he merely followed, knowing that he had to rid himself of all outward influences and concentrate on a way to find his son. And the only way to do that was out here where there were few houses and less people to distract him.

His land, when he reached it, was shrouded in a cape of snow. Unlike the city pavements it still retained its virgin state. He hunched over the fence, the rain dripping from the peak of his cap to trickle down his nose. Every attempt he made to produce a line of thought was invaded by the sound of the raindrops embedding themselves in the white blanket. He stood there for a long time, trying to force his mind into submission, but the noise of the rain grew louder, driving him to distraction. His only accomplishment would seem to be earning himself a severe chill.

The snow was beginning to succumb to the onslaught; pitted by the rain it took on the appearance of a huge slab of tripe. He stared at it for some moments longer, then straightened and looked about him despairingly. He was surrounded by a white wilderness. Going back to the track he considered the trail of distinctive footprints in the snow, the outside edge a good inch deeper than the inner. There were two sets of Catch's footprints, going in opposite directions; one going, one coming back. Patrick disregarded the set of prints that went towards York and followed the other with his eyes. Quite suddenly he found that he was soaked to the skin. Catch's cabin was only a mile or two down the track. Unconsciously, he permitted his feet to fill Catch's bootprints and took their lead.

'Tha must have a slate loose comin' out on a day like this!' The old bachelor waved him inside and reshot the bolts that secured his small fortress. 'Can't be too careful, there's a lotta queer folk abaht. By gum, look at state o' thee!' He pushed a shivering Patrick in front of the fire. 'Get them be-ats off. No! Don't sit in that chair, tha's soppin' wet. 'Ere!' He threw a pile of sacking onto the chair. 'Now tha can sit down.' He watched Patrick unlace his boots and hold his stockinged feet to the blaze. 'I allus knew tha were cracked. Surely tha didn't come up 'ere to do any work?'

Patrick took off his cap and shook his head. 'I just wanted to get some peace.' He flicked his wrist, unleashing a spray of droplets which made the fire hiss and its smoke waft out into the room.

Catch grimaced. 'Way tha's goin' on tha'll have plenty o' that – an eternity of it. If tha don't catch tha death o' cold Ah'll eat me hat.'

There was a large can dangling from a homemade

contraption over the fire. Catch took a poker and swung it wide of the blaze, pouring the water that was in it into a teapot. 'Ah knew minute Ah put tea on to brew somebody'd smell it. It's allus way. Folk must think Ah'm med o' brass, brewin' tea for half o' county.' He put his hand in a drawer and brought out the first item he laid his hand on. 'You watch – Ah'll 'ave another half dozen hammerin' on me door in five minutes.' He inserted the fork into the teapot, gave it a brisk stir, tapped it noisily on the rim and threw it aside. Finding two pewter mugs he filled them and passed one to Patrick.

'Blinkin' 'ell, look at thee!' He pointed to the Irishman's steaming clothes. 'Tha's like a hoss what's just run Derby.' He reached behind him as he sat down, adjusting the squashed patchwork cushion.

Patrick cupped grateful hands to the mug. 'I'm sorry to inconvenience ye, Catch. I don't know why I came really. I'll just get thawed out an' I'll be off.' He glanced around him at the typical bachelor's lair – the curtains fixed over the windows with six inch nails, permanently drawn; nails hammered here, there and everwhere on which to hang saucepans, coats, anything that would hang up; an oil can on the table, plus a selection of nuts and bolts; a row of wooden boards with moleskins stretched out to dry; the boots on the ash-covered fender; every corner of the twelve feet square room put to good use, and most of it taken up by the old man's bed next to the fireplace. It was a primitive lifestyle, but remarkably warm and comforting to Patrick as he sat here nursing his troubles.

Catch opened his mouth to sample his tea when there came a knock at the door. 'What did Ah tell thee?' he exclaimed vociferously. 'Buggers round 'ere can smell a brew before it hits cup.' His bandy legs carried him to the door where he struggled with the three bolts and opened it an inch. 'Oh, it's thee is it?' He opened it wider. 'Well, don't just stand there lettin' all warmth out, away in.'

Sonny stamped the snow from his boots and stepped into the snug cabin. 'I thought I might find you here, Father.'

Patrick looked up in surprise. 'I thought ye were helping your mother at the store. Here, come by the fire, boyo an' get yourself a warm.' He drew in his long legs to make way for his son.

Sonny stepped into the gap and held out his hands. Unlike Patrick's his clothes were barely damp; the rain had eased. 'Mother sent me to find you – no thanks, Catch.' He refused the tea.

'Tha might as well have one whilst tha's 'ere,' insisted Catch.

'Oh, all right, thank you – just half a cup though, I'll not have time to drink a full one.' He turned back to Patrick. 'We had a visitor at the store, Dad. A policeman.'

Patrick came out of his benumbed state and set aside the mug eagerly. 'They've found Dickie?'

Sonny thanked Catch and grasped the pewter mug. 'They think they have . . . at least they've found someone who matches the description we gave them.'

Patrick picked up the mug again to cover his apprehension, and with the gulp that he took came a sense of foreboding. 'Get it over with, son.'

'Well . . . if it is Dickie . . .' Sonny glanced at Catch, then back at his father. 'He's dead . . . I'm sorry, Father.' He watched Patrick's face drain of colour. 'They asked if someone could go and identify him. Mother couldn't . . .'

'Of course she couldn't.' Patrick rose swiftly then, remembering his boots, ducked to the hearth and began to pull them on, tussling with the saturated leather. His mind screamed its horror, but when he opened his mouth the words came out evenly. It was as though another person were speaking. 'How is your mother, Sonny?'

'She's as one might expect after receiving such news,' answered the other. 'I didn't like leaving her but there was no one else to send for you. Josie's seeing to her.'

'So she's at home now?'

'Yes, I insisted she close the store for the remainder of the day. She was, in no fit state to continue.'

Patrick finished securing his laces. 'Have ye come in the gig?' Sonny replied that he had. 'Then I'll drop you off at home while I go down to the whatsit.' Mortuary, he thought. Say it! *Mortuary, mortuary, mortuary.*

'I thought you may be glad of some support,' said his son.

'That I would, but your mother will need ye more. I can manage on me own.'

'No need,' said Catch, grabbing his coat. 'Ah'll go wi' thee.' He was familiar with the latest drama in the Feeney family. Patrick was inclined to divest himself of his problems whilst toiling the land, and the old man provided a ready ear whose owner was not inclined to blab.

'There's no call for you to drag yourself out in this weather, Catch,' said Patrick. 'It won't be a very pleasant task either.'

'Don't argue, I'm off.' Catch damped down the fire, twined a scarf around his neck and pulled on a woollen hat. 'Tha can bring me back, mind. No doubt it'll be a wasted journey.'

'I pray to God you're right,' said the Irishman, but was sure deep down that it would not be.

When they all stood outside Catch locked the door and climbed onto the cart, squeezing himself beside Patrick and his son. Sonny clicked his tongue and flapped the reins and set off towards York.

Once there they dropped Sonny outside his front door and carried straight on. Patrick wanted to get this thing over with as quickly as possible, and face it squarely. Thomasin's tears would not stand him in very good stead for his coming ordeal. He took control of the reins and steered the gig towards the mortuary.

A bitter draught whistled down the corridor where he and Catch sat waiting. Patrick stared at the reflection in the brown tiles and saw an old man sitting bolt upright, hands gripping knees, fingers flexing and unflexing, the mouth a rigid gash in the white face and a nervous tic playing round the right eye. At first he thought it was Catch, then saw another, much shorter, old man sitting alongside it, and realised with a jolt that the first old man was himself.

Catch nudged Patrick. 'Get tha pipe out, lad. If nowt else it'll help to get rid o' this blasted stink. God's truth, what the hell is it?' His wrinkled face screwed up in distaste.

Patrick had come across death many times in his life and knew very well what the smell was. He searched for his pipe and put it to his mouth, then pulled out a box of matches, but his fumbling, cold fingers spilled the whole lot over the floor. The policeman who had shown them in poked his head around the corner at the noise. The look on his face caused Patrick to abandon his idea.

Catch sniffed in disgust. 'They leave thee sittin' 'ere in this draughty blessed hole for half an hour, never a cuppa tea, an' they won't even let thee tek comfort in tha pipe.'

'It doesn't matter.' Patrick finished collecting the matches and put them and the pipe back into his pocket. 'I wish they'd hurry up. What the hell are they doing in there?'

''Ave tha thought about what tha's purrin' in that top corner next year?' Patrick looked askance. 'Tha crops, man! Tha'll have to be more careful o' that carrot fly. Don't be so heavy-handed wi' t'seed so's tha don't have so much thinnin' out to do. That's when buggers get in, tha knows.'

Patrick couldn't believe this. 'I'm sitting here waiting to identify me dead son an' you're talking about carrot fly!' he accused.

Catch looked offended. 'Nay, Ah thought tha might be interested, seein' as how tha lost half yer crop last year.'

'God!' sighed Patrick with feeling. 'I don't know what help I thought I'd get from you when I brought ye along – ye've no children of your own, how could I expect ye to understand what I'm going through? But at least I thought ye'd place human life above bloody vegetables!'

The old man rose stiffly. 'Ah came along 'cause Ah thought Ah might be able to tek tha mind off t'ordeal. But all thou seems to want to do is to wallow in tha misery. Don't fuss abaht givin' me a lift home – Ah'll walk!'

Patrick groaned and buried his head in his hands. 'Oh,

Jazers, Catch ye know I meant no disrespect.' He dragged his fingers down over his cheeks leaving red tracks on the pale skin. ''Tis all this infernal waitin'. I thank ye for trying to take me mind off things, but nothing can do that. God, I wish they'd hurry up.'

Patrick's entreaty was answered by the sound of footfalls echoing down the corridor. Both men looked up enquiringly as an attendant came round the corner. 'Mr Feeney?' Patrick stood up. 'This way, please.' The man moved off. Patrick turned fearful eyes to Catch who gave him an encouraging shove.

'Come with me, Catch,' begged the Irishman. 'I need somebody.'

The attendant was waiting by an open door as they rounded the corner. Patrick walked slowly towards him, the bandy-legged rustic hobbling by his side. The corridor seemed endless. The sound of their boots bounced back and forth off the tiled walls. The sound enhanced his trepidation.

'In here, sir.'

Patrick gagged at the smell and moved no further than the doorway. The tiled room was empty save for what looked like a table spread for tea. But there were no knives and forks, and there was an ominous undulation in the creased cloth.

'If you'd like to step closer?' The man waited.

Patrick felt Catch's hand cradle his elbow and at the insistent pressure stepped up to the table, the bile souring his throat.

'Now, I'll simply lift a corner, sir and you can tell me if it's him.'

The cloth peeled away. Patrick's jaw sagged. He took a staggering step backwards and Catch had to steady him before he fell. He forced himself to look again. The youth could have been asleep but for the mark at his throat that bespoke his violent death. Like a piece of ripped linen, frayed pink at the edges. Patrick quickly averted his eyes from the wound to those of the boy; closed, the dark lashes like the spread bristles of an artist's brush, resting upon the waxen cheeks, thick and luscious like a girl's. The ebony hair fell in soft curls over the passive forehead. The bloodless lips curved into a peaceful smile – a far cry from the tortured wreck that had been wheeled in here, thought the assistant proudly.

Patrick felt the tears burn his eyes. The boy's face became blurred. When the fog cleared the sheet was once more in place. He could have imagined it all.

'Well, sir?' asked the attendant gently.

Patrick took a deep lungful of air as his eyes came up from the shrouded form. The attendant tried to guess what his response would be. The pale-blue eyes were moist with sympathy, pain – and relief.

'That's not my son,' whispered Patrick gratefully. 'It's not Dickie.'

CHAPTER THIRTY-THREE

Since his brother's disappearance Sonny had found himself back in the grocery full-time. Things were far too hectic what with deliveries and book-keeping for him to have the afternoons off for his painting. He didn't know if he could be bothered to paint anyway. Enthusiasm didn't figure in his moods lately. Not even the fact that he'd sold quite a few of the pictures that hung in the store could lift him. He could not say what his feelings had been when his father had come home and broken the news. He wasn't sure that he felt anything. Even his parents' relief was short-lived; Dickie was still missing. However, they were more inclined to believe that their son had been the victim of an abduction rather than a murder and were convinced that if they found the Fallons they would also find their son. Thomasin returned to the store too, where both she and her younger son plunged themselves into its running, in the hope that it would take their minds off other things.

Sonny was perched in the window, making lukewarm attempts at a new display while his mother pandered to the inconsistencies of her loquacious patrons. He wondered where on earth they found the breath for their non-stop gossip, then cursed as his display fell to bits in his fumbling hands. He was about to start from scratch, when he happened to glance up and saw Clancy striding purposefully along Goodramgate, his face set in a determined scowl, and had no illusions as to where the man was heading.

It wasn't Clancy's first visit. He had called at their house a dozen times. Up until now the Feeneys had managed to keep their son's disappearance a secret, but judging from the look on his face, someone had not been so discreet. Sonny's first thought was to hiss a warning to his mother, then decided against it. Why should he? Let them fight and bicker among themselves and leave him out of it.

Thomasin had just scraped three and a penny change from the till and was handing it over when Clancy burst through the knot of customers to confront her, ignoring the women's twittering grievances at being jostled. 'Somebody's just informed me that that snake-eyed brat o' yours has pulled a fast one! Is it right?' Thomasin rebuked him for his behaviour. He ignored her. 'I said is it right?'

'If you refer to my son's disappearance,' she snapped, 'then yes, you were informed correctly. Now, could you wait 'til I've served these ladies?'

'I've a daughter at home with your son's child bustin' her belly an' you tell me to wait!' yelled Clancy.

There was a chorused gasp from the customers. A lot of clandestine titters were exchanged.

Thomasin was mortified. 'Really, Mr Clancy – do you have to speak so plainly?'

'Really, Mr Clancy!' mimicked the Irishman. 'Listen, if that schemin', lyin' worm o' yours thinks he's goin' to welsh on his promise just by runnin' away then he can think again.'.

'He hasn't run away,' protested Thomasin, wishing Sonny would come to her aid. But the young man merely observed from his window-seat. 'We think he's been kidnapped.' It sounded absolutely ludicrous.

Clancy thought so too. He opened his mouth and roared while the customers listened to this exchange with unconcealed interest. 'Kidnapped? Jazers, that's the best joke I've heard all year. Who'd want to kidnap a useless backslider like him?'

'You were keen enough for him to marry your daughter,' was Thomasin's glacial response.

'An' I still am.' Clancy placed large, meaty hands on the counter and breathed beer fumes into her face. 'So, if ye catch up with him before I do ye can tell him this: either he gets his arse into that church before my girl gets much fatter, or Peggy gets herself a nice new pair o' dangly earrings – made from your son's balls.'

There were more gasps of condemnation as he barged out, then every eye turned on Thomasin who smiled weakly and wished she were dead.

When Patrick was informed of the incident he was all for sorting the matter out in his usual fashion. 'The pie-eyed poltroon! I'll teach him to threaten my family.'

'Cool down!' Thomasin, calm once again, flicked out her table napkin and covered her skirt. 'The days have gone when you can go around thumping people. Anyway, that'd only make matters worse.'

'Hah! How could they be worse?' Patrick wanted to know. He took a mouthful of soup then pushed away the bowl, his appetite blunted.

'They can be worse if you upset Josie by not eating the meal she's been slaving over all afternoon,' replied his wife. She pushed his bowl back towards him. 'The Lord knows I don't feel like eating either but you have to keep up your strength. I can't have you flaking out on me.' She eyed Sonny who was staring down into his soup. 'You too.' He blinked at her, then picked up his spoon uninterestedly. 'And where were you this afternoon when I needed you?' enquired his mother. 'Sat in the window like

403

some . . . dummy. Were you waiting until he got his hands round my throat before you decided to move?'

'I'm sorry, I assumed you could handle it,' muttered Sonny.

'And so I could. But it would've been nice if my son had shown some sort of filial concern.'

'Your son!' he retorted, laying down the spoon. 'And which son would that be, Mother?'

'I only see the one here.'

'Oh, forgive me,' he replied sarcastically. 'I quite forgot for the moment that you had two sons. I thought you referred to the one who's always getting up to his mischievous little tricks. Playful things, like deception and lechery. The one who makes a hobby of stealing other people's girls. The one who's been occupying your thoughts for the past two months so that you don't give a damn about anyone else!'

'That is quite enough!' Patrick pushed back his chair and flung his napkin onto the table. 'Jesus, Mary an' Joseph, what's got into this family?'

'I can't speak for Mother but I can tell you what's got into me,' was the brittle answer. 'Two months ago I was making wedding plans with Peggy, then suddenly overnight I find my life in ruins. And does one of you really care about that? No! You're all too busy searching for my dear brother.'

'It might look that way . . .' began his mother.

'It is that way!'

'No! Now be quiet,' commanded his father, coming round to his side of the table. 'To accuse me and your mother of favouritism is absolutely preposterous. After all the trouble Dickie caused us . . .'

'Yes! After all the trouble he's caused you and still all you can think about is if he's alive or not. Never a thought for my unhappiness – and what about Peggy?'

'What about her?' asked Thomasin without thinking.

'Exactly! If I hadn't seen you weeping and wailing I could almost think you were glad my brother has disappeared so that she'd no longer have any claim on this family. You've never liked her, never wanted me to marry her, and now you've got the excuse to be rid of her because with Dickie gone there'll be no wedding, will there? And what about Dusty? There was no complaint about Dickie marrying her, was there? No trying to talk him out of it like with me and Peggy. And we all know the reason for that, don't we? Dusty was bringing property with her – not like poor old Peggy. That was the crunch, wasn't it, Mother? You weren't so fond of Dusty as of her money.' He suddenly found himself spreadeagled on the carpet with his father towering over him and the taste of blood in his mouth.

'Don't you ever speak to your mother like that again!' warned Patrick, his pointed finger quivering with passion. 'D'ye hear me? Never! Let me put a few facts your way, boy. Firstly, there is no favouritism in this house. Of course we're worried about your brother, we love him, he's our son, despite all the hurt he's caused us – but we worry just as much about you. Secondly, your mother and I welcomed Dusty for her own sake, not because of her father's business. She's a nice girl; we liked and respected her very much. She would've been a great asset to this family. As for Peggy . . .' he frowned, dropped his hand to his side and took a pace backwards, giving his son room to pick himself up; but Sonny stayed where he was, a thread of scarlet running to his chin. 'Personally speaking I was ready to accept the girl – even if she did talk as though she had a mouthful o' plums. But your mother . . .' he paused to allow Thomasin her say.

'I didn't think she was right for you, Sonny,' she told him candidly. 'It's as simple as that. No other reason – certainly no monetary one. And I've been proved right about her, haven't I?'

Sonny thumped the carpet. 'But you will insist on laying all the blame on her when you know it lays with Dickie!'

'Oh, come on, let's be right Sonny,' parried Thomasin. 'She had her eye on him ever since you first brought her to this house. I wonder you never noticed – and I did try to warn you. How can you defend her when she's hurt you so?'

'Damnation! Don't you think she's been hurt as well?' volleyed Sonny, springing up and angrily wiping the blood from his chin. 'Can't you see that? Are you both blind?'

'You're the one who's blind, lad,' said Thomasin reciprocating his exasperation. 'And yes, you were right when you said I was relieved you weren't going to marry her; she would've made your life a misery.'

Sonny sighed heavily and was about to reply when the door opened a fraction and Josie's wary face peeped around it, bearing a note before her. 'I'm terribly sorry to intrude, sir,' she said to Patrick. 'But I've just found this note shoved through the door. I thought it might be urgent.'

Patrick thanked her as she backed out. He roughly unfolded the note which was without an envelope. The others watched his face which remained unreadable as he scanned the sheet. When he had finished he passed it to Thomasin who read aloud the badly composed and misspelt letter.

To feeny this is ofishal an if I do not get a repli I am goin to the Law if you think I am goin to pay for this bastad yor son as planted you can think agen my dorter reseevd a propsl of marrij from yor uther sun so if the won wot did the damij as cleerd off then the won that propsd will hav to marry her if he dont I will get onto him for breech of promis expectin a promt repli – CLANCY.

'I don't think we need concern ourselves,' said Thomasin, passing the note to her son. 'I'd hardly class it as a legal document. Besides, it'd never stand up in court when the truth was known, even if Clancy could afford the legal fee.'

'Nevertheless, our Mr Clancy could cause a whole lot o' trouble,' speculated Patrick.

'No, he won't.' Sonny, having read the letter, ran his

finger and thumb along the crease and filed it behind the clock on the mantelshelf.

'How can you be so sure?' asked his mother.

'Because I'm going to do as he asks,' replied her son simply. 'I'm going to marry her.'

'Really, Sonny there's no need,' panicked Thomasin. 'Clancy has neither the nous nor the money to take you to court. Even if by some miracle he did then you know we'd stand by you. There's not the slightest reason why you should kowtow to blackmail.'

'Yes there is, Mother,' replied Sonny, fixing her with his solemn grey eyes. 'You see, I love her.'

All the hurt and betrayal were magically washed away when Sonny beheld his enchanting little bride. She looked so vulnerable and innocent that his heart surged with love as he walked to the altar with her. He had had time to do a lot of thinking in the past two months and had come to the conclusion that if you really loved somebody you could forgive them anything – and he really did love her. He just couldn't bear to spend the rest of his life wondering what he had missed, and so he accepted his brother's leavings.

There was precious little merriment at the wedding – it was a furtive and hasty affair – but Sonny didn't mind; he had what he craved for. Thomasin, strongly against the marriage – more so than ever – had threatened to withdraw her former offer of a settlement, but Sonny was not ruled by thoughts of money as was his brother. 'You'd surely not see your own son rely on others' charity,' he had taunted, and she had given in – but not completely. He could bring Peggy to live in the family house where she, Thomasin could keep an eye on her, but the settlement would not come until Sonny's mother was satisfied as to her daughter-in-law's motives.

'I don't deserve anyone as noble as you, Sonny,' Peggy told him as she sat up in bed waiting for him later that night. 'After I wronged you so, I wonder that you even wanted to see me again.'

He stationed himself by the bed, feeling awkward and conspicuous in his nightshirt. 'How could I think that?' he answered gruffly. 'I love you, Peg.'

'After what I did?' she asked with hooded eyes.

'All you did, Peggy, was to be led astray by someone who didn't give a toss for the consequences. I couldn't go on blaming you for Dickie's treachery.'

'Oh, Sonny!' She threw aside the sheet, allowing him to discard his modesty. 'I'm sorry I hurt you, and I promise I'll be a good wife.'

He slid into bed beside her and took her in his arms, felt himself harden at the soft assault of her swollen breasts which pierced their two nightgowns. The warm feminine scent at the base of her throat acted as balm to his uncertainty, and he began to apply his lips tenderly to her musky hollows, tugging gently at the bows on her nightgown. He ran his hands down the sweep of her back, cleaving her to him. He murmured that he loved her dearly, and she responded by hoisting up both their garments so that the full heat of her body was upon him. And gently, very gently he entered her as though his brother's defilement had never taken place.

Later, drenched in contentment, Sonny fell asleep, his scarlet head pillowed on his wife's flawless shoulder. Peggy lay awake for much longer, bitterly regretting the scheming that had landed her in this mess. At first she had genuinely considered Sonny as a suitor – oh, she didn't love him, but his obvious wealth made him a very attractive prospect indeed . . . until she had been introduced to his brother.

It wasn't the first time she had heard the name Richard Feeney; his reputation as a ladies' man was well-broadcast and it was easy to see the reason women fell for him as both had run an admiring eye over the other. It had then become her idea to test each brother out, see which one was the best candidate for marriage then opt accordingly. She had desperately hoped it might be Dickie, but after only one secret assignation she had come to recognise a nature as unscrupulous as her own – this one did not intend to offer marriage or anything else come to that –

so she had regrettably decided that it must be the boring, if steadfast, one for her husband. Still, she hadn't allowed that to handicap her enjoyment. The arrangement had seemed like a perfectly reasonable one and she had seen no wrong in accepting the more honourable son's proposal whilst rutting with his kin.

Then she had found herself pregnant. She hadn't bothered telling Dickie, aware that it would make no impression, but instead had continued with her plan to marry Sonny. Of course, that was before her mother had noticed her condition and her father had started to throw his weight about, nearly spoiling everything. There had been a brief flash of optimism when he had ordered Dickie to marry her, but that hadn't lasted long. Dickie was gone and here she was landed with his brother.

She moved her head around as far as his own would allow. He moaned in his sleep and snuggled up closer. Peggy supposed she should be grateful, but she just couldn't help comparing her husband's clumsy love-making with his brother's experienced throes. Her body throbbed, unsatiated. Sonny mumbled her name in his sleep. Poor Sonny, despite the bitter disappointment she would try to be a good wife to him. She would try dreadfully hard.

CHAPTER THIRTY-FOUR

Unfortunately for everyone there was little conviction in Peggy's resolution. The brilliant sunshine that marked St Patrick's Day did nothing to brighten the fractious atmosphere that her arrival in the house had created. Oh, she had tried; for three whole weeks she had been wifeliness personified. But, as Thomasin had predicted to herself on witnessing this attempt, the mode of perfect spouse was short-lived.

Peggy became bored with her role. She had expected that marrying into such a wealthy family would bring her everything she had always wanted, plus a servant to wait on her hand and foot. Oh, what a delight to play the part of lady for once, instead of overworked maid. But she had reckoned without her mother-in-law. Thomasin made it clear that Peggy was expected to assist with the household chores; albeit small ones, this was not what Peggy had had in mind when she had laid her plan. Her husband, she found out, was totally under his mother's rule. It would appear that her inauguration to lady of the manor would have to be attained by drawing on his sympathetic nature. So, one morning, under pretext of a debility brought on by her condition, she had stayed in bed and had remained there ever since.

At one point it looked as if her subtle workings would be spoilt by her father; Clancy had not been invited to the wedding and neither had any other member of that family. It was quite bad enough, said Thomasin, having one of them living with her without having to entertain a dozen such monstrosities. Clancy, though, had had other ideas. His daughter was not to be the only beneficiary of the marriage – he wanted a piece of it for himself. However, his belligerent attempt at blackmail had been thwarted before it had taken root. The only money he had squeezed from the Feeneys had been the amount needed to mend his broken jaw when Patrick had dished out his answer to this blackmail. Happily for everyone, Peggy especially, this had been the last visit Clancy had paid to the Feeney house.

Thomasin helped herself to a honeycomb and observed her son over the breakfast table. 'Are we not to have the pleasure of Peggy's company again this morning?' Why, oh why could she not keep the twinge of acerbity from her voice when speaking of her daughter-in-law? It was hardly Sonny's fault that she was as she was, and it must hurt him to hear his wife spoken of in such scathing tones. She must try to practice tolerance.

'I would've thought you might have a bit of sympathy

for her, Mother,' said Sonny, slicing a piece of toast. 'Having borne two children of your own you must know what she's going through.'

'Is she still getting the sickness?' Thomasin tried to make the concern genuine. 'She should be over that by now.'

'Yes, it is rather worrying,' frowned Sonny. 'She was all right at first. The sickness came when, by rights, she could have expected it to be over with. I've been debating whether to call in the doctor.'

'I don't think there's any need for that,' assuaged his mother. 'The midwife had a look at her and is perfectly satisfied.'

'But midwives can't know as much as doctors,' he replied worriedly. 'There may be something seriously wrong.'

Thomasin chuckled. 'I shouldn't let the midwife hear you saying that. She carries a pretty sharp pair of scissors in her pinny. Don't worry, lad. If she can't cope she's had my firm instructions to send for the doctor. I had the two of you without any medical help so there's no reason why Peggy can't.' A vision of Dickie's fluffy head cradled in her arms intruded on her thinking; she thrust it aside.

At her words Patrick, too, got the vision. Oh, son, son! If only we knew ye were all right and not lying rotting in some back alleyway. He and Sonny had made various trips to surrounding villages in an effort to sniff out the tinkers' trail, but the Fallons had vanished completely.

'She can't eat anything,' Sonny rambled on. 'I asked Josie to take up a tray after we'd gone to Mass; it came down untouched. It must weaken her, not eating.'

'Look, will you stop worrying,' said Thomasin. 'Wearing yourself to a frazzle isn't going to help her. It's perfectly natural, having babies. She'll be right as rain in a few weeks, you see.' She reached for the cream jug and tipped it towards her cup. There was a delicate ping as the two pieces of china accidentally kissed.

'Perhaps she might have an appetite now,' persevered Sonny. 'Maybe if I ask Josie to take up another tray.'

'Really, Sonny you're getting like a broody old hen,' reprehended his mother. 'If you are forced, you may ask Josie to take something up, but go and ask your wife if she wants anything first. I don't want poor Josie tramping up and down three flights of stairs for nothing.'

'I'd hardly call it nothing,' objected Sonny. 'My wife's ill and . . .'

'Oh, Sonny for pity's sake!' Thomasin covered her brow with her hand. 'Act as you must, but do stop treating that girl as if she were made of porcelain. You're making a rod for your own back there, I tell you.'

Sonny shoved his chair under the table and marched out, ruffled.

'Eh, she's got him like that!' Thomasin clenched her fist and shook it. 'Can't he see she's just having him on a bit of string? All she wants is attention.'

'An' what's wrong with that?' asked Patrick cheerfully. 'I'd welcome a bit more attention meself at times.'

Her visage became even more severe. 'Would you care to enlarge on that remark?'

'Jazers, woman ye're always biting these days. All I meant was we'd all like more attention than we get.'

'No, you didn't. That jibe was directed at me. I want to know what it meant. You don't go short of anything, do you? There's always a meal on the table when you come home, isn't there?'

He rose, his face smilingly-patient and, coming round the table, took hold of her hands and pulled her gently from her seat. 'Woman, you're so damned bristly lately. I know you're worried about Dickie – we all are – but snapping at me isn't going to make him reappear. All I meant was I don't see as much of ye as I'd like to these days. You're always busy at your work. I love ye, Tommy. I miss your company. You're right, I don't go short of anything – but there are occasions when I hanker after the old days.'

'Don't try to tell me you'd swap all this for that poky old house, because I'd not believe you.'

'If I thought it'd bring me more o' your company then

412

I'd do it this minute,' was his honest answer. 'All this is very fine, an' if you're happy with it then so am I. But you know me – I'm all for the simple life.' There had been less and less of that over the past couple of years. His visits to Walmgate had tailed off after the humiliation of Erin's wedding; he could not bear to face Molly. But, as he said now, 'It wouldn't worry me if I were back in Walmgate tomorrow if you were with me.'

She smiled lovingly then. 'Forgive me, love. I have been a bit of a maungy cat lately. It's that wife of Sonny's, she'd drive a saint to murder. And I'm sorry if it looked like I've been neglecting you in favour of the store. I shall make a definite effort to be a more dutiful wife to you.'

'Dutiful – you?' he laughed. 'Begod, 'tis not miracles I'm askin' for. No, all I want is the old Tommy waiting for me when I get home from work on an evening. Give me that an' I'll be happy.'

'Eh, he's easily pleased is lad!' Thomasin gave him a smacking kiss. 'Very well, sir – your complaint will be rectified forthwith.'

But though they laughed, secretly they both knew that she would be unable to fulfil the promise, for the old Tommy no longer existed.

Sonny gripped the brass knob in his square, competent hand, twisted gently and peeped into the bedchamber. Someone had opened the drapes and the bright sunshine streamed into the pleasant room so that the fourposter with its yellow spread was a soft blur of gold. He crept over to the bed and looked down at his sleeping wife. She looked radiant with the sunbeams striking her passive features. Peggy gave a sigh and began to open her eyes, closing them again quickly as the sunlight dazzled her. Sonny went solicitously to the window and tugged at a curtain to shade the light from her face, then returned to sit on the bed.

He bent over and kissed her lips, and would have liked to press his suit had she not turned her head away. 'How's our patient? Did you have a nice rest while I was at Mass?'

She groaned and spoke through her fingers. 'I feel awful. Did anyone mind very much that I wasn't at church?'

'I did,' said her husband. 'I missed you like anything.' He stroked the tousled hair from her face. 'Father Kelly asked after you.'

'Did he? I trust you acquainted him with my state of health.'

'He understands,' replied Sonny, wishing the same were true of his mother. A fool could see that the girl was undergoing enormous suffering. He made his voice deliberately bright to raise her spirits. 'Is there anything I can get for you? Could you face some breakfast if I send Josie up?'

She groaned again. 'Maybe later I might be able to keep something down. Just now all I want to do is sleep.'

He kissed her and rose. ''Course. It was selfish of me to wake you in the first place.' He cupped her cheek with his hand and gazed at her lovely face. 'You sleep now. I'll ask Josie to pop in later.'

When the door had closed behind him Peggy listened for the creak of the stairs. Then, satisfied that he had gone, she leaned forward, punched at her pillows and made herself comfortable. Retrieving the box of chocolates which had been in danger of melting under the bedclothes, she stuffed two into her mouth and went back to the magazine through which she had been thumbing before she had been so rudely interrupted.

'You just tell me what Miss Peggy wants, Mr John an' I'll whisk it up any time,' said Josie. 'Poor lamb, it must be awful to be in such a happy condition and yet feel so wretched.' It was no secret that Miss Peggy was in a delicate state and that Mr John had stepped into the breach to save her being labelled a loose woman. It was a grand thing for any man to do – marry a girl when the babe she carried wasn't his – but that was just like Mr John. She straightened the cloth on the tray and laid a setting. 'What d'you think she'd fancy?'

Sonny ballooned his cheeks. 'Oh, I'll leave it to you, Josie. I'm not very well informed on what might tempt a sluggish palate.' He glanced down at the bucket of shamrock at his feet, imported for this special day. 'You might decorate the tray with a bit of that – make it look pretty so that she doesn't feel left out of the celebrations.'

'Don't you worry, Mr John.' Josie bustled about the kitchen. 'I'll do it up right special and see that she gets something down her.'

A short interval later Josie boiled an egg, placed it in a silver eggcup on the tray along with some strips of bread and butter, some pieces of honeycomb, a cluster of grapes, cream jug, sugar bowl, cup, saucer and teapot. She didn't really have a lot of time to spare as there was the St Patrick's Day luncheon to see to, but if she couldn't manage a few minutes for Mr John's wife then it was a bad show. She wound her way up three flights of stairs, stepping lightly so as not to disturb Peggy if she was still sleeping. Laying down the tray outside the bedroom door she carefully twisted the knob and inserted her head round the door. Two dimples punctuated her artless expression. 'Why, Miss Peggy I'm so glad to see you're feeling better!'

Peggy, caught on the hop, had no time to conceal the half-eaten casket of chocolates as she had done at Sonny's approach. In her anxiety she clipped the box with her fumbling hands and tipped the contents onto the floor.

'Oh, here, let me!' Josie rattled in with the tray and set it on the bedside table.

'Would it not have been more mannerly to knock before you entered?' demanded Peggy waspishly, watching Josie scrumple up the empty chocolate cases and return the uneaten ones to the box.

'Well, I didn't like to, Miss Peggy.' Josie heaved up her ample proportions and, putting the chocolates aside, started to rearrange the bedclothes. 'Mr John said you might be asleep an' I didn't want to wake you. Let's make you comfy, shall we?'

'For Heaven's sake stop doing that!' Peggy struck out

at Josie's ministerings. 'And please afford me my correct status. I am not Miss Peggy but Mrs Feeney.'

Josie remained cheerful. 'Well, I just thought it'd save confusion.' She laid the tray on Peggy's lap. 'I mean, we won't know who we're talkin' about with two Mrs Feeneys in the house.'

'Nevertheless I insist that you have the courtesy to use my proper title,' snapped Peggy, then pointing at the tray: 'What's all this?' she picked at the sprigs of shamrock that bordered the tray and held one up between thumb and forefinger. 'One would think this family was still treading the Irish bogs!' She threw it and all the other pieces of shamrock onto the floor.

'I'm sorry you don't like it, Miss . . . Mrs Feeney,' said Josie, still even-tempered, attributing Peggy's foul mood to her condition; women could be a bit odd at such times. 'Mr John an' I thought . . .'

'Mr John and I?' mouthed Peggy imperiously. 'My husband has been discussing our private affairs with the servant?'

'He simply suggested that I make the tray look pretty so's you'd eat something,' explained Josie.

'And this constitutes pretty, does it?' Peggy viciously smashed the top of the egg with a spoon. 'One over-boiled egg and the leftovers from the breakfast table. Well, if you think I'm going to eat that muck you're mistaken.' With one violent movement she hurled the tray onto the floor, plastering the Axminster rug with butter, smashed honeycombs and steaming tea.

'Oh, Miss Peggy I'm sure there was no call for that!' Josie clasped her hands to her cheeks and stared down at the mess.

'I beg your pardon?' Peggy, undergoing a remarkable recovery, leapt from the bed and confronted Josie face to face. 'Just whom do you think you are addressing?' Josie gaped. 'It seems to me that people in this house have been far too lenient with you. You are much too familiar with your superiors. Well, I for one will not be spoken to in such a fashion.'

'I apologise, Mrs Feeney,' answered Josie contritely. 'I'm sure I didn't mean to upset you.'

'You do not upset me,' snarled Peggy. 'You annoy me greatly. Now please be quick to clean up that mess and get out!' She flounced back to bed glaring as Josie tried to rehabilitate the Axminster, using her apron as a mop.

When she had done her best the maid curtseyed and asked: 'Will you be coming down to lunch later, ma'am or will you require a tray?'

'You can fetch me something on a tray,' replied Peggy ungratefully. 'And make sure it's more edible than the previous offering. Now go and leave me alone.'

When Sonny returned from the store at lunchtime he intercepted Josie on her way upstairs with another tray. 'Oh, she's still in bed then? I was hoping she'd be over it by lunchtime, that's why I persuaded Mother to close so we could all take lunch together.'

She took in his look of disappointment. 'Well, babies can cause an awful lot of trouble, Mr John; they have minds of their own.' Like some people I could mention, but won't.

'How did the breakfast go down?' he asked.

'Oh, she really went to town on it,' replied Josie, without so much as a blink.

'Splendid. I knew you could be relied upon to produce something effective, Josie.' He reached for the tray. 'Tell you what, I'll take that up, save your legs. I was going up to see my wife anyway.'

'Very good, Mr John.' Josie handed it over. 'I hope Mrs Feeney finds something there to her satisfaction.' Though I wouldn't think so if she's been stuffing herself with chocolates all morning. What a performance! Josie had been quite hurt by the young mistress' attitude – though she wouldn't mention it to Mr John. He had enough troubles and would be in for some more if he crossed swords with his wife, which he would if he knew how she had treated the maid. He was a very fair young man was Mr John – the way he had seen no wrong in taking the tray up himself advertised this. Mindst, the poor girl had been through a lot and they all had to make allowances for her. She'd be a bit more pliable when the baby arrived.

Sonny issued a cheerful greeting as he elbowed his way into the bedroom with the tray and saw that his wife was awake. 'Glad to see you've livened up since this morning. Josie tells me you enjoyed some breakfast.'

She fastened wary eyes to his face, but seeing no hint of satire answered, 'Yes, it went down a treat.'

'I'm so glad. D'you think you could tackle some lunch?' He lifted the lid that covered the plate. 'There's a lovely bit of fish pie here. She's an expert at pastry crust is Josie – even better than Erin; but keep that to yourself.'

'It looks too stodgy,' was Peggy's unkind reply. 'Though I may attempt a forkful of vegetables – just to please you.'

Sonny sat by her while she picked over the meal. She caught him staring at her. 'What's the matter?'

'Oh, nothing.' He started and smiled. 'I was just thinking how I'd love to paint you in that pose.' His wife had such expressive eyes.

'Then why don't you?' she asked, before sliding a regiment of peas between her lips.

'I'm afraid I have to go back to the store this afternoon. I promised Mother I'd do the ordering for her.'

'Oh, Mother, Mother! What about me? I'm your wife. Surely it wouldn't harm your mother to do without you for one afternoon – and it is St Patrick's Day; it would have been more respectful not to have opened the store at all.'

'Well . . .'

She leaned over and grabbed his hand imploringly. 'Stay with me, Sonny. I'm so bored being stuck up here alone.' And the magazines had all been read; the chocolates eaten.

He stroked her fingers. 'Maybe you'll feel strong enough later to get up; then you could take a little walk to the store and keep me company.'

'Oh, no!' She fell back against the pillows. 'I'm much too weak. Please, Sonny, stay and paint me. You always said you would.'

'I know but . . .'

418

'What's the matter? Don't you think I'm pretty enough at the moment?' she pouted. He was quick to set that matter straight – she was radiant, he told her. 'Then please, please stay and paint me.'

He chewed on the idea for a moment. Mother had not arrived home yet; maybe she had changed her mind about closing for lunch. If that were the case he would not be able to let her know he wasn't coming back this afternoon. Still, he stared at Peggy's pleading face, his wife must come first. With mixed feelings he capitulated and went to dig his equipment from the cupboard. Mother couldn't possibly mind if he spent the afternoon with his sick wife.

In his absence Peggy gloated; that was another point she could safely award to her score. The stake which she had inserted between mother and son was slowly being driven further home. Soon the bond should be severed completely and Peggy would have her way.

Thomasin waited until Patrick was out of the room before approaching Sonny that evening. She had suffered a prick of alarm when he had not turned up after lunch, coloured by the abduction of her other son. All through the afternoon she had worried. When she had arrived home to find he had been here all the time she was livid. It had taken great restraint to control her temper until now.

'You might have sent word that you didn't intend to come back after lunch,' she censured. 'I was very concerned about you. Yes, concerned!' she lashed at his sceptical smile. 'Can't you imagine what went through my mind when you didn't turn up? All these weeks you've watched me worrying over Dickie and it's taught you nothing. Didn't you realise how frightened I'd be?'

'Not frightened enough to close the store and come looking for me, though eh, Mother?' He relented at once under her glare. 'No, I'm sorry – you're right, it was remiss of me. I just didn't think . . .'

'Oh? I don't see an Out of Order sign round your head. I mean, presumably some things get the old cogwheels turning – I don't need to ask who.'

'Peggy asked me to stay with her . . .'

'Oh, how surprising!'

'I didn't think you'd mind as she's so ill.'

'Is she really so ill, Sonny? She's having a baby, that's all. It's a perfectly natural thing to happen to a woman. You shouldn't let her make an invalid of herself.'

He lost his temper. 'I resent that! If you took the trouble to go up you'd see straight away how pale she is.'

'Small wonder she's pale if she's bunged up in that stuffy room all day and every day. It can't be good for her nor for the child. Tomorrow you ought to insist that she comes down and has a breath of fresh air and a stretch of her legs. She might feel more like eating if she gets some exercise. And another thing! I don't want Josie traipsing up and down stairs a dozen times a day. She's got quite enough to do.'

'Good God! What d'you expect poor Peggy to do – drag herself downstairs just to save the maid's legs?' At this point Josie entered to clean up the pots, catching as she did so Sonny's comment, and smarting at the way he referred to her. She had always supposed that she and Mr John were friends. However, she covered her hurt and said to Thomasin, 'I couldn't help overhearing, ma'am, and I don't mind taking trays up, honestly I don't.'

'Well, we'll see,' hedged Thomasin. 'No doubt Peggy will soon be well again then we can all function correctly.' She gave a meaningful look at her son.

But hopes for a change in Peggy's conduct faded when the summer arrived. Her few appearances at the breakfast table sparked off so many incidents that most members of the household felt glad when she stayed in bed. She was now enormously fat, due not only to her pregnancy but to the vast amounts of confectionery she consumed. As soon as breakfast was over and the rest of the family had gone to work she would summon up Josie and demand that the maid go out and purchase her customary requirements.

Previously she had relied on her husband to supply her with these, but Sonny, in his maddening fashion, had asked his mother if so many chocolates could be good for the invalid whereupon the service was promptly curtailed, leaving her to rely on the maid.

At first Josie had put up a stand when told to take the money from the housekeeping allowance, but the tantrums which followed such resistance were so frightening that Josie, fearing that the baby might be harmed by the outbursts, gave in. The trouble was that Peggy craved so many chocolates and magazines that it became a great strain on her budget. She began to experiment with cheaper cuts of meat, and sometimes a course less than usual, hoping that her mistress wouldn't notice. Poor Mr John was in his mother's bad books already for marrying the girl, of this Josie was well aware, so if the mistress discovered Peggy's latest recalcitrance then Mr John would suffer even more.

Such optimism that the cut in rations would go undetected was pitiable. On the evening that the events were to come to light she was entrenched in clearing the dinner plates. Thomasin and Patrick were holding a conference about the merits of adding to their labour force, when Patrick, noticing his son's dejection, tried to induce him into the conversation.

'Ye must try to curb this multiloquence, Sonny,' he teased. ''Tis burnin' me ears off.'

Thomasin's lower jaw dropped. 'Multi . . . ? Josie, you'll have to stop serving all these dictionaries for dinner,' she joked. It was one of Patrick's pleasures to drop a word such as this into their laps just to show how his vocabulary had progressed. 'Ah! Which leads me on to a point I've been meaning to mention . . .' Josie's heart skipped a beat. 'Now, I don't want you to take this as criticism, Josie but I couldn't help noticing that this is the fourth evening you've served boiled bacon. Is there any special reason for this?'

The maid felt her face go hot and she kept on working. 'No, ma'am!' It would be dreadful if the mistress thought she was scrimping on the meals to line her own purse.

'Isn't the housekeeping adequate?' asked Thomasin.

'Oh, yes, ma'am. I'm getting a bit absent-minded lately. It must've slipped my memory that I've done it so many times – the bacon I mean.'

'That's not like you, Josie,' replied Thomasin, but let the matter rest for now. She could see how flustered the question had made Josie. It might be that she was embarrassed to speak in front of Patrick and Sonny. Thomasin would consult her in private, for there was definitely something amiss. She then suggested they should all go into the other room, where Patrick picked up a newspaper and perused it lazily for a while before becoming excited.

'Here, listen to this!' He rustled the paper into a more readable position. 'There's a piece here about Appleby Horse Fair; 'tis comin' up in a couple o' days.'

'Can't you buy a horse round here without trailing all the way over the country?' quizzed his wife. 'What about Barnaby Fair?'

'I don't want another horse ye eejit. I'm thinkin' o' the Fallons. They're nowhere round these parts for sure, but they might be up there. I don't know whether they deal in horses or not but 'tis one o' the biggest gypsy gatherings around an' surely worth a try, don't ye think?' He turned to his son. 'Will ye come with me, Sonny?'

Sonny gave the immediate response: 'What about Peggy?'

Peggy, Peggy, bloody Peggy, sighed Thomasin to herself. He's obsessed with that girl and she's turning him into a proper dullard. He used to be so good-natured and conscientious towards his family; now he seems to consider no one but his wife.

'We can be there and back by the time she's ready for birthing,' promised Patrick. 'I can ask Catch if he'll keep an eye on the land while I'm away. It'll not be for long, an' there's nothing much wants seeing to except a little hoeing now and again.' He spoke to his wife. 'You'll be able to cope here without me for a couple o' weeks?'

Thomasin suppressed a smile at his assumed indispensability. 'Well, you'll be sorely missed, but if there's a chance you might find Dickie then you must go of course. Anyway, as I was saying before, I've been tickling with the idea of taking on two assistants. It'll give me more time to be at home – I want to be here when you find him – and I shall start looking tomorrow.' She saw the struggle that was taking place in her son's mind. 'Don't fret about Peggy,' her voice was warm. 'Josie'll take good care of her through the daytime and when I come home I'll make sure she's not ailing. This is a real chance of finding your brother; we can't pass it up, can we?'

'Oh, no,' responded Sonny. 'We must think of Dickie.'

Thomasin permitted the snipe to pass. 'Right. Well, I'll leave you two to make your plans. I've something I want to discuss with Josie.'

In the kitchen she presented the question again. 'Now then, about that housekeeping money – and let's be having the truth this time, Josie.'

The maid, while relieved to have the matter out in the open, could not conceal her trepidation and played with the hem of her apron, pleating it through her nervous fingers. 'Oh, Mrs Feeney, I hope you don't think I've been fiddlin' you 'cause I'd never do a thing like that.'

'I don't recall saying the slightest thing about fiddling, Josie,' overruled Thomasin. 'Besides, you don't own a violin, do you?'

Josie couldn't find anything to laugh about. 'But you must think ... what with the meals being a bit ... and ... oh!' She nibbled at the screwed-up apron.

'Do you imagine that if I had the slightest doubt as to your honesty I'd've entrusted you to pay the food bills? Not many maids have that privilege, you know.' She had given Josie this task to see how she coped, with the further intention of promoting her to housekeeper if she performed well. 'Now come on, lass, stop eating your pinny, pull yourself together and tell me what's been happening to that money.'

The words spilled from Josie's lips. How Peggy ate so many chocolates that Josie could hardly keep up with her demands – those, and the stack of books and magazines she ordered. 'She sends me out every day, ma'am, and you know how expensive they can be. I had to make ends meet somehow. I even added a few shillings from my own purse.'

'You never did!' exhaled Thomasin.

'Oh, I'm not worried about that, ma'am. It doesn't matter. I just didn't want you thinkin' I was pilferin', that's all.'

'It does matter, Josie! It matters a great deal. Tell me, did you keep a record of how much of your own money you spent?'

Josie nodded. 'I wrote every single item in the budget book – just in case.'

'Wise girl. Let me see.' Thomasin leafed through the account book. 'Godfrey Norris! You've spent all this on chocolates? But you must have used all your wages, girl. Why on earth didn't you tell me about it? Surely you didn't think I'd be angry with you?'

'It wasn't so much that I was frightened what you'd think, ma'am – though I was. It was ... well, I didn't want to go telling tales, like. And as long as I have enough money to send home to Mam I'm not bothered about spendin' any on meself.'

'Telling tales my elbow. I'm not having you spending all your hard-earned cash on that little parasite.'

'Oh, please I don't want no trouble for Mr John!' blurted Josie.

Thomasin stopped ranting and regarded the maid with new eyes. 'And why should it cause trouble for my son?'

'Well, he thinks the world o' Miss Peggy – or rather Mrs Feeney, ma'am. I wouldn't like to be the cause o' Mr John being upset.'

'And that's another of her fads, is it – having you call her Mrs Feeney?' Thomasin nodded grimly. 'Well, I've got news for her: there's only one Mrs Feeney what gives orders around here, and that Mrs Feeney is damned if she's eating boiled bacon every day of the week just so's her rotund lodger can stuff her face with chocolates.' She patted Josie's plump hand. 'You leave everything with me, lass. Mr John will be off on a short trip with his father in a couple of days, so there'll be no danger of him being upset. On the other hand,' she smiled wickedly, 'I know someone who is about to get a nasty surprise.'

PART FOUR

1872–1874

CHAPTER THIRTY-FIVE

The mist had lifted, leaving the blankets of wild pansy and meadow vetchling sparkling with diamonds. He was glad that the icy mornings were over now – it was good to look out onto bejewelled pastures when one awoke. The life he led was harsh; not the least of it having to squat in an ice-hardened ditch and peer through the hawthorn hedge while the farmer trudged across the snow to feed his flock. There could be a long wait for the fellow to leave, after which, Garret Fallon would spring across the white coverlet and quickly bundle up the hay to take for his horses. It was hard luck on the sheep, but then who would look out for the Fallons if not themselves?

Garret tugged on the reins and jumped from the caravan, preparing to hitch up another horse to haul them up that last big hill to Appleby. The deft harnessing took but a few seconds and he was soon boarded again, moving lazily up the incline. The road was lightly-laden now, but soon it would be packed with vardos and wagons, their horses straining against the traces, many with leggy foals trotting loose at their sides. He craned his neck back down the slope to see how the others were getting on. When he had alighted at the foot of the hill so had they – no use the horse having to pull all that extra weight – and now they were far behind with Con leading the column of variegated horseflesh, plodding faithfully after his brother. Even old Mother walked, though she was a long way behind now. He would wait at the crown of the hill for her to catch up. There was only one person who remained in the caravan, and their weight would not affect the horse's pulling power.

They came here every year. Garret, especially, would not miss it. For the Fallons were not tinkers in the occupational definition of the word – *tincaerd* – tin-maker. Although they did make a few pots and pans their income came mainly from horses.

Once at the crest of the hill, he took the opportunity to cogitate, visualising the scene here by midday. There would be tinkers and Romanies stripped to the waist, knee-deep in the river, preparing their nags for the sale. When they had finished, the river would be topped with foam from their painstaking latherings. The horses would stand there, ever-patient, while their owners soaped and twisted their tails into frothing plumes, manes too, allowing the indignities for the reward of feeling the cool water lap around their aching fetlocks. Afterwards, with the dust of many days' travel added to the river's silt, their feathered legs soft as baby hair and gleaming white, they would be pounded up and down before the cheering spectators.

Garret glanced down as Conor came alongside with his charges. 'Is Mother far behind?'

'She says for us to go on,' replied his brother, with no hint of the exertion he had undergone. 'She might sell a few pegs on the way.'

Hitching his horses to the back of the van he climbed up beside Garret and they made their rumbling way in the direction of the river.

The Irishman and his son emerged from the public house to a cacophony of shouting and whinnying. Patrick felt his hopes slide as he looked at the tumult of gypsy life before him. The place was overrun with swarthy-complexioned buyers, haggling in the time-honoured custom. Was it too much to hope that amongst the Smiths, Lees and Moores there might also be two Fallons?

Sonny had on a knowing expression, which Patrick could have done without. He did not need his son to tell him that it had been a waste of time their coming. Trying to find the Fallons here would be like seeking a ladybird on that gypsy wench's red, polka-dot dress. The girl he was admiring tossed a lofty eye in his direction, and he looked away. 'Come on,' he said, slinging his jacket over his shoulder. 'We may as well make an effort now we've come all this way. It's stupid to admit defeat without giving it a go.'

The crowd parted with the quick sweep of a curtain as a skewbald stallion thundered proudly through their midst, mane flowing like silk, great legs pounding up the dust. The gypsy youth perfectly balanced on its back needed neither saddle nor bridle, his gangly legs jutting out like coat-pegs.

The midday heat intensified the smell of horse and man. Patrick and Sonny pushed their way through the hubbub, examining each face. His son had pointed out that Patrick had never seen the Fallon boys, so how would he know what to look for? This had been no deterrent to Patrick who had replied: 'When I see them, I'll know.'

Long into the afternoon they searched, with the sun beating down cruelly, baking their throats, until the crowd began to thin. Feeney was about to admit he was beaten, and prescribe adjournment to the inn, when he sensed Sonny's tension and followed his gaze. His son's waning vigilance had been refuelled by a young tinker who stood not a hair's breadth away.

Garret Fallon maintained a grip on the horse's tail while the bidding was going on, the latter consisting of much spitting and slapping of palms. Not until the final, acceptable bid was made did Garret permit his hand to be grasped in a firm handshake. The money changed hands. Garret, with no more horses to dispose of, was about to pack up for the day when both his arms were linked and he found himself being pressured through the crowd.

'I'd warn ye not to struggle,' growled Patrick in the tinker's ear as they marched. 'Arms tend to snap very easily.'

Garret, apprehensive but not unduly so, gave a derogatory laugh. 'Is it a fool y'are? There's a thousand men'd cut ye down before ever ye reached the edge of this crowd. If 'tis money you're after I have to tell ye I'm a poor man.'

'Don't bother with the coddum,' Patrick cut him short.

'I've just seen the amount that fella paid ye. 'Tis not your money I'm after. Just show me the way to your caravan.'

'Sure, ye're not thinkin' to steal me home, are ye?' joked Garret.

'I'm not. But there's something o' mine gone missing an' I'm thinkin' I'll find it in your caravan.'

'I can't think what that could be,' frowned Garret. 'But if ye're bent on goin' d'ye think ye could let go of me arms?' He addressed this to both parties and then, looking at Sonny a second time, had no further reason to ask what it was his tall assailants were after. He said no more.

Dympna Fallon was sitting on the grass by the caravan when the three men came. She saw Garret first and noticed he was empty-handed. 'I thought ye was bringin' me a quart of ale,' she said in Shelta, the tinker dialect.

'Sure, an' I was, but the mood hopped off me like water off a duck's back,' he answered witheringly, forgoing the Shelta in favour of English. 'Can't ye see I was otherwise engaged?'

She too dipped into her reserves of English. 'What did ye bring them wid ye for? We've little enough to paint our ribs with as it is – an' somethin' tells me they'd not be very partial to hedgehog.'

'We don't want your food, mother,' said Patrick, releasing the tinker now he had reached his destination. 'I've come for my son.' He studied the brightly-painted wagon with its lace curtains, its odd chimney – a large black worm, frozen in its searching gyration to the sky.

The woman crooked an eyebrow at Garret for interpretation. 'I think,' he told her, rubbing his arms, 'he be talkin' about the bloke that had the fling with our Lucy.'

Her wrinkled face darkened – like a bitter old walnut, thought Patrick. 'Then ye've had a wasted journey,' she snapped abruptly. 'He's not here.'

'I don't believe ye,' replied Patrick stubbornly. 'I want to look in the caravan. Dickie! Are ye in there, boy?' His cry was answered by a frail ribbon of sound. Patrick looked sharply at the tinkers then, before Garret could stop him, he leapt up the steps and into the caravan.

430

Inside, Dympna came silently up beside him. 'Aye, that's your son's get,' she spat at him as he stared down at the unhappy, red-faced bundle in the reed basket. 'The one that kilt me daughter.'

Patrick stared at the babe for a long time until the woman shoved past him and picked it up. It ceased crying immediately, searching with gaping mouth for something on which to affix itself.

'Where is my son?' asked Patrick again, his eyes still on the infant.

'The divil knows. He could be dead for all we care,' said Garret, joining them in the surprisingly roomy wagon, followed by Sonny. 'Ah, we did have it in mind to bring him here, but we finally decided against it.' He proceeded to tell Patrick the sparse details. He and his brother, Garret said, had been very fond of their sister. So when she had told them of her predicament and that she wanted to marry the buffer who had seduced her they had discounted the fact that he was not of their tribe – and that neither would Lucy be if she married him – and had set out after him to put matters to rights.

Dickie's reluctance had proved a bit of a handicap, he said, and he and Con had had to get a bit mean. 'That was when we realised what a mistake we'd be makin' in allowin' our sister to give up her way o' life for such a creature. Ah, he was a good–lookin' animal I'll agree, but a gutless specimen all the same, pissed hisself before we touched him. So, we found it more to our advantage to leave him where he'd fallen.'

Patrick felt the hair on his body stand to attention and he took a step forward. But Garret held up a seasoned palm to ward off the assault.

'Oh, ye needn't worry about his health – though I dare say I would if he was related to me – we didn't harm a hair on his pretty head. One look at them knives was enough for that young bucko.'

'Tell me,' growled Patrick.

'He fainted,' came the grinning answer.

*

Patrick felt a deep sense of shame under the tinker's supercilious grin. He was in a quandary of what to believe. If he took the tinker's word then his son had opted for the coward's way out. If he chose not to believe Fallon . . . that meant they had killed him. He was unsure which was worse.

'And your sister?' he said, after a long silence.

'Dead,' replied Garret. 'She died giving life to your son's bastard. Her screams come back to haunt me every night.'

'I'd like to make amends for my son's callousness,' said Patrick. There was little else he could say.

'We don't want none o' your sympathy,' said Dympna. 'Just hop it.'

He wanted to comply, but was faced with another problem. The rag-wrapped infant in the tinker woman's arms was his grandchild and in no way could he allow it to remain with them. 'I want the child,' he told her. ''Tis my grandchild an' I want it.'

'Take it,' said Garret casually, but his mother retreated, clutching the child to her sagging bosom. 'Ye'll take me first!'

'Ma, aren't ye always goin' on about how ye can't stand the sight of it?'

She turned on Garret. 'Nor can I! It kilt my Lucy. But give it up an' I lose half me income. Use your brain, son.'

Garret now understood the reason for her show of maternity; people were more likely to part with their money at the sight of a hungry baby – especially when, given a nip, the child would cry most convincingly.

'What does she mean, lose half her income?' enquired Patrick. Garret told him. Feeney was incensed. 'You're using my grandchild for begging?'

''Tis mine too,' retorted Dympna. 'I've more right to it than you, an' I can do with it what I want.'

'I won't permit this!'

'I don't see as ye've any choice,' said Garret lazily. 'It seems the mammy has her mind made up.'

'I'll pay ye for it,' said Patrick impulsively, reaching into

432

his pocket. 'I'll give ye all the money I have on me – nearly twenty pounds.'

Garret whistled, and would have held out his hand but Dympna slapped it down. ''Tis not enough. The child'll bring me a good two years' income yet. I'll not let it go for a measly twenty pounds.'

Patrick sounded out his son. 'Do you have anything, Sonny?'

The other tested his pockets. 'About four guineas, and a few pence.'

'That's nearly twenty-five pounds I'm offerin',' said Patrick, referring himself to Garret who seemed more approachable. 'Please, the child means nothing to you. Let me have it.'

'Still not enough.' Dympna shook her head emphatically.

'I can bring ye more later,' he pleaded. 'If ye let me have the wean.'

She snickered unpleasantly. 'I can just see ye comin' back wid more money once ye get your hands on the child. Oh, yes!' She hushed the infant who was still mewing.

'Dammit! I won't allow my grandchild to live like this. You're treating it no better than an animal. I'll wager ye treat your horses better.' He made to take the baby from her but she clutched it roughly, squeezing from it a frightened wail.

Garret now stepped between the intruder and his mother, his stance threatening. 'I think ye'd be wise to pocket your money an' be on your way.'

'Need any help, Gary?' The daylight was temporarily extinguished by Conor Fallon's meaty frame. Patrick felt the chill of reincarnation; the younger Fallon was a replica of his murdered father.

'Everything's fine, Con. The man here wants to buy the babe an' Mother has a fondness for it all of a sudden, 'tis all.'

'Look, you're sensible men, I'm sure.' Patrick made one last attempt. ''Tis an awful lotta money – ye'd surely not throw it away so lightly?'

Garret reached casually into his pocket and pulled out a wad of banknotes, splicing Patrick with scornful black eyes. 'See that?' He waved the collection of fivers under Patrick's nose. 'That's good tinker money, that is. We don't need no buffer thinkin' he's doin' us a favour.' He spat.

Patrick's anger soared. 'You bloody wretches! Ye've money like that an' you're using the child for mere coppers?'

'We've not always the horses to sell,' replied the man defensively.

'An' why shouldn't we take what's going?' demanded Dympna.

''Cause 'tis a filthy way to make a living that's why!' Patrick gave them a long, hard look, a muscle twitching perilously in his jaw, then, angrily pocketing the money, he shoved his way past Conor and ran down the caravan steps, closely flanked by Sonny.

'What do we do now?' posed his son, pacing alongside Patrick. 'Go home?'

'Sure, ye don't think I'm giving up that easy, d'ye?' said his father. 'That's my grandchild they have there. I don't intend to leave without it.'

Later at the inn they discussed the child over a meal and a pair of frothing tankards. Patrick dipped a chunk of crusty bread into his soup and opened his mouth. 'We've got to create a plan to lure them tinkers away from the caravan,' he said, munching. 'If we've only the old woman to deal with, it'll be a lot easier.'

'You do realise that this could be construed as kidnapping?' returned Sonny, stirring a spoon through his thick broth.

'I see it as rescuing a member of my family,' said Patrick. 'There's no judge'd blame me for taking that child away from such a life.'

'Supposing,' said Sonny, 'that we succeed in getting the babe. What do you propose to do with it?'

Patrick replied with a vacuous stare. 'Why, take it home.'

'And who is to look after it? Mother's out at the store

434

all day, Josie won't have time to tend to the house and a baby as well. That leaves me and Peggy. I trust you aren't suggesting that I be saddled with another of my brother's bastards?'

'That's a rotten thing to say, Sonny,' accused his father quietly.

'But true nevertheless. Isn't it enough that I've agreed to bring up one of his offshoots without landing me with another?' Sonny drank angrily from his tankard.

'We could hire a nurse,' his father propounded. 'Or maybe Erin an' Sam would care for it. Erin loves children.' He spooned up the last drop of soup, wiped the bowl with a morsel of bread and leaned back against the wall. 'Course, 'tis all mere notion at the moment. We have to get the wean back yet.'

Patrick had overlooked the trick a summer's night had of catching one napping; the climate now would have done justice to Christmas Eve. Despite his coat he shivered as he lay on his belly behind a grassy hillock, looking down on the Fallons' wagon. There was still a number of caravans about, roosting by the sparkling river, their bowed roofs outlined against an indigo sky. Providently, the Fallons' home was stationed a short distance from the rest; their task would be easier if they did not have to deal with a whole brigade of travelling folk.

Beside him, Sonny, his chin resting on a moss-covered stone, wondered what had persuaded him to be party to this madness. Mother was hardly going to offer salutations when they brought another of his brother's by-blows into her house.

Together they watched the wild activity that was taking place in the gypsy encampment. There were many people silhouetted by the light of the numerous small campfires, singing, dancing. Patrick wondered if the Fallon brothers were among them. He tapped Sonny's arm.

'Come on, we'll get a bit closer so we can see what we're up against.'

They slithered and clawed their way nearer until the

435

faces – eerily intimidating in the fireglow – were clearly discernible. The Fallons were not here; obviously not the social type.

'We must draw them out o' that caravan,' breathed Patrick. 'Listen – if you saw your neighbour's house on fire would ye rush to help put it out?'

'I would,' murmured his son. 'But then, I can't say how these folk would react.'

'I'd say they'd react the same way any man would,' replied Patrick. 'They're a closely-knit people. Look, see that campfire with no one near it? D'ye think ye could sneak down an' grab a piece of it? We'll have to fire one or two so's they've plenty to think about.'

'We can't go setting fires indiscriminately!' hissed Sonny, beginning to think his father had lost his reason. 'There may be people in them – children!'

'I'm not that daft. We'll take a look inside them first, make sure they're empty. Come on!' And he was off before Sonny could voice any more objections.

There was the familiar quickening of the heart, the blood-tingling invigoration, the sensation of a deadly spider creeping over one's skin. They crawled furtively down towards the fire. Patrick flattened himself to the ground as a gypsy appeared to look right at them, then, slowly unfurling himself, he stretched out a hand to the fire and tugged at a piece of kindling.

Equipped with burning brands father and son trod stealthily between the wagons, avoiding the leaping lights from the campfires and, after peering into each, finally selected those far removed from the ones containing slumbering children. They rammed home the flaming torches then broke away, long legs jetting them at the nearest hedgerow where they hurled their bodies under its cover to wait for their deed to be noticed.

It did not take long. The caravans made fine tinder, crackling, sparking and lighting up the whole area. A company of travellers started to run towards them, communicating the danger in their ancient tongue. Patrick's eyes, uninterested in the frantic gestures of the

436

gypsies, remained fixed on the Fallons' caravan, urging them to come out.

A face appeared over the half-door, drawn by the smell of blistering paint and the commotion of his fellow travellers. Garret Fallon flung himself down the steps, shouting to his brother. Both ran to volunteer as links in the human chain to the river.

Now was the time. Patrick and his son set off at a crouching run and reached the Fallons' wagon in seconds. They burst straight in. Dympna sprang up as Patrick accosted her. 'I want the child! Where is it?' He looked about him feverishly. There was no sign of the infant.

She leapt at him and raked his face with her nails, drawing blood. He drew in a pained breath and threw her onto a bunk. 'Y'old bitch! Where's my grandchild?'

'Ye'll not have it – I've kilt it!' she screamed, and launched herself at him again.

Sonny was furiously lifting cushions, tossing them to right and left in his search for the child. 'It's here!' A tiny whimper had directed him to a cupboard. He tore open the doors and there it was, almost stifled under a pile of crocheted blankets, its green limbs trying to fight them off.

'Grab it an' let's go!' cried Patrick, fending off the woman who was hurling everything she could lay her hands on.

'We'll never make it, Dad,' replied Sonny, hoisting the basket. 'As soon as we leave she'll alert the others.'

'Then we'll have to take her too! You take the babby – an' hush it up, will ye?' Patrick bundled the struggling, kicking woman down the caravan steps while Sonny rocked the basket frantically. Outside, he took in the action with a nervous glance. The travellers still formed a human chain from the river, slopping buckets of water between them to be tossed at the fiercely burning wagons. Dympna dug her heels into the ground to hamper their escape.

'I'll let ye have it if I have to, woman,' grunted her captor. 'Now walk!'

Sonny was the first to reach the gig, parked under cover of a group of trees, well away from the encampment. He dumped the Moses basket and its complaining contents safely inside, then grasped the reins and jumped on board. 'Hurry, Dad!' He looked back down the slope at the medley of colours; raging flame had changed the colour of the sky to a bruised plum, clouds of pink and orange smoke splayed across its pained backcloth.

The woman still struggled and kicked. 'I'm going to let ye go now,' gasped Patrick. ''Tis no good screaming; they'll not hear ye from up here.' He clamped his teeth over a howl as the hand that he had been too slow in removing from her mouth took a nasty nip. Pushing her from him he clambered up beside his son. She flew at the carriage, scrawny arms flapping under the shawl like an evil black crow. Patrick prised her hands loose from the shiny paintwork and shoved her to the ground; she deserved no courtesy, this one. Sonny whipped up the horse then they were off.

Dympna jumped up and stumbled after them, screaming and cursing. 'Ye filthy, stinkin' varmints! Ye'll be sorry ye ever set eyes on the Fallons. May the Divil take your louse-ridden hide. A curse on ye! D'ye hear me?'

She fell further and further behind as the gig outdistanced her and sank, gasping, to the stony ground. 'A curse on all your kin!' Her voice cracked, but still had enough impact to make Patrick shiver as the carriage bobbed over the brow of the hill.

'What pap,' muttered Sonny, slapping the reins on the horse's rump.

His father, brought up on Celtic superstition, said nothing.

CHAPTER THIRTY-SIX

There were more than a few raised eyebrows when they reached home. It was Sunday and their arrival coincided with the usual stately exodus to church.

'Good day to ye, ma'am!' Patrick gave his son a sly wink as he raised his hat to one of his more snobbish neighbours. ''Tis a wondrous mornin' ye have for your worship.'

The woman treated him to an abrasive glare before ascending into her landau. Really! this was too much. She had believed the notorious Feeneys could not lower the tone of the neighbourhood any more than they had with their incoming but one look at father and son this morning told her differently. They were as bold as brass, the pair of them, like two brawny Irish labourers in their crumpled shirtsleeves, with a week's growth of beard on their chins and dirt-smudged faces. If that man expected her to return his greeting he had another think coming. She ordered the coachman to drive off.

Patrick blithely ignored the disapproving expressions and, instructing his son to stable the horse, picked up the Moses basket and kicked at the front door. 'Hullo! Anybody about?' He kicked again, then cocked an impish face at the neighbours who had paused to gape openly.

There came the sound of hurrying footsteps and the door was finally opened by Josie who stood there nonplussed for quite a span. 'Why, Mr Feeney – I didn't recognise you, sir! Whatever's happened to your face? Have you been involved in an accident?' One side of his face was divided by three angry weals where Dympna had gored him, and around the hand she had bitten he had knotted a bloodstained handkerchief.

'That's the way to win friends, Josie. Come on, are ye going to keep me standin' on me own doorstep or will ye give us a hand? I feel like I'm in a circus with that lot gawkin' at me.' She opened the door wider for him to enter and he struggled past her with the basket. 'Where's me wife?'

Her eyes were glued to the Moses basket, but Patrick's height made it impossible for her to see the contents. 'She's just got back from church, sir. She's in the drawing room with Mr and Mrs Fenton and Mr and Mrs Teale.' She stood on tiptoe, trying to see into the basket.

Patrick's spirits flagged when he heard of his mother-in-law's presence. 'An' here's me thinking I'd left trouble behind me. Jazers, 'tis a mite early for them to be callin' isn't it?' Josie informed him that they had stayed the night. He lowered his voice. 'D'they know I'm here I wonder?'

'Well, I should be surprised if they hadn't heard your arrival, sir.' Josie finally managed to glimpse the inside of the basket. 'Oh, sir! A baby!' she cried delightedly.

'Ssh! Quiet, woman, d'ye want to get me hung drawn an' quartered?' He gestured at the crib. 'Will ye tell me where's the best place to put this – as long as it's not a rude answer. I want it to be a surprise d'ye see?'

Unfortunately, Josie's exclamation had penetrated the door of the drawing room and a curious Thomasin came out to investigate. 'What sort of racket is this on the Sabbath?' she began, then, 'Pat, you're back!' She rushed for him but then seeing he was alone, froze, her joyous expression fading. 'You didn't find him,' she said pathetically.

'I'm sorry, love.' He stood there, still holding the basket. 'We did catch up with the Fallons, but he wasn't with them.'

A look of alarm passed across her face and her fingers played worriedly at her collar as she said in a small voice, 'They've killed him.'

He began to deny it.

'Yes!' she insisted. 'If he wasn't with them then they must've killed him and buried him somewhere along the way. Oh, Dickie!' She pressed her fingertips to her lips. Her eyes grew large with fear. Patrick held onto his knowledge for the time being, unable to decide which was the worst eventuality for a mother to handle – to believe her son dead, or to learn that the 'kidnap' had been of his own connivance. It was cruel, he knew, to keep her in limbo, but what would it do for her if she knew the truth. Dickie was better off dead as far as she was concerned.

The front door opened and in walked a dishevelled

440

Sonny. Thomasin turned clouded eyes on him. 'Look at you both,' she chided tearfully. 'You look like a couple of tinkers yourselves.'

'That's a fine welcome for all our trouble,' said her son and kissed her, glad to be home. 'What do you think to our surprise? Not very much by the sound of it.' Too late he caught his father's grim warning: the tight lips and vee-d brows. 'Sorry, I thought you would've told her by now.'

'Told her what?' The eyes were no longer tearful but suspicious. Then she spotted the basket in Patrick's arms. 'What have you got in there?'

'It's a baby, ma'am,' said Josie happily. 'Come and look. It's beautiful.'

'A what!' Thomasin stepped forward and thrust her face into the lowered crib to be rewarded by a dimpled smile.

Alerted by the sound of raised voices Erin, Sam, William and Hannah came into the hall and now clustered round the tableau, crooking their necks over Thomasin's shoulder.

'Oh, Daddy!' Erin's face lit up and she elbowed her mother aside to dip her hands into the basket. 'It's gorgeous!'

'I wouldn't get too close,' warned Patrick as they crowded round. 'It stinks like a cartload o' maggots.'

'Oh, the poor little soul.' Thomasin softened as Erin plucked the baby from its bed, leaving a dark stain where it had lain. 'How long has it been like that? It's absolutely plastered. Didn't you even know to change it?'

'Sure, I tried me best,' said her husband, laying aside the vacated crib. 'But, t'was a funny thing, I clean forgot to pack a fresh set o' baby clothes.'

'Soft 'aporth!' Thomasin slipped back into the old vernacular. 'What is it anyway? Boy or girl? We can't keep referring to it as "it", can we.'

Patrick shared a silent joke with Sonny. It had been some hours before he had even thought of looking. They had stopped, that first night, at a halfway house to hire a bed and clean themselves up – though one would never have guessed it from their appearance now. It was only when Patrick was struggling over a name for the baby, that he realised he didn't even know its sex and, even more pressingly, that it desperately needed changing. He had put the baby in the bowl of water which he had used to wash himself and tried to clean up the mess as best he was able, his big hands slipping and sliding round the naked little body. But as soon as he had done so and had used his only spare shirt to wrap it in – which accounted for his scruffy manner of dress now – the baby had returned the compliment by emptying its ever-regular bowels with noisy precision, drawing great merriment from the other patrons of the inn.

'She's a girl,' he smiled as his reverie ended. 'And her name is Rosanna.'

'Well, if you know her name you must know who she belongs to,' said his wife, watching Erin and Josie clucking over the child.

Patrick felt his son's eyes on him, but did not return the stare. 'I know her name because I gave it to her,' he disclosed, the smile levelling into seriousness. 'Well, I thought I had a right to,' he paused – here goes. 'Seeing as how I'm her grandfather.'

For the next few seconds the only sound was the gurgling of the baby while they digested his startling confession. Then pandemonium broke out with Hannah the driving force, demanding to know how this child could be a relative and her unaware of its existence until now. They had tried to keep her in the dark about Dickie and the tinker girl, quoting some feeble excuse for his vanishing trick. But it would all have to come out now.

'Then . . . this must be the Fallon girl's child,' guessed Thomasin rightly.

'It is. The child's mother died giving birth to her.'

Erin crossed herself with her free hand and placed her cheek against the baby's peachy-soft one.

Patrick set sail on his revelations. 'We found the tinkers at Appleby Fair all right. They were . . .'

'Tinkers!' screeched Hannah, aghast. 'You have the audacity to bring a tinker baby into my daughter's house?'

'I do have a small claim to ownership too, Hannah,' replied her son-in-law tartly. 'I am your daughter's husband.'

'Oh, no!' Hannah sprang into action. 'You may have had some claim until recently due to an archaic law which robbed the wife of her rights, but all that is about to change, and not before time, I say. This house was left to my daughter and you have no right to fill it with your foundlings. Thomasin, you have suffered years of humiliation at the hands of this man – and now this! You must tell him enough is enough. Yes! Sell up and move away to where no one will be aware of your previous misassociation. Cast him out into the gutter – him and his tinker baby!'

'Hannah, you appear to have missed the point,' said Patrick, well-used to her melodramatics. 'If I am this "tinker baby's" grandfather, by my reckoning that would make Thomasin its grandmother.' He paused for the wicked thought to sink in and saw it register itself on her horrified face before he grinned widely and said, 'Why, dear me, that'd make you its great-grandmother, Hannah!'

'It most certainly would not! Thomasin, you are not going to allow him to disgrace this family with his ludicrous notions. The very suggestion that you or I could be related to such a waif is preposterous.'

'Oh, shut up, Mother,' said Thomasin, as was the usual comment when Hannah was on one of her high-handed launchings. 'And they just dumped the child on you, just like that?' she asked Patrick.

'Not ... exactly.' He looked at Sonny uneasily.

'How ... exactly?'

'We kidnapped her, Mother,' Sonny answered for his father, enjoying the impact of his lightly-delivered words. 'What d'you think to that?'

'I think,' said Thomasin weakly, 'we'd all better go and sit down.'

The rims of Hannah's nostrils were white with indignation. 'I do wish someone would tell me just how this child is supposed to be related to my family – and don't you think it would be wiser for someone to clean it up before anything else is said? Apart from the atrocious smell it must be infested.'

William prodded Rosanna's cheek with a nicotine-stained finger. She sighed and dimpled. 'She might stink to high heaven, but she's a canny lahl bugger.'

'Well, one might have expected that from you,' snapped Hannah, and stalked back into the drawing room.

Josie and Erin took the baby away to clean her up, cooing like two broody doves.

'How's Peggy been?' Sonny suddenly asked his mother before she followed Hannah.

'Oh, I clean forgot! The midwife's with her. She started getting her pains a few hours ago.'

'Mother, why didn't you tell me at once?' Sonny made a dash for the stairs.

'Knock before you go in!' Thomasin shouted after his fleeing figure. 'That nurse is a right old battleaxe.' She turned and went after her mother and father. 'Come along, Patrick Feeney, we shall have words.'

But Patrick hung back and ambushed Sam before he too joined the others. 'Can I beg a word in private? I thought I'd best put it to you before I said anything to Erin so's not to raise her hopes if ye feel ye couldn't stomach it. I'll put it to ye straight, son. We need someone to care for the baby. Tommy can't do it 'cause she'll be out most o' the day. We could hire a nurse, but I'd prefer the child to have proper parents. I know Erin loves the weans, an' I wondered if ye'd be willing to foster Rosanna?'

'I'm sorry you asked me that, sir,' replied Sam gravely. 'Because I have to say no.'

Patrick was caught off-balance by this short and candid reaction, but remained amiable. 'Which, of course, you're entitled to do ... Would ye care to tell me why? I thought ye wanted a dozen children.'

'So I do – my own,' said Sam firmly, then looked embarrassed and pulled at his earlobe. 'This really is most awkward for me to say.'

'Ye don't owe me any explanation, Sam. Perhaps I

shouldn't have asked ye in the first place.' Patrick started to move away.

'No, wait! You were perfectly within your rights to ask it,' answered his son-in-law. 'And I'd like the opportunity to speak to someone. You might understand better than I do. You see, I'm afraid that if I let Erin foster Rosanna then she'll never want any children of her own.'

'Now ye've lost me.' Patrick reached into his pocket for pipe and matches and leaned against the wall to light up.

'I find this very difficult.' Sam presented his back, the better to form his words without Patrick witnessing his discomfort. The lobes of his ears were pink as he spoke. 'You see . . . what usually happens on people's wedding nights . . . well . . . it didn't happen on ours – it's never happened.'

'But ye've been married over a year!' Patrick blurted out thoughtlessly his breath extinguishing the match.

Sam threw a brief, pained look over his shoulder, then turned away. 'You don't have to remind me of that. Four-teen months to be more correct. Four hundred nights of shattered dreams. Hoping each time it would be different, that she wouldn't cringe and cower when I approached her . . . and those terrible screams.' He spun round accusingly. 'The screams which you once explained away by saying she couldn't stand the sight of blood.'

Patrick lowered his eyes, replaced the dead match in its box and turned the unlit pipe through his fingers. 'I didn't deliberately mislead ye, Sam . . . 'tis just that we couldn't think of a more valid explanation. I mean, the screaming stopped as soon as ye cleaned yourself up, didn't it? I genuinely thought I was giving ye the truth.'

'Well, I now know it *not* to be the truth. I'm not in the habit of going to bed in my butcher's togs. It's that . . . you know . . . *that*, what's worrying her. Soon as I go near her she starts to cry an' tremble . . . it's awful.'

'Sam, this is terrible! Maybe if Thomasin talked to her . . .'

'Huh! What do you think Erin's been payin' all these solo visits for? But when she gets home an' I ask if she's got it sorted out, she makes some excuse sayin' her mam was too busy to talk, or there was someone else in the room ...'

'Has she given ye no explanation for her behaviour, Sam?' asked Patrick.

Sam shook his head. 'She just says she's frightened. Well, I could understand that – at least, her being nervous, but she seems really terrified. I mean, you'd understand it if I'd forced her, but I'd never do that.'

Patrick couldn't distract a certain thought from his brain. At last he decided to share it with Sam. 'Look ... has she ever mentioned anything about her childhood?'

'Naturally.' Sam frowned.

'About Jos Leach?'

A shake of the head. 'Who's he?'

A slight pause then: 'He was the imbecile who tried to rape her when she was six years old.'

After Sam had gasped his shock he asked for the full story.

'There's not much more to it. She was locked in a slaughterhouse with this big strapping butcher's lad who had a mind younger than her own. He didn't know it was wrong ...'

After Sam had digested the tale he said, 'No, she never told me.'

Patrick nodded. 'Tommy was right then. She said Erin wouldn't remember that far back. 'Twas just the thought of you an' him being butchers, see ...'

Sam shook his head. 'She never mentioned it. It can't be that.'

'Oh, God I wish there was something I could do to help yese.'

'You can,' replied Sam. 'Please don't tell Erin about the adoption. Her need for a child is the only thing I have left to play on. If she has Rosanna it could smother that need, an' then we're lost.'

Patrick tried to be helpful. 'D'ye think spending more time with her would make a difference? I mean, she

446

doesn't see ye all day, ye only have the evenings an' Sundays together. It takes time to get to know someone.'

'You could be right,' allowed Sam. 'How can I expect her to want to ... with a stranger. She's never been overjoyed at me workin' at the butchery.'

'Well, who knows – if ye leave it might just be the thing to help. Washing them bloody aprons won't make life any easier, will it?'

'She doesn't wash them,' divulged Sam woefully. 'I leave them for Mrs Simons to do. She's very understanding about it. I'd take your advice if I thought I could get a job nearer home.'

'Haven't I heard ye mention that ye'd like to go into dairy farming?'

Sam laughed weakly. 'I can't see that happening for a few years.' He had managed to scrape enough together for one cow.

'Me an' Tommy'd help,' urged his father-in-law.

Sam looked interested then, but offered a feeble refusal. 'I couldn't really expect ... you've given us so much.'

'Rubbish. Listen, ye don't mind if I tell the girl's mother about the other, d'ye?' Sam shook his head. 'See, if Tommy knows, I'm sure she'll agree with my suggestion. Leave it to me. I'll talk to her when everyone's gone.'

Just then, they were interrupted. Sonny had not been allowed in to see his wife and slouched mopishly down the stairs. Sam slipped away to join the others in the drawing room. Patrick let him go and accosted his son.

'Before ye go in there, Sonny, I'd ask ye not to tell your mother what we learned about Dickie, understand?'

'I do; but she'll have to find out some time. Don't worry though, I won't sprag.' He was about to move on, but Patrick put a hand out, the other rubbing his chin thoughtfully.

'Can ye spare another minute?'

'I can spare any amount of minutes. Honestly, you'd think that midwife owned the place the way she's carrying on.'

'I want to talk to you about Rosanna,' said Patrick.

'Now, I've approached Sam and it seems he isn't too keen on fostering her.'

'Who would be?' said Sonny cruelly. 'No need to ask what's coming next, is there? How d'you expect Peggy to cope with two babies?'

'We can hire a nurse to help her. I just want the baby to have a stable upbringing, Son, she's not had a very good start in life, has she? 'Tis no good me sayin' I'll foster her, I'm too old; she needs someone young like yourself . . . an' she needs brothers an' sisters.'

'And she's already got one on the way up there, that's what you mean, isn't it? All right, all right! I know. Don't go on,' said Sonny resignedly. 'I'll take her. I can't see what difference another'll make anyhow.' He began to walk away, laughing ironically to himself. 'God! D'you think I've set some sort of precedent? Here I am, eighteen years of age, with two children – and neither of them mine.'

She was a pretty little thing when they had washed and dressed her in one of the nightgowns meant for Peggy's imminent baby. Her hair was black and very thick for such a young child, and far from being miserable as might be the case after having led so wretched a life, she had the most infectious smile one could imagine, showing off the beginnings of her first two teeth. But the eyes that peeped out from under the lacy bonnet, so blue and laughing, were her selling point as far as her grandmother was concerned – they were Dickie's.

Thomasin rose instantly as the two women brought her in, and reached out her arms for the baby.

'There! Isn't she beautiful?' asked Erin, handing her over.

'She certainly is.' Thomasin smiled and kissed the downy cheek, balancing Rosanna's bottom in the crook of her arm. 'Oh, Pat look at her. Isn't she just like Dickie?' She proudly paraded her grand-daughter before the gathering.

Hannah, now fully conversant with Rosanna's

parentage, sniffed. 'Well, I for one find the whole affair completely distasteful. What your neighbours must think with two illegitimate children in the house I dread to imagine – and I'm sure we shouldn't be discussing this at all with the maid present.'

'I think we'll have some refreshment, Josie,' said Thomasin, giving the maid a way out without being made to feel like an outsider. She waited for Josie to slip away then turned to Hannah. 'Tell me, Mother – just where are these two illegitimate children you're talking about?'

'What about the girl upstairs?' said Hannah. 'Just because one of your sons was gentleman enough to marry her does not cover up the fact of the other son's philandering. People are going to put two and two together; they know that it takes nine months to produce a child and that John and that girl have only been married five.'

Sonny was annoyed. 'I wish you'd stop referring to Peggy as "that girl". I didn't marry her out of courtesy, but because I love her.'

'And as for what the neighbours think of it all, Hannah,' said Patrick congenially, 'we'll never know – seeing as how they never talk to us anyway.'

'And who is to blame for that?' retaliated Hannah. 'Certainly not my daughter. There is nothing in Thomasin's character which attracts discredit. Indeed, if she were not lowered socially by her marriage then her triumph in the business world would have the neighbours falling over themselves to invite her to tea.'

'Please! Please!' shouted Thomasin, pacing up and down, jiggling the baby. 'Let's not get started on that again. Mother, I'm sure everyone is quite aware of your views on our marriage by now. Do you think we could direct our energy into planning what's to be done with Rosanna's future?'

'That's all sorted out,' Patrick told her. 'Sonny says he'll have her.'

There came an involuntary cry of disappointment and everyone looked at Erin. 'But that seems so silly,' she argued. 'Peggy will have enough to fill her day without

449

another young baby to look after. It would be a much better idea for me an' Sam to have her.' She took the baby from a surprised Thomasin and cuddled her acquisitively, throwing a pleading look at Sam.

'I suppose you have a point there,' said her mother, but Patrick jumped in swiftly.

'I'm sorry, lassie, but I think it best Rosanna goes to Sonny and his wife where she'll have a brother or sister.'

Erin beheld him with condemnation in her flashing eyes. 'She'll have brothers and sisters with us – won't she, Sam?' She beseeched her husband who continued to stare at the carpet.

'Erin, I know she's a bonny little creature, an' anyone in their right mind would want to keep her,' conceded Patrick. 'But what'll happen when ye have children of your own? Will Rosanna be as dear to ye then? Ye see, that child upstairs, when it's born, will be Rosanna's half-sister or half-brother. A point in favour, wouldn't ye say, of placing her in Sonny's guardianship?'

'Your father's right, love,' said Thomasin, not understanding the reasoning beneath this exchange but detecting from the firmness in Patrick's voice that it was done in Erin's interests. He must know something Thomasin didn't.

Erin glared censoriously at her husband, at his failure to reinforce her case. Then, as his eyes came up to look at her, she saw in them the reason for his non-alliance, and felt her body go limp. Poor dear Sam! What must he be going through. How selfish and cowardly she was, wanting babies and not prepared to give anything in return. And he was so kind and patient, never forcing himself upon her. She would try tonight, honestly she would. She would make a huge effort to trap that scream within her heart and offer herself to him. God give her strength, she would.

She handed the baby back to her mother and clasped her hands behind her back so that no one would see her fingers twising out their torment on each other. 'Hadn't we better think about getting her something to eat?' she

450

put forward as the baby started to grizzle. 'She must be hungry.'

Thomasin gently pinched Rosanna's cheek. 'What about it, Treacle-face? Shall Granny get us some din-din?'

'Oh, for Heaven's sake,' breathed Hannah disgustedly.

'Eh, I forgot,' said Thomasin to the baby. 'We have to talk proper in great-grandmother's presence.' She thrust her tongue into her cheek, procuring a grin from her husband. 'Erin, will you go and ask Josie to make some pobs for our little Rosie? Eh, listen to me – poetry! I wonder what those tinkers fed her on? She'd certainly never get any mother's milk if her mother died giving birth, an' she'll not get none here neither, poor little devil.' Out of sudden interest she asked her husband, 'How did you manage to feed her on the way home, by the way? I assume you wouldn't let her starve.'

'She had the same as us,' he answered.

'Which was?'

'Bread, soup, cheese . . .'

'Oh, Patrick!' she admonished. 'She's not old enough to be weaned by rights and there you are giving her bread and cheese.'

'Ye make it sound as if I was stuffing her with great wadges o' the stuff,' he said sheepishly. 'They were only little pieces – an' I dunked them in me ale first to soften them.'

'You did what?'

'We-ell, she lapped it up. An' we never got no sleepless nights with her, neither.'

'I should think you didn't. The poor mite must've been sozzled,' said his wife drily. 'It makes you wonder how she survived the tinkers' welfare, because I don't suppose they went out of their way to meet her needs.'

'Well, whatever she's had she's certainly thrived on it.' Patrick pointed to the baby's healthy cheeks, then took her from his wife and cuddled her fondly. She was an endearing little person. 'What do you make of her, Billy?' he consulted his father-in-law whose silence during the conversation was very unrepresentative.

451

'Woah, she's a menseful lahl goblin!' William chucked the baby's chin in his rough and ready fashion. Rosanna displayed her gums. 'We've hardly had a peep out of her yet. 'Ere, Hannah don't tha want to hold tha great grandbairn? First of her kind.'

'Certainly not!' But it was too late, William had plonked the child in Hannah's lap. 'Oh, dear.' She held Rosanna gingerly, unable to hide her dismay, then all at once her face went crimson and she held the baby at arm's length. 'Take her back, please.'

'Nay, tha's not had her for two seconds! Don't tha want a good cuddle?' William fitted his horny hands round the baby's body, lifted her and immediately began to rock with laughter.

'And what pray is so amusing?' said his wife stiffly, hands spread over her lap.

'Nay, it's no good tryin' to 'ide it, lass!' he chuckled, gesturing at the damp patch on Hannah's dress. 'She's just med it reet plain what she thinks o' thee.' He handed the child back to Patrick. 'By, tha's gorra grand lass there, Pat an' no mistake. She's never gonna let anybody say things not without gettin' her own back. That'n's gonna get what she wants out o' this world, no doubt abaht it. She's got reet outlook: if tha can't impress folk by bein' friendly – piss on 'em!'

CHAPTER THIRTY-SEVEN

It was early afternoon before Sonny was allowed access to his wife. He had made use of his spare time by cutting a great bunch of flowers from the garden, much to his mother's annoyance, and now as the midwife opened the door he burst into the bedroom, arms piled with pink and purple daisies.

'Peggy, oh how I've missed you!' He dropped the

flowers onto the bed and stooped over her eagerly. The midwife made a diplomatic exit.

'An odd way you have of showing it,' she replied sulkily, not returning his kiss. 'Leaving me here to be bullied and used by your mother and the servant.'

Instantly he wanted to know all that had transpired and Peggy took great enjoyment from enlightening him. 'The moment you left this house I was at their mercy. They dragged me out of bed when they knew how ill I was. I could hardly walk and almost fell down the stairs, but did they show mercy? No! They forced me to walk up and down the garden until I almost fainted. That is only the beginning.' She paused for breath. 'After two days of this they said I was well enough to help around the house and made me stand for hours in that stupid kitchen of all places, making stupid pastry with that idiot of a maid guarding me to see I didn't escape. Imagine it! Me, forced to do servant's work by my own husband's mother.'

'She might've thought it'd help you to get up for a while, to take your mind off your discomfort,' placated Sonny, not wanting Peggy to work herself up at this stage; she had enough to face.

She started to weep. 'She hates me! I know she does. Her and that spiteful fat slut of a maid.'

'Eh, come on, Peggy.' Sonny stroked her hand. 'You know that's untrue. Mother doesn't hate you and neither does Josie. What reason could they have?'

'Your mother hates me because I've taken her son,' sobbed his wife. 'And the maid hates me because she wants you for herself.' She caught his negating smile. 'It's true! I can see it in her eyes.'

'Peggy, you are daft,' he smiled and pulled her to him, rubbing her back soothingly. 'As if I'd look at a plain old thing like Josie when I've got an angel for a wife. Here, use this.' He produced a handkerchief and dabbed at her eyes.

She took it from him to blow her nose. 'I don't know how you can say that of me at the moment. Look at me – I'm grotesque!'

453

'No, you're not. You're just a bit plump because you're about to have a baby, that's all. Why, in a few days' time you'll be able to wear all those becoming dresses again.'

'Oh, I was hoping you might buy me some new ones.' Her voice was plaintive. 'It doesn't seem much to ask in return for what I'm about to go through. Aagh!' She arched her back suddenly, mouth and eyes wide open. 'Oh, help me! It's getting worse. Help me, Sonny, help me!'

He gripped her hands, teeth gritted, sharing her pain as her fingernails cut into him. After a few writhing moments she relaxed and took a deep breath. 'See? See what I have to face? And this is just the start.'

'Oh, Peggy, you'll have your new dresses, of course you will.' He coaxed the stray hairs from her forehead. 'And anything else you might want.'

'Then stand up for me, Sonny,' she begged him. 'Tell your mother that you won't allow your wife to be treated like a servant.'

'Of course I'll speak to her . . .'

'And you must get rid of the maid, too. She frightens me – I daren't eat anything she prepares for fear it's poisoned.'

He started to laugh, then curbed himself at her pained expression. 'I'm sorry, Peggy, but that really is being silly. As if Josie would do a thing like that.'

'She's got to go!' she screamed.

The midwife returned to the room with a pile of linen over her arm. 'Right me laddo, let's be havin' yer.' She tapped her foot and indicated the door with a toss of her head.

'Is it time?' he enquired anxiously.

'Nay! D'yer think I'd let you in here if it were that close? She's barely started yet.'

'But the pain seems so bad.' Sonny was loath to move from the bed, let alone the room.

'Aye, well. Some make more fuss than others,' said the nurse scathingly. She'd had a bellyful of this little madam already, fetching and carrying, wanting this, than an'

454

t'other. She'd be no less relieved than Peggy when it was all over. 'Happen I might let you in later – if the young lady behaves herself.'

Sonny rose. 'You're not going to leave me with her?' Peggy clung to him, dragging on his arm.

'I really can't stay.' He eyed the dragon of a midwife. 'And you'll be perfectly safe I'm certain. Nurse will take care of you, won't you, nurse?'

'I will indeed,' she replied darkly and began to gather up the flowers from the bed. 'Yer'll have to tek these out o' me road an' all. Can't have 'em cluttering up t'place.' She pushed them into his arms and manoeuvred him from the room.

'Sonny!' yelled Peggy. 'You'll remember what I asked you to do?'

'I'll take care of it, don't worry!' He craned his neck around the midwife's bulk as she tried to shove him out. 'Trust me! I love you!' The door was slammed in his face. He stood on the landing for a while longer then went downstairs to confront his mother.

'You couldn't wait for me to close the front door before it started could you, Mother?' he opened, on finding her alone in the dining room. She and Erin had shared the task of feeding Rosanna. Meal over, Erin had taken her upstairs to have a nap.

'Before what started?' asked Thomasin, engaged in wiping a creamy stain from her dress where Rosanna had dribbled the bread and milk. She sniffed the spot and wrinkled her nose. 'Pooh! We'll have to get some bicarb on that.'

'The persecution of my wife!' Sonny had her full attention now. 'Peggy's just told me how you and Josie bullied her out of bed when she was unwell and made her tackle the baking.'

'Oh, she has, has she?' answered his mother. 'And did she also tell you how she's been forcing the maid to embezzle money from your mother? How, when we finally managed to haul her fat carcase out of bed she called me every name in the book – and I don't mean the good one neither! And as for baking, well – after seeing what a performance she made of that I decided that perhaps bed was the best place for her after all!'

'What's all this nonsense about forcing Josie into embezzlement?' he demanded. Thomasin passed on everything that the maid had told her and his face showed unbelief. 'I think you're just making that up!'

'Are you calling your mother a liar?' She pulled herself up to her full height which, though not very tall, could be very imposing.

He reddened at his impulsive blunder. 'Of course not. I apologise. It's just so hard to believe this of Peggy, especially when you say it happened some time ago and it's the first I've heard about it.'

'Well, you'd hardly expect Josie to say anything,' retorted his mother. 'When she's so taken with you.'

He frowned. 'That's what Peggy said. I told her not to be so daft.'

'It's you that's daft. That lass idolises you, it's as clear as day. Though I'm not surprised you never noticed, you're that besotted with that wife of yours.'

Sonny puckered his eyebrows thoughtfully. 'That will make it all the harder then.' Thomasin waited for enlargement. 'Peggy wants us to sack her. She says Josie is trying to poison her.'

'Oh, my God!' Thomasin could have laughed if it wasn't so serious. 'That's a load of bunkum,' she snorted. 'And you know it.'

'Yes, I've got to agree on that score. I think it's just Peggy's condition that's making her like this. But she is awfully upset Mother, and I'm afraid it will harm the baby if Josie stays. It would be best if we hired a new maid.'

'Oh, would it? Well, we're not going to. Now, look here, my lad.' Thomasin came to stand directly in front of him and though she had to look up there was nothing subservient in her manner. 'Let's just get a few things clear. When you've got a household of your own you can run it in any way you please. But this is my house and I'll be damned if I'll have anyone telling me what to do with my staff. Josie has been very patient with your wife – I doubt anyone else would've put up with her for so long – and I'll not throw her out just because of one of Peggy's spiteful whims.'

Sonny's face was the colour of his hair. 'Right! Now we all know where we stand I can go back and tell my wife that she has less status in this house than a servant. Hah! And that's a good one about running my own household when you know very well I'll never be able to afford one. Oh yes, very rich. No wonder my dear brother escaped – he knew he'd never see any charity from you!'

Fortunately Thomasin missed the deeper meaning of the word 'escape'. 'That is totally unjust!' she cried. 'Not every mother would've allowed her son to bring a pregnant woman into her house.'

'You know as well as I that your action wasn't born of benevolence, Mother,' volleyed Sonny. 'On the contrary, you retracted your promise of a settlement knowing that I'd be unable to afford my own house without your assistance and would have to bring Peggy to live here – where you could keep her under your dictum. Don't try to deny it.'

'I wouldn't dream of denying it,' rejoined his mother angrily. 'It's perfectly true and its fortunate for you that I did because anyone who'd stoop to forcing a poor maidservant to defraud would have no scruples about duping her husband. If I had given you the money as promised she would've juggled it from you in days.'

'She wouldn't have had to juggle it from me!' he shot back. 'I'd have given it to her gladly – because I love her. But you wouldn't understand that, Mother, you're far too busy guarding your money to worry about a paltry thing like love.'

His words came like a slap in the face. 'How can you speak so?' came the wounded reply. 'Was there ever a moment when I gave you cause to doubt my fondness for you?'

He was still too incensed by her treatment of Peggy to show any compassion. 'If you did love me you wouldn't

457

treat my wife as you do, knowing how it hurts me. Even admitting that your invitation for us to live with you was made out of pity, that emotion has not been sustained. Peggy just cannot do a thing right here; if she as much as asks the maid to serve one of her favourite dishes you think she's trying to displace you as mistress.'

'But, Sonny! Can't you see that *everything* Peggy does is manufactured to cause mischief? Why are we arguing now? Because she told you a pack of untruths which she knew would have you crying for my blood. I did give her every opportunity to help in the running of the place when she first came, but did she take advantage of it? No.'

'Because you insist on questioning her motives!'

'No! . . . oh, very well, yes I do sometimes – but really, Sonny your wife would take over the whole house if I allowed it. I must keep a little authority; it is my house.'

'Mine, mine, mine!' hurled Sonny. 'That's the crux of the argument. Everything's yours – the money, the servant, the house.' He could see that he was not going to incur any sympathy for Peggy here and turned about, flinging a final retort. 'Well, you needn't worry about us any more, Mother. As soon as Peggy's given birth I'll be sure to have her up and about so that we can all get from under your feet. Then you'll have your precious house all to yourself!'

'Damn!' hissed Thomasin, then picked up two cushions and threw them at the wall. 'Damn, damn, damn!'

Sonny was spared from having to relay that Peggy's request had been vetoed by the sudden speeding up of his wife's labour. He was forced to sit on the landing, listening to her screams and the low, patient commands of the midwife. It was horrific to witness. The house was filled with shrieks and yells and the vilest of language. Poor Peggy, whom he had never heard utter one swear-word, must be in appalling agony to resort to such profanities. There was no reason for him to sit here and listen to it – he could just as easily spend the next couple of hours out of earshot in the alehouse as most men were relieved to do – but by being here outside her door he felt at least as if he were

458

somehow taking a bit of her pain onto his own shoulders; helping her. Curse his brother for heaping all this suffering upon her.

He was still sitting there, propped against the wall, several hours later when Erin, Sam and his grandparents had gone home and his parents came up to bed. Thomasin faltered and looked down at him as if to speak, but he refused to even look at her, confining his goodnight to his father alone. By the small hours the noisy screams had dimmed to horrible, painfilled groans, and still Sonny sat there, his head nodding, only to jerk awake with each of his wife's contractions. He looked up, bleary-eyed, as someone padded along the landing and flopped down beside him on the carpet.

'I couldn't let ye sit out here all on your own.' Patrick, clad only in his trousers, smiled through the half-light. 'I've been through it meself. I know what it's like listening to the woman ye love goin' through hell an' not being able to do a damn thing about it.'

'It's not quite the same though, is it?' asked Sonny, battling with his lassitude. 'You were waiting for your own child to be born – I'm waiting for someone else's. Oh, take no notice of me,' he returned his father's smile, 'I'm glad you came. It's comforting to know somebody cares.' There came another weary moan from Peggy.

'Your mother cares too, son,' answered his father softly. 'I know she badly wanted to come an' sit with ye herself but pride, or pig-headedness, call it what ye will, stopped her. That's why I came in her stead; to tell ye that she loves ye an' she doesn't want ye to go packing your bags. She's already lost one son, she doesn't want to lose you, too.'

Sonny gave a slanted smile on recalling his impulsive declaration. 'I don't think there's much danger of that the way my bank balance stands.' He turned fully round to face his father. 'I can't understand it, Dad. Why *does* she hate Peggy so? Can you tell me?'

'Now, would ye take one bit o' notice of anything I said if it were not in Peggy's favour?' asked his father. 'No, I

459

thought not. Then 'tis no good me saying anything, is it? Apart from telling ye that anything your mother says is purely for what she sees to be your own good and not out of spite. She loves ye, Sonny. It'd be awful nice if I were able to go back an' tell her she's forgiven. Can I?'

Sonny set his head at a weary angle. 'I'm sure we both said things that need to be forgiven. Father . . .' He picked at the cloth of his trousers. 'Do you feel the same way as Mother? Do you think I did wrong in marrying Peggy?'

'Ah, the girl's young yet,' said Patrick evasively. 'Any failings she has will right themselves with age.'

'But you don't really like her,' said Sonny, then was diverted by an ear-splitting staccato of pain. 'Oh, Christ!' A sudden renewal of energy brought him leaping to his feet and he began to pound at the bedroom door.

'What's happened? What's happened?'

Presently the door opened and a tired-looking midwife filled the doorway carrying a bowl of water. 'Can't you shout any louder? Don't you think I'm deaf enough already wi' listening to that lot in there? What's happened, you say. Your son's happened, lad – an' a right load o' truck he's caused in gettin' 'ere an' all!'

Because the midwife refused to let him in until Peggy had had some sleep, Sonny used the five hours that followed to rest his own throbbing head. When he woke he rushed down some breakfast then went back upstairs to demand entry.

'Aye, you can come in now,' granted the nurse, wiping her hands on a towel. 'I'm off home. I'll be back tomorrow to see how things are.'

Sonny had expected to feel nothing for the child his brother had sired, had not even thought of it as a separate entity; but when he bent his head over the lace-draped crib and eased aside the covers he was greatly surprised to find his vision blurred by tears. There was nothing about the child to suggest his paternity – no thick, black curls like Rosanna's – only a delicate, pale-gold cap, a

460

button of a nose and puckered pink lips that, even in sleep, went through sucking motions.

'Peggy, he's marvellous,' he breathed, glancing up adoringly at his wife. 'Just like you.'

Peggy seemed to be donating more interest to her manicure than the child.

'Well, don't you think so?' he urged.

She shrugged and continued to file her nails. 'If you say he is then he must be.'

He attributed her lack of zeal to fatigue. 'I'm sorry. Here I am paying all this attention to the baby and none to the wife who gave him to me.' He took a final warm look at the baby, then came to sit on the bed. 'Was it very rough?'

She spread her fingers then, satisfied with her efforts, folded away the manicure set and regarded him frostily. 'If you are truly interested it was agony – sheer agony. I never want to go through it again. And I would have thought that the least my husband could do was to show some consideration while I was passing the night in purgatory.'

Sonny took the rebuke to heart. 'You know I would've been here if I'd been permitted. The midwife . . .'

She bared her teeth. 'I'm not talking about that! I refer to what we discussed yesterday when I asked you to dismiss that maid and you said you would. And what is the first thing that greets me after my tribulation? That great fat, lumpish prig bringing in my breakfast – so much for your promises.'

'Oh dear.' So that was the reason for her cool manner; she thought he had let her down – and he had.

'Precisely. Oh dear!' replied Peggy. The way his ginger hair clashed with the gold bedspread vexed her beyond reason. She pushed him off the bed with the excuse of wanting to straighten the covers.

'I did talk to Mother about it. In fact we had quite a row. She made it clear that we're only guests in her house and aren't going to tell her what to do with the servants.'

'I'd like to tell her what to do with them,' said Peggy

vindictively. 'And I suppose you just stood there and took it?'

'I tried my best! I even said that as soon as you were on your feet we'd get a place of our own.' He caught the spark of hope in her eye and felt impotent at having to douse it. 'But I'm afraid it won't be up to much. I've a bit of money saved but it's not going to provide anything as big as this.'

'So we're stuck here,' she countered.

'It looks like it – but only till I get enough. Besides,' he looked uneasy, 'there's something else you should know.' He told her about finding Rosanna, finishing with, 'And as the two babies are half-brother and sister Father suggested it'd be kinder to keep them together.'

'Father! Mother! Don't you do anything off your own bat?'

Her vehemence shook him, but he remained firm. 'I happen to agree with him. She can't help her beginnings, and she's a likeable little thing – though not as much as ours.' He looked fondly at the crib. He had never found babies in the least attractive until now.

'I don't know how you expect me to cope with two babies,' she replied badtemperedly. 'Though I don't suppose it'll concern you unduly, regarding the fact that neither of them are yours. Why don't you go scouring the country in search of all your brother's bastards? Then we can have a whole houseful.'

'What a rotten thing to say! And so bloody unfair. Where would you have been if I hadn't agreed to marry you?'

'Oh, so I'm going to get that thrown in my face every five minutes, am I?'

'Oh hell! I didn't intend it to sound that way. You know why I married you – not because of the baby but 'cause I love you. Haven't I told you often enough?'

The baby, woken by hunger and their quarrelling, crumpled his face and started to whimper. 'Pass it over, will you?' said Peggy unforgivingly. 'I suppose I must feed it much as it disgusts me. After all, we can't have your mother forking out for a wet-nurse can we? You're sure

462

you wouldn't like to bring the other one up so I can have one stuck on each side?'

'There's no call for such crudity,' answered Sonny, gingerly picking up the infant and placing him in her arms. What on earth had come over her? She was like a different person. 'Besides, Rosanna is weaned; she's not going to cause that much trouble. If you like, Josie can see to most of her needs while she's tiny. Honestly, Peg, I wouldn't have agreed if I thought it was going to upset you like this. You know I wouldn't do that for the world.'

'Oh, I can't see it making much difference,' sighed Peggy lethargically, undoing the ribbons of her nightgown, then she bristled again. 'But it would've been nice to be consulted for once. I don't have any standing in this house whatsoever.'

'That's not true, Peggy. You're the most important person in my life.'

For a moment her face softened as she looked down on her newborn son. Once again there was the Peggy he'd fallen hopelessly in love with. 'Yes, I believe you mean that, Sonny. You're much too good for me, you know.'

'Rubbish!' he laughed awkwardly.

'Yes, you are. There's not many would have had me after what I did to you, and look upon the baby as their own.' She put a finger to the infant's cheek; the mouth was instantly open. She laughed softly and put her face close to his, breathing in his scent. Strangely, this display made him feel even more pushed out. But he was glad to see her looking happier and said as much.

She sighed. 'I would be even happier were it not for your domineering mother.'

'I do wish you'd try to make an effort to get along with her, Peggy,' he begged.

She reverted to her defiant profile and the radiance he had witnessed a moment ago evaporated. 'Like you do, you mean? Knuckling under, never standing up for your rights, or your wife's rights – never taking a decision unless Mother agrees. Hah! Now I understand why they call you Sonny – you're just a weak little boy. Now, will you please go? I'd like to do this privately.' She had finished undoing her ribbons, and waited.

Sonny, mortally wounded, slunk from the room. Looking back, he would remember this as the time he began to come awake from his false idyll.

CHAPTER THIRTY-EIGHT

The ensuing years brought great change to the house in Monkgate. Some for the better, some much worse. The mutual dislike of the two Mrs Feeneys continued to hang like a shroud over what might have been a pleasant family atmosphere. But Thomasin still refused to give in over the settlement. It was hell living with Peggy but she would be even more on edge if Sonny and his wife moved out of her control, not only because she knew Peggy would take charge of her hard-earned cash, but also for the babies' welfare, for Peggy was no mother. It was as well this was a large house and the two could keep out of each other's way, only meeting at mealtimes. Sometimes Sonny feared he was going to crack under the strain of it all.

Peggy had insisted after the birth of the child that she had to have a room to herself. It was very tiring bringing up two children and she claimed that Sonny disturbed her when he came to bed. Mother had not been very pleased, but for once Sonny had insisted on his wife's rights to privacy, even though Peggy's request had cut him deeply.

The state of their marrige deteriorated. It was as though they were merely lodgers in the same house. He had tried very hard to understand his wife's attitude – it was said that some women behaved apathetically after parturition, and he would have liked to believe this to be the contributing factor to her treatment of him. But he sensed that she somehow held him to blame for her unhappiness. She could be very cruel at times; making excuses to keep him from her bed. Yet at others there would be the old Peggy whom he had wooed and courted in the front parlour, delighting him with her attention and welcoming him into her bed for nights of sensuous pleasure.

At first poor unsophisticated Sonny was far too appreciative to notice that these passionate nights coincided with a request from Peggy for clothes or money. When he did connect the two, the realisation hurt even more.

There was only one way he could find solace in his loneliness and that was in his painting. Things being more settled at the store, his mother had once again granted him the afternoons off. She felt so desperately sorry for her son, despite the hurtful words he'd flung at her. She knew that it was Peggy speaking and not her son. He was able to paint quite openly now. Patrick had returned home one rainy day to catch his son in the act. After a few harsh words about why Sonny was not at the store helping his mother, Patrick was made to realise by his son's answer just how important Sonny's painting was to him. He knew that all was not as it should be with the boy's marriage, but had not imagined that it was so bad.

'Ye've floored me, Sonny,' he gasped. 'I never knew it was as rough as that. By God man, ye want to take her in hand.'

Sonny shook his head tiredly. 'If she doesn't want me then I'll not force myself on her.' He looked up earnestly. 'It's just . . . I can't understood what I've done wrong.'

'Now there's no blame to be laid at your door, Sonny,' replied Patrick. ''Tis not for me to say why she's doing this to ye, but I know an' you know that ye've done that girl proud. How many men would marry a girl who was carrying their brother's child; set her up in a big house with a servant at her beck an' call; place her on a pedestal almost? No, 'tis nothing you've done. I've a mind to go tell that young lady just how lucky she is.'

'No! Please leave it, Dad, it'll only cause a row an' could make matters much worse. It's my problem; I must sort it out for myself.'

Problems, problems, sighed Patrick to himself. God,

what's happening to this family? I've a son disappeared off the face o' the earth, another whose wife has reduced the marital act to a bargain basement, and a daughter who's too terrified to let her husband touch her. Where did we go wrong?

He had looked at his son then, sat like a forlorn child at his easel, painting away his sorrow. What right had Patrick to take away this last scrap of comfort? Leaning nearer the unfinished painting he stroked his chin thoughtfully. 'This was your mother's idea, ye say? You taking the afternoons off to paint.'

Sonny played with a palette knife, pushing and pulling at the patches of colour on the wooden board. 'She gave me her permission, yes, but I hope you're not going to wait for her to come home then pounce on her. If you want to have a go at me then do so, but Mam was only trying to help me; she knows how things are.' They had stitched up the wounds each had inflicted on the other; things were tranquil between them at the moment. 'I wish she'd thought to share it with me,' said his father. There was a time when they had had no secrets from each other. But lots of things were different between them these days. And he had his own secrets.

'Well, I dare say she knew how you'd react,' replied his son.

'How long's it been going on?'

'A couple of years or so. My pictures have been selling very well actually.'

'I thought your mother was only selling the ones ye'd done ages ago. I didn't realise you were having to take the afternoons off to provide her with stock.'

'I suppose that's that then, is it?' Sonny fetched a large cloth and draped it over the canvas.

'Take it off.'

Sonny looked enquiringly at his father.

'Take it off,' repeated Patrick. 'An' for Christ's sake, Sonny – stop trying to be some sort of bloody martyr. Ye really know how to make a father feel guilty, don't ye? What's happened to ye? Where's your fight gone? Ye used

466

to be such a spunky kid – even as a five year old ye were never afraid to argue with me.'

'I'm still not afraid,' sighed Sonny. 'I just can't be bothered.'

'Christ, she's really done a magic trick on you, hasn't she? Why d'ye stand for it, if she's upsetting ye like this? Is it that you're nervous o' chucking her out? 'Cause I can tell ye ye needn't be. We'll be right behind ye, Sonny.'

'There's none of you understands, is there? I don't want to throw her out, I love her.'

'God! How can ye love anybody who treats ye like she does?'

'How the hell do I know? I just know I do.'

'Will ye stop putting them bloody painting things away! For God's sake stand up for yourself, lad. That bloody woman's making a sop of ye. Ye want me to say it? All right I will: I was wrong to stunt your ambition, wrong about your pictures, wrong about every bloody thing. Now take off that bloody cover an' get on with it!'

So Sonny did.

Patrick himself had experienced changes. Catch had been correct in saying that his was too much land for one man to work, so apart from having the old molecatcher help him from time to time he had also taken on a labourer.

Domestic matters too had not escaped modification. Josie had been promoted to cook-housekeeper, with two young girls to help with the chores. Peggy – well, Peggy was just as lazy and slovenly as ever, using the children as an excuse to get out of any work and sitting in the park all day reading her magazines.

The only thing which flourished in this uneasy atmosphere was Thomasin's business, which had built up a very fine reputation for itself. The demand for home-baked produce was now so considerable that Thomasin had hired an experienced pastry-cook. Added to William and his apprentice, the boy who had taken over Dickie's mobile grocery and the other female assistant she had taken on, this brought the strength of her shop staff to five, not counting Sonny. All of which enabled Thomasin to spend more time touring the city drumming up business and sniffing out a good deal. Which is how she found out about the vacant property in Parliament Street.

This particular day had been pleasing in all aspects. She had just clinched an important deal. Her opponents had been obstructive to her proposals in the beginning, but after lunch by the riverside with a capful of wind whispering through the treetops and an attractive female bargainer, they had finally come around to Thomasin's way of thinking. Immensely pleased with herself, Thomasin had shaken hands on the deal and had taken a cab, intending to squeeze in another commitment before the sun went down. But as the cab steered slowly in and out of the parked vehicles along Parliament Street she spotted it.

Asking the cabbie to wait a while she alighted from the hansom and peered up at the estate agent's sign, then back down again at the property. It was ideal; much bigger than her present store, and in not too bad a shape, either. It wouldn't need as drastic treatment as had *Penny's*. An opportunity such as this would not come twice; she must take instantaneous action.

Excitedly, she leapt back into the cab and demanded to be taken to Davygate where her accountant had his premises. Once there, she paid the cabbie and almost ran up the steps to Mr Cowthorpe's office, only to be told that the accountant was engaged.

'He'll see me,' she told the secretary firmly and marched straight past him.

Mr Cowthorpe nearly fell from the chair in which he had been dozing, a handkerchief over his face. 'My dear Mrs Feeney! What a pleasure to see you.'

'I've seen a property in Parliament Street and I want it,' she told him without prelude and placed a piece of paper on his desk. 'There. I've written down the estate agent's name. Find out the details, will you? Time of auction, approximate asking price.'

'Just like that, eh?' he smiled. Dear Mrs Feeney, she was so impulsive at times.

'Well, there's nothing spoiling here, is there?' she said wrily. 'You don't appear to be too busy to me.'

'You're a slavedriver, madam, but I shall do my utmost to fulfil your request.'

'Aye, well when you've done that I shall ask you to do me another favour. Hah! What am I talking about – favour? God knows you cost me enough, so I may as well have my moneysworth.'

He laughed, used to her candour. 'What is it, dear lady?'

'I'd like you to bid for me. I'm too excited to behave rationally and I'll probably come away with the wrong property or half a ton of cheese or something equally daft.'

He pulled a face. 'The likelihood of that happening to the astute Mrs Feeney is so unimaginable that should it be so I promise here and now to eat every last crumb of the said cheese.'

'Don't make such rash wagers – I'm so excited anything could happen. Anyway, I'd be too much on edge to stand about waiting to see if someone was going to outbid me. Will you do it?'

He bowed and said he would inform her of the details when he learnt them. 'And a fine move if I may say so – the property I mean. An ideal site for a business such as yours.'

Thomasin's family were a little less enthusiastic. 'But you're slap-bang in the marketplace, Mother,' Sonny pointed out. 'It'll be a struggle from the start – besides the competition from the other grocers.'

'An' it sounds an awful big place,' added Patrick. 'Are ye sure you're ready for it?'

'By, you're like a couple of damp squibs, the pair of you! Of course I'm ready for it. I've never been more ready. There's a pile of cash in the bank sat doing nowt. It's all right this little shop making money but once you've made it you have to plough it back into something else. Expand.'

'Will ye listen to the woman,' joked Patrick. 'Yesterday it was "an emporium", today 'tis "a little shop".'

'Stop making fun! I'm serious.' His wife wagged a finger. 'Firstly, you've got it wrong about the market being a struggle, Sonny. The only struggle will involve who can get to my counter first. Don't you see? On market days there'll be all these country people flocking into town to sell their produce and *buy*, Sonny, buy! They're not going to take any custom from me, they're going to add to it. As for your point about competing with the other grocers, well, I'm not even going to try. My aim is not simply to run a grocery, but to have all sorts of commodities under the one roof. You'll have seen I've been working towards that for some time.'

'Yes, we had noticed,' affirmed Patrick, looking at the callouses on his hands.

'Now, you know there's no need whatsoever for you to be working in those fields,' she chastened. 'You could quite easily hire a couple more labourers, leaving you free to do more important work.'

'An' what sort of important work would I be doing, tell me?'

'Have you considered that with another couple of hundred acres you could grow not just enough to keep us in produce but a lot of other businesses as well?'

'A wholesale business, ye mean?'

'It's a start. I always intended to have one some day.' And very likely would have done, she thought, if Dusty had still been with us. 'We could begin with the green-grocery and see how it progresses before going the whole hog.'

'Gob, woman, ye'll be meeting yourself coming back if ye aren't careful,' said her husband. 'Who was it always telling me not to go rushing into things when I was in business for meself?'

'That was entirely different,' she replied. 'You and John wanted to take on too much too early. I've had seven years' experience, and no one could accuse me of moving too fast. In fact my accountant is always telling me how reticent

470

I am. All this aside, have you ever known anything I've turned my hand to to meet with failure?'

He had to admit that she had taken to this life like someone born to it. ''Tis a pity we didn't know what an expert we had in our midst when I was struggling to keep out of jail.'

Sonny felt the light-hearted atmosphere suffer a drop of ten degrees. Poor Father, it was such a blow to his pride that a woman had succeeded where he had failed.

Thomasin fought back the answer she had been about to thrust at him: *who was it got you out of jail?* Like her son, she understood Patrick's divided emotions. On the one hand she knew he was glad that her ventures had met with more success than his had; on the other, he thought that it was the husband who was meant to be the bread-winner, so with her success came his failure. 'If I'd offered my advice then would you have taken it, Patrick?' she asked quietly.

He gave a rueful smile. 'Was I ever one to take advice? Especially when it was sensible advice. I'm sorry, Tommy, the previous skit was uncalled for; I take it back.' His smile widened as Josie brought in the children for a goodnight kiss before they changed into their nightgowns. 'Ah, hosanna, Rosanna!' He swept up his three year old grand-daughter and dandled her on his knee. Facially, she was so like Erin had been as an infant, but her character was oh, so different. There was no shyness here, nor stubbornness. Rosanna, even at this early age, knew that these were not ways to win her beloved grandfather. Instead, she used the wiles inherited from her natural father – charm and cajolery. Grandfather was as malleable as dough in her baby hands.

Thomasin cuddled the much quieter and less wilful Nicholas. They were both such lovely children. It was a crime their mother did not show them more affection. The little bit that was going was reserved for Nick; poor Rosie received none at all. Still, the other members of the family made up for Peggy's lack.

'Where's my wife, Josie?' asked Sonny, enjoying the

471

warm feeling that the children had produced. He had come to love them both as his own.

'She's lying down, Mr John,' said the maid, enjoying too the sight of the children being cosseted.

'Had a hard day at the park, I suppose,' said Thomasin caustically.

Sonny let the snide remark go over his head. He had long since given up defending Peggy, though he still loved her as much as ever. 'Can I hold him for a while, Mother?' He stretched out his arms. Thomasin set the little boy on his feet and he ran straight to his father, falling at the last minute, his legs becoming tangled with his frock. Sonny caught him laughingly and swung him onto his lap, breathing in his fresh baby smell; then began to bounce the child in time to Patrick's mellifluous voice as he broke into tune.

This was not one of the nasal Gaelic laments that the Irishman sometimes entertained them with, but as lively a ditty as the young lady it was composed for.

I was dan-d-lin' a pretty Irish colleen on me knee,
When a prosp'rous-lookin' stranger comes a strollin' up to
* me,*
Says he, 'Kind sir a favour I would beg ye if I dare,
Could I poach a tiny snippet from your lady's bounteous
* hair?*

''Tis just the very colour that I've been lookin' for,
An' I never saw the like of it in a thousand miles or more,
I'll pay ye very kindly with a pot of fairy gold,
An' once taken your fair colleen will never to grow old.'

Well, then I get the notion that he's of the leprechaun,
An' I cling to her so tightly for I know what is to come.
The moment that his scissors flush across her silken hair
She'll be taken for a fairy an' I'll see my love no more.

Says I, 'Well thank ye kindly an' I've no wish to offend,
For I know ye need the hair your fairy coats to mend,

But I tell ye little stranger, this is not the stuff for you
For 'tis rough an' thick an' sure to break your needles all
*   in two.'*

Now, ye may think 'tis a slander of my darlin's wondrous
*   hair,*
But I tell ye I would say it twice if I thought it would save
*   her,*
For there's no one who is dearer be it woman, child or man,
If she asked I'd surely die for her, my darlin', sweet Rosanne.

The little girl laughed and clapped delightedly as she always did when Patrick showed her the tiniest amount of attention, and complained noisily when Josie took her and Nick off to bed.

'They're grand weans, Sonny,' said Patrick, his eyes bright with love. 'An' you're doing an admirable job o' raising them.'

'I'd heartily agree with your first comment, Dad, but I can't accept the credit for the latter – that's more down to Peggy and Josie.'

Mostly Josie, thought Thomasin bitterly. The other slut couldn't give a damn what happened to them. It was Josie who collected them from their beds in a morning, Josie who put them back there on an evening, and Josie who saw to all their needs in between. If Thomasin had been their mother she knew she would have been intensely jealous, but not Peggy. All the children meant to her was an excuse to escape work. 'Oh, I'm sorry, Mother-in-law I can't possibly do that! I must give the children their fresh air and exercise.' Thomasin dreaded to think what took place when they arrived at the park, for Peggy would probably let them run riot and wouldn't even miss them if they were to fall in the lake.

She changed the subject; she always grew bad-tempered if she dwelled on Peggy for too long. 'Well, shall we have a glass to celebrate our coming venture?'

'I'd not say no to a drop o' the ould poteen,' said her husband, in better spirits now.

'Those were the days, eh, Dad?' smiled Sonny.

'Aye, and thank God they're behind us is all I can say,' remarked Thomasin, pouring out the sherry. 'Now, raise your glasses, gentlemen. I give you Mrs Feeney, your succour and salvation, may she ever be as humble.'

'Hey, ye can't toast yourself,' Patrick pointed out.

To which his wife responded: 'Well, if I don't, no bugger else is likely to, are they?'

By the following week Thomasin had been furnished with all the relevant details of the property and had also been taken on a tour of the interior. In about five minutes she had decided exactly where everything was to go. There, would be provisions; and there, fresh produce; over there, baked items . . .

The place was even roomier than she had anticipated, allowing her another inspirational gesture.

'What if,' she suggested to Sonny and Patrick who had been dragged along to share in her delight, 'we put some chairs and tables in that corner and serve refreshments? People'll think it's a lovely idea – being able to do all the shopping in one place, have it delivered *and* get a cup of tea into the bargain.'

'Not all the shopping,' said Patrick. 'Ye've no meat department, remember? Though knowing yourself I'm sure you're working on it.'

'What a grand idea! Why don't we ask Sam . . .' She roared with laughter at her husband's face. 'I'm only kidding. I don't think Sam would appreciate us carving up his young ladies.' A private joke: true to his promise Patrick had, with his wife, bought Sam ten Shorthorn dairy cows to start him off on his ambition, plus another fifty acres to keep them in. Sam had soon grown devoted to each beast. However, neither Patrick nor Thomasin knew if the gesture had produced any results in the way of Sam and Erin's marriage. Sam was rarely on his own for Patrick to ask him, and Thomasin knew that it was a question Erin would not welcome, so the parents remained ignorant. They did notice, though, that there seemed less tension between the couple.

'But look, you two,' Thomasin continued. 'Can't you just see it? When it's painted in a decent colour and with a few of Sonny's pictures on the walls ... I mean, they're selling well enough at the old store but if we arrange them cleverly where the customers are sat drinking their tea and they have a chance to study them, well, they could do even better here.'

'Speaking of the old store,' said Patrick. 'What's going to happen to that?'

'Nothing's going to happen to it. I'm keeping it on. We'll move all the main equipment here naturally, as there's more room for a proper bakery, but Goodramgate will trade as normal. There's no point in disposing of something that's making money.'

'But how can ye look after two stores?' protested her husband.

Sonny's heart dropped: she was going to put him in charge of the smaller shop.

But no. 'I thought I'd divide my time equally between the two. With all the coffee-roasting paraphernalia and the bakery at this place there won't be much to supervise at Goodramgate. However ...' here she looked at Sonny and he knew his fear had been half-right, 'I am going to need a lot of extra help in getting this place in order and supervising the new staff. I'm sorry, Sonny but I'm going to have to ask you to forgo your free afternoons for a while – not forever, just till we get into a routine.'

He managed to deliver his answer gracefully, though it took great willpower.

'Good lad.' She patted his hand. 'It won't be for long, I promise. Oh! but isn't it absolutely grand.' She clapped her hands with glee. 'If I don't get it I'll just die.'

'I see every reason for optimism,' said her accountant when they met to discuss what her ceiling price should be. 'With a bid of that stature there are few who could beat you.'

She wrung her hands as he climbed into his carriage.

'Do please get word to me the minute it's ours,' she begged anxiously.

'Trust me, Mrs Feeney. I shall get it for you with a few pence to spare.'

Thomasin, unable to concentrate on her work, spent that morning either wringing her hands or casting nervous glances at the clock. Josie, on being asked for the tenth time for a tray of tea, became nettled with her employer. 'Mrs Feeney, ma'am, I don't want to get above myself but wouldn't it be more sensible for you to occupy yourself rather than sit here drowning in tea? I can see you're all of a twitter about something an' I don't mean to pry, but . . .'

'I'm waiting to hear if I've been successful in my bid for a new store, Josie,' Thomasin divulged. 'And you're right!' She leapt up and tugged at her bodice. 'I can't sit here for another second not knowing whether I've won or lost.' She glanced at the clock for the umpteenth time. 'It's almost eleven. It'll take me about fifteen minutes to get there and by that time it should all be over.' She patted Josie's well-covered shoulder as she moved quickly past in a swish of crêpe de chine. 'Sorry I've been under your feet this morning, dear. I just couldn't settle to work.'

'It's your home, ma'am. If you can't sit in your own drawing room I don't know who can.' She ran after Thomasin, overtook her in the hall and opened the front door. Her mistress rushed through it. 'Good luck!'

Thomasin's reckoning was accurate. When she reached The Black Swan where the auction was being held it was all over. There was a slow trickle of disaffected bidders leaving the inn. One of them spotted her and raised his hat as she alighted from the cab to a mixture of wind and rain.

'Congratulations, Mrs Feeney. I'm sorry to say you beat us all – again.'

'You mean I've got it?' she said elatedly, grabbing hold of her hat as a gust threatened to tear it from her head. 'Are you sure?'

'Positive. I like to know who my rivals are. I was standing

very close to the rostrum and heard the buyer's name quite clearly – although it was a gentleman who tendered your name. Perhaps your husband?'

'My accountant,' said Thomasin. 'I was too keyed-up to do my own bidding. Oh, how perfectly lovely! Thank you.' She bade him a hasty good-day and escaped from the foul weather, pushing her way through those who had stayed to drown their blighted hopes in a tankard. She sought out Mr Cowthorpe, inclining her head to right and left at the murmurs of congratulation. When she finally found him she snatched at the hand that was about to reach for a tankard. 'I ought to crown you! Sitting here supping when you should be haring down Monkgate with the good news – Oh, never mind! Thank you.'

He looked askance. 'My dear Mrs Feeney, I am much discomfited to tell you that you have been unkindly misled. We were unsuccessful in our bid.'

She frowned and dropped his hand abruptly. 'But I've had people congratulating me right, left and centre. They can't all be mistaken. One of them actually told me he'd heard my name put forward.'

Cowthorpe's perplexity dissolved. 'Ah, I can see now how the misunderstanding came about. It grieves me to have to tell you they were wrong, Mrs Feeney – although it was true to say that the successful gentleman's name is the same as your own. In fact, there he is at the bar right behind you – perhaps you are related?'

Thomasin turned quickly to inspect the handsome usurper – and felt herself sway.

'Hello, Mam,' grinned Dickie.

CHAPTER THIRTY-NINE

The last time she had felt like this was when, as a child, she used to twirl round and round a dozen times then stop suddenly and watch the room still spinning around her. But now, instead of slowing as it used to do, the room continued to whirl until everything went black.

The oblivion was followed by a buzzing noise, then a low mumbling and an acrid smell. She coughed and pushed away the smelling salts, fighting her way dizzily to her feet. They clustered round her, all eager to lend a helping hand. She took a deep breath, then permitted herself to be placed onto the chair that one of her attendants had procured.

'Well, you certainly know how to time your entrance,' she breathed, staring at the apparition in front of her. Seeing him on the street she would have had to look twice to recognize him as her son. In her mind he had remained the gangling eighteen year old, tall and slim, but the affluent-looking man before her would be three years older, and his frame had filled out to be more like his brother's. Sonny – it came as a jolt. What was Sonny going to say when he knew?

Her son smiled widely. 'Well, aren't ye going to welcome home the prodigal?'

'I get the impression that you've just helped yourself to the fatted calf.' She shook her head, unable to digest his presence even now. Then she threw her arms about him. 'You're alive! Oh, God you're alive!'

'Alive an' kicking.' He showed surprise at her welcome.

She wiped her eyes with a gloved hand, laughing and crying. 'Oh, but you've changed,' she breathed, examining every new line on his face.

He grinned. 'So have you.' His eyes roved about the hair that peeped from under the kingfisher-blue hat. Like most auburn hair past its prime it had not undergone the gradual and unattractive greying process, but had turned pure, gleaming white in a relatively short period. The only hint that her hair had ever been otherwise was in the pale russet tips that lay hidden within the chignon, as if reluctant to let go of the last shreds of youth.

She raised self-conscious fingers to her temple, then her voice hardened as she suddenly realised that if he was alive that meant he had been walking around for the last three years without ever a word to his family. 'Can you wonder? Can you? All these years of thinking you were dead . . .'

'Ah, I'm sorry about that,' offered her son.

'Oh, you look extremely sorry, I'm sure,' whispered Thomasin as the crowd around them diplomatically thinned. 'You stand there in your finery, having put me and your father through not months but years of uncertainty and expect me to be satisfied with "Sorry"?'

'I'm so . . .' He laughed and held out his hands. 'Well, there's not much else I can say.'

'Oh yes there is – and you're going to say it!' She seized his arm and piloted him to the exit. 'If you think you can just appear as if from nowhere and fob me off with an "I'm sorry" you must have lost your memory while you've been away. I want to know the full story. Why, why did you not let us know you were safe, for pity's sake?'

The grin was still there. 'Shall we wait until Father's present before we kick off on explanations? 'Tis a long story an' wouldn't bear telling twice.'

She frowned, still shaken, then once on the pavement, allowed him to hail a cab and assist her inside. 'It'd better be good,' she warned as the carriage pulled away.

He smiled and crossed his palms over the knob of his cane. 'Oh, I should think it'll be quite illuminating.'

By an act of Fate every single member of the family was present in the dining room that lunchtime. Patrick, rained off again, was seated at the head of the table with Sonny on his right and Peggy to his left, the children by her side where she could keep their table manners in check. Josie, aided by Abigail, was serving out the meal. They all looked up expectantly as Thomasin entered. Patrick and Sonny pushed back their chairs.

'Did ye get it?' they both asked simultaneously, laughed, then looked serious again at her odd expression. Josie noticed it too and sent Abigail off for another place setting.

'Sorry . . . what? Oh, no. No, I didn't get it,' replied Thomasin absently, then looked directly at Patrick. 'You know that prosperous-looking stranger you were singing about the other night? Well, prepare yourself for a shock.'

She stepped aside and waited for the outburst at Dickie's sweeping entrance. Yet, oddly, there was none. Not a sound. Patrick returned the gaze of the elegant-looking man who had taken off his hat and now balanced it on his cane.

'You don't seem surprised,' exclaimed Thomasin slowly, at Patrick's refusal to shake his son's offered hand. He steered his pale-blue eyes upon her and she read them true. 'You knew, didn't you?' she breathed. 'You knew all along he was alive and you didn't tell me.'

'I didn't tell ye, Tommy because I was ashamed. Disgraced by his dastardly behaviour.' He watched his elder son as he spoke. 'Did he tell ye what occurred on the day he went missing?'

'No, but I wish somebody would.' She wheeled to take in Dickie.

'Are you going to tell your mother, or will I?' asked Patrick darkly.

'Oh, pray continue,' said Dickie, seemingly unmoved.

Patrick's jaw muscle twitched. His eyes still on his son, he revealed the details of Dickie's cowardice. 'The Fallon boys told me they had it in mind to force Dickie to do right by their sister. However, when they cornered him, d'ye know what he did? He pissed his pants! That cowardly, irresponsible wastrel pissed his pants an' then he fainted. Quite understandably the Fallons wanted nothin' more to do with him after that. What took place afterwards was of his own making. The one truism is that he allowed us to think he'd been abducted or killed so's he could escape from his other responsibilites at home.'

Dickie threw up his hands in a helpless gesture to ward off the host of scandalized glares then, indicating Peggy with a nod, said, 'Well, it looks as if everything turned out for the best.'

Sonny blew up. 'How you've got the nerve to show your face in here after the most abject cowardice ... do you fully grasp what you've put everyone through? Can you

480

imagine what it was like for Father being asked to identify a body he thought to be his son's? Can you? And was this what it was all for?' He slapped Dickie's shoulder with the back of his hand. 'A set of fancy clothes that makes you look like some popinjay.' His scornful eyes washed over the brocade waistcoat under the immaculately-tailored green suit. 'Always a touch flamboyant for my taste.' He roughly pushed his brother round to examine his back view. 'D'you not think the colour a mite ostentatious? Green and yellow.' He simulated repentance at his brother's puzzlement. 'Oh, sorry! Sorry – I thought that yellow streak down the back was part of the outfit.'

Dickie took the baiting in good part, and turned to face his brother again. 'That's cruel, Son – but I expect it was coming to me. Is it too much to ask that ye accept my apologies for all the damage I've done ye?'

'You're damn right it is!' Sonny whirled away to comfort Nicholas who had begun to whimper at the harsh voices. Rosanna retained a lively interest.

Dickie noticed now that there were two children at the table with Peggy. He moved after his brother. 'Which . . .' he began, then stopped himself.

'Which one's yours, you were going to say,' said Sonny cuttingly.

'I meant no harm,' mollified Dickie. 'I'd just like to thank ye for stepping in for me. Ye make a much better father than I would.'

'Well, that's one thing on which we can agree!' Sonny's voice was raised again. 'And while you're thanking me for looking after one you can thank me for taking the other one in, too. Aye!' He nodded at Dickie's bafflement. 'That one's yours as well. Regular little industry, aren't you?'

Dickie frowned at the children, trying to decipher the riddle. Thomasin solved it for him. 'The little girl is the child you fathered on Lucy Fallon,' she said coldly. 'Your father rescued her and brought her home where she'd be properly treated – not that I'd expect you to be interested in her welfare. Sonny agreed to adopt her.'

Dickie's glib tongue deserted him on this occasion. In

fact he was quite touched at his brother's compassion. 'You're a good man, Son, looking after my children,' he said quietly.

'Don't you dare refer to them as your children!' shouted Sonny. 'You relinquished any claim on them when you deserted them.'

'That's a bit strong,' complained Dickie concernedly. 'They weren't even born then.'

'Oh well, that makes it all right for you to walk out on them,' came the sarcastic response. 'It doesn't matter about walking out on embryos.'

Dickie decided to call a halt to what he considered calumny, and backed away murmuring, 'Well, thank ye anyway . . .'

But the battle was not over. 'God dammit I don't want your bloody thanks, you leech!' hurled Sonny. 'And I wish everybody'd stop telling me how noble I've been. I married Peggy because I love her – something you'd never understand.' He spoke now to Thomasin. 'Mother, I know this is your house and I can't stop you bringing into it whoever you like – you made that very clear. But if he isn't gone by the time I get back, then I must tell you I'll never enter it again.' He aimed one last stab at Dickie. 'And while you're here, just keep your hands off my wife or this time – I *will* kill you!' He stormed out.

'And how's Peggy?' asked Dickie, injecting his voice with a false lightness.

Peggy scowled and gathered up the children. 'Josie, set three places in the kitchen – there's something about this room that makes me lose my appetite.'

'Sure, it'd do ye no harm to lose a couple o' pounds!' shouted Dickie as the door slammed. 'Well,' he smiled tightly as he was left alone with his parents, 'I never expected to see the bunting out, but I wasn't prepared for all this. May I sit down to recover?'

'Ye might as well,' growled his father. 'We're due an explanation, young man an' if it's going to be as long as I suspect we'd all better sit down.'

Dickie laid his hat on the table but kept his cane with

him as he settled in a chair. His fingers played with the ivory handle, composed of a hand clasping a snake. 'It'll not be very interesting, ye know.'

'Oh, I don't expect the one we're going to hear will be,' agreed his mother, adding shrewdly, 'but I'll bet the true one would interest us greatly – if we were ever privy to hear it.'

He laughed then and leaned back, the old Dickie grin on his tanned face. 'Tut, tut, Mother! Are ye making out I'd string ye a pack o' lies?' He stalled another rebuke. 'No matter – I can see ye'll not settle till I've told ye. So, will ye all gather round an' I'll tell yese me tale!'

When Dickie had awoken from that life-saving swoon to find himself cold but virtually unscathed, he had seen it not as a miraculous intervention by his guardian angel and a warning to change his lifestyle, but as a means of solving all his problems. He had hidden in a disused pigsty until dark – he was too well-known around these parts to risk being seen in daylight and must make his 'kidnap' look convincing.

When dusk had fallen he had exchanged his hideout for one nearer the marketplace where the following day would see the Martinmas Hirings. With a little Irish luck he would be hired to some out-of-town gentry and by mid-morning be well on the way to forging a new identity.

He cursed the recklessness that had made him hand over all his cash to the Fallons; when examined, the pocket of his trousers yielded nothing more lucrative than a farthing that had escaped his panicked fingers. The urine had dried to a stiff and stinking patch that chafed at the insides of his thighs. They had taken his topcoat as well, the bastards. He shivered and gripped his upper arms to ward off the freezing cold. He must get some money from somewhere if he was to survive the night. The very thought of food set his stomach immediately a-rumble.

On reaching Pavement, which verged on the market-place, he searched for a place to spend the night and found it in the ancient church of St Crux. It was the safest place he could think of, being an extremely unlikely venue for any of his Catholic acquaintances. The pew on which he laid his punished frame could not compare with his comfortable bed at home, and the church was like an icehouse. His fingers were drawn to his forehead, which felt strangely tight, and they found a patch of encrusted blood. He hoped they hadn't scarred his face too badly. Finally he dozed off.

His slumber ended prematurely sometime before three o'clock when he awoke shivering, his fingers and toes numb with cold. Dragging his stiff body from the pew he stumbled up the aisle tucking his hands into his armpits in an effort to thaw the blood. Perhaps there might be some garment, anything, that he could borrow till morning. The only items of clothing to be found were the clergyman's vestments which Dickie had no compunction in donning forthwith, though the light cotton surplice and flowing cassock made a negligible difference to his state.

He fumbled about in the darkness for something more substantial and his hand fell on a trunk. It was locked. He groped around for something with which to open it and in his search came across a candle and a box of matches. With a little more grubbling and the added illumination Dickie found a key, inexpertly secreted over the sacristy door lintel. He unlocked the trunk and threw back the lid, holding the candle over its contents and drawing in his breath as the glint of gold struck him in the eye. A blob of wax from the guttering candle fell onto the treasure and burnt a hole through his trance. Placing the candle on a ledge he tucked his hands into the trunk and cupped them around a golden chalice whose bowl was encrusted with precious stones. There were several such items in the chest, all of which were in turn reverently handled.

For one heart-thudding moment Dickie entertained the idea of prising loose one of the stones; it would be foolishness to steal the whole chalice but a missing stone would pass unnoticed for maybe months. He was searching for some way of removing the stone when a faint noise from the direction of the main door alerted him and he hurriedly piled the treasure back into the trunk. Locking it he replaced the key in its original place.

He listened with his ear to the door. After that initial sound there had been only silence. In his avaricious fantasy, the coldness had been momentarily forgotten, but now once again the freezing draught began to rise from the stone floor. He beat his hands about himself. This was no good at all. He would have to find some cover for himself even if he had to borrow the altar-cloth. What irony to escape the wrath of two fiery tinkers then freeze to death in a place of sanctuary.

With great caution, Dickie turned the iron ring on the door and re-entered the main body of the church. His boots made hollow echoes as he slowly advanced on the altar. His eyes had fallen on the curtains at the altar-rail which looked as though they might allow him a decent rest for the remainder of the night. Purposefully, he strode towards them, laid his hands upon the brass curtain-rings that secured one of them to the rail and began to unhook it. His frozen digits were all thumbs and he swore under his breath. He pulled and tugged at the curtain badtemperedly. With a sudden rent it parted company with the brass rings and hung limply in his hand.

But Dickie had lost all interest in the curtain. He was transfixed by the ghostly face which loomed out at him as the curtain fell away. He gulped in a breastful of cold air and backed away, his free hand held out before him to ward off the evil-eye.

'Oh, forgive me, Reverend!' The girl leapt from her hiding-place and threw herself at his feet, clutching at the hem of his cassock and making his palpitations ever more erratic. 'I didn't mean no harm. It's such a cold night out there. I didn't mean to steal owt, honest.' She knelt at his feet, looking up with pleading blue eyes.

Dickie's heartbeat gradually regulated itself as he realised that this was no spectre. He laughed at himself for being so easily scared. Like as not he wouldn't be needing that curtain now; here was some real flesh and blood to warm him. He adopted a saintly expression and, bending, extricated the girl's fingers from his vestments. He pulled her to her feet before she had time to notice his unReverend-like boots.

'Oh, Reverend – you've hurt yourself!' She pointed to his forehead.

'Ah, 'tis nothing, my child. I bashed my head on a low lintel.'

But she insisted on tending it, cracking the thin veil of ice on the font and dipping in the rag that she pulled from her sleeve. She dabbed tentatively until the encrusted blood fell away. 'It's left a nasty mark,' she told him. 'An odd shape; just like the letter L.'

Dickie shrank and closed his eyes. L for Lecher. He opened them again and smiled. 'That must surely be a mark of God's love – seeing as how it was a lintel in the church I banged it on.' He laughed and surreptitiously pulled the cassock over his boots which were once more in danger of giving him away.

But in the end it was not so much his boots that revealed him as his irreverent behaviour during the remainder of the small hours. By daybreak the poor girl, worn out with fighting off his numerous attempts on her chastity, huddled like a bedraggled sparrow in a corner and watched the handsome imposter with heavy-lidded eyes. 'What's your name?' she mumbled as he yawned noisily and scratched his ribs under the crimson curtain.

'Didn't I tell ye? The Reverend O'Donnel.' He arched his back away from the hard pew.

'You're the queerest parson I've ever known,' came the sceptical reply.

He threw off the curtain and put his boots to the stone floor, grinning. 'Don't ye know us priests are worse than any normal man? We're the very devil when it comes to women an' liquor.' He stepped from the pew into the aisle and in his sleep-befuddled state automatically genuflected to the altar, crossing himself.

'There, I knew it!' She sprang from her corner. 'No vicar I ever saw did that. Them's papist ways. Right! I'm off to the police station an' tell them there's an imposter here who's masqueradin' as a clergyman so's he can steal the silver an' ravish the congregation. You probably murdered the poor vicar an' all.'

'Ah, will ye shut your gob,' he grumbled unconcernedly. 'I can't be doin' with all this blatherin' of a mornin'.'

'You think I'm bluffing, but I'll do it!'

He spoke with strained patience. 'An' what will ye say when I tell the Constable you're my accomplice?' He nodded at her shocked face. 'Now, will ye stop your ranting an' go do something useful like finding us some food.' He slouched up to the font and splashed icy water onto his face, dabbing it dry with the priest's robes. He glanced at her incredulous stare. 'Well, can ye get me something to fill me stomach or not? I've not had a bite past me lips since yesterday morning. Or are ye going to be as uncooperative in that quarter as ye were in the other?'

She blushed deeply. He smiled then and walked up to her. Gripping her arms he planted a kiss on her cheek. 'Well?'

She wriggled free. 'Have you no sense of propriety? We are in the house of God, yer know. I can't think what possessed me to linger here with such a rogue. I should've departed hours ago.'

'Then why didn't ye? Nobody's stopping ye. I'll tell ye why ye didn't go: because ye found my company so irresistible ye couldn't bear to leave it.'

'Ooh, you're insufferable!'

'I'm also hungry – now do I get some breakfast or don't I?'

She glared at him. What a pompous oaf to suggest it was his presence that kept her here, and totally wrong of course. It was not his self-supposed magic that held her but the fact that last night she had crept into this hiding-place and now dared not leave it. She had decided when she had met him last night that though she found his company obnoxious it was better than no company at all. The streets were no safe place for a girl on her own – though the sanctuary offered by the church had not been much safer. However, he was obviously not an out-and-out rogue; a big man like him could have ravished her with ease if he had been so disposed. She looked at him. He was smiling. If he were not such a lout there was no denying that he was extremely handsome – unbearably so, thought Sally. She wondered where he had really got that wound on his head; probably from some irate husband or father. She supposed he had all the girls eating out of his hand, the little fools. Sally had more sense than that. The sort of companionship he was offering was the very reason she had absconded from her previous employment as a potwench. She was heartily sick of the pawing and nipping that went on in that smoke-filled prison and having to work like a slave for a wage that would not keep a mouse alive. Last night, when a drunken customer had broken into her room she had decided it was time to make her break. Filling her apron with as much food as she dare take, plus a bottle of wine, she had climbed out of the window, skimmed across a couple of low rooftops and shinned down a drainpipe. What lay ahead she could only guess, but she was going to put herself up for hire at the Martinmas Fair today. She began to pull at the knot in her apron. Her fingers were mauve, the nails white and deathlike.

'What are ye scratting about at now, woman?' demanded a ravenous Dickie.

'Yer want summat to eat, don't yer?' she retorted sharply.

Swiftly he snatched her bundle and began tearing at the knot.

'Careful! Yer'll have it all over t'deck.'

He unfastened the apron and spread it on the floor. Inside were two small loaves sprinkled with seeds, a slice of meat pie, two capon wings, an apple and two honey cakes. Dickie set upon one of the loaves, ripping it between his large hands. 'I suppose ye didn't think to bring any butter?'

She had to laugh at this audacity. 'Pardon me! If I'd known I was going to dine with a gentleman I would've brought the roast swan.' He was now biting into the meat pie. She grabbed the other loaf and a capon wing before they went the same way.

After they had feasted she pulled out the bottle of wine from under a pew and offered it to him. 'My, but you're a real handy sort to have around.' He took a long pull at the bottle, then passed it back. 'Beautiful eyes ye've got,' he added matter-of-factly.

'Have I?' She raised a hand to her face, wonderingly.

'Has no one ever told ye before? I'm surprised. Now, would ye like to tell me how come I have the pleasure o' such dainty female company?'

To her own incredulity she found herself telling him not only the story of her escape from the tavern but her whole life story. Perhaps, she decided, she did like him after all. She had been annoyed at his bestial approaches last night, but now, with the thin strands of morning striking his face with the colours of the stained-glass windows, added to the compliments he had begun to pay her, she quickly warmed to this rogue. She asked him how he had happened to be dressed in clergyman's garb.

'Well, I'm in a similar position to your sweet self,' he reflected sadly. 'I came to York to put meself up at the Statties.Me mother died, ye see, leavin' me to fall back on my uncle's mercy. She left the house to him in the hope that he'd care for me. But, him bein' the old skinflint that he is, chucked me out on the streets. Gave me a good beating too, so's I wouldn't go back – that's how I got this.' He touched his brow. 'Well, I know it was wrong but I snuck in here an' borrowed the priest's clothes. I thought he'd rather have me do that than have a frozen corpse on his hands.'

Sally was horrified. 'Didn't yer uncle even give yer money for food?'

'If he had d'ye think I'd be relyin' on your handouts? No, he's a hard cruel man is Uncle.' He sighed melodramatically.

'Haven't yer any other family? What about yer father?'

'I never knew him,' he replied tragically. 'I hope ye aren't shocked by that. 'Twasn't Mother's fault; she was taken advantage of. She did marry later but her husband, my brother an' sister all perished in a fire some years ago, and the youngest only three years old. I think that's what kilt poor old Mother in the end, the heartbreak.' He covered his face with his hand.

She thrust the wine bottle at him. 'Oh, don't distress yourself so! Have another drink, it'll soothe your pain.' She placed a hesitant hand on his shoulder and he snuggled up to her, laughing heartily inside. 'We'll stick together, you an' me,' she promised. 'At least 'til we get ourselves a job. I've got no one I can turn to, either.'

After returning the vestments to their rightful place Dickie spared a covetous glance for the trunk of precious metal then followed Sally outside. The elegant cupola that crowned the church was shrouded in November mist. Nearby, in the Shambles, the butchers had started to display their wares on the hooks outside their poky medieval shops. In the summer this quaint street abounded with flies; today the meat went unmolested.

Sally answered Dickie's lament that he did not even have tuppence to buy a pipe by crossing the road to a tobacconist's where she spent the last of her money on a clay pipe and a plug of tobacco. Dickie hovered outside a woollen merchant's, wondering what occupation he could lay claim to at the Hirings. It was customary for shepheds to wear a piece of fleece in their hats or for workmen to carry their implements so that a prospective employer could see at a glance what he was getting without having to waste time asking each one. What could Dickie display? He was unversed in any skill – at least the sort that employers would be after. However, he could cope quite well with horses now, and though he would never succeed as an ostler would pass as a competent stable lad or carriage driver.

He watched Sally trip back across the road as the grey streets began to come alive. What was she going to hire herself out as – a maid of all work? He examined his own clothes. Even without his topcoat he looked a darned sight smarter than any of the country bumpkins who were making their way into Parliament Street just around the corner, where the Hirings were to be held. Maybe he could pass for a gentleman's valet or something equally worthy.

'Ah, God love ye, Sally!' He bent his face to her cheek as she handed him the pipe. 'Ye know I've been thinkin': perhaps we might get ourselves employed at the same place – you as maid, me as groom. If so then I can repay your kindness out o' me first wages.'

She smiled enthusiastically. 'That'd be nice, Dickie – working together I mean.' How extraordinary; last night she had found him repulsive but today when she looked at him she felt all warm and excited at her future.

They made their way with the burgeoning throng into Parliament Street where young men and girls were already being driven away by their new masters. The long street was packed with carriages and delivery wagons, gaitered farmers who toured the rows of apprehensive labourers looking for a good strong lad, men in leather aprons trying to make their deliveries, jostling their handcarts between the bartering participants. It was busy enough now but in an hour or so there would be twice or three times as many people. It would be a near-impossibility to drive a carriage between them, and the invariable sideshows that accompanied these proceedings.

In the thick of the crowd now and keeping a firm hold on Sally, Dickie eyed the poor peasants disdainfully. What a fall in status he thought dismally – me, who was going to be rich. Ah well, I suppose this'll not be forever, I'm only a young man. There's still time to make that fortune.

An hour passed and still he had not found a position. He had stolen a whip from a parked carriage in the hope of advertising his profession but it did not seem to bring him any luck. He began to be irked by these ignorant yokels who did not know a good thing when they saw one, saying they wanted no flash coves in their employ. His irritation was tinged with a soupçon of fear. The longer he stood here, the more likely the chance of someone coming along who knew him.

Sally had received a dozen offers and had declined them all on account of him. She would wait, she said, until they were both offered a position at the same place. God willing that would not be too long. She stamped her feet. The soles of her slippers drew the Arctic conditions like a magnet and inside them, her toes were pinched and tingling. She hugged her cloak more tightly around her shoulders. Only her red nose showed beneath the voluminous hood.

'I'll not stand for this much longer,' declared Dickie. There had been but one offer for his services, and even that had been withdrawn on hearing his Irish accent.

He was blowing on his hands and rubbing them together when a shifty-looking character caught his interest. The man was ogling a group of hopeful maids a short distance away. Dickie noticed as he approached them that each girl would shake her head. He watched alertly and slowly an idea began to form itself.

He suddenly turned to Sally. 'Look, I know we said we'd like to get a place together, but it looks like I'm being a burden to ye. No one wants to employ an Irishman, so if ye stick with me ye'll never get a job. I say, the next person that asks ye to go with them ye must take your chance. We could be standing here till next week if not.'

'But what about you?' she enquired worriedly, having no wish to leave her handsome partner now.

'Don't worry about me, I always land on me feet,' he promised. 'But I'll not have you standing here in this climate after ye've been so good to me.' At the very instant he spoke yet another person approached Sally. It must be her honest appearance, thought Dickie acidly.

She turned the job down. 'I'll wait,' she replied obstinately, and the man moved on.

'Look, ye can't go on like this.' Dickie bounced up and down on the spot to boost his circulation. 'Tell ye what, I'll do a bit o' touting meself, it'll do more good than stood here like a couple of icicles. That seems a smart-lookin' fella over there.' He pointed to the man he had been watching a few minutes earlier. 'Will I go over an' ask if

492

he's got a job for the pair of us? If I put on me best Yorkshire twang I think I can fix it.'

Sally was dubious. 'I don't like the look of him somehow. There's summat about him. He might be a villain.'

'Sure the cold's gone to your head! How can ye tell what he is when ye've never even spoken to the fella? I expected a more enlightened answer from a charitable person like yourself.' He saw her weaken. 'Let me try him at least,' he pressed. 'It's all right for you being choosey but I'm going to die if I stand here much longer.'

She was at once apologetic. 'Oh, I'm so selfish. I didn't spare a thought for you. You must be absolutely frozen with no coat. Go on then, ask him if yer like. It can't do no harm.'

'Good. If ye see me give this signal,' he held up crossed fingers, 'then ye'll know I've worked it. All right?'

Sally watched him force his way through the crowd towards the shifty-looking man. When he arrived he touched a finger to his forelock and inclined his head towards the man's ear. She tried to make out what he was saying, but Dickie's face was turned away from her. After some confabulation he sought her out with his eyes then held his fingers aloft in the specified signal. She primed herself, pulled her cloak tighter and struggled through the swelling ranks, being rudely pushed this way and that.

She paused to stand on tiptoe in order to see if she was moving in the right direction. There was the man waiting for her, but Dickie had momentarily disappeared. He must be somewhere near, though. She pressed on, finally reaching the place where he ought to be; but he wasn't. She looked startled as the man took her hand and threaded it through the hook of his arm. 'Where's Dickie?'

'Who? Oh, he's gone, has me laddo.' The man put his face close to hers, his reasty breath making her draw back. 'Away then, let's be off. Can't tarry here all day, we've a long way to go.'

'I'm not going anywhere without Dickie!' She shook him off, the panic rising, and tried to escape into the crowd, but it was too closely packed. He dashed after her and grabbed her cruelly, his eyes hard. 'What the hell d'yer think you're at?'

'I don't want to come with you!' She tried to wriggle free, twisting and turning in his brutal grip. 'I've changed my mind.'

'Nay, too late for that, m'dear,' he informed her bluntly. 'I've just paid seven bob for thee.'

CHAPTER FORTY

At this moment, Sally was the furthest person from Dickie's mind. After leaving her to her fate he had bought himself a second-hand topcoat and a bag of hot chestnuts and positioned himself at the far end of Parliament Street under the market bell, where he had shortly been approached by a man. Spotting the whip under Dickie's arm the man had asked if he was for hire. It transpired that the fellow's coachman had been taken ill and was unable to drive his master back to Leeds.

Though the elegant carriage and four greys were a little different from a horse and cart, Dickie had welcomed the chance to escape the marketplace, and was now rolling down the Mount towards Tadcaster Road feeling pretty smug at the way he was coping with the job. There was not much more to this than driving one nag.

'Whip them up, man!' bawled his passenger, Rycroft. 'We'll never reach Dringhouses at this rate.'

Before long they were out in open country. Dickie slapped the reins and the horses increased their speed, silver manes flowing over the lovingly-polished harness. Dickie grew over-confident and his mind began to wander. He thought of Dusty, of her dear laughing face, of her gentle bossing. What sort of marriage would theirs have been, he wondered. He felt her wild, springy hair in his fingers, her breath against his cheek, baby-sweet. Oh,

Dusty! There was a frightened whinny and one of the lead horses started to jump and buck in the traces. The rabbit which had caused it to shy vanished into the opposite hedgerow and the horse set off at full pelt, dragging its partners with it.

'*Whoa!*' Dickie hauled on the reins, bracing his boots against the footrest whilst trying to keep his balance. But this wasn't old Polly he was dealing with. The highly-strung greys, all four infected by the panic now, plunged down the narrow road at breakneck speed, totally ignoring his invocations.

'What the devil's going on?' shouted Rycroft, bouncing about inside the carriage. 'I meant to get there in one piece.'

Dickie heaved and cursed, but the horses charged on. They were coming up to a stiff bend. 'Stop! For Christ's sake, stop!' Dickie yelled and applied all his strength to the reins. The horses took the corner, but the carriage didn't. It careered, broadside on, its wheels shooting sparks, teetered for a couple of seconds, then crashed over onto its side, wheels still spinning.

Dickie was flung clear and landed in a frozen ditch. The horses galloped on up the road, dragging after them the clanking carriage shaft. Then, having run out their panic they stopped to nose at the frosty verge, their nervous sweat manifesting itself in great steaming clouds on the cold air.

Dickie dragged himself from the ditch in time to see his dazed passenger emerging from the upturned carriage, and began to walk towards him. 'Are ye all right, sir?'

Rycroft looked as if he were about to commit murder. He strode to meet Dickie, stooping to pick up the fallen whip on the way. 'You damned imbecile! I thought you said you could handle them.'

'Sure, it wasn't my fault.' Dickie rubbed at his bruised shoulder. '"Twas a rabbit what scared the horses.'

Rycroft advanced on him swinging the whip and beating him about the head and shoulders. 'Numskull! Dolt! Ninny! Buffoon! How am I going to get home now? Look!

Look at my carriage. I might have known something like this would come of hiring a damnfool Irishman. You're all the same – incompetent, addlebrained shirkers.' He beat time with the whip on Dickie's bent spine, then stepped back, panting. 'There's a farmhouse over there.' He pointed across a field. 'Go there and fetch all available hands forthwith and ropes with which to right the carriage.'

'Yes, sir,' said Dickie, and risked a glance from his crouched position. 'About my fee . . .'

'What!' The man laid into him again. 'You have the audacity to mention a fee for ruining my carriage? Get you gone before you forfeit more than your fee!'

Dickie lurched across the field as if making for the farm. But once on the other side he took the lane that ran behind it. That ungrateful bugger could drum up his own crew, for Dickie would be damned if he was wasting his time with no recompense at the end of it.

Towards evening he knocked on a farmhouse door and asked for a drink of water. 'My carriage has overturned a couple of miles back,' he told the farmer's wife. 'My coachman is staying with the team. I said I would press on and try to find myself lodgings. Unfortunately on my way here I was set upon by robbers who stole every penny I had. If you would be so kind as to spare me a sup of water to sustain my journey I would be eternally grateful to you.'

Inevitably he received the farmer's sympathy and was invited in for a meal and a bed for the night. The following day, bearing a napkin full of freshly-baked bread and a wedge of cheese, he set off looking for work, with the promise that he would repay their hospitality when he finally reached home.

It was another couple of days before he found means of earning himself a few shillings. By this time he was famished, so he would have taken on anything. It was the sound of the explosion that alerted him. Hearing it, he stepped up to a hedgerow, peered through its frost-furred spines and saw, away across the field, a group of navvies blasting their way into a hillside. Searching for a weak spot in the hawthorn he squeezed through and set off in the direction of the scene.

The foreman's ferret face sneered over him. 'An' why would I want to hire a ponce like you?' he asked inhospitably, leaning his tattooed forearm on the handle of a shovel.

'What's wrong with me?' Dickie wanted to know. 'If 'tis me face ye've taken a dislike to I'll not be workin' with that but me hands.'

'Let's see 'em then!' The other man held out a hand like a dinner-plate.

Dickie displayed upturned palms. 'Hah! Smooth as a babby's arse. Yer'll carry two bucketfuls o' muck then start whining about yer hands bein' sore.'

'I can take hard work!' Dickie started to strip off his coat and shirt, flexing lean but muscled arms.

The foreman, Standish, made a swift jab at Dickie's abdomen and the youth doubled over with a grunt of pain. Standish guffawed. 'I'd not give yer hundred to one in a lard competition. Still,' he rasped a hand over his unshaven jaw, 'I could use another pair of hands. I've lost three men this mornin'.'

Dickie paused in his dressing. 'Killed, ye mean?'

'Nah! Buggered off,' declared Standish. 'Couldn't stand the bloody pace, lazy sops. I don't suppose you'll last long either. Well, it's three bob a day. Now, see that baldy fella over there? Go see him an' he'll tell yer where to stick your rubble.'

Dickie was given a barrow and a shovel and sent into the winding intestines of the hill. His job was to scrape up the loose rock caused by the explosion and barrow it out. The first two trips, though hard work, were not too gruelling, but by the third barrowful Dickie was thinking that he might have made a mistake in leaving the road back there. By the sixth he felt as if his back was breaking and by the tenth he wished he was dead. Belying the cold weather, the sweat trickled down his dirt-caked forehead and into his eyes, stinging them into blurred pools as he strained under the weight of the rock-laden barrow. The journey to daylight was at a slight incline and his thigh muscles screamed their protest at the tortuous haul. The barrow wheel became wedged against a rock. He put his shoulder behind it and strained, his face screwed up with pain.

'Come on, Mary-Ellen!' Standish came strutting over. 'Don't be pullin' a face to mek it look as if yer workin'. Put some bloody muscle behind it.'

Dickie grunted and pushed. 'S'no good!' he gasped. 'Could ye just kick that rock out from under me wheel? I'll be able to manage then.'

'Me, lad?' Standish was affronted. 'I'm not 'ere to wipe your bloody arse. Now, get the bugger shifted.'

Dickie heaved once more, his hands juddering as though from a bad attack of nerves. The barrow keeled over, spilling out two hundredweight of rubble.

Standish leapt deftly out of its path and aimed a kick at Dickie who had collapsed with it. 'Yer useless, lazy pillock! Yer like a spare prick at a wedding. Gerrup an' start shovellin' that rubble back into barrow else your morning's wage goes up the creek.' He towered over the fallen youth, kicking him till he rose.

Dickie dragged himself upright, set the barrow straight and started to spade the rubble back in.

'I could do it quicker wi' a bloody teaspoon,' growled Standish. 'Come on, put some weight behind that shovel.'

'I'm doin' me best,' Dickie stopped to say.

Standish cuffed him. 'I've just had an example of your best – nearly broke me bleedin' foot. Now I'm gonna be watchin' you all day, an' every time I think you're slackin' tuppence o' your wage goes in my pocket. Yer'll be lucky if yer've a bob left at end o' day. Now get crackin'.'

After this Standish shadowed him all day, tongue-lashing and belittling. 'Who's carved his initial on yer bonce, then?' He prodded the L on Dickie's forehead. 'Yer fancy-man? The L must stand for Lucy, does it? Come on, Lucy, yer can shovel quicker than that. Mind yer don't get them pretty little hands dirty. Aw! diddums has cut his po' likkle finger. Eh, don't bend down lads,

Lucy's around. Whoops!' Dickie took it all, too weak to offer any form of resistance, even verbal. But at the end of the shift, with his hands torn to ribbons, unable to straighten his spine and every tendon of his body shrieking, he knew that if he stayed here he would be dead before he had a chance to make even one thousandth of his fortune.

He went off to look for his topcoat. Someone – it didn't take much guessing who – had tossed it into the latrine. It was beyond redemption. Wearily he limped off to join the queue for wages. While he waited he wondered what to do next. One thing was certain, he would not be undertaking any physical work for a while.

When it came to his turn to receive his pay Standish greeted him like a long-lost friend. 'Why, if it isn't Lucy Locket come for his money! Easiest day's pay he ever earned.'

Dickie grimaced. 'Aye, so easy ye'll not be seein' me tomorrow.'

Standish gave an ugly laugh. 'Ah, I said it'd be too much for yer. Well, Lucy,' he counted out the money, 'here's yer brass an' don't go spendin' it on owt naughty like beer or women – oh, I forgot – there's no danger o' that, is there, lads?' There were few laughs; no one liked the foreman.

Dickie stared down at the pittance on his bleeding palm. 'What d'ye call this?'

Standish bent forward. 'I can understand that an impoverished bugger like you might not have come across it afore, but that there, lad, is called money.'

'I meant,' snapped Dickie irritably, 'there seems to be some missing. Ye told me three bob.'

'I know what I told yer. I also told yer that every time I caught yer slackin' I'd dock tuppence.'

'On no occasion have ye caught me slacking, Standish . . .'

'Mr Standish to you,' growled the other.

'. . . I've been sweating my balls off all day . . .'

'Oh, I didn't think he had any, did you, lads?' came the smug reply.

'Are ye going to pay me my full wage?' persisted Dickie angrily.

Standish grinned. 'An' what are yer gonna do if I say no?'

Dickie glared at the sneering face. A quick glance around him told that he would get no support from his fellow workers. He pocketed the coins sullenly and began to move away.

'Eh, hang on, Lucy!' Standish called him back. 'Sign this little chitty to say yer've had yer brass.'

'But I haven't, have I?' replied Dickie.

'Sign it! The gaffer wants every penny accounted for. If yer can't write yer can put yer mark. Let's see, yer could put a little flower or a loveheart.'

'I can write!' Dickie snatched the stub of pencil and scribbled on Standish's form, then strode away rapidly.

Standish patted his pocket, his voice raised to cover the widening distance between them. 'Night, night, Lucy! I shall enjoy spendin' your wages tonight.' He dropped his grinning face to look at the form where Dickie had written his name, and his amusement paled to a puzzled gawp.

In very large, untidy lettering for all who followed to see was: HUGH CUNT.

He forsook the main road in favour of the fields and the little tracks that dissected them and travelled until dark when, unable to find any farm building or cottage at which to curry sustenance, he spent the night under a hedge. Hungry, worn-out and without his topcoat, he was in danger of succumbing to exposure. In the morning, long before the mist had lifted, he crawled from his insubstantial bed of crackling leaves and rags to set off down the track again, this time allowing it to lead him back to the road and a far-off cluster of buildings, just discernible through a quivering swathe of poplars.

He had been walking, or more correctly limping, for half an hour when the mist finally lifted and gave way to glorious and unexpected sunshine. He began to feel happier, even to the extent of pursing his lips into a tuneless whistle. There was a movement on the road ahead, far in front of him, as a vehicle trundled over the horizon. He shaded his eyes. It was going in the wrong direction, but perhaps the people on board might not be averse to his company, and there again, which way *was* the right way?

Carrying on towards it he was about to raise a hand in a friendly wave when suddenly the continued approach of the vehicle brought with it the dreadful realisation of what it actually was. He hurled himself over a drystone wall and made himself as small as possible, heart thumping as the wagonwheels ground nearer. The rumbling and clanking grew louder as the tinkers' caravan drew alongside, then began to recede as it continued along the road.

Dickie cautiously unwound his cramped body to peer over the top of the wall at the retreating wagon, then heaved a large sigh and sat back on his heels in relief. He brought up a hand to push back his hair, and jumped nervously as a movement caught his peripheral vision, relaxing when he recognised the movement was caused only by his shadow.

'I've heard the saying but never given it much credence before!'

His jolt was accompanied by a cry of alarm and he spun round to face the owner of the voice – but whether it was man or woman he could not decipher. The person making the observation was well past middle-age. The clothes were a man's – shabby, patched trousers, knee boots and a filthy, wine-coloured frockcoat – but the face belonged to a woman. It was smooth and round, the cheeks with the bloom of advancing years, her eyes like two periwinkles beneath a pork-pie hat.

'Whassat?' Dickie stared.

The other patiently repeated the statement. 'I said, I always thought it were only a saying – jumping at your own shadow – but I've just witnessed it with me own eyes. Somebody's got you real wound up I'd say.'

He relaxed a little then. "'Tis right y'are there, ma'am,' he paused for the objection to his premise of her gender and when none came pressed on. It *was* a woman after all – but as strange a one as he had ever seen. 'I was just keeping out o' the way o' them tinkers. I had a nasty bit o' truck with them lately, and I'd as soon not repeat the experience.' He held out his hand. 'Richard Feeney's the name. Dickie for short.'

'Victoria Hughes. Torie for short.' The woman had a surprisingly strong grip. 'Where're you heading?'

'Oh, nowhere in particular. I'll just go where the road takes me an' where I can find a job. Ye wouldn't be wantin' any work doin' in exchange for board an' lodgings, would ye?'

'I might.' She encompassed him with shrewd eyes. 'That depends on what sorta work you'd be willing to do.'

'Oh, I'm a strong worker, ma'am! Ye knew where they're laying the railway over yonder? Well, I been workin' there for six weeks now. But the thing is see, they're cutting down on labour an' I was forced to quit.'

'You're sure it wasn't for any other reason?' asked Torie, viewing him strangely.

'What other reason could there be? I wouldn't attempt to kid ye, ma'am. Wherever I've worked I've always had the best references.'

'And you got on with your fellow workers?'

'Like bees and honey, ma'am. The foreman and me were like twins – in fact I'll bet he's still shedding tears over the way I had to leave him.'

She made a noise in her throat. 'So, when did you leave the diggings, then?'

'Yesterday evening.'

'And what have you been doing since then?'

He flung his arm in a random direction. 'There was a farm a few miles back. They let me stay the night but there was no work, see.'

She made the noise in her throat again. 'Have you ever worked with animals?'

'Yes.'

'Cows?'

'Yes.'

'And you don't mind hard work?'

'I thrive on it.'

'Right! Come along then.' Torie set off at a march across the field of turnips, the tattered frockcoat flapping around the calves of her boots. Dickie ran to catch her up, loping along beside her. 'How much does the gaffer pay, if ye don't mind me askin'?'

'That depends on what she thinks you're worth,' replied Torie.

'She?'

'I'm the gaffer, lad. There's only me you have to please.'

'What about your family?' he asked.

'Have none. Leastwise, not now. Lost 'em all in one fell swoop. Husband and three sons. Fever.'

'I'm sorry.'

'No, you're not. You didn't know them, so what call have you got to be sorry?' He gave a shrug. 'Wasn't out here they caught it, mind,' she added. 'We never see nobody from one week to the next out here. No, they went along to the market as per usual to sell some cattle. Stopped the night at a lodging house, thought they'd have a bit of fun before they came back to my nagging. Couple o' weeks later they were all dead, every one.'

Dickie looked around to see where her home might be but failed to spot anything. 'Looks like we're in the same boat; I'm all alone too. How do ye manage on your own? Is it a big place ye've got?'

'Middling. That's it over there on that hill.'

Dickie strained his eyes. He could see the hill with something on it that could have been a house but he could not tell from this distance.

'But that's miles off!'

She dismissed his concern with a flap of her hand. 'Nah! We'll be there in half an hour.'

His body groaned. When he had met her by the road he had assumed that she lived somewhere nearby and said as much.

'Been to see my neighbour,' she explained. 'He's getting on a bit. I call every morning to see he's all right. Come on now, stop dawdling, there's work waiting!'

It was all he could do to keep up with her. He felt as though he had walked ten miles. 'Don't tell me ye have to slog up and down here every day?' he puffed when they finally reached the top of the hill.

'You get used to it. Best place for a house I reckon. I miss nowt up here. Anyways, I thought you were supposed to be fit?' She took the last few steps to her back door and opened it. Dickie, some yards behind, paused to catch his breath, then dragged himself to the doorway and went in after her.

The kitchen was like a menagerie. Torie was surrounded by cats which jostled to arch against her boots, tails held high. There were ginger tabbies, grey tabbies, blacks, whites, tortoiseshells leaping from their comfortable seats to see what Mistress had to offer. Perched on the dresser and the table, trying to find a foothold between the stacks of screwed-up paper and stale food, was an assortment of hens. Torie, still enmeshed in a slinky tangle of feline adoration, paced slowly over to the hearth rug where lay the motionless form of a huge grey cat. She stooped over it and curved her fingers round its chest.

Dickie's eyes darted round the kitchen. It was strewn with clutter. Every available surface was coated with hen-droppings and pieces of bacon rind which the well-fed cats had scorned, stale bread, congealing pools of spilt milk, feathers. The inglenook was two inches deep in ashes. Living here, he decided, would be like living in a midden. But there seemed little choice open to him at the moment. Certainly he was not going to attempt walking back down that hill until he had had a decent night's rest and a good meal.

'She's dead.' Torie looked up from the hearth rug whose colours had been lost beneath the layers of grease and cat-hair. 'Old Spittler.'

'Have ye had her a long time?' asked Dickie without interest.

'Ten years, but she was much older. Found her half-dead in the yard. Been scrapping with a fox what had tried to take her kits. Half o' those are hers.' The sons and daughters of the old cat resumed their positions and observed the scene with dead-pan green eyes. Torie ran her hand over the grey fur; there was no answering purr.

'Have ye no dogs?' Dickie scooped a cat from a spindled chair and took its place. 'I would've thought ye coulda done with one, living here on your own.'

'Can't stand 'em!' spat Torie, inserting her hands under the limp body and lifting it gently. 'Fawning, lickspittle creatures. Anyway, I can look after myself well enough. Right now, you can start your employment by going out and giving her a proper burial.' She extended her arms bearing the floppy corpse.

'Jazers, can't it wait till I've got me breath back?' he pleaded.

'No,' came the flat reply. 'And that's the first and last time you'll use the Lord's name in vain in my house. I don't hold with such talk. This is a Christian household. Now, behind the barn you'll find a row of graves. Dig another – and make it deep enough; I don't want no mangy fox coming and digging up my Old Spittler. When you come back I'll have a pot of tea ready.'

Dickie exhaled impatiently but did as he was ordered. He had assumed Torie to be a soft touch; a woman on her own. How wrong could one be?

When he returned there was a mug of tea awaiting him. 'Have you done it proper?' Torie enquired.

'I have.' He pulled out a wooden stool and sat down. 'I even made a little cross out of twigs like the others have. Does that please ye?' He reached into his pocket for his pipe.

'It's no more than I'd expect – and you can put that away too!' She pointed to the pipe. 'I don't hold with filthy habits neither.' She went to the door and opened it. 'I'll go and inspect your work. I daresay you'll have finished your tea by the time I get back.'

505

'Don't ye trust me, then?' He sipped the scalding tea as she turned on the threshold.

She gave him one of her strange looks and went out. Dickie's stomach juices sizzled acidly and he looked around for something to eat. Pushing himself from the chair he sauntered over to the dresser and scattered the clucking hens. 'What sorta place is this?' he mumbled to himself, sweeping the rubbish onto the floor. 'I've been in some holes in my time but this beats all.' There was a biscuit barrel on the shelf; as it was the only thing pertaining to food he lifted it down. He inserted his hand – but instead of the crisp feel of shortbread his fingers encountered something cold and hard. He withdrew them quickly and peered into the barrel. It was almost full of gold and silver coins.

It took him only a few seconds to recover from his pleasant shock. When he did he began to pour the money into his pockets as fast as he could. Before Torie came back he would be gone. With the biscuit barrel empty and his pockets weighing heavily he turned to go. But something stopped him in his tracks – a small black hole aimed directly between his eyes.

CHAPTER FORTY-ONE

'I thought that might be your little game!' Torie squinted down the barrel of the ancient musket, her finger curled around the trigger.

Dickie swallowed, took a step backward and gripped the edges of the dresser. 'That's some gun ye've got there, Torie. I've never seen one like that before. Very old, I'd say.'

'If you're asking does it work – just walk over to that door and see how far you get.'

'I'd rather not.'

'Then just put my money back where it belongs,' she said menacingly.

'I wasn't stealing it.' He hurriedly tipped the coins back into the biscuit barrel.

'No, I know – you were just taking it down to the river to wash it,' she answered scathingly as he threw in the last coin. 'Now turn out your breeches pockets too.'

He pulled out a handkerchief and the money that he had earned yesterday. 'This is mine; it's what I got from the diggings.'

'I don't believe you, put it back!'

He defied her withering scrutiny. 'But 'tis mine I tell ye!'

She cocked the gun. '*Put – it – back.*'

Sullenly he threw the florin and pennies into the jar. 'All right! But I still say 'tis mine an' I worked bloody hard for that.'

'One more curse and I'll rip your tongue out! I'll have you know I worked hard for that money you were about to steal. I don't want no dirty little thief working for me. You can get out.'

'Call me a thief!' he threw at her in desperation. 'Why, you're as bad, taking my money and throwing me out tired and hungry. Call yourself a Christian?'

The gun wavered. His mouth went dry as Torie continued to hold him in her sights for what seemed like an age. Then she uncocked the gun and set it down. 'You're right – wouldn't be a very Christian thing to do, even to a thief.'

'I'm not really a thief, Torie.' He watched her put the gun in a corner, the saliva beginning to rush back into his mouth. 'S'just that when I saw all that money I sorta lost me head. I thought – sure, what does Torie want with all that money and her no one to spend it on, and there's me poor ould mam at home, bedridden, living the life of a pauper. The things I could buy her with that money . . .' his voice trailed away wistfully.

'Where does your mother live?' asked Torie distrustfully.

507

'Leeds. I couldn't get a job there that paid enough to keep us so I've been navvying like I told ye.'

'Aye, an' you also told me that you were all alone.'

Damn! He had slipped up there – that was most unlike him. It must have been that gun. 'I meant I was travelling alone,' he said hurriedly. 'That's all.' Torie fixed him with a cockatrice eye but said nothing. He stared back at her, wondering what lay behind that pensive squint. 'What're ye going to do?' he ventured, when her silence grew too much to bear.

'I don't know,' she answered ruminatively. 'I haven't decided yet.'

He used her indecision to his advantage. 'Torie, if ye keep me on I promise I'll never try anything like that again. I don't know what came over me. It must've been the thought of me poor ould mam, starving, that overcame my normal honesty. But say, you're not the kind to go round shootin' folks, Torie. I'll stake my life that the gun wasn't even loaded.'

She thrust out her lower lip noncommittally, then turned abruptly and shuffled over to retrieve the gun. She picked it up in her right hand, her index finger stroking the trigger, and pointed it calmly at the ceiling.

There was a snowstorm of plaster, coinciding with an earth-shattering bang. The livestock scattered in a rush of fur and feathers. 'Does that answer your question?' she asked pleasantly, and propped the gun back in its corner. 'There's a lesson in the imprudence of gambling, son. Never stake anything on what Torie might or might not do – especially your life.' She moved to the dresser where she rummaged noisily in the cutlery drawer. 'But, all said, happen I might give you a second chance. Though you'll have to prove your worth if you're to work here. I want no namby-pamby dealings but an honest day's toil.'

Dickie, though his ears still rang and his face was bloodless, moved into action. 'Ah, God love ye, Torie! I knew ye were a charitable body an' wouldn't turn a fella out because o' one slip. I'll do anything. Anything. Just name it.'

She found what she had been looking for in the drawer and shuffled back up to him. 'You'd likely see the pigsty when you went to bury Old Spittler?'

His heart sank, but he nodded eagerly. 'I did. Will ye be wanting it cleaned out?' Back to shovelling shit, he thought dismally. What a let-down.

But she shook her head. 'That was done this morning. It's the pig that needs attention.' She made a swift movement and the knife clattered onto the table, sending the hens jumping. 'Go kill it.'

He gave a disbelieving laugh. 'I can't do that!'

'Why not? Is it too much for you to stomach?'

'Well, no but . . . I've never done it before, ye see. I'm not sure . . .'

'Don't you want to stay here, then?'

'Of course I do.'

She picked up the knife and pressed the handle into his hand. 'Then go out and do as you're bid, then when I see what sort of job you make of it I'll decide whether or not to overlook your dishonesty.' She scattered the hens from the table and began to slice some carrots into a cooking-pot. 'Take that there pot with you to catch the blood. When you've done we'll have some dinner – if you've still got an appetite.'

Dickie looked down at the knife in his hand, swallowed, then reluctantly turned and went outside to find the pigsty. It was still perilously cold. He reached the pigsty; it had split doors. He stared at them for a second, then unlatched the top half to peer inside. Out of the straw rose the biggest pig he had ever seen. It sniffed the air suspiciously, sitting on its haunches like a large pink toad, and skewered him with pink-rimmed eyes. He crossed himself, tested the sharpness of the knife on his thumb, then unbolted the bottom half of the door.

The pig raised itself and began to shamble about, swishing idly through its bedding. 'There's a good piggy,' he murmured, edging towards it, knife-hand outstretched. The pig watched him get nearer, then moved slowly out of reach into a corner. Dickie pursued it doggedly, pushing the pot along the floor with his foot. 'Go-od piggy.' The pig allowed him to touch a hand to its head. It sat there like a dog while his fingers slipped behind its ear, scratching, and the other surreptitiously brought the knife under its chin. The point was almost touching ... just a wee bit closer ... nearly there ... and – the pig was on him, biting and slashing with sabre-like tushes at the arms that had flown up to protect his face. The knife had gone, lost somewhere in the straw, so he had nothing with which to protect himself. The pig's diamond-hard trotters pounded at his chest, rolling him this way and that in the dung-fouled straw. His legs scrabbled and lashed out at the pink belly, trying to escape those wicked fangs. Its stinking breath was hot on his face. He saw those evil, salivating jaws bearing down on him ... Oh, God he was done for ... he felt them crushing his bones ...

'All right, Percy, that's enough!' Torie waded in, swinging her besom down upon the wide body. 'Back! Back, I said!' She beat the pig about the head until he retreated grunting and grumbling into a corner to watch maliciously as his victim scrambled to his feet and was out of the pigsty like a tautly-coiled spring.

'Mother o' Christ, Torie!' he panted, displaying his badly-gashed arms. 'I coulda been kilt!'

'Nay!' She laughed uproariously and bolted the sty door. 'I was watching all the time. Ready, in case Percy got carried away.'

'Ye were there? Well, why didn't ye come in sooner?' He sank to the grass, cold as it was, and rolled about in agony. 'Oh, Jazers, I'm dyin'!' She brought the broom down on his elbow and he howled louder. 'What was that for?'

'I've told you about blaspheming! I let the other one go unpunished but don't imagine you'll get away with any more.'

'You're a wicked woman, Torie.' He held up his slashed arms. 'Please, help me, I'm bleedin' to death.'

'Don't make such a meal of it, it's nobbut a scratch.' She hauled him to his feet and took him into the house

510

where she set about cleaning the bites on his arms, rubbing in some pungent-smelling ointment that made him dance about. When she had bandaged him up and poured the bloody water into the yard he asked, 'Torie, have ye anything I could wear? My clothes are covered in pig muck.'

'Tsk! A bit o' good manure never hurt no one. You're too soft, my lad. A townie through and through. Oh well, I daresay I could find something.' She rifled another drawer and came up with a pair of trousers and a shirt. 'Try those on, though I don't suppose they'll fit – you're a big lad. How old are you?'

'Eighteen, nearly nineteen.'

'Oh, I'd've taken you for older if you weren't so green.'

He took the clothes from her. 'Where shall I . . . ?'

'Pooh! Proper shrinking violet now, aren't we? Oh, go on upstairs if you must – but don't you dare touch so much as a pin, mindst!'

When he came down she laughed heartily at his appearance; the trousers flapped halfway up his calves. 'Oh well, they'll do 'til I get your own washed. Give us 'em here!' She snatched the bundle of dirty clothes and thrust them into the copper. 'Now, sit down if your hands are clean. Let me see.' She caught hold of his arm and inspected his upturned palms. 'Filthy! Go stick them under pump.'

After washing his hands in the freezing cold water he sat down at the table. 'I'm sorry I didn't sort the pig, Torie. I don't suppose ye'll be keeping me on now?'

She guffawed and leaned over a steaming cooking-pot. 'My life! You didn't think I meant it, did you? I knew you'd never get near Percy in a month o' Sundays. A prize boar like him isn't for bacon, laddie. He earns his keep in a different fashion.'

He didn't understand. 'Then why . . . ?'

She turned a grinning face on him. 'Retribution.'

'For thinking to steal your money? I did apologise for that, Torie,' he looked reproachful. 'I mean to say . . .'

'I don't think you know what you do mean to say, lad,'

511

she cut in sharply. 'You tell that many lies you don't know what the truth sounds like any more.'

'Lies?'

'Yes, lies! Thou Shalt Not Bear False Witness. You've got to learn that in this house lies don't go unpunished – nor any other broken Commandment.'

'But what lies have I told?' he objected.

'Almost everything you've said since you came into this house has been lies.'

'No, it hasn't.'

'That's another!'

''Tis not!'

Torie spread the fingers of her left hand and counted off the untruths with her right. 'Lie number one: you said you'd spent last night at a farmhouse a few miles back. There isn't one farm nor cottage on the road that you'd've taken from the diggings.'

'I didn't take the road, I came over the fields!'

'Lie number two: you haven't been navvying for six weeks like you told me. If you'd been working the diggings that long them hands'd be hard as nails, apart from which I happen to know that you were only set on yesterday morning.' His jaw dropped as she went on. 'Lie number three was the one about your poor old mother when you'd all but told me you were an orphan. Are there any more you'd like to get off your chest while you have the chance?'

He was amazed, mostly at how she could possibly have known he only signed on at the railway cuttings yesterday, when she lived so far from anywhere.

Torie smiled wickedly and crooked a finger, beckoning him over to the window. She handed him a heavy brass spyglass. 'Fix your peeper to that.'

He swung the telescope slowly over the landscape – then back quickly as a familiar figure blocked the aperture. The magnification was tremendous, he could make out every gesture that Standish made as he swore and drove the navvies to work.

Torie gave a knowing smirk as he lowered the telescope in disbelief. 'He really didn't like you very much, did he, that old weasel-face. Well, I shouldn't take it too much to heart; he's like it with most people. I could've put my boot up his backside many a time for treating folk like dirt.' She took the spyglass from Dickie and put it to her own eye, talking from the side of her mouth. 'It's amazing what you can see through this. Wouldn't be without it. Spend hours every day watching people that don't realise they're being watched.' She lowered it and replaced it on the windowsill. 'So, now you know how I saw through all your lies; I've had my eye on you since yesterday. Good worker you said? Tut, tut!'

He shook his head, the beginnings of a smile in his eyes. 'But if ye knew I was givin' ye a load o' coddum why did ye bring me here in the first place?'

'Now that I can't answer.' Torie scratched her head and went to search out two sets of cutlery. 'Happen I felt sorry for you – leastwise I did 'till you pocketed my life-savings.'

He hung his head and observed her beseechingly through the curly forelock that had tumbled over his brow. 'I didn't mean it. Honest. It was just the sight of all that money.'

'Well, God be praised! The boy's got a whole sentence out without lying.'

He gave a scandalised laugh. 'So, ye got your own back with the pig? Why, you wicked old . . . I coulda been torn to pieces in there.'

'And serve you right.' She began to ladle stew onto two plates. 'Now we both know where we stand I don't need to expect any more hanky-panky do I?'

'Chr . . .' he saw the warning look on Torie's face and changed his comment to 'Crumbs! Ye mean I can stay?'

'For a while.' She sat opposite and clasped her hands. 'Dear God, we give Thee thanks for the meal Thou hast provided.' She pushed a plate of bread at him. 'Aye, you can stay – but it might not be for long. I'm getting on a bit. Fifty-six. That's the main reason I brought you here. Wouldn't like to think I might die all of a sudden and have no one to tend my animals.'

A lump of potato dropped from his fork and splattered

gravy onto the borrowed shirt. He wiped it and did a quick mental calculation. This could be his El Dorado. Torie had no family; if he got well in, gained her trust, it just might be that she would leave everything to him as Mr Penny had done Mother. The only snag being that Torie could live another thirty years with her spirit; he couldn't face that long away from civilisation. But all said, she was a clever old stick. He admired the way she had got the better of him, and his stay here would at least be entertaining.

'Do you think you can manage it?' she asked, chewing. 'Or more relevantly, can you be *trusted* to do it?'

'I think so,' he told her. 'As long as ye've no more Percys tucked up your sleeve.'

She smiled. 'No, it's mainly the land I'll be needing you for. S'too much for me now. Can't handle the plough like I used to. I can't bear to see it choked with weeds. And I'll need the cow milking – I only keep the one now. I get this queer tingling in my fingers, they go all numb when it isn't even cold. Can't feel what I'm doing with 'em. The cow doesn't think much of it either. Your soft townie hands should be just up her street. In return you'll get good wholesome meals and two shillings per week.'

'Two shillings!' he cried. 'Oh, Torie, that's a bit stingy isn't it? I mean, there's me poor ould mother to consider.'

She eyed him sharply, then saw the twinkle in his eye. 'Tell me, have you really got a mother somewhere?'

'I have – and a father and brother and a sister.' And a couple of children somewhere, he reflected.

'I'll ask you to tell me more later,' said his host, finishing her meal and leaning back in her chair. 'But right now I've a few jobs I'd like you to do.'

'What did your last slave die of, Torie?' But there was no malice in his comment.

In the evening, when the pigsty and byre were locked up for the night and a candle glowed on the still-cluttered table, Dickie told the widow all about himself, withholding those parts which he thought might be detrimental to her hostelry. After unburdening himself he asked, 'Enough o' the jawing. Have ye any cards, Torie?'

'Cards?' she answered spikily. 'Cards? I don't have none o' that Devil's recreation in my house.'

He sighed and crossed his ankles before the radiant peat fire. 'What *do* ye do for pleasure then, Torie?'

'I read,' she provided, rising to lift a heavy Bible from a shelf. 'And that's what you'll do if you're to stay here. If you ask me you could do with a few examples from the Good Book.' She laid it open on the table and moved the candle closer. 'Come on!' she gestured to Dickie.

'Me?' He fingered his chest.

'Well, unless there's some miracle taken place the cats can't read. Your eyes are younger than mine. Come on, boy, stir yourself! Chapter twelve of this page, verse seventeen.' She pointed a yellow-nailed finger at the passage.

Dickie's thick eyebrows came together as he struggled over the tiny print and began to read falteringly. 'He who speaks the truth gives honest ev ... ev ...'

'Evidence,' she prompted.

'... evidence, but a false witness utters deceit. There is one whose rash words are like sw ... sword ...'

'Sword,' she pronounced correctly.

'... sword thrusts but the tongyew ...'

'Tongue,' she interrupted his stilted narrative yet again.

'... tongue of the wise brings healing. Tru ... truth ...'

'Truthful lips endure forever but a lying tongue is but for the moment.'

He voiced his irritation. 'If ye know it off by heart why do I have to read it?'

''Cause I like to hear it,' said Torie simply. 'And who knows, after a couple of repetitions it might just sink in.'

CHAPTER FORTY-TWO

If Thomasin and Patrick could have seen their son at this
time they would never have recognised him. He rose at
five to milk the cow before breakfast, then went on to
tackle all the repair jobs, of which there were many.
Though Torie was a tough old bird she was no carpenter
and the outbuildings had been left to rot. With the demise
of her family Torie had sold three hundred acres of her
land – there was no way a woman on her own could work
it – but even the two, twenty-acre fields which she had
kept for herself had been allowed to run rampant, and
Dickie's intention to bring every inch of soil back to
profitable use was an ambitious project. However, he set
to work with borrowed horse and plough, amazing himself
with his discovered virtuosity. He was even more surprised
to find that he was actually happy and made more so when
he found out that one of his worst fears was not to be
realised. Torie, though deeply religious, did not hold with
churches – 'Heathen places' she called them. So, thankfully he would not have to face the fifteen-mile trek to the
nearest place of worship every Sunday.

Of course, had she wished it he would have gone. There
was no sense in antagonising the old girl over such a
meaningless item as religion. Indeed, every one of Torie's
wishes was carried out with conscientious aptitude. The
only job he would on no account tackle, even at the
expense of risking Torie's displeasure, was cleaning out
the pig.

The fact that he only earned a florin per week for all
this work did not seem half so important as it had done.
He was so tired after his day's toil that he would fall asleep
immediately after supper, so there was hardly any time in

which to spend it. Torie usually had a struggle to wake him in order to read her a passage from the Bible.

Despite all this, he had not completely forsaken his old pursuits. On the one day a week when he tramped the fifteen miles to the nearest village to attend the market, he usually managed to summon the energy with which to partake of a dainty morsel. Well, he had to do something to make Torie's harsh standards bearable.

All in all it was a demanding life, but with his sights set on the contents of the biscuit barrel and the unspoken promise of the farm on Torie's death, he was sure he could bear it. Wasn't he working towards his fortune?

The seasons rotated. A year, eighteen months passed. They grew accustomed to each other, he to her Bible-strict living, she to his habitual tall stories – on hearing one she only had to mouth the word 'Percy' and he would quickly recant. And never once did he lift the lid from that biscuit barrel.

Now, Dickie laid his face against the cow's smooth, warm flank, dreaming of his last conquest as he gripped the teats and squeezed. Apart from that one day per week he had to suffice with dreams now. Such sacrifice would never have been imagined in the old days. Unused to such celibacy he frequently rebelled and swore that this was definitely the last time he was mucking out the byre, and that tomorrow he would be off to find himself a more accommodating landlady. But the vision of that money was invariably stronger than those of bodily needs and his threats remained unfulfilled.

The cow lowed mournfully, lancing his thoughts. There was nothing happening. He inclined his head towards the cow's ruminous gaze. 'What's up, coween, aren't I doing it right for ye?' The cow swung her head round to the manger, snatched a mouthful of hay, then fixed him again with baleful eyes. 'Come on, Tilly, I've no time for shenanigans tonight.' He replaced his cheek against her warmth and squeezed again. There was the sharp ping of milk hitting the bucket. He smiled, closed his eyes and began to tug mechanically, sinking back into his dreams. He had not known her name but boy! had she known how to jig-a-jig. He hoped she'd be there again tomorrow when he went to market. Yet even as he thought of the girl her face metamorphosed to Dusty's; his dear, plain, bossy girl. Likely by now she would have married someone else. The thought made him angry, mainly at himself. To have a prize like that and lose it for a slut like Peggy was sheer idiocy. He suddenly realised he was once again pulling on empty teats and groaned. Straightening his spine he peered under the cow. 'What! Half a bucket, is that all ye can do? Sure ye won't half be in for it when I tell madam. Let's try the others.' He changed teats but apart from a token trickle there was nothing.

It was then that he noticed the sore on his wrist. As he reached down for the bucket it peeped out from the cuff of his shirt. He examined it closely, feeling a cold hand clutch at his guts. It looked like an erupted blister, large and angry. He had seen something like that before. Something he had hoped never to see on his own flesh.

'Oh, Christ!' he whispered. 'Oh, Mother o' God, tell me I'm mistaken.' He stared at the mark, then slowly pulled up his sleeve. There were two more. He could not snap his eyes away from them. His heart thudded. The filthy bitch! The filthy, pox-ridden bitch. He pulled down his sleeve to cover them, then, as if hoping that the act had made them disappear, pulled it up again to inspect the arm. They were still there, of course. Consumed by fear he stood up quickly, accidentally kicking over the bucket, and swore, but made no move to stop the precious milk from seeping into the straw. Then he draped his arms over the cow's bony back and buried his face in her red hide. 'Oh, sweet Jesus tell me what to do.'

He was in this same pose when Torie entered the byre. 'What's keeping you, lad? Away now, your supper'll get cold else.'

He stooped quickly to pick up the fallen bucket, as he did so tugging down his sleeve to hide the tell-tale sores. 'The cow's gone dry,' he said dully, his back to her. 'Will I take her to be served?'

She came alongside and ran her hand over the cow's white-flecked hide. 'No, she's too old for breeding now, aren't you, Tilly? We're two of a kind her and me. It'll break my heart to part with her but I'm not wrowt o' brass. I can't be payin' thee to grow fodder for t'winter and getting no return. You'd best take her to market tomorrow. We'll have to make do with what bit o' milk we've got.'

'Will I buy us another while I'm at the market?'

'You will not! I'd not trust you to buy a bucket o' water. Them's fiddling demons at that market; put rouge on the udder so's it looks nice and plump then when you get home all you got's a bag full o' wind. No, I'll go meself to Turner's place next week an' see if he's got anything. Come on now, let's get them boggles locked out and take our sup.'

'I'll just wash me hands.' He paused at the pump. She made to work it for him but he refused her help tonight and watched her go in before he rolled up his sleeves. They were still there.

He took similar care at the table, dropping his hands to his lap between each mouthful, though he did not actually feel like eating at all. What the deuce could he do? He had heard it went away for a spell and you were lulled into thinking it was cured, but there was no cure that he knew of. It eventually sank its claws into your brain and all but tore it out, reducing a once-virile man into a slobbering lunatic. He shuddered.

'What's up with you tonight, lad?' Torie leaned across the table and prodded him with her fork. 'Just 'cause the cow's gone dry ain't no call for long faces.' He was usually full of himself at this hour of the day, when all his work was done, and though she found his humour a bit on the bawdy side she had grown very, very fond of him.

He jumped and slid a hurried forkful into his mouth. 'Sorry, Torie. I was just thinking ... oh, nothin' in particular; just what they might be doing at home.'

She filled her mouth with vegetables, to cover her dismay. 'You're not going to tell poor Torie you're leaving her? Not after all this time?'

He produced a strained smile. 'Leave me favourite girl? Ye must be joking.' Then his frown returned. 'I can't help wondering about them, that's all.' Will I ever see any of them again? he wondered hazily.

'You'll go back someday then?'

'Probably.' He sawed at his mutton. 'When I'm rich enough to stop them ordering me about.'

'Takes more than money, lad,' Torie told him. 'Experience, that's what counts. Anyway, where d'you suppose you'll be making this fortune? I hope you haven't got your eye on my savings again.' Her voice was hard but he had known her long enough to interpret that spark in her eye. She knew very well why he stayed with her, and did not mind in the least. 'I'll wager the minute I'm dead you'll ... hey, what's that?' Her hand shot out and grasped his own, making him drop his fork. She tugged it up to her face in order to examine the sore that had caught her eye. His heart turned a somersault. What would be Torie's Old Testament retribution for this unspeakable sin? Would she cast him out, making all his work in vain? Christ, what was he talking about? It was already in vain. He would probably not live to spend it. He gulped and awaited his fate.

'Have to see to that after supper,' she grunted and dropped his hand to resume her meal.

'Ye mean ... ye mean ye know how to cure it?' he hardly dared to hope.

'S'only cowpox, lad, not Black Death. You been rubbing noses with Tilly each and every day, what else did you expect?'

'Cowpox!' he almost shouted, then laughed out loud and sprang up, grabbing Torie's arm and lifting her from her seat.

'You soft dunnock, what're you playing at?' She lost her fork and slapped at him. 'Put me down!'

'Ah, Torie, you're a miracle-worker.' He swung her round the litter-strewn kitchen in vast relief. 'Ye oughta have yourself more fun, ye know. 'Tis no life ye lead all alone here. Here – let me teach ye how to dance.' He set

520

her down and clasped her around the waist with one long arm, demonstrating with his feet. Unfortunately, when he whisked her past the window his elbow caught the telescope and dashed it to the ground.

'Wisht!' She pushed herself free. 'Now look what you've done! The glass is cracked. You'll have to take it to get mended tomorrow – and you're paying for it, mind. And will you stop all that cavorting. I've told you I'll have none o' your heathen ways in this house. Go draw me some water to wash these plates.' She tutted once more at the broken spyglass and laid it aside.

'Work, work, work! That's all you ever think about, Torie.' He danced along beside her as she fought her way to the sink, his eyes twinkling. 'Ye know what you are, don't ye? You're an old tyrant; but ye've just made me the happiest fella in the whole bloody world – an' that's swearing for ye. Go on, clout me, I don't care, nothing ye could do would upset me tonight. An' d'ye know another thing?' He crushed her frail body against his, ignoring her protests to plant a smacking kiss on her cheek. 'I love you, Torie Hughes – will ye marry me?'

Torie watched the pair of them set off down the hill, the youth and the cow, and experienced something she had not felt in years; the something which her own sons had evoked. Though her voice was sharp her periwinkle eyes had a maternal shine to them. 'And don't be coming home with a handful o' beans in exchange for the cow!' she bawled after him. 'I've heard enough o' your fairy stories without getting a beanstalk in my garden.'

He laughed heartily and flung over his shoulder: 'Sure, what giant would be fool enough to climb down into your garden? He'd want his head seeing! Come on, Tilly!' He tugged at the cow's halter. 'I know you're in no hurry to get there but I am. Now that I know me rod an' tackle's in fine working order I can't wait to catch meself a pretty little minnow.'

At the halfway stage he employed a milestone to take the weight off his feet while the cow took the opportunity to graze. 'Aye, you do that,' he told her, his words emerging on a cloud of tobacco-smoke. 'Poor bugger, ye'll not be getting much o' that where you're going.'

After ten minutes' rest he was sufficiently revived to continue his journey and, walking as briskly as the cow would allow, eventually reached the village. He took no time at all to complete the main business, his slick tongue – a little rouge and a bucketful of milk pinched from someone else's cow – earning him much more than Torie had expected for the beast. But instead of spending it all on himself as he might once have done, he decided to use some of it to buy Torie a present, if only for the good news she had given him last night. Cowpox! Jaze, he had been laughing about it all night. Now, what could he buy her? She didn't go in for ornamentation or gewgaws. He passed a stall selling confectionery and back-tracked to it. If Torie had one weakness it was her sweet tooth – what was left of it; he doubted she had an undecayed tooth in her head. Purchasing a quarter-pound of the bull's eyes he pressed on, keeping his eyes peeled for a mate.

When the hour came around when the market traders began to pack away their unsold wares he had imbibed several quarts of ale, had purchased a pair of woollen stockings to go with Torie's sweets and had tested his 'tackle' successfully three times.

He whistled all the way home, grinning at himself for the way he regarded Torie's home as his. It was a fact that he felt more at home with her than he had ever done with his own parents. Very odd indeed, for she was a stubborn old cuss and kept an even stricter control over him than they had done. But something in her makeup – perhaps it was the way she always got the better of him – had earned his grudging affection, and it was probable that he thought as much about Torie as he had ever done about anyone. Gob, she was a funny old bird and no mistake. But she had treated him as he imagined she would one of her own, and last night when he had jokingly said he loved her it wasn't so far from the truth.

In the time it took him to reach the foot of the hill the

sun had turned to orange and his rumbling guts told him it was nearly time for supper. He fingered the stockings in his pocket and wondered what Biblical anecdote Torie would dish out at his choice of gift. She would likely think the stockings much too familiar a present. He was sure she wouldn't refuse the bull's eyes, though. The thought brought a smile with it.

His giant strides had eaten up most of the slope – he was pretty fit these days – and had just taken him through the lengthening shadows towards the back of the house, when he heard the grunts and scuffles. His primary reaction was – Christ! the pig's got out and killed her! But when he reached the corner of the wall and peeped cautiously round it he saw that it was not Percy who was attacking Torie but two men; looming shadows against the burnished sky, punching and slapping her about the face and body. The grunts were coming from Torie as each vicious punch forced the breath from her. His immediate reflex was to slip back out of sight.

'Where is it, damn you?' One of the shadows put his fingers round her throat and shook it. 'We know on good authority you got money here some place.' He slapped her twice across the face.

Dickie's hand flew to his own face as Torie's lip burst open under the assault, but much as he felt he should help her he could not move.

'There's nowt here! I'm a poor widow woman!' screamed Torie, fighting his grip. 'Do I look like I've got money?'

'You can't bluff me, you old crow,' growled the man holding her throat.

'I don't know who told you I had money, but he's lying,' came the strangled reply. 'Not here anyway – it's all in the bank. You'd best be gone before my lad gets home. He's twice the size o' you two. He'll kill you for what you're doing to me.' Behind the wall Dickie cringed in fear and self-abasement. She had said that about him, and here he was letting those men hit her.

'I'll ask you one more time, missus!' The man tightened his grip and hauled her face close to his. 'Where is it?'

Torie's answer was to shoot a glob of spittle into his face. The man appeared to go insane. Dickie cowered as the plucky old woman fell back under a particularly vicious punch. And then both the men began hitting her, pulling her about by the thin, wispy hair, tossing her from one to the other and laughing as if it were all a huge joke. 'You'll tell us, missus! Oh, you'll tell us.'

Dickie hugged the wall, hamstrung by terror, wanting to stop her punishment but too afraid to move. There were two of them, both big men, and he could not take on the pair of them. He would end up getting beaten – like Torie was. Oh, Jesus please stop this! He averted his face but he could still hear the blows raining down on her poor body.

'You'll not have it, you bastards!' It was the first time he had heard her swear. 'My boy didn't work his fingers to the bone for you to steal it all from him.' The defiance terminated in a sharp cry of pain.

Oh, my God! she was doing it for him. She wasn't bothered about them stealing it from her but because of all the work he'd put in. Yet even in this knowledge he couldn't bring himself to run out from his hidey-hole and tell them where it was. He just sat there shivering, listening to the sound of flesh hitting flesh. He covered his ears to blot out the sound, but the vision was still in the front of his mind. He had often imagined scenes like this with himself as the hero, rescuing some under-dog from a gang of cut-throats. The swashbuckling victor remembered that now in this craven reality and felt worse than ever. And still he made no move to help her.

As he took his hands away from his ears to see what was happening there came the sound of a body slumping to the ground, followed by footsteps over the gravelly yard. He stole a swift glance round the corner of the wall. They were going into the house. Panic rose. Had she told them where it was while Dickie had feigned deafness? Still rooted by fear, his horrified gaze affixed itself to the inert, crumpled figure lying among the farmyard droppings, while his ears listened to the sounds of ransack coming from the house.

Eventually they came out and without sparing a glance for their victim came straight for Dickie's hiding-place, faces dark with bad temper. One of them carried the musket which Torie had not had time to snatch up as they vaulted over the wall and surprised her on her way back from the shippen. Dickie pulled his face sharply away from the edge of the wall and ran, spurred by panic, towards the nearest hideout – the pigsty. He quickly let himself in, pleading, coaxing, entreating the animal to behave itself, leaned over the lower door and bolted it, then pulled the top flap as close as he could. Percy's disdainful sneer made itself felt even in the darkness as he crouched in the reeking straw and waited.

The encroaching footfalls renewed his trepidation. He pressed himself further into the recess of the sty. He stopped breathing and listened. There was sudden rush of orange light as the top door was flung open, then the sound of the bolt being grated through its socket, followed by voices.

'D'yer think there's owt worth pinchin' in here? Nice lookin' pig; fetch a few quid.'

The door creaked on its hinges. Dickie's heart stopped. He crammed his knuckles into his mouth and bit down on them. He felt positive that the men could hear the nervous belches that kept bubbling up his windpipe. A shadow fell over him. 'Well, what have we 'ere?' The man set one foot towards him. Dickie felt his whole body dissolve – and then the pig struck.

There was uproar as the enormous pig launched himself at the first intruder, sinking his teeth into a considerately-placed thigh. The man screamed for his partner to help him, but the other was halfway down the hill by now. Percy slashed and tore like a maniac, driving his victim from the sty, squealing in porcine delight. Then they were out in the open and running, all three of them, down the hill.

Dickie had almost passed out when the pig had charged but now in his relief he fell over into the stinking straw, listening to the shrieks of the robbers as they fled with the manic pig snapping at their heels. He tried to control the shaking, but couldn't. The sound of those blows on poor Torie's head kept rebounding through his brain. He must go to her. But he daren't, he daren't. What if they should come back? They had the gun, hadn't they? They could shoot the pig and come back for him.

The thing that finally decided him was the faint sound of grunting as Percy made his vainglorious return, a tatter of blue serge caught on one of his tushes. Dickie edged his way out of the sty and around the perimeter of the house as Percy stopped to root happily in the yard.

He stared down at Torie's immobile, twisted form and knew that she was dead. Such a pitiful, tragic sight ... her hair, without its pork-pie hat, plastered with glistening black fluid, one leg buckled at an abnormal angle, obviously broken, the periwinkle eyes dulled by the glaze of death, and the face that had smiled so fondly at him this morning streaked with blood and dirt. He knelt down and pulled out his handkerchief, gently wiping the blood from her temple. 'I'm sorry, Torie.' His breath caught in a sob. 'I'm so sorry.' He remembered the stockings and sweets and brought them from his pocket. 'I was bringing ye these an' all ... God, what am I going on about? Ye can't hear me, can ye?' He laid the offerings at her side, then stood up quickly and turned his steps towards the house.

The kitchen had been all but demolished. Dead chickens mingled with the broken crockery. Among the debris sat sixteen deeply offended cats, fur puffed out, tails twitching.

But he spared no thought for any of this. Instead his eyes flew to the place where the biscuit barrel normally stood. It was lying on its side. The lid was somewhere with the other pieces of smashed pottery. He did not need to go further to see that it was empty.

The rage seethed up in him and emerged in a stream of curses. 'The shit-necked, whore-pigs! They've taken my bloody fortune!' He slashed and clanked about amongst the rubble searching for a stray coin, but found not one. They had taken it all. His fury magnified. He lashed out at the cats, dislodging them from their chairs and booting them in all directions.

'Out, you bastards, out!' He picked up a dead hen and ripped off its wings, tearing frenziedly at its feathers in uncontrollable rage, his teeth bared like some rabid animal, then flung it with all his strength at the window off which it bounced with a sickly plop. The fact that the window remained unbroken seemed to infuriate him further. He picked up a chair and hurled it. There was a noisy splintering of glass as the chair leg did its work then ricocheted back into the room. He picked it up again and lifted it over his head, bringing it down upon the flagstones time and time again until each leg was snapped off.

His temper took half an hour to re-harness. Still trembling, he dashed the tears of injustice from his cheeks and went outside to bury Torie alongside the graves of her cats, the idea of sending for a doctor never occurring to him. She was dead after all – anyone could see that. He was suddenly assailed by an unfamiliar feeling of guilt and shame as he picked her up – emotions he had never experienced in all his twenty years. She weighed next to nothing in his arms. How could he have stood there and let them do it to her? He could have told them where the money was, for had they not found it in the long run? And Torie had had to suffer for nothing. Poor old darlin'. He turned in the direction of the cats' graves, feeling a deep loathing for himself. 'What is happening to me? What kind of a shit am I?' he asked out loud.

Later, he took a broom and swept up the mess in the house, apologising to the cats who had reclaimed their territory and now sat glaring at him. He ran the broom along the dresser, sweeping everything off it, both whole and smashed, onto the floor and did similarly with the table, collecting everything into one big mound on the stone floor. The swines had even overturned the last jug of milk. He went to fetch a shovel and began to scrape up the rubbish. The biscuit barrel, still unaccountably in one piece, evaded his broom and cruised across the floor.

'Now where d'ye think you're off to?' He stooped to rescue it. 'You're the first to go in the bin, you bloody useless piece o' trash!' He dashed it to the ground where it finally shattered and was swept up with the rest.

The kitchen was tidier than it had ever been. He looked around for something to eat, picked up one of the dead hens and half-heartedly began to pluck it, then decided that would take too long and carved himself a thick slice of bread in its place. He clamped it between his jaws while he put the kettle on to boil. This done, he stared out of the broken window munching his meagre supper. There was something missing from the scene; what was it? Ah, gob! it was the spyglass. That was another point against him. If he had not acted the fool last night it would still have been there and Torie would have seen the two men coming a mile off and been ready for them. But it was lying in the shop awaiting repair and there it would stay. He watched Percy enjoying his freedom, lumbering about in the gloaming. 'Now how am I going to get that brute back in his sty?' he asked himself.

After the kettle boiled and he had drunk his black tea he went out into the dusk to try and corner the pig, taking a lantern with him so as to be able to see every move the animal made. Surprisingly, and for the first time ever, Percy offered no violence, trotting into his sty as meek as any lamb. 'You're a contrary old swine, ye know that?' said Dickie. 'You're no good for nothing except pork pies. D'ye hear me? PORK PIES! Still, I suppose I oughta thank ye for getting rid o' those two villains. The thieving poltroons. Well, Percy I'll away to me bed now, an' in the mornin' we'll have to think of our future. Both of us. Ye realise we can't stay here now that Torie's gone? Shall I tell ye something, Perc? I'll bloody-well miss the old crow, an' I guess you will too.' Grateful for the pig's cooperation he divided some food from amongst the smashed pots and threw a handful into the sty. 'Who knows, I might even surprise the both of us an' muck ye out tomorrow – there's no one else'll do it now,' he added sadly.

It was Dickie who was the recipient of the surprise. At dawn with no cow to milk and accustomed to rising at this hour, his first task after a cold breakfast was to clean out the pigsty. Coaxing Percy into the yard with a bucket of swill he nipped into the vacated sty and closed the door firmly behind him, just so the pig wouldn't sneak up on him – it was not above himself, thought Dickie, tossing the straw about.

The surprise came when his pitchfork delved into a corner to rake at the straw and made a tinny clank. Teasing aside the stalks he came across a box – the box into which, after that first day's temptation, Torie had transferred her savings, plus her bank-book and the deeds to the farm, and had hidden them in the safest place she could think of.

Dickie had found his fortune at last.

Neither Patrick nor his wife had interrupted Dickie's story up till this point, still dazed by his sudden reappearance, but now the former asked, 'What happened to the farm?'

Dickie extracted a gold hunter watch and flicked open the lid. 'I sold it. Look, I didn't realise this would take so long in the telling – can we continue it later? I've an important appointment in half an hour with my stockbroker.'

'Oh, *my* stockbroker is it?' His mother rose with him. 'We are distinguished, aren't we? Well, I'm afraid your stockbroker will just have to wait; I need to know more about this. How could you sell the farm? It didn't belong to you.'

'An' who knocked it into shape, might I ask?' enquired Dickie. 'Who sweated . . . listen, when I first went there it was nothing more than a glorified shed in the middle o' forty acres o' weeds. I spent fifteen hours a day ploughing, planting, joinering, milking, breaking my back . . . it belonged to me as much as anybody.'

'But not legally,' argued his mother. 'She never left a will. You had no right.'

'Stuff legally,' retorted Dickie. 'I spent two hard years on that farm. I'm damned if I'm having some lawyer crossing that out with a stroke of his pen just 'cause she never left a will. Anyway, she meant it for me. I held the deeds in my hand. No one was going to tell me it wasn't mine.'

'I don't like it, Dickie,' said his father gravely. 'You burying her without first calling a doctor.'

'Dad, we were out in the wilds! D'ye think a doctor would be very pleased to travel all that way out just to issue a death certificate?' He turned his back. 'Besides, I wanted to get her buried as quickly as possible. She was very dear to me, ye know. I couldn't bear to look at her after the pig had savaged her like that.' This was one of many points where the story had transgressed from the truth. Rather than relate his cowardice he had concocted a fictitious attack by the pig, whereupon he, Dickie, had come home to find her already dead. 'He was a terrible animal, ye know,' he told them, rolling up his sleeves to add truth to his story. 'See! That's what he did to me on me first day. I tell ye, the first thing I did was to send him off to market.' That at least was true. Percy had been the first to go, then the hens. The cats had been allowed to stay until he had found a buyer, for deprived of their plentiful diet they served to keep the rats down. He couldn't abide rats. It had broken his heart when the bank had refused to release Torie's savings to him. He had not pressed the matter for fear of attracting too much attention. He had had to suffice with the money that the farm had brought and the contents of the box in the pigsty. Which was no mean sum, but the thought of all those hundreds going to waste in the bank was almost unbearable.

'So,' said his mother, following the lines of his immaculately turned out appearance. 'You're a rich man.'

'I am indeed.' After selling up he had gone to the nearest city and found himself a room at the best hotel.

Apart from two sets of expensive clothes this was the only luxury he had permitted himself. He was rich in comparison to his former state but with a little gambling on the Stock Exchange he could be even richer. Despite Torie's views on the detriments of gambling, his flutters, with professional help, had paid off. He was now prosperous enought to return to York without fear of repercussion from his previous digressions. Clancy was a brute of a man, but Dickie could buy his sort of power a thousand times over. Money was the real strength. Men like Clancy didn't frighten him any more.

Besides all this, he had a score to settle with his mother. He had in fact been in York for some weeks but it was only when the whisper had come to him of Thomasin's interest in the Parliament Street property that he had decided to show himself. He had not expected the opportunity for revenge to come so quickly but when it had, he grasped it in his usual predatory fashion.

'I really must be off,' he told them, reaching for his topper from the circular table.

'I've not finished!' Thomasin waylaid him again. 'What are you going to do with that building you've just bought?'

He appeared somewhat baffled. 'Oh – I hadn't really thought about it. I just bought it on a whim, really.'

'Your mother had set her heart on it,' Patrick informed his son, stepping forward to put his arm around his wife's waist. 'She was going to expand the business.' He looked at Thomasin when he next spoke. 'Perhaps Dickie might like to . . .'

Before he could finish his sentence Dickie had severed it with a laugh. 'God, no! I'm afraid the grocery trade isn't up my street at all.' He smoothed the wrinkles from his gloved fingers. 'But, if Mother has her heart set on it, who am I to steal her dream? The building means nothing to me.'

'You mean you'll let me have it?' said Thomasin guardedly.

He smiled but there was no pleasantness in it. 'At a price.'

Her face immediately hardened and her hand came up, but Patrick tightened his grip on her waist and she put aside the idea of striking her son. 'How much?'

He named a sum that exceeded his buying price by five hundred pounds.

'Why, you little bloodsucker!' cried his mother, and whirled away in disgust.

'Mother, I thought ye'd set your heart on it,' he answered mildly. 'I know if I wanted anything that badly I'd be willing to pay any price. I thought my offer was quite reasonable.'

'This is your mother, Dickie, not a business opponent,' said Patrick sternly. 'Ye've no right to do this after everything else ye put her through.'

'There's a lotta talk about rights being bandied about,' said Dickie, his smile gone. ''Tis a pity no one in this house gave a thought to my rights while I was here before. Now, I'm not stayin' to argue. Mother, if ye want the place ye can have it – at the price stipulated. I'll call back later for your answer.'

'Don't bother!' spat Thomasin. 'You can have it now.' She went to the bureau and scribbled out a cheque.

The ease of her submission rather took the spark out of Dickie's triumph. He had expected her to fight harder than this.

'Tommy, are ye sure ye know what ye're doing?' asked her husband gravely as she handed over the cheque to her son.

'Oh, I know all right,' was her bitter reply as Dickie, grinning again, pocketed the cheque. 'I'm paying him off. That's the only money he'll ever see from us. The minute he goes from here I'm off straight to my solicitor to alter my will. I still held out some hope, you see,' she enlightened Dickie spitefully. 'Never had the heart to amend it after you disappeared. Oh, when I think of all the years of anguish you've caused us,' she hissed at him. 'All this time when we didn't know whether you were dead or alive, and you never sent so much as a letter to put our minds at ease – and you dare to talk about rights! You

532

forfeited those with your scurrilous treatment of those closest to you. And now this. Knowing the way your mind works I suppose you see it as a way of getting your own back – though God knows what for. You brought your troubles on your own shoulders, my lad. Well, now you've had your revenge you can get out and don't bother to come back. You're not welcome in this house. As far as I'm concerned you *are* dead.'

Dickie looked to Patrick. 'I wonder what Father has to say – or does she keep you in tow as well, Dad? You're a fair-minded man, are ye going to let a woman dictate what goes on in your house?'

Patrick had had much experience in fighting down his temper; he was not going to allow a shallow character like his son to rile him. 'Nobody dictates to me, Dickie, least of all you. It so happens that your mother took the words right out o' my mouth – only I'd've probably made them a mite stronger. You're very adept at your chosen subjects I'll grant ye – a liar, a cheat and an opportunist. But I can tell ye this and it'll not cost ye a penny – you're a dead loss as a son. Now, take your misbegotten rewards and get out of my house, for nobody in it ever wants to see you again.'

1874

PART FIVE

1874

CHAPTER FORTY-THREE

The fact that she had had to pay more for the store than she had bargained for had no effect on Thomasin's enthusiasm for the project – though her son's underhandedness had obsessed her for a long time afterwards. Many a private tear was shed before she was able to shove Dickie to the back of her mind and get on with her life. If he wasn't dead before he might as well be now, she told her family. But it wasn't quite true. He was her son and she still thought about him.

Thank God she had her work to take her mind off things. The Parliament Street store was open for business now and everything here was as she had pictured it. The service area was three times larger than the one in Goodramgate and looked very grand with Sonny's pictures hung on its walls. She had been correct about those too – they were selling even better in this setting. She hoped it wouldn't be long before she could release Sonny from his bargain and let him get on with producing some more. He was as miserable as sin being stuck here all day. Come to that, he wasn't much happier when he got home. She wondered, as the two of them took the cab home that evening, if there was some way she could cheer him up, and was provided with the answer when a poster caught her eye in Church Street.

She tapped Sonny's arm. 'Ooh, look! That looks like a good play on at the theatre! Why don't you take Peggy tonight?'

He studied the poster until the carriage took it out of view. 'I don't know that I can be bothered. I'm worn out.'

'What – at your age! Come on, don't be such a stick in the mud. It'll make a nice change – I'll buy the tickets.'

'Well . . .'

But his mother was already banging on the cab roof and giving the driver a change of directions. 'We'll call at the theatre on the way home and see if there's any tickets to be had.'

There were. Thomasin purchased two in the Dress Circle and pressed them into her son's hand before telling the cabbie to move on. 'It's ages since you had a night out. It'll do the pair of you good.'

Peggy thought otherwise. 'But you know very well that Thursday is my sewing circle!' she berated when he told her about the tickets.

'All right!' he shook his head vigorously. 'There's no call to jump down my throat. Mother just thought it would be a nice change for us, that's all. And so do I. Can't you miss your sewing circle for once?'

'No!'

'What's so special about a sewing circle?' enquired Thomasin, nettled that her treat had met with such ingratitude. 'I'm certain Dora and the others would forgive you for wanting to spend the evening with your husband instead. You never go out together these days.'

'What business is it of yours, Mother-in-law?' Peggy demanded. 'And yes! I'm sure my friends would understand if I wanted to spend the evening with my husband – but I don't.'

'Peggy, I'd ask you to speak more civilly to my mother,' warned Sonny. 'She's only concerned that the two of us don't get very much enjoyment these days.'

'And whose fault is that?' declared Peggy. 'I'm stuck here on my own with no company except for two screaming children, and when you come home in the evening what do you do? You paint!'

'Is there any wonder when he has to listen to all this carping?' cut in Thomasin. 'All the more reason, I would've thought, for you to jump at tonight's offer. And if you're as bored as you say you are during the day there's plenty of work needs doing at the store or even at home. I suggest that you take up your husband's invitation before the time comes when he grows tired of asking.'

'Come on, Peg,' coaxed Sonny. 'Say you'll come. If I'd known how you felt about my painting I wouldn't've spent so much time on it.' Maybe that was the problem.

'It's not in my nature to deprive you of something that's so vital to you,' she said pettishly.

'Nothing's as important as your happiness,' he told her. 'Please come with me tonight. I promise you'll find it more exhilarating than your sewing circle – it's a comedy.'

'The others'll be expecting me,' wheedled Peggy. 'I can't let them down.'

'But you'd let your husband down,' observed Thomasin coolly.

'Oh, very well!' snapped Peggy. She might as well give in. They were all against her, damn them. She went upstairs to change, seeing in her mind's eye Edward tapping his cane with impatience, waiting on the steps of the Assembly Rooms. He was the third so far in what was to be a procession of meaningless affairs. They had started a few months ago with a chance meeting in the park. There had been nothing handsome or charming about that first man, in fact he was positively base, but the baseness in him had stirred the intrinsic sameness in her, and had set the wheels in motion. She had, from that point, taken to leaving the children at home when she went for her constitutional; they were too mischievous and bright to risk taking them with her. The knowledge that she was depriving the children of their walk had not come to light as yet. With Sonny having to work in the afternoons she was quite safe. Though Josie and the other maids had complained that the little imps were always under their feet none of them had taken their complaint higher than the children's mother. However, because of their repeated griping, Peggy had been forced to turn to other methods to contain her charges.

She braked in her motion of dragging the brush through her hair and rose from her seat to study her figure in the mirror. On her face were all the signs, the reasons for her extreme irritability. She wondered how long it would take for her dear mother-in-law to notice and congratulate

Sonny, thereby letting the cat out of the bag. Though it would be more like a tiger than a cat; she hadn't allowed Sonny near her for ages, he would know immediately. She really must make an effort to rectify the situation. But it certainly wouldn't be the solution she had contemplated in her first attack of panic; she would rather risk being thrown out than face death at the hands of a crone.

Turning sideways, she still posed before the glass, running a hand over her abdomen. At least there was nothing showing there yet. That gave her time to carry out her plan. Sonny wouldn't know the difference – he would be too pleased at regaining admittance to her bedroom to notice he had sired a seven month baby.

For once she did not ring for Josie's help in dressing – she was already laced – and selecting her prettiest dress, put it on. When Sonny came up to change she called to him as he passed her open door, begging assistance with her buttons. Without speaking his fingers fumbled their way up the row of blue buttons. On reaching the last one they were about to move away when she stayed his hand with one of hers.

'I'm sorry, Sonny.' She pressed her lips to his captive hand. 'I was an utter fishwife down there. I really don't know what came over me. After all, I'm forever complaining about Dora, aren't I?'

Sonny's surprise at this unexpected softening transmitted itself to his face, then was swept aside by his love for her. Here was his old Peggy as she had been before Dickie had got his filthy hands on her – soft and gentle. He pulled her around to face him. 'I do worry about us, you know, Peggy. I think the world of you ... but if I thought it was me who was making you unhappy then I wouldn't keep you to this marriage. You're free to go whenever you want.'

She fell against him, though the action was caused more through dread than sentiment. That was the last thing she wanted; him to let her go at this stage. 'Oh, Sonny, Sonny! It's not you. If it weren't for your mother I know our marriage would be truly wonderful. She comes between

540

us, Sonny, you know she does. If only we could be on our own ...'

'Then we will,' he said impulsively. 'We've waited long enough for Mother's settlement – it's never going to come. Well, she can keep it. I'll get a loan, and you'll choose wherever you want to live.'

This was more than she could have hoped for. 'D'you mean that?'

'Yes. I think you're right, Peggy. It is living here that's made us fall apart. I'd do anything to have things how they used to be.' He touched his lips to the curve of her shoulder. 'I'll go see the bank manager the first chance I get tomorrow.'

She found it difficult to stop her hopes soaring, having had them stamped on too many times by his mother. But this time she felt pretty confident that he would carry out his promise. She jumped from his embrace. 'Oh, Sonny I do love you! Come. Don't let's waste time discussing such boring things as money. Let's go celebrate with a night on the town.' She grabbed her wrap and purse, then ran helter-skelter down the stairs.

Sonny, with the feeling that he was taking part in someone else's dream, pursued her.

The evening at the Theatre Royal transcended his grandest hopes. The play, as he had told Peggy, was a comedy, but it was not the actors' amusing poses that made him laugh and laugh until his stomach ached. The happiness that had eluded him for so long was now sitting next to him in the shape of his lovely wife, who giggled and heaved out her appreciation of the play on his shoulder. Afterwards, bowing to Peggy's decision that it was far too early to go home, Sonny escorted her to a dance where they waltzed and reeled until the early hours and their bursting lungs screamed for mercy.

Once home, like two naughty children, they crept upstairs laughing and shushing until they arrived at Peggy's bedroom door. And there, Sonny's prayers were answered

541

as she put her arms around his neck and drew him into the darkness.

Peggy screwed back the lid on the pot of moisturising cream, gave her cheeks a brisk rub to heighten their bloom, then rang for Josie to tighten her stays. The housekeeper, having to break off her work, came huffing and puffing into the bedroom.

'There are another two maids already up here who could've done this, Mrs Feeney,' she reminded Peggy, grasping the laces of the corset and straining with all her might. 'It's not really my job.'

'But I sent for you,' replied Peggy with a grunt as the stays bit into her waist.

– Aye, and we all know why, thought Josie, heaving and sawing with the laces. Because there's only me what's strong enough to squeeze this load o' flab into a twenty-two inch waist.

Once laced, Peggy examined her wardrobe. 'I think I shall wear the beige today.' She pointed to a beige gown, criss-crossed with cream braid over the bodice which, when it was donned, made her look like a bakewell tart in Josie's estimation. She'd never have as much style as Miss Erin or Mrs Feeney senior, who was more than twice her age but still had a better figure.

'Very well, that will be all.' Peggy stabbed a marcasite pin through the straw hat.

'Could I enquire if madam is going out?'

Peggy turned cold eyes on the maid. 'If it is any of your business I shall be out for the remainder of the day.'

'What about the children, ma'am?' asked Josie, knowing full well what the reply would be.

'You have no need for concern,' answered Peggy, pushing a curl into place. 'I shall make sure they do not become a nuisance to you.'

– I'll just bet you will, thought Josie angrily. We'll never hear a peep out of them bairns all afternoon. In fact I'll have the Devil's job of even waking them to get them ready for bed. The girl kept persuading herself that it was none of her affair, but all the same she knew that it was; it was everyone's affair. She really ought to do something about it, but just what she had not decided. One thing was certain; Mr John would not like it. No, he wouldn't like it one little bit what she was doing to them kids.

After Josie had gone, Peggy reached to the back of her wardrobe and brought out a wad of stockings. Unravelling them, she carefully plucked the bottle and spoon from their folds and threw the discarded garments on the bed. Then she went to the nursery.

'Oh, Mam!' complained Rosanna, the minute she saw the bottle being tipped towards the spoon. 'Not today. Me an' Nick are playing a good game. We don't want to go to sleep.'

'Hush, Rosie. You must have your nap in the afternoon to keep you healthy and strong. Come, open wide.' Peggy pointed the spoon at the child's mouth and the hard expression in her eyes brooked no resistance. Rosanna had tried that once, to her cost.

Ugh! but it was foul. The gooey draught stuck to her teeth and she knew from experience the taste would still be with her when she woke. Nick dutifully received a similar dose and the two were stripped of their clothes and put to bed. Peggy tucked them in and kissed them before departing.

'Be good and I might bring you a sugar mouse when I come back.'

A sleepy Rosanna didn't hold out much hope; Mam was always promising to bring them presents but usually forgot. She yawned, cuddled up to a drowsy Nick and was very soon asleep.

Peggy wound the stockings back around the bottle and replaced the bundle at the back of her wardrobe, then went off to meet her lover.

From her seat in the counting house, which was separated from the main store by a glass partition enabling her to keep a check on business, Thomasin could see the back of Sonny's head and wondered what was so interesting in the conversation he was having with the dapper man to keep him so long from his work. He had gone into the main store to check on a price for her and had ended up being there for fifteen minutes at the very least.

There had been a significant change in his mood since last night. That it was to do with his wife Thomasin was well aware, for having the bedroom directly below Peggy's she had come to distinguish whether the bed held one occupant or two. She was equally aware that if Peggy was showing some wifely devotion there was some chicanery behind it.

Oh, God what had that poor lad done to deserve such a partner, she sighed, twiddling the pen through her fingers. Such a decent, upright lad he was – but not any more. Peggy had made sure of that.

She frowned and raised herself a little way out of the chair in order to catch a glimpse of his conversation partner. Quite obviously it was Sonny's paintings that was the subject of their talk for the man kept referring to the exhibition as he spoke.

The implication of what Sonny had just heard set the tingle of excitement whirring in his breast. He asked the man, who had introduced himself as William Lewis – though introductions were superfluous for the man's reputation as a great artist was well known to Sonny – to repeat his offer. He was unable to believe what he had just been told: that the great William Lewis was inviting him, a virtually unknown artist, to put on an exhibition of work at the other's gallery.

The man smiled and directed his gaze over the heads of the tea-drinkers to study the paintings once more. 'Is it so incredible? All the great artists were unknown once upon a time. Some whom I consider to be the greatest of all are still not recognised today. But Mr Feeney, the one point where you differ from them is that you will not have to wait until you are dead for recognition. Another point to your favour is that you are apparently not influenced by any of them – no heroes. There are plenty of competent Van Eycks, Rembrandts and Gainsboroughs around today, all churning out admirable but boring copies of their idol's work. Your style, however, is most distinctive. I should like to see a wider example of it, hence my offer.'

'But to grant me an exhibition without seeing the rest of my work . . .' Sonny was mesmerised.

'No need, my dear chap – if the two dozen or so I see here are indicative of your collection.'

Sonny pushed a noisy breath of wonder through his teeth. 'Good heavens! I still think somebody forgot to wake me this morning.' He flapped his hands against his sides.

The man noticed two customers leaving their table and asked if he and Sonny might take their places so that he could study the young man's brushwork more closely. Sonny steered him to the table under a landscape of the Dales, painted in his college days. 'I can recommend the coffee, sir, the beans were freshly roasted this morning.'

'Thank you, no.' Lewis put his eye close to the painting and made respectful noises. Finally he straightened and said, 'I'd like to purchase this one if I may?'

Sonny, just escaping from the vortex of excitement was plunged back in. 'You? You want to buy it?' Then took control of his manners. 'Why, certainly, sir . . . of course!'

The man inserted his hand into his inside pocket. 'Is there anywhere a little more private where we may do business?' Sonny rapidly escorted him into the counting house, introducing Lewis to his mother. 'Charmed, Mrs Feeney.' William Lewis bent over Thomasin's hand. 'I'm delighted to meet the mother of such a talented young man.'

'Mr Lewis wants to buy one of my paintings, Mother. Imagine it!' Sonny held up the landscape which he had removed from the wall. 'And you'll never guess . . . he's also promised to arrange an exhibition of my work at his very own gallery.'

Thomasin was effusive in her congratulations. 'Didn't I always say you'd be famous?'

'Well, it's early days yet, Mother . . . oh, Mr Lewis I beg your pardon! Am I keeping you waiting?' Sonny had noticed the man's glance at the clock.

'As a matter of fact I'm already late for my appointment,' said Lewis. 'But all in a good cause. I was strolling past your store, spotted your work and came for a closer look. Actually it was that one which drew me.' He nodded at the painting in Sonny's hands, ready to write out the cheque. 'I grew up around Wensleydale and recognised that stretch of water immediately. A most prepossessing place, Semmerwater and excellently captured here. Are you conversant with the legend?' Sonny said he was. 'I recall staring into its grey depths as a child, trying to spot the submerged city. Never did.' He smiled. 'So, how much do I owe you for my nostalgia?'

Sonny pointed to the price ticket on the corner, holding his breath: was it too high? Normally Sonny's pictures sold for between two and five guineas but he was loath to let this large masterpiece go for less than ten. No one had wanted to pay it of course ... until now. Lewis handed over the cheque without complaint. On the contrary: 'You could be earning much more if you undertook commission work, young man.'

'People would never pay more than that!' laughed Sonny.

'You'd be surprised at what some people will pay for a portrait of their favourite horse,' smiled Lewis. 'Especially from an artist of your calibre, unknown or not.'

'But how do I get these commissions if no one knows me?' protested Sonny.

'They soon will, once you've exhibited at my gallery,' replied Lewis. 'I don't like to see talent going to waste. You'll soon make a name for yourself. Here's my card, should you wish to get in touch before I see you again. Good day.'

William passed the man on his way out. Finished with his coffee roasting he was visiting the counting house before he went home. 'I see we've sold another.' He nodded satisfiedly at his grandson. 'How much?'

'Ten guineas,' Sonny informed him.

'Ten ... bloody 'ell, he must be puddled! Ten bloody guineas for a picture?'

'Aye, it took me by surprise as well,' laughed Sonny and turned to his mother. 'Ten guineas!' Then the significance of the piece of paper in his hand made him pensive. He had been wondering how to ask for time off to go and see the bank manager and now he had been given the excuse.

'D'you think it would be all right for me to nip to the bank and pay this in? I'd sooner not have it lying around the shop.'

'Afraid it'll find its way into the till, are you?' asked Thomasin.

'He wouldn't be far wrong, I'll bet,' mocked her father.

'Eh, you'd better hop it before I dock your wages,' warned Thomasin, then grinned at Sonny as the old man left with a rude retort. 'Oh, I'm really pleased for you, Son. It's time you had some good luck. Go on then, you'd better take it to the bank so it doesn't get lost.'

'Oh, thanks.' He moved to the door.

'Er, if it's not too much to ask would you find me that price before you go?'

He laughed and clapped a hand to his face. 'Sorry! I clean forgot about it. I'll do it now.' He was gone about thirty seconds and bounced back into the counting house. 'It's one and three ha'pence! God, I still can't believe this . . . I can't wait to tell Peggy.'

She wrote down the price, then laid aside her pen. 'Well, if you just can't wait tha'd best go now.'

'But you need me here, don't you? I'd feel so guilty . . .'

'Guilty be tickled! You'll be no use to me whatsoever till you've got this out of your system and I'm sure I can cope for one afternoon. Go on! Take that cheque to the bank then go home and tell milady all about it. I'm sure anything to do with money will alter her features and that'll benefit us all.'

He was her loving son again. 'Oh, thanks, Mam!' and knocked her head sideways with a rough kiss before dashing off.

At the bank he paid in his cheque, but found that the manager would be engaged for some hours yet and so made an appointment for the following Monday when he knew his mother would be round at the other store doing the weekly ordering. Then he caught a cab, the sooner to be home and tell his wife the great news. This was just what they had been waiting for. Now he was no longer dependant on his mother!

CHAPTER FORTY-FOUR

But sadly when he arrived home there was no sign of Peggy. Never one to ring for a maid when his legs would serve him just as well, Sonny went through to the kitchen to question Josie.

All three domestics, who had been taking a short break from their chores, stood at his entrance. He waved them down, but Josie maintained they had been chatting long enough and sent the underlings on their way. They giggled as they passed him, knowing how their master was coveted by their superior.

'I just came to ask if you know where my wife is,' said Sonny, having the grace not to comment on her blushes – perhaps because he never noticed them.

She turned away to lift a heavy tin from a shelf and place it on the table in the centre of the kitchen. There was a note of disapproval in her answer. 'She's gone out, sir. She usually does of an afternoon.'

'Oh . . . she's gone to the park, I suppose. There goes my surprise.' He watched her struggle to open the can with hammer and chisel. 'Here, let me do that.' She passed over the implements and complimented him on his deft opening of the can. 'You'd think somebody would invent a better method of opening cans than this, wouldn't you?' he said, passing back the tin. 'You could do with me in here all the time I'll bet; have me on a shelf alongside the tins so's every time you needed to open one you'd only have to lift me down.'

She giggled. 'Oh, Mr John you are funny!' He was in high spirits today, Josie thought and she knew the cause of it. When Abigail had made Miss Peggy's bed she had found Mr John's clothes in a pile on the carpet and had taken great delight in telling Josie. Well, at least he's happy again, thought the young housekeeper, and if he is then so am I . . . No, I'm not! I could smack her stupid face, messing him about like she does.

'Well, as I'm not to have the company of my wife I must find something else to occupy me,' said Sonny. 'It's a pity she takes the children with her; I haven't had a game with them in ages.'

'Oh, she doesn't take them with her any more, Mr John,' Josie informed him, thankful for the excuse to speak on the subject. 'Miss Peggy says too much exercise is bad for them. She's taken to putting them to bed for the afternoon.'

'Well, yes – I suppose that's sensible. Still,' he winked, 'I can't see it doing much harm if I wake them for once, and I'm sure they'll be glad to see me.'

Josie was about to add something as he made his exit from the kitchen, but decided not to bother, anticipating his swift return.

When he did reappear his face was worried and puzzled. 'I couldn't rouse them. I know it was wrong of me but I even picked Rosie up by the shoulders and shook her and still she wouldn't open her eyes. She was just like a little rag doll – Nick, too. D'you think I ought to call the doctor?'

She caught her lip between her teeth. He noticed her reluctance to speak. 'Do you know what's the matter with them? Come on, girl! If you do then say so, for Heaven's sake. They look dreadful.'

'There's nothing exactly wrong with them, Mr John,' she began.

'Is my wife aware of their malady?' he asked. She didn't respond. He became stern. 'Josie, if you know what ails those children I demand that you tell me now!'

'It's really not my place . . .'

'Tell me!'

549

'Well . . . oh, I shouldn't say this.' She put a hand to her cheek. 'Miss Peggy'll think I've been spying on her. I didn't mean to find it, honestly. I thought it were just a bundle o' mucky washing – then I felt summat hard and found the bottle wrapped up in the bundle.'

He sprang to the wrong conclusion and his face was aghast. 'D'you mean to tell me my wife's been drinking?'

'Oh no, sir . . . It was a medicine bottle. I took the stopper off an' sniffed it. It smelt o' treacle. Then I remembered she – that's Miss Peggy, sir – she asked me for some treacle a long time ago. I thought it were a strange request but I gave it to her. Of course, I didn't know what it was she wanted it for then.'

'Josie,' he shook his head perplexedly. 'What is all this leading to? All this nonsense about treacle?'

'Well, you see, Mr John, I heard that sometimes when babies are fractious people dose 'em with treacle an'. . . an' summat else.'

He sighed exasperatedly at her longwindedness. 'What summat else?'

She hesitated, then said, 'Opium, sir.'

'Op . . . Jesus, Mary an' Joseph! How long has this been going on?'

'A couple o' months at least, Mr John,' replied Josie, then blurted, 'An' if you don't mind my saying so I don't think it's right. Not right at all. I grant it could've been partly my fault, but . . .' Here he interrupted to ask for an explanation. 'Well, sir, when Miss Peggy took to leavin' the bairns at home I told her they was being a nuisance. I didn't mean it,' she told him hastily, 'I just made it an excuse so she'd start takin' 'em again. They missed their walks. I don't know why she stopped taking them all of a sudden. They can be little devils I know but . . . Anyway, she didn't take the bait, just started putting them to bed. I didn't catch on at first, kept wonderin' why they were all listless at teatime, and their breath smelt . . .' she screwed up her nose, '. . . well, not normal, like. Then when I found the bottle I knew straight away.' She reached out and clasped his arm unthinkingly. 'You must stop her, Mr

John. She doesn't know what harm she's doin'. I tried to tell her but you know what she thinks of me.'

He laid his fingers over those resting on his arm, and for an instant she felt the heat from his skin transfer itself to her. Then he released her and said resolutely, 'Thank you for telling me, Josie. I shall put a stop to it, of course. And if my wife has some reason why she can't take the children with her when she goes out then I must put a stop to that, too.'

'No, Mr John I'd rather you didn't! Oh, dear, I'm ever so sorry.' She blushed. 'I'm forgetting myself. It's not my place ...'

'Forget about your place for once, Josie,' he replied kindly. 'What were you about to say? Come on, I regard you as a friend, you can speak your mind without fear of chastisement.'

A friend, she thought miserably – that's the most I can hope for. 'Well, sir, by all means put a stop to Miss Peggy dosing the children – that's only right – but I'd rather you didn't stop her going out. She ... well, I think we both know that your wife doesn't hold me in very high regard. If you cut off her pleasure she'll take it out on me.'

He might once have answered: 'Don't be silly!' But not now. He had got to know his wife too well. 'But it doesn't seem fair that you should have to look after the children, Josie – you've got your own job. If my wife finds it too taxing then we must hire a proper nanny.'

'Oh, no please!' She started forward. 'Don't do that, Mr John. I'd never see them at all then, an' I wouldn't like that. They're wonderful bairns, I love 'em as much as anyone in this house. I can quite manage to fit in my own work between looking after them – even though that Miss Rosanna is like a drop o' quicksilver.'

He smiled and patted her arm. The shiver went through her again. 'Yes, I've noticed how fond you are of them, Josie and how well the three of you get on together. Very well, if it won't be too much of an imposition ... though I shall definitely speak to my wife about the opium. Don't worry though, I shan't say how I came to find out – and thank you once again for telling me.'

She flushed at the warmth of his voice. 'Mr John, if you've nothing better to do I was just going to put the kettle on for a pot of tea; I'd be honoured if you'd join me.'

He was still in the kitchen when Peggy returned from her jaunt. When the bell sounded from the drawing room he begged leave of Josie – treated me just like a lady, she would think afterwards – telling her not to answer its summons for he wanted to speak to his wife alone.

He was stunned by her appearance as the surprised face flew up at his entry – her disarrayed hair and enlarged pupils, the flushed cheeks and bruised, pouting lips. He had only ever managed to produce that result once, but knew exactly what it meant. He did not need to ask now why she had left the children at home. She had been with a man.

'Why, Sonny dear – I didn't expect to find you here!' She held out her arms and pecked his cheek. His nostrils flared at the musk that wafted from her heated body.

'Mother let me go early,' he finally stammered. 'I came home to see you.'

'Oh, what a shame.' She found herself a seat. 'I've been to visit *my* mother – she's so ill, poor dear. I had to stay with her all afternoon.'

His gorge rose at this deceit but he fought it down. 'Is that why you never took the children with you?'

'Naturally. I didn't want to subject them to infection.'

Oh, Peggy, how could you? he raged inwardly. After last night. Such a wonderful night. He had thought, hoped, that this was to be the start of their reconciliation. They had talked long into the night, discussing how they might soon be able to afford a place of their own; how they would add another child to their family.

'Sonny, what are you staring at?' she asked vexedly.

'Nothing.' He sat down before his shaking legs betrayed him. 'Peggy, I want to speak to you about the children.' He could not look at that mottled face.

'What about them?' she said carefully. 'They haven't been causing trouble, have they?'

'They'd hardly be doing that in the situation in which I found them when I came in earlier. My intention, when I found that you had left them behind, was to spend the afternoon playing with them. Unfortunately I was unable to wake them.'

'You should know better than to disturb a child's sleep, Sonny,' she rebuked, though still even-tempered.

He looked at her sharply then. 'Had it been a normal sleep perhaps I wouldn't have done. But I was worried for their safety.'

'Safety?' she laughed uneasily. Damn him, he knew! How had he found out?

'Please, Peggy,' he said wearily. 'I know what you've been doing and I want it to stop.'

'I don't have the slightest idea . . .'

Impatiently he grabbed her arm and marched her up to her room where, after a brief search of the wardrobe, he brought out the bundle of stockings containing the bottle of opium. 'Now, deny that you've been doping them every day with this!' He thrust it under her nose.

'How dare you accuse me of such an act!' she cried indignantly. 'Dope my own children? Why, I had no idea that bottle was even there. Who has been spreading malicious lies?' She narrowed her eyes at his silence. 'Why, it's that maid, isn't it?'

'Peggy . . .'

'Don't you Peggy me! You knew exactly where to look. You believe the word of that trollop against that of your own wife.'

'That's not true. Josie has nothing to do with this . . .'

'Don't lie! I know her – she's still trying to get her hooks into you by blackening my character. The truth is that it was most probably her who planted that bottle in my wardrobe just to vilify me. I can see it all now. She's waited until my back was turned then doped the children to keep them out of her way. She was always complaining about them, and now she's trying to blame it all on me.'

'Don't be ridiculous!'

'I've caught her before rifling through my belongings, looking for things she can steal.'

'She wouldn't!'

'Oh, no! of course she wouldn't,' sneered his wife. 'She couldn't do anything wrong, our dear Josie, could she? Only steal another woman's husband!'

He seized her by the shoulders and shook her. 'Peggy, you're getting yourself all worked up over nothing. Josie doesn't mean a thing to me; she's only a friend. You're my wife, I love you. Didn't I make that clear last night?'

'Then why won't you believe me instead of her?' she demanded.

'Because . . . oh, I don't know what to believe any more.' He ran his fingers through his hair in an act of defeatism. 'What's happened to us, Peggy? We were happy once, weren't we? It wasn't all in my imagination – or was it?' His eyes came up to confront her. 'Was last night just a pretence? You go on about Josie trying to steal me, yet you don't want me yourself, do you? Not really. Come on, admit it.' He could not bear to say the rest; still felt sick at the image of another man's hands on his wife's beautiful breasts, her thighs . . .

She became afraid then, seeing the plentiful life slip from her grasp. Who would support her if Sonny should throw her out? Certainly not Edward. 'I do want you, Sonny!' she started to sob. 'I do!'

'Then why?' he beseeched her. 'Peggy, I know . . . I can see . . .'

'See what?' she flashed, the tears miraculously dry. 'If I am to be pilloried about some other crime then you must try to be more articulate. But I warn you, if it is another of that maid's . . .'

'I can see you've been with another man!' he yelled at her. 'Is that bloody articulate enough for you? How can you stand there and swear that you want me when you've just come from someone else's bed?'

She glared at him breathlessly, her plump breasts heaving. 'Tell me I'm wrong!' he barked. 'Tell me!'

Slowly, her enraged frown melted into futility. 'I can't,' she said flatly, and turned her back on him.

He spun her round to face his attack. 'I told you!' he shouted. 'Didn't I say last night that if you were unhappy with me then you were quite at liberty to leave; that I wouldn't hold you to this marriage? Why, *why* do you continue to live with me if you so obviously feel nothing for me?'

She gave up her pretence. 'Do you really have to ask that? You've seen what sort of home I come from. Would you want me to go back to that?'

He was visibly shaken; even though he had been the one to bring it into the open he had expected her to deny it. 'Are you telling me you only married me for what I could give you, and to give your child a name? Is that all I ever meant to you?'

She did not answer, just stared at him with those black treacle eyes full of nothing.

He made a little knowing sound in his throat. 'Well . . . !' He thrust his free hand into his pocket and stared down at the bottle in the other. Then, slowly, he turned and made for the door. There, he managed to accomplish his original command. 'You may not care for your husband, but you will have a bloody thought for the health of our children. This is going where it belongs – in the dustbin. I don't expect to find another in this house.'

Not even as he left did he remember he had not shared his exciting news. But later he would remember, and would cancel his appointment at the bank; he would not leave this house now.

Peggy keeled over onto the bed as he closed the door and put a hand to her throbbing temple. It was all going wrong. She hadn't meant to blurt it out, he just made her so mad – and it was all the fault of that fat prig of a maid.

After this, it was only natural that he should lean towards Josie – if still only for friendship. It appeared to a depressed Peggy, annoyed and on edge, that every time she encountered her husband he was in the girl's company.

555

The more Peggy fumed and raged at him the more he turned to Josie for comfort. One thing that should have pleased her was the discovery that her pregnancy had been a false alarm. It should have, but didn't; all it meant to her was that all that play-acting had been for nothing. One thing that did gratify her, though, was that her cruel taunts and insinuations continued to hurt him; she could see it in his eyes. She wondered how any man could be so stupid as to still love her when he was fully aware of the reasons for her daily outings. Any other man would have thrown her out, but thankfully not Sonny.

Josie, too, was watchful of the situation and hated what it was doing to Mr John. Though she didn't want to be accused of breaking up a marriage she did nothing to discourage his casual and numerous trips to the kitchen. Besides, what marriage? It was a sham. Mr. John should never have married that martinet. Apart from which, thought Josie sadly, the young master saw her only as a shoulder to cry on; only his wife put sexual connotations on the relationship. Yet, as things were to turn out, it was Peggy's jealousy which was to be Josie's greatest ally.

There came a day in midsummer, when the air was heavy with the threat of an electric storm. There was the rumble of distant thunder and the odd spur of lightning, but as yet the swollen nimbus remained unperforated, as it had done since yesterday, waiting for the right moment to strike. The impending storm had kept Peggy from her rendezvous, which was more, thought Sonny acidly as he watched her restless passage, than her husband was capable of doing. Wordlessly he finished his lunch then went off to his room to lose himself in his painting. Since Mr Lewis' visit his mother had once more repealed the embargo on his painting; the afternoons were again his own.

Peggy was like a trapped panther, pacing from room to room. First the nursery then, when the children began to grate on her nerves, the drawing room, then back to her own room. Back and forth, back and forth, all afternoon, furiously wafting her fan against the cloying heat. By four o'clock she was almost on the point of screaming with boredom and, on impulse, decided to pay her husband a visit. He got quite tetchy about being interrupted while involved with his painting; an argument would at least ease the monotony.

But when she made her theatrical entrance she was disappointed; he wasn't there. On the easel was a half-completed study of Thomasin which Sonny intended as a birthday surprise for his mother. He had really excelled himself with this one and had captured his mother completely. To add to the surprise he planned to include this in his coming exhibition. When his proud mother accompanied him on the opening day she would, in the foyer, be confronted by her double. He couldn't wait to see her face. Nearly everything was ready; framed and catalogued – and priced. Apart from the dozen or so pictures still at the store everything was here, neatly stacked and waiting to be transported to Lewis' gallery during the coming week.

Peggy strolled about the room, arms folded, fingers itching. She came across a portfolio of sketches and casually picked loose the string that bound them. Perching on Sonny's bed she sifted through them without much interest, tossing them carelessly to float hither and thither about the room. Suddenly, her mouth dropped open. She tugged out the offending sketch and stared at it. It was of a very pretty girl, done in pastel, Sonny's first attempt in this medium. But the thing of interest to Peggy was not Sonny's diversion from the usual oils, but that the girl depicted was completely naked. Her eyes roamed over Dottie's curves for some time, then her lips clamped together as she screwed and twisted the picture to shreds.

The darts of jealousy began to stab at her again. She left the fragments where they had fallen and charged off to find her husband, having no need to ask where he would be. The kitchen door was ajar. There were two figures at the table, and though they sat on opposite sides the act of leaning on their elbows brought their faces close together. Like his children in times of need, Sonny turned

557

to Josie to share his sorrows and his joys. When his wife had robbed him of his glory, the day he had made the discovery that there was another man, he had instead shared it with the girl. She had expressed great interest in his talent, much more than Peggy had ever done. He found in her a ready ear for his ideas.

'I do so admire your paintings, Mr John,' she had said wistfully, that first time. 'I wish I was as clever as you.'

'I had no idea you'd seen my work, Josie,' he had returned her interest. 'D'you mean the ones hanging in the store?'

'No, sir ... I mean the ones in your room. I'm sorry, I couldn't help noticing them, what with having to make your bed an' that. I didn't touch anything, honest. Just stole a peep if you happened to have one on the whatsit.'

'The easel,' he provided.

'Yes. There's one I particularly like. It's a view of Skip-with Common ...'

'You recognised it?' he broke in delightedly.

'Oh, yes, sir. There was no mistakin' it. I spent a marvellous afternoon there once with my mam an' dad an' our Cissie. I well remember that lovely avenue of trees, all gold an' russet – 'cause it were autumn, like. I could've carried on down that path forever.'

Sharing her memory, Sonny smiled. 'Yes, it is an evocative place. I've been there many times – and you recognised it without being told where it was! You're a great morale booster, Josie.'

'Well, I couldn't help but recognise it, it was so skilfully done. How you get the bark o' them trees just right ... an' the colours ... oh, you're so clever!'

'That does it!' He had banged on the table. 'The picture is on sale at the store right now but directly I get there tomorrow I shall take it down and you shall have it.'

'Oh, no!' She clapped her hands to her cheeks.

'Oh, yes! Praise like you've just given me deserves its reward – if it doesn't sound too big-headed to call one of my paintings a reward.'

It did not matter that the painting in question was one

of his finest and would have fetched a good price; true to his word he had brought it home and it now hung on the wall opposite her bed and was the last thing her eyes saw before she went to sleep, dreaming of its donor.

Nowadays, before he as much as touched brush to canvas and knowing how she shared his love of colour, Sonny would display each of his preliminary sketches to Josie and they would discuss them together.

It was one of these they were poring over now as Peggy glared in on them. But she did not see it. All she saw were their two heads brushing.

Sonny murmured something inaudible and Josie emitted a low, soft laugh. They were completely unaware of her presence.

Quietly she slipped back upstairs. Her angry trembling had given way to a determined calm. There was plenty of time. What she had to do would wait until tomorrow.

Somewhere through the grumbling sky the sun rose, but no one saw it. The storm had still not broken and the sullen clouds brought a timely backdrop to the events that were to take place that day.

After everyone had breakfasted and gone to work, Peggy checked on the whereabouts of the children and the domestics before carrying out her plan. A quick survey of the kitchen found Rosanna and Nick being tutored in the art of apple pie baking by Abigail. Judith, she knew, was in the master bedroom changing the sheets, there was only her arch rival to pinpoint and then she could set to work. She would teach him. Teach the pair of them.

On encountering Judith on the stairs she enquired as to Josie's presence and was informed that the housekeeper was checking on the contents of the linen cupboard. 'Shall I tell her you want to see her, ma'am?' asked the sparrow-like maid, cocking her head.

'And what makes you think I want to see her?' replied Peggy icily. 'About your work, girl!'

She watched the maid scurry off, then turned in the direction of Sonny's room. She closed the door behind her and leaned on it momentarily 'til she decided where to start. Then with no particular method she began to pile the canvases into manageable stacks.

Struggling under the weight of a section of them she made an ungainly descent down the staircase, passing Judith once again and charging her to be silent with a narrow-eyed glare. The maid watched, open-mouthed, as Peggy stumbled past her with a pile of canvases and marched across the hall.

Three more startled faces watched her flit across the kitchen window, but she carried straight past them and on into the garden, her brow shining with the effort. Reaching the lawn she threw down her load and retraced her steps for another.

It took three trips to move all the paintings, then another to collect every tube and every bottle she could lay her hands on. On her final journey she paused to regard the portrait of Thomasin on which her husband had been toiling most of the night in order to complete it. It was still wet; the paint came off on the edge of her palms as she lifted it from the easel. She didn't notice the smears of colour that spoilt her pink gown as she tucked it under her arm and ran down the stairs, clutching the tubes and bottles to her bosom, dropping many of them along the way.

Her face was bright red when she reached the garden. There were patches of perspiration under her arms. Her feet were sliding about in her slippers. She noticed none of this.

Taking Thomasin's portrait from beneath her arm she gave it pride of place on the bonfire. 'You can be Guy, Mother-in-law dear!' she smiled viciously.

Uncorking a bottle of turpentine she sprinkled it over the pile of canvases. There was still a pall of black clouds overhead. She stared up at them. 'Don't you go raining on me till I'm finished,' she threatened, then touched a lighted match to Thomasin's face, and waited.

Josie spotted the smoke curling past the bedroom window and, frowning, went to peer out. It was not until she saw what Peggy was using for faggots that she threw open the window and shouted at the top of her voice, 'Stop, Miss Peggy, stop!' But Peggy chose not to hear her. She shouted again more stridently – then careened down the staircase past a startled Judith and flew out into the garden.

'Miss Peggy, don't!' She began to tussle over her friend's paintings. 'For God's sake don't do this to him!' She seized the edge of a canvas that jutted from the fire and hauled it from the flames. 'It'd be like burning his children!' She threw the singed canvas on the ground and attempted to rescue another. Peggy thrust her to one side, amazingly strong in her madness, and hurled the salvaged painting back onto the fire.

As quickly as Josie rescued the paintings Peggy threw them back on, enraging the normally placid housekeeper. 'I won't let you do this to him!' Josie screamed and clung fiercely to the canvas that Peggy tried to wrest from her. But her grip slipped from the frame and she fell over, her splayed fingers plunging onto red-hot bubbling paint. She screamed in pain and staggered back, unable to do any more to rescue poor Mr John's pictures, forced to watch as Peggy flung them one after another onto the blaze. 'Please, Miss Peggy, I beg you!' She started to weep at the sight of his long-awaited exhibition going up in a cloud of madness. 'Oh, don't. How can you be so cruel?'

'Cruel?' The saliva frothed at the corners of Peggy's hysterical mouth, like a hydrophobic bitch. 'You dare to label me cruel after you've done everything in your power to snatch my husband away from me. You slut!' She struck the helpless housekeeper across the face then stood sentinel over the merrily-dancing bonfire. 'Well, this'll teach you – and him – what happens to marriage-breakers!'

When Sonny came home at lunchtime the two kitchen-maids observed him with dumb expectancy. He asked politely where his lunch was and received only frightened looks. Exasperatedly he enquired after Josie.

'She's not here, sir,' volunteered Judith, round-eyed.

'Daddy, is it Bonfire Night?' interrupted Rosanna from her seat at the table. The maids swapped nervous looks. 'Where's the fireworks?'

'Rosanna, please don't butt in when I'm speaking to someone; I've told you that before,' said Sonny, annoyed, but more from the heat of the unbroken storm than at his daughter. The sweat was pouring off him. All he was asking for was his lunch and here he was faced with riddles. 'Would someone kindly tell me where Josie is?'

'But we always have fireworks on Bonfire Night, don't we?' whined Rosanna.

'For Heaven's sake it's the middle of summer!' cried her overheated father.

'Can we have our dinner, then?' asked Rosanna. 'We haven't had anything yet an' we're starving, aren't we, Nick?' She started to thump on the table with her fists. 'We want our dinner! We want our dinner! Come on, Nick.' He joined her. 'We want our dinner, we want our dinner!'

'Silence!' roared Sonny, crashing his own fist onto the table. The two children ceased immediately. 'Now, will someone – anyone – tell me: *where is Josie?*'

'Mam gave her a sack of something to take home,' Rosanna informed him. 'She came up to tell us she was going home and she wouldn't be here to get our lunch. When's she coming back, Father? My tummy's telling me off.'

Sonny turned his attention to the maids and demanded to know what had gone on. 'It's right what Miss Rosie said, sir,' replied Judith. 'The young missus sacked her.'

'Where is my wife now?' he exploded, and on being told rushed out into the clammy heat. 'Peggy! Peggy, where are you?'

He saw her then, standing by the charred remains of the still-smouldering bonfire. He dashed up to her. 'What on earth's going on in this house? I come home for a quiet lunch to be told that you've dismissed Josie and find my

562

daughter with the mistaken belief that it's Bonfire Night. What've you been burning? Just what's been going on?'

She continued to gaze down at the smouldering heap. He looked down also. A tiny square of unburnt canvas caught his eye as it levitated from the hot ashes and settled like a feather upon his boot. He stooped to pick it up – and icy fingers stroked his skin.

'She tried to stop me so I sacked her,' said Peggy, by way of explanation before he could speak.

'You've burnt my paintings!' It came out as a whisper as he turned the piece of canvas over and over in his fingers.

'Yes – every frigging one!' she spat.

'You bloody cow!' His hands reached for her throat, his expression one of fury. But her choking objections pierced his blind rage and he shoved her to the ground.

Peggy set up a mad baying as he ran pell-mell towards the house to see for himself, dreading what he would find . . .

Only the easel remained, grotesque in its nudity. Every single painting that he had painstakingly catalogued, every sketch, every tube of paint – gone. She had destroyed him. Seizing the easel he hurled it down again with a crash, swearing and damning her. Then he swayed to the window and saw through a red mist his wife still poised by the smoking bonfire as large drops began to bang against the window. How could she? How could anyone sane commit an act of such savagery?

But then Peggy wasn't sane. She was quite, quite mad. There she stood in the pouring rain, prodding at the sizzling heap of ashes with a stick, like a witch at her cauldron.

Regathering some composure, he pivoted swiftly, went downstairs, rifled purposefully in the bureau then ran out of the house. With that one crass, selfish deed she had succeeded in killing his love where everything else had failed. As the prongs of lightning scratched the surface of the bruised sky and the rain began to fall even faster he hailed a cab and climbed into its womblike darkness.

In his pocket his fingers curled round a scrap of paper. On it was scribbled Josie's address.

CHAPTER FORTY-FIVE

She had been such a comfort to him, cupping his face with her poor bandaged hands and telling him he'd replace all those pictures his wife had destroyed.

'It's not just the pictures, Josie,' he sighed loudly. 'Though God knows that's bad enough. It's me she's destroyed, pretending she loved me, setting me against my family . . . I feel so bloody awful for the times I've ranted at Mam on Peggy's behalf. She was right all along, but I was too besotted to see it.'

'People often do things which're against their natures when they're in love,' soothed Josie. She had been surprised – not to say overjoyed – when he had turned up at her little terraced house.

He nodded desolately, then frowned. 'I still can't see why she had to go this far. She could've gone on living in the same house . . . I would've gone on supporting her . . . why, *why* did she have to pick on the thing I prized most?'

Josie looked away. 'I think I'm to blame.'

'Because she thought you and I were . . . ?'

She faltered, then nodded. 'I'll never forgive myself. I tried to rescue your pictures but she was too strong. I tried to tell her there was nothing between you an' me . . .'

'But there is, isn't there, Josie?' he said unexpectedly.

Slowly she lifted her face to his, then nodded. 'I feel I'm to blame for all this . . . I show my feelings too easily.'

He took one of her bandaged hands gently between his. 'You're not to blame. If anybody's at fault it's me for not seeing what was under my nose. You and me . . . we share a lot of things, don't we? I feel . . . sort of comfy with you.

I can talk about my paintings and you understand straight away what I mean ...' He sighed.

'What about your exhibition, Mr John?'

A bitter laugh. 'What exhibition? Everything's gone.'

'What about the paintings at the store?'

'Hardly sufficient for an exhibition,' he said lifelessly. 'There's only a dozen or so.'

'Nonsense! People'll only have to see one painting to know how talented you are – and you can have the one you gave me. I brought it with me.'

He was unconvinced. 'Oh ... I don't think I'll bother about the exhibition now, Josie. I haven't really got the heart. In fact I doubt I'll ever have the heart to paint again.'

'Now enough o' that rubbish!' she chastised sternly. 'I'm not going to allow all that talent to go to waste 'cause o' one upset. I'll stand behind you with a whip if I have to.' She saw the sad smile. 'I mean it! I won't let go, John.' John, she had called him John. 'This exhibition was to be the most important event in your life an' I'm going to see it happens.'

'Oh, you're a nice girl, Josie,' he said in earnest. 'I don't deserve such support after being so bloody stupid.'

'Then you'll go ahead with it?' she persisted.

He nodded rather reluctantly. 'If you're behind me I think I can do it.'

'Oh!' She collapsed in relief. 'Well, that's a load off my mind. I'd never've forgiven myself if I'd been responsible for ruining your career.'

There was a period of silence. She chose that moment to offer the hospitality she had overlooked in her shock at seeing him. 'Would you care for some tea?' He smiled and said he would and settled back into the sofa to survey the homely room.

He stayed throughout the afternoon, just talking, getting rid of his pain and his anger. When the time came for him to go he felt a great deal better. Her words had gone a long way to restoring his confidence in himself. He stood ready to take his leave. 'Well . . . I'd better go home and tell Mam and Dad what's happened.'

'You'll give the master and mistress my apologies for leaving them in the lurch?' asked Josie.

'I will, but there's no need. I feel I should apologise to you for the way I let Peggy treat you.'

'Oh, that doesn't matter . . . but if you would thank the master an' mistress for being so decent.'

'Mother'll probably want you to come back, you know.'

'I'm sorry but it just wouldn't work.'

'I agree,' he said. 'And anyway I don't want you to come back.' At her look of hurt surprise he smiled and tapped her shoulder gently. 'When I see you again I'd rather it be here where Peggy can't hurt us.'

Us. Her lips parted. 'You want to see me again?'

'Well, didn't you mention something about standing behind me with a whip? You can hardly do that if we don't see each other can you?' He smiled. 'Oh, Josie, you've been so good . . . and listen! You'll have to come to my exhibition too. I'll send a carriage for you.'

'What about Miss Peggy?' she asked doubtfully.

His sombre mood returned. 'It's all over between us, Josie. Anyway, she's not likely to be at the exhibition, is she?' He saw her again at the bonfire. The sting of his wound was still fresh, but it was futile to be angry any more. 'No, I want you there, Josie.'

'I'd love to come, John.' She smiled her affection. 'An' I know it'll be a great success.'

'Yes,' he pondered thoughtfully. 'Suddenly, I think you're right.' He smiled again and turned to the door, opening it.

Before saying goodbye she voiced her feelings on leaving his children. 'Oh, dear – I am going to miss them.'

'There's no need. I'll bring them to see you.'

'Oh, would you? I'd love to have them.'

'Tell you what,' he gestured at the pouring rain, 'if this lot has stopped by tomorrow I think we should take a picnic, all four of us.' What the hell had made him say that, he didn't know; his world had fallen around him and

566

here he was suggesting picnics! But it would take his mind off things, and maybe he might just buy a few tubes of paint on the way home . . .

Josie was overwhelmed; all she could answer was, 'That'd be nice.'

'I'll call for you at three, all right?'

'Shall I not expect you if it's still raining?' she asked apprehensively.

He smiled. 'As long as you don't see old Freddie Gash you can expect me,' he promised.

'Who's Freddie Gash?'

'Never mind. Just expect me.' Suddenly he kissed her, then dashed off into the pouring rain.

No one had ever seen Thomasin so angry as when Sonny had told her of his tragedy.

'May God forgive me for saying this, Sonny, but say it I will: if you'd listened to me none of this would have happened! That evil bitch! How could she? Wait till I get my hands on her.'

Her son had physically to restrain her from leaving the room. 'Whatever you're going to do to her, Mam, it won't make one scrap of difference. Can't you see she's ill? Sick in the head.'

'She will be when I've finished with her!' roared Thomasin, trying to free herself. 'Sick you say? She isn't the only one. You must be sick in the head to let her get away with this. She's not sick, she's evil -- evil!'

'Look -- if I can accept it philosophically, why can't you? They were my pictures she destroyed, yet I'm not ranting and raving, crying for revenge.'

'No, you aren't and I can't for the life of me understand it,' replied his mother hotly. 'If it were my exhibition she'd burnt I'd be after chucking her on the bloody bonfire.'

'D'you think I haven't contemplated that?' sighed Sonny. 'God, when I saw what was left . . . but gnashing my teeth and tearing my hair won't bring them back, will it? So I'll just have to buckle down and start again.' As easily as that – he could almost smile about it, but really it was no joke.

Patrick had been as shocked as his wife at the news, for despite his former reservations he had come to recognise Sonny's talent and had been immensely proud of the coming exhibition. However, he gravitated towards clemency. 'Much as I want to throttle her meself,' he told his wife, 'I'm inclined to agree with Sonny; she is sick. She has to be to do a thing like this. We can't just chuck her out on the street, we must show some sort of responsibility.'

'I would've thought that fell to her own family,' replied Thomasin stiffly.

'Oh aye, I can just see Clancy welcoming her back,' said Patrick.

'So what are we supposed to do with her?' demanded Thomasin. 'All right, Sonny you can let me go now, I promise I won't throw another bobbery.' Her son slackened his grip on her arms and smoothed out the wrinkles his fingers had made in the silk. 'And to cap it all!' went on Thomasin, 'she has to sack Josie. The cheek of it! She's been dying to do it all along. Well, that's something I can at least remedy. I'm going to fetch that girl back.'

'I'm afraid she won't come, Mam,' Sonny told her and passed on Josie's message.

'Oh, so you went after her?' she said with interest.

'Well, I thought one of us had better offer apologies for Peggy's treatment of her. And while we're on that subject I'd like to say I'm sorry to both of you. I've said some bloody disgusting things, especially to you, Mam . . .'

She silenced him. 'God knows we all do and say some stupid things when we're in a passion.' Patrick silently agreed with his eyes.

Sonny nodded his thanks as his mother said despairingly, 'Well . . . now that the passion's over, it looks as though we're stuck with her – for the time being anyway.'

After prolonged discussion it was decided that the best thing to do about Peggy was to have her examined by a doctor and for each member of the family to watch her carefully in case she should turn her wrath on the children.

Despite her tantrum when the doctor came, he was unwilling to certify her, saying that in his opinion she was as sane as he was but was just susceptible to bouts of hysteria, rather like a spoilt child. For this condition he prescribed a sedative, leaving the bottle in Thomasin's keeping.

However, it was not found necessary to use this after a week or two. Peggy's mood changed course and if anything she became rather introverted, keeping herself very much to herself and upsetting no one – so the bottle was forgotten, to gather dust on the medicine cabinet shelf.

As far as the exhibition was concerned things were not nearly so bad as they might have been, for at Lewis' insistence and with the support of Josie and his parents Sonny went ahead with the display. Not only did he sell every picture, but received enough commissions to provide him with two years' work, which he would carry out at the studio that Thomasin had obtained as consolation for his loss and also to avoid the risk of a recurrence. At last his star was beginning to shine.

Thinking Peggy was her only worry Thomasin was lulled into a false calm by the uneventfulness from this quarter. It was Friday morning. She had been almost ready to go and inspect the modernisation work that was to result in her second-floor department when her stepdaughter turned up carrying a large bag.

'Erin, what pleasure to see you! But so early.' She laid aside the hat that she had been about to put on and hugged the visitor. 'Where's Sam? You look as though you've come for a couple of days.' She pointed at the bag.

Erin pressed her cheek against her mother's in greeting, then moved away. 'I'm on my own. I thought I might take a few days' holiday.' She tugged at her gloves then removed the felt and feather hat from her black hair.

Thomasin at once sensed the tautness behind the remark. 'Has there been trouble between you two?' She moved to the sofa, sat down and patted it.

Erin, never one to hide her emotions, let her face crumple. 'Oh, Mam!' She flung herself into Thomasin's arms and sobbed heartrendingly. 'We had a terrible row last night. I couldn't stand it any more. I want to come home – for good.'

Thomasin fought her dismay. 'That's a bit drastic, isn't it? Anyhow, I always thought Sam was so placid. What made him lose his temper?'

'He's a different person lately,' Erin sniffed. "Everything's gone wrong.'

'Oh, not everything, surely?' soothed Thomasin. 'Come on, tell me what's amiss.'

Erin went crimson and pulled away. 'I can't. It's too personal.'

'Even to your mother?' encouraged Thomasin. Then her wits sharpened. 'Erin, you don't mean to tell me that you two still haven't bedded together?'

Erin sat bolt upright. 'How do you know about that? It was Sam, wasn't it? It must've been. Oh, how awful! I'll bet he's told everbody how stupid I am.' She burst into fresh tears.

'No, no,' Thomasin consoled her. 'Only me and your father know about it.'

'Father knows as well? Oh, how embarrassing!'

'Sam was forced to tell him when the question arose about who would foster Rosanna. He was afraid if you got her you wouldn't want his child. But, love – surely it's not still the same way between you two! I mean, we thought that was sorted out by now. You seemed to look a bit more settled with each other after Sam finished at the butchery and spent more time at home.'

Erin shook her head woefully. 'We made an agreement: we'd live together as friends and sleep in separate rooms. If I seemed happier then it was only because that pressure was off me. But Sam decided that he didn't want to live as friends any more. He thought after I'd had a rest I'd be willing to try again. I was . . . but it was still the same. I'm afraid he's finally got sick of my stupidity. That's why I'm here. He's told me that if I won't be a proper wife I must go and live somewhere else. He doesn't want me now.'

'I'm sure that's not true. But the question is, do you want him?'

Erin lifted a red-mottled face. 'Yes. That's the most confusing part of it all. I *do* love him and want him . . . but I can't, I just can't . . .'

'D'you remember Jos Leach?' asked Thomasin suddenly.

There was no reaction, only a frown. 'No, who's he?'

'Doesn't matter, only a thought. Look . . . I know it's a bit delicate for you to talk about and I'm not asking for details, but just what is it that makes you afraid? I mean, you said you knew what was expected of you. You told me not to bother when I tried to give you fair warning before your wedding night. It wasn't just because you were too embarrassed to listen, was it?'

'No, no, I did know really. But knowing doesn't make things any easier, does it?'

Thomasin sighed. 'I can't say as I've ever had that problem, it just sort of came naturally to me. Eh dear, I don't know how I'm going to help you.'

'Could I stay here awhile? Not for good, just for a few days if you'll have me.'

'Daft 'aporth, of course we'll have you – but that won't solve anything, will it, love? Some time or other it's got to be faced or you'll have a long, lonely time ahead of you. And I don't think you want that do you?'

'No, I love him as much as ever . . . but I'm so frightened, Mam.' Erin leaned her head on her stepmother's shoulder.

'Then you'll have to make up your mind which frightens you most,' said Thomasin firmly. 'Being a proper wife – or losing him altogether.'

Patrick found it hard to reconcile himself to Erin's defection. 'A woman's place is with her husband,' he informed her. 'All the argument you put up in favour of Sam an' now ye go leave him in the lurch.' He looked at his wife. 'If we appear to condone her behaviour, let her hide behind her parents then we're as much to blame as she is if the marriage fails.'

'Daddy, please don't send me away,' begged Erin.

'I'm not about to send ye anywhere,' replied Patrick calmly. He had been as shocked as his wife to learn that Erin's apparent reconciliation had been but a charade. 'But I do think that we should inform Sam where you are and tell him to come over and sort matters out once and for all.'

Thomasin endorsed his view. 'He'll be worried, Erin.'

'He knows where I am,' argued their daughter, dismayed by their lack of support. 'I've been here for three days – if he'd wanted me he'd've been here. He's made it patently clear by his absence that he wants nothing to do with me.'

'Clear?' said her grandfather who had come to invite them all to the birthday tea that Hannah had organised for Sunday. 'It's all as clear as a pile o' bloody sheep doddins to me.' He had unwittingly asked about Erin's presence and Patrick, to his daughter's horror, had involved him in the argument. 'If somebody'd tell me what cause of Erin leavin' was, happen I could add my superior judgment, but I'm not sidin' wi' anyone without knowin' all facts.'

'No one's asking ye to take sides, Grandad.' Erin glared at her father, daring him to let her secret out.

Patrick cleared his throat. 'Aye, well perhaps I was wrong to involve ye, Billy. 'Tis a bit delicate-like.'

'None o' my bloody business tha means,' said William.

'It's none of anyone's business,' exclaimed Erin. 'But Mother an' Father seem to be making it theirs.'

Thomasin would not allow this. 'Now wait on! You involved us when you came running here, tail between legs.'

Erin was at once contrite. 'I know, I know. I'm sorry.' She stopped measuring the carpet to sit down with a bump. 'An' I know this discussion is only designed to help, but you're confusing me further with your suggestions.

I've got to have time to sort this out for myself. I'd like to do it here, but if ye want me to leave I will.'

'Eh, Erin Feeney-as-was you're an independent cat.' Thomasin crossed her arms. 'You know very well we wouldn't chuck you out.'

'Look, if nobody's gonna tell us what this is all abaht can I ask if any o' you buggers are gonna come to this 'ere party or not?' requested William impatiently. 'Our Hannah's rushing round at 'ome as if her arse is on fire. There'll be hell to pay if no bugger turns up. Besides,' he grinned, 'I've got this special present what I want everybody to' see.'

'By the look on your face I can't wait,' said Patrick. 'What is it?'

'Ah, keep tha neb out! Tha'll know soon enough. I'm not spoilin' surprise.'

They were no wiser when it was unveiled by the recipient at the Sunday birthday tea. Hannah held the metal contraption this way and that, and theorised on its purpose. 'It's a very well-made gift, William, I'm sure,' she told her husband. 'But ... what exactly is it?'

'I knew it'd flummox thee.' William slapped his knee. 'But tha were right when tha said it were well-made. Does anybody else know wharrit is?'

Thomasin took the article from her puzzled mother and applied pressure to the metal strips. It was shaped something like a helmet, but the bands ran full circle and there was no way one could get it over one's head.

'I think it's a birdcage,' she announced, and passed it to her husband.

'Nay, I hope you can show more initiative than that, Pat,' said William, and pressed for an answer. 'Away! What d'yer think it is?' His face was elfin-like.

Patrick disagreed with his wife. 'Well, it's definitely not a birdcage – look at the spaces between the bars. Anyway, even if it were big enough to house a parrot I doubt Hannah would allow one in her house if you had anything to do with training it to speak. But, I can't for the life of

573

me provide a better solution to your riddle. I might have said a helmet ...'

'Tha's gerrin' nearer,' pronounced William happily.

'That was my first thought,' contributed Thomasin. 'But what would Mother want with a helmet? Always considering she could get it on her head in the first place. It's the queerest thing I've ever seen.'

After Sonny, Peggy and the children had passed it amongst themselves and failed to guess its purpose, it was offered to an uninterested Erin, whose head was filled with her own problems.

'I've really no idea what it is.' She was about to pass it back but as William's face fell she made herself look brighter than she felt to please him, examining the object more thoroughly. 'Well, it can't possibly be a helmet because ... oh, yes look – it's got a lock here. This piece must come open somehow.' She tugged at it.

'It waint open, lass.' William, his face devilish, dangled a key between thumb and forefinger.

Hannah was beginning to grow suspicious. 'If this is one of your insidious jokes ...'

'A chastity belt!' provided Patrick instantaneously.

'Nay, nay!' guffawed William, his eyes red with suppressed tears. 'Tha's got wrong end. First answer was warmer.'

'What a birdcage?' said Sonny.

'Nay, a bloody helmet, whoops! Sorry children present.' William cupped his hands over Rosanna's ears.

'Oh, come on,' protested Thomasin. 'Let us out of our misery. What is it?'

William held his breath, surveyed each expectant face, then blurted out the answer in a rush of wind. 'It's a scold's bridle! Hah, ooh!' He could say nothing more for laughing.

'A what?' Patrick laughed with him, as did the others.

'A scold's bridle!' The tears, unleashed, streamed down the wrinkles on William's screwed-up face. 'I ... ooh, God! I saw this contraption hangin' outside a blacksmith's last time we went to pay our Erin a visit. I were stumped, same as thee, couldn't mek head nor tail on it. I just had to go an' ask smithy what it were – eh, I'm glad I did! Well, when he told me I nearly split me sides. Said he'd seen a picture o' one in a book an' thought it were a good idea to mek a copy to shut his wife up. 'Course, he never used it tha knows, just hung it there as a threat, an' it worked!' He grabbed the metal contraption from Erin and inserted the key, opening the back.

'See, this 'ere bar goes over her head, an' this little square bit goes in her mouth to press her tongue down. An' when it's all locked up she can't get no words out, see? Well, when I saw it I sez I'll have to have one o' them – it'll mek a perfect present for our Hannah!'

'Oh, William!' cried his wife. 'This is the most despicable thing you have ever done to me. Indefensible. I shall never speak to you again.'

'Aye, that were t'general idea!' roared William as she rushed from the room.

'Oh, Dad you are awful,' giggled Thomasin, and the others joined her laughter. The present was so wickedly apt.

Even Erin was incited to join in as her grandfather heaved and coughed and brayed, his eyes screwed shut in gleeful agony. 'Ooh, I'm a wicked owd bugger an' no mistake! I won't half suffer for this. It'll be bread an' watter for months.' He rocked back and forth, gripping his knees, not knowing which part of himself to clutch first as the laughter stabbed him from all angles. His mouth open, he bent double, cradling his aching ribcage. 'Ooh, hah! God, that's the best one I've played on her for a long while. Oh, somebody get me a drink to calm me down!' His old shoulders pulsated with mirth and he jerked upright to catch his breath, then flopped back into the chair, mouth agape in the jolly face, ready to emit another belly laugh.

It took some seconds for the laughing onlookers to realise that William was dead.

'Mother! Mother, come quickly!' The urgency in her

daughter's voice impelled Hannah to throw off the cloak of self-pity and come uncertainly to the top of the stairs.

'What is it?' She clutched a damp handkerchief as she looked down on Thomasin's white face.

'It's Dad ... you'd better come down ... oh, Mam.' Thomasin's stalwart expression crumpled, then vanished as its owner moved swiftly back to attend her dead father.

There was the clatter of hurried footfalls on the stair and a breathless Hannah, straight as a stick with no hint of her rheumatism, stood clutching the handkerchief, gazing with horror at the scene before her. Then the handkerchief flew up to her mouth. 'William! William!' She rushed up to his chair and began to shake him by the shoulders. The children, frightened but dry-eyed, watched her, fascinated.

Patrick broke off from comforting his wife to take his mother-in-law in hand. 'Hannah, I'm sorry ... there's nothing you can do ... he's dead.' It was so hard to believe. The swiftness of it ...

Hannah, face set in a waxen mask, let herself be eased gently away from the chair. She fell back to join the conclave of mourners, but perversely when the situation demanded true grief Hannah's eyes were dry. It was one of her idiosyncrasies that any upset, however mild, could divine a river of tears; the lack of histrionics made the scene all the more poignant. Her eyes were drawn back to the birthday present on which William still retained a loose grip. 'I told him I'd never speak to him again,' she said feebly.

'He knew you didn't mean it, Hannah,' placated Patrick, one arm around her shrunken shoulders, the other round his wife's. 'He was having a really good laugh about it ... you know Billy ...'

'Yes. Yes, I know William,' whispered Hannah, her glassy eyes fixed to his chair. 'Hadn't someone better go for the doctor?'

Patrick released her. 'I'll go, if ye can tell me where I'll find him.'

Sonny stepped into the breach. 'I'll go, you stay with

Grandma; you're more use than I am.' He checked to see if Peggy and the children were all right. He needn't have worried. Peggy was unmoved by the event, and Erin was comforting the children infected by the sounds of grief from their grandmother and aunt. Armed with his grandmother's instructions he departed to look for the doctor's house.

Patrick examined Hannah's face concernedly. She was taking it awfully well – too well, in fact. There was Tommy and Erin hollering their eyes out, the children too, while Hannah sheltered under an umbrella of dignified calm. But the dam would break sooner or later he knew.

Hannah's hands, the skin loosely draped over the bony phalanges and marbled with liver-spots, played absently with the tongue of lace that fell from the neck of the dress she had made herself for her birthday. He touched her arm. 'It was very quick, Hannah. The way he would've wanted to go. If ye've got to go I can't think of a better way than to die laughing.'

'But I wasn't with him,' she replied vaguely. Then all at once the eyes, till now dry, brimmed over as she looked at him. Her mouth discharged one long, heart-rending moan and she broke down in a paroxysm of grief.

'Tommy!' commanded Patrick, shaking his wife. 'Ye've had your turn, come an' look to your mother while I go see if I can get any brandy. Erin, you too!'

His daughter raised her head from the children's and followed Patrick's flying exit with distraught eyes. Oh, Sam, Sam, how I wish you were here. Eyes and nose streaming, she went blindly to where she knew the smelling salts were kept, for Hannah had now collapsed in a dead swoon. Erin prayed earnestly for the same kindly oblivion to overtake her and blot out all this unbearable misery. But no one heard her plea.

As was usual in such emergencies, any animosity that might pass between Hannah and Patrick was put aside; they acquired a state of unity during times of stress. So, when Hannah tearfully declared that nothing could persuade her to spend the night here alone with her beloved William, Patrick made the kind offer that he knew, even as he said it, he was later going to regret.

'Of course we wouldn't expect ye to stay here on your own, Hannah.' He helped his mother-in-law on with her coat while Thomasin packed a small case with her mother's belongings. 'Ye must go home with Tommy an' the others. I'll take care of things here.'

'But all the funeral arrangements,' said Hannah weakly.

'Don't you fret yourself, I'll take care of it all.'

'He must have the best,' ordered Hannah.

'I wouldn't dream of arranging anything other than the best for Billy, you know that.' Patrick would miss his father-in-law. He recalled, as one does at the death of a friend, their first meeting. How Billy had welcomed the marriage between his daughter and the Irishman; had made him feel part of a family with his down-to-earth humour and lack of pretensions. He instructed his son to see the womenfolk safely home while he tended to matters here.

'Hadn't someone better let Dickie know?' Sonny found that he could say his brother's name without the usual taste of rancour. He assumed it to be because Peggy was no longer of any importance to him.

But his mother could not dispose herself so kindly. 'No one will inform Dickie,' she told him, her face dead of expression. 'Doubtless he'll get to hear of it. If he does then he's welcome to come to the funeral, but I'm damned if I'm going out of my way to tell him. His actions have robbed him of any right to membership of this family.'

Sonny turned his attentions to his sister who comforted Nick on her lap. 'If you like I can ride out and tell Sam, to save you going home then having to come straight back.' He had no idea of the turmoil his offer caused her, nor of the reason behind his sister's visit.

Erin formed her lips into a 'no', but Thomasin jumped in first. 'That's good of you, Sonny. Tell him to come as soon as he's able.' The sooner the better, she thought emptily. She had had her fill of her children's troubles; Erin, for one, must be made to face her own.

CHAPTER FORTY-SIX

He could not look at her, nor she at him. When he had turned up at Monkgate, bedraggled and weary from his eight-mile journey on an open cart in the pouring rain, it had not been his wife who had administered tender concern but Peggy. It was she who had shown him up to his room, providing him with a towel, commandeering the maids to fetch up a bath of hot water and issuing him a set of warm, dry clothes belonging to Sonny. Even when he had returned to the gathering there had been nothing from Erin.

All the way there he had practised what he was going to say. He had been going to be oh, so strong; tell her she must come home right this minute else she could stay with her parents for good – that was before he had met with his brother-in-law in a similar state of saturation coming to tell him of William's untimely demise. He couldn't say all those things now, could he? When he and Sonny had arrived Sam had tried to offer his condolences, but she had merely nodded and moved away, leaving Thomasin to welcome him. He had lamely apologised for his drenched clothes and for not having brought any more suitable attire. 'I was halfway here, you see when I met Sonny and he told me . . . I really don't know what to say. I was awful fond of Grandad.' He had pulled at his dripping things. 'I'm going to look a bit out of place at the funeral, aren't I?'

That was when Peggy, surprising everyone with her concern, had assumed command of the situation, taking Sam and her husband away to dry them off.

Now, he stood amongst the funeral mourners, his head

held low so that he did not have to look at Erin, the trousers, much too long, bagging round his ankles. 'You'll be able to change back into your own clothes when you get back,' Peggy told him. 'I've seen to it they've been aired and pressed. I'm sorry all the men in this house appear to be giants.' She looked down at the baggy trousers.

'You've been very kind, Peggy,' he answered, and looked pointedly at Erin, who turned her head away swiftly. 'It's a sad business. I'm sure we'll all miss Grandad very much.'

The room was filled with William's relations. It had been decided to hold the funeral from Monkgate as Hannah's little house would not take all the mourners; the old man had been very popular. All Thomasin's sisters were here with their spouses, shedding tears of remorse that they had not been more regular visitors to their father's home. But Thomasin knew that their tears were more for themselves and would dry much more rapidly than either hers or her mother's. Apart from his immediate family, probably the most genuine grief came from William's young apprentice, a lad of sixteen – the two had been great pals.

Hannah looked out of the window, waiting for the hearse to arrive. She looked old and frail standing there, bowed with the pain of her rheumatism, the black dress, due to a damp storage place, freckled with mildew. This was how she would look all the time now, thought her daughter sadly. The dragon's fire had been doused; in its place was a weary old crow with moth-eaten feathers, just waiting for her turn to come.

All eyes turned to Hannah as she spoke. 'I think I'll just go and say goodbye before the carriage arrives.' She limped into the other room where her husband was laid out. The men rose as she left.

Soon after this the funeral cortège with its plumed horses rolled up and the men departed with their sad load, leaving the women behind closed curtains. When they returned in sombre mood everyone sat down to a salad lunch, Sam next to Erin where his mother-in-law firmly steered him. Even juxtaposed their incommunicativeness remained unbroken – though no one but Thomasin and Patrick appeared to notice, their own conversation sparing, and by the time the meal was over only about five minutes had been dedicated to speech.

Thomasin herded everyone from the dining room, keeping Erin and Sam under her strict control and making certain they ended up with similar seating arrangements in the drawing room; they were going to have to speak to each other some time. After she had drunk her coffee, Erin, unable to bear this silence any longer, excused herself and went to sit in the cool of the lavatory, where she could put her words into perspective before she delivered them. She realised that one of them was going to have to back down, and it should be her. When she emerged everything was clearer in her mind; she would take Sam out into the garden where she might explain her feelings in private. Sadly, when she returned to the drawing room he had forsaken his seat and was now, in more relaxed pose, joking and laughing with Peggy by the window.

'This *is* supposed to be a funeral!' she hissed under her breath as she passed them. 'Think what your insensitivity does to Grandma.' She went to reclaim her seat. Sam looked after her guiltily, then turned back to Peggy, his voice suitably lowered.

'It'll do no good giving him murderous looks.' Thomasin spoke behind her cup. 'That lad's in a right old state with himself.'

'He looks fine to me,' muttered Erin angrily. 'Look at him flirting with Peggy, and never a word for his wife.'

'You didn't exactly make him feel welcome,' said her mother. 'And if it wasn't Peggy it'd be someone else. I've been watching him closely; his eyes have been on every female in this room – excluding your grandmother of course.' Her attempt at humour belied her heartache. Her father's death had affected her more than any of them knew.

But Erin could see nothing humorous. She turned surprised eyes on her mother. 'What, even you?'

Thomasin cocked an eyebrow. 'Aye, even me! I'm not past it yet, you know.'

'Sorry, I didn't mean it to sound like that.' Erin sighed. 'Well, he seems to have singled Peggy out for his attention.'

'That's only because she's shoving herself at him,' said Thomasin. 'I should take care if I were you – that lad's so hungry for it that anyone who treated him half like a man would do. He doesn't know where he is. A piece of paper tells him he's married but he's not getting from that status what he should be – and if you think that's being coarse that's your look-out. It's the truth.'

Erin looked startled. 'D'ye think he'll ... d'ye think anything'll happen between him and Peggy?' She knew that Sonny's marriage was all but over.

'Not under my roof it won't,' said Thomasin emphatically. 'But it's not really my place to see that it doesn't – it's yours. You must try, Erin, you really must, because whichever way he turns, it can only be in the wrong direction.'

Sam wriggled his way out of Sonny's clothes and folded them neatly over a chairback. The mourners were long since gone. Only the little apprentice had lingered and in the end had had to be politely turned out.

He pulled a nightgown over his head and climbed into bed. Clasping his hands behind his head he stared at the ceiling through the darkness. He had not meant it to be like this. He wanted her back, truly he did; for all she tortured him he still loved her. Even though he had said nothing at the funeral he was only waiting for some of the pain to heal before having matters out with her. He thought of the warmth of Peggy's reception and compared it to his wife's frigidity. She had not even spared a look in his direction, apart from administering that waspish remark after the meal. It was only talking to Peggy that had made the afternoon bearable. He closed his eyes in

582

annoyance as he began to feel a stirring under the sheet. Blazes! it was pathetic when just the thought of a woman could bring on an erection. He moved a hand down over his body and pressed against the hardness, fighting it. Then flung himself over onto his side and brought his knees up to his chest.

A slit of light on the wall was the first indication that someone had entered the room. The person slipped inside and hastily closed the door. Wide awake, he lifted his head from the pillow. He had known somehow she would come. The way she had looked at him before, her eyes unashamedly dropping to the lower half of his body. He had nearly disgraced himself there and then. There was a flurry of movement as the figure padded across the room.

'Erin!' The surprise in his voice conveyed the fact that he had expected someone else. He pulled himself into a sitting position as the waif-like figure in the white night-gown came to rest by his bed.

'Well, who did you expect?' There was defiance there, but her voice caught with apprehension and she fell on the bed. 'Oh, Sam forgive me! It was all my fault. I've been so stupid, so childish, an' I've missed ye so; I can't bear to tell ye how much. Please speak to me; I can't stand this silence. I can't bear the way ye looked at Peggy all afternoon – ye were expecting her, weren't ye? I'd die if ye turned to her. I love ye, Sam. Oh, I love ye – an' I'm here to be a proper wife, if ye still want me.'

In his joy he flung aside the covers and pulled her eagerly into bed, pressing her slight body to his inflamed hardness. She felt him against her belly and immediately began to tremble. Oh, Blessed Virgin it was going to be like all the other times . . .

'It's all right.' He kissed her and smoothed the hair from her face. 'Everything's going to be fine. Trust me, I won't hurt you, I promise. Oh, Erin I love you so much!' His hands travelled rapidly over her thin body. He was too eager; he must calm himself or he would frighten her off for ever – and he had waited so long for this. Thoughts of Peggy's voluptuous body vanished as he clutched the woman he loved, hugging her, feeling her, loving her. 'Erin, Erin, my love.' His lips burnt down on hers – but there was no response. He drew a halt to his fevered lovemaking and looked down at her, his eyes suffused with passion, gleaming in the darkness. Her eyes were squeezed shut, her lips compressed and the body beneath him trembled with uncontrollable terror.

'For pity's sake!' He made an exasperated exit from the bed, kicking out at the tangled covers and strode across to the wardrobe where the maid had hung his newly-pressed clothes.

Erin's head shot up as he savagely thrust his legs into the trousers. 'What are ye doing?'

He did not answer; the words remained strangled in his throat. Not until he had donned the rest of his clothes and she had reiterated her query several times did he stride back to glower over the bed. 'What sort of creature do you think I am, Erin Teale?' he barked, his voice on the point of breaking. 'Blazes! If I wanted a sacrificial lamb I can get one anywhere. You come in here offering yourself up like the pieces of dead flesh I used to see at my work and expect everything to come right?'

She was sobbing now. 'I thought you wanted me!'

'I do! But not like that. If I just wanted something to stick it into I could go to a brothel again.'

She flinched at his bluntness, then realised what he had said. 'Again? You've been to one of those places?'

'Well, what did you think I was made of?' he shouted. 'My wife doesn't want me, what am I supposed to do?' It was all lies; he had only said it to punish her.

'Oh, Sam!' she wept. 'I do want you, I do!'

'Then show it to me, Erin. Love me,' he begged, leaning over her.

'I can't! I can't!'

He glared at her distorted face shining with tears, then straightened and marched to the door. 'Where are you going?' she screamed after him.

'Anywhere! Away!'

'But it's the middle of the night. What will I tell people?' She wiped her face on the sheet.

'Tell them what you like,' he answered, the door opening under his violent pull. 'Tell them how I've done everything that's humanly possible to please you. How I've given up my job because you wanted me to – how I've never abused you as some men might – or is that what you want? Someone who'll knock you about and take his rights? Well, you won't get that from me, I'm afraid, Erin, I'm no animal. I'm a man, with feelings, and I can only take so much. What d'you imagine all this does to me? To know that my body horrifies you. The way you look at me . . . you make me feel . . . loathesome . . . unclean.' He was almost sobbing now.

The desperation of his words invoked her maternity, her compassion. 'Oh, no you're not, you're not!'

He shook his head, not hearing. 'It's no good . . . every time I see you I want you . . . I've got to get away.'

'Sam, I love you, please don't leave me!'

'I'm not leaving, I'm going home. When you've made your mind up what it is you want perhaps there'll be a place for you, too.'

Miraculously, the fear vanished, replaced by the greater threat that she was about to lose him for good. 'Sam, come back!' She leapt up, falling from the bed, her feet imprisoned in the nightgown. 'I know what I want. I'm all right. I'm not afraid now. Look!' She swiftly wrenched the garment over her head and stood there in the centre of the room, naked and shimmering, in the rays of morning light that came creeping through the curtains.

Her beauty screamed out to him to go back; to plunge his body into that sweet-smelling flesh. But still he smarted over the way she had offered herself, as though making love to her husband was some sort of painful duty. He wanted her to feel the way he had felt on the hundreds of occasions she had rejected him – inadequate. Maybe then she would truly understand what it felt like, needing someone and having them throw your love back in your face. The remembered humiliations stronger than his need, he swallowed and said thickly, 'It's good that you're not afraid of me any more, Erin. But I'm sorry, I've been disappointed too many times to trust you now. I'm going. It'll give you time to think – to see whether you really do want me. If you decide that you do, I'll be at home.' Then he was gone.

Naturally it had to be Peggy who commented upon Sam's absence from the breakfast table the next morning, though her wording was ambiguous.

'Did anyone hear the din last night?' she enquired lightly, dabbing her lips with a napkin. 'Someone was having a right old thunderstorm somewhere.'

Erin blushed and reached for the milk jug. 'I'm sorry if we woke you, Peggy.'

'Woke us? I wouldn't be surprised if you woke them up in Sheffield, the ding-dong you were having. What was it all about? Anything I can help with?'

Having to share a bedroom with her husband last night had not made her any sweeter. Especially since Sonny had shown he found it just as distasteful.

'I shouldn't imagine so,' said Erin, keeping her voice under control. An argument was just what Peggy wanted.

'If you have matrimonial problems perhaps I . . . '

'All right Peggy, I think ye've said your piece,' warned Patrick, spreading a knob of butter over his toast. 'Erin has enough to contend with – she doesn't need your unkind remarks.'

Peggy bridled. 'Why, I was only trying to help, I'm sure.'

'Well, you're hardly the one to assist with problems of a matrimonial nature, are ye?' said Patrick, with a sideways glance at his son. How long was this false marriage going to go on?

Peggy, still annoyed that Erin and Sonny between them had foiled her plans for last night, left the table and flounced off to her room.

Thomasin itched to find out just what had occurred during the night, but as Hannah was still at the table she fought down her inquisitiveness.

Unfortunately, Peggy had stirred Hannah's curiosity also. 'Where is Samuel? I thought he was to stay the night?'

Erin looked down at her plate and let Thomasin answer for her. 'He did, Mother, but he left early this morning.'

'Without saying goodbye? And why has Erin not accompanied him?' Hannah's rheumatic hand trembled under the weight of the cup.

'Erin is staying on for a few days,' said Thomasin brightly. 'I've decided she's looking peaky and needs a rest. Living in the country can be hard work, Mother, as you well know.' She deftly enlarged on this. 'You never got used to it, did you? Being away from civilised society.' William had taken her to share his weaver's cottage when they were first wed, but Hannah had eventually talked him into moving back to the city.

'Indeed I did not,' sighed Hannah. 'It was only to please your poor father that I went there in the first place. I would never have endured such spartan living conditions for anyone but William.'

Thomasin saw that her mother was going to cry, and said quickly, 'Well, you can stay here as long as you want, Mother. Have you any idea of how long that might be? Just so I can arrange the laundry and such; the maids like to be kept up to date.'

The cup rattled in its saucer as Hannah put it down. 'But I thought I made my position clear . . . I understood that was why you and Patrick brought me here. I could never go back there, Thomasin dear, never. The memories . . . it would all be too painful.'

Patrick froze in the act of stirring his tea and looked at his wife. 'Ye mean ye'll be staying with us . . . for good?'

She turned autocratic eyes on him, the Hannah they were familiar with. Thomasin had been wrong in her assessment yesterday; here she was, as rampant as ever. 'Am I to understand that the offer is withdrawn?'

'Oh no, Hannah,' he replied swiftly. 'But ye see . . . well . . . we didn't expect . . . I mean, you're welcome to stay of course . . .'

'Good, that's settled then.' Hannah reached for a piece

of toast as Patrick stood up dazedly to wander up and down, the spoon still in his fingers. What had he let himself in for?

Thomasin tried to change her mother's mind. 'Are you sure you won't regret leaving your own little house, your independence? The memories aren't all painful ones, surely?'

'Impossible,' said Hannah, snapping the toast with her swollen fingers. 'William's ghost would be there, always. Besides, I am a gregarious creature. Living alone I would waste away. No, you have plenty of room here, Thomasin, and I'm sure you would not begrudge your mother this little comfort after all she has done for you.' The toast crumbled and fell to the plate. 'Really! I shall have to take your domestics in order – this toast is like charcoal.'

'Mother, I hope you aren't going to interfere in the smooth running of my house?' put in her daughter.

'Interfere? I would not dream of it – though I feel it is time someone did. If this were my household I would hire someone who can cook. This meal was appalling.'

'Yes, well I did intend to hire another cook until all this upset,' said Thomasin, and turned away to hide a smile as she caught sight of Patrick standing directly behind his mother-in-law, moving the spoon in a circular direction above her head. They were in for a lot more stirring if she were not mistaken.

Thomasin finally captured her daughter when Hannah and Sonny had left the table. 'At last! Now we can talk.' She noted Erin's look at her father. 'Oh, pretend your father isn't here. He knows all about it anyway, and I'm certain he's as curious as I am to know what the Devil went on last night.' She made a waving gesture as Erin opened her mouth. 'Well, it's palpably clear what didn't go on! What's wrong with you, girl? Can't you get it past your stubborn fear just how lucky you are to have a partner like Sam? Look at Sonny – what sort of a marriage has he got? Look at poor Grandma; she's just lost her husband. You've got a good marriage there, Erin – and all you can do is throw it away.'

Patrick frowned at his wife. 'There's no need to treat the girl so hard; she doesn't need you to tell her, I know.'

Erin raised a hand. 'It's all right, Father. She's got a right to be annoyed after we made such fools of ourselves last night.'

Thomasin shook her head and covered Erin's hand. 'You know I don't mind you smashing the house to bits if it resolved anything – but did it? That's all I want to know.'

Erin looked from one to the other, at their expressions of loving concern, then she allowed her mouth to turn up at the corners, moved the hand under Thomasin's and gripped it reassuringly. 'Yes, it did,' she said quietly. 'I'm going home.'

'Bairns!' snorted Thomasin when she and Patrick were left alone. 'Nowt but trouble – as if we haven't enough. And to have Mother on top of all that.' She groaned. 'I'm sorry, Pat love. I did try.'

'Ah well,' he replied. 'I suppose ye could say I brought it on meself. 'Twas me who was playin' Lord Bountiful.' He accepted her offer of more tea. 'Aye, thank ye. That's one thing I like about being a master: ye don't have to worry about being late for work.' He scoured the advertisements on the front page of the newspaper. 'Though with Hannah in the house I'm not sure I'll be master for long. I'll probably be glad of somewhere to escape to.'

'Is that new lad framing any better?' She was glad Patrick was seeing sense now and not trying to do all the work himself. Though if she could persuade him to take on even more help she would, that's what the money was supposed to be for – to make life easier. Patrick tended to do the opposite; this last year had seen him add a further hundred and fifty acres to his land. And he had plans to buy more – if the work didn't kill him first.

'He's better than he was, as long as Catch is there to keep an eye on him. These young uns are all the same ye know, won't have work.' His eyes roved the page. He touched his cup to his lips and, replacing it in the saucer, turned over the leaf.

'Well, it sounds as if our Erin has got herself straight,' said Thomasin smiling, then her happiness turned to something nearing confusion. 'And have you noticed Sonny's started looking a lot happier, too? It must be his painting – it certainly isn't Peggy, there's nothing so sure as that. Eh, that wife of his! I do believe if she hadn't been forced to double up with Sonny last night she would've been in with Sam like a shot. Did you see the way she was looking at him yesterday? It's a wonder his clothes didn't catch fire – oh, which reminds me! Have you taken that bottle of sedative from the medicine cabinet? I noticed it was missing the other day . . . are you listening to me?'

He looked up vaguely from the paper. 'What? Sorry, I didn't . . . ' He looked back down at the print.

'What is it?' His wife leaned forward concernedly. 'Patrick?' She stared at him worriedly. Now, when did he grow old? she asked herself with surprise, looking at the lines that dissected his tanned face, his grey hair. Time had always seemed to stand still for Patrick, it was she who had been the one to age – but now he had joined her, looking incredibly earth-weary.

'Listen to this.' He began to read from the newspaper. 'The headline reads: **Victory Over House of Ill-Repute**. *"Several charitable bodies were today celebrating the closure of that infamous building 'Traveller's Comfort' after a successful battle in the police court. Magistrates told the brothel-keeper,"* ' here he paused for effect, ' *"Richard William Feeney,"* ' Thomasin gasped as he continued, ' *"That his house was a vile slur on this fair city and the continued referral of his courtesans to the magistrates' proceedings would no longer be tolerated. An order was made that the house must be closed within twenty-four hours or Feeney would be faced with more serious charges. The true purpose of this supposed lodging house came to light when a known woman of the town, Maria Stanton, was witnessed by a police officer accosting several gentlemen in Spurriergate. After several such instances Stanton persuaded one of the gentlemen to go with her. The officer followed them to a house in Micklegate where on gaining entry he found all of the upstairs rooms occupied by persons of opposite gender, some of* *whom were in an advanced state of undress. Stanton was taken to the police station and subsequently charged with wandering abroad and indecency. Further to this, two police officers visited the said establishment two days later and found a man and a woman in an upstairs room. The man, Richard William Feeney, was arrested and charged with keeping a bawdy house. In his defence Feeney – whose mother owns a number of grocery stores in the city,"* ' Thomasin groaned, ' *"emphatically refuted the charge and said that he was simply the proprietor of a legally-registered lodging house. He did admit that the woman, Stanton, was in his employ, but argued that it was in the capacity of chamber-maid; if she had committed an act of indecency then it was from an independent stance and not of his instigation. Of the initial police visit to his house, Feeney provided evidence that he had not been present on the night in question and therefore could not be held responsible for his staff's behaviour in his absence. He had, he told the court, been forty miles away in Scarborough and produced a receipt for bed and breakfast at the Grand Hotel and also a railway ticket. Cross-examined, the arresting officer, Sergeant Rhodes, agreed that the defendant had indeed not been present during the raid and the woman concerned had admitted that she was responsible for her own misdemeanour. However, there had been other instances of girls in Feeney's employ appearing before magistrates and despite his plea of ignorance Feeney was found guilty of permitting his house to be used for immoral purposes . . ."* ' Patrick had read enough and tossed aside the paper in disgust, then looked at his wife.

What the newspaper account did *not* mention was that a member of the bench had met with an unfortunate experience in the said house – a five pound note had been stolen from his trouser pocket while he was being entertained. Being, supposedly, a pillar of society the magistrate had little redress, but he now grasped this opportunity to get his own back by ordering the brothel to be closed down. Dickie, fearing a long sentence, decided not to make any cheeky comment. Even the regular instalments that Dickie paid out for police protection were useless in this case. The high ranking officer, finding himself in danger of demotion by his involvement, backed down. Dickie as usual was on his own.

Thomasin was rendered mute. Leadenly she reached for the paper that Pat had discarded and read the rest of the article for herself. '... *sentence was waived in order for Feeney to carry out the magistrates' ruling. A spokesman for the York Society for the Prevention of Youthful Depravity praised the bench's bold decision and said: "There is still a long way to go before the respectable people of this city can walk its streets without fear of molestation, but today's closure marks a great triumph for decency."* '

'Why's he doing this to us, Tommy?' cried Patrick from the heart. 'I thought he was supposed to be a rich man? Men of his position don't need to descend to that level to earn their living, do they?'

'Of course not,' came the wooden response. 'He's just doing it to spite us; drag our name through the mud. Who else do you think told them about his mother owning a number of grocery stores? I trade under the name Penny, so they'd hardly have drawn the connection unless he'd told them. He wants to make sure we all suffer with him.'

'But what has he got to be spiteful about? Sure, I would've thought he'd had enough out of us.'

'Nothing's enough for Dickie,' she said quietly, laying down the paper. 'And I have the feeling that this isn't the last we're going to hear of our son.'

At about the same time that Patrick had read the paragraph from the county press to his wife, another person's eyes had also been drawn to it. Detective Sergeant Scholes Nettleton snipped deftly around the column of print with a pair of nail scissors and, after re-reading it, folded it into his inside pocket. There might of course be no connection here, but then again it was worth following through; there wasn't much else brewing at the moment. He would have words with his superior later.

Leaning over the arm of his office chair he reached down to pull out a drawer. From here he took a file and laid it open on his desk, glancing through the details with which he had become well-acquainted: '*Deceased – female, approximate age – sixty years . . . cause of death – multiple fractures to the skull . . .*' He skimmed over the rest of the details to the paragraph at the foot of the page: '*Discovery of body in shallow grave . . . several other graves . . . all found to contain the skeletal remains of animals.*' He recalled the look on that chap's face, the one who had discovered the fingers sticking out from the earth after a particularly heavy downpour, and had launched a murder hunt.

Subsequent enquiries had determined that the deceased had taken in a lodger some years previous to her death and it was the lodger who had been responsible for the sale of the farm – or at least so it appeared. The present owner had not minded that the transaction hadn't been entirely legal, having paid a low price for the farm. He did not, however, relish being implicated in a murder. When he had come across the body he had told the police all he knew about the other party, including a good description. Added to this, the man produced a bill of sale bearing the lodger's name. The same name as was in this newspaper article. Whether or not he had used his real name in his nefarious activities was debatable – probably not if he had killed the old woman – and even if he had, it was a very common name among the thousands of immigrants in the big cities. Nevertheless, the case of the brothel-keeper in York would bear investigation.

Nettleton drummed his fingers thoughtfully on the file, then closed it and replaced it in the drawer, under H for Hughes.

CHAPTER FORTY-SEVEN

'But, Dickie where we gonna go?' pleaded Lally, her naked legs draped over the chair arm. 'You know we love it 'ere with you.'

'Lally, my pet I don't rightly know where you're going to go, but go ye must.' Dickie twirled a diamond cravat pin thoughtfully. 'Love me or not, I won't go to jail for anyone. Ye can blame that silly cow who thought she'd try to make an extra quid on the side – as if I didn't pay her enough. I hope she enjoys her fourteen days.' He rose and crossed the ostentatious room, heavy with ormolu and gaudy trappings, to check on his appearance in the mirror, fixing his cravat pin as he went. 'And just let that bastard Sleetham come looking for his free jump . . .' Sleetham was the policeman who had normally helped in such matters.

She started to moan again and he grimaced. 'Look, Lally – we all had a good time, but 'tis over now. No amount o' bellyachin' is going to change things.' As ever when before a mirror he traced the faint, but still legible *L* on his brow.

She sighed regretfully. 'I reckon so, only I don't know where I'm gonna find a place as good as this.' She swung her legs to the floor and padded over to him seductively. 'How about a last bit o' fun, Dickie my love?'

He finished preening and spoke to her reflection in the cherub-laden mirror. 'Ye had your check-up yesterday – what did the quack say?' Not for Dickie the bad reputation of the lower class brothel-keeper; at first sign of disease his girls were pensioned off. 'Was it a clean bill o' health he gave ye?'

'Clean as yer muvver's.'

He spun round, checking his watch. 'All right then – but make it quick, I've a lotta sorting out to do.' Women came so easy to him these days that he had no need to waste his charm, especially on a pro.

'You really know how to make a girl feel wanted, you dog.' But even so she led him over to the four-poster bed.

Afterwards, Dickie was preparing once again to take positive steps in the sale of his property when the front doorbell sounded. 'Oh, Mother o' God.' He ripped off the lopsided cravat and threw it onto the bed. 'Lally, will ye get your fat backside up an' answer that. Don't they know we've been closed down?'

Lally scissored her bare legs and leapt out of bed, throwing on a flimsy peignoir. 'What if it's the beak?' she asked jokingly.

'Then I'll trust you to keep him happy while I get out the back way.' The bell rang again. 'Woman, will ye please answer it? An' then go see if the others have packed. I'm supposed to have sold up lock, stock an' barrel by now, an' there they are fancying themselves up as though 'tis business as usual. I could smell 'em in Scarbro' with all that bloody scent they're chucking about. That's probably what's drawn the customer; he's just followed his nose.'

It wasn't a customer, neither was it a magistrate. Dickie swore as Lally came back into the bedroom. 'Blessed Mary! How can I tie this cravat when you keep prancing in and out. Who was it anyway?'

'Somebody wantin' to see you – a girl.' She unfastened her peignoir which was coming loose, wrapped it more tightly around her and retied it. 'I told her you were busy but she pushed right past me. She's now in the hall refusing to move.'

He tutted exasperatedly. 'Here, can you do this? It was perfectly all right 'til you got your dirty hands on me.' She came over, snatched the violet cravat and had it tied in a flick of her wrist, topping it with the diamond. 'Ah, a true professional.' He smiled now and slipped into his silver-grey frockcoat. 'Well, I'd best go see what she wants, we don't want to throw her out if she's brought us some money.'

Lally stepped out of his way. 'That's hardly likely, lookin' at her.'

The shabby figure in the hall sprang from her chair at the sound of his boots on the stairs. 'Well, as I live an' breathe – Amy Forsdyke!' He made his approach slowly, looking her up and down. 'An' what can we do for you?'

'Oh, yer do remember me, then?' His mother's former maid took a newspaper from the folds of her cloak and waved it at him. 'I saw your little piece in the paper; thought I'd come an' get meself a job.'

'Christ! the woman's off her head. There's me trying to get rid o' the half-dozen girls upstairs an' this one askin' for a job. Can ye not read?'

'Oh, I know what it sez,' replied Amy, turning up her nose. 'But I didn't think you'd be takin' any notice of it; you who can talk yer way out of owt.'

He took her arm and tried to coax her to the door. 'Listen, Amy, 'tis nice to see ye but ...'

'But yer can't wait to get rid o' me!' she snapped. 'You'd see me starvin' an' not chuck a carraway seed in my direction.'

'Now, you're not going to tell me you're starvin', 'cause I'd not believe ye.'

'Near as dammit. An' it's all your fault. I reckon you owe me.'

'How d'ye work that one out?' he asked. 'An' what happened to the domestic line o' work that ye want to throw it over to come an' work here?'

'It's not out o' choice I do it but necessity,' she retorted. 'Yer don't think anybody else was gonna employ a maid what's been sacked without reference, d'yer?'

He made a noise of understanding.

'An' who was it got me sacked?' she added pointedly.

'I'm sorry, but I don't see how I can help ye, Amy. Like ye read in the paper, I have to have everyone out in twenty-four hours, or else.'

'Yer'll not be livin' in the middle of a field, will yer?' she argued. 'Yer'll need a maid wherever yer goin'.'

'Well, I suppose ...' He stroked his chin, drawing her attention to the difference in his appearance since the last time she had seen him. His exploits had detracted nothing from his handsomeness. What lines he had accumulated were mostly around the eyes, enhancing the twinkle in them when he smiled. He had grown side-whiskers, which was a shame for they hid one of his best features; the strong, determined jaw inherited from his father.

'Look at me!' she said harshly. 'It's you what brought

me down to this level. Haven't you got one ounce o' conscience?'

He laughed aloud. 'Ah, God I'm sorry but that's really funny coming from your lips.' Then, with a quick consultation of his watch said. 'All right, Amy, ye've twisted me arm. It's to your advantage that I have to go out an' haven't time to argue.'

'Oh, thanks, Dickie!' She jumped at him and kissed his cheek. 'Where shall I put me things?'

'Christ, not here! There might be spies about; they see girls moving in instead of out an' I'm jail fodder. Now, if I can get a quick sale I'll require your services in a couple o' weeks. Though at this pace I'll never get it sold.' He pushed her to the door. 'Where will I find ye?'

'I'm stoppin' at Mrs Sykes down Friargate – but don't wait too long before yer send for me: I owe three weeks rent an' might be out on me ear if yer leave it too long.'

'Don't worry, I want to get things settled as much as you do.'

She lingered on the doorstep. 'Yer sure you aren't just sayin' it to get rid o' me? Only if I thought . . .'

'Amy, Amy, please!' He clapped a hand to his brow. 'I'm not gonna be able to send for ye at all if ye don't let me go about my business. Now, I promise as soon as it's done I'll send word; ye can be sure o' that. Goodbye.'

'Dickie!' She foiled his attempt to shut the door. 'D'yer think yer could see your way to givin' me an advance in wages? Just so's the old sow don't chuck me out.'

'Jazers, everybody's after me money.' He dug into his pocket. 'Wherever ye go it's pay, pay, pay. Here – an' now I'm really going. Goodbye!' He slammed the door.

Amy grinned and savoured the jingle of coins in her clenched fist. 'Oh, you haven't finished payin' yet, Dickie boy; not by a long chalk.'

With his scuppered brothel duly sold, but for the signature on the contract which would be undertaken tomorrow, Dickie sought relaxation at The King Willie. It was laughable that, for all his money, whenever he hungered for company his feet always brought him back to the area of his childhood. That was one point on which his father had been right; money or no, the gentry wanted nothing to do with the Irish.

He asked for a whiskey. The landlord spoke confidentially as he poured it. 'We had a slop in here last night looking for you.' He pushed the glass towards Dickie. 'No uniform, but it didn't take much guessing.'

Dickie's ears pricked at this. 'A bogeyman, ye say? Did he ask for me by name?'

'Well, how else would he ask for yer, silly bugger.' The landlord took a cloth and wiped the beer spills from the bar-top.

'He could've had a photograph.'

'Oh aye . . . no, he asked for you by name. But I don't reckon he knows yer personal-like. I hear he's been doing all the pubs.'

'Ye didn't tell him I'm a regular?' said Dickie cautiously.

'Would I do that?'

Dickie was grateful. 'Thanks, Sam. Will ye give me a nod if ever I'm in here an' he's standing next to me?'

The landlord inclined his balding head and refilled the proffered glass. 'You'll hardly be able to miss him though; he had half his ear'ole missing. I got him talking about it so's I could catch his accent. Said he had it chewed off in an affray. West Ridin' fella my own ear told me.'

'That's puzzlin'. Did he say what he wanted with me?' Dickie pushed a shilling at the landlord. 'Have one for yourself, Sammy.'

'Oh, ta. I'll have the same. No, he was quiet on that score, just asked where he might find yer.' He handed Dickie his change. 'Good health to yer.'

'*Sláinte.*' Dickie washed the whiskey around his teeth. A man came alongside and ordered a stout. 'Hello to ye, Mr Bearpark.' Dickie saluted with his glass. 'How's business?'

Isaiah Bearpark, 'Growler', as the Feeneys had nicknamed him in their childhood for his guttural monosyllables, perused Dickie from top to toe, then picked up his drink, hawked and spat in the lead-lined spittoon at the foot of the bar and moved away to sit near the fireplace. Dickie smiled sweetly at the landlord and clicked his tongue. 'He's a lovely fella.'

'Don't you go riling him,' warned Sammy. 'You know you can't handle it.'

'All I said was hello.'

'You're well aware you don't need to say anything else to spark off a brawl. After I've done you that favour an' all,' he added peevishly.

Dickie grinned and slammed his empty glass on the counter. 'Aye thanks for the tip-off, Sammy, I owe ye one. Well, I came in for some company but if the law's after me here an' all I'd best make meself scarce. Don't get drunk.' He worked his way between the closely-packed tables. At one point the gap between the drinkers was so narrow that he had to place his hand on someone's shoulder to steady himself. He continued past, until the someone gripped his arm. He looked down at the seated individual. It was Growler.

'You touched me!' The statement was made with shocked affront.

Dickie was immediately contrite. 'I humbly beg your pardon, Mr Bearpark.'

The man rose to his full height. 'I don't like being touched.'

'Yes, I know that, Mr Bearpark – but it was an accident.' Dickie, poised for flight, waited for Bearpark's fingers to begin stroking his bulbous nose, for he knew that after a few moments of hypnotising his intended victim those same fingers would fork out like two bolts of steel into his opponent's eyeballs.

'I'm truly sorry, Mr Bearpark,' he said again, urgently. 'Can I buy ye a drink by way of recompense?' And was relieved to see that the fingers stayed twitchingly at Bearpark's side. The man made a growling sound in his throat and, after a speedy trip to the bar, Dickie placed a full bottle of whiskey on the table. 'A bottle of Scotch with my humble apologies. Good health to ye.' May God rot your ugly balls, he thought grimly as he made his swift exit. As if I haven't enough troubles.

Dubious of visiting any of his other regular hostelries for fear of running into the detective, he sauntered idly around the streets, speculating on what property to invest in next. He was looking into a goldsmith's window, with his eye firmly fixed to a gold signet ring furnished with a single, but large, diamond, and did not see her reflection at first. Then all at once, between the trays of glittering jewellery, materialised two brighter-than-bright emeralds in slanting, cat-like settings. He turned round quickly, sweeping off his hat in delight. 'Dusty!'

'Hello, Dickie,' she said. It could have been yesterday; she had not altered one bit. 'Got yourself in another spot of bother, I see.'

His eyes drank her in. 'What?' God, she was marvellous! Look at her.

'I read about your escapade in the paper.'

His trance was broken and he dropped the doting expression to sigh, 'Gob, is there anyone who hasn't seen it?'

She gave a brief smile, then began to walk away. He started, then kept pace with her, watching her face all the while.

'You're going to trip over something if you continue to stare at me.'

'Sorry!' But he didn't turn his face away. 'I just can't get over meeting ye like this. 'Tis so good to see ye, Dusty.' They walked in silence for a short distance, then he said, 'How is everything with you?'

'If you mean businesswise, extremely well,' Dusty informed him. 'If, on the other hand, you refer to my personal life . . . my father died last year.' She caught the look that flicked directly to her left hand. 'No, there's no ring, Dickie. I've decided I shall never marry.'

'That's a shame; ye'd make somebody a good wife.' She looked at him sharply. 'I'm sorry, Dusty,' he said genuinely. 'For everything.'

'Don't flatter yourself that you're responsible for my

spinsterhood,' came the tart reply. 'The business takes up so much of my time that I'd have none to spare for a family. Besides, that's all in the past now, isn't it?' She looked through him to stare into another shop window. 'How is Peggy, by the way?'

His black eyebrows met. 'Same as she ever was I suppose.'

'And . . . and the baby? Well, it won't be a baby now, will it?'

He understood now. 'Dusty, I didn't marry Peggy, I thought you'd have heard.'

She lost interest in the shop window and turned on him. 'You ran out on her?'

'If ye want to put it like that, I did.'

'Is there any other way to put it? You used her then you ran out on her – like you ran out on me.' Her hopes that he might have changed were dashed. She moved off, her pace more urgent this time.

He hurried beside her. 'Dusty, there's an awful lot ye don't know . . .'

'And if that press account is anything to go by I've no desire to!'

'Please, Dusty allow me to tell ye! My brother married Peggy.'

She was almost running while his long legs pursued her at an easy gait. 'Well, it's probably a great relief to her that she's married to a decent dependable man and not a brothel-keeper!'

'Ye don't understand! That was only a bit of a joke.'

She stopped abruptly then, causing him to retrace half a dozen steps. 'A *joke*?'

He shrugged helplessly. 'Well, I thought 'twas a bit of a lark at the time. Thought it might knock Mam an' Dad off their pedestal; take them down a peg or two for trying to palm me off with that slut.'

'I have never heard such spurious outpourings in all my life!' panted Dusty, eyes blazing. 'I imagined when I saw you that you had grown up, but I see now the maturity was only skin-deep. You're still a child in a man's body.

As childish as ever. Like a little boy who says: if I can't have my own way I'm spoiling your game. Your parents may have had their faults, but nothing they've done could warrant inflicting such shame upon them. And slut though Peggy undoubtably is I should not be too quick to call her it if I were you, for she would be quite within her rights to hurl the male equivalent of that insult at you!' Her tiny bosom rose and fell. She seemed about to say more, but turned away in frustration and walked off.

He stood for a second, digesting her condemnations, then rushed after her. 'You're right!' He caught up with her. 'Everything ye say about me is right. I am a slob. I've only ever been interested in meself, I admit it.'

'Small consolation to those you've hurt,' muttered Dusty, the skirts of her gown frothing with the rapid movement of her legs.

'But, Dusty ye said yourself ye thought I'd grown up — well ye weren't wrong; I have. I've begun to see how silly my joke was: it's only brought me more trouble.'

'Your penitence is touching but still a little stained by self-indulgence.'

'Dusty, please listen to me! There's so much I need to say to ye, but I can't say it out here.'

Her eyes widened. 'If you think I'm coming back to that bawdy house . . .'

'No, no! I wouldn't dream of suggesting it. But will ye talk to me on neutral ground?'

'There's little point . . .'

'There is! Look.' He snatched at her arm to stop her. 'I can't keep this up; 'tis wearin' me lungs away. There's a tea shop over there . . .'

'Dickie,' she begged. 'I've only just got over . . . I don't really want it to start up again.'

'Dusty, I'm only askin' ye to take tea with me,' he pleaded. 'Just to give me room to explain. Come on now, for old time's sake. Unless,' he taunted, 'ye'd rather not have folk see ye in the company of such a notorious villain.'

'Since when have I cared for what people think?' She searched his beseeching face. Was his repentance genuine

– or just another of his ploys? She finally condescended. 'Oh . . . all right. If it'll give me the opportunity to knock some sense into that bonny head of yours about this feud with your parents. Come on.'

CHAPTER FORTY-EIGHT

It became their regular meeting place during the following weeks; the little tea shop blanketed in the shadow of York Castle. She hadn't wanted it to happen, but of course it had – as she had known it would when she had seen his reflection in the goldsmith's window. The ache had begun again.

Having disposed of the sprawling building in the centre of town, Dickie had purchased a more sedate dwelling on the outskirts of the city, leaving ample surplus with which to gamble on the Stock Exchange. His one regret was that Dusty would never come here. It was as if she was afraid to be alone with him, always seeking the safe cloisters of the tea shop. He knew that she had not yet forgiven him, but hoped that day would come – for under no circumstances would he permit her to escape again. He intended to ask her to marry him. In the meantime, he had to take his pleasure where he could find it.

'Come on, Amy.' He pushed his thigh against that of the maid. 'Let's be having ye. I've an important engagement at two.'

'Isn't it funny that once yer've had what yer wanted you always have an important engagement,' complained Amy, rolling out of bed. 'She must be prettier than me, Dickie.'

'Who says it's a woman I'm meeting?' He punched at his pillows and leaned back, his face looking more tanned than ever against the whiteness of the linen.

'I do, you old lecher.' She pulled on her chemise and

tucked it into her drawers, tugging sulkily at the drawstrings.

'Is that any way to speak to your employer?' He watched her put on the rest of her clothes, an act that always fascinated him, then followed her with amused eyes as she flounced to the door. 'Hey! and remember, it's sir in front of my guests and not Dickie; you raised a few eyebrows last night. Oh, and fetch me up a bath, will ye?'

'Yes, *sir!*' she flung at him, and slammed the door.

He hauled himself out of bed, stretching, and folded a brocade dressing gown around him, knotting the sash over his well-defined stomach muscles. When Amy and Laura, the other maid he had hired, brought up the bath some twenty minutes later, he flung off the robe, unabashed, and stepped into the steaming, perfumed water. 'Which of you's going to scrub me back?'

'You can scrub your own bloody back, two-timer!' shouted Amy. 'Lest yer want a bleedin' wire brush takin' to it.' And stalked out, pulling Laura after her.

He shook his head and shouted. 'I don't know what the lower classes are coming to these days!' Then ducked into the water as she came back to throw a towel at him.

An hour later he went to keep his appointment with Dusty, swinging his ivory-handled cane to a jaunty rhythm. It was on Nessgate corner that he made the totally unexpected meeting.

Thomasin scowled at him as he doffed his hat. She could hardly claim not to have seen him, them being on the same footway.

'Good day to ye, Mother! Father. 'Tis a blustery day to be takin' a walk. That wind's sharp enough to hang your coat on.'

'Dickie,' acknowledged Patrick, but said no more.

Thomasin looked up at her elder son's face, feeling his daughter's warm fingers curl around her own. 'It might feel cold to them as blood runs thin. Some of us have consciences to keep us warm. I don't know how you've got the nerve to face us after you've dragged our good name through the dirt.'

He gave an awkward laugh, then dropped to his heels to speak to Rosanna. 'And who might we have here, then?' he said in a light tone.

'My name is Rosanna Feeney, sir,' she told him politely. 'What's yours?'

He grinned. 'Richard Feeney esquire at your service, ma'am.'

The child consulted her grandmother. 'His name is the same as ours.'

When Thomasin made no comment, Dickie said, 'That's right, child, I'm . . .' He saw the flash of warning in his mother's eyes and frowned. She surely didn't think he was going to lay claim to the child now, did she? 'I'm your Uncle Dickie,' he told Rosanna, and on sudden impulse caught her tiny pointed chin in the crook of his finger. Something happened then. He could not say what it was, but a feeling ran through him as he gazed into those alert, blue eyes, bringing with it an extraordinary melancholy; a feeling of desolation, as if every other person had vanished from the street, leaving him here quite alone. He stared back at the child for an age, then stood abruptly, and asked his father to introduce him to the child the older man carried. Patrick noted with curiosity the seriousness that had taken over his son's expression.

'We'll have to go,' said Thomasin suddenly. 'The children will be catching a chill.'

'Mother!' He stepped in front of her impulsively and caught her hand. 'I'm sorry.' It took a devil of a lot of saying after so many years waiting to get even.

She regarded him with disdain. 'And for which bit in particular are you sorry, Richard? Extorting from your mother, cuckolding your brother, or defaming the entire family with your filthy goings-on?' She was about to pull away, then added cruelly, 'Or for not turning up at your grandfather's funeral?' She went then, dragging the child after her.

Patrick studied his son's shocked face closely, then followed his wife. 'Ye shouldn't've done that, Tommy,' he said grimly when he caught up. 'It was plain that was the first he'd heard of Billy's death.'

Thomasin didn't trust herself to answer. She knew without being told that it was a terribly cruel thing to have said to a boy who, however callous, had thought a great deal of his grandfather. She had just felt compelled to get back at him for all the hurt he had brought her.

Only Rosanna looked back. Dickie stared as the child's mouth turned up in a sudden smile and she raised her hand in a farewell salute. By the time he thought to wave his own they were round the corner and out of sight. Grandad, dead!

He told Dusty about the meeting. She reached across the table and laced her fingers with his. 'It's hardly surprising the way you've treated them,' she said softly, as the waitress brought the tea.

'But I was trying to atone,' he replied. 'Doing what you said. I wanted to make everything right between us. Grandad dead. God, I can't believe it. I always felt he'd live forever – an' she didn't wait for me to say I was sorry or anything; just marched off, after dumping that on me.'

She withdrew her hand to lift her cup. 'Sorry is a sadly inadequate word, Dickie, to cover all your crimes. You've hurt them deeply. It would come as no shock to me if they never forgave you again.'

He suddenly recalled the day when, hard up for a few coppers, he had pawned his grandfather's beloved watch, and heavy-heartedly told her about it.

'Oh, Dickie!' Her green eyes were full of reproach.

'I know. I'm a right bastard, aren't I?' He tested the tea and, finding it too hot for his taste, put down the cup. 'No wonder they don't want anything to do with me. If only I could get it back; but it'll be long gone by now, I suppose. Sonny always wanted that watch, ye know. I knew that. I could've sold it to him rather than pawned it, but then that was me all over in those days – didn't give it a second thought. He's probably not forgiven me for that, either.'

'I don't expect he has,' agreed Dusty sadly.

'D'you feel that way too, Dusty?' he asked suddenly. 'I thought ... well, I hoped maybe you ...'

'Dickie, it's only been three weeks,' she answered. 'Three weeks since you turned up looking like you'd never been away. If you knew what I went through ...'

'I do know! I went through the same – not that I expect ye to believe it. Oh, but I've changed, Dusty.' He pushed aside the cup and put both hands on her wrists. 'I truly want to make amends.'

'Part of you has changed,' she granted. 'But which part? And no funny quips.'

'I wasn't about to make one; it's too serious for that. I'll tell ye what hasn't changed, though: the part of me that wanted to marry ye – still wants to marry ye.'

'It's too soon. I don't want to get involved again only to be hurt.' She dabbed at her lips with a handkerchief and started to rise.

He pulled her down. 'I won't hurt ye again, Dusty, I promise.'

'No, Dickie, it's too early to make serious plans. Let it lie.'

'Very well,' he sighed resignedly. 'Save your answer. But know this: I love you, Dusty, I always have, despite the pain I've brought ye. An' I'll wait until ye've forgiven me ...'

'I've forgiven you already. You were very young, after all. It's just that I can't bring myself to trust you, Dickie. I couldn't stand being hurt like that again. You'll have to be content with my friendship for the time being. Let me go now, I've a lot of work to catch up on.'

He held onto her. 'You're not going to turn up tomorrow, are ye? I can see it by the way you're avoiding looking at me.'

She forced herself to meet his eyes, and immediately gave up the fight. It was no use trying to fool herself, she would never be free of him, even if she walked out now. Still, she had to try for her own self-respect. 'We're becoming too close ... I can't ...'

'Please, please, Dusty I'm begging ye! I'll go down on

607

me knees, anything, but please don't leave me. Say ye'll be here tomorrow.'

She opened her mouth to say no, but it didn't come out that way. 'Very well; I'll be here at two as usual.' Then she smiled.

'There's a man what wants to see yer, Dickie.' Amy took his hat and cane as he returned from his rendezvous with Dusty.

'How many times have I asked ye not to call me that?' He strode up to the door of the drawing room. 'Is he in here?'

'Aye – a Mr Nettleton.'

Dickie, unfamiliar with the name, paused to think, then went back to whisper, 'What's he look like?'

'Don't look like owt.' Amy brushed his coat and hung it on a mahogany stand.

'Come on, come on!'

She nipped her nose. 'Well, he's just an ordinary sort o' fella. Bit short on top . . .'

'Has he got an earlobe missing?' came the sharp interruption.

'How the hell would I know? I don't give all your guests the medical once-over. Next yer'll be askin' me if he's cut his toenails this week.'

He frowned and instead of the drawing room made for the stairs.

She bustled after him. 'Where're you off to?'

'I'm off to pack a bag. I think I'll spend a couple o' nights at The Black Swan, Coney Street.'

She adjusted her lace cap. 'An' what'll I tell him?' she called.

He leaned over the balustrade. 'Ye won't have to tell him anything if ye keep shouting off your big gob like that. Wait till I'm out o' the house before ye make my excuse.'

'Will yer be comin' back then? Only who's gonna pay me and Laura if yer not?'

He was thoughtful then. 'I can't say; probably not.'

'Oh, that's lovely that is! Leavin' us 'ere without a job.'

608

'Here!' He screwed up a ten pound note and threw it down at her. 'That will more than recompense ye both. If ye call at The Mucky Duck I'll have references for ye, only I haven't time to write them now.' He dashed off to his room.

There he pulled open the jaws of a bag and threw in some clean underwear and shirts then, as an afterthought, tipped in the entire contents of his valuables case. Reaching to the windowsill he grasped a pelargonium by the stem and ripped it, along with its dried-out rootball, from the plantpot, then shook out the hundred or so sovereigns he had hidden there for such an emergency. One had to be devious with a maid like Amy. He knew she had been taking his possessions since the day she arrived but had not worried as long as they did not amount to anything more valuable than odds and ends. Poor kid, he had given her a rough deal in the past. After throwing in the sovereigns he tossed a few toiletries after them and snapped the bag shut, then made for the stairs. He stopped on the landing. There were voices in the hall.

'I thought I heard your master come in,' Nettleton was saying. Dickie peeped out to grab a look at the man who so plagued him.

'No, that weren't him,' lied Amy. 'He's still out. That were the coalman.'

'Does the coalman always use the front door?' enquired Nettleton.

Amy skipped over the question. 'Yer welcome to stay 'til he does come back. Shall I show you back into the drawin' room?'

Nettleton's brow dropped. He looked up the stairs. Dickie pressed himself into a corner. 'I'll wait here.' The detective was deuced certain Feeney was in the house.

'Yer'd be more comfy in there,' pressed Amy, casting nervous glances up the staircase. 'He might not be in for ages.'

Silly bitch! cursed Dickie – she's all but told him where I am with her eyes wavering up here all the time. The detective had taken a chair. Dickie clenched his fist. Blast!

He looked to his right, then his left, seeking another way out. There were only the windows. It was a long climb down to the garden. Oh well, he tiptoed back to his room, he had done this sort of thing before.

Sliding up the sash as softly as he could he leaned out to take stock. The drop was longer than he had thought. He picked up his bag and after a moment's hesitation dropped it to the flower bed below, cocking his ear to see if anyone came running at the dull thump. He looked down ruefully at his smart clothes – too bad it couldn't be avoided – then slid his leg over the sill and grasped hold of the drainpipe. His boots grated on the brickwork as he slithered down. At one point came a bodeful creaking and he clung on grimly, staring into the grinning face of an iron cherub. 'S'all right for you, ye bastard,' waiting for the pipe to break free of its brackets. He felt the sweat trickle down his temple as he risked a look down. It held. He continued his descent and jumped the last few feet to the garden. Brushing off his clothes with his hands he snatched up his portmanteau and made for the wall at the bottom of the garden.

Nettleton, lured back into the drawing room by some sixth sense, spotted him through the window as he straddled the high wall. The detective opened the window to shout his name. Dickie looked up, startled, then was gone.

Nettleton turned his bile on the maid who had appeared at his shoulder. 'I could have you for collusion!'

'Keep yer hair on,' she said mildly, placing a tray on the table bearing two cups and saucers, a pot of tea and milk jug. 'I daresay you'll have time for a cuppa tea before we begin our little game.' She seated herself on a chaise longue and spread out her legs.

'And what game might that be?' asked the detective warily.

'The one where we see how long it takes you to hit on the right amount I'll accept to tell you where he is,' grinned Amy.

But Dickie, his shrewd mind telling him what he would

have done in Amy's position, had changed venues, checking instead into The Old George Hotel as R. Freemason. Once in his room he found it hard to venture out again, but forced himself to visit the bar later in the evening. If he stayed cooped up in that room all the time he'd go mad.

However, feeling conspicuous in the bar's lack of patronage he decided to risk going further afield and visit his usual haunts. Even if the detective caught up with him it was unlikely that Dickie would be trapped in a place he knew so well. The sobering vision came flashing back of a cornered youth in a blind alley, cowering with wet pants. Never take anything for granted, Dickie boy, he told himself as he looked to right and left before leaving the hotel. And remember, you're at a disadvantage now; the man's seen your good-looking face.

He reached his destination without mishap. 'Large Irish, Sam!' He leaned on the bar, his chin resting on his chest, glancing furtively about him.

'The slop's been in again,' said the landlord. 'Don't worry,' he added hastily to Dickie's worried expression, 'it were a few hours ago; he's not here now.'

'I've seen him already.' Dickie knocked back his drink and asked for another. 'A bit too close to home for my liking.' He took his refill, then looked around again. 'Oh, Christ! I see Growler's in again; I could've done without that tonight.'

Sammy grimaced. 'Please, try not to touch him. We had a stranger in here last night what spilled ale on him – that's his blood on the wall.'

Bearpark slouched up to the bar and growled his request. Dickie moved away slightly and offered no greeting. Bearpark turned a basilisk eye on him. Dickie gave a tight smile, but still no comment.

Of all the people, it had to happen to him. Some clown, laughing over a joke, shoved his friend in the chest and he fell back into Dickie who brushed against Bearpark. The drink he was holding splashed over the sides of the glass and speckled Bearpark's tattooed hand. The man looked down dumbly at the affront, then slowly raised his eyes to Dickie who had whipped out a handkerchief and was dabbing furiously whilst muttering apologies. The landlord sighed heavily and began to remove the breakables from the bar top.

Bearpark was still staring at him. He growled out, 'I thought you knew: I don't like people touching me.'

'Ah, sure it wasn't my fault, Mr Bearpark.' Dickie jabbed a thumb over his shoulder. 'This here fella behind me was the one who did the pushing.' He looked around; the man had gone. When he turned back Bearpark's fingers had risen to his face and had begun to rub at the crenellated nose.

But before those same fingers could gouge out his eyes, Dickie's knee shot upwards and caught the drunkard in the crook of his legs. Bearpark doubled over with a grunt – when he raised his bloodshot eyes the bar was completely empty.

'What're you so nervous about?' enquired Dusty. Dickie's head had swivelled round every time the doorbell sounded.

'If ye'd been with me last night ye wouldn't have to ask.' He told her about Bearpark and the detective, how he had escaped and was having to stay in an hotel.

'But what does the policeman want with you?' she demanded.

'I didn't wait to find out. Could be any one of a number o' things.' His head moved in a semi-circle as the doorbell tinkled again.

'But you can't live the rest of your life as though you've got a nervous tic,' she told him. 'And I'm certainly not going to spend my life watching the door.'

Her implication did not strike him at first; when it sunk in he said wonderingly, 'Does that mean what I think it means?'

'That depends on what you think I mean it means,' she answered coyly.

He laughed then. 'We could be here forever playing that game. Come on, Dusty, are ye saying ye'll wed me?'

Her eyes were warm and shining. 'I've not decided yet; don't push me.'

But he could tell by her expression that she had decided, and grabbed her hands, squeezing them tightly. 'Now don't be having me on a bit o' string, as me mother would say.'

'Talking of your mother,' she became serious. 'Have you seen any more of her?'

He released her and shook his head. 'I was thinking of payin' them all a visit of peace until this lot came up. She'll not thank me for taking any more trouble to her door – always supposing she'd let me get that far.'

'Well, I'm glad you've decided to show her a little consideration at last. Look,' she pleaded, 'why don't you go down to the police station and see what they want with you? I'll come with you if you like.'

'God love ye, is it mad ye are? They could slap me in the Castle for some of the naughties I've got up to.'

'But surely it's better to risk that than be wondering if someone's following you all the time?' she said earnestly.

'What, risk being parted from you for another three years or longer? I think not.' He pulled gently at one of her chestnut curls. 'Look, love, I hate to leave ye already but I'd best be on me way. The longer I'm on the streets the more chance I have o' being collared.' He pushed out his chair and paid the bill, waiting while she collected her things then moving to the door. On the pavement he pecked her cheek and looked down at her fondly. 'Will ye be waiting for me tomorrow?'

She bit her lip. 'Me – and half the police force. Oh, Dickie I do wish you'd go down to the station and get it sorted out. I shan't be able to sleep for worrying whether they've got you locked up.'

He shook his head firmly. 'They'll not lock me up. I went to a fortune teller the other day and she told me I'd be going on a long journey – d'ye fancy Botany Bay for your honeymoon, Dusty?'

She slapped his arm. 'Stop joking! Anyway, they don't send people there nowadays.'

'Then stop worrying your bonny little head. It'll be neither summat nor nowt, to quote me mother again. I'm more anxious to know whether you'll be here tomorrow or not.'

She rose onto the balls of her feet and rubbed her nose to his. 'Deranged as I am I'll be here. Two o'clock as usual – and don't be late else I shall think all sorts.'

'Am I ever late?' He smiled and watched her fade into the distance before turning to go, replacing his hat as he swivelled on his heel. With his other hand gripping his cane he had no way of stopping it. When Bearpark's two-pronged thrust came he took the full force of it in his eyes.

CHAPTER FORTY-NINE

The hotelier gave him an old-fashioned look as he staggered past reception and up the stairway to his room, groping his way along the wall. Once inside he locked the door and, going to the enamel bowl on the wash-stand, lowered his face over it, spashing his swollen eyes with cold water. Apart from the excruciating pain he could barely see. Drying them tenderly with a corner of the towel he peered into the mirror. His slit-like vision saw two, ugly purple masses staring back at him. With a groan he made his way over to the bed.

He did not know it, but Nettleton was touring the city's hotels, asking to examine their registers. At the moment that Dickie collapsed onto his bed the detective was entering The King William.

Nettleton turned his feet to the bar and requested a measure of light ale. 'You here again?' said the landlord, fulfilling the order. 'You've had a wasted journey.'

'Ah, one never knows.' Nettleton took the tankard over to a table and sat down. He was none too pleased that the

614

maid's tip had proved a dud; but he could wait – he was good at that. The way Feeney had run had proved his guilt. Nettleton was never one to give up easily.

The saloon was quiet today; there was only a morose-looking man by the fire and two others sitting at the table next to Nettleton's. After a few pulls at his ale the detective struck up a conversation with the nearest man, starting with the weather and progressing to the salient factor. 'You wouldn't happen to know if Richard Feeney will be in at all?' he asked casually. 'Only, I owe him a jar and I like to pay my corner.'

The man caught the slight shake of head from the landlord. 'Richard Feeney, you say? Would that be the fella with the one eye?'

'No-o!' said his partner, sensing the drift. 'That's Freddie Feeney. Richard is the one with the wooden leg an' the wolfhound.'

Nettleton, guessing he was being set up, retreated to the bar for replenishment. When he turned back to his table the man who had been hugging the fire had moved. The policeman downed the tankard on the table and asked good-naturedly, 'Can I buy you a drink?'

Bearpark growled. 'I'll have a stout.'

Nettleton purchased a glass of stout and took it back. 'Cheers.'

'You wanted to know about Feeney?' said Bearpark, lacking the other's niceties. 'How much you prepared to pay?' Nettleton placed two coins on the table and the other pocketed them. 'You'll find him at the café near the gaol, two o'clock tomorrow afternoon.' With that, he poured the whole glass of black liquid down his throat, pierced the detective with a fanatical look, then left the bar.

Nettleton downed his own tankard and called, 'Land-lord! fetch me a brandy. I'm beginning to feel lucky.'

The long but fitful sleep had done nothing to ease Dickie's discomfort. Moreover, the eyes were even blacker and swollen, their corners encrusted with yellow pus. He felt his way from the bed and staggered to the jug of fresh water which the chambermaid had placed in his room earlier and poured it into the bowl. He dabbed at the tender, puffed flesh, easing away the crusty discharge, raised his dripping face to the mirror, groaned, then went downstairs to purchase something to eat.

A blurred glance at the clock showed he had only half an hour before he saw Dusty. Summoning a maid he procured a ham sandwich and went out eating it.

It took ten minutes to get to the arranged meeting place. When he did he could see, despite his poor vision, that Dusty was in her normal seat – early, as she usually was. She had not noticed him yet, would not be expecting him for twenty minutes or more. He was about to go in when he caught sight of someone else. Nettleton sat holding a paper in front of him and looking highly conspicuous. Dickie backed away and moved on hurriedly, walking in no particular direction. Damn the man! He was everywhere.

Having plenty of time to play with he decided to walk around for ten minutes – Nettleton's presence in the café might be just a coincidence. When he went back, Dusty was still there. So was the detective. Dickie was forced to walk straight past, and trod the streets for another fifteen minutes. But his return to the café met with the same result.

On his third trip past he caught sight of Dusty's worried consultation of the clock just above her head, and was gripped by indecision. He couldn't possibly go in there – but he had to see her; if he didn't she would think he had stood her up. Once again he doubled back to tread the pavements, then made a last effort.

Nettleton was still there, ordering another cup of tea. This time Dickie continued walking, it was pointless hanging round. His feet carried him over Castle Mills Bridge, under Fishergate Postern and up George Street to Walmgate. He had decided now to spend an hour in a pub, giving Dusty time to get home or go back to the warehouse, then go and see her there and explain. She would not like it, he knew, him not turning up like that. He could feel her reaction now.

He downed anchor at The Lord Nelson, bought a tankard and a meat pie and sat down to wait. During the afternoon the faces of the clientèle mutated. Dickie's weeping eyes flitted to the door each time it swung open. The clock on the wall said ten past four. Dusty would be at home now, or at the warehouse. He would try both places shortly. He was curious to know whether Nettleton's presence at the café had been a coincidence, or had somebody tipped him off? If the latter were true the detective would in all probability follow Dusty when she left. That made things rather precarious. He would have to tread very carefully when he went to call on her himself.

He went over to the bar for another drink and glanced up as an argument developed between the landlord and a slattern who had been pestering the customers.

'Haven't I warned you before not to do your touting in here? You'll have me out of business.'

The woman leaned drunkenly over the bar and looked at him pleadingly. 'I was only after someone to buy me a drink.'

'And who's going to waste their money on a decrepit sot like you?' the landlord wanted to know.

The woman's raddled cheeks flushed even deeper. She pulled herself upright in the manner of drunks. 'I'm not stayin' here to be insulted – I'll go to The Black Horse.' She hoisted her nose at the landlord's laughter and swayed past Dickie who, feeling a pang of unaccustomed pity, offered to stand her the drink she wanted.

She courted him gratefully. 'You're a gennleman, sir – I'll 'ave a gin.'

'You're scraping the bottom of the barrel, aren't you?' said the landlord as he handed Dickie the drinks. 'Take my advice, son, don't pay for anything else but drink – she's riddled with it.'

Dickie smiled and, going to the table she had chosen, handed the dirty old harlot her gin which she saw off expertly then shivered. 'Oh, thank yer, sir! I fair needed that.'

'Would ye like another?' He surprised himself, and her also.

'You are indeed a gent. I'll 'ave another o' them.' When he passed her the second drink she asked his name and he told her. 'Mine's Bertha. Bertha Sunday.' She caught his look of recognition and misinterpreted it. 'I'll bet you're thinkin' what a bloody silly name, aren't yer?'

He shook his head disbelievingly. Could this jaded old slattern really be the same who had conducted his initiation to manhood?

'You're lookin' at me funny,' she slurred. 'Whasamatter?'

'Don't ye know me?' he asked incredulously.

'Cor! the men I've been with I can't be expected to remember all on 'em. Customer, were yer?'

He nodded. 'Ye could say.'

She squinted at him closely. 'Must say, my memory fails me badly. I'm sure if I'd had an 'andsome toff like you I would've remembered.'

'It was a long time ago.' He buried his inexplicable disappointment in the tankard.

'What did yer say yer name was?' she asked again, scratching her knotted hair. He repeated it. 'Dickie. Dickie.' The lines of concentration stood out on her forehead. 'Nah! Can't for the life o' me recall yer.'

'I was fourteen an' you were seventeen,' he prompted.

She cackled. 'Blimey, it were a long time ago!' Then was suddenly serious. ''Ang on a mo, it's comin' back. You're not the cocky little devil what had no brass, are yer?'

'The same.' Dickie grinned widely, ridiculously pleased that she had remembered.

'Oh! Now it all comes back to me.' She clutched his knee and her hand remained while she reminisced. 'By, what a time we had, didn't we? Aye, I do remember yer now. Had my eye on yer at the fair, I did.'

'Yes, an' when ye discovered I had no money ye weren't too pleased!'

'Gerraway!' She nudged him. 'I knew all along you had

nowt. Yer don't think I'd let meself get taken in like that, d'yer?'

'Ye mean, ye let me think I was getting away with a free ride when that's what ye had in mind all along?' He began to laugh, forgetting for the moment about Nettleton. She joined his laughter. He propped his chin with his palm and stared at her closely. It was pitiful. She was only three years older than himself – about twenty-four – and already her profession had added fifteen years or more to that figure. She looked older than his mother.

'Dickie.' She snuggled up close to him. 'How about you an' me goin' someplace for a reunion?'

He flinched, then pulled away. 'Sorry, Bertha, I've got things to see to.' He changed the subject. 'Hey, did ye ever get that place ye promised yourself? The cottage at Dringhouses?'

'Does it look like it?' she replied sombrely, and took a pull of her gin. 'I haven't even got the place up Cross Alley now; got chucked out. I tried gettin' off the game once. Went to the Refuge in Bishophill, but I couldn't stand it. They were really strict and I like a bit o' fun.'

'Where've ye been living since then?' he asked, snatching a glance at the clock.

'Here an' there,' she replied noncommittally, then: 'Eh, your eyes aren't half a mess. How did yer get 'em? Somebody's given you a right purler by the looks of it.' He told her the culprit's name. 'Oh, my good Christ!' she murmured fearfully. 'Then I hope he doesn't come in 'ere an' catch the pair of us together 'cause he's after me an' all.' He asked the reason. 'He's my bully – leastwise he was, self-appointed, like. I got sick of him beating me up so I never went back one night. Took all the money I'd earned an' all.' That couldn't be much, thought Dickie, looking at her pitiful appearance.

'But you're in the wrong place if ye don't want to see him, Bertha. He's a regular of all the pubs down this way.'

'Blimey! I didn't know that; I haven't seen him for ages. I normally stick to the Nessgate pubs but they got sick o' me an' turfed me out.' She finished her drink. 'I'd best get goin' while I'm still in one piece – you an' all if yer don't want another brayin'.'

'No, I've had all I'm going to get,' said Dickie, emptying his tankard. 'Once Growler's dished out his punishment that's it – finished with.'

'Not if he sees yer with me, it isn't. I'm off, are yer comin'?'

He stood up. 'Where will ye go?'

'I dunno.' She eyed him plaintively. 'I thought yer might take pity on me, us being old flames, like.'

He sighed inwardly. This was the last thing he wanted to be lumbered with. 'Sorry, Bertha, I'd like to but I can't. I'm staying at the George in a single room – an' pretty soon I'll be getting wed. It wouldn't look too good to my fiancée if she found me with another woman, would it?'

'Oh. No, I suppose not,' she replied disappointedly, then recovered herself. 'Oh well, congratulations, Dickie. Be happy. I'll mebbe see yer sometime. Thanks for the drinks.' She gave him one last desirous look, then left.

Shortly after her departure Dickie left also, making his way back to the hotel with the intention of having a meal then visiting Dusty. But before this could happen, something else occurred.

He had just eaten and returned to his room to change when there was a frantic tapping at his door. 'Don't smash the door down, come in!' he shouted, pulling on his boots and getting up from the bed. He sauntered over to the mirror as the person burst in. Her reflection made him spin round in shock.

'Good God, woman what're ye doing here? More to the point, how did ye get past the sentinel downstairs?'

'I sneaked past the desk an' asked a maid what number your room was,' panted Bertha. 'Oh, Dickie you've got to help me!' She fell against him and he reeled at her strong odour. 'He saw me in the Spread Eagle tonight. I managed to get away but he ran after me. This was the only place I could think to run.'

Dickie didn't have to ask who he was. 'Ye led him here? You bloody stupid fool!' He shoved her out of his way in order to lock the door, but the reflex came too late. Bear-park, with no warning knock, thrust his way into the room. He had barged thus into every room on his way up until he had reached the correct one.

'Look, Mr Bearpark you're making a . . .' Dickie stumbled back as the man swept him to one side.

'I don't want you, I want her!' The intruder strode up to a whimpering Bertha and grasped a handful of her hair, snapping her head backwards. 'You thieving little slug! Think you can do the dirty on me?'

'Isaiah, please . . . *agh!*' The plea was cut off as his hand squeezed her jaw.

'Very naughty girl to run away like that. I shall have to teach you a lesson.'

Dickie crouched by the bed, watched Bearpark's hand rise and fall. Bertha screamed his name, then sagged as the blow caught her cheek. She swung by her hair from Bearpark's fist. His hand came up again, the fingers bunched. Bertha moaned, 'Dickie!' The word emerged in a bubble of blood.

He cowered there seeing history replay itself. Seeing not Bertha but Torie falling under the merciless blows. Seeing himself cringing like a coward while his friend was beaten to death. Bertha moaned again as Bearpark's fist smashed into her body, the aimless punches landing anywhere with painful effect: breast, stomach, face. She began to retch. The vomit spilled from her bleeding lips and dribbled down the ragged bodice. He continued to hit her.

Dickie's stomach rebelled at the sound of the blows on her misused, defenceless body. Why could he not move? Help her! his mind shouted. He's too big, he argued back, he'll hit me. Get him! Get him! Now, while his back's turned. You can take him by surprise. He searched around frantically for some weapon. His swimming vision landed on the enamel jug. He leapt for it, tipping the water onto the floor.

Bearpark stalled as the jug came down on the back of his skull. But he remained on his feet. His face came round to look at Dickie, wearing an expression of bemused disbelief. Dickie hit him again swiftly and waited for him to go down. He didn't. Dickie started to back away as Bearpark dropped his hold on Bertha and stumbled after him. He held up the jug again and clanked it down on Bearpark's temple. The man stopped dead – then staggered on. Judas! why wasn't he going down? thought Dickie, filled with panic. He sought wildly for something else, some more effective weapon, backing away as Bearpark came on. There was nothing.

His back was pressed to the wall now. Frantic, he threw the jug at Bearpark ... who came on. In a last fit of desperation Dickie grabbed the bowl of water from the washstand at his side and flung the contents into Bearpark's face, then with all his remaining strength crashed the enamel bowl over the bullet-shaped skull. Bearpark's eyes glazed over – but he was still vertical. Dickie held his breath. The man took a tottering step forward, raised his arm – then went down, his head striking the corner of the brass fender with a stomach-churning crack.

Dickie slumped down the wall into a quivering heap beside the unconscious Bearpark, his breath coming in rapid hiccups, his shirt saturated with the sweat of undiluted fear. Bertha moaned and rolled over. He ran the back of his hand over his mouth and scrambled up to help her, lifting her onto the bed and taking out his handkerchief to mop her bleeding face. She whimpered as the linen touched her smarting lips.

'It's all right, Bertha.' He pressed her down as, suddenly conscious, she tried to rise. 'I've knocked him out. He won't bother us for the moment.' He dabbled the handkerchief in a puddle of water on the linoleum, and tried to clean her face. She moved her head away feebly and took it from him. 'I'll do it. Thanks, Dickie – for stoppin' him, I mean.' She craned her neck to look at Bearpark's sprawling form. 'I'd best get away while he's still out.' She swung her legs over the side of the bed, rose – then flopped back. 'Ooh, I feel giddy.'

'Stay there a minute,' he told her. 'If he wakes up I'll

crown him again.' He laughed despite his trembling hands. 'Blood and sand, he takes some putting to sleep.' He began to stuff his clothes into the portmanteau, lifting the edge of the linoleum to retrieve the long row of sovereigns he had hidden beneath it. His valuables he took from various corners of the room. Bertha watched him, her hand pressed to her head. 'Where will yer go now?'

'God knows.' Between Bearpark and the detective he didn't know which way to turn. He only knew he had to go from here. 'Are ye ready to move?'

She stood up carefully. 'Aye, I think I'm all right now.'

He busied himself with his packing. 'What about you? Where will you go?'

She shrugged. He reached into his pocket. 'Listen, I've got an address of a place in Leeds.' He copied from the notebook onto a scrap of paper. 'The woman there owes me a favour; she'll see to it ye come to no harm. Take this as well.' He gave her four sovereigns. 'Sorry I can't give ye any more but I need everything I can lay me hands on.'

'Oh, Dickie!' She twined her arms round his neck.

'You're welcome. Now come on, we'll have to disperse before Growler wakes up.' He pushed her to the door, bending over the unconscious Bearpark before he left. He placed his fingers to the man's temple, then looked up at Bertha wearing a discommoded grimace. 'Oh, shit!'

'What's wrong?' she asked worriedly.

'Nothing, nothing. Everything's fine. You get going.' He stood up and pushed her out, then locked the door and leaned on it, staring down at Bearpark. Now where the hell did one hide a body around here?

Nettleton blew his nose and moved out of the way as a grubby creature brushed past him in the reception area, then turned to watch her rapid exit. Without checking on his notes he had lost count of the hotels he had visited. If Feeney wasn't here it was most likely that he had left the city altogether. This theory had been strengthened by Feeney's non-appearance at the tea shop. Maybe this search was futile, as that episode had been, but as he had done most of the city's hotels he might as well complete the task.

'Yes, sir can I be of any assistance?' The hotelier paraded an obsequious smile, which Nettleton did not return.

'Have you a man named Richard Feeney staying here?'

When the hotelier showed reluctance to divulge this information Nettleton produced identification. The man dropped his servile attitude and consulted the register, flicking back through the pages. 'No ... no, there's no one of that name here.'

'Mind if I take a look for myself?' Nettleton reached for the register without waiting for permission. He ran a finger down several columns, then retraced its path. R. Free-mason. He tapped the name thoughtfully, then looked up at the hotelier. 'Can you give me a description of this person?'

'I cannot divulge any personal information about one of our guests,' replied the man then, as Nettleton impatiently placed a coin between them, grabbed it and said, 'Tall chap, Irish, very suave, dark hair ... oh! and two black eyes.'

Nettleton's interest was instantly stirred. 'What room is he in?'

'Thirteen,' said the man. 'It isn't his lucky day is it?' He referred to a number of keys which hung on a board behind him. 'His key isn't here so he must be in. Do you want me to send someone up?'

'No need to trouble yourself,' said Nettleton, moving to the staircase. 'I'll find him.' R. Freemason – R. F. – Richard Feeney. They never learned, did they?

Outside room thirteen he paused, then put his ear to the wood, tapping lightly. There was no sound from within. He knocked again, waited, then tried the handle; it resisted his pressure. From amongst the fluff in his pocket he pulled a strip of metal, bent at one end into a right angle. With this he gained entry to the room.

The curtains had been drawn together, making the room

very dim, but after a glance at the bed, he could see there was no one here. He started across the floor. His foot kicked something which rolled along the linoleum and at the same time encountered the puddle of water and he skidded, an involuntary curse escaping his lips. Righting himself he looked around for signs of Feeney's occupation; a suitcase or something. There didn't seem to be anything.

Nettleton went across to the wardrobe and flung open the door – and came eye to eye with a corpse.

CHAPTER FIFTY

This climbing down drainpipes was becoming a habit, thought Dickie as he sat nursing a tankard in the Spread Eagle. It was all very well escaping, but where did he go now? All his money was tied up in the house or at the bank. He still had a great deal of money on him, plus his valuables – watch, cravat pin etcetera – but was loath to leave his long-awaited riches behind. Yet he must decide one way or another. Oh, Dusty I've gone and done it again. He lifted his hands from the tankard to cradle his reeling head. What the hell am I going to do? Suddenly he felt a hand on his shoulder and his head shot up.

'Good grief! What the devil's happened to your eyes?' Sonny would never have known his brother had it not been for the lazy grin that followed the initial apprehension.

Dickie balanced his chair on its back legs. 'Well, well, if it isn't my little brother. The eyes? Ah well, 'tis a rough hole is this, anything can happen to ye. I trust ye had the foresight to notify your next of kin before ye ventured in?'

There was the ghost of a smile from Sonny who placed his drink on the table. 'Can I sit down?'

Dickie touched his chest. 'With me?'

Sonny ignored the satire and pulled out a stool. Just lately, he'd been plagued by an urge to meet with his brother again. He had looked in a lot of places before this one.

'You're the last person I expected to meet in a place like this,' said Dickie, watching him drink. 'I thought ye'd gone on to better things.'

Sonny eyed the other's expensive clothes. 'And who was the one who was always saying he'd be out of this slum the first opportunity he got?'

Dickie surrendered a grin and sampled his drink. 'Truth is, I don't feel at home anywhere else. Now, what's your reason for coming?'

'To see you,' said his brother. 'I thought it was high time we made our peace.'

'Why now all of a sudden? Not that I don't welcome it,' hurried Dickie. 'But what brought about the change of heart?'

'I've had one or two changes of heart lately,' replied Sonny seriously. 'The most important one being about Peggy. I'm going to divorce her, Dick. I know it won't be easy, but I feel it's for the best, as you are wont to say. Our marriage is in ruins – taking for granted we ever had a marriage in the first place.'

'I'm sorry about that, Son,' said Dickie honestly. 'I truly am. I know I behaved like a right bastard to ye . . . if there was some way I could make it up.'

Sonny silenced him. 'I'd prefer not to resurrect all that. Let's just say I realise now there was wrong done on both sides. I couldn't believe what people were saying about Peggy – or wouldn't.'

'But ye do now?'

'There's no need to listen to others now. I've seen for myself what she is.' Haltingly he told Dickie all about his wife burning his paintings. Even his brother was shocked at this display of viciousness. 'There'll be hell to pay, naturally, when I broach the question of divorce, from the church and from Peggy herself, but I'll see to it that she's well provided for.'

'Yes, I heard about your piece o' good luck,' said Dickie.

'Didn't I always say we'd have someone famous in the family one day?'

'Did you? I thought you were talking about yourself.' Sonny smiled. 'Or in your case read *in*famous. Are you still consorting with your nymphs of the pave?'

Dickie made a circle of his mouth. 'Please, don't drag that up, I'm still haunted by it. So, what will ye do after the divorce?'

'I'm going to start a new life.'

And me also, brother, pondered Dickie, knowing now where the route of his escape would take him.

'I've got someone else,' Sonny continued. 'After the divorce we'll marry.'

'Anyone I know?' enquired his brother.

Sonny's grey eyes held a spark of mirth, knowing that there was no danger in imparting his sweetheart's identity. 'Yes, it's Josie.'

'The maid? Ah well, each to his own, I always say.' Dickie finished his drink.

'I realise she wouldn't fit your lordship's idea of a companion,' said Sonny. 'But she happens to be one of the nicest people I know. She's been a good friend to me when I needed one. I feel comfortable with her . . . and she adores the children. She's been more of a mother to them than Peggy ever has.'

'Won't there be a few shocked expressions when ye tell them you're going to wed the maid?' asked Dickie.

'Why should there be? However far we rise we're still someone's servant.'

'I was thinking of Grandma,' replied Dickie.

'Well, let's be realistic – no one would be good enough for Grandma,' grimaced Sonny. 'Can you imagine what it's like living with her permanently? I'm glad of my studio I can tell you. Anyway, I've a sneaking feeling that Mother already knows about Josie and me. She never got on with Peggy so I daresay she'll welcome the change. Can I buy you a drink?'

'I'd say yes, but I haven't time to tarry here,' said Dickie.

'As a matter o' fact I was just thinking o' going when you came in.'

'Anywhere special?'

'America.' Dickie laughed at his brother's face.

'America? Hell, why there?'

'Why anywhere?' shrugged Dickie. 'Because it's the farthest place I can think of. Listen, Son, not to put too fine a point on it I'm in a spot o' bother.'

'Same old Dickie.' But Sonny smiled as he said it.

''Tis a bit more serious this time. D'ye think ye could see your way clear to cash me a cheque? I've a bit o' money, but not enough for what I need an' I can't get to the bank right now.' Nettleton would be waiting there — if he wasn't at the railway station.

'Certainly.' Sonny reached into his inside pocket. 'How much?'

'Ooh, say... five hundred.'

'Five ... you must be having me on! I don't have that sort of money, and even if I did I'd not be carrying it on me, not round this den of thieves.'

'Well, how much can ye manage?' asked Dickie hopefully.

Sonny counted all the money in his possession. 'Four pounds, seven shillings and ninepence.'

'God, such affluence – could I give ye a cheque for it?'

'Surely,' said Sonny, puzzled, then joked, 'I hope it won't bounce.'

Dickie found it hard to smile when he thought of all that cash in the bank, virtually lost to him but he managed to conjure up an expression of gratitude. 'Thanks, you're a pal.'

'I'm your brother,' said Sonny.

'Yes, you are,' replied Dickie, and clasped his arm. 'I'm sorry I never gave that fact its proper value before. I always learn too late, don't I?' He stood quickly. 'Now I must go.'

'Hang on, Dickie, I'm going to ask something of you.' Sonny stood with him. 'That's a long way you're going; we'll maybe not see each other again. I think you ought to come home and say goodbye to Mam and Dad before you go.'

'Sure, they'll be glad to see the back o' me. Won't give tuppence for my goodbyes.'

'Listen, listen! They've been talking a lot about you lately . . . well, not exactly directly about you,' he corrected himself, 'but your name has been creeping into their conversations.'

'Oh, I can quite believe that. I'll bet it wasn't my given name, though.'

'Seriously, I think they'd like to see you. It's a long way to go to find out they want you to come home. Think about it.'

'I am thinking. I'm thinking you're mad to believe they want me home after all the trouble I've caused.' He stared at his brother for a while, then blurted, 'Oh, what the hell! They can only throw me out. Come on then, Son, lead the way.'

Sonny suggested that they walk to Monkgate, the more time in which to patch up their differences, and in spite of Dickie's fear of bumping into the detective he agreed.

'How're the bairns coming along?' he asked conversationally.

'They'd be a lot better if they had a mother who cared for them,' said Sonny. 'Still, they'll have that when I marry Josie. I can't see Peggy wanting custody . . . well, she might want Nick, but not Rosie. I hope she'll see things sensibly, I couldn't stand a nasty court battle.'

'Ah well, they have a good father in you,' said Dickie. 'An' they're real bonny kids, the pair o' them. Ye know, when I saw that wee girl with Mam I could almost have taken her home. Ah, don't fret yourself,' he reassured his brother, 'I'll not be layin' claim to them now. Even if I could take them where I'm going I know in my heart they'd be better off with you.'

'One never knows, you might have a family of your own someday,' replied Sonny, reaching into his pocket for a penny to give a destitute child then, realising he had given all his ready cash to Dickie, smiled apologetically to the urchin. Dickie noticed the gesture and tossed a sixpence into the air. The urchin caught it, and tugged his forelock.

'One never knows,' echoed Dickie with a smile. Oh, Dusty Miller, what shall we do about you?

'I can see you're mellowing,' said Sonny as they passed Stonebow Lane. 'There was a time when you wouldn't even have noticed that little beggar, let alone given him anything.'

'Ah well, I guess ye could say I've been doing some growing up lately. Gob, I think I've aged fifty years in the last couple o' weeks.' He wrapped an arm over his brother's shoulder like he used to do. 'Hey, d'ye remember the things we used to get up to when we were young an' innocent?'

'You were never innocent,' returned Sonny.

Dickie laughed aloud. 'Ah, those long-gone dog-days! I often hanker after them. D'ye recall the time you, me an' Bones went on that picnic? Poor old Bones; I wonder what form he'd be in now if he was still with us . . . an' that girl; what was her name? Bonny? Sarah . . . oh, I can't recall her name, but I can see her as plain as day. I wonder what she's doing today?'

Sonny's ginger head bobbled alongside the black one. 'Her name was Beth, and who knows? she's probably a millionaire by now if what she did to us was anything to go by.'

'Aye, right mugs weren't we?' laughed Dickie, and gripped his brother affectionately. 'So, we part as friends, do we? I'm forgiven for my sins?'

'Was there ever a time when I didn't forgive you?' answered Sonny. Dickie grinned in his devilish manner and gripped the shoulder more firmly. They continued with their reminiscences all along the way, and reached Monkgate far too soon.

Dickie sniffed the air. 'Somebody's burning old socks.'

Sonny reflected his grin. 'I hope Peggy hasn't found her way to my studio.' It was odd how that episode had stopped hurting now he had Josie.

But as they neared home his smile was displaced by a

look of concern. 'It's somebody's house on fire, Dick – look at the smoke.' Ominous black clouds were seeping out from the closed doors and windows. 'God, save us! It's our house ... Mam!' He set off at a gallop, Dickie after him. They were met by their parents and grandmother who were enveloped by an excited throng of neighbours on the pavement. Erin and Sam were there too; here to deliver some heartwarming news – but this was not the time. They, too, had arrived to find smoke pouring from the building and their frantic parents making desperate attempts to get into the house.

'How did it start?' Dickie overtook his brother and was the first to reach the scene.

Patrick spoke to him as though he had merely been down to the corner shop; showed no surprise nor welcome. 'I don't know!' He was coughing. 'Your mother an' me had taken your grandmother to the solicitor's. When we got home we found the door locked an' the house full o' smoke.' He grasped Sonny's arm as he thudded up to them. 'Son ... Peggy's still in there – with the children. At least we think they are. We don't know where the maids are.' He broke off coughing again.

Sonny blanched, and Dickie shouted, 'Bugger the bloody maids, my children are in there!' He dashed to the door and started to kick at it. 'What about the windows?'

'They're locked too,' shouted Patrick.

Sonny had flinched at Dickie's possessive term and now ran after him to join in the battering of the door. 'Out of the way, Dickie! It's my family in there.'

Dickie continued to ram the door. 'This is no time for arguin' whose children they are. They belong to both of us.'

The door caved in and a great wave of heat swept over them, belching black smoke far out into the street. 'Let me be the one to go in!' cried Dickie, but Sonny grabbed him. 'No! It's got to be me.'

Patrick saw that if he didn't intervene they were going to lose them all. He grappled with Sonny. 'For Christ's sake let him go!'

Before Sonny could object his brother had leapt into the smoke-filled house. It seeped into every orifice of Dickie's head. His eyes, already suffering, streamed as he fought his way into the dining room. He began to cough and gag. This room was empty. He ran through the other downstairs rooms and into the kitchen where the smoke had not yet reached, the door being shut against it. Here it was cool and tranquil. He took breathing space to look around. There was no sign of any maids. Quickly he pulled a towel from the airer above the fireplace and doused it in the sink then, draping it over his head and around the lower half of his face, he shut the kitchen door and ran back through the house to the stairs where the fire was crackling and spitting. He could hear Patrick and Sonny arguing by the front door, behind the wall of smoke.

He tried the first bedroom – it was empty. The second was more productive – what he saw there made him hang in the doorway for precious seconds. Then he was away and skimming up another flight of stairs.

He eventually found them in the nursery; two terrified children huddled wide-eyed and whimpering by the window. He grabbed them, one under each arm, and fled back to the landing where the flames were licking the banisters and the smoke had grown even more dense. The children choked and retched as they encountered the clogging vapour, heads jiggling about as he leapt down the stairs three at a time.

Nick put his hands to his racking face, smearing the mucus over his cheeks in an effort to clear it. Rosanna did likewise – allowing the box of matches she had been clutching to drop, unseen, to the floor.

She hadn't intended to be naughty. It was just a trick to play on Mam, who had started to give them that horrid medicine again so she could go out without them. When their mother had come in with the bottle she had sneaked from the medicine cabinet, Rosie and Nick had taken it dutifully and climbed into bed like good children. But when Mam had left, Nick, as Rosanna had instructed him to do previous to Peggy's expected visit, pulled the removable head from his wooden soldier and had spat the medicine into the hollow body, replacing the head after Rosie had rid herself of her own spoonful. They had thought themselves extremely clever to hold the nasty stuff in their mouths for so long, and had giggled at their own audacity. Then they had waited for their mother to go out. When the door had slammed Rosie had dragged Nick down to the kitchen and poured them a glass of milk to take away the claggy taste. They had sat for a while dangling their legs from the kitchen stools and nibbling biscuits – then Rosie had spotted the matches. She knew how naughty it was of her to take them, but grand-daddy wouldn't be cross when she kissed him and told him she hadn't really known it was bad.

It had only been a little fire to begin with. She couldn't have foreseen it would grow like that. When the blaze had spilled over from the cupboard into the hall they had become frightened and had gone looking for the maids to own up. But when they had seen their mother asleep in her bed when she was supposed to have gone out they decided silence would be more prudent. Perhaps if they shut themselves in the nursery the fire would go out of its own accord.

In a strangely adult attempt to keep out the smelly smoke Rosanna had stuffed the gap under the nursery door with dolls' clothes, earning them a lucky reprieve until their natural father had found them.

Dickie felt as if he would collapse any minute. His head was about to burst open like a water-filled balloon. And just when he thought that all was lost he found himself on the pavement and the jubilant crowd swarming round him.

He looked blearily at the sobbing children in his arms, then kissed each heartily and handed them over – one to Thomasin, one to Sonny. 'There's no maids, but your wife's still in there, unconscious,' he informed his brother. 'I'm off back in.'

'No!' Sonny started to hand over Nick to his father. 'That's my place, Dickie, come back!'

But Dickie, giving Thomasin a hasty, but sincere peck on the cheek and patting his father as he passed, was already on his way.

'I'm certain he'll come to no harm, Mrs Feeney,' consoled Mrs Price, one of the neighbours who had up until now scorned them. Typical how it took a tragedy to bring them rallying, thought Thomasin, but was grateful for her support even if it was a little late, and smiled weakly, hugging Rosanna protectively as she stared up at the smoking building.

It seemed the neighbour had no sooner spoken these words than there was an almighty roar and the crowd was driven back into the road as a giant fireball ripped through the house, ballooning high into the street in a huge flower with petals of orange, crimson and gold. Women and children screamed. Horses whinnied shrilly, prancing and bucking in their harness.

'*Dickie!*' Patrick ran towards the raging inferno but was dragged away by his neighbours as the roof, showering red sparks, finally gave way and plummeted down, down in a seething mass of flame.

No one could comfort her. After the fire brigade had arrived and had reduced the blazing house to a shell of hissing embers, neighbours had vied as to whose hospitality the Feeneys should accept. In the end they had been led to Mrs Miles' stately Georgian residence to receive succour: cups of sweet tea laced with cognac.

Thomasin sat rigidly with her cup and saucer on her lap, staring glassily at the wall. She supposed she should have salvaged some consolation out of all this: her son had redeemed himself in the end – he had been coming home. And Erin, dear Erin and Sam had tried to soften the blow with their news of the baby. They kept telling her that she would feel better if she cried, but the tears wouldn't seem to come. Everyone else had cried – Erin, Sonny, Mother, even Patrick, great anguished sobs – but not Thomasin.

'Ye've got to hand it to him, Tommy,' said her husband dazedly. 'He went out in a blaze o' glory.'

'Oh, Patrick your choice of words!' burst out Hannah.

'Tommy understands what I mean, don't ye, love?' said Patrick softly. 'He went out the way he lived – larger than life – an' he proved us all wrong, didn't he? When it came down to it he was the most courageous o' the lot of us. Oh damn!' He caught his breath. 'I could kill meself for all the rotten things I said to him.' Thomasin nodded dumbly.

Erin squeezed Sam's warm hand. This had been meant to be such a happy day. She comforted herself with the thought of her husband's loving body pressing down on hers. How odd that that which had been so terrifying could be such a source of support now.

Sonny picked at the loose skin on his thumb. 'I feel so guilty . . . if I hadn't persuaded him to come home . . . It should have been me in there.'

'Enough o' that talk,' said Patrick firmly. 'He did what he did 'cause he wanted to. You know Dickie, he never lets himself be coerced into anything.' With a stab of pain he realised he had referred to his son in the present tense and the tears pricked his eyes. 'At least he was coming home.'

Sonny saw no need to mention that the reunion was to have been brief, that Dickie had come home only to say goodbye. That it would have been such a final goodbye . . . He cleared his throat. 'Where will we sleep tonight, Mother? Mam . . .'

Patrick touched Thomasin gently and she turned fathomless eyes on him. 'What?'

'Sonny was just asking where we'll live now.'

She shrugged indifferently.

'Maybe one o' your sisters . . .' Patrick began, then broke off as Mrs Miles came in.

'Mr Feeney, Mrs Feeney, I regret having to intrude on your bereavement but there is a gentleman here to see you.'

'Not at all, Mrs Miles.' Patrick rose, as did the other males in the room. 'This is your house. I'm sorry I omitted to thank you for taking us in . . .'

She smiled sympathetically, feeling guilty for her previous snobbishness. The man was not at all as she had expected him to be – really very polite – and his poor wife looked positively devastated with grief. 'It is the very least I can offer after your terrible tragedy, Mr Feeney, and naturally you will be most welcome to stay here until you find more suitable accommodation. I shall show the gentleman in personally.'

The man, leaving his hat with the maid in the hall, stepped into the room and looked around at the collection of grief-stricken faces, then walked up to Patrick. 'Mr Feeney? This won't take a minute, sir. Detective Sergeant Nettleton . . .'

Patrick frowned. 'A policeman?'

'Yes, sir. I've just heard about your ghastly experience. May I offer my deepest regrets.' Patrick moved his head. 'I've no wish to impose at such a time but it's imperative I get one or two facts clear. I understand from your hostess that someone died in the fire. Two people, she said.'

'That's correct,' said Patrick, lowering his gaze from the policeman's mutilated ear. 'My son and my daughter-in-law.'

'Could you tell me your son's name, sir? Just for the record.'

'I've already notified the police of both the victims' names,' said Patrick. 'Why do you only want my son's?'

'Please, sir,' persisted Nettleton.

'It was Richard, Richard William.'

Nettleton felt swamped by anticlimax as he pocketed his notebook. 'Thank you, sir. I shan't have to trouble you any more.'

'Won't there have to be an investigation into how the fire started?' asked Patrick, watching the detective's passage to the door.

'I expect so, sir, but that's not my department. That'll be the local police and fire brigade. I'll be on my way, then. And I'm very sorry . . .' this to everyone.

He was in the hall when he heard the noise. It was born as a low moan and rose swiftly to a crescendo of unbelievable pain. He brushed past the maid and out through the front door. The sound pursued him into the street. It was a mother's realisation of grief.

'My baby!' keened Thomasin heartrendingly. 'My son!'

EPILOGUE

A squall of gulls had shadowed them from Liverpool, screaming and dipping into the foam-lashed waves each time the ship evacuated another load of refuse. But now the gulls had gone, signifying that they had left the mainland well and truly behind them.

The girl held her face to the elements, shaking her head as the spray-laden breeze whipped and tossed her unrestrained blonde locks about her pretty features. She leaned on the rail, twirling her pink parasol against her shoulder and pretended to find something profoundly captivating about the sea, when all the time her interest lay in something more tangible; someone who was casting a mutual display in her direction. She caught his eye, smiled, then looked away, seeing from the corner of her vision the young man's casual approach.

He propped his elbow on the rail and scanned her admiringly. 'Ye want to be careful, ma'am if I might make so bold. A slip o' gossamer like yourself could get caught up by this damnable wind and carried out to sea. What you need is a strong arm to anchor ye down.'

She parted her lips and her laughter was lost on the wind. She was about to speak then, seeing his diverted attention, followed his eyes and with a regretful shrug strolled off along the heaving deck.

The other woman observed his sheepish advance, her slanting, feline eyes bright with loving reproach. 'You never alter, do you?' She tucked her arm into his and they followed the girl's path along the deck, feeling light-headed with the rush of salt-spray at their nostrils.

He gave a reparatory smile then swung his eyes out to sea over her wild, chestnut head and relived those vital seconds that had enabled his escape.

He had wondered at Nettleton's absence from the railway station – expecting to have to face this last obstacle – but when he weighed the facts carefully he surmised what must have happened. They had found the second body in the house, the one sprawled by the door of Peggy's room, hands clutching in a vain attempt at escape before he had been overpowered by the smoke, and had assumed it to be his; a last, heroic attempt at redemption. He wondered how long it would be before the truth was discovered; not that it mattered, for he would be out of their jurisdiction by then.

He wondered, too, how long Peggy had been entertaining her men friends in her husband's house, and also if Sonny knew about it. At least that explained the absence of the maids; Peggy had obviously given them the afternoon off, leaving only the children and the wallpaper to witness her adultery. That had been the sight that had arrested him on his breathless dash to the nursery; Peggy's white body, naked and ungainly, hanging head down from the bed, her lover slumped by the door. They must have been dozing for the smoke to have taken hold so quickly. When they had woken their lungs were too weak to take them further than the door.

When he had gone back into the blazing house it was not for the purpose of rescuing Peggy, but because his primary inspection of the kitchen had revealed a way for him to rectify everything. On his second trip – minutes before the fireball had ripped through the house – he had gone, not upstairs, but directly to the kitchen, seeking out the cellar door. He had felt the intense heat scorch the back of his neck even in the coolness of the cellar as the house volcanoed overhead. In the remaining seconds all his efforts were focused on that one spark of hope – the coal shute.

When he had reached the bottom of the garden, cool and serene while back there the world erupted, he had looked back to watch the burning building collapse, knowing what assumption they would draw. But there was no going back – even if he wanted to. Then, he had vaulted over the wall.

The roaring of the waves brought him back to the present. He felt her eyes upon him, and smiled into their loving depths. She had left everything behind – for him. Gripped by a rush of feeling he drew her into his arms and kissed her upturned face. 'Well, Mrs Feeney – and how does it feel to be a married lady?'

Her fingers went unconsciously to the band of gold on her finger, her own mother's wedding ring – one of the few things she had been able to bring. Then she put her arms round him and leaned her face against the burgundy jacket. 'We've not been married but ten minutes ...' Literally – the Captain had just performed the ceremony. 'I go to our cabin, and when I return what do I find? You're at it already.'

He smiled and kissed the tip of her nose. 'Sure, you're not jealous? I was only talking to her. Ye should know me by now: I can't resist a pretty face. But 'tis you I love. Honest, Dusty, I truly love ye.'

She moved her untamed hair beneath his chin, pulling him closer to add weight to her words. 'And I love you. But hear this: if ever I catch you doing more than talking ...'

The girl to whom he had spoken earlier stood by the rail, watching the newly-weds attentively.

He hugged his wife tighter and cried out in a pained voice, 'Dusty! As if I'd ever ...' – and winked at the girl with the pink parasol.